OBSOLETE

ANNOTATED TEACHER'S EDITION

G·L·O·B·E
LITERATURE

Robert R. Potter

Globe Book Company
Englewood Cliffs, New Jersey

PURPLE LEVEL

Globe Literature...

Globe brings the world within reach of

- A superb collection of classic and contemporary literature
- Consistent, easy-to-use, beautifully illustrated format
- Literature-based composition using the writing process

Blue Level, Grade 7

Red Level, Grade 8

Purple Level, Grade 9

Green Level, Grade 10

# of fine literature every student.

- Fully integrated skills program
- Comprehensive teaching materials

Teacher's Resource Binder for each level

Silver Level, Grade 11 (American Literature)

Gold Level, Grade 12 (English Literature)

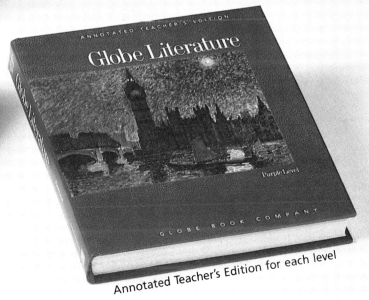

Annotated Teacher's Edition for each level

Colorful, exciting Unit Openers capture students' interest

Selections in the Student Editions are organized into Units that reflect a theme (grades 7–10) or literary period (grades 11–12). Every selection represents the very best in classic or contemporary literature. Students will discover a wide variety of genres—fiction, nonfiction, poetry, and drama—all from a rich diversity of authors.

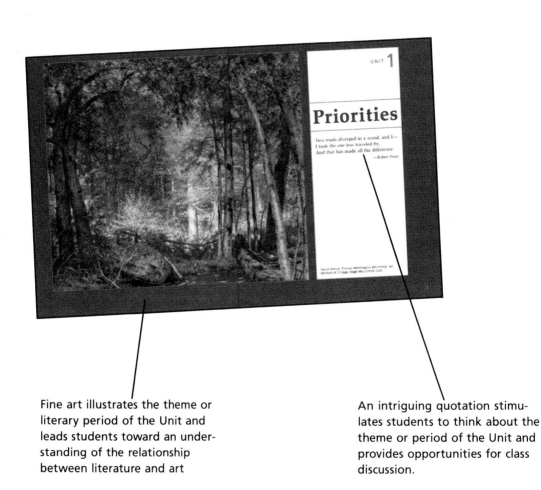

Fine art illustrates the theme or literary period of the Unit and leads students toward an understanding of the relationship between literature and art

An intriguing quotation stimulates students to think about the theme or period of the Unit and provides opportunities for class discussion.

An informative introduction explores ideas related to the Unit's theme or period and discusses how the selections in the Unit are related to one another.

Motivational questions help students relate the themes and ideas of literature to their own lives.

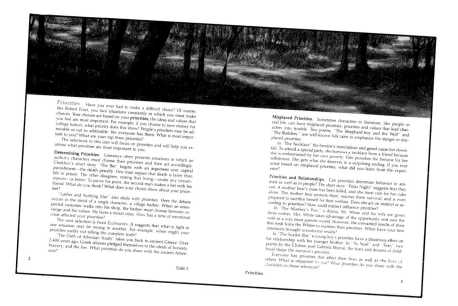

For Active Reading...

Previews of the selections in the Unit create anticipation and excitement. Students will look forward to reading the selections to discover more about the relationships and ideas presented in the literature.

A consistent lesson format delivers

All selections are carefully chosen to be readable, appropriate, and interesting to both improving readers and those performing on grade level. Students quickly become familiar with the easy-to-follow, carefully paced lesson format: skills instruction, literary selection, and follow-up skill activities.

Lessons begin with an explanation of the literary skill examined in the selection.

Skills instruction precedes the selection to establish an active reading direction for students.

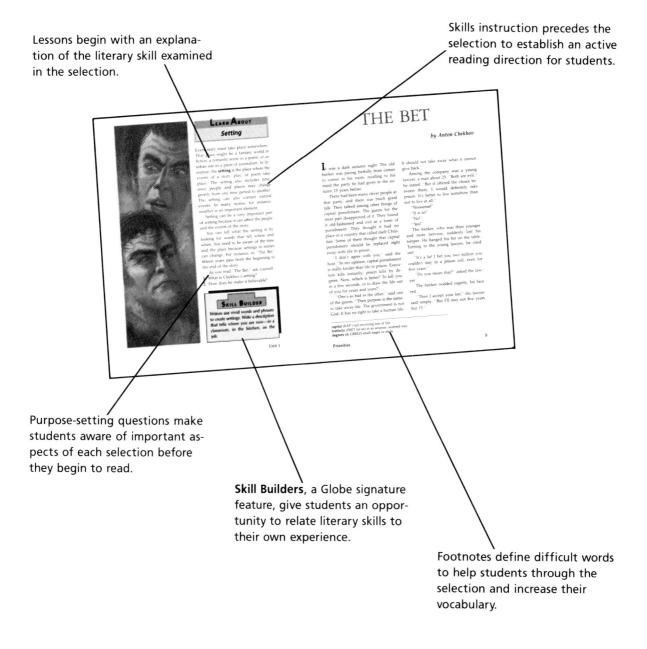

Purpose-setting questions make students aware of important aspects of each selection before they begin to read.

Skill Builders, a Globe signature feature, give students an opportunity to relate literary skills to their own experience.

Footnotes define difficult words to help students through the selection and increase their vocabulary.

comprehensive coverage of essential skills.

Comprehension questions challenge students' recall ability, inferential capability, and higher-level application skills.

In **Write About the Selection**, students use the writing process to explore the meaning of the selection.

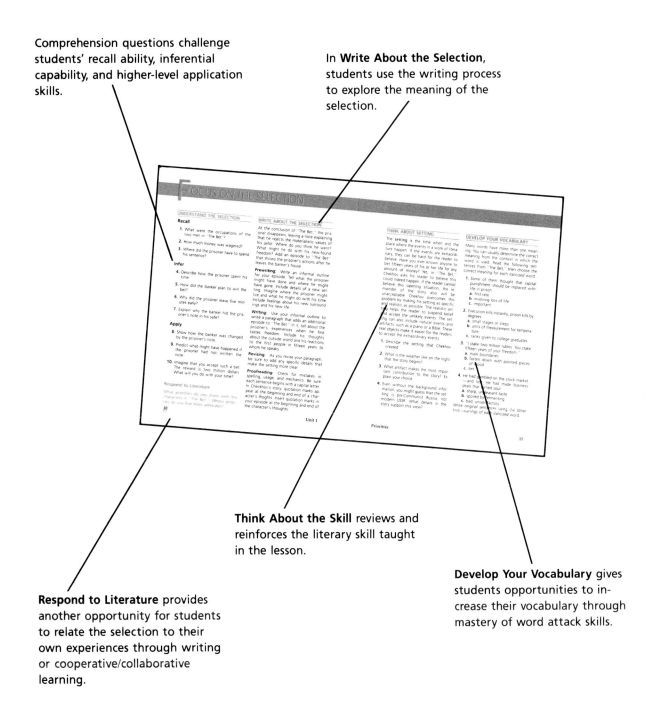

Think About the Skill reviews and reinforces the literary skill taught in the lesson.

Respond to Literature provides another opportunity for students to relate the selection to their own experiences through writing or cooperative/collaborative learning.

Develop Your Vocabulary gives students opportunities to increase their vocabulary through mastery of word attack skills.

Explore Genres...

Only in Globe Literature will you find these lessons—two
pages of comprehensive instruction in the elements of a
genre followed by an annotated selection in that genre.
There's a lesson in every Unit to help students develop a
better and fuller appreciation of fine literature.

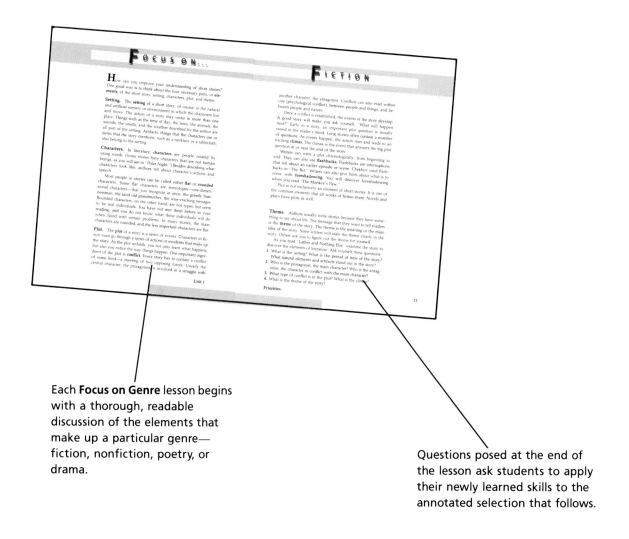

Each **Focus on Genre** lesson begins
with a thorough, readable
discussion of the elements that
make up a particular genre—
fiction, nonfiction, poetry, or
drama.

Questions posed at the end of
the lesson ask students to apply
their newly learned skills to the
annotated selection that follows.

give students a close-up look at the
and how they work.

The annotated selection helps students master the
steps in active reading.

Useful **Study Hints**, a Globe signature feature, guide students as
they read.

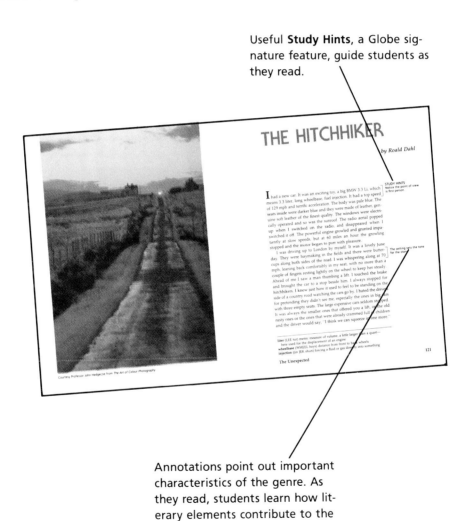

THE HITCHHIKER

by Roald Dahl

I had a new car. It was an exciting toy, a big BMW 3.3 Li, which means 3.3 liter, long wheelbase, fuel injection. It had a top speed of 129 mph and terrific acceleration. The body was pale blue. The seats inside were darker blue and they were made of leather, genuine soft leather of the finest quality. The windows were electrically operated and so was the sunroof. The radio aerial popped up when I switched on the radio, and disappeared when I switched it off. The powerful engine growled and grunted impatiently at slow speeds, but at 60 miles an hour the growling stopped and the motor began to purr with pleasure.

I was driving up to London by myself. It was a lovely June day. They were haymaking in the fields and there were buttercups along both sides of the road. I was whispering along at 70 mph, leaning back comfortably in my seat, with no more than a couple of fingers resting lightly on the wheel to keep her steady. Ahead of me I saw a man thumbing a lift. I touched the brake and brought the car to a stop beside him. I always stopped for hitchhikers. I knew just how it used to feel to be standing on the side of a country road watching the cars go by. I hated the drivers for pretending they didn't see me, especially the ones in big cars with three empty seats. The large expensive cars seldom stopped. It was always the smaller ones that offered you a lift, or the old rusty ones, or the ones that were already crammed full of children and the driver would say, "I think we can squeeze in one more."

STUDY HINTS
Notice the point of view is first person.

The setting sets the tone for the story.

liter (LEE tur) metric measure of volume, a little larger than a quart—here used for the displacement of an engine
wheelbase (WHEEL bays) distance from front to back wheels
injection (in JEK shun) forcing a fluid or gas down or into something

The Unexpected

121

Courtesy Professor John Hedgecoe from The Art of Colour Photography

Annotations point out important
characteristics of the genre. As
they read, students learn how literary elements contribute to the
form of the genre.

Each Unit concludes with four pages of review and writing activities. Two pages of literature-based activities teach skills in all areas of language arts, and two additional pages of innovative activities expand critical thinking, speaking, and study skills.

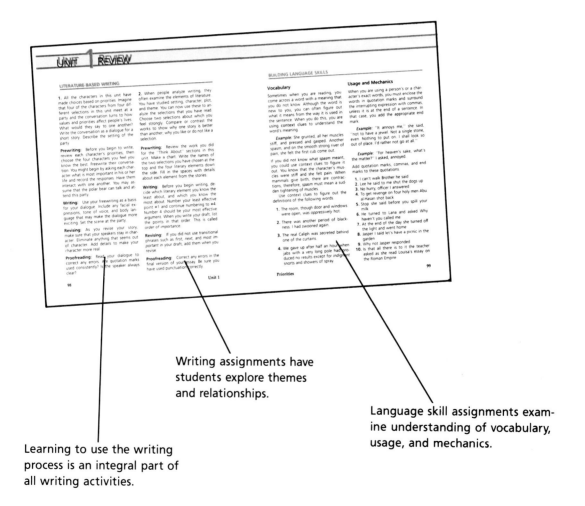

Writing assignments have students explore themes and relationships.

Learning to use the writing process is an integral part of all writing activities.

Language skill assignments examine understanding of vocabulary, usage, and mechanics.

...Extend, Express

see literature as a whole language experience.

Speaking and listening activities motivate students to analyze and evaluate literature through oral interpretation.

Critical thinking activities help students find connections between their own experiences and knowledge and the literature they've read in the Unit.

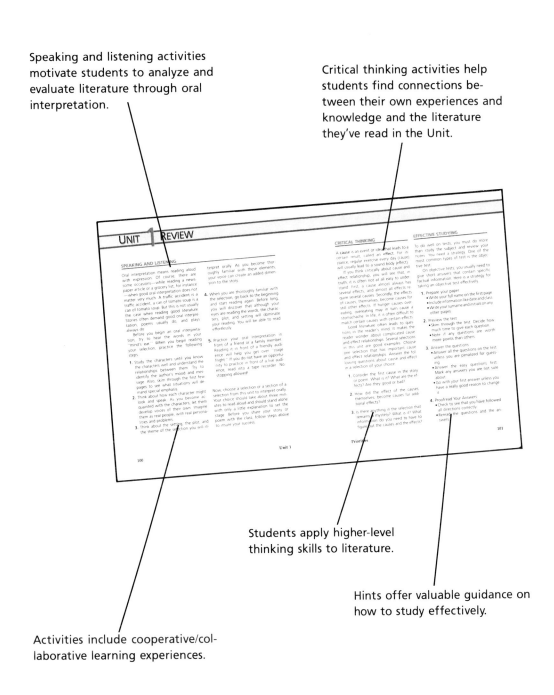

Students apply higher-level thinking skills to literature.

Activities include cooperative/collaborative learning experiences.

Hints offer valuable guidance on how to study effectively.

Complete Support...

The ANNOTATED TEACHER'S EDITION provides a success in

The easy-to-use "wraparound" format puts teaching helps right next to the corresponding students' page. Complete Teaching Strategies guide you in using the program in the most effective way.

To help you enrich and vary students' learning experiences, there are creative suggestions on research activities, cross-cultural activities, and interdisciplinary lessons.

the help you need to make GLOBE LITERATURE your classroom.

An overview of the Unit's selections and lists of skills covered and Unit objectives prepare you for teaching the Unit. Teaching helps at the end of the Unit (not shown) include answers, motivational suggestions for the writing, speaking, and listening assignments—plus a special feature on careers related to the themes or content of the literature and a "Mini-Quiz" for a quick check of student learning.

Strategies, background on fine art in the Student Edition, activities, and lists of audiovisual materials give you suggestions for introducing the Unit and stimulating interest in the theme or literary period reflected in the Unit.

With a Wealth...

Teaching suggestions include background information; ideas for discussion; cooperative/collaborative learning activities; and activities to build critical thinking, literary, speaking, and listening skills.

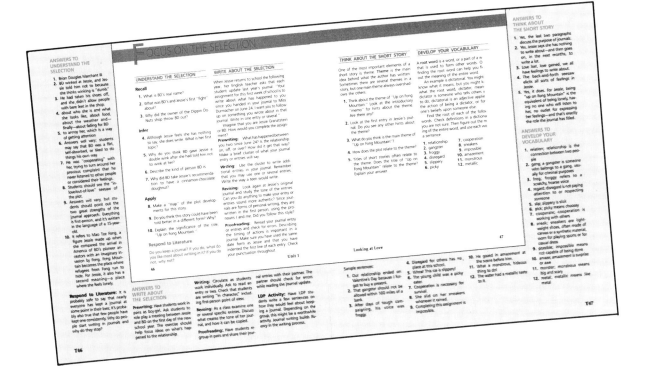

The variety of teaching suggestions lets you tailor a strategy to students' needs and abilities.

Every selection is accompanied by suggestions for teaching language diverse populations (LDP).

Answers to all questions make it easy to quickly and accurately evaluate students' work.

Teacher's Resource Binders give you worksheets, tests, and suggestions for additional activities—all in one convenient package of Blackline Masters.

The Teacher's Resource Binder includes:

Language Enrichment Workbook
Test Book
Comprehension Workbook
Writing Process Worksheets
Reinforcement Activity Worksheets
Usage and Mechanics Worksheets
Critical Thinking Worksheets
Literary Analysis Worksheets
Reading in the Content Areas Worksheets
Speaking and Listening Worksheets
SAT Preparation Worksheets (grades 11 and 12)
Unadapted Selections (grades 11 and 12)

Tests for each selection cover knowledge of the reading material as well as vocabulary, thinking skills, and the writing process.

The **Language Enrichment Workbook** has been specifically developed to enhance learning in language diverse populations (LDP) with special attention to techniques and activities that encourage LDP students to learn English.

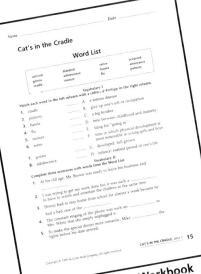

The **Comprehension Workbook** teaches and reinforces vocabulary and comprehension skills that complement the corresponding literary selections.

Writing Process Worksheets support the composition assignments in the Unit Review.

CONSULTANTS

Barbara Benson
English Teacher
Watauga High School
Boone, North Carolina

Suzanne Chavez
Teacher
Palos Verdes United School
District
Palos Verdes Estates,
California

Mariann Cholakis
Reading Specialist
New York City Board
of Education
New York, New York

Mary Contreras
Fellow of UCLA Writing
Project
Rancho Buena Vista High
School
Vista, California

Patricia Devaney
Reading Resource Teacher
Board of Education
City of New York
New York, New York

Ellen Flanagan
Principal
St. Brigid School
Brooklyn, New York

Josephine Gemake
Associate Professor
School of Education
St. John's University
Jamaica, New York

Francine Guastello
Assistant Principal
P.S. 312K
New York, New York

Margaret Haley
Reading Specialist/
Special Programs Instructor
St. John's University
Staten Island, New York

Nelda Hobbs
ECIA Coordinator/Language
Arts
Social Studies Coordinator
High Schools of North
Chicago
Public Schools
Chicago, Illinois

Barbara Milhorn
Los Angeles United School
District
Los Angeles, California

Mary M. O'Brien
Reading Specialist
Head of Reading Department
Hazelwood West Junior and
Senior High Schools
Hazelwood, Missouri

Anthony V. Patti
Full Professor and
Chairman of Secondary
Adult, and Business Education
Herbert H. Lehman College
City University of New York
New York, New York

Evelyn Pittman
Supervisor of Language Arts
Paterson Board of Education
Paterson, New Jersey

Judy Rios
Secondary Language Arts
and Resource Teacher
West Allis—West Milwaukee
School District
West Allis, Wisconsin

Robert J. Scaffardi
English Department Chair
Area Coordinator (K–12)
Cranston High School East
Cranston, Rhode Island

Richard Sinatra
Director, Reading Clinic
St. John's University
Jamaica, New York

Beth Craddock Smith
Reading Specialist
Durham County Schools
Durham, North Carolina

Sheila Byrd Smith
Language Arts/Reading
Teacher
St. Paul School
Staten Island, New York

Benjamin Stewart
English Teacher
Pine Forest Senior High
School
Fayetteville, North Carolina

Judith E. Torres
Coordinator/Limited English
Proficiency Programs
Yonkers Public Schools
Yonkers, New York

Paula Travis
Language Arts
Department Head
Newton County High School
Covington, Georgia

O. Paul Wielan
Associate Professor
School of Education
St. John's University
Jamaica, New York

G·L·O·B·E
LITERATURE

Robert R. Potter

Globe Book Company
Englewood Cliffs, New Jersey

PURPLE LEVEL

CONTENTS

Printed in the United States of America   10 9 8 7 6 5 4 3 2 1

ISBN: 1-55675-173-7

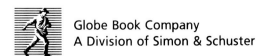

Globe Book Company
A Division of Simon & Schuster

GLOBE LITERATURE SERIES
INTRODUCTION

OVERVIEW

Language is everywhere in our lives. Students use it every day as they read the sports section, talk with friends, or jot down a note. The better students can use language, the more effectively they can deal with life. Literature is language, and the Globe Literature Series is designed to help students to read, speak, and write more effectively.

The Globe Literature Series provides a complete literature program of high-interest classic and contemporary literature with thoroughly integrated skills. The selections are carefully chosen and presented in such a way that they are accessible to students who may read below grade level or who may be part of the language-diverse population. The strong literature-based writing strand grounded in the writing process teaches fluency, form, and correctness while encouraging critical and creative thinking. Strong student support, which features preteaching of literary skills and annotation of specific literary selections with study hints, insures student success.

The Globe Literature Series provides everything you need to teach your students to analyze, appreciate, and enjoy literature.

ORGANIZATION

Each book of the series has six sections. In the blue, red, purple, and green levels, these are organized around a theme. The silver and gold levels are organized chronologically, with sections that cover a time period. Students will enjoy reading the stimulating plays, poems, short stories, and nonfiction in each section. In addition, each unit focuses on a particular genre in order to teach students the elements of literature. The uniform instructional format provides the consistency required for effective teaching and learning.

All units begin with a fine art illustration that represents the theme or time period. An intriguing quotation draws students into the section. A unit discussion follows. There, students are presented with a thorough examination of the theme or time period and are guided to consider it through purpose-setting questions. Each selection, or group of selections, is introduced with an explanation of the literary skill studied in the lesson. Then students are asked to make an immediate application of the skill to their real-life experiences. As students read the selection, any difficult vocabulary is noted at the bottom of the page, where the students have immediate access to it. Following the selection are two pages of activities that concentrate on comprehension, literature-based writing, literary skills, and vocabulary. Unit reviews give students opportunities to see literature as a whole-language experience.

SPECIAL FEATURES

Skill Builders. Practical application of skills instruction gives students the opportunity to relate the literary skill to their own experience.

Focus on the Genre. Students comprehensively examine the elements of fiction, nonfiction, poetry, and drama in two readable pages. This thorough discussion of each genre promotes fuller appreciation of literature.

Study Hints. Each unit annotated selection helps students master the steps in active reading. The informative study hints lead students to recognize important characteristics of the genre as they apply to a specific selection.

Respond to Literature. Students have the opportunity to consider the selection in light of their own experience and culture through writing or cooperative/collaborative learning activities.

End of Unit Features. Unit reviews give students opportunities to see literature as a whole language experience. The unit concludes with a review emphasizing two literature-based writing assignments; one stressing themes and relationships and the other, literary analysis. Students extend their understanding of literature with Speaking and Listening activities, vocabulary, literature-based usage and mechanics exercises, study skills, hints, and critical thinking activities.

TEACHING SUPPORT

Annotated Teacher's Edition. The wraparound format of the teacher's edition is designed for your quick reference as the lesson is taught. Information and ideas are right where you need them—next to the slightly reduced student pages. On-page answers make evaluating student work easier. The three articles that begin the Annotated Teacher's Edition present an in-depth overview of special techniques for teaching language-diverse populations and promoting comprehension through guided reading.

TEACHING THE UNIT

Before the Unit. In addition to useful synopses of the literary selections, there are ideas for unit assignments, cross-cultural activities, and interdisciplinary lessons that offer you creative alternatives for enriching and varying learning activities. If you wish to extend student reading on a theme or time period, a list of related literature is included.

Teaching the Selection. Specific selection-by-selection teaching suggestions offer strategies for planning and evaluation. These can be used on a daily basis. In the side-columns are objectives to aid in preparation of every lesson. Discussion prompts, motivational activities, fine arts notes, and practical teaching suggestions provide emphasis, direction, and enrichment. There are suggestions for adapting selections for language-diverse populations to help you with students who speak English as a second language.

End of Unit. Besides giving answers to questions and offering motivational suggestions for the writing and speaking and listening assignments, the end of unit wraparound columns present two special features: Careers to Consider and the Mini Quiz. Careers to Consider provides

information about professions related to the themes or content of the literature while the Mini Quiz offers a quick check of student learning.

THE TEACHER'S RESOURCE BOOK

The Teacher's Resource Book includes thirteen ancillaries that are designed to supplement the Globe Literature Series. These ancillaries make it possible to teach literature and attendant skills in the most comprehensive way possible. All the activities and worksheets are blackline masters that make it easy for you to reproduce the ones most useful in your classroom.

Comprehension Workbook. Each worksheet teaches a comprehension skill that complements the corresponding literary selection. Students learn valuable reading skills that will aid them in understanding literature as well as in improving their reading ability.

Test Book. The test program offers tests for each literary selection. Students are tested not only on their knowledge of the selection but also on vocabulary. Students are asked to use higher-level thinking skills and to show mastery of the writing process as they respond to literary questions.

Reinforcement Activities. These blackline masters supplement the Learn About literary skills lessons in the text. Student learning is reinforced by reteaching important literary ideas that are presented before each selection.

Writing Process. The writing process activities are designed to expand on the two composition assignments in each Unit Review. Each stage of the Unit Review assignment is examined with the writing process in mind. These worksheets provide structure as well as models and examples in order to ensure student understanding. Careful attention is given to peer response and cooperative/collaborative activities, thus increasing involvement. This step-by-step progression through the writing process guarantees student success.

Usage and Mechanics. Since the correct use of language is best taught not in a vacuum but in relation to reading and writing, usage and mechanics activities are presented in relation to the literature being read.

Language Enrichment Workbook. Specifically created to enhance learning in the language-diverse population but also applicable to less advanced students, the Language Enrichment Workbook teaches not only vocabulary but other language skills in relation to the literature the students are reading. Special attention is paid to specific techniques, cooperative/collaborative opportunities, and cross-cultural activities that encourage LDP students to learn English.

Critical Thinking Worksheets. Specific techniques for critical thinking teach students more about reading effectively. These critical thinking activities help students develop critical-thinking strategies to encourage them to analyze and evaluate material that they have read. By relating critical thinking skills to literature they have studied, the students develop reading and test-taking skills valuable not only in an English class but in other situations as well.

Literary Analysis. Students have the opportunity to demonstrate what they have learned about literary genre and elements as they annotate, with the help of guided questions, a new literary selection.

Reading in the Content Areas. Students apply the reading skills they have developed to other disciplines by analyzing articles in social studies, science, and mathematics that have themes and ideas related to the units studied in the Globe Literature Series.

Speaking and Listening. The Speaking and Listening activities are designed to complement those in the Unit Review. Worksheets provide students with a means of reinforcing and mastering the communication skills covered in the text as well as demonstrating their understanding of the literature in a creative way.

SAT Preparation. A successful score on the SAT is one of the most important factors in college admissions. The verbal portion of the examination is mostly a test of vocabulary and comprehension skills. The Globe Literature Series is a program designed to foster student interest in words and appreciation of reading through a variety of literary experiences. However, to ensure good performance on the SAT examination, the TRB includes instruction and practice in exercises that simulate the actual examination.

Unadapted Selections. Included in the TRB are original literary selections from which Globe's adaptations were written. Teachers may use these unadapted pieces along with the text, instead of the text, as a point of comparison, or in many other ways. The flexibility provided by this alternative will enhance any literature program.

Answer Keys. Answers to all questions in the TRB are included. When the question allows for divergent responses, sample answers are suggested.

The Globe Literature Series is designed to help students develop a better understanding and command of literature and language through exciting selections with a strong skills approach. This series supplies you with complete support, not only in general strategies for planning and evaluation, but also with specific selection-by-selection teaching ideas for use on a daily basis. The Globe Literature Series provides you with the help you need to give your class the best.

SUCCESSFUL EXPERIENCES
IN LITERATURE
FOR LIMITED ENGLISH PROFICIENT STUDENTS

by Alfredo Schifini, Ph.D.

THE COMPLEXITY OF THE ISSUE

Rapid demographic changes in the United States have had a direct impact on public schools. Every year an increasing number of students come to school with a primary language other than English. Limited English Proficient (LEP) students lack the language skills to benefit from instruction geared for native speakers of English.

All students, including those whose primary language is other than English should have access to challenging content material and literature. Yet all youngsters do not bring the same world knowledge and language skills to school. Some LEP students may never have been in school in their homeland. Others, before coming to the United States, may have had the benefit of a rich educational experience which has afforded them a high level of literacy in their native language. In addition to dealing with the needs of LEP students, teachers may also encounter native language speakers of English who demonstrate similar difficulties manipulating literary or academic language.

EDUCATIONAL APPROACHES

English as a Second Language

In recent years students in American schools who are totally non-English proficient have been able to gain immediate access to literature and basic subject matter through instruction in their mother tongue while they are in the process of learning English. All LEP students, regardless of the extent of instruction in their mother tongue, should be provided a rigorous program of English as a Second Language (ESL) lessons. As student proficiency in English increases, the dependency on primary language instruction decreases. A strong ESL program provides the necessary foundation or "launching pad" in the language to ensure future success in subject matter instruction taught in a mainstream context.

Content ESL

In addition to beginning level ESL courses geared toward functional fluency, other ESL classes that incorporate content material, i.e. math, science, and social studies, have been designed for intermediate speakers. These content area ESL courses teach the terminology and key requisite concepts needed to provide a broader linguistic and experiential base for second language learners.

Sheltered English

Recent advances in language acquisition theory have made it clear that language is acquired by receiving meaningful input in a low anxiety environment. Language is more effectively learned when conscious language learning is not the focus of the lessons. It follows, therefore, that if subject matter can be made comprehensible through a variety of means, such as by demonstrations, visual aids, hands-on material and manipulation of the content, student language development will be expanded, and requisite subject matter concepts will be acquired. Thus, the popularity of "Sheltered English" content courses delivered by mainstream teachers in a more language sensitive fashion.

The Globe Literature Series

The Globe Literature Series integrates language and content instruction using a variety of literary selections. Instructional strategies are designed to build on students' prior knowledge or install schema, background knowledge with regard to the study of literature. Activities such as brainstorming enable the students to capture the broad meaning before studying details. Vocabulary is acquired through interactive activities that are contextual in nature. Learning strategies such as organizing and summarizing and a wide range of questioning techniques are included which prepare students to meet the challenge of cognitively demanding subject matter. In short, the Globe Literature Series provides a theoretical sound approach to integrating language development and literature study. It enables students to successfully engage in a wealth of experiences with literature that are appropriate to their evolving language and literacy levels. The subject matter presented in this language sensitive fashion not only provides increased familiarity with masterworks of literature, but develops the requisite language skills necessary for academic achievement.

Suggested Strategies

When working with LEP students teachers might consider the following strategies:

• Simplify the language used with youngsters who are new to English by utilizing a slow but natural rate of speech; enunciating clearly; defining troublesome idiomatic expressions and multiple meanings before reading, and limiting the teaching of vocabulary to those that are key to comprehension of the passage to be read or to the discussion at hand.

• Use context clues wherever possible. Context clues give meaning to oral language for LEP students. Common context clues already used by most teachers are: paralinguistic clues (gestures, facial expressions, acting out meanings, etc.); props, graphs, visuals, real objects, bulletin boards, maps, timelines and visual and word associations. Pre-reading discussion of visuals and other features in the text that capture the essence of the piece to be read also greatly aid in comprehension.

• Check frequently for understanding by asking for clarification and expansion of student statements. Utilize a variety of oral questions that are commensurate with the evolving language proficiency of the students. Provide opportunities for teacher-student and student-student interaction.

• Tap and focus the prior background knowledge of the students regarding the theme to be presented in the text by asking open-ended questions such as: "have you ever had this experience or been in this situation," or "how would you feel if _____ would happen to you?" Use real objects or visuals to stimulate pre-reading discussion and provide an opportunity for students to share what they already know about the topic to be read. Allow students to respond in their primary language, if necessary, while sharing.

• Make activities student centered by utilizing different grouping strategies that allow students to try out their newly acquired English skills in a safe environment. By negotiating with their peers, students must rephrase their thoughts and correct their own errors so that they can be understood by others.

• Keep in mind that affect is a crucial element to consider and that language development is accelerated when students are engaged in activities that enable them to experience success. Direct error correction, especially in the initial stages of acquiring a new language, should be held to a minimum. Accept phonological inaccuracies in the beginning. Accents ameliorate over time with meaningful input and proper modeling. In cognitively demanding situations, emphasis should be on what is said, rather than on form.

• Remember that language acquisition takes time.

TEACHING IN THE LANGUAGE DIVERSE CLASSROOM

by Dan Fichtner, Ph.D.

I want to do what's best for my students, but they just don't get what I'm doing in the class. They don't know English very well, so they can't get the ideas that I want to teach them. What can I do?

RATIONALE

As teachers we want to be successful in our mission to prepare our students for the life they will choose to lead, channeling them in correct directions; advising them so that they will not go astray. This is where our success as teachers lies—drawing out each student's full potential, building upon what is already within the individual. Success for the students lies in the process through which they are becoming better educated persons and more valuable citizens in the communities in which they live. All students should reach their highest academic potential. This should in no way interfere with their freedom to enjoy and share with others their cultural and linguistic heritages. The education process can enhance the opportunities for those with cross-cultural experiences.

More than English is involved in teaching reading: psychology, sociology, science, geography, culture, and mathematics also play a part in a person's learning to read. Reading cannot be taught in a vacuum. The concepts learned through reading should be useful to the students. If students feel that reading is useful in their daily lives, they will be motivated to read.

The opportunity to teach a class with a language-diverse population (LDP) is fortunate: all the elements for a rich mixture of experiences are present. The teacher needs only to draw out, channel, and help organize the wealth of individual experiences that the LDP students possess. The teacher needs to "conduct" the students. Robert Louis Stevenson said, "To travel hopefully is a better thing than to arrive, and the true success is to labor." We must continue on the right path in our endeavors to educate all of our youngsters.

CHANGING POPULATIONS

We in the United States live in a pluralistic society. The fabric of the U.S. is forever in flux. We are indeed a nation of immigrants. This is as true today as it was two hundred years ago. As our American culture continues to adopt newcomers, the social and cultural quilt that is America incessantly adapts itself in those areas that are not essential, but retains those cultural elements that are necessary, to the American way. The story of the American people is an unfinished story.

This heterogeneity of the American nation is evidenced in the diversity of the origins of people from many ethnic, cultural, linguistic, racial, and religious heritages. However, from our founding as a nation, we always have been united in the common ideals of equality, opportunity, and freedom. This story of the American people is thus the unfinished story of a nation growing and becoming richer with each new wave of immigration while continuing to share the high ideals and aspirations of democracy. The pluralistic character of the American nation is unusual in the world with its people representing a multicultural, multiracial, multiethnic, and multireligious society. Our national heritage and future is at once both pluralistic in origins as well as united as one nation.

James Dimitriou, Jan., 1989
Palos Verdes Peninsula Unified School District
Philosophy of Multicultural Education, draft

As teachers, we have the awesome responsibility to be central figures in this enculturation/acculturation process. Our goal is to "Americanize" our students—to help them find out who they are and how they fit into the "fabric of America." What happens in the schools and classrooms has wide-ranging ramifications. A school experience that offers all students the chance to be successful in their lives, living and working with each other in a variety of linguistically and culturally different settings, is what our profession is all about. You may ask how this can be done. This Globe Literature series will offer some suggestions to help in this important mission.

CONSIDERATIONS

In order to meet the needs of a language diverse population best, teachers must have an awareness of the **process** of acquiring a second language. Once that is understood, a working knowledge of some specific teaching techniques that are especially beneficial to second-language learners is essential. The strategies employed should match the language skills of the students, always making sure that the teachers stretch their skills by having high, but realistic, expectations. Knowing and understanding the stages in second-language acquisition make it possible for teachers to tailor the language demands of their content area to fit the English-language skills of their students. Teachers can have attainable goals as they guide their language diverse population students on their way to mastery of the English language. We will meet with success if we keep students *progressing* through the process of learning the language skills of English.

Another area to be familiar with when working with LDP students is the acculturation process that they are going through. The situation of these students is a sociolinguistic one. They are learning to "fit in" with the values of a new culture while they are also "learning the lingo." What is valued in their home culture may not be highly prized in the American educational system. These are things that will bring about conflicts in the students themselves and also among family members. Intergenerational conflicts are certain to arise as the younger more "culturally pliable" students become acculturated to the American way while their parents become Americanized more slowly and selectively. Classroom cross-cultural activities that allow an opportunity for the LDP students to explore the changes in their value systems are a needed part of their acculturation process. They need the chance to reflect on how they are changing and becoming hyphenated Americans, to consider which of their values and beliefs are remaining and which are changing over time.

Teachers need to be culturally sensitive and aware of the differences in the cultures of their students so that differences in behavior are not incorrectly diagnosed. One difference that is very evident in certain cultures is the mode of discourse. Differences in how people speak to one another are very important to members of a society. American schools and American society at large is very **direct** and **linear** in its conversations. Americans want the other person to tell them what he or she wants to say and also to draw conclusions and reasons for saying what is said. The need to do this may indicate that Americans do not always feel a relationship with their listeners and want to make sure they are "with them" in their thoughts. The American pattern of speech looks something like this

If you think this and,
if you think that,
then probably you believe thus.

The speech pattern of some other cultures resembles a shotgun blast. There is no need to draw conclusions for the listener or even to state a reason for speaking. If you listened to Colonel Qadafy as he spoke about the U.S. planes that attacked Tripoli, you will have a good example of this mode of discourse. He spoke about the planes, Great Britain, international waters, etc. To many Westerners he sounded very "unconnected." Yet he did not worry about being understood. His audience knew exactly what he was saying because there was a bond between him and his people. When we get flustered, which is usually in the privacy of our homes, we, too, can speak like this to our intimates with no fear of being branded "scatterbrained." They may say that we are, but they don't brand us as such. (Don't try it at work though!)

The visual model for such discourse looks like this:

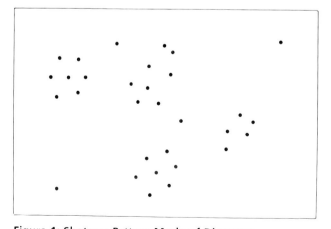

Figure 1: Shotgun Pattern Mode of Discourse

A third possibility is a circumlocutory pattern of discourse, one in which many words are used to say what one or a few words could say. To use this mode of discourse would indicate that speaking to the other person was at least as important as the message that was being conveyed. The relationship with the listener is cultivated by speech so that more words are used and discussions are roundabout rather than straightforward and direct. Hispanic culture values this type of discourse. When a teacher asks an Hispanic student to retell a story, the student will embellish the story with many minor details, and the teacher gets impatient, thinking the student slow, when in actuality the student is operating under a different set of rules for discourse. The important thing is to be speaking with the teacher, not necessarily getting the main idea out immediately. The teacher in desperation demands that the student "get to the point!"

A visual representation of the circumlocutory mode is:

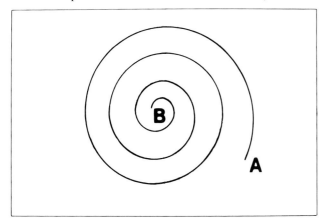

Figure 2: The Circumlocutory Mode of Discourse

Pupils who operate in this mode all of the time in a classroom will be considered to be this:

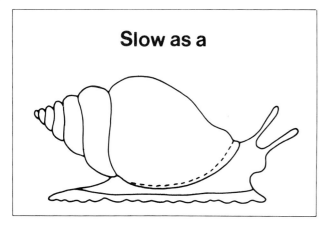

Figure 3: Slow as a . . .

Often we suppress this creativity in our students, only to try later to revive it in a "Creative Writing" course in high school. Wouldn't it be better to allow all of these modes to operate in our classrooms? All have a place in human interactions.

When writing, we need to go through a writing *process*. In prewriting exercises we must feel uninhibitedly free to brainstorm—to be a little scatterbrained—in order to get the "creative juices flowing." The shotgun pattern has a place at this point in the writing process. But, in order for us to brainstorm, we must feel relaxed with our fellow brainstormers!

Then when we start to cluster all our ideas into some sort of order, we need to have someone to listen to them before they are "jelled" or "set in concrete." This is the circumlocutory mode of discourse in action. Indeed, most poetry could be placed into this category of writing/discourse because poetry leaves much to interpretation by the reader/listener.

Once the prewriting has taken place and we are sure of what we want to say (main idea), it is time to work on the *message*, to make sure that it is not misunderstood by a reader. The audience determines the exactness of the message. Thus, business letters and contracts must be written in a much more technical way than a personal letter. The main idea must be unequivocally clear, with supporting details in place. The reader cannot mistake the meaning in the business letter or the contract. Here is the niche of the direct or linear mode of discourse in the writing process. Here is where clearly defined statements need to be and should be used. Japanese businessmen have said that they prefer to do business in English because it is so direct and allows the precision that makes business dealings so businesslike. "I want 1,000 TP-7 units by April 25, 1990, or else there will be a 5 percent reduction in the cost." Are there any questions about what is happening in this transaction? Perhaps this is why English is becoming the international business language. But our whole lives don't run this way!

Being aware of these three different modes of discourse and their relation to different cultures and to the writing process may help teachers to understand why LDP and other students write and speak the way they do. Knowing that, the teacher can develop lessons that will gradually acculturate the LDP students to the American educational system and to America's pluralistic society.

Let us now discuss the process of acquiring a second language.

NATURAL APPROACH TO LANGUAGE ACQUISITION

The Natural Approach to Language Acquisition has four main stages through which students go before they become fluent in a second language: 1. the preproduction, 2. the early production, 3. the speech emergence, and 4. the intermediate fluency stages. The Natural Approach to Language Acquisition also considers all four of the language skills: listening, speaking, reading, and writing. Listening and reading are somewhat passive skills, and develop more quickly than speaking and writing, which require much more comprehensible experience with the language. Thus, students who are not fluent in English are able to understand much more from listening, reading, and interacting in a classroom with English as the language of instruction than they can produce as speech or writing. Teachers with such language-diverse classrooms need to develop skill in evaluating, using alternative methods that are not totally language dependent. Using alternative evaluation methods permits the students to be more successful in the classroom because it gives them the chance to provide this comprehension of the subject matter without having to have fluency in the English language.

To illustrate this point, an LDP student after being engaged in comprehensible classroom activities will understand the concept that there is conflict between man and nature in the Jack London story "To Build a Fire." The LDP student can even use the word in a phrase but is not yet at a stage in his or her English development to be able to write an essay on the conflict. This student can be required to produce a collage or an illustration or to act out in some

STAGE Time Frame	EXPECTATIONS I can expect students at this stage to:	ACTIVITIES What activity will produce a product as proof of acquisition of intended skill?
Pre-Production "Silent Period" 10 hours to 6 months	1. Respond physically to cues in the target language and realia 2. Listen to simple descriptions of pictures and to realia 3. Answer simple yes/no questions and questions with names of students	1. Teacher gives commands. Students point, draw, look, touch, write simple words, and make things. 2. Teacher acts out situations as a model. Students mimic, combine and/or develop own situations as directed by the teacher. 3. Teacher describes pictures and realia and asks simple questions that require yes/no answers or one-word answers (names of students). Students listen to descriptions and demonstrate comprehension by body gestures or by answering yes and no. 4. Teacher gives composition booklets to students and writes target vocabulary on the board (literacy skills in L1 a prerequisite). Students write the new vocabulary and any personally useful words in the "personal dictionary" with the help of the teacher, aide, picture dictionary or peer tutor.
Early Production 6 months to 1 year	*All of the above plus:* 1. Give one- or two-word answers to *who, what, where, when,* and *either/or* questions 2. Fill in the blanks in sentences 3. Make lists	*All of the above plus:* 1. Teacher describes and discusses neighborhoods, countries, continents, etc., and draws maps, graphs, and diagrams to help explain. Students draw maps, etc., to help explain their neighborhood and answer questions about it with one- or two-word answers. 2. Teacher describes a situation using verbal and other cues, then reviews the material, leaving blanks where some of the target vocabulary belongs. Students fill in the missing word or words. 3. Teacher elicits vocabulary from the students and writes it on the board. Students then list (categorize) the vocabulary in some predetermined way, e.g., noun, verb, adjective; living, nonliving; plant, animal, mineral; etc.

Figure 4: Expectations and Activities Appropriate to the First Three Stages of Language Acquisition

way the conflict of the story. Not knowing English fluently does not mean inability to learn in English if the instruction is "language sensitive" and if alternative non-English evaluation methods are used. Let us now look at the stages in the Natural Approach to Language Acquisition. In this way we will be able to see how language progresses and what we as teachers can expect our students to be able to do when they reach the different stages. This will allow us to meet their needs in the instructional mode of our lessons and to keep our expectations high and reasonable, thus forcing them to become even more proficient.

The chart "Expectations and Activities Appropriate to the First Three Stages of Language Acquisition" has three columns: stage/time frame, student expectations, and activities that are appropriate for the stage. Acquiring a second language (L2) is dependent on many factors. Three of the most important are: skill in the primary language (L1), personality, and age.

Transferability: Primary language skills are transferable into a second language (L2). If students can read and write in L1, then they can be easily taught to read and write in an L2, because the reading skills of decoding, encoding, inferring, etc., do not have to be taught. They are transferred into the new language. The better developed the primary language skills, the higher the level attained in the second language.

Personality: Risk takers get much more practice in the second language than nonrisk takers. They, it seems, move through the beginning stages more rapidly than the meeker students, but when it comes time to polish up on the finer points, they may be at a disadvantage.

Age: When age is considered a factor in language acquisition, it is a fact that younger students have less complicated

STAGE Time Frame	EXPECTATIONS I can expect students at this stage to:	ACTIVITIES What activity will produce a product as proof of acquisition of intended skill?
Speech Emergence (Intermediate Stage) 2–3 years	*All of the above plus:* 1. Give three-word or short-phrase answers. 2. Answer *why* and *how* questions 3. Complete sentences 4. Ask simple questions	*All of the above plus:* 1. Teacher develops with the students a list of questions for interviewing a person. The teacher interviews a volunteer. Students then interview a partner, using the list of questions, and introduce their partners to the whole group, orally and/or written. 2. Teacher describes pictures using target vocabulary and passes out other pictures or magazines with pictures. Students in groups then look for pictures to describe, using the target vocabulary. 3. Teacher models some role play examples and passes out papers with different situations for pairs of students to role play. Students read the situation, practice their role play, and then present it to the class. 4. Teacher explains the rules of a game and plays with the students for a while. Students then continue on their own to play the game and refer to the teacher when questions about the rules come up. 5. Teacher writes or says the first part of some sentences, e.g., "My favorite sport is . . . ," "I like it because . . . ," "One thing about my homeland that I will never forget is . . . ."
Intermediate fluency 2½–4 years	1. Perform as well or better than an average speaking student in all of the language skills (listening, speaking, reading, and writing)	1. Teacher tailors the instruction to fit the needs and abilities of the students. Sheltered classes in content areas, if possible.

*Involvement is the key

Figure 5: Expectations and Activities Appropriate to the First Three Stages of Language Acquisition

language patterns to acquire, and thus, for them, learning an L2 is a much quicker process. Their age-appropriate language is internalized more rapidly because it is so much less complicated.

Having discussed three of the factors in the learning of a second language, let's now look at the four stages in the acquisition of a second language and some appropriate questions and activities for students at each of the stages.

Stage One—Preproduction

The first stage in the development of a language is the preproduction stage, often referred to as the "Silent Period." During this period the language learner is usually linguistically passive, listening to the language but producing no language or very little language. The "silent period" lasts for about ten hours to six months, during which time the student can **listen** to simple descriptions of illustrations and realia, **respond physically** to directions, and **answer yes/no** questions and **use the names of students** to answer questions. You will notice that all of these activities involve very little, if any, language per se, but rather allow understanding to be manifested through physical actions. TPR (Total Physical Response) is a method of teaching English as a Second Language that requires students to show comprehension of language cues by using some type of physical action. For example: "Stand up!" The student stands up. "Put the box with the crayons under the table." The student puts the box with the crayons under the table. Much English can be learned by students and checked by the teacher in this manner without requiring the student to produce any oral English. Looking at the chart will disclose some other activities appropriate for students at the preproduction stage. A student at this stage needs an extremely language-rich environment with much student-student or student-teacher interaction in order to progress to the next stage, Early Production.

Sample questions for comprehension at the preproduction stage:

- Point to the picture of _____ .
- Take the picture of _____ .
- Put the picture of the _____ (on, under, over, etc.) the _____ .
- Is he, she, or it a _____ ?
- Is the _____ in picture 1, 2, or 3?
- Does the _____ have a _____ ?
- Draw a picture of the _____ .

Stage Two—Early Production

The early production stage averages six to twelve months and is different from the preproduction stage because L2 learners can answer "who," "what," "where," "when," and "either-or" questions with one- or two-word answers. Students at this stage can also fill in blanks and make lists. This means that, starting at this stage, students who are literate in their primary language or have some literacy in English can actively participate in cooperative or collaborative prewriting activities. They will be able to contribute to a group effort. This will enhance their self-esteem, an important element to consider in the education of children and adults. Activities for students at this second stage of language acquisition will take into account the fact that students are now able to produce one- and two-word answers: labeling illustrations, making and categorizing lists (one of the easiest and most success-building activities), filling in the blanks, brainstorming, and starting word clusters (semantic mapping or word webbing). All of these activities, if done with partners or in groups, will greatly increase the chances for practice in the second language. Students will gradually enter into the third stage, speech emergence, as they interact with their teachers and peers. They will be experiencing "whole language" activities, activities in which listening, reading, speaking, and writing are used to produce an interesting, meaningful, and learning environment. The students cull from these experiences the necessary ingredients to move to the next stage on their way to fluency. This all takes time, patience, caring, and work.

Sample questions for comprehension at the early production stage:

- What is this?
- Is he, she, or it a _____ or a _____ ?
- What are they doing?
- The dog is drinking _____ .
- Where is the _____ ?
- Make a list of all the things you can _____ in the picture.
- Who is _____ ?
- When is this happening?

Stage Three—Speech Emergence

The time frame for this third stage is about two to three years. During this time L2 students gain experience in the second language and begin to use short phrases. They also can now answer "why" and "how" questions because these require a short phrase for an answer. At this point they can complete sentences like "In the story *Tom Sawyer,* Tom was a clever boy because _____." Another skill they develop is asking their own questions, thereby allowing them individually to gather information that they feel is pertinent to their purposes. Their language skills are increasing dramatically as they learn to gather facts and information to synthesize some knowledge for basing decisions. No longer are students developing mostly intercommunication skills; they are now actively involved in **learning in** the second language. They are learning the language, as well as the content of their courses. This is the main theory behind "Sheltered English" classes, which we will discuss at greater length in another section of the introduction.

Sample questions for comprehension at the speech-emergence stage:

• Why did the _____ do that?
• Write (if literate) or talk about the picture/person.
• What do you think will happen next? (good reading strategy)
• What do you think would happen if _____?
• What do you think would have happened if _____? (done in context of a story)
• What would you do or say if something like that happened to you?
• Has something like that ever happened to you? Tell about it.

Stage Four—Intermediate Fluency

The fourth stage lasts two to four years. Throughout this stage L2 students will be able to perform almost as well as, and occasionally in some areas better than, average native speakers. Teachers with students at this stage of language development must continue to be "language sensitive" to the needs of their students, constantly monitoring their progress, and adjusting strategies to meet the students' needs. Only a teacher who has close and continual contact can adequately assess the needs of particular LDP stu-

dents. Thus, teachers with LDP students must regularly evaluate the students' language skills. This does not have to be done formally through special tests, but should be done informally through attention paid to the errors most often made in speech and writing. In this way a program can be developed to meet the individual needs of the L2 learner. The questions used to check for comprehension by students at the intermediate fluency level are the same as those used with a general L1 population. More time for answering, for illustrations, and for other aids to comprehension may be used throughout.

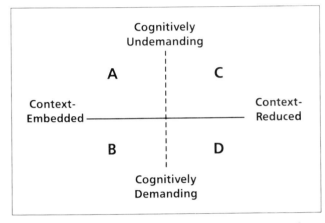

Figure 6: Range of Contextual Support and Degree of Cognitive Involvement in Communicative Activities

Figure number 6 is Cummins' *Model of Language Proficiency.* The vertical axis represents the academic difficulty of the subject matter, with the upper quadrants easy (cognitively undemanding) and the lower quadrants more difficult (cognitively demanding). The horizontal axis represents the number of context clues embedded in the subject matter. Those on the left have a greater number of context clues possible in lessons than those on the right. In classes with LDP students, teachers should attempt to give as many context clues as possible, so as to make the material comprehensible to the students. The teachers' challenge is to take cognitively demanding concepts and make them comprehensible through activities that have students and teachers **show**, **try**, **tell about**, and **do** what is to be mastered. Figure number 7 is a graphic illustration of this concept by Northcutt and Watson. [L. Northcutt and D. Watson, **Sheltered English Teaching Handbook** (Carlsbad, CA.: 1986) page 31.] For example, in an art class the teacher can demonstrate a technique the students are to learn. Cognitively undemanding and highly context-embedded courses can be *shown* to the learners. Art and

Slide Show Diagram Chart Film Overhead Visual Aids Computer Graphics (SHOW) **A**	Textbook Tapes Reference Books Overheads Guest Speaker Computer Text (TELL) **C**
B	**D**
Dramatization Computer Simulations Manipulatives Pocket Charts (TRY)	Workbooks Worksheets Computer Applications Tests (DO)

Figure 7: Tools to use for Show, Tell, Try, and Do within the Cummins' model.

Physical Education teachers have fewer problems with LDP students than do the science and social science teachers. One of the reasons is that many of the objectives of the quadrant A classes can be demonstrated, modeled, or diagrammed for the students, thus aiding the LDP students' comprehension. Quadrant B activities include: clustering, semantic mapping, discussing, role playing, experimenting, and reciting. In all of these activities the teacher or the students themselves are *trying* to do a more cognitively demanding activity that has many context clues. When the material to be learned is not too cognitively demanding, but has few clues as to the meaning, Quadrant C students can watch a film or video, read the text, or listen to a lecture. The learners can have others *tell* them in some manner what they are to learn. Quadrant D activities, that is, activities that are cognitively difficult and have few context clues, include: worksheets, workbook exercises, tests, homework, and the writing of paragraphs. In order to help students, especially LDP students, to succeed in Quadrant D activities, students and teachers should first have done activities from the first three quadrants. In that way the activity will not be completely new to the students. They will have been actively working with the concepts in a "sheltered" environment before they are asked to *do* their own work in the form of an essay, or test. That is, they will

have done some clustering of main ideas and filled in a chart with information before they are asked to write a paragraph on the topic or the theme of the lesson.

So Cummins' Model of Language Proficiency and Northcutt and Watson's repetition of the Cummins' model, with Show, Tell, Try, and Do incorporated, both show visually what it is that we as teachers should be trying to do in order to help our LDP students grasp concepts in their content-area classes.

Natural Language Acquisition: Summary

A brief review of the main ideas of the section on the Natural Approach to Language Acquisition would indicate that: **1.** language acquisition is a process with specific stages that learners go through; **2.** much more is understood in a second language that can be explained using that language; **3.** this means that alternative evaluation techniques need to be fostered in classrooms with LDP students, so that LDP students can show comprehension of concepts in nonlanguage-dependent ways; **4.** language skills are transferable; **5.** probably the most important thing to remember about L2 learners is that lack of skills in the language of instruction does not mean inability to learn; **6.** teaching techniques must match the skills of the learner; and **7.** lessons that are thematically organized help in the acquisition of vocabulary and language skills germane to the subject or content area.

What is it that we need to do to make the classroom instruction and other related activities comprehensible for our LDP students? To answer this we need to take a look at "Sheltered English"—a process of educating LDP students in which concepts in the content areas are developed, as well as scholastic and communicative language skills.

TECHNIQUES USEFUL IN LDP CLASSROOMS—SHELTERED ENGLISH

Let's first start out with a definition of Sheltered English and look at where it fits into the educational program for LDP students. It is only one part of a comprehensive and effective program to meet the needs of Language Diverse Populations. As was mentioned before, the learning of L2 skills is positively affected by having corresponding L1 skills. Therefore, if it is at all possible to teach age-appropriate L1 skills as part of a comprehensive language development program, it should be done. It makes pedagogical sense. Sheltered English is a valuable tool for teachers, especially those with students who are making the transition from classes in their native language to regular English-only classes. The following is a synthesis of Sheltered English definitions that were developed during workshops with teachers of Sheltered English classes:

Sheltered English is an eclectic process, the techniques of which include development of content-driven, activity-based lessons for students at their appropriate grade level, regardless of their language ability. This is accomplished through extensive use of
1. context clues
2. peer interaction
3. modeling of skills
4. whole language experiences

In order to understand Sheltered English, we must first discuss the components of language. Language has two components that develop in the L2 learner. These are

1. **BICS** - basic interpersonal communication skills

2. **CALP**s - cognitive academic language proficiencies

The BICS, all the skills that one needs to "get around" in the L2 environment, are the first to be acquired. For example, one must be able to ask permission to leave a room or excuse oneself for doing something rude. CALPs, on the other hand, are the language skills that are needed to learn concepts in a subject area. For example, in order to take part meaningfully in a reading lesson, students need to know how to infer meaning from text, learn the meaning of vocabulary through context clues, and find the main ideas of paragraphs. These are cognitive and academic skills, as opposed to the interpersonal communication skills needed to ask permission to leave the room or the skills required to excuse oneself or to find out a partner's telephone number.

In Sheltered English classrooms, the teachers are aware of both of these elements of language in the acquisition of a second language, and they develop lessons that produce both types of language proficiency in the L2 learner.

Lessons are comprehensible to LDP students if the content and delivery are "language sensitive" and the anxiety level is low, but not completely absent. "Language sensi-

tive" lessons are those that include class activities that involve students in tasks that take into account their expanding language skills; i.e., they continue to review the skills the students already have while they "stretch" them and increase their competencies. It is natural for students to want to take in information, work with it, and share the insights and knowledge of their work with others, especially their peers. Students will want to explain, analyze, and conceptualize in a classroom that allows them freedom to experiment with their new language in a nonthreatening environment.

A student who feels comfortable enough to ask, "Teacher, I don't know what's that? A elephant?" will learn concepts and language from a teacher who is willing to model for, and unobtrusively monitor, the L2 learner. Good content teaching increases language acquisition; the "special language" of the particular subject area is developed. The LDP student is not threatened by a lack of L2 skills, but rather feels challenged to pursue an attainable goal—learning some subject area content and English.

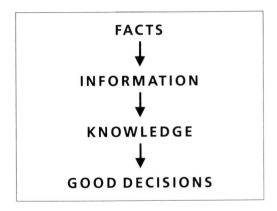

Figure 8

Teachers control, as tightly or loosely as they desire, the facts that students in their classes are able to work with as information. Facts remain facts unless they are brought to someone's attention. At that point they become information. Information becomes knowledge through processes of critical thinking—synthesis, evaluation, categorizing, etc. Without working with the information in some meaningful manner, the information remains information. After they have produced some knowledge from the facts that they have gathered, students can then make informed decisions based on that knowledge. We as teachers should be looking for the best ways to help students wade through the vast sea of facts to get the information they need to produce the knowledge to make informed decisions. This is a hard task, and it becomes even more challenging when students are not fluent in English, the language of instruction.

The following is a short explanation of the whys and wherefores of Sheltered English. Skill in a language includes the ability to explain, analyze, and conceptualize in the target language. Students with survival skills in a target language, in our case English, are ready to start to learn in the language. Things to consider when developing lessons for such students are

1. modeling
2. contextual clues, built-in redundancy
3. age-appropriateness
4. humor
5. equal-status activities
6. cooperative/collaborative activities

Modeling refers to the visual or auditory examples used to explain what is expected of the students. If rhyming is the concept being taught, then the students should see, read, and hear many examples of rhymes before they are asked to produce one of their own. Modeling can be done by the teacher, other students, or an audiovisual aid. The main idea is that the LDP students see or hear, in some comprehensible manner, the material that they are to master.

Context clues and built-in redundancy help Sheltered English lessons become more comprehensible because they increase the chances for students to understand the concepts that the lessons are designed to convey. Use of realia, pantomime, and gestures, and connecting the familiar with the unknown provide students with a schema, or frame of reference, upon which to build new knowledge. By repeating, paraphrasing, restating, and using synonyms, the teacher gives students many chances to understand the material. These "redundancy-producing methods" increase the chances for students to learn the content of the lesson and the specific grammar and vocabulary of the academic subject. Varying the teaching methods and types of activities will insure that the diversity of general learning styles and language learning styles will be met. All students will be challenged in their most appropriate mode at least some of the time, and they will be able to receive help from their partners when the teaching mode is not a perfect match with their learning style.

Age-appropriateness refers to keeping a task **reasonably** difficult for students. *Reasonably* is boldfaced and underlined because it is very important to make expectations high but attainable. Eighth graders should be required to write seven to ten sentence paragraphs with topic sentences, supporting details, and a concluding sentence. A twelfth grader, on the other hand, should be learning to write a longer, more involved essay. The task to be performed should be one that can be done by age-mates. Thus, one can see that the older the LDP students, the more difficult the task of helping them to reach their age-appropriate performance levels. The older LDP students will usually develop the skills required at the younger stages more rapidly because they will often already have the skills in their primary language. The skills will transfer from L1 into English. But, if the students do not possess these skills in their primary language, it will take a little longer to build up the background skills necessary for their more difficult age-appropriate skills. As teachers we must be ever-conscious of the difficulty level of the tasks we ask our students to perform, always looking for ways to "stretch" the skills the students already possess and leading them to the possession of the full range of age-appropriate language skills.

Humor is another extremely important factor in an interesting, exciting, and effective classroom. Causing others to laugh is a skill that can be developed by compiling a file of humorous examples to use in the classroom and by practicing them in the classroom. Use of humor will lower the anxiety of the LDP students and thus increase their chances for success. In teaching homonyms, there are ample chances for humor to enter the lessons. Save the best examples from your students' work as models for use in the following semesters' classes. Another possible activity is reading humorous columnists such as Erma Bombeck, Art Buchwald, and Andy Rooney. These can give students and teachers alike a much needed boost. Both silent and oral reading skills can be enhanced through humor. Depending on the students' abilities, they can do silent reading of Mad Magazine, Bill Cosby, or Mark Twain and then report on the articles they have read as proof of comprehension. As an oral reading exercise, students can perform dialogues of famous comedy routines, such as the "Who's on First" routine of Abbott and Costello. This will strengthen their oral reading ability. Thus, it can be seen that humor does play a role in a success-driven reading classroom.

An interesting way to mix humor with modeling is to

keep a file of some of the writing exercises your students do through the semester and then periodically allow them to review their former work. (If you keep the files, it is a safer bet that they will not disappear. This has worked well with tenth and eleventh graders. When they looked at their first attempts, they would start to giggle and laugh at their earlier errors. But then they realized how much they were progressing, because they saw how they had started to write topic sentences and supporting details. It was a real eye-opener for them. They could *see* evidence of their growth in the area of writing. They could tell that learning is a process! There was humor, but also learning.

Equal-status activities are tasks that require two-way, cooperative interactions between and among learners. Examples of such activities include reciprocal peer tutoring, inclusion of students' interests and experiences as part of the curriculum, and instructional and testing practices. Making the students the center of active learning will increase the motivation to learn; locus-of-control moves toward the students. They will experience an increase in their effectiveness at learning and, thus, be more willing to take part in the activities that are mutually planned. In reading/literature classes, students should work with each other in activities that require all parties to provide necessary information for the proper completion of tasks. Cross-cultural activities in which each student must explain something about his or her own culture offer ample opportunities for equal-status cooperative interactions. For example, if students are required to gather information on the status of women in different cultures, they need to work with students of other cultures to obtain the information they need. Each participant has some necessary information for the others involved in the activity. Therefore, each is operating as an equal in the activity. In such situations, the English used might not be perfect, but when the other students solicit the information, they can ask questions to clear up anything that is unclear. This offers some unobtrusive monitoring and modeling for the LDP student—it offers a chance to communicate. Cooperative and collaborative teaching techniques offer many opportunities for equal status interactions between students. This leads us to the next important element in "Sheltered English" lessons—cooperative and collaborative learning.

The benefits of **cooperative learning (CL)** and **collaborative learning** techniques have been identified and proven. When there is a positive interdependence plus individual accountability built into lessons and testing, both higher achievement and a higher retention of material is achieved than when students learn individually. Furthermore, the gap between high- and low-achieving students narrows from pre- to post-test in CL classrooms. By discussing and reflecting on how well they worked together as a group and setting goals for improving their collaborative efforts, students are able to increase even more radically their achievement and retention of material over those who study individually or cooperatively without reflecting on the process. [S. Yager, R. Johnson, D. Johnson, and B. Snider, **"The Impact of Group Processing on Achievement in Cooperative Learning Groups."** *The Journal of Social Psychology,* Volume 126, 1986, pages 389–397.] All students benefit from using CL strategies, but even more importantly, the low-achieving students do better. This fact suggests that CL techniques should be used in "Sheltered English" classrooms and other classrooms with LDP students in them. Both social and academic benefits are derived from cooperative learning activities. Every teacher's "bag of tricks" should include at least some CL techniques. In this introduction we will discuss and suggest five of the many CL structures available for use in a reading/literature classroom: roundtable, corners, numbered heads together, color coded co-op cards, and partners. These will be explained in the section on Cooperative Learning.

Sheltered English Lessons

A Sheltered English lesson should have the following components in order to meet the needs of the language-diverse population in a classroom:

Theme/Topic:—This helps to organize the thinking needed to learn the concepts.

Key Concepts—These focus the learning process on the main reason for studying the particular theme or topic. They also give an organization to the learning process.

Essential Vocabulary—This consists of the terms that are absolutely required to attain the key concepts determined for the lesson. This section can also be incorporated into the next section, the Set. Learning the vocabulary can also build some of the background necessary for an understanding of the material.

Set (T←→C)—Here is where the teacher finds out if the students have, and builds if necessary, the background knowledge required to make sense out of the key concepts determined for the lesson. Hence, the (T←→C) mark indicating an interaction between the teacher and the class.

Input (T←→SS)—Included in this section of the lesson are all the activities the teacher does with the students either in groups or as a class (T↔SS), in order to provide, in a comprehensible manner, the facts they need to start the learning process. Activities may result from the text, realia, audiovisual materials, etc.

Guided Practice (T↔SS)—In this part of the lesson groups of students should be interacting with the text, with the targeted vocabulary items, with each other, and with the teacher in order to practice their growing knowledge of the concepts of the lesson. At this point the teacher can monitor the students' progress and adjust the lesson accordingly.

Follow-up Activities (T↔S)—These include any independent activities that the students might do in order to practice the skills they have been developing throughout the lesson. This is a chance for the teacher to do a formative evaluation, to ascertain if the students are ready for their final evaluation and if they have met the objectives of the lesson.

Evaluation (T↔S)—At this stage of the lesson the students have had ample practice working with the concepts and vocabulary of the lesson. In sheltered lessons the students might be asked to show mastery of the concepts in a nonlanguage-dependent manner, that is, by making a collage, through role play, by developing a semantic map to answer essay questions rather than writing the essay, or by using previously developed semantic maps or outlines to write an essay answer. In this last case, the students should be ready to write essays. The method used to evaluate should match the stage of language development of the students, but must hold them accountable for the academic concepts they were to have learned.

Again we can see that a knowledge of the stages in language acquisition and of the corresponding activities that language learners are able to perform at each stage is invaluable to the teacher with students of diverse language backgrounds when developing lessons. Lessons must take into account the language skills of the students in both the learning and the evaluation processes. In order for success to be built into the lessons, *high* and *realistic* expectations must be set for the students. In this way students will be challenged in a meaningful manner and meet with success in both their academic and linguistic development.

Sheltered English: Summary

In summary, Sheltered English is a system of techniques that develop content-driven, activity-based lessons for students at their appropriate grade level and appropriate stage of language skills development. Teachers of language diverse populations need to develop lessons that have modeling of the targeted skills, have redundancy built into them, are age-appropriate, are not lacking in humor, and, most importantly, have the students working together collaboratively to finish the academic tasks. Developing lessons using the format explained above will help the students to focus on the essential material in a lesson and also help the teacher to keep track of what and how well the students are learning. Focusing on the essentials enables both teacher and student to work on developing the content-area concepts and the specific language skills necessary for their attainment. It gives both students and teachers a chance to succeed in the education process.

Now that we have inspected some of the elements of Sheltered English classrooms and looked at the parts of a Sheltered English lesson plan, it is time to discuss Cooperative Learning techniques that are useful in the reading/literature class.

COOPERATIVE/COLLABORATIVE LEARNING

The LDP Annotations of this literature series make suggestions for five different types of Cooperative Learning (CL) structures. These activities were incorporated into the annotations because the benefits of Cooperative Learning in education have been proven as a way to prepare our students with the skills they need for a productive and meaningful life. Today's schools have students with a socio-cultural diversity that was not as prevalent in years past. Spencer Kagan, a Professor of Psychology and a member of the Cooperating Faculty with the School of Education at the University of California, Riverside, has written:

> Changing economic, demographic, and [social] structures have led to a crisis in education, a crisis which is felt particularly in the domains of minority academic achievement [socialization] and race relations. And it is in these domains that cooperative learning has proven most effective.
>
> *S. Kagan*
> **Cooperative Learning Resources for Teachers**
> Laguna Miguel, CA 92677: 1987, page 11

Kagan continues to describe the "New Majority" and the achievement gap that exists between the old and new majorities.

By year 2000 the breakeven point will be past: over 53% of the state of California will be "minority;" Hispanics will be the single largest "minority" group in California. . . . And the New Majority is about to have a tremendous impact on public education.

The new majority does not come to school with the same values and background as did the old majority. Nonwhite students are not responding well to traditional educational structures. . . . [T]here is little or no difference in achievement scores at or near entry to school; by the end of elementary school nonwhite students are about half a grade behind white students in math and a full grade behind in reading. By the end of junior high, the gap had doubled . . . .

Kagan, 1987, p. 18

One reason that is proposed for this achievement gap is that traditional classroom structures are biased in favor of a more competitive social orientation. Hispanic students are more cooperative in their social orientation, and there is evidence to show that they and all other students have achievement gains in cooperative classrooms over traditional competitive ones. Educators should attempt to best meet the educational needs of all our students so that they can cope with the demands of an increasingly interdependent social and economic world. Include some Cooperative Learning experiences in your classrooms, and you will help in the endeavor to close the education gap.

Some comments on Cooperative Learning by sixth graders may help to illustrate how students view Cooperative Learning: one member of the team *The Smart Dudes* defines Cooperative Learning as "a way that makes it easier to learn and work because you do these things in a group of people, which is faster and funner [sic]"; an insightful member of *The Brainy Bunch* states, "Cooperative learning is being trusted enough by your teacher." Thus, it is apparent that more than just learning academic material is achieved by using CL techniques in the classroom.

The Cooperative/Collaborative Learning Structures

Included in this series are references to the following five CL structures. These five strategies have been chosen by teachers who went through a Cooperative Learning teacher training program with Dr. Kagan and Shelly Spiegel-

Coleman. We consider these five strategies among the most powerful to use and the easiest to implement.

They are:

1. **Roundtable**—a team-building structure
2. **Corners**—a class-building structure
3. **Numbered Heads Together**—a mastery structure
4. **Color-Coded Co-op Cards**—another useful mastery structure
5. **Partners**—the simplest of the task specialization strategies

We will now go through a discussion of the techniques and a reading/literature application or two of each. To reiterate, these five particular structures were chosen both for their efficacy and their ease of implementation. If you wish to learn further strategies, you may consult one of the books listed at the end of this introduction or another book on the subject. A further suggestion is to look for a Cooperative Learning workshop in your area. In such a workshop, you can be instructed personally in the "ins and outs" of the process. Having another teacher at your school who is teaching a similar subject will help greatly, too, because you will have someone with whom you can bounce ideas around. When things are going well, there will be someone to share the joy; when things are not going so well, as does happen when we try something new, there will be an interested person to solve problems with. You can coach each other. This introduction is meant as just that—an introduction to some of the easiest and most useful of the CL techniques. Once you have tried some of the techniques, you will want to learn more. Let's look at them now.

1. **Roundtable**—this structure is most often used at the beginning of a lesson to get both content and activities going. It can be used in any subject matter, and it has the added benefit of providing some team building among the students. In CL activities the feeling of "team" is very important. Unless the students feel part of a team, they will not wholeheartedly enter into the activities. This type of activity also implies that the team can create more answers to the problem than can one person alone. Many students may feel that they will be at a disadvantage if they work in teams. A member of the *Gigglers* defined CL as "helping each other with classwork because four heads are better than one." The social and academic benefits of CL activities will become apparent to the students as they gain more experience in doing them. Give them a chance to

experience the *joys* and *difficulties* of learning together. Their lives will be richer for it. And they will thank you for affording them the opportunity.

There are two steps to a Roundtable exercise. First a problem with many possible solutions is posed to the class. An example could be to name as many emotions or feelings as they can in one minute. Or, if the selection being studied is one about anger, they might be asked to list ways in which anger is shown by people. During the second part of the Roundtable exercise, one by one, the students in their teams write and answer on a sheet of paper and then pass the paper to the next person on their team. Thus the name *Round*table; the paper makes the rounds. To insure that each student writes an answer and contributes to the team effort, the teacher can require that each student on the team use a different color pen or pencil. The types of questions that you pose to the students can very easily be related to the theme or period of the unit you are studying at the time. This type of exercise is well suited for the SET portion of the lesson, where you start students thinking about the topic or theme of the lesson.

You can also increase the amount of time students are permitted to work on the problem. They might be asked to engage in a roundtable exercise on the past tense verbs in a selection or even to finish a story for which you have supplied a beginning. Obviously one minute would not be enough time to finish such a task. One rule of thumb, though: It's better to give too little time than too much. You can easily extend the time allowed, if necessary. *Realistic high expectations* in an atmosphere conducive to learning freely will have wondrous results. Also, be sure to give genuine praise to those teams that have done well. You may wish to keep scores from day to day. The manner in which this is done will not be discussed in this introduction. You can refer to Kagan's book or another of the ones listed at the end of the introduction. Be creative with this structure! Allow the students to come up with some of the problems used in the exercises. You'll be surprised both with the creative ideas they come up with and the willingness to work in groups that will be fostered with this simple exercise.

One other note before we start to discuss Corners. Team spirit will be greatly aided by having team names. The process for such an activity is to tell the student teams that there are only three rules in picking a name: the name must be positive, all members must have a say in the process, and all members must consent to the name. In this way a team unity is beginning to form in the process of finding a name for the members. In summation, round-table exercises can be used as a team identity builder and as an anticipatory set for a lesson. It is a very strong CL structure, with many applications.

2. Corners is a class-building structure. When teacher and students talk about "our" classroom, it is a positive step toward building a class identity. A class project that is shared with other classes is one way to accomplish this. Another way is by having students make choices. In Corners, the teacher names up to four possibilities for students to choose from and then designates a corner of the room for each possible choice. The students go to the corner of the room corresponding to their selection from among choices posed by the teacher. An example might help to illustrate: the topic is individual preferences and the teacher tells the students to go to corner one if they like vanilla ice cream best, corner two for chocolate, corner three for strawberry, and corner four for mint chocolate chip ice cream. It is usual to have four choices in this activity because a classroom traditionally has four corners. The students are given some time to make their decision and once in their corners, students discuss with a partner the reasons for their choices. A sampling of each corner's students is polled so that all the class hears some of the reasons for all of the choices. Then the teacher will ask some students to paraphrase the responses of the other corners' choices. This activity offers many chances for active listening and speaking—a necessary element of lessons for the language diverse students.

Let's not take an example for a reading/literature class. Your class has read the selection *Moby Dick* and has discussed the story elements of setting, protagonist, antagonist, and conflict. Ask the students to go to the corner representing the most important element of *Moby Dick*. Students are to discuss with partners the reasons for their choices. This would take about three to five minutes. Then choose one or two students from each corner to paraphrase their partners' reasons. The teacher or a student can keep notes on the board for later use in a related writing exercise. In this way, all students will hear the reasons others thought differently from themselves. You may also wish to have students from different corners paraphrase the responses of one of the other corners, again requiring active listening.

After this exercise students could then start mapping or clustering as a prewriting exercise. They should have a fairly good idea of where they stand on the topic of Moby Dick's most important story element(s) and be able to give some support for their choice(s). The Corners exercise has modeled what is expected of the students.

3. Numbered Heads Together is a chance for all students to help each other review and master facts and information that have been worked on in class through direct instruction or with written material. All members of the teams should have a number from 1 to 4. The teacher then asks a question of the class and tells them they have a certain amount of time for all the students to know the answer (individual accountability). The students then put their heads together to make sure that everyone on the team has a correct answer to the question (positive interdependence). At the end of the time limit (Be sure not to give too much time!), the teacher randomly calls a number and all students with that number raise their hands to answer. A spinning wheel or a four-sided die (available from any toy store that sells *Dungeons and Dragons*) makes the activity more gamelike and frees the teacher from the possibility of being biased in calling the numbers. The teacher then judges whose hand went up first and calls on that student for the answer. If there is more than one correct answer, other students with the same number should be given the chance to suggest them. A point system can be used to reward each right answer and an appropriate praise given to the best team overall.

A variation of the activity is Simultaneous Numbered Heads Together. All steps are the same until it is time to answer the question. The number is called and all the students with that number are allowed a chance to answer at the same time (simultaneously): coming up to the board and writing the answer; holding thumbs up for yes and thumbs down for no; or writing the answer on a piece of paper and then holding it up for the teacher to see. In this way there is more activity and more students are involved in the process.

Let's take an example. The class had read a selection of five or six poems on different types of love. Convergent questions might be to name the title and author of the poem that dealt with the love between mother and child or between best friends. These would be easily done using the Simultaneous Numbered Heads Together because the answers would be short and easy to write down on the board or a piece of paper. It could also be done as a true-false type of question where the persons whose number was called would hold thumbs up or down according to whether the title and author matched correctly or the theme was correct or not. The time given to answer these would not be as long as if the questions were divergent, allowing for more variation in the answers.

Some divergent questions to pose for this material would be to suggest what type of person would appreciate the poem about mother-child love and why that person would think so. Again, if teams have an answer different from the first one, they should be given a chance to offer it. The idea here is to generate thinking and speaking about the topic, **not** to find one right answer. A good mix of convergent and divergent questions will enable students of all linguistic abilities to answer the questions correctly, thus keeping them a part of the class. The key is to keep things going, keep things lively. This activity is useful as a way to review material the day before a test or quiz. With an activity like this as a review, you will find that more students will "have a handle" on the material. Their teammates will have helped them to master the information.

4. Color-Coded Co-op Cards is another mastery structure that is quite helpful to students in memorizing basic facts and information they need to know. The Color-Coded Co-op Cards strategy provides a method to attain a strong information base from which students can go on to higher level thinking; applying, analyzing, synthesizing, and evaluating the information to come up with new knowledge applicable to their lives.

The following is a condensed version of Kagan's Color-Coded Co-op Cards structure. No attempt is made to discuss all the elements of the structure. This introduction does not allow for a full-scale explanation of the technique. The essential elements, however, have been culled from the complete structure and are written here.

Students take a pretest on the material for the unit and then make cards for the items they missed on the pretest, putting the question on front and the answer on the back. Each student on the team uses a card of a different color or marks the corners of the cards with his or her special color so that it is easy to separate them when they are mixed. The flash card game now starts. There are three rounds to this part of the activity: the Maximum Cues, the Few Cues, and the No Cues rounds. The students partner off, with one half of them becoming the tutors and the other half the tutees. The tutees hand over five of their cards to the tutors who then show and read the front and then the backs of the cards to the tutees. The tutor then turns the card around and asks for the back. Ninety percent of the answers should be correct since short-term memory is being used. Praise is given for correct answers, and the card is won back by the tutee. If a wrong answer or no answer is given by the tutee, the tutor and tutee work together to find a way for the tutee to remember the correct answer. The card is placed back in the pile for another run. Once all five cards are won back, roles are reversed. (If students missed less than five words on the pretest, they should work on special bonus vocabulary. Everyone has space to grow.)

Round two, Few Cues, starts after both of the students have won back their five cards. The same basic rules are followed this time, but fewer cues are given—perhaps only the fronts of the cards are read, and the backs must be given by the tutee from long-term memory. A correct answer will bring about a praise and the return of the card. (Encourage students to exaggerate and be creative with their praises; for example, George Bush will be asking for you to join his Cabinet as Secretary of Education.) An incorrect answer will mean that some help to master that piece of information is given by the tutor. Again, once tutee #1 wins back all the cards, the roles reverse.

In Round three no visual cues are given to the tutee. The vocabulary word or the term is read out by the tutor and the tutee must then give the answer. The same rules prevail, with praise or help given after each answer. After this round, the students should be ready for a practice test on the material, and again the missed items should be practiced, following the above steps preparing them for the final test on the facts and information. Special recognition should be given to teams that do well. With your class you can decide what the criteria for doing well should be. Perhaps teams that have all members score 80 percent or better on the final test will receive a 5 percent bonus on the test or some other academic or social recognition. The recognition can be as simple as you wish (e.g., all students applauding for the teams that deserve praise), but it is important to reward the students for their positive achievements.

Using the Color-Coded Co-op Cards is very useful in a classroom with LDP students because it focuses students' attention on their most needed work, it gives students immediate feedback regarding their improvement, and it makes the memorization process a more interesting drill. The co-op cards exercise should be done over the period of a few days rather than in one period. This encourages a better retention of the material. It also gives an opportunity for extra work on the information at home. It would be helpful if the students kept one large and two smaller

envelopes to keep their co-op cards in. One of the two smaller envelopes should read "I know these" and the other "I'm learning these." Both of these then can be kept in the larger envelope.

In a reading class, Color-Coded Co-op Cards are extremely useful in the memorization of vocabulary. The vocabulary term goes on the front of the card while the meaning and/or the word in a sample sentence goes on the back. The learning of synonyms and antonyms is also facilitated by the use of the co-op cards, as is the mastery of the elements of prose and poetry, titles, authors, themes, etc. Using the Color-Coded Co-op Cards is highly recommended when teaching the vocabulary in this series. It will meet with success because it has varied rewards; it is multimodal—offering visual, auditory, and kinesthetic input; and it lowers the affective barrier and makes learning with a teammate more enjoyable.

5. Partners is the simplest of the task-specialization strategies. Kagan describes the strategy in a nutshell. He came up with the idea after learning about another new task-specialization structure that a teacher had developed. As he thought about Telephone, he mused:

> Why not split the learning unit in half, have two members on each team working on one part, the other two working on the other part, and afterwards have them teach each other. The pairs or partners could sit on opposite sides of the rooms. As soon as we tried this, an exciting possibility opened up—the partners, sitting next to partners from other teams working on the same material could consult each other. Thus Partners was born.
>
> I especially like the process: Barbara who had trained with me trained Carol who in turn came up with a structure which led me to a new structure.
>
> *Kagan, 1987, p. 184*

Let's now take a look at the Partner's process. Team members are split up into partners. A high- and a low-achieving member can be partnered. There will be two A partners and two B partners per team. The assignment is explained to the class, with each partner responsible for either section A or B of the assignment. The class then divides into two camps, section A and section B, whereupon the materials are distributed to the individuals. The students work on their assignments and consult with other students with the same work to do. Once the work is done, the partners decide how best to present the material to their teammates. They must analyze the material and decide on a teaching strategy to use. They also must figure out a way to determine if their teammates are understanding their presentation. After this stage, the teammates reunite and the teaching occurs—Partners A teaching Partners B and vice versa. After the teaching, there is time for quizzing and tutoring of the teammates. When this is completed, it is suggested that the teams take a look at how they did as teachers and how they could do a better job the next time. Then the students are ready for their individual assessments. All the students must be aware that their partners have to master the material from their teaching. This is the positive interdependence that is fostered in the cooperative learning experience. The students help each other to gain knowledge for which they are individually accountable. The team members must learn their material so well that they can teach it to their partners. We know our material best when we have to teach it to others!

Partners is a very useful strategy in teaching literature. If a class is working on a section of poetry, the two different partner groups can analyze different selections and then report to each other. Or if the selections have many examples of alliteration and onomatopoeia, the two partner groups can each take one of these and look for examples from the selections. After students have seen semantic mapping done in the class, the partners can also produce semantic maps for different topics related to selections. Mapping is a very interactive way to check for comprehension and meaning. Main ideas, mood, main concepts, and essential words are all required to produce a proper semantic map. All the same-section partners can take part while they brainstorm to create the map. The semantic maps will help them organize their new knowledge and will also make them more familiar with the transitional words needed to connect the elements of the map, or cluster. Thus, we can see that the Partners structure lends itself to many uses. One is limited only by one's imagination. The teamwork makes the work lighter, covers more content, and allows more growth, both academically and socially.

CL Structures: Summary

The five CL structures that have been discussed here have been chosen for their ease of use and their breadth of utility. All the structures will create chances for students to show, try, tell, and do. Students will be afforded opportunities to *listen, speak, read,* and *write* in a context that will

have both social and academic consequences. Debriefing will allow the students the chance to reflect on their activities and decide what went well, what could have gone better, and what might improve their future performances. Isn't that why we're teachers? Don't we want to help our students to become the best they can be? Try some of the activities. Talk over the results with the students and with other teachers who are also interested in Cooperative Learning. Go to a Cooperative Learning workshop. Read up on Cooperative Learning. Your students will be glad you did—and so will you! You will begin to tap into the natural inclination of youngsters to take in information, explain, analyze, and conceptualize it, and then share their insights with their peers. You will be truly educating—leading out from the students, taking them to new places. Who knows to what heights they will climb?

LDP ANNOTATIONS IN THE GLOBE LITERATURE SERIES

Teachers using this literature series have a two-fold goal. They must work with their language diverse population in order to develop: **1.** basic English skills, and **2.** academic literary skills. Charles Suhor states that:

> the central job of the English teacher is to elicit from students language that helps them to shape and give meaning to their individual experiences and the experiences of others—others whom they meet in the real world and in the imagined worlds of literature.

> *Charles Suhor*
> *"Content and Process in the English Curriculum"*
> Content of the Curriculum
> *1988 ASCD Yearbook, p. 49*

The teacher is charged with the duty of helping students to process the content of English through proper oral and written language. All the language skills should be involved in the process, and by involving all the language skills in the learning process, we strengthen the basic skills for *all* students. The practice, the doing, of the language affords all the students opportunities to learn **about** the language **through** the language. Motivation will be high and success strong. The main thrust of lessons should be on communicative competence. Grammar instruction should focus on actual problems that are revealed in the students' work, and should be done in the later stages of the writing process. Students can be considered to know English if they can show over a protracted period of time that they can: **1.** take an active part in class discussions, stating their ideas clearly and logically; **2.** proceed powerfully through the writing process with some sense of style; and **3.** read for enjoyment and insight. In order to accomplish this we as teachers must

1. **build upon** the students' strengths and interests and also help to better their critical thinking skills
2. make extensive use of **discussions** in the process, using both large and small groups
3. give students chances to "**do**" English: to read critically and with pleasure, to state main ideas clearly in discussions, and to write with some style

The ATE of this Globe Literature Series is set up to give ideas to the teacher about how to do these very things. The **science of teaching** proves that these things are pedagogically sound practices. The **art of teaching** is what keeps many of us in the profession. The art of teaching is why some classes at the college level fill up on the first day of registration. The special LDP annotations are attempts to give some ideas on how to approach the content of the lessons for your LDP students. They are meant to be suggestions upon which you will build to make the lesson most pertinent to your students. Only you can provide the many opportunities that students need to become successful listeners, readers, speakers, and writers.

The sections of the ATE that are especially pertinent to LDP students are marked with an LDP in the margin. At least one special LDP activity per selection has been included. It is included after the *More About Vocabulary* section and is geared specifically to help the LDP students. Often it is a Cross-Cultural activity in which there will be equal status interactions between the LDP students and the English Only (EO) students in the classroom.

It is suggested that Color-Coded Co-op Cards be used to help students master the vocabulary for each selection. The *Reading Strategies* are also often especially marked for the LDP students with suggestions that will help them to better understand and interact with the material.

In the *Write About the Selection* sections the activities have often been modified so that the activity is at least partially applicable to LDP students. The LDP students should all be able to take part in any prewriting activities, especially those that are cooperative or collaborative in nature. Remember to "stretch" their writing skills by demanding work that is "doable" by them. Only you can monitor their

progress as closely as is needed to do this. You will be able to tell if their skills have reached a point at which they should be required to write a first draft of an essay or only a cluster or semantic map on the topic.

The special *LDP Workbook* has exercises that build and expand upon necessary background for the LDP students. Remember that **interactions** are the key to communication, and communicative competence is what we are trying to develop. Therefore, whenever all the students can be included in an activity, it should be done. Feel free to modify any of the suggested activities to fit your students' needs. Be creative!

OVERALL SUMMARY

Whom are we trying to help? This special section of the Globe Literature Series is written to help those teachers who have linguistically and culturally diverse students. The California Office of Bilingual Bicultural Education has set forth three objectives for programs that are designed for such students.

. . . Regardless of the approach taken, at the end of the treatment period, language minority students should exhibit: **1.** high levels of English language proficiency, **2.** appropriate levels of cognitive/academic development, and **3.** adequate psychosocial and cultural adjustment.

Schooling and Language Minority Students: A Theoretical Framework
Sacramento, CA: Office of Bilingual Bicultural Education p. iii.

Following the suggestions in the Introduction and the Annotations will give the students ample opportunities throughout the year to work on and accomplish these three objectives.

In addition these three suggestions are also pertinent to teachers of LDP students:

1. Learn where your students are in their progress in acquiring English proficiencies. In this way you can keep your lessons comprehensible and the learning anxiety of your students bearable.
2. Capitalize on cultural similarities and differences between your students. In this way all your students' lives will be enriched.

3. Attempt some of the Cooperative Learning techniques suggested to help build both the cognitive/academic proficiency and the language proficiency of your LDP students.

We at Globe Publishing Company wish you the best of luck in your endeavors. Remember, we are all on a road to success!

BOOK LIST

Dishon, D. and O'Leary, P.W. *A Guidebook for Cooperative Learning; A Technique for Creating More Effective Schools.* Holmes Beach, FL: Learning Publications, Inc., 1985.

Graves, N. and Graves, T. *Getting There Together: A Sourcebook and Desk-top Guide for Creating a Cooperative Classroom.* Cooperative College of California, Santa Cruz, CA 95060, 1988. (Although written for use in elementary classrooms, many of the activities can be adapted for older students.)

Johnson, R.T. and Johnson, D.W. (Eds.) *Structuring Cooperative Learning: Lesson Plans for Teachers.* Minneapolis, MI: Interaction Book Company, 1984.

Kagan, S. *Cooperative Learning Resources for Teachers.* Laguna Miguel, CA 92677, 1987.

Northcutt, L., and Watson, D. *Sheltered English Teaching Handbook.* Carlsbad, CA: Northcutt, Watson, Gonzales, 1986.

California State Department of Education. *Schooling and Language Minority Students: A Theoretical Framework.* Sacramento, CA: Office of Bilingual Bicultural Education, 1984.

PROMOTING COMPREHENSION THROUGH GUIDED READING LESSONS

by Josephine Gemake, Ph.D.

The scene is common in schools—teachers staring at blank pages in plan books, wondering how to make literature written a hundred years ago meaningful to students. Of course, there are no absolute answers. The Globe Literature program, however, offers broad, flexible, lesson formats that have been developed with today's students and teachers in mind.

Each literary work included in the program has been carefully selected and presented to expose students to the classics of their own literary heritage as well as the historical and literary environments that produced these literary works. Each work is preceded by a concise explanation of a literary element directly related to the work. As students read each selection, guided reading questions are provided for the teacher so that pertinent connections between the work, literary elements, and historical contexts are immediate and clear.

Information about unknown and difficult words is provided at the bottom of the pages on which the words appear. In this way students can learn meanings and pronunciations of words at the most relevant time possible.

Follow-up questions and writing activities have been designed to deepen students' understanding of the literary work and to help students identify the human themes that have made a work timeless. Students are encouraged to discuss these universal themes and to consider how they apply to their own lives.

Teachers' Editions are designed and annotated with similar attention to clarity, immediacy, and relevancy. Detailed support is provided for activities and discussion before reading, during reading, and after reading.

Before Reading: This part of the lesson builds the foundation for understanding and interpreting text. Students are given time to recall past learnings to facilitate development of new ideas. Traditionally, teachers lectured about political, economic, and social influences which shaped the authors' style, message, and intent. They also explained the literary significance of selections chosen for reading. While this information is still necessary for students to know, the emphasis on teacher as "information giver" has changed.

Currently students are introduced to a time period or a theme in literature, and then they are invited to become active participants in building requisite understandings. Through activities such as brainstorming students list what they know—or think they know—about a theme or a literary period. Their ideas are classified into categories and recorded on a graphic organizer.

Graphic Organizers are diagrams which illustrate connections among ideas. They may be webs, maps, time lines, arrays, or idea clusters. Graphic organizers visually display associations and properties of topics. When a class develops an idea cluster through brainstorming and sharing, active comprehension occurs as students dictate ideas for recording. The resulting diagram is a picture of the collective knowledge of the group on a topic. Students reach into their experiences and generate meaning as they develop the diagram. As students read assigned selections and learn additional, relevant details, these graphic organizers become more factual and grow in size to include new facts and details.

In generating and recording ideas for graphic organizers, teachers can take dictation from students, or alternatively, students can be divided into smaller discussion groups and develop their own maps, time lines and arrays. While building graphic organizers, teachers can introduce new or difficult vocabulary so that students learn words in relation to relevant ideas recorded in the graphic organizer.

Students need to have purposes for reading and analyzing selections, as well as basic background information. Students will be helped in their appreciation of selections by explanations that show how ideas and situations in literature reflect and reveal life at a given period. They can better understand how the literature transcends that time to record messages and yield insights about human nature and behavior still relevant today.

Another way of directing students' attention and building needed background information is the use of **anticipation** or **prediction guides**. Using these guides, the teacher writes statements about selections to be read. Students respond to these statements within predictions about what they think will happen in selections assigned for reading. Statements are written so that thinking is stimulated at literal, interpretive, and applied levels. These guides are not marked for accuracy of their predictions and ideas. This prereading focus enables students to think about topics and concepts and fosters purposeful reading as they judge, evaluate and change their ideas.

Prediction strategies can be used also in connection with learning logs and response journals. Rather than reacting to teacher-prepared statements in anticipation guides, students have time to preview the selection to be read. Then they record their own prediction statements about the selection in their logs or journals. These predictions change daily as students read and gain information. Some teachers ask students to write in their logs or journals questions about the selection chosen for study. Students generate questions about setting, mood, characters, problems, conflicts, episodes, climax, resolution and theme. Thus students can focus their inquiries on any of the major elements of narrative discourse in which they are interested.

During prereading time, strategies necessary for reading and interpreting selections are taught in specific directed ways. These lessons have clear objectives and students are told why it is important to learn the objectives. Teacher modeling through "think alouds" is an important part of the procedure in skill development lessons. "Think alouds" enable students to watch how the teacher uses the objective being taught to gain meaning from text. The teacher modeling which occurs in "think alouds" demonstrates appropriate, sequential text processing. This type of modeling is important because otherwise unexplained mental operations become accessible to students so they can then employ similar techniques to gain meaning from text. Students model their thinking under the guidance of the teacher in this type of reciprocal learning.

Finally, vocabulary necessary for reading the chosen selection is taught. Words which students must know to understand authors' ideas must be presented in relevant contexts so that students can infer meanings for them. One good technique invites students to infer a meaning for unknown words from text. Then, after a "guesstimate" of the word, this approach provides time for them to check their dictionaries for correct meanings. Students can be taught to use specific elements of text such as context clues to improve their inferences about word meanings. Graphic organizers are often used in vocabulary development to display synonyms and associations.

During Reading: There are several ways to guide silent reading for comprehension. In traditional directed reading activities, students read silently to find answers to questions posed by teachers. In this method, teachers divide selections into meaningful sections. Then, purpose-setting questions are posed for each section. Students are directed to read to answer the teacher's questions. Discussion follows silent reading as teachers ask students to provide information and opinions and substantiate their ideas by reading pertinent text out loud. Questions which stimulate inferential and critical thinking are preferable to those that require literal recitation of details, and discussion among students about answers is valuable. In these types of whole class lessons, teachers are responsible for guiding and directing thinking and explanation of text.

Other methods of guiding silent reading encourage students to pose their own questions about events and ideas in the text. In these methods, students working in small discussion groups of five or six list questions about the text. Next, students read to find answers to their own questions. In this way, students set their own purposes for reading as they use their questions to guide silent reading. To use this method, teachers must help students form relevant questions about text. Teachers can ask questions that focus on narrative elements and literary techniques used by authors to convey meaning. Students discuss and evaluate purpose-setting questions as well as answers to these questions in this method.

A third method of guiding silent reading encourages students to form hypotheses about ideas and events that will occur in discourse. Students make educated guesses about what they think will happen in the text. Small group or whole class formats are used in this method so that students interact and share ideas about text. First, students are asked to predict what they think will happen in a story. Next, hypotheses about story events are recorded on the chalkboard or on chart paper as students set their own purposes for silent reading. After students silently read the text, they discuss and evaluate narrative events, compare these events to their predictions, and evaluate and change their predictions. This approach mirrors the process mature readers use when they read text independently. Thus, reading progresses through several sequential steps for which students are responsible—predicting ideas and events that may occur in text (hypothesis setting); indepen-

dent silent reading to determine text ideas and events (information gathering); discussing ideas that occur in text and comparing and contrasting these ideas to hypotheses (hypothesis testing); evaluating original hypotheses and making new predictions (hypothesis evaluation and restatement). To use these methods, students must learn to use literary clues—foreshadowing, rising and falling action, genre elements, etc.—to anticipate outcomes. Once again, discussions are used to clarify ideas and evaluate thinking as students become responsible for directing their own reading.

A fourth method of guiding silent reading in purposeful ways requires that teachers prepare and write study guides. Study guides are used to divide reading selections into meaningful pieces. These guides set purposes for reading and direct students to the pages they must read to gather relevant information. Thought-provoking questions and vocabulary activities lead students through the selections and support comprehension. Guides can be written so that, as students answer questions and respond to statements about text, they are directed through the discourse in logical and purposeful ways. Questions and statements in these study guides should not only require literal answers, but evoke opinions and value judgments. These guides, although teacher-prepared, allow students to read and respond to selections at their own pace.

During reading time, lessons to build literary appreciation skills are taught. Pertinent portions of text are used to develop specific objectives. These lessons are brief and teach not only a skill, but through "think alouds," also teach techniques for applying the strategy.

Graphic aids such as story maps, time lines, and arrays can be developed to illustrate conflict, sequence of events, character descriptions, cause-effect interactions and other narrative dynamics. This way, students can see how discourse elements relate to one another.

Discussion in whole group or small group formats is used throughout the lesson so that students can share ideas and opinions about text and learn from their peers. These discussions have a particular focus, and students present their conclusions to the whole class at the end of discussion time. Discussion gives teachers and students the opportunity to share, clarify and extend ideas. In discussions, students share points of view and refine beliefs and opinions. Discussions have specific goals and purposes and relate to readings and assignments. In whole class discussions, the amount of student talk increases as the teacher guides, elicits and summarizes. Roles in the lesson change as the teacher changes roles from lecturer to reflective listener who provides insightful comments that enable students to clarify and change ideas. In small group formats, students rotate roles as leader and analyze questions about text posed by teachers or classmates. After forming summary statements, students reassemble as a whole group to share their responses.

Whether students keep response logs or literary journals, free writing that expresses personal ideas is as important as structured and purposeful essay writing. After recording their ideas, students are asked to share their written comments. As they listen to their peers' viewpoints, students hear that classmates share similar thoughts and feelings. Thus, sharing becomes less threatening as they realize that each of them has something valuable to share.

After Reading: After reading activities extend and evaluate ideas developed during reading lessons. Now, content which is important to retain for subsequent lessons is summarized and reviewed. Skills necessary for literary interpretations and appreciation are practiced, and mastery of these skills is evaluated through worksheets and tests. Attitudes and understandings emanating from readings are discussed. Vocabulary is recalled and reviewed. Generalizations about themes are made. Concepts and skills which will be transferred and used in subsequent lessons are reinforced.

After reading time is generally used for formal and informal evaluations. To demonstrate understanding and promote integration of ideas, students can compose opinion essays, prepare graphic organizers to summarize related ideas, write reviews, and talk about what was meaningful for them in the lessons. Students can demonstrate their learnings in a variety of ways other than traditional tests.

Comprehension monitoring skills promote the development of reader self-awareness. Students are asked to read aloud portions of text which are difficult for them to decode and interpret during independent reading. They explain why portions of the text were hard to understand and demonstrate how they worked with text to analyze discourse to create meaning. Common problems of word recognition and text interpretation emerge when hard spots are isolated and students are encouraged to reveal coping strategies. Students learn strategies for getting meaning from print. They also gain confidence as they realize that comprehension problems are not uncommon, and that these difficulties can be overcome with deliberate strategies.

Writing is an important component of every lesson. Students are encouraged to write reaction journals and response assignments. They are given time to note brief analyses of basic story elements of problem, characterization, climax and resolution as well as personal opinions and review of text.

In planning guided lessons, teachers must consider students' reading and thinking abilities in relation to the difficulty of the text they will be required to read. Complex sentences, sophisticated vocabulary and remote concepts create problems with comprehension and dampen students' interest. For this reason, activites which explicate text occur before, during, and after reading, and in whole class as well as small group settings.

In summary, there are many ways students can be guided in their readings of stories, plays, essays, and poems. Choice of methods and activities is related to students' interest and abilities and the difficulty levels of texts they will read and interpret. Students' learning styles and teachers' preferences for various methods influence lesson planning. The techniques described here will help students to develop comprehension skill. These techniques have the added advantage of being easily adaptable to existing curriculum structures.

SCOPE AND SEQUENCE OF SKILLS	UNIT 1	UNIT 2	UNIT 3	UNIT 4	UNIT 5	UNIT 6
READING COMPREHENSION						
Analyzing Information	✓	✓	✓	✓	✓	✓
Antagonist						
Author's Purpose	✓	✓	✓	✓	✓	✓
Author's Use of Language	✓	✓	✓	✓	✓	✓
Cause and Effect	✓	✓	✓	✓	✓	✓
Character Traits	✓	✓	✓	✓	✓	✓
Comparing and Contrasting	✓	✓	✓	✓	✓	✓
Critical Reading	✓	✓	✓	✓	✓	✓
Details	✓	✓	✓	✓	✓	✓
Drawing Conclusions	✓	✓	✓	✓	✓	✓
Fact and Opinion	✓	✓	✓	✓	✓	✓
Fantasy vs. Realism		✓			✓	
Farce						
Figurative Language	✓	✓	✓	✓		✓
Finding Evidence	✓	✓	✓	✓	✓	✓
Gothic Romance						
Humor	✓	✓			✓	
Implied Main Ideas	✓	✓		✓		
Inferring	✓	✓	✓	✓	✓	✓
Letter						
Main Idea	✓	✓	✓	✓		✓
Making Judgments	✓	✓	✓	✓	✓	✓
Oath						
Personal Response	✓	✓	✓	✓	✓	✓
Predicting	✓	✓	✓	✓	✓	✓
Protagonist	✓	✓	✓	✓	✓	✓
Sentence Meaning	✓	✓	✓	✓	✓	✓
Sequence	✓	✓	✓	✓	✓	✓
Speech/Oration					✓	
Summarizing				✓		
Symbols		✓	✓	✓	✓	✓
Using Experience	✓	✓	✓	✓	✓	✓

SCOPE AND SEQUENCE OF SKILLS	UNIT 1	UNIT 2	UNIT 3	UNIT 4	UNIT 5	UNIT 6
Verifying Conclusions	✓	✓	✓	✓	✓	✓
Willing Suspension of Disbelief						
LITERARY SKILLS						
Autobiography				✓		
Biography	✓	✓	✓	✓	✓	✓
Characterization	✓	✓		✓	✓	
Comparison and Contrast	✓	✓	✓	✓	✓	✓
Conflict	✓	✓	✓	✓		
Drama	✓	✓	✓			
Epigram						✓
Essay						
Fiction	✓	✓	✓	✓	✓	✓
Figures of Speech	✓	✓	✓			
Alliteration		✓	✓			
Metaphors	✓	✓				
Onomatopoeia		✓				
Personification	✓	✓				
Similes	✓	✓	✓			
Synecdoche						
Flashback					✓	
Folktales/Fables/Legends						
Foreshadowing	✓	✓			✓	
Imagery	✓	✓		✓		✓
Irony	✓		✓		✓	
Journal/Diary/Almanac	✓					
Mood		✓		✓		
Mystery/Suspense		✓	✓	✓	✓	
Myth					✓	
Nonfiction	✓	✓	✓	✓	✓	
Novel						
Plot Elements		✓	✓		✓	
Action						
Climax/Turning Point		✓	✓		✓	

SCOPE AND SEQUENCE OF SKILLS	UNIT 1	UNIT 2	UNIT 3	UNIT 4	UNIT 5	UNIT 6
Complication		✓	✓			
Conflict		✓				
Crisis						
Denouement/Conclusion/Resolution		✓	✓		✓	
Exposition		✓	✓			
Falling Action		✓	✓		✓	
Rising Action		✓	✓			
Subplot						
Poetry	✓	✓	✓	✓	✓	✓
Epic					✓	
Heroic						
Lyric					✓	
Narrative		✓				
Sonnets						
Point of View	✓	✓	✓	✓	✓	✓
Rhyme	✓	✓		✓		
Rhythm		✓			✓	✓
Satire						
Setting		✓	✓	✓	✓	
Style/Techniques	✓	✓	✓	✓	✓	
Surprise Ending	✓	✓	✓			✓
Symbols		✓	✓	✓	✓	✓
Theme	✓	✓	✓	✓	✓	✓
Tone/Attitude	✓		✓	✓	✓	✓
VOCABULARY/WORD ATTACK						
Antonyms						✓
Archaic Words	✓	✓				
Base/Root Words	✓	✓	✓		✓	
Compound Words			✓			
Connotation/Denotation		✓	✓			✓
Context	✓		✓	✓	✓	✓
Contractions	✓	✓		✓	✓	
Dialect						

SCOPE AND SEQUENCE OF SKILLS	UNIT 1	UNIT 2	UNIT 3	UNIT 4	UNIT 5	UNIT 6
Dictionary Pronunciation Key				✓		
Etymology		✓			✓	✓
Figurative Language	✓	✓	✓	✓	✓	✓
Homographs						
Homophones (Homonyms)	✓				✓	✓
Letter Sounds	✓	✓		✓		✓
Meanings of New Words	✓	✓	✓	✓	✓	✓
Multiple-Meaning Words	✓	✓	✓	✓	✓	
Parts of Speech	✓	✓		✓	✓	✓
Adjectives	✓	✓		✓	✓	✓
Adverbs				✓	✓	✓
Articles						
Conjunctions		✓				✓
Nouns	✓	✓	✓	✓	✓	✓
Prepositions				✓		
Pronouns	✓		✓	✓		✓
Verbs	✓	✓	✓	✓	✓	✓
Phonetic Respellings						
Prefixes		✓				✓
de-						
dis-		✓				✓
fore-						
il-						✓
im-		✓				✓
in-		✓				✓
ir-						✓
mis-						
non-		✓				
re-						
un-		✓				✓
Roots		✓				
Shades of Meaning	✓	✓		✓	✓	
Slang						✓

SCOPE AND SEQUENCE OF SKILLS	UNIT 1	UNIT 2	UNIT 3	UNIT 4	UNIT 5	UNIT 6
Suffixes						
-able	✓					
-acy						
-ard	✓					
-ation						
-ence		✓				
-ery						
-ful	✓					
-ible						
-ic	✓					
-ion						
-ish	✓					
-ity		✓				
-less	✓					
-ly				✓		
-ment						
-ness		✓				
-tion						
-tude		✓				
-ward						
Syllables	✓					✓
Synonyms	✓	✓	✓	✓	✓	✓
Technical/Occupational/Jargon						
Word Parts		✓				
RESEARCH AND STUDY SKILLS						
Dictionary	✓	✓	✓	✓	✓	✓
Encyclopedia					✓	
Following Directions	✓	✓	✓	✓	✓	✓
Glossary						
Reference Sources			✓			
Special Dictionaries		✓	✓		✓	
Thesaurus			✓	✓	✓	

SCOPE AND SEQUENCE OF SKILLS	UNIT 1	UNIT 2	UNIT 3	UNIT 4	UNIT 5	UNIT 6
PROCESS WRITING						
Prewriting						
Brainstorm/Chart Ideas	✓	✓	✓	✓	✓	
List:						
Actions/Events			✓			
Causes/Conditions/Factors				✓		
Character Traits			✓			
Characteristics				✓		✓
Descriptions			✓			✓
Emotions/Thoughts	✓		✓	✓		✓
Examples						
Explanations			✓	✓		
Facts			✓	✓	✓	✓
Ideas	✓	✓	✓	✓		✓
Literary Elements	✓			✓		✓
Points/Reactions		✓	✓		✓	✓
Priorities						
Qualities/Abilities			✓			✓
Questions/Answers		✓			✓	✓
Reasons	✓		✓			
Responses			✓			
Similarities/Differences	✓		✓			
Solutions			✓			
Words/Phrases			✓			
Write:						
Conversation						✓
Notes	✓	✓	✓	✓	✓	
Outline	✓	✓	✓		✓	✓
Additional Episode	✓	✓	✓	✓	✓	
Character Sketch						
Comparisons	✓	✓			✓	✓
Composition	✓	✓	✓	✓	✓	✓

SCOPE AND SEQUENCE OF SKILLS	UNIT 1	UNIT 2	UNIT 3	UNIT 4	UNIT 5	UNIT 6
Description	✓	✓	✓	✓	✓	✓
Dialogue		✓	✓		✓	✓
Essay			✓			
Explanation		✓	✓	✓	✓	✓
Firsthand Report		✓	✓	✓	✓	✓
Journal/Diary Entry	✓					
Letter	✓	✓		✓		
Narrative	✓	✓				
Newspaper Article		✓				
Oath						
Opinion	✓	✓	✓	✓	✓	✓
Paragraphs	✓	✓	✓	✓	✓	✓
Persuasion		✓			✓	
Play			✓			
Poem	✓	✓		✓	✓	✓
Review	✓			✓		✓
Speech			✓		✓	
Story	✓	✓			✓	✓
Talk-show Discussion						
Television Report			✓			
Timeline						
Writing Process (General)	✓	✓	✓	✓	✓	✓
Revision						
Include:						
Character's Thoughts/Ideas/Feelings			✓			✓
Description	✓	✓			✓	✓
Details	✓	✓	✓	✓		✓
Dialogue					✓	✓
Literary Elements						
Observations			✓			
Quotations			✓		✓	✓
Reasons/Examples			✓			
Topic Sentences	✓			✓	✓	

SCOPE AND SEQUENCE OF SKILLS	UNIT 1	UNIT 2	UNIT 3	UNIT 4	UNIT 5	UNIT 6
Transition Words				✓	✓	
Maintain:						
Believability				✓		
Consistency	✓	✓	✓	✓	✓	✓
Clarity	✓	✓	✓	✓		✓
Proofreading						
Correct:						
Capitalization/Punctuation	✓	✓	✓	✓	✓	✓
Grammar	✓	✓	✓	✓		✓
Letter Form						
Paragraphing		✓			✓	✓
Rhythm/Rhyme						
Spelling	✓	✓		✓	✓	✓
CRITICAL THINKING						
Facts/Opinions		✓		✓		
Generalizations						✓
Inductive/Deductive Reasoning	✓					
Inferences					✓	
Observation						
Syllogisms			✓			
Themes						
CRITICAL THINKING AND DRAMA						
Adapting a Play for Movies/Radio/TV		✓				
Comparing and Contrasting Characters	✓		✓			
Interpreting the Effect of Imagery	✓					
Making Inferences About Characters	✓	✓	✓			
Predicting Outcomes				✓		
Recognizing Causes and Effects	✓	✓	✓			
Summarizing a Play						
CRITICAL THINKING AND FICTION						
Analyzing the Effect of Setting		✓	✓	✓		
Analyzing Sequence in a Story	✓	✓	✓	✓	✓	✓
Analyzing Solutions		✓	✓		✓	✓

SCOPE AND SEQUENCE OF SKILLS	UNIT 1	UNIT 2	UNIT 3	UNIT 4	UNIT 5	UNIT 6
Comparing and Contrasting	✓	✓	✓	✓		✓
Drawing Conclusions	✓	✓	✓	✓	✓	✓
Identifying Causes and Effects	✓	✓	✓	✓	✓	✓
Identifying Exaggeration						
Making Inferences	✓	✓	✓	✓	✓	✓
Making Inferences About Characters	✓	✓	✓	✓	✓	✓
Paraphrasing		✓	✓		✓	
Recognizing Relevant Details	✓	✓	✓	✓	✓	✓
Understanding Plausibility	✓	✓	✓	✓		
Using Narration to Draw Conclusions	✓	✓	✓	✓	✓	✓
CRITICAL THINKING AND NONFICTION						
Comparing and Contrasting Words		✓	✓	✓		
Evaluating Biographical/Autobiographical Subject				✓		
Evaluating Historical Inferences				✓	✓	
Finding Relevant Evidence	✓	✓	✓	✓	✓	
Inferring a Writer's Purpose		✓	✓	✓	✓	
Recognizing Generalizations			✓	✓	✓	
Recognizing Persuasive Techniques		✓	✓		✓	
Separating Details	✓	✓	✓	✓	✓	
Separating Fact From Opinion		✓	✓	✓		
Summarizing an Essay						
Understanding the Sequence of Events		✓	✓	✓	✓	
CRITICAL THINKING AND POETRY						
Interpreting Figures of Speech	✓	✓	✓			✓
Interpreting Sensory Words	✓					
Interpreting Symbols	✓	✓		✓		✓
Making Inferences About Theme	✓	✓	✓			✓
Making Inferences About the Speaker	✓	✓	✓	✓	✓	✓
Paraphrasing Poetry	✓	✓	✓	✓		✓
Recognizing Assertions	✓	✓	✓		✓	
Understanding Cause and Effect	✓	✓	✓	✓	✓	✓
EFFECTIVE STUDYING						
Analyzing Poetry	✓					

SCOPE AND SEQUENCE OF SKILLS	UNIT 1	UNIT 2	UNIT 3	UNIT 4	UNIT 5	UNIT 6
Encyclopedias						
Note Taking				✓		
Reading Techniques						
Reference Books			✓			
Remembering Information						
Study Habits		✓				
Test-Taking Strategies						
Essay Tests						
Objective Tests					✓	✓
SPEAKING AND LISTENING						
Character Talks						✓
Characterizations						
Extemporaneous Speeches				✓		
Group Presentations						
Imaginary Interviews					✓	
Improvised Dialogue						
Poems	✓					
Plot/Theme Discussions			✓			
Readings						
USAGE AND MECHANICS						
Conjunctions: Coordinating/Subordinating						✓
Modifiers: Adjectives/Adverbs						
Punctuation: Quotations					✓	
Punctuation: Word Series		✓				
Punctuation Marks						
Sentence Fragments/Complete Sentences						
Sentences						
Subject-Verb Agreement	✓		✓	✓		
Syntax						

G·L·O·B·E
LITERATURE

Robert R. Potter

 Globe Book Company
Englewood Cliffs, New Jersey

PURPLE LEVEL

CONSULTANTS

Barbara Benson
English Teacher
Watauga High School
Boone, North Carolina

Suzanne Chavez
Teacher
Palos Verdes Unified School
District
Palos Verdes Estates, California

Mariann Cholakis
Reading Specialist
New York City Board
of Education
New York, New York

Mary Contreras
Fellow of UCLA Writing Project
Rancho Buena Vista High School
Vista, California

Patricia Devaney
Reading Resource Teacher
Board of Education
City of New York
New York, New York

Ellen Flanagan
Principal
St. Brigid School
Brooklyn, New York

Josephine Gemake
Associate Professor
School of Education
St. John's University
Jamaica, New York

Francine Guastello
Assistant Principal
P.S. 312K
New York, New York

Margaret Haley
Reading Specialist/
Special Programs Instructor
St. John's University
Staten Island, New York

Nelda Hobbs
ECIA Coordinator/Language Arts
Social Studies Coordinator
High Schools of North Chicago
Public Schools
Chicago, Illinois

Barbara Milhorn
Los Angeles Unified School District
Los Angeles, California

Mary M. O'Brien
Reading Specialist
Head of Reading Department
Hazelwood West Junior and
Senior High Schools
Hazelwood, Missouri

Anthony V. Patti
Full Professor and
Chairman of Secondary
Adult, and Business Education
Herbert H. Lehman College
City University of New York
New York, New York

Evelyn Pittman
Supervisor of Language Arts
Paterson Board of Education
Paterson, New Jersey

Judy Rios
Secondary Language Arts
and Resource Teacher
West Allis—West Milwaukee
School District
West Allis, Wisconsin

Robert J. Scaffardi
English Department Chair
Area Coordinator (K–12)
Cranston High School East
Cranston, Rhode Island

Richard Sinatra
Director, Reading Clinic
St. John's University
Jamaica, New York

Beth Craddock Smith
Reading Specialist
Durham County Schools
Durham, North Carolina

Sheila Byrd Smith
Language Arts/Reading Teacher
St. Paul School
Staten Island, New York

Benjamin Stewart
English Teacher
Pine Forest Senior High School
Fayetteville, North Carolina

Judith E. Torres
Coordinator/Limited English
Proficiency Programs
Yonkers Public Schools
Yonkers, New York

Paula Travis
Language Arts
Department Head
Newton County High School
Covington, Georgia

O. Paul Wielan
Associate Professor
School of Education
St. John's University
Jamaica, New York

G·L·O·B·E
LITERATURE

BLUE LEVEL

Annotated Teacher's Edition
Teacher's Resource Binder

RED LEVEL

Annotated Teacher's Edition
Teacher's Resource Binder

PURPLE LEVEL

Annotated Teacher's Edition
Teacher's Resource Binder

GREEN LEVEL

Annotated Teacher's Edition
Teacher's Resource Binder

SILVER LEVEL

Annotated Teacher's Edition
Teacher's Resource Binder

GOLD LEVEL

Annotated Teacher's Edition
Teacher's Resource Binder

CONTRIBUTING WRITERS
Allen Gilbert
Marcia Mungenast
Steven Otfinoski
Kathy Welsh

PHOTO RESEARCH
Cover: Lisa Kirchner
Text Interior: Ouarasan
Unit Openers: Rhoda Sidney

COVER DESIGN
Marek Antoniak

FRONTISPIECE
Rocks and Sea, Milton Avery.
Bettmann Archive

COVER PHOTO
Big Ben, André Derain. The Granger Collection

ABOUT THE COVER
Big Ben, André Derain (1880–1954). In many of his paintings, Derain attempted to identify color with sensation instead of with objects. For the artist, color had to convey the emotional truth of an experience, not merely its appearance. Derrain's exaggerated color and the departure from natural drawing techniques aroused reactions from conventional critics and the public. His style marks the transition from Impressionism to Fauvism.

Printed in the United States of America.   10 9 8 7 6 5 4 3 2 1

ISBN: 1-55675-172-9

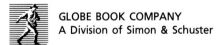

GLOBE BOOK COMPANY
A Division of Simon & Schuster

CONTENTS

Make literature a part of your life.

The Unit Openers will start
you thinking.

Discover the theme or time period
in the exciting unit opener.

Fine art suggests the theme or
period of the literature
in the unit.

See how the quotation relates the
theme to your life.

Set the Stage...

Enjoy reading the best in classic
and contemporary literature.

Explore ideas about the theme or
period.

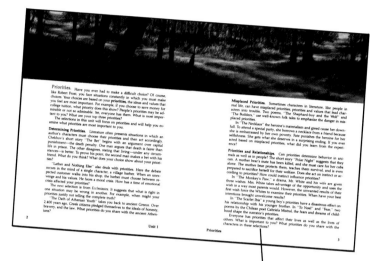

...For Active Reading

Preview the selections to see how
they relate to the theme.

Read actively with the help
of skills instruction.

Discover the characteristics of
literature by studying the lesson
before you read.

Relate the literary skill to your
own experience by using the Skill
Builder activity.

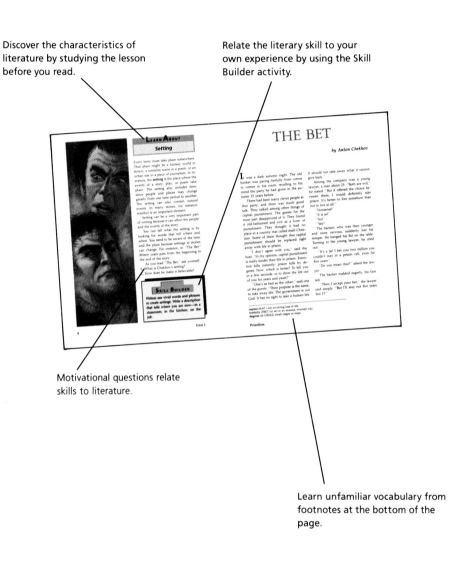

Motivational questions relate
skills to literature.

Learn unfamiliar vocabulary from
footnotes at the bottom of the
page.

...While Building Skills

Develop your skills with
creative activities.

Exercise all your thinking skills
with comprehension questions.

Explore the selection's meaning
by writing about it.

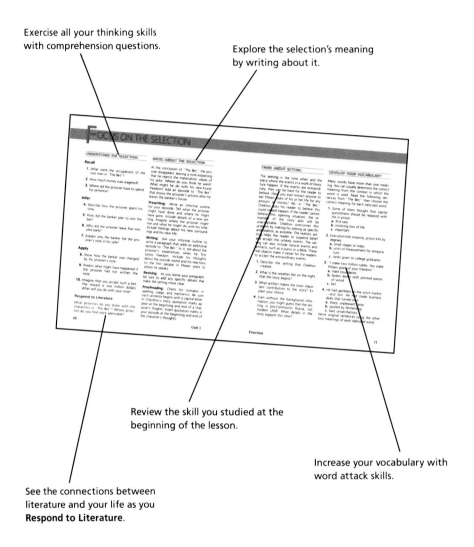

Review the skill you studied at the
beginning of the lesson.

Increase your vocabulary with
word attack skills.

See the connections between
literature and your life as you
Respond to Literature.

Explore Genres...

Explore the elements of fine
literature as you focus on
the genre.

Learn about elements of fiction,
nonfiction, poetry, and drama.

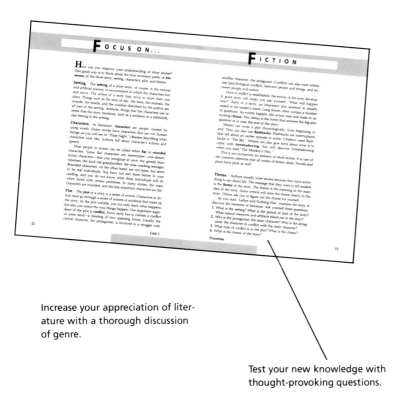

Increase your appreciation of literature with a thorough discussion
of genre.

Test your new knowledge with
thought-provoking questions.

Develop your reading skills
with study hints.

Master the steps in active reading
as you read the annotated
selection.

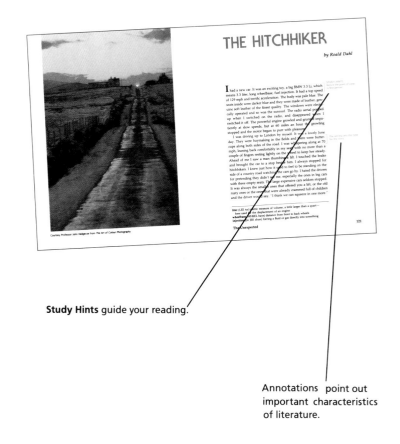

Study Hints guide your reading.

Annotations point out
important characteristics
of literature.

Review, Enrich...

Improve your language
skills with literature-based
activities.

Make language connections
through the Unit Review.

Explore themes and relationships.

Use the writing process.

Enrich your vocabulary.

Practice writing correctly.

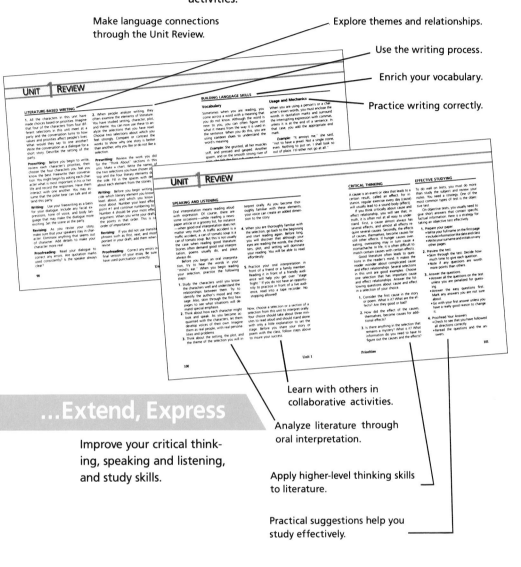

...Extend, Express

Improve your critical thinking, speaking and listening,
and study skills.

Learn with others in
collaborative activities.

Analyze literature through
oral interpretation.

Apply higher-level thinking skills
to literature.

Practical suggestions help you
study effectively.

UNIT 1: Love

UNIT ACTIVITY

One of the selections in this unit, "Up On Fong Mountain," is written in the style of a journal. This provides an excellent opportunity for students to become familiar with keeping a journal and to try their hand at journal writing.

Explain to students that a journal is like a diary. It is a way of recording the events of their lives, as well as the feelings and thoughts that they experience. Point out that writing in a journal is similar to writing to a friend. Very often, problems and feelings become much clearer once they have been examined. Writing in a journal can also help a person decide what is or is not really important.

Have students keep a personal journal as they read this unit. Encourage students to relate each selection that they read to events and feelings in their own lives. You may wish to have students write in their journals every day, or you may ask them to write only after reading each selection. The important thing is that the response to each selection should be integrated with the student's life and experience. Ask students to be especially aware of selections that seem to relate to their personal experiences. For example, a student who has just broken up with a boyfriend or girlfriend may find special meaning in one of the poems about ending a romance.

You may wish to allow some class time for journal writing, or you may wish to have students do their writing as a homework assignment. Some general questions that will help students in writing their entries include:

What is the most important thing that happened to you today?

Did you do anything today that was unusual or out of your normal routine?

What kind of mood are you in? Did anything happen today that caused you to have strong feelings?

Given the kind of day that you had, how did the selection affect you? How does the selection relate to events happening in your life right now?

Does the selection bring up memories of past experiences? What are those memories?

Did you have any other thoughts and feelings about the selection?

If your class requires more structure, you may wish to pose a question for each selection. Some possible questions include:

"The Love Letter"
Are you a sentimental person? Do you dream of finding the "perfect love"?

"Black American Folk Poem"
What do you think love is like?

"First Person Demonstrative"
Do you sometimes have trouble expressing your feelings? What do you do instead?

"What Is Once Loved"

"Spring"
Do you find yourself always trying to dominate a relationship?

"Up On Fong Mountain"
How has writing a journal helped you thus far?

"Romeo and Juliet"
Have you ever loved or wanted to be friends with someone who was not acceptable to your family or peer group? What did you do?

"Grey Day"

"Here—Hold My Hand"

"Finis"
How do you feel when you are separated from the people you love?

"Housecleaning"

"Where Have You Gone?"

Have you ever been the one to end a relationship? How did it make you feel?

"Where Are You Now, William Shakespeare?"

Have you ever lied about something and later regretted it?

"I Dream a World"

"Reflections"

What problems in the world, your school, or your community make you unhappy?

Ask the class to help you decide who should read their journals. In "Up On Fong Mountain," the teacher does not read the students' journals, but just makes sure that the assignments have been done. This is one option. Another option is to give each student a choice as to whether or not you will read the journal. Yet another option is to have students exchange journals with classmates of their choice.

After the unit has been completed, have students discuss their journal writing assignment. Did they find it difficult or pleasurable? What did they learn about themselves and the selections? Ask for volunteers to share one or two of their journal entries with the class.

"The Love Letter"
by Jack Finney   **(page 5)**

SELECTION SYNOPSIS

A young bachelor purchases an old desk and finds in it a secret drawer. The drawer contains a love letter from a young woman who lived in Brooklyn long ago. Although the woman is long since dead, the bachelor finds himself falling in love with her. He decides to answer the letter that she has written. After he answers the letter, he finds another secret drawer in the desk—and another letter that seems to answer the one he wrote! The young man writes a second letter, then finds another secret drawer. This time the drawer contains a picture of the woman whom he has come to love. The bachelor goes on a search of Brooklyn to find out where the woman must have lived. Finally, the young man finds the woman's tombstone at the cemetery. Inscribed on the stone are the words, "I Never Forgot."

The young man, who has revealed himself as quite a romantic, will never forget either.

SELECTION ACTIVITY

"The Love Letter" is fiction, but the time and place in which Helen Elizabeth Worley lived are real. In this activity, students will conduct research to gain additional information about Brooklyn, New York, in the 1880s. In preparation for the activity, you may wish to collect encyclopedias and other reference books, and make these available to students during class time. Or, you may wish to assign the activity as homework and have students do research on their own.

To begin the activity, ask students to imagine they have found a letter written by a young woman (or man) who lived in Brooklyn in the 1880s. They want to learn as much as possible about what life was like in Brooklyn at that time. Have students suggest some things they would like to know:

What did Brooklyn look like?
Was the population large or small?
What were the houses like?
What were the neighborhoods like?
How did people dress?
What kinds of stores and other buildings were in the city at that time?
What were the schools like?
How far did most people go in school?
What kinds of things did people do for a living?
What did people do for fun?

Next, have students list the facts that are contained in the short story, "The Love Letter." These include descriptions of the old Post Office, of Varney Street as a "typical residential street," of women's clothing that the young bachelor found in the library book, and the way Helen Worley was dressed in her photograph.

At this point, divide the class into small groups. Each group should decide how to proceed with its project, and what they want their finished report to be. For example, a group may decide that they want to title their project "Life in Brooklyn in 1880." They may want to include in their project a written report plus drawings and photographs. Another group may decide to give an oral presentation in which each group member talks about a different aspect of life in Brooklyn.

Emphasize to students as they work that they must verify their facts. If something in a reference book is suggested but not stated clearly, students must note that in their presentations.

Once the projects are completed, allow ample class time for them to be presented and displayed. Class discussion should focus on how all of the information that has been gathered provides a picture of life in Brooklyn in the 1880s.

"Untitled"
Black American folk poem   (page 21)

The subject matter of this poem is love. The message of the poem is that a lot of significant things can happen in life, but nothing is more important than falling in love.

SELECTION ACTIVITY

Have students work in pairs or groups to create songs and lyrics that reflect the message of this poem. Students can use the actual lines of the poem, or they can create their own lyrics. Tape recorders may be helpful to students as they complete their songs. You may also wish to enlist the assistance of a music teacher in your school.

"First Person Demonstrative"
by Phyllis Gotlieb   (page 26)

The subject matter of this poem is the unwillingness of the speaker to express feelings of love. An underlying message of the poem is that the speaker really *wants* to express her feelings.

SELECTION ACTIVITY

Divide the class into small groups. Challenge each group to create a dramatization of this poem. Students may find it helpful to realize that a lot of action is suggested in the figures of speech used by the poet.

"What Is Once Loved"
by Elizabeth Coatsworth   (page 31)

"Spring"
by Carole Gregory Clemmons   (page 31)

The theme of the first poem is that it is possible to hold onto what is loved in one's own thoughts and feelings. The theme of "Spring" is that when a person loves the second time around, certain things may be done differently—but that will cause the lovers to succeed.

SELECTION ACTIVITY

Both of these poems give advice about love. The first poem points out that the love a person has for another can never be taken away. The second poem talks about how one might approach a love relationship the second time around—especially with regard to struggles against domination and the desire to dominate.

Point out to students that the kind of advice given in these poems might appear in a newspaper column such as "Ann Landers" or "Dear Abby." Challenge students to create a "love advice" newspaper column, using one or both of these poems as the "answer" to several letters.

Have the class assist you in deciding how the columns will be written. One way would be for each student or small group to write the letters and answers for a typical column. Another, and probably more interesting, way would be for several students to write letters for another student "advice-giver" to answer. Yet a third way would be for each student in the class to write a letter; then have students randomly pick the letters they will answer in their newspaper columns.

When students have completed their columns, display them on a bulletin board. Allow time for discussion about the similarities and differences in the "love problems" that were written about. Also discuss the various interpretations that may have been given to the two poems.

"Up On Fong Mountain"
by Norma Fox Mazer   (page 35)

SELECTION SYNOPSIS

Jessie, a fifteen-year-old high school girl, begins keeping a journal as an English assignment. (Her journal entries make up the story.) At first, Jessie finds little except food to write about. But as she becomes interested in a boy called BD, she begins to record the course of their relationship in her journal. As Jessie and BD become better acquainted, she grows increasingly distressed at BD's insistence on having his own way in everything. Even though Jessie knows she may enjoy the dates BD has planned, she minds not having a voice in deciding what they do. The situation worsens, and Jessie and BD finally quarrel and break up. Depressed and bored after the quarrel, Jessie decides to get a parttime job in a donut shop. Soon after, BD turns up at the shop and demonstrates in comic fashion his willingness to attend to Jessie's wishes. They agree to be friends again. Jessie hands in her journal and receives a "Pass."

SELECTION ACTIVITY

Many of the events described in "Up On Fong Mountain" are humorous. Many of Jessie's descriptions are also humorous, for example, the way Anita's boyfriend dresses. In this activity, students will make cartoons inspired by various entries in Jessie's journal.

Begin by discussing with students the things that make a good cartoon. Some of these include telling a story or communicating a message, exaggeration, and humor. Students will understand these aspects of cartoons better if they can look at examples of clever ones from newspapers, magazines, or books.

Emphasize that a cartoon must tell a story or communicate a message. A person looking at the cartoon should be able to see at a glance what the cartoon is about. There may be a caption line or a "balloon" showing the words or thoughts of people in the cartoon, but these will be no more than a sentence or two. The picture itself must do the job of communicating what the cartoonist wants to say.

Also point out that a cartoon must be an exaggeration. If, for example, a student decides to draw a cartoon of BD with bare feet, the feet should be exaggerated in some way—either in terms of size, or by making some feature of the feet, such as the toes, very prominent. If an emotion such as anger is being shown, the body language and facial expressions of the characters must be exaggerated by huge frowns, great splashing tears, a mouth wide open in yelling, a large fist raised in the air.

Finally, a cartoon must be funny. It may not be a great joke, but it should make the viewer smile or chuckle. Usually a cartoon is made humorous by exaggeration, by the subject matter itself, or by the little "twist" that the cartoonist gives to the subject matter. For example, a cartoon of Jessie writing in her journal might show a thought "balloon" filled with cake, hamburgers, and other rich foods. Tossed carelessly on the floor might be a copy of the latest book on dieting. The cartoon is humorous because it says that, while Jessie would like to lose weight, all she thinks about is food.

After students have discussed the elements that make up a good cartoon, have them make a list of episodes or descriptions from Jessie's journal, which could be used in a cartoon. Some of these include Jessie's description of herself in the first entry, Anita acting as if Jessie does not exist when Mark is around, Jessie's discussion with BD about winking, the episode with BD's bare feet in the donut shop, and the day BD ran up behind Jessie and yelled "Kiss! Kiss!"

Make a class display of the students' completed cartoons. Allow time for discussion in which students can react to each other's drawings and the messages they can discern from them.

"Romeo and Juliet" (Adaptation)
by William Shakespeare (page 49)

SELECTION SYNOPSIS

The story of Romeo and Juliet takes place in Verona, Italy. Two prominent families, the Capulets and the Montagues, have had a long-standing feud. Lately, new violence has erupted. When the first act of the play opens, Romeo Montague is unhappy because he is in love with a woman named Rosaline, who does not love him. Romeo's friend Benvolio tells him not to worry—he can meet some pretty girls at a party being given by Capulet. Because of the feud between the families, Romeo must go to the party in disguise. It is at this party that he meets Capulet's daughter, Juliet. Juliet is supposed to marry a young man named Paris, but she is drawn to Romeo. Romeo and Juliet fall in love almost at once. They know, in a certain sense, that their love is doomed because of the family feud, but their passion is so great that they vow to go on loving. In the second act of the play, Romeo goes to see Friar Lawrence, a Catholic priest. The friar agrees to marry the pair, hoping that the marriage will end the fighting between the families.

The marriage takes place secretly, in Friar Lawrence's private room. In Act III, there is a terrible fight between the Capulets and the Montagues. Romeo's friend Mercutio is killed, and Romeo, in his distress, killed the Capulet who killed his friend. Romeo is banished from the city for murder and is thus separated from Juliet. Meanwhile, Juliet's parents tell her that she must marry Paris in three days. Juliet feels she must kill herself. Friar Lawrence, however, comes up with a plan. He tells Juliet that she will take a potion that will make her appear dead. Her body will be taken to the Capulet family tomb, and there Romeo will meet her. When the potion wears off, the two lovers will flee to another city. The plan goes awry when a letter from Friar Lawrence informing Romeo of the plan does not reach him in time. Romeo hears only of Juliet's supposed death and vows that if she is dead, he, too, must die. Romeo goes to the tomb and, seeing that Juliet appears to be dead, takes a bottle of poison and dies. When Juliet awakens and realizes what has happened, she stabs herself and also dies. When the parents of both lovers arrive at the tomb, they find that their grief is greater than the hatred that exists between their families. The feud is ended as Capulet extends his hand to Montague, and Montague vows to build a statue in honor of Romeo's beloved Juliet.

SELECTION ACTIVITY

In this activity, students will become familiar with the story and music of *West Side Story*, a musical that became popular in the 1960s. Many of the songs from *West Side Story* are still popular today.

If possible, obtain a video or rental film of the movie version of *West Side Story*. Show the film to your class. (You may need to do this over several class periods since the film is about two hours long.) You may also wish to borrow from the library the book of the musical, as well as a copy of the musical score, and a record or tape cassette of the songs. Your school music teacher may be able to help you obtain some of these items.

Explain to students that the plot of *West Side Story* is similar to that of *Romeo and Juliet*—only the setting is different. In *West Side Story*, Tony, of Polish descent, and Maria, a Puerto Rican, fall in love. They quickly discover that their love is doomed because their friends and siblings are members of rival gangs in New York City's Upper West Side.

Once students have viewed the film and have had a chance to look at the other materials you have obtained, divide the class into small groups. Ask each group to choose some aspect of *West Side Story* to use as a basis for a group project. Some possible group projects include:

1. A paper and/or oral presentation comparing and contrasting the setting, theme, plot, and characters of *West Side Story* and *Romeo and Juliet*.

2. A presentation of several of the songs from the musical, using instruments such as guitar or piano, as well as singing. This project could include teaching one of the songs to the class.

3. A dramatization of one or more of the scenes from *West Side Story*, with or without the music.

After each group has had a chance to present its project to the class, close the activity with a discussion about the timelessness of Shakespeare's plot, and how human nature seems to have changed very little in the last 400 years. Encourage students to share experiences they may have had in which they were caught between two families or groups who were at war with each other.

"Grey Day"
by Maya Angelou   **(page 81)**

"Here—Hold My Hand"
by Mari Evans   **(page 81)**

"Finis"
by Waring Cuney   **(page 82)**

SELECTION SYNOPSES

These three poems deal with some of the sad and frustrating aspects of romantic love. In "Grey Day," the speaker is sad because her lover is away. The speaker in "Here—Hold My Hand" is frustrated because verbal communication does not seem to work with the person she loves. The poem "Finis" speaks rather wistfully about a relationship in which two people have drifted apart—and one of them vows never again to love "overmuch."

AUTHOR BIOGRAPHY

Have students read the short biography of Maya Angelou on page 83. Then have students read at least a portion of Angelou's well-known autobiography, *I Know Why the Caged Bird Sings*. Have students write a short summary of what they have read. Since this book was made into a screenplay, it may be possible to obtain a film or video version that can be shown to the class. If this is the case, show the screenplay and then have students discuss the various events that were important in the life of this writer.

"Housecleaning"
by Nikki Giovanni   (page 87)

"Where Have You Gone?"
by Mari Evans   (page 87)

SELECTION SYNOPSES

Both of these poems deal with the end of a relationship. The viewpoint of the speakers, however, is quite different in each poem. The speaker in "Housecleaning" is the one who has decided to end the relationship. It is clear from tone of the poem that the speaker has no regrets and has not had to struggle very much to come to this decision. In "Where Have You Gone," the speaker is the one who has been left by another. The speaker is suffering a great deal and feels very much the victim. One can infer from the poem that the person who left did so very abruptly and perhaps without warning.

SELECTION ACTIVITY

Most students have probably listened at least once to a radio talk show. A popular format for these shows is to have a well-known psychologist or other expert in human behavior on the air live for a certain period of time. During this time, listeners call in and talk to the expert. Usually the purpose of these calls is to obtain advice about a personal problem. Most of the problems center around human relationships. Very often, the expert uses a person's call to give the audience general advice about a particular type of situation.

Divide the class into small groups. Tell each group that their assignment is to present a ten to fifteen–minute segment from a radio talk show. Encourage them to let their imaginations run freely. The only restriction is that at least one of the speakers in the poems in this selection must be used as a telephone caller.

Discuss with students how the two speakers represent two different personality types. For example, the speaker in "Housecleaning" seems to have no trouble ending a relationship, finding it as simple as cleaning out the refrigerator or sweeping the house. One gets the feeling that this speaker's life will go on as usual without the relationship. The speaker in the second poem, on the other hand, is a typical victim. She has been abandoned by her lover (whom she still loves) and has also lost out on at least part of her financial support. She faces problems that are both emotional and practical. It is likely that she will suffer for awhile before pulling her life back together—unless her lover returns.

Ask students to think about what each speaker might say when calling a radio talk show for advice. For example, perhaps the speaker in "Housecleaning" is being criticized by friends for being cold-hearted or irresponsible, and calls to justify her behavior. Perhaps the speaker in the second poem feels overwhelmed by her problems, or she may want advice on how to get her lover back. An interesting variation on the theme is the possibility that the speaker in "Where Have You Gone" has been abandoned by the speaker in "Housecleaning." If this is the case, she might complain that her lover acted as if getting rid of her were no different than vacuuming the rug.

Have each group present their finished talk-show segments to the class. An interesting extension or variation of this activity would be to have one student act as an expert who is on the air, and have other students spontaneously "call in." In this version of the activity, both the calls and the expert's responses would be unrehearsed.

"Where Are You Now, William Shakespeare?"
by M. E. Kerr   (page 91)

SELECTION SYNOPSIS

The Shakespeare in the title of this autobiographical sketch is a ten-year-old playmate of Marijane, the narrator. A bit of a tomboy, Marijane likes to climb trees and ride bicycles with Billy. But she also likes to play house with a neighborhood girl named Dorothy. The game is always essentially the same: The girls are preparing dinner for their movie-star husbands. Dorothy always prepares a dinner of meat loaf and mashed potatoes for Spencer Tracy. Marijane varies her menu and changes the movie star from time to time. All this is before the girls go to see "Brother Rat," starring Ronald Reagan. Both girls fall in love with Reagan, and the dinner preparations in the playhouse become tense. Both girls decide to write to Reagan. In hopes of getting a better letter than her friend, Marijane tells Reagan that she is crippled and has to go to his movies in a wheelchair. When Reagan's reply comes, Marijane's father learns of her trick. He forces her to confess her lie to her idol in another letter.

In this activity, students will write their own versions of the letter that Marijane's father made her write to Ronald Reagan. Students can work in pairs to create their letters, or they can work individually.

Discuss briefly with students some of the things that the letter might contain. Also remind them that it is being written by a ten-year-old child, not a teenager or an adult. The style of the letter should reflect the way a ten-year-old would speak.

After students have completed their letters, have them "send" them to a classmate to read. Ask each student to imagine being Ronald Reagan reading the letter. If time permits, you may wish to have students respond to the letters as they think Ronald Reagan might have responded to Marijane.

"I Dream a World"
by Langston Hughes (page 101)

"Reflections"
by Vanessa Howard (page 101)

SELECTION SYNOPSES

The subject matter of both poems is the many social problems that cloud our world. The tone of each poem, however, is quite different. The speaker in "I Dream a World" hopes for a day when things will be better—when all people will be free and when love will be in evidence everywhere. Although he sees the problems at hand, he also sees them as solvable. The speaker in "Reflections" is much less optimistic. If she hopes for a better world, she does not say so. She speaks only of the negative things that she sees: hate, sorrow, and war. She feels that the world is in such bad shape that it should run away and hide.

SELECTION ACTIVITY

Many social and economic problems affect the world in which we live. In this activity, students will choose a current social problem and determine some ways in which the problem might be solved or changed.

Begin by having the class suggest some important social concerns. These concerns may be local or national. For example, perhaps there is a crisis in your town because there is not enough housing senior citizens can afford. Perhaps your city is concerned about drug traffic or large numbers of homeless people. People all over the country may be concerned about terrorist activity and its impact on airline flights, or about crime, or about the lack of equality between people that still exists in many places. List on the chalkboard all of the students' ideas.

Ask each student or group of students to choose one social problem that interests them. Then have them complete these four steps.

1. Define the problem and its scope. This means reading newspaper and magazine articles or using current reference sources.

2. Find out what is already being done to eliminate the problem. This would include any laws that have been passed or that are pending, and any volunteer or professional organizations that have been set up to work on the problem.

3. Express your own ideas about what more could or should be done about this problem. How do you feel about what is being done so far?

4. Offer several suggestions of contributions the average person can make right now to eliminate this situation. This might include volunteering time, donating money, writing a letter to a Congressperson, voting for certain laws, or encouraging adults to vote for them.

Have each student or group present their information to the class in the form of an oral report. Encourage the class to respond to each presentation. Emphasize the significance of this activity by saying that it is important to identify problems and to be idealistic about their solution. It is also important, however, to take practical and informed action against a problem.

STUDENT READING LIST

Byars, Betsy. *The Summer of the Swans*. New York: Viking, 1970.

Davis, Ossie. *Langston*. (A play about Langston Huges) New York: Delacorte, 1982.

Fox, Paula. *A Place Apart*. New York: Farrar, Strauss, & Giroux, 1980. Paper, New American Library.

Kerr, M. E. *If I Love You, Am I Trapped Forever?* New York: Harper, 1973. Paper, Dell.

Henry, O. *The Gift of the Magi and Five Other Stories*. New York: Franklin Watts, 1967.

from Globe Classroom Libraries:

The Teen Years: If I Asked You, Would You Stay? by Bunting; *The Love Letters of J. Timothy Owen* by Greene.

OVERVIEW OF THE UNIT

Love is the theme of this unit. The selections—which include poems, short stories, a drama, and a story told through journal entries—are organized into the categories of "Love Found," "Love Lost," "Love for Friends and Family," and "Love for the World."

In "The Love Letter," a lonely New York bachelor finds "Ms. Perfect"—only she's been dead for many, many years.
Literary skill: point of view
Vocabulary: revise archaic words and phrases
Writing: an unresolved aspect of the story

An untitled black American folk poem compares love to a lizard, and warns of the pitfalls of falling in love.
Literary skill: rhyme
Vocabulary: words as nouns and verbs
Writing: a description of love

A modern-day look at what's expected when you fall in love is offered in the poem "First Person Demonstrative," the annotated selection in this unit.
Literary skill: tone
Vocabulary: figurative expressions
Writing: humor

Two poems, "What Is Once Loved" and "Spring" deal with the lasting influence of love.
Literary skill: metaphors
Vocabulary: contractions
Writing: abstract thoughts or feelings

A series of journal entries written for a high school English class shows the highs and lows of adolescent love in "Up on Fong Mountain."
Literary skill: the short story
Vocabulary: recognizing root words
Writing: journal entries

No unit on love would be complete without "Romeo and Juliet." An adapted version with the play's important scenes is offered here.

Literary skill: similes
Vocabulary: archaic words
Writing: a letter of advice

Love lost through separation or breaking-up is described in the poems "Grey Day," "Here—Hold My Hand," and "Finis."
Literary skill: imagery
Vocabulary: using context clues
Writing: images that express feelings

The poems "Housecleaning" and "Where Have You Gone" offer two different approaches on what to do when a relationship ends.
Literary skill: tone
Vocabulary: slang
Writing: a reply to a poem in first person

The short story "Where Are You Now, William Shakespeare?" takes a look at young love, this time from an adult's perspective.
Literary skill: more about tone
Vocabulary: homophones
Writing: a reply of friendship

The final poems in the unit, "I Dream a World" and "Reflections," present love in the real world.
Literary skill: theme
Vocabulary: synonyms
Writing: a poem in first person

Unit Opener

Looking at Love

How do I love thee? Let me count the ways.

—Elizabeth Barrett Browning

Birthday, Marc Chagall, 1915. Oil on cardboard, 31¾ x 39¼". Collection, The Museum of Modern Art, New York. Acquired through the Lillie P. Bliss Bequest.

UNIT OBJECTIVES

After completing this unit, students should be able to
- understand the elements of poetry
- understand tone and theme
- use context clues in defining new words
- develop further the plot or characters of a story
- describe abstract feelings in writing
- identify and use images
- recognize slang and archaic usages
- find homophones and synonyms.

Fine Arts Notes

Marc Chagall (1887–1985) lived nearly a century, and in that century profound changes happened in all aspects of life, including art. Chagall's style is linked with the modern art movements of Cubism and Surrealism; some of his works are considered the earliest examples of the latter movement. "Birthday" is an example. Surrealism gives free expression to the unconscious, and the viewer is asked to interpret the message behind the artist's use of unconventional forms. Is the man in "Birthday" swept off his feet in an expression of love for a woman on her birthday? How are we affected by his snake-like twisting? What does their kiss signify? Chagall, born in Russia, lived most of his life in France and the United States.

Teaching Strategy: Elizabeth Barrett is addressing her husband-to-be, Robert Browning, in the quotation opening this unit. What might the answer to her question be? How many ways are there to love people? Explore with the class various kinds of love: love for a parent, love for a boyfriend, love for a movie star, love for a pet, love for people suffering misfortune. Does the word "love" mean the same thing to all people?

AUDIOVISUAL MATERIALS

Love Letters (Metacom, Inc.), performed by Joseph Cotten and Barbara Eiler. A woman suffering from amnesia is saved by a man. Audio tape.

Love Tapes (Mystic Fire Video or Filmmakers Library), by Wendy Clarke, 1981. People express their feelings about love. Video tape.

The Cat Who Went to Heaven (Random House), by Elizabeth Coatsworth. Audio tape.

Dear Bill, Remember Me (Listening Library), a collection of Norma Fox Mazer short stories. Audio tape.

Romeo and Juliet (Paramount: Paramount Home Video), 1968; directed by Franco Zeffirelli. Video tape.

I Know Why the Caged Bird Sings (Random House), Maya Angelou reads from her book of the same title. Audio tape.

If I Love You, Am I Trapped Forever? (Random House), by M.E. Kerr. Audio tape.

Poetry and Reflections (New York, Caedmon), performed by Langston Hughes. Audio tape.

Looking at Love.

Why do writers always write about love? Why do singers always sing about love? Why does the U.S. Postal Service put L-O-V-E on a stamp?

It must be because love is a theme always on people's minds.

Do we know, however, what love is? The poet Elizabeth Barrett Browning obviously had an idea and was able to count the ways she loved someone.

Are we all so lucky? Does everyone find love? What happens when we lose love? Is love for friends, family, and the world a totally different kind of love from what is felt between a boy and a girl?

The selections in this unit are about love and its power over people.

Love Found. Are you searching for Mr. or Ms. "Right"? Jake Belknap in "The Love Letter" was, and he found her—only she existed in another century.

An untitled black American folk poem describes love as "a lizard" and calls it "the great fall." The poem is simple and direct, yet powerful.

Poet Phyllis Gotlieb knows she loves someone in "First Person Demonstrative," but she is unable to do all the little things people expect from someone in love. Elizabeth Coatsworth reintroduces romance in "What Once Is Loved," while Carole Gregory Clemmons in "Spring" thinks she will be more realistic about "second" love.

Do not be fooled by the title of "Up on Fong Mountain." It has nothing to do with mountains, but everything to do with love—as told in a journal a student is assigned in an English class.

A classic love story in the English language is William Shakespeare's *Romeo and Juliet.* An adaptation appears here. Romeo and Juliet are bound

by love, yet their families are divided by hate. Love is found, but also lost in death.

Love Lost.   When you are apart from someone you love, or love begins to unravel, it is easy to become depressed. Maya Angelou describes her feelings in the poem "Greyday." Mari Evans suggests a solution to the problem of not being able to communicate with someone you love in "Here—Hold My Hand."

Waring Cuney in "Finis" sees his relationship ending and warns that the next time he loves, he will not love "overmuch." In "Housecleaning," Nikki Giovanni thinks the way to end a relationship is the same way she cleans house. A relationship has ended for Mari Evans in "Where Have You Gone," but she feels lonely and hurt rather than confident.

Love for Friends and Family.   Shakespeare reappears towards the end of the unit in M.E. Kerr's "Where Are You Now, William Shakespeare?" However, this is not the same Shakespeare of "Romeo and Juliet." The subject of the story is love, but the characters are even younger than Romeo and Juliet were. As you read it, ask who the characters really love.

Love for the World.   The last two poems in the unit, "I Dream A World" by Langston Hughes and "Reflections" by Vanessa Howard, talk about love (and hate) between different kinds of people rather than just love between individuals. How do you translate your feelings of love for individuals into love for people of different races and countries? How can hate exist in a world where everybody talks about love?

What is love? Come, discover!

Looking at Love   3

New York Street in Winter, 1902, Robert Henri. The Granger Collection

LEARN ABOUT
Point of View

Have you ever read a story that seems so personal and real that you feel you know the characters first-hand?

Perhaps the author told the story through a character; that is, the author used the first-person pronoun *I.* Perhaps the story was told from the outside.

The position from which a story is told is called **point of view.** The **first-person** *I* is one of the most common forms of point of view. In this form, the author not only uses *I* but often takes part in the story's action. So, the storyteller is both "narrator" and "participant."

First-person writing can be very vivid since the storyteller is a character in the story. You feel you have a special view of what is going on, as in "The Love Letter," the next selection.

Point of view can quickly give a story a certain "feel." As you read "The Love Letter," ask yourself:

1. How do you know the story's point of view?
2. How does the point of view make you feel about the story?

SKILL BUILDER

Think of something interesting or amusing that happened to you today. Write three sentences telling about it. Use the first-person point of view.

4

Unit 1

T4

The
LOVE LETTER

ADAPTED   *by Jack Finney*

I've heard of secret drawers in old desks, of course—who hasn't? But the day I bought my desk, I wasn't thinking of secret drawers, and I know very well I didn't have the least premonition or feel of mystery about it. I spotted it in the window of a secondhand store near my apartment, went in to look it over, and the proprietor told me where he got it. It came from one of the last of the big, old, mid-Victorian houses in Brooklyn; they were tearing it down over on Brock Place a few blocks away. He'd bought the desk along with some other furniture, dishes, glassware, light fixtures, and so on. But it didn't stir my imagination particularly; I never wondered or cared who might have used it long ago. I bought it and lugged it home because it was cheap and because it was small. It was a legless little wall desk that I fastened to my living-room wall with heavy screws.

I'm twenty-four years old, tall and thin, and I live in Brooklyn to save money, and work in Manhattan to make it. When you're twenty-four and a bachelor, you usually figure you'll be married before much longer. I'm reasonably ambitious and bring work home from the office every once in a while. And maybe every couple weeks or so I write a letter to my folks in Florida. So I'd been needing a desk; there's no table in my phone-booth kitchen, and I'd been trying to work at a wobbly little end table I couldn't get my knees under.

So I bought the desk one Saturday afternoon, and spent an hour or more fastening it to the wall. It was after six when I finished. I had a date that night, and so I had time to stand and admire it for only a minute or so. It was made of heavy wood, with a slant top like a kid's school desk, and with the same sort of

---

premonition (PREE muh nish un) a warning in advance
proprietor (pruh PRY uh tur) owner

Looking at Love   5

Reading Strategy: You might ask students to reread Paragraph 3, focusing on the description of the desk. It is fairly exact, but make sure students understand what is meant by "a kid's school desk," "pigeonholes," "roll-top," and "scrollwork."

The Letter, Mary Cassatt. Courtesy of the Library of Congress

space underneath to put things into. But the back of it rose a good two feet above the desk top, and was full of pigeonholes like an old-style, roll-top desk. Underneath the pigeonholes was a row of three, brass-knobbed little drawers. It was all pretty ornate; the drawer ends were carved, and some fancy wood scrollwork extended over the back and out from the sides to help brace it against the wall. I dragged a chair up, sat down at the desk to try it for height, then got showered, shaved, and dressed, and went over to Manhattan to pick up my date.

I'm trying to be honest about what happened, and I'm convinced that includes the way I felt when I got home around two or two-thirty that morning. I'm certain that what happened wouldn't have happened at all if I'd felt any other way. I'd had a good-enough time that evening. Roberta Haig is pretty nice—bright, pleasant, good-looking. But walking home from the subway—the Brooklyn streets were quiet and deserted—it occurred to me that while I'd probably see her again, I didn't really

pigeonhole (PIJ un hohl) a small, open, boxlike space in a desk
ornate (awr NAYT) showy, or flowery
scrollwork (SKROHL wurk) spiral designs on wood or paper

6   **Unit 1**

care whether I did or not. And I wondered, as I often had lately, whether I'd ever meet a girl I desperately wanted to be with—the only way a man can get married, it seems to me.

So when I stepped into my apartment I knew I wasn't going to feel like sleep for a while. I was restless, and I took off my coat and yanked down my tie, wondering whether I wanted some coffee. Then—I'd forgotten about it—I saw the desk I'd bought that afternoon, and I walked over and sat down at it, thoroughly examining it for the first time.

I lifted the top and stared down into the empty space underneath it. Lowering the top, I reached into one of the pigeonholes, and my hand and cuff came out streaked with old dust; the holes were a good foot deep. I pulled open one of the little brass-knobbed drawers, and there was a shred of paper in one of its corners, nothing else. I pulled the drawer all the way out and studied its construction, turning it in my hands; it was a solidly made, beautifully fitted little thing. Then I pushed my hand into the drawer opening; it went in to about the middle of my hand before my fingertips touched the back. There was nothing in there.

For a few moments I just sat at the desk, thinking vaguely that I could write a letter to my folks. And then it suddenly occurred to me that the little drawer in my hand was only half a foot long, while the pigeonholes just above the drawer extended a good foot back.

Shoving my hand in the opening again, exploring with my fingertips, I found a secret drawer which lay in back of the first. There was a little sheaf of folded writing paper, plain white, but yellow with age at the edges, and the sheets were all blank. There were three or four blank envelopes to match, and underneath them a small, round, glass bottle of ink. There was nothing else in the drawer.

And then, putting the things back into the drawer, I felt the slight extra thickness of one blank envelope, saw that it was sealed, and I ripped it open to find the letter inside. The folded paper opened stiffly, the crease permanent with age, and even before I saw the date I knew this letter was old. The handwriting was obviously feminine, and beautifully clear. The letters were

---

sheaf (SHEEF) bundle

Looking at Love

7

Literary Focus: What is about to happen at the end of Paragraph 5? Is this foreshadowing, especially the last sentence?

Critical Thinking: As the narrator leads us through his actions step by step, in Paragraph 6, note to students that the construction of each sentence begins with "I" and is followed by an active-voice verb. The different construction of the last sentence breaks the "rhythm" of I and draws the reader's attention to the all-important drawer opening in the desk.

Literary Focus: Just when the narrator thinks there is nothing else in the drawer, he finds something. (Paragraph 7–9) The plot seemed to be going nowhere, but now, all of a sudden, there is a new development: the sealed letter.

Enrichment: Can you, or a student, write in fancy script on the chalkboard? (Paragraph 9) Few people today view handwriting as an art, but in 1882 it was.

perfectly formed and very ornate, the capitals, especially, were a whirl of dainty curlicues. The ink was rust-black, the date at the top of the page was May 14, 1882, and, reading it, I saw that it was a love letter. It began:

Dearest! Papa, Mama, Willy, and Cook are gone to bed. Now, the night far advanced, the house silent, I alone remain awake, at last free to speak to you as I choose. Yes, I am willing to say it! Heart of mine, I crave your bold glance, I long for the tender warmth of your look; I welcome your ardor, and prize it; for how else should these be taken but as sweet tribute to me?

I smiled a little; it was hard to believe that people had once expressed themselves in elaborate phrasings of this kind, but they had. The letter continued, and I wondered why it had never been sent:

Dear One: Do not ever change your ways. Never address me other than with what consideration my utterances should deserve. If I be foolish and whimsical, deride me sweetly if you will. But if I speak with seriousness, respond always with care, to let me know you think my thoughts worthy. For, oh my beloved, I am sick to death of the indulgent smile and tolerant glance with which a woman's fancies are met. I am repelled, as well, by the false gentleness and nicety of manner which too often ill conceal the contempt they attempt to mask. I speak to you of the man I am to marry; save me from that!

But you cannot. You are everything I prize; warmly and honestly ardent, respectful in heart as well as in manner, true, and loving. You are as I wish you to be—for you exist only in my mind. But, figment though you are, and though I shall never see your like, you are more dear to me than he to whom I am betrothed.

I think of you constantly. I dream of you. I speak with you, in my

---

curlicues (KUR lih kyooz) fancy curves
crave (KRAYV) desire
ardor (AHR dur) passion
tribute (TRIB yoot) an expression of appreciation
utterances (UT ur un suz) spoken words
whimsical (HWIM zih kul) humorous in an odd way
deride (dih RYD) make fun of
indulgent (in DUL junt) too kind to the wishes of another
tolerant (TOL ur unt) willing to accept views different from your own
fancies (FAN seez) ideas, notions
repelled (rih PELD) put off
figment (FIG munt) something imagined
betrothed (bih TROHTHD) engaged to be married

Unit 1

mind and heart; would you existed outside them! Sweetheart, good night; dream of me, too.

With all my love, I am,
your Helen

At the bottom of the page, as I'm sure she'd been taught in school, was written, "Miss Helen Elizabeth Worley, Brooklyn, New York." As I stared down at it now, I was no longer smiling at this cry from the heart in the middle of a long-ago night.

The night is a strange time when you're alone in it, the rest of your world asleep. If I'd found that letter in the daytime, I'd have smiled and shown it to a few friends, then forgotten it. But alone here now—a window partly open, a cool, late-at-night freshness stirring the quiet air—it was impossible to think of the girl who had written this letter as a very old lady, or maybe long since dead. As I read her words, she seemed real and alive to me, sitting—or so I pictured her—pen in hand at this desk, in a long, white, old-fashioned dress, her young hair piled on top of her head, in the dead of a night like this. Here in Brooklyn, almost in sight of where I now sat. And my heart went out to her as I stared down at her secret, hopeless appeal against the world and time she lived in.

I am trying to explain why I answered that letter. There, in the silence of a timeless, spring night, it seemed natural enough to uncork that old bottle, pick up the pen beside it, and then, spreading a sheet of yellowing old notepaper on the desk top, to begin to write. I felt that I was communicating with a still-living young woman when I wrote:

> Helen. I have just read the letter in the secret drawer of your desk, and I wish I knew how I could possibly help you. I can't tell what you might think of me if there were a way I could reach you. But you are someone I am certain I would like to know. I hope you are beautiful, but you needn't be; you're a girl I could like, and maybe ardently, and if I did, I promise you I'd be true and loving. Do the best you can, Helen Elizabeth Worley, in the time and place you are; I can't reach you or help you. But I'll think of you. And maybe I'll dream of you, too.
>
> Yours,
Jake Belknap

I was grinning a little sheepishly as I signed my name, knowing I'd read through what I'd written, then crumple the old

Looking at Love 9

Discussion: Do students understand Helen's letter? Review any new vocabulary, and, then, briefly discuss the letter's contents. The third paragraph is particularly important. Here, the role of imagination is addressed. Ask students, What is meant by the phrase "for you exist only in my mind."

Literary Focus: The setting—late at night—is used to create an air of romance. Under its spell the narrator explains what seems to be an irrational act (answering Helen's letter).

Critical Thinking: Compare the style of Jake's letter to Helen's. Only once does Jake "borrow" from her vocabulary, when he uses the word "ardently." Ask students, "Does Jake's letter seem out of place? Is there a mocking tone? Or is it totally sincere?"

Critical Thinking: (Paragraph 19) Again, the narrator sees a need to explain something; it's become a sure hint he's about to do something other people might find irrational. Suggest to students that he is asking the reader to trust him, to continue the story and to understand what he was thinking, feeling, and doing.

Enrichment: (Paragraph 22) The narrator is reaching back into his own past to establish a link to Helen Worley; the connection is an 1869 stamp he'll put on his letter to her.

sheet and throw it away. But I was glad I'd written it—and I didn't throw it away. Still caught in the feeling of the warm, silent night, it suddenly seemed to me that throwing my letter away would turn the writing of it into a meaningless and foolish thing; though maybe what I did seems more foolish still. I folded the paper, put it into one of the envelopes, and sealed it. Then I dipped the pen into the old ink, and wrote "Miss Helen Worley" on the face of the envelope.

I suppose this can't be explained. You'd have to have been where I was and felt as I did to understand it; but I wanted to mail that letter. I simply quit examining my feelings and quit trying to be rational; I was suddenly determined to complete what I'd begun, just as far as I was able to go.

My parents sold their old home in New Jersey when my father retired two years ago, and now they live in Florida and enjoy it. And when my mother cleared out the old house I grew up in, she packed up and mailed me a huge package of useless things I was glad to have. There were class photographs dating from elementary school through college, old books I'd read as a kid, Boy Scout pins—a mass of junk of that sort, including a stamp collection I'd had in grade school. Now I found these things on my hall-closet shelf, in the box they'd come in, and I found my old stamp album.

It's funny how things can stick in your mind over the years; standing at the open closet door, I turned the pages of that beat-up old album directly to the stamps I remembered buying from another kid with seventy-five cents I'd earned cutting grass. There they lay, lightly fastened to the page with a little gummed-paper hinge; a pair of mint-condition, two-cent, United States stamps, issued in 1869. And standing there in the hallway looking down at them, I once again got something of the thrill I'd had as a kid when I acquired them. It's a handsome stamp, square in shape, with an ornate border and a tiny engraving in the center: a rider on a galloping horse. And for all I knew, they might have been worth a fair amount of money by now, especially an unseparated pair of stamps. But back at the desk, I pulled one of them loose, tearing carefully through the perfora-

---

mint-condition (MINT kun DISH un) brand-new
perforation (pur fuh RAY shun) a hole, especially in paper

tion, licked the back, and fastened it to the faintly yellowing old envelope.

I'd thought no further than that; by now, I suppose, I was in almost a kind of trance. I shoved the old ink bottle and pen into a hip pocket, picked up my letter, and walked out of my apartment.

Brock Place, three blocks away, was deserted when I reached it. Then, as I walked on, my letter in my hand, there stood the old house, just past a little shoe-repair shop. It stood far back from the broken, cast-iron fence, in the center of its wide, weed-grown lot, outlined in the moonlight, and I stopped on the walk and stood staring up at it.

The high-windowed old roof was gone, the interior nearly gutted, the yard littered with splintered boards and great chunks of torn plaster. The windows and doors were all removed, the openings hollow in the clear wash of light. But the high old walls, last of all to go, still stood, tall and dignified in their old-fashioned strength and outdated charm.

Then I walked through the opening where a gate had once hung, up the cracked and weed-grown brick pavement toward the wide old porch. I brought out my ink and pen, and copied the number carefully onto my envelope: *972* I printed under the name of the girl who had once lived here, *Brock Place, Brooklyn, New York.* Then I turned toward the street again, my envelope in my hand.

There was a mailbox at the next corner, and I stopped beside it. But to drop this letter into that box, knowing in advance that it could go only to the dead-letter office, would again, I couldn't help feeling, turn the writing of it into an empty, meaningless act. After a moment, I walked on past the box, crossed the street and turned right, suddenly knowing exactly where I was going.

I walked four blocks through the night. I turned left at the next corner, walked half a block more, then turned up onto the worn, stone steps of the Wister postal station.

It must easily be one of the oldest postal stations in Brooklyn; built, I suppose, not much later than during the decade following the Civil War. And I can't imagine that the inside has changed much at all. The floor is marble; the ceiling high; the woodwork dark and carved. The outer lobby is open at all times, as are

---

gutted (GUT id) having the interior removed

Looking at Love　　　　　　　　　　　　　　　11

Literary Focus: Rich description is used to help the reader "see" the old Worley house. (Paragraphs 24–26) The house might look decrepit, but the narrator makes it seem romantic.

Reading Strategy: Can the class guess the significance of the Wister postal station? (Paragraph 28) It wasn't that conveniently located, so why would Jake go there to mail his letter?

Discussion: Ask students how *they* would feel the next morning if they had done the same thing. Foolish? Pleased?

Enrichment: The New York Public Library is, after the Library of Congress in Washington, the largest library in the United States. (Paragraph 32)

Enrichment: Columbia University, one of the Ivy League universities, is located in New York City. (Paragraph 33)

post-office lobbies everywhere, and as I pushed through the old swinging doors, I saw that it was deserted. As I walked across the worn stone of its floor, I knew I was seeing all around me precisely what Brooklynites had seen for no telling how many generations long dead.

I pushed the worn brass plate open, dropped my letter into the silent blackness of the slot, and it disappeared forever with no sound. Then I turned and left to walk home, with a feeling of fulfillment, of having done, at least, everything I possibly could in response to the silent cry for help I'd found in the secrecy of the old desk.

Next morning I felt the way almost anyone might. Standing at the bathroom mirror shaving, remembering what I'd done the night before, I grinned, feeling foolish but at the same time secretly pleased with myself. I was glad I'd written and solemnly mailed that letter, and now I realized why I'd put no return address on the envelope. I didn't want it to come forlornly back to me with NO SUCH PERSON, or whatever the phrase is stamped on the envelope. There'd once been such a girl, and last night she still existed for me. And I didn't want to see my letter to her—rubber-stamped, scribbled on, and unopened—to prove that there no longer was.

I was terribly busy all the next week. I work for a wholesale-grocery company; we got a big new account, a chain of supermarkets, and that meant extra work for everyone. More often than not I had lunch at my desk in the office and worked several evenings besides. I had dates the two evenings I was free. On Friday afternoon I was at the main public library in Manhattan, at Fifth Avenue and Forty-second.

Late in the afternoon the man sitting beside me at the big reading-room table closed his book, stowed away his glasses, picked up his hat from the table, and left. I sat back in my chair, glancing at my watch. Then I looked over at the book he'd left on the table. It was a big, one-volume pictorial history of New York put out by Columbia University. I dragged it over, and began leafing through it.

I skimmed over the first sections on colonial and pre-colonial New York pretty quickly, but when the old sketches and draw-

---

pictorial (pik TAWR ee ul) containing many pictures

12

Unit 1

Davis House, Edward Hopper. Collection of Harriet & Mortimer Spiller. Buffalo, New York

ings began giving way to actual photographs, I turned the pages
more slowly. I leafed past the first photos, taken around the
mid-century, and then past those of the Civil War period. But
when I reached the first photograph of the 1870's—it was a view
of Fifth Avenue in 1871—I began reading the captions under
each one.

I knew it would be too much to hope to find a photograph of
Brock Place, in Helen Worley's time especially, and, of course, I
didn't. But I knew there'd surely be photographs taken in
Brooklyn during the 1880's, and a few pages farther on I found
what I'd hoped I might. In clear, sharp detail—and beautifully
reproduced—lay a big, half-page photograph of a street less than
a quarter mile from Brock Place; and, staring down at it there in
the library, I knew that Helen Worley must often have walked
along this very sidewalk. "Varney Street, 1881," the caption said,
"a typical Brooklyn residential street of the period."

Far down that lovely, tree-sheltered street—out of focus and
distinct—walked the retreating figure of a long-skirted, puff-

Looking at Love

13

Discussion: (Paragraph 36) Ask students if they've ever felt this way: wanting to "walk into" a photo and enter a different era.

Literary Focus: Notice how the author again relies on the night to create a mood of romance. (Paragraph 37) All his "experiences" with Helen Worley take place at night.

sleeved woman, her summer parasol open at her back. Of the thousands of long-dead girls it might have been, I knew this could not be Helen Worley. Yet it wasn't completely impossible, I told myself; this was a street, precisely as I saw it now, down which she must often have walked. I let myself think that, yes, this was she. Maybe I live in what is, for me, the wrong time. I was filled now with the most desperate desire to be there, on that peaceful street—to walk off, past the edges of the scene on the printed page before me, into the old and beautiful Brooklyn of long ago. And to draw near and overtake that bobbing parasol in the distance; and then turn and look into the face of the girl who held it.

I worked that evening at home, sitting at my desk. Once more now, Helen Elizabeth Worley was in my mind. I worked steadily all evening, and it was around twelve thirty when I finished; eleven handwritten pages which I'd get typed at the office on Monday. Then I opened the little center desk drawer into which I'd put a supply of rubber bands and paper clips, took out a clip and fastened the pages together, and sat back in my chair. The little center desk drawer stood half open as I'd left it, and then, as my eye fell on it, I realized suddenly that, of course, it, too, must have another secret drawer behind it.

I hadn't thought of that. It simply hadn't occurred to me the week before, in my interest and excitement over the letter I'd found behind the first drawer of the row; and I'd been too busy all week to think of it since. But now I pulled the center drawer all the way out, reached behind it and found the little groove in the smooth wood I touched. Then I brought out the second secret little drawer.

The night is a strange time; things are different at night, as every human being knows somewhere deep inside him. And I think this: Brooklyn has changed over seven decades; it is no longer the same place at all. But here and there, still, are little islands—isolated remnants of the way things once were. And the Wister postal station is one of them; it has changed, really, not at all. I think that there, in the dimness of the old Wister post office, in the dead of night, lifting my letter to Helen Worley toward the

---

parasol (PAR uh sawl) an umbrella used as a sunshade
remnants (REM nunts) little bits; fragments

old brass door of the letter drop—I think that I stood on one side of that slot in the year 1959, and that I dropped my letter, properly stamped, written and addressed in the ink and on the very paper of Helen Worley's youth, into the Brooklyn of 1882 on the other side of that worn, old slot.

I believe that—I'm not even interested in proving it—but I believe it. Because now, from that second secret little drawer, I brought out the paper I found in it, opened it, and, in rust-black ink on yellowing old paper, I read:

> Please, oh, please—who are you? Where can I reach you? Your letter arrived today and I have wandered the house and garden ever since in an agony of excitement. I cannot conceive how you saw my letter in its secret place, but since you did, perhaps you will see this one, too. Oh, tell me your letter is no trick or cruel joke! Willy, if it is you; if you have discovered my letter and think to deceive your sister with a prank, I pray you to tell me! But if it is not—if I now address someone who has truly responded to my most secret hopes—do not longer keep me ignorant of who and where you are. For I, too—and I confess willingly—long to see you! and I, too, feel and am most certain of it, that if I could know you, I would love you. It is impossible for me to think otherwise.
>
> I must hear from you again; I shall not rest until I do.
>
> I remain, most sincerely,
> Helen Elizabeth Worley

After a long time, I opened the first little drawer of the old desk and took out the pen and ink I'd found there, and a sheet of the notepaper.

For minutes then, the pen in my hand, I sat there in the night staring down at the empty paper on the desk top. Finally, then, I dipped the pen into the old ink and wrote:

> Helen, my dear: I don't know how to say this so it will seem even comprehensible to you. But I do exist, here in Brooklyn, less than three blocks from where you now read this—in the year 1959. We are separated not by space, but by the years which lie between us. Now I own the desk which you once had, and at which you wrote the note I found in it. Helen, all I can tell you is that I answered that note, mailed it late at night at the old Wister station, and that, somehow it reached you, as I hope this will, too. This is no trick! Can you imagine anyone playing a joke that cruel? I live in a Brooklyn, within sight of

---

comprehensible (KOM pree HEN suh bul) understandable

Looking at Love   15

Discussion: Review any new vocabulary and discuss Helen's second letter. (Paragraph 41) How is it different from the first? Can it possibly be a response to Jake's letter? What is a more rational explanation for its contents?

Discussion: Does Jake seriously believe his letter reached Helen Worley? Why else would he write a reply? (Paragraph 45)

Reading Strategy: What do students think Jake will write?

Enrichment: The current population of New York City, including the borough of Brooklyn, is about 7 million. Brooklyn Bridge, finished in 1883, connects Brooklyn and Manhattan. It was a marvel of modern engineering when built and is still considered by many as America's most beautiful bridge. Brooklyn itself retains an architectural grandeur in many neighborhoods, such as Park Slope, Flatbush and the Heights.

Discussion: In his second letter to Helen, what does Jake reveal about how he thinks he "communicates" with her? They aren't really exchanging letters, are they?

your house, that you cannot imagine. It is a city whose streets are now crowded with wheeled vehicles propelled by engines. And it is a city extending far beyond the limits you know, with a population of millions, so crowded there is hardly room any longer for trees. From my window as I write I can see—across Brooklyn Bridge, which is hardly changed from the way you, too, can see it now—Manhattan Island, and rising from it are the lighted silhouettes of stone and steel buildings more than one thousand feet high.

You must believe me. I live, I exist, seventy-seven years after you read this; and with the feeling that I have fallen in love with you.

I sat for some moments staring at the wall, trying to figure out how to explain something I was certain was true. Then I wrote:

Helen: There are three secret drawers in our desk. Into the first you put only the letter I found. You cannot now add something to that drawer and hope that it will reach me. For I have already opened that drawer and found only the letter you put there. Nothing else can now come down through the years to me in that drawer, for you cannot now alter what you have already done.

In the second drawer, in 1882, you put the note which lies before me, which I found when I opened that drawer a few minutes ago. You put nothing else into it, and now that, too, cannot be changed.

But I haven't opened the third drawer, Helen. Not yet! It is the last way you can still reach me, and the last time. I will mail this as I did before, then wait. In a week, I will open the last drawer.

Jake Belknap

It was a long week. I worked, I kept busy daytimes; but at night, I thought of hardly anything but the third secret drawer in my desk. I was terribly tempted to open it earlier, telling myself that whatever might lie in it had been put there decades before and must be there now, but I wasn't sure, and I waited.

Then, late at night, a week to the hour after I'd mailed my second letter at the old Wister post office, I pulled out the third drawer, reached in, and brought out the last little secret drawer which lay behind it. My hand was actually shaking, and for a moment I couldn't bear to look directly—something lay in the drawer—and I turned my head away. Then I looked.

I'd expected a long letter; very long, of many pages, her last communication with me, and full of everything she wanted to

---

silhouettes (sil oo ETS) outline drawings filled in with a color, usually black

say. But there was no letter at all. It was a photograph, about three inches square, a faded brown in color, mounted on heavy, stiff cardboard, and with the photographer's name in tiny gold script down in the corner: Brunner & Holland, Parisian Photography, Brooklyn, N.Y.

The photograph showed the head and shoulders of a girl in a high-necked dark dress with a cameo brooch at the collar. Her dark hair was swept tightly back, covering the ears, in a style which no longer suits our idea of beauty. But the severity of that dress and hairstyle couldn't spoil the beauty of the face that smiled out at me from that old photograph. It wasn't beautiful in any classical sense, I suppose. The brows were unplucked and somewhat heavier than we are used to. But it is the soft, warm smile of her lips, and her eyes—large and serene as she looks out at me over the years—that make Helen Elizabeth Worley a beautiful woman. Across the bottom of her photograph she had written, "I will never forget." And as I sat there at the old desk, staring at what she had written, I understood that, of course, that was all there was to say—what else?—on this, the last time, as she knew, that she'd ever be able to reach me.

It wasn't the last time, though. There was one final way for Helen Worley to communicate with me over the years, and it took me a long time, as it must have taken her, to realize it.

Only a week ago, on my fourth day of searching, I finally found it. It was late in the evening, and the sun was almost gone, when I found the old headstone among all the others stretching off in rows under the quiet trees. And then I read the inscription on the weathered old stone: Helen Elizabeth Worley—1861–1934. Under this were the words, *I Never Forgot.*
And neither will I.

---

cameo brooch (KAM ee oh BROHCH) a large pin, usually worn at the
   neck, containing a stone with carved figures
serene (suh REEN) calm; undisturbed
headstone (HED stohn) tombstone

Looking at Love   17

Discussion: Is the ending satisfying? disappointing? Ask students, Which is more important—a plausible plot or skillful storytelling?

MINI QUIZ

Write the following questions on the chalkboard or overhead projector and call on students to fill in the blanks. Discuss the answers with the class.

1. Jake lives in _____ .
2. The desk Jake bought had _____ little brass-knobbed drawers.
3. The time Helen Worley wrote her letters was the _____ .
4. Jake wrote his letters with _____ _____ _____ .
5. Jake found the old photograph of Varney Street in _____ .

Answers to Mini Quiz

1. Brooklyn
2. three
3. late 1800s (1882, to be exact)
4. pen and ink (he found in the old desk)
5. a book at the public library

T17

ANSWERS TO
UNDERSTAND
THE SELECTION

1. from a secondhand store, which had gotten it from an old Brooklyn house
2. None; the envelope was blank.
3. It was from his old stamp collection.
4. Romantic; looking for the "perfect" girl.
5. He wanted the exact address of the house the desk had come from.
6. The post office existed when Helen Elizabeth Worley wrote her letters, and it hadn't changed much.
7. He was anxious, excited, and could think of little else except what he might find.
8. Answers will vary. Sample answer: Read it, looked for other letters, and then probably showed all my friends what I had found.
9. Answers will vary. Sample answer: No. I'm not the kind of person who likes to be kept in suspense about something.
10. Answers will vary. Sample answer: Spooky, but a little romantic.

Respond to Literature: Students' answers to whether the "perfect" person exists for them will vary. Probe their responses by asking, Do only romantics believe in finding the "perfect" person? Might your idea of the "perfect" person change in time?

ANSWERS TO
WRITE ABOUT
THE SELECTION

Prewriting: Discuss with the class what might realistically happen to a "dead" letter. Then point out the peculiar characteristics of this letter: written on very old stationery, sent with no return address, and having an old, possibly valuable stamp. Is it likely the letter was simply thrown away?

T18

UNDERSTAND THE SELECTION

Recall

1. Where did Jake get the desk?
2. What address was on the first love letter's envelope?
3. How did Jake get the old stamp?

Infer

4. When he discovered the love letter, Jake says his feelings influenced what he did. Describe how he felt.
5. Why did Jake go to Brock Place before he mailed his letter?
6. Jake mailed his love letters from the Wister post office. Why?
7. Describe Jake's feelings before he opened the third secret drawer.

Apply

8. What would you have done if you had discovered a love letter in the old desk?
9. Could you have resisted opening the third secret drawer immediately?
10. How does the inscription on Helen's headstone make you feel?

Respond to Literature

"The Love Letter" suggests that the "perfect" person for anyone might exist, but it is probably impossible to meet him or her. Do you agree with that idea?

18

WRITE ABOUT THE SELECTION

Do you wonder what happened to the two letters Jake mailed to Helen Elizabeth Worley? They could not possibly "reach" her, could they? Yet, can you imagine them simply getting thrown away at the dead-letter office?

See if you can add something to the story about the letters. You could put it at the end of the story, or somewhere else if you like.

Prewriting: Brainstorm for ideas about where you think the letters went. Write down anything that occurs to you, no matter how ridiculous it seems. Next, decide which explanation has the most possibilities. Then, brainstorm details about your choice. Make sure your explanation is believable.

Writing: Use your prewriting to write one or several paragraphs about Jake's letters. Present your additions to the story in chronological order. Keep in mind the point of view. You must tell "your" story through Jake's eyes.

Revising: Try to add words or phrases that might add feeling to your story. Look back to see what words the author used to create mystery and romance, and consider using similar words.

Proofreading: Reread what you have written and check for errors. Have you capitalized the first word of each sentence and all "proper" nouns? Correct errors in spelling, usage, and mechanics.

Unit 1

Writing: Circulate as students work individually on their explanations. Make sure they are using first-person point of view.

Revising: Point out particular passages in the story that evoke specific feelings. Discuss as a class how those feelings are created.

Proofreading: Have students work in pairs and exchange papers for proofreading.

THINK ABOUT POINT OF VIEW

The first-person point of view makes a story seem immediate and personal, but it limits action to what the narrator takes part in, sees, or learns about.

1. Look at the story's first paragraph. Does the point of view add to the story's interest?

2. First-person point of view emphasizes the narrator. Details about him or her are important to the story. Find one place in "The Love Letter" where the narrator gives information about something personal.

3. The narrator also uses description to tell us how he or she sees things and feels about them. Find an example where you learn something about the narrator through a description he provides.

4. Is there information the narrator does not provide that you would like to have? What is it?

5. Imagine that this story was written with *he* substituted for *I*. How would it be different?

DEVELOP YOUR VOCABULARY

Helen Elizabeth Worley's first letter probably sounded very "stiff" to you. That is because the words people use and the way they use them change.

The definitions of unfamiliar words were given in the story. However, do you understand how the words were used?

Below are several sentences from the story. Each has at least one "new" word. Rewrite the sentences the way *you* would write them in a love letter.

1. Heart of mine, I crave your bold glance.

2. If I be foolish and whimsical, deride me sweetly if you will.

3. But, figment though you are, and though I shall never see your like, you are more dear to me than he to whom I am betrothed.

4. If you have discovered my letter and think to deceive your sister with a prank, I pray you tell me.

5. I am repelled, as well, by the false gentleness and nicety of manner which too often conceal the contempt they attempt to mask.

LDP Activity: Have LDP students use their sentence describing their "ideal lover" in a letter to that "lover," being sure to mention what the person does specially to warrant such affection. Teach specific letter writing format.

ANSWERS TO THINK ABOUT POINT OF VIEW

1. The story seems immediate and personal as told through a narrator—almost as if the reader feels a personal and secret involvement.

2. Examples: the second and fourth paragraphs.

3. The sixth paragraph, in which Jake examines the desk: His description reveals he is a thorough person who likes to analyze and discover things.

4. Answers will vary. Sample answers: I'd like to know what happened to the letters Jake sent; I'd like to know why Helen Worley chose as her epitaph "I Never Forgot."

5. Sample answers: The reader would no longer feel as though he or she were a participant in the story. Jake's actions might not seem quite as plausible if someone else were explaining them.

ANSWERS TO DEVELOP YOUR VOCABULARY

Sample answers:

1. Dearest, I love when you look right at me.

2. If I get silly and strange, you can make fun of me, gently, if you want.

3. You are only a dream, and even though I'll never see anyone like you, you're more important to me than the man I'm engaged to.

4. If you found my letter tell me and don't try to fool your sister.

5. I resent how your phony niceness is only a way to cover up how much you look down on me.

After completing this selection, students will be able to
• understand rhyme
• see how rhymes are used in everyday life
• talk about feelings associated with love
• write a description of love
• analyze different kinds of rhymes
• recognize words used as both nouns and verbs.

More About Rhyme: Advise students that "end rhyme" occurs when similar-sounding words are at the end of lines; "internal rhyme" when these words are within lines. Point out that there are many different rhyming patterns. The pattern in the upcoming folk poem, for example, is broken only once. Then, note that certain rhyming patterns within a set number of lines make up a specific form of poem. A **limerick**, for example, contains five lines; the end-of-line rhyming pattern is first-second-fifth lines, and third-fourth lines.

Cooperative/Collaborative Learning Activity: Divide students into groups of four or five. Have them share their lines from the Skill Builder. Then, ask each group to pick what it considers the best rhyme. Write these rhymes on the board, and as a class analyze which lines would most effectively sell a product. Ask students to save their rhymes for the next Cooperative/Collaborative activity.

Sidelights: The concept of folk poems might be new to students, but that of folk songs is probably not. True folk songs, like folk poems, have obscure origins; little is known about who wrote the lyrics. Today, the definition of a folk song is often stretched to include a new, often faddish style of music, but authentic folk music still endures and continues to come anonymously from "the folk."

LEARN ABOUT
Rhyme

Many, but not all, poems are written in rhyme. Why is rhyme a popular technique?

Our brains seem to remember things that are repeated. Rhyme is the repeating of the same sound, so this repetition says to us "Hey, take notice of this and remember!"

The next selection is a poem with no title. It is a **folk poem,** a term that means no one is sure who the author is. It was popular with African Americans, and no doubt rhyme helped people remember its message.

The pairing of words by rhyme can help to communicate the feeling and meaning of a poem. An imaginative rhyme can make you smile or gasp with immediate understanding.

As you read the folk poem, ask:
1. What are the rhymes, and where are they?
2. Do the rhymes occur regularly?

SKILL BUILDER

Rhymes are all around us, not just in poetry. Imagine that you work for an advertising company. You just have been told to write a rhyme that advertises a product. Choose a product, and write a rhyming advertisement for it.

UNTITLED

Black American folk poem

Love is a funny thing
Shaped like a lizard,
Run down your heart strings
And tickle your gizzard.
You can fall from a mountain,
You can fall from above,
But the great fall is
When you fall in love.

Folk Singer, Charles White. Courtesy Heritage Gallery, Los Angeles.
Harry Belafonte Collection

---

gizzard (GIZ-urd) [Colloq.] the stomach; usually a humorous usage

Looking at Love

21

Vocabulary: Preteach the vocabulary words. See the Comprehension Worksheet in the TRB.

More About Vocabulary: Write the new vocabulary word, *gizzard*, on the chalkboard or overhead projector. Then, ask students to guess why the poet may have used it in a poem about love. (You may want to hint at an end-rhyme association with **lizard**.)

MINI QUIZ

Write the following questions on the chalkboard or overhead projector and call on students to fill in the blanks. Discuss the answers with the class.

1. This selection is a _____ poem.
2. Love, shaped like a lizard, _____ _____ a person's heartstrings.
3. Love can tickle your _____ .
4. Two places you can fall from are _____ and _____ .
5. The great fall is _____ _____ _____ _____ _____ .

Answers to Mini Quiz

1. folk
2. runs down
3. gizzard
4. a mountain, above
5. when you fall in love

Motivation for Reading: Ask students, What animal would you choose to help describe the way love affects people? For example, can you compare the idea of love with a dog, a cat, or even—as in the next selection—with a lizard!

More About the Thematic Idea: Doesn't the expression "fall in love" seem a bit odd to describe becoming involved with someone? A "fall" usually refers to an accident, sometimes painful. Is that what falling in love is—a painful accident?

Purpose-Setting Question: How does love make you feel?

Reading Strategies: Have students read the poem through without stopping, just for the sheer fun of its language. Then go through it line by line.

Literary Focus: Similes are comparisons formed by using "like" or "as." They provide description through images—unlike direct statements, such as the first line of the poem.

Clarification: "Heartstrings" are covered in the "Understand the Selection" exercises. They, too, are an image—a metaphor for one's emotions.

Critical Thinking: "Fall" is used four times in four lines. Discuss with students how this repetition produces unity and focuses attention on the final line.

Discussion: What would be a good title for this poem? Brainstorm ideas as a class, and then try to reach a consensus on just one.

T21

ANSWERS TO UNDERSTAND THE SELECTION

1. lizard
2. heart and gizzard
3. Falling in love.
4. love, and what it's like
5. Through the lizard, the concept of love seems slippery and able to move anywhere.
6. No, they don't exist; they are an image for emotions.
7. not so much "humorous" as "strange" or "unpredictable"
8. Answers will vary. Sample answer: I'd compare it to a panda bear—hard to produce, always hungry, and very cute.
9. The word, "fall," compares three different experiences that have the same meaning —a downward spiral.
10. "Fall" usually means an action beyond your control.

Respond to Literature: Refer to the questions posed in "More About the Thematic Idea." Ask students whether they like the feeling of being "swept off their feet" by emotion, or whether love is like "a painful accident." Have they ever been swept away by another emotion—such as pride, or anger?

WRITE ABOUT THE SELECTION

Prewriting: Encourage students to consider all kinds of images for a comparison for love. Suggest some other ideas: a snowstorm, a high-tension wire, falling leaves.

Writing: Circulate as students work individually. For those who need assistance, guide them into focusing on the relationship between love and the thing they've chosen to compare it to.

Revising: Discuss as a class when rhyme is effective. Point out to students that rhymes created simply for the sake of rhyming rather than for connecting ideas are usually distracting to the reader.

UNDERSTAND THE SELECTION

Recall

1. Love is compared to an animal in the poem. What animal is it?

2. Two parts of the body are mentioned in the poem. What are they?

3. According to the poem, what is the greatest fall of all?

Infer

4. What is the theme of the poem?

5. Why do you think love is compared to an animal?

6. What is meant by "heart strings"? Do they really exist?

7. The poem calls love "a funny thing." What is meant by "funny"?

Apply

8. If you had to describe how love felt, what description might you use?

9. How is falling from a mountain or from "above" like falling in love?

10. Why do you think the word "fall" is used to describe what happens when you first love someone?

Respond to Literature

Do you believe people "fall" in love or is it an old-fashioned idea? Have you ever fallen in love? What did it feel like to you?

WRITE ABOUT THE SELECTION

What is love like for you? What can you compare it to?

Maybe, it is like a broken-down car that will not start, a stereo set at maximum volume, or an alarm clock that always seems to go off too early. Perhaps you think love is like the flowering plant on your window sill.

What does this thing look like? What does it do to your attitude toward life? How does it make you feel?

Try to write your own description of love, by comparing it with something real in your life.

Prewriting: In the middle of a piece of paper, write down the thing with which you will compare love. Around it, cluster ideas about its relation to love.

Writing: Use the cluster to write a paragraph comparing love to the thing. Make sure you make clear the connection between the thing and love.

Revising: Turn your paragraph into poetry. Consider using rhyme to add emphasis or to make imaginative connections between ideas. You may prefer free verse so you can form lines and verses as you wish. Perhaps you want to try a concrete poem where the lines form a recognizable shape.

Proofreading: Reread what you have written and check for spelling errors. If you are rhyming words, a mistake in spelling could confuse the reader.

Proofreading: Once students have proofread their own papers, have them write a list of 10 words they use in their poems. Before exchanging the list with a partner, they can purposely misspell a word. Their partners then look for errors. The partner gets a point for every misspelled word he or she finds and spells correctly. The writer gets a point for every misspelled word that isn't caught.

THINK ABOUT RHYME

What counts as a rhyme? Do you consider *thing* and *strings* a rhyme in the poem? Most poets would, although strictly speaking the words do not rhyme. The final *s* on *strings* makes the sounds slightly different.

1. **Poetic license** usually allows rhymes between words that "almost" rhyme. Think of an example.

2. Rhymes often occur at the end of lines, but they also can occur within the same line. Find an example of **internal** rhyme.

3. The best rhymes are those that link interesting words or ideas. What is your favorite rhyme in the poem, and why?

4. Eliminate one of the rhymes in the poem by substituting another word. Reread the poem. How does it sound now?

5. Without looking back, try to recite the poem. Which lines, if any, are easiest to remember?

DEVELOP YOUR VOCABULARY

A **noun** is a word that names a person, place, idea, or object. A **verb** is a word that expresses an action or state of being. Poets often use both forms of a word in a poem to make a connection between two ideas or feelings.

In the poem you have just read, *fall* is used as both a noun and a verb. Which *fall* is a noun and which is a verb?

In the sentences below, decide whether the *italicized* word in the sentence pairs is a noun or verb. Find the dictionary definition that fits the meaning of the word in the sentence. Then, use both words in original sentences.

1. **a.** You can *fall* from a mountain.
   b. The great *fall* is love.

2. **a.** She took a *turn* down the street.
   b. I *turn* cartwheels when I see her.

3. **a.** *Love* is a book with blank pages.
   b. We *love* creating new things.

4. **a.** The *shape* of my feelings is square.
   b. I *shape* my life around you.

Discuss with students the ideas contained in the first three paragraphs of the "Elements" section. Then, point out the importance of understanding poetry as a "concentrated" genre: The poet attempts to get more out of less. Language is used creatively and energetically, with the poet sometimes speaking in what might seem like code. A poem must be read several times, the meanings of words and phrases explored, and the connections between ideas made clear.

Suggested Questions

Use the untitled black American folk poem to explore the elements of a poem.

Who is the character in the poem? There is no "I" speaker, perhaps reflecting the poem's unknown origins. The "you" of the poem refers to the reader.

Where is imagery used? Think of how a lizard running down your heartstrings might feel.

What is the theme? If students thought of a title for the poem, remind them of it and discuss how it might relate to the theme.

What is the tone? The image of love "shaped like a lizard" helps make it much less than serious—even though the theme might be very serious indeed.

Can the rhyming structure be "improved"? One suggestion: Try making the one unrhyming line (the one ending in "mountain") rhyme with another line.

What figure of speech is used prominently in the poem? Think of the comparison of love and lizard; how can love even have a shape?

F OCUS ON...

Many people do not like poetry. Others think poetry is still the world's most powerful form of communication—whether it be a sixteenth-century Shakespearean sonnet or a modern age lyric by Stevie Wonder.

The poet uses language in a very different way from prose writers. To understand a poet's message, you need to learn the elements of poetry.

Character. Character in poetry refers to the speaker. If the poet uses *I*, you usually learn about the poet him- or herself. The poem can be very personal, as in "Finis." However, sometimes the *I* is a speaker very different from the poet.

Often the poet addresses an unidentified "you," as in "Where Have You Gone." This person is an absent character whom we know only through the speaker.

Imagery. Poets often use language to appeal to any or all of your five senses. They use images to help you see, hear, smell, feel, or taste what they are writing about.

The author of "Greyday" uses images from the Christian religion of "a crown of thorns" and "a shirt of hair" to help you feel the heaviness she is describing.

Theme. The idea or meaning of a poem is its theme. The poems "Reflections" and "I Dream A World" both have themes about the world. In the first, the poet expresses the idea that there is only hate, not love, in the world. The author of the second poem might agree with that idea, but he also expresses hope that "love will bless the earth."

Tone. The poet conveys to you an attitude when writing. That attitude is called tone. Tone is a clue to meaning.

Maybe the tone is earnest yet light-hearted, as in "First Person Demonstrative." The tone also can be sad, as in "Finis."

You can determine a poem's tone by simply asking yourself, "How does this poem make me feel?" Do not be afraid to give

POETRY

Ask students to point out examples of poetry in everyday communications. Song lyrics are an obvious example. Some advertising slogans use poetry. Many popular expressions use poetry. Some politicians also occasionally use poetry in speeches. Suggest that students research their local newspaper's calendar of events for scheduled poetry readings, which they could then plan to attend, either individually or as a group.

more than one answer, for often tone creates many feelings.

Rhyme. Rhyme is repetition of the same sound. If it comes at the end of a line, it is called **end rhyme.** If it comes within a single line, it is called **internal rhyme.**

End rhyme is the more common type. The untitled black American folk poem uses it. Notice the rhyming of *lizard* and *gizzard,* and *above* and *love.*

Figures of Speech. When you use an expression that says one thing to mean something else, you are using a figure of speech. Common figures of speech are metaphor, simile, personification, and hyperbole.

The author of "Spring" talks about a "wishbone," yet she does not mean that she and her "second man" actually will find a wishbone and make wishes. "Wishbone" is a **metaphor** for the hopes that she and her partner will have.

The comparison of one thing to another through the use of *like* or *as* is a **simile.** In "I Dream a World," for example, *joy* is described as being *like a pearl.*

Another line in "I Dream a World" is an example of **personification,** or the giving of human qualities to nonhuman subjects. In this line the poet talks of a world "where wretchedness will hang its head." The poet has given a human quality to an abstract idea in order to express his idea more forcefully.

Another way to express ideas forcefully is to exaggerate by using **hyperbole.** In "First Person Demonstrative," the poet says she would rather "wrench off an arm than hug you." She uses hyperbole to exaggerate her feelings.

As you read the next selections in this unit, look for the elements of the poems. Ask yourself these questions:

1. How do the elements of poetry such as imagery and figures of speech strengthen a poem?
2. Is the theme of a poem always easy to determine? What can I do if a poem confuses me?

Looking at Love

25

More About Tone: Suggest to students that the best way to determine the tone of a poem is to ask yourself how it makes you feel. Then, ask students to write down the first feeling that comes to mind after they've read "First Person Demonstrative." A discussion of initial reactions is likely to point to the tone of the poem.

Cooperative/Collaborative Learning Activity: First, ask students to divide into small groups. Next, have them read to one another the advertising rhymes they wrote for the previous Skill Builder. Ask the groups, How important is tone in advertising? Then have them choose their best rhyme, present it to the class, and explain how its tone could influence advertising sales.

First Person Demonstrative

by Phyllis Gotlieb

STUDY HINTS
Can you imagine anyone heaving a brick rather than saying, I love you? The speaker is exaggerating her feelings, using hyperbole.

Notice the speaker's appeal to your sense of touch. She uses imagery to describe how she feels.

The speaker fears showing her emotions. She speaks in first person. Her character is frank and open.

This series of "if" descriptions uses "body language." The poet is being sarcastic, making fun of usual expressions about feelings. The tone is serious yet mocking.

The "message" is the theme of the poem. The speaker wants to make sure that the reader "gets" her main idea. If you do not, read it again, she says, in a lighthearted yet earnest tone.

I'd rather
heave half a brick than say
I love you, though I do
I'd rather
5   crawl in a hole than call you
darling, though you are
I'd rather
wrench off an arm than hug you though
it's what I long to do
10 I'd rather
gather a posy of poison ivy than
ask if you love me

so if my
hair doesn't stand on end it's because
15 I never tease it
and if my heart isn't in my mouth it's because
it knows its place
and if I
don't take a bite of your ear it's because
20 gristle gripes my guts
and if you
miss the message better get new
glasses and read it twice

---

posy (POH zee) a flower or bouquet
gristle (GRIS ul) tough, elastic white animal tissue
gripe (GRYP) to cause sharp pain in the bowels

Vocabulary: Preteach the vocabulary words. See the Comprehension Workbook in the TRB.

More About Vocabulary: Write the three new vocabulary words—posy, gristle, and gripe—on the chalkboard or overhead projector. Pronounce and define the words, then ask students how these words help establish the tone of the poem. Suggest that

students read the poem several times before deciding, in exact terms, on its tone.

LDP Activity: Partners: Have the LDP students discuss with their partners differences in how people show their feelings. Some are very emotional and others are very controlled. Have students discuss if one type or the other has more feelings. Have LDP students list

people they know of as examples of other types. Have students identify if they are more comfortable with one type or the other.

MINI QUIZ

Write the following questions on the chalkboard or overhead projector and call on students to fill in the blanks. Discuss the answers with the class.

Her World, Philip Evergood. The Metropolitan Museum of Art, Arthur Hoppock Hearn Fund

1. The speaker would rather throw a _____ than say "I love you."
2. The word that might make the speaker crawl in a hole is _____.
3. The speaker's _____ doesn't stand on end.
4. Her _____ isn't in her mouth.
5. The speaker suggests anyone not understanding her message should read the poem _____.

Answers to Mini Quiz

1. brick
2. darling
3. hair
4. heart
5. twice

Sidelights: Phyllis Bloom Gotlieb is a Canadian writer who writes both poetry and prose. She once said that the most help she ever got in developing her writing was from her husband, who is a computer scientist. Could "First Person Demonstrative" be addressed to him? It seems unlikely, but maybe . . .

Motivation for Reading: Is it easy to express deep feelings? Discuss with students generally whether they find it easy or hard to

UNDERSTAND THE SELECTION

Recall

1. What would the speaker rather do than call someone "darling"?

2. What plant is mentioned in the poem?

3. What instructions does the speaker give at the end of the poem?

Infer

4. Does the speaker love the person to whom she is talking? Explain.

5. Why do you think poison ivy is mentioned in the poem?

6. What connects all the "if" expressions in the second half of the poem?

7. What is the "message" of the poem?

Apply

8. The theme of the poem is repeated a number of times. Point to at least three examples, and explain them.

9. Which of the statements of the theme seems clearest to you?

10. Do you think this poem was written recently, or a long time ago? Why?

Respond to Literature

Do you show your feelings? Maybe you are like the speaker in "First Person Demonstrative." Perhaps you are somewhere in between. Describe your personal style of expressing feelings.

28

WRITE ABOUT THE SELECTION

Phyllis Gotlieb uses humor in "First Person Demonstrative," even if the theme of the poem is serious. She exaggerates, using hyperbole to make her point. She mocks, poking fun at figurative expressions that are used to describe strong emotions.

Can you use humor to make some point about your feelings? Write a poem to express your feelings in a humorous way. You may choose a feeling other than love.

Prewriting: Pick a feeling, or several feelings, you would like to write about. Write the feelings in the middle of the page. How do having these feelings make you feel? In other words, do you become strong when you are angery or afraid, or shy when you care about someone? Cluster ideas around the feeling or feelings. Think humor!

Writing: Use the form of "First Person Demonstrative" to write several lines of poetry about your subject. Substitute your ideas for the poet's, if you like. Study how she uses hyperbole, and see if you can do the same.

Revising: Have you used any imagery? Add an image appealing to one of the five senses, or try to strengthen any images you have.

Proofreading: Writing a poem in the first person means you will be using a lot of pronouns. Reread what you have written and make sure you are using all pronouns correctly, and your verb forms agree. Also, be very careful to check the punctuation in your poem.

Unit 1

THINK ABOUT POETRY

Poetry shares some elements with other types of literature. However, because a poet wants to create a strong feeling with only a few words, he or she also uses special language techniques. Characters in poetry are usually the speaker and the listener. Poets use images to appeal to their readers' senses. Poems, like stories and plays, have themes—ideas—to communicate. Poets convey their attitudes toward their subjects through tone. Rhyme is the repetition of the same sounds at the ends of words. Poets use rhyme at the end or inside lines of their poems. Figures of speech are expressions that compare two or more unlike things.

1. Who is the speaker in "First Person Demonstrative"? Who is the listener?

2. What is your favorite image in this poem? Explain.

3. What is the poet's theme?

4. Identify the tone. How do you know?

5. Give an example of a figure of speech.

DEVELOP YOUR VOCABULARY

Figurative expressions are groups of words that have a special meaning. The meaning usually is quite different from the meanings of the individual words.

Phyllis Gotlieb uses several figurative expressions in "First Person Demonstrative." They use "body language" to make their point.

Below is a list of the expressions that Gotlieb uses in her poem and some others. What does each mean?

1. hair standing on end

2. heart in your mouth

3. keep an ear to the ground

4. look down your nose at someone

5. put your foot in your mouth

6. cross your fingers

7. to jawbone someone

8. a lump in your throat

9. catch your eye

10. bite your lip

Now write five sentences that use figurative expressions to make the point.

The Equatorial Jungle, Henri Rousseau.
National Gallery of Art
Washington, D.C.

LEARN ABOUT

Figures of Speech

Poetry allows you to use language in a free and creative way. Figures of speech give you a special kind of freedom. They allow you, the poet, to make connections between things that normally you might not connect.

The connections allow the reader to transfer knowledge of one thing to another. It is as though you, the writer, are carrying a torch lighting new paths for the reader.

Metaphor is one of the most common figures of speech. A **metaphor** shows the connection between two ideas without using the words "as" or "like." An example is "The sun was a golden shield hung in the sky." Other figures of speech are simile, which compares using the words *like* or *as*; personification, which gives human qualities to nonhuman things; and hyperbole, which exaggerates a quality or element.

As you read "What Is Once Loved" and "Spring," ask yourself:

1. What metaphors are used?
2. What is the purpose of the metaphors?

SKILL BUILDER

People use figures of speech all the time, both in writing and speaking. Create your own metaphor.

30

Unit 1

What Is Once Loved

by Elizabeth Coatsworth

What is once loved
You will find
Is always yours
From that day.
Take it home
In your mind
And nothing ever
Can take it away.

Spring

by Carole Gregory Clemmons

the second man I love,
we'll find the wishbone
and make our wishes,
I won't even try for the strongest end,
because this time when the bone breaks
either way I'll be in.

Guide students to an understanding that these poems are related because both speakers have already found love. In "What is Once Loved," the poet speaks generally of the value of loving someone; she couldn't have written the poem without having felt love herself—even though no specific relationship is mentioned. In "Spring," the poet had found a first love, but that relationship has ended and she is reflecting on what a second love might be like.

Purpose-Setting Question: Does love for somebody stay with you, even after the relationship has ended?

Reading Strategy and Literary Focus: After students have read the first poem, help them to analyze its structure: it is two sentences, each broken into four lines. You might then want to point out the main theme: The memory of love can never be taken from you. Note also that there is no rhyme in the poem, and that the language is simple.

Critical Thinking: Ask students, How important is memory as a function of human intelligence?

Critical Thinking: In "Spring," the speaker doesn't want to discuss her first love. From the start, she indicates that in a new relationship hopes and wishes come first. Ask students, Do you think this is true of first love?

Enrichment: In "Spring," the speaker takes for granted that some sort of break will occur. Her first relationship has made her more realistic.

MINI QUIZ

Write the following questions on the chalkboard or overhead projector and call on students to fill in the blanks. Discuss the answers with the class.

1. When you love something, according to Elizabeth Coatsworth, it is _____ yours.
2. She also advises to take _____ what you once loved.
3. Carole Gregory Clemmons opens her poem by describing the kind of relationship she'll have with the _____ _____ she loves.
4. She and her new man will find a _____.
5. She's sure that eventually the bone they hold will _____.

Answers to Mini Quiz

1. always
2. home
3. second man
4. wishbone
5. break

ANSWERS TO UNDERSTAND THE SELECTION

1. love, or "what is once loved"
2. "in your mind"
3. "the second man I love"
4. Could be either or both. The past tense is not used for any of the verbs, just the indefinite time adverb "once."
5. The poet uses "home" as a metaphor for the human mind because home is the most personal place we have.
6. It is a metaphor for love and its joys and problems.
7. She won't try to dominate the relationship.
8. uncertain; it could refer to anything because it's not defined in the poem
9. Spring represents a new beginning; it is a metaphor for a new love.
10. Answers will vary. Sample answer: One break won't necessarily end the relationship. People in love learn they must give and take.

Respond to Literature: Is the poet's main theme true? Is the mind—even though intangible, invisible and finite—the most precious possession of all human beings?

WRITE ABOUT THE SELECTION

Prewriting: Brainstorm as a class. Write on the chalkboard or overhead projector as many feelings as students can think of.

Writing: Circulate as students work individually. For students having difficulty, review their notes with them and discuss ideas they could develop.

Revising: Return to the list of feelings the class brainstormed. Take one of the feelings and ask the class to think of metaphors describing it.

UNDERSTAND THE SELECTION

Recall

1. What "is always yours"?

2. Where should you keep what "is always yours"?

3. Who will be at the other end of Carole Gregory Clemmons's "wishbone"?

Infer

4. Do you think Elizabeth Coatsworth is talking about lost love or an existing love in "What Is Once Loved"?

5. Explain the phrase "home in your mind" in "What Is Once Loved."

6. What does a wishbone have to do with love in the poem "Spring"?

7. Explain why the speaker says she will not "try for the strongest end" in "Spring".

Apply

8. Does the word *what* in "What Is Once Loved" refer to people, things, or both?

9. Why do you think Carole Gregory Clemmons chose the title "Spring"?

10. Explain the last line "either way I'll be in" in the poem "Spring."

Respond to Literature

Do you believe that you can *always* carry in your mind "what is once loved," or is that an exaggeration of the power of memory?

WRITE ABOUT THE SELECTION

What is it like to carry something "in your mind"? It is an odd expression. You can never carry a "thing" in your mind, just abstract thoughts.

Poets try to make abstract thoughts, particularly feelings, become real. You will do the same. How can you turn a feeling into something real? Try using a metaphor; it might help.

Prewriting: Brainstorm to find a feeling to describe. Choose one of your ideas, and jot down a few notes about it. Think about what you associate it with; perhaps a specific color, a special place, a wonderful song, or a valued posession. Write about experiences with the feeling, give examples, and compare it to other things.

Writing: Use your notes to describe the feeling. Try to write in poetry form, but use prose if you can not.

Revising: Have you used a metaphor to describe the feeling? Try to add one if you have not. Make your ideas clear by using specific words and vivid phrases. Eliminate any dull, boring, or overused phrasing.

Proofreading: Reread what you have written and check for mistakes in verb-subject agreement. Singular nouns take singular verbs, and plural nouns take plural verbs. Be careful with punctuation at the end of lines if you wrote a poem. You can use punctuation more creatively in poetry, but do not confuse your readers.

Proofreading: Review verb-subject agreement rules. Point out how punctuation is used in the two poems. Clemmons doesn't follow strict punctuation and capitalization rules, yet what punctuation she does use is used clearly and effectively.

LDP Activity: Have LDP students use their list of descriptive words and phrases to write a short paragraph about their lost love. Discuss the requirements of a good paragraph.

THINK ABOUT FIGURES OF SPEECH

Carole Gregory Clemmons used a metaphor to relate love to a wishbone in "Spring." She also could have used a **simile**, which is distinguished from a metaphor by the use of the words *like* or *as:* "Love is *like* a wishbone."

Phyllis Gotlieb used hyperbole, a figure of speech, again and again in her poem "First Person Demonstrative."

A fourth common figure of speech is **personification**. Human qualities are given to a nonhuman subject in the following example: *The broom stared at my empty hands.*

1. What human qualities are given to the broom?

2. How can personification be used to describe a car or something a car does?

3. Use a simile to express the kind of love Phyllis Gotlieb describes in "First Person Demonstrative."

4. Do you think hyperbole is used in "What Is Once Loved"? Think back to your answer to the discussion question in "Understand the Selection."

5. Use a metaphor to describe weather.

DEVELOP YOUR VOCABULARY

A **contraction** is a shortened form of two words. One or more letters have been omitted, and these are replaced by an apostrophe (').

> *Examples: he + is = he's*
> *they + will = they'll*

Only one contraction requires a spelling change:

> *will + not = won't*

Write the two words that have been joined, or contracted, to form the *italicized* contractions.

1. *We'll* find the wishbone.

2. I *won't* even try for the strongest end.

3. Either way *I'll* be in.

4. *I'd* rather heave a brick than say I love you.

5. If my hair *doesn't* stand on end *it's* because I never tease it.

6. If I *don't* take a bite of your ear *it's* because gristle gripes my guts.

Write an original paragraph or poem that uses five contractions.

After completing this selection, students will be able to

- recognize the elements of a short story
- determine if specific selections are short stories
- discuss journal-keeping
- update a story character's journal
- identify the main theme of a short story
- recognize root words and use them to define new words.

More About The Short Story: Many of the selections in this book are short stories. In this unit alone, students have already read two. The next selection, "Up on Fong Mountain," is an adaptation of the short story form. The author uses a series of journal entries to tell her story, which is written from a student's point of view. She opens the story with a memo from the student's teacher, explaining the journal assignment.

Cooperative/Collaborative Learning Activity: Begin with a brief synopsis by the class of the O. Henry selection. Then, as a review of the elements of a short story, ask volunteers to name the four elements and write them on the chalkboard. Next, divide the class into four groups. Assign a different element to each group, directing them to analyze the O. Henry story only from the standpoint of their element. Ask, How—in specific terms—is the element made evident throughout the story? Then, ask the groups to present their evaluation, in detail, before the class.

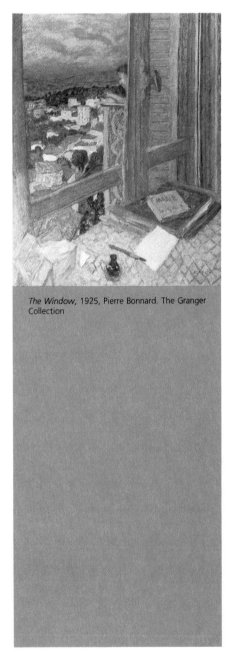

The Window, 1925, Pierre Bonnard. The Granger Collection

34

LEARN ABOUT
Short Story

A short story is everything a story is, only short. It can be read in one sitting.

What is a **story?** It is a piece of prose (not poetry) with the following four elements: setting, characters, plot, theme.

A **short story** contains the same basic parts. Usually a short story is fiction, meaning it is made-up.

A short story can take different forms. For example, it can be presented as a folktale, as a dream, or as an account of some event.

In "Up on Fong Mountain," the story is presented as a series of entries in a student's journal. Nevertheless, all the elements of the short story are present.

As you read "Up on Fong Mountain," ask yourself these questions:

1. Why do you think the author used journal form to write the story?
2. How does the first-person point of view affect the way the story is told? Think of specific examples, such as choice of words and development of the plot.

SKILL BUILDER

Think about "The Love Letter" by Jack Finney, in this unit. Is it a short story? Why or why not? Write down reasons to back up your answer.

Unit 1

More About Vocabulary: Point out to students that although this is a long selection, there are relatively few new vocabulary words. Discuss why that is in terms of the author's point of view. Review the new words, and then ask students to use each of them in a sentence they might write in a journal. You might also ask students to give some slang words and phrases that are currently "in" with young people, that might add variety to a journal.

LDP Activity: Group Discussion: Have LDP students discuss why it was so important to Jessie that Miss Durmacher not read her journal. Have students discuss how they would feel and why.

Vocabulary: Preteach the vocabulary words. See the Comprehension Workbook in the TRB.

T34

UP ON FONG MOUNTAIN

by Norma Fox Mazer

DATE: Feb. 3

TO: All Students Taking English 10
MEMO FROM: Carol Durmacher

Your term project will be to keep a weekly journal. Purchase a 7¾ × 5-inch ruled, wire-bound notebook. Date each entry. Note the day, also. Make a minimum of two entries each week. The journal must be kept to the end of the school year. It is to be handed in June 24th.

I will not read these journals—only note that they have been kept. There will be two marks for this project —Pass and Fail. Only those students not handing in a journal or disregarding the few rules I have set down will receive a Fail.

In writing in your journal, try to be as free as possible. This is *your* journal: express *yourself*. Use the language that comes naturally to you. Express your true feelings. Remember, I will not read what you have written (unless you ask me to). Once I record your mark I will hand the journal back to you. You may be present while I check.

These journals are for YOU. To introduce you to the joys of record-keeping. To help you think about your lives, the small events, the funny, sad, or joyful moments. Record these as simply and directly as possible.

A moment recorded is a moment forever saved.

journal (JUR nul) a written daily record; diary
entry (EN tree) thing written in a book or list
minimum (MIN uh mum) smallest amount; lowest

35

Sidelights: Journals are popular teaching tools because they furnish students with a ready-made subject to write about: themselves. However, it's sometimes hard for people, especially adolescents, to believe that their lives contain anything of interest to write about. Norma Fox Mazer addresses this in several of the journal entries in "Up on Fong Mountain." By writing from a student's point of view, the author creates empathy for the journal writer's constant question, "What to write?" She then provides the answer through an entertaining and sensitive commentary on teenage love. The author's message to students, conveyed through a student, is "There's a journal writer in every one of us."

Purpose-Setting Question: Can a class assignment really inspire a deeper sense of one's own feelings of love?

Clarification: Point out that the terse style of the opening paragraph of the memo is just what a teacher might use in making an assignment.

Discussion: Ask students how they would feel if handed this assignment. Are the instructions clear enough? What might their first entry be? Point out that the memo really serves as exposition for the story.

Motivation for Reading: Read or, if possible, show on an overhead projector the memo that opens "Up on Fong Mountain." Ask students, Can the teacher's memo be accurate? Is there "joy" in recording–keeping?

More About the Thematic Idea: Do people express their feelings of love more easily in a personal journal? As Phyllis Gotlieb pointed out, love is often a hard thing for many people to demonstrate. Ask students, Do you keep a journal in which you express—in addition to other things—your feelings of love? If so, How has it helped in understanding those feelings?

T35

Enrichment: The opening entry is almost like a "free write," yet it provides important information about the main character. Look at the style of writing: The simple sentences, all of them beginning with "I" or "My," tell us Jessie is an uncomplicated person, yet she's observant.

Critical Thinking: We learn something about the dynamics between Jessie and her sister in this offhand, honest observation. (February 8) Concise narration—"I didn't exist"—is so much fresher than saying, "I really got pushed aside by my sister whenever her boyfriend Mark came over."

Literary Focus: Small details— such as the exact dinner menu— add realism and humor to the story. (February 12)

February 6, Thursday

I don't know what to write really. I have never kept a journal before. Well, I better write something. I have to do this two times in the next three days. Miss Durmacher, you said, "Write your true feelings." My true feelings are that I actually have nothing to write. Well, I'll describe myself. My name is Jessie Granatstein. I'm 15 years old. My coloring is sandy (I think you would call it that). I ought to lose ten pounds. My eyes are brown. I have thick eyebrows that my sister Anita says I ought to pluck. My father says I'm stubborn as a bulldog.

February 8, Saturday

Anita and I made a *huge* bowl of popcorn tonight, then ate it watching TV. Then we were still hungry, so we made a pot of spaghetti. We had a good time till Mark came over, then Anita acted like I didn't exist.

February 12, Wednesday

Lincoln's birthday, also my parents' anniversary. Mom made a rib roast, baked Idaho potatoes, and strawberry shortcake. I stuffed myself like a pig. It half rained, half snowed all day. Why would anyone want to get married on Feb. 12, in the middle of winter? Mom just laughs when I ask her, and looks at Dad.

February 14, Friday

I don't have anything to write. I'm sorry, Miss Durmacher, but all I seem to be writing about is food. Mom says not to worry about my weight, that I'm "appealing." She's nice.

February 18, Tuesday

Yesterday I was talking to Anita and we got called to supper right in the middle of a sentence. "Girls!" That's my father.

But, anyway, that wasn't what I was going to write about today. I was going to write about Brian Marchant—Brian Douglas Marchant III. Kids call him BD. I'm pretty sure he was watching me in class today. Fairly sure, although not positive. What I am positive of is that *I* was watching *him*. In fact—well, I'm not going to write any more about it. I thought I wanted to, but I take it back. And that's all I have to say today.

Feb. 21, Fri.

Well, Miss D., it's a Friday, it's winter, I feel sort of depressed. I wish I had someone I could really talk to. It snowed again today. I've always loved snow. Today, for the first time ever I didn't like it. I *hated* it. And that depressed me even more.

And to tell the truth, Miss D., while we're on depressing subjects, I just can't believe this journal. Almost three more *months* of my real thoughts and feelings —that's depressing!

Monday, February 24

Brian Marchant borrowed paper from me, and winked at me. I have always hated winking boys.

Feb. 28, last day of the month, Friday

BD winked at me again.

I said, "Why are you winking at me?"

"What do you mean? I'm winking at you because I feel like winking at you."

"Don't," I said.

"Don't?" He looked at me in amazement. I mean it, Miss Durmacher, like nobody ever said *don't* to him before.

"I think winking is dumb," I said.

He stared at me some more. Then he gave me a double wink.

March 3, Monday

I saw BD in the cafeteria today. I said, "Hi." He said, "Hi." I said, "Have you given up winking?" He said, "What?" Then he laughed. He has a nice big laugh.

Tues. Mar. 4

BD and I ate lunch together today. No winking.

Thursday, March 6

Lunch again with BD. I forgot to bring mine, and didn't have any money with me. BD brings *enormous* lunches. Two peanut butter jelly sandwiches, one tuna fish with pickle relish, one salami with cheese, one bag of chips, an apple, an orange, a banana, plus he bought three cartons of milk and two ice cream sandwiches. And parted with one of the pbj's for me. Also, he gave me half his apple.

And that makes *three* entries for this week, Miss Durmacher. Not bad, huh?

Tuesday, March 11

BD walked home with me and came in for cocoa. Then we went outside and he looked up at the tallest tree around. "I think I could climb that, Jess," he said.

"Don't, BD," I said.

"Why not? I like to climb trees."

"I don't like heights, and it might be slippery."

"*You* don't have to climb it," he said. And up he went.

Looking at Love

37

Literary Focus: Here's the plot complication: She's falling for Brian Douglas Marchant III, otherwise known as BD.

Enrichment: Jessie wants someone to talk to about her feelings, yet the journal is providing exactly that kind of outlet. The entry is ironic. (February 21)

Enrichment: The journal form is ideal for quick, staccato bursts of information such as the entry about "winking boys." (February 24)

Reading Strategy: This is the first time direct conversation has been used at some length in the journal. Does that affect the way students read the entry? Does direct speech add or detract from the tone that's been established? (February 24)

Literary Focus: The detail of this paragraph puts the reader right in the school cafeteria when BD opens his lunch. Notice also— as Jessie does—that she writes three instead of two entries this week; what might that mean? (March 6)

Literary Focus: This is simple narration, a story within a story. Direct speech is used to tell much of it. (March 11)

When he got nearly to the top he yelled, "Jess-eee! Jess-eee!" I yelled back, "I hear you, Beee-Deee!" Then he came down, laughing all the way.

Wednesday, March 12

Anita said she thought BD was funny-looking. I said I didn't think he was any funnier-looking than most human beings.

She said, "You have to admit he's shorter than you. Green pop eyes, like a frog. Also, a big mouth which looks like he could swallow your whole face when he kisses you."

"How do you know he kisses me, Anita?"

"Well, sister, I hope he kisses you!" She laughed.

Are you reading this, Miss Durmacher? Don't, please. The truth is, I have only been kissed a few times—well, not even a few. Three to be exact—at parties. But I'm not going to tell Anita that.

March 21, Friday

Anita doesn't stop making cracks about BD's looks. I just don't understand it. Her boyfriend, Mark Maloff, is supposed to be super-good-looking, but I really can't stand him. He wears pink ties and has a little green ring on his left hand. It's true BD looks as if he never thinks about what he's wearing. Nothing ever matches. But something about him really pleases me.

Saturday night, March 22

Miss Durmacher, don't read this—you said you wouldn't. I think I love BD!

Wednesday, March 26

Mom thinks she and I are alike. She's always saying it. *But* I'm not like her *at all. I'm not sweet.* I became aware of this because of BD. I have been noticing that he likes things his own way. Most of the time he gets it. I have noticed, too, that I don't feel sweet about this at all!

March 29, Sat. afternoon

BD came over last night and said we were going bowling. I said why didn't we do something else, as we went bowling last week. He said he liked bowling and what else was there to do, anyway? I said we could go roller skating. I like roller skating. BD said, "Jessie, why are you being so picky? Why are you being hard to get along with?" I thought, Right! Why am I?

And we went bowling. And then, later, I realized he had talked me out of what I wanted to do and into what he wanted to do.

Monday, March 31, last day of the month

I don't even mind writing in here anymore, Miss Durmacher. I have plenty to write all the time. That favorite subject, Myself.

Also, today, I noticed that BD is another one whose favorite subject is—myself. That is—*himself.* The thing is, I really like to listen to him because, mainly, I like him. But if he never wants to listen to me, I get this horrible lonely feeling. I think that's it. A lonely feeling. Sad.

April 2, Tuesday, no I mean, Wednesday

A dumb fight with BD today. He got going on his ancestors who came over here about 200 years ago. *Pioneers,* he said with a big happy smile. As if because they got on a boat about 150 years earlier than my family this made them really special. So I said, "Well, BD, I think there's another word for your ancestors. *Thieves.*"

"Thieves!" His cheeks puffed up.

"They stole Indian land, didn't they?" (I have just become aware of this lately from history class.)

BD whipped out a map of the Northeast. He stabbed his finger about a dozen places all over Maine and Vermont. "Here's Marchantville, Jessie. Marchant River. Marchant's Corners. East Marchant! West Marchant, and Marchant's Falls!" He looked at me very triumphantly.

"BD," I said, "I've seen all that before." I burst out laughing.

"You think thieves were the founders of all these places, Jessie? You think that's why all these rivers and towns were named after the Marchants? They were *pioneers,* Jess—" And he got that happy look on his face again at the mere sound of the word. "*Pioneers,* people who had the intelligence and foresight to go to the new country, the unexplored—"

"Now listen, BD," I said. I had to talk loud to slow him down. "Suppose a boatload of people came over here tomorrow from China and pushed us all

out. And they say to us, 'From now on, we're going to call this Fong City after our leader, Mao Tze Fong. This river here, this is going to be Fong River, and over here we've got Fong Mountain—'"

"Jessie, that's dumb," BD yelled. "That comparison just won't work—"

Well! I can yell, too. "*Like I was saying,* BD, although we don't know it, the Chinese have developed this ray gun. Instant death. Okay? Now—"

"No, it's not okay. We've got atomic weapons, an army, police—"

"So here comes Mao Tze Fong," I

---

mere (MIR) nothing else but; simple

Enrichment: In the same entry, Jessie sets forth a revisionist history of the European settlement of America succinctly and vividly. Her specific example, given to illustrate her point, also informs us about the title of the selection. "Mao Tze Fong" is a play on the name of the late Chinese leader, Mao Tse-tung.

went on, "and all the others with him. They've got these ray guns which we can't do *anything* against. They kill off a bunch of us, take over our houses and land, and the rest of us run to hide in the mountains—"

"Fong Mountain, I presume?" BD said.

"Right! We're up on Fong Mountain. From there we would try to get our homes back. But after a few years, we'd have to agree to anything they said. Because, remember, we have just a few old hunting rifles against their ray guns. They, after a while, would let us have some land they didn't care about, some swamps and stuff. They'd stick us all on it and call it a reservation. And meanwhile, *meanwhile*—BD, are you listening?—they'd have been wiping out all the old maps and making new ones. With Fong Mountain, East Fong, West Fong, Fong's Corners. And that's it, BD, if you don't want to understand the point of what I'm saying!"

April 3, Thursday

In class today: "How're your famous ancestors, BD?"

"How're things up on Fong Mountain, Jessie?"

April 6, Sunday

I talked to BD on the phone. We were peaceful. That's good. Because we have been fighting a good bit lately.

April 12, Saturday

Mom came into my room with a sweater she'd washed for me. "Oh, by the way, honey," she said (which is always the signal that she's going to be serious), "aren't you and Brian seeing an awful lot of each other?"

"Me and BD?" I said. "You don't have to worry, Mom. No one is going to carry me away."

Tuesday, April 15

Thinking about me and BD. At this point in my life, the way I feel is—I don't think I have to know why. It's just the way I feel.

Sunday, April 20

A fight with BD last night. Please don't read this, Miss Durmacher! It's private and personal. BD said I was being mean. He said I was being selfish, and also unfair. I didn't know what to say in return, so I just got mad. He won't even let me get mad in my own way!

Monday, April 21

Miss Durmacher, you didn't say how long or short the entries had to be. I'll describe the weather today. Gray air and the smell of garbage everywhere.

Tuesday, April 22

Today, in school, I saw BD in the halls, and I saw him in class, and I saw him in the cafeteria. We looked at each other. He didn't say anything, and I didn't say anything.

After school I started home. After a few blocks I felt someone was following me. I turned around. There was BD behind me. I started walking again. Then I turned around. He was right behind me. He grabbed me in a big hug, knocking

Clarification: Make sure students understand the allusion to "Fong Mountain." (May 4)

my books every which way and said, "Kiss! Kiss!" I was sort of shocked, but I couldn't help kissing him back. And then he laughed and laughed.

Wednesday, April 30

Today I tried to talk to BD. He says it's my fault we fight so much. He says I pick the fights, that he's peaceful. This might be true. He *is* peaceful when he gets his way. He says I'm a prickly character. He's started calling me Porky, short for porcupine.

Sunday, May 4

Last night BD and I went out. I had the feeling that I was up there on Fong Mountain again. And I was all alone. And I thought, Oh! I wish I had someone to talk to.

Saturday, May 10

I have kind of a problem here. What I want to write about is BD and me, but I keep thinking you'll read this, Miss Durmacher. So this is going to be my second entry for the week.

Looking at Love

Friday, May 16

Oh, BD, you mix me up . . . I love you . . . but . . .

Friday, May 23

BD came over last night. I thought we could just walk around, buy ice cream, and maybe talk. Be restful with each other. It was a nice night, warm, and I didn't feel like doing anything special.

But the minute we set foot on the sidewalk, BD said, "We're going to the movies," and he starts walking fast, getting ahead of me.

So I just kept walking along at my usual pace. I said to his back, "How do you know that's what I want to do?"

"There's a new movie at the Cinema," he said. "You'll like it."

"How do you know that?"

He turned around, gave me one of his smiles. He really has the nicest smile in the world! But he uses it unfairly. "Oh, listen, Jessie, if I like it, you'll like it. Right?"

"Wrong!" I yelled.

"Say it again, Porky. They couldn't hear you in Rochester."

"Very funny, BD. And I told you not to call me *Porky!* I don't believe I'm going to any movie," I said. "I haven't made up my mind what I want to do tonight. Nobody asked me what I wanted to do, only told me what they wanted to do."

"They," BD said. "There's only one of me."

"Oh, BD," I said, "no, you're a whole

government. You're a president, vice-president, and secretary of defense all rolled into one."

"What are you talking about?"

"You know what I'm talking about, BD. How you always have to be Top Banana. The Big Cheese. Always telling me. You're a regular Mao Tze Fong! We're going to do this. We're going to do that. We're going here. We're eating this. Don't you think I have a mind of my own?"

"You're being difficult tonight," he said. He was smiling. Only not his regular beautiful smile, more of a toothy mean smile, as if he would like to really bite off my arm instead of talking to me. "You've been difficult just about every time we see each other lately. Now, do you want to see that movie, or don't you?"

"I don't care about the movie," I said. "What I care about is that I have a mind of my own. I am a free person also, and I don't want to be in any dictatorship relationship!"

"Dictatorship relationship," he said. And he laughed. Hee-hee-hee. "You mean a *dictatorial* relationship. *Dictatorial*, not *dictatorship*."

I stared at him. Then I turned around and walked in the other direction. And he didn't come after me, and I didn't go back after him.

Wednesday, May 28

I guess everything really is over with

---

dictatorial (dik tuh TAWR ee ul) forcing one's beliefs upon
someone else

BD and me. We really have broken up. I never would have thought it—breaking up over grammar!

June 2, Monday

I know I missed making a couple of entries, Miss Durmacher, but I was sort of upset. I'll make some extra ones to make up for it. Anita has a job after school at the telephone company. Mom has been going over every day to help Aunt Peggy, who just had her fifth baby. I don't have anything to do except hang around the house, feeling crummy.

June 4, Wednesday

Sometimes, thinking about BD, I think I was the biggest fool in the world. I never loved a boy the way I loved BD. Then I go over everything in my mind, and I don't see what else I could have done.

June 5, Thursday

Why should I miss someone who all I could do was fight with, anyway?

Friday, June 6

I'm sick of hanging around the house. I'm sick of thinking about BD. Two whole weeks is enough. I'm going to get a job.

Saturday, June 7

Everyone at every place I go says, "Leave your name, we'll call you." Or else, "Fill out this application." Then they ask you a hundred questions about your whole life for a job which they don't mean to give you, anyway.

Sunday, June 8

I got a job!

It happened just by accident, this way. Yesterday, I stopped into Dippin

DoNuts. Just out of habit I told the lady behind the counter I was looking for work.

She looked me over. I sat up straighter. She said, "Are you prepared to start next week, and then work all summer?"

I said, "Sure!"

She looked me over again. She asked me how old I was. She asked me where I lived. She said she was Mrs. Richmondi and she owned the place. She needed someone right away. I start tomorrow afternoon.

Sunday, June 15

I've worked a whole week, every day after school from four to seven. (Then Mrs. Richmondi comes in for the last three hours and to close up.) And I worked all day Saturday. I'm a little bit tired today, but I like working. Yesterday morning I got up at five o'clock. Everyone was asleep. I crept around the house and let myself out as quiet as I could. The streets were empty. Not even one car. And the houses all quiet. It was nice. I was never out early in the morning like that.

Monday, June 16

I have to wear a horrible uniform, orange with white trim. But other than that, I really like my job. Mrs. Richmondi is nice, too, but she *hates* bare feet. She's got a sign on the door: NO BARE FEET.

Wednesday, June 18

I see BD every day in school and we never say a word. We just look at each other and then keep walking.

Mom came in to Dippin DoNuts today and ordered coffee and a jelly

Reading Strategy: The June 19 entry, the longest in the journal, contains the story's climax. Have students approach it as a short story by itself, noting especially the verbal interaction between Jessie and BD.

Clarification: Jessie, the 15-year-old journal writer, tries to capture the tone of her interaction with BD by using a loose phonetic spelling of "cup of coffee." She's quite taken by the writing aspect of keeping a journal.

doughnut. Then a bunch of kids came pouring in yelling orders. Before I'd really taken in who was there, I thought—BD's here! And my hands got sweaty.

Thursday, June 19

BD came into the doughnut shop today.

It was 6:30. At first I almost didn't recognize him. He was wearing a funny-looking hat that was too big for him. And huge red-and-white sneakers.

He sat down at the counter. I wiped my hands down the sides of my uniform. "Yes?" I said, just like I did to anyone who came in. "Can I help you?"

"Cupacawfee," he said.

I poured coffee into the orange mug. "Would you like a doughnut?" I said.

"Yup," he said.

I was nervous. Some of the coffee spilled. I wiped it up. "Cinnamon, plain, sugar, jelly, chocolate, banana, peach, orange, cream, or cinnamon-chocolate?"

"What kind would you recommend?"

"Whatever you like."

"What do *you* think is the best?"

"That depends on your taste," I said.

"Well, what is your taste? What is your favorite?"

"The cinnamon-chocolate."

"Then that's what I'll have," BD said. "Cinnamon-chocolate."

"I thought you didn't like chocolate, BD," I said, putting the doughnut down in front of him.

"Everyone needs an open mind in this world," he said. "I haven't eaten chocolate in quite a few years, so I might

just as well try it again. Don't you agree, Jessie?"

I stared at him. I wanted to say, "BD, is that you?" I had missed BD an awful lot. I had thought about him nearly every single day. Sometimes I had loved him so much that I could hardly stand it. Sometimes I had hated him just as hard. Now here he was, not more than two feet from me. And all we were talking about was doughnuts.

"Cooperation, ma'am," he said, putting on a Western accent. "We strive to co-op-erate. For instance, how do you like my hat?"

"Your hat?"

He took off the hat, twirling it on his fingers. "My hat. This antique, genuine gangster hat. You don't like it, do you?"

"Well—"

"No, I can tell. You don't have to say anything. You think it's an ancient, grungy piece of junk. Okay, Jessie, if that's what you think, then I don't want to wear this hat." And he opened the door and flipped the hat through. I could see it sailing out into the parking lot. "That's what I mean by cooperation, Jessie."

"You dope, BD," I said. "I liked that hat all right, it's your sneakers I'm not so wild about."

"My sneakers? These genuine red-and-white All-Americans? Jessie! That's all you have to say." He kicked off his sneakers and sent them sailing into the parking lot where they joined his hat.

"You're crazy, BD," I said. "You're

---

grungy (GRUN jee) shabby or dirty

really impossible."

And just then my boss, Mrs. Richmondi, parked her car outside in the lot. I looked down at BD's bare feet and then at the sign tacked on the door. NO BARE FEET.

"BD, here comes my boss," I said, sort of fast. "You better leave." My voice was froggy. I felt kind of sick. Because BD and I hadn't said anything real. "My boss hates bare feet. BD, you better just go."

Mrs. Richmondi was coming to the door now.

"But, Jessie—"

"BD, she's coming!"

Mrs. Richmondi pushed open the door with her shoulder. And the first thing she saw was BD's feet. "Young man! You have bare feet. You shouldn't have let him in, Jessie. I've told you, no bare feet!"

"I didn't come in with bare feet," BD said.

Mrs. Richmondi glared at him. "Out!" She pointed to the door.

"I'm going," BD said, "but don't blame—"

"Out!"

BD left. I watched him through the window, cutting across the parking lot. Mrs. Richmondi was talking to me.

"I'm sorry, Mrs. Richmondi," I said. "Excuse me, please." I bolted through the door. I snatched up BD's sneakers and hat and ran after him. "BD! BD!" I thrust the sneakers into his hand and clapped the hat on his head. "Perfectly good sneakers, BD," I said, which wasn't what I wanted to say, at all.

"If you don't like 'em, Jessie, I don't want 'em."

Oh, BD, I thought. Oh, BD! I knew I had to go back in the shop. Mrs. Richmondi was watching us through the window. But we still hadn't said *anything*. Neither of us. And we were just standing there, looking at each other.

"BD," I said. "BD, do you want to be friends?"

"That's what I mean," he said. And then he gave me a smile, that terrific smile which I'd missed all this time. "That's what I really mean, Jessie."

Friday, June 20

Today I hand in my journal.

When I started writing it way back in February, I didn't even know BD. It's funny. Odd, I mean. So much has happened. And now, this is the last time I'm writing here. I'm not going to do it anymore. I don't care about the past that much. Not when there's tomorrow to look forward to! So, Miss Durmacher, this is it. Please remember your promise not to read this journal. I trust you, Miss Durmacher.

Pass
Carol Durmacher

---

bolt (BOHLT) run away fast
thrust (THRUST) push with force

Looking at Love

45

Enrichment: In her last entry, Jessie sums up the situation simply and accurately. (June 20)

Discussion: What happened between Jessie and BD? Does being "friends" again mean that they are back together? Ask students, Even though she finished her assignment, should Jessie go on with her journal?

MINI QUIZ

Write the following questions on the chalkboard or overhead projector and call on students to fill in the blanks. Discuss the answers with the class.

1. Jessie must keep a journal for her _____ _____ class.
2. Jessie is _____ years old.
3. BD scares Jessie when he climbs a tree because _____ _____.
4. BD says his ancestors were pioneers, but Jessie calls them _____.
5. BD orders a _____ doughnut when he visits Jessie at the Dippin DoNuts shop.

Answers to Mini Quiz

1. English 10
2. 15
3. Jessie doesn't like heights (and worries the tree might be slippery).
4. thieves
5. cinnamon chocolate

ANSWERS TO UNDERSTAND THE SELECTION

1. Brian Douglas Marchant III
2. BD winked at Jessie, and Jessie told him not to because she thinks winking is "dumb."
3. He had taken his shoes off, and she didn't allow people with bare feet in the shop.
4. about who she is and what she looks like, about food, about the weather and—finally—about falling for BD
5. to annoy her, which is a way of getting attention
6. Answers will vary; students may say that BD was a flirt, self-absorbed, or liked to do things his own way.
7. He was "cooperating" with her, trying to turn around her previous complaint that he never listened to other people or considered their feelings.
8. Students should see the "in-love/out-of-love" seesaw of the plot.
9. Answers will vary, but students should point out the two great strengths of the journal approach: Everything is first-person, and it's written in the language of a 15-year-old.
10. It refers to Mao Tze Fong, a figure Jessie made up when she compared the arrival in America of BD's pioneer ancestors with an imaginary invasion by Fong. Fong Mountain becomes the place where refugees from Fong run to hide. For Jessie, it also has a second meaning—a place where she feels lonely.

Respond to Literature: It is probably safe to say that nearly everyone has kept a journal at some point in their lives; it's probably also true that few people have kept one consistently. Why do people start writing in journals and why do they stop?

T46

UNDERSTAND THE SELECTION

Recall

1. What is BD's real name?

2. What was BD's and Jessie's first "fight" about?

3. Why did the owner of the Dippin Do-Nuts shop throw BD out?

Infer

4. Although Jessie feels she has nothing to say, she does write. What is her first topic?

5. Why do you think BD gave Jessie a double wink after she had told him not to wink at her?

6. Describe the kind of person BD is.

7. Why did BD take Jessie's recommendation to have a cinnamon-chocolate doughnut?

Apply

8. Make a "map" of the plot developments for this story.

9. Do you think this story could have been told better in a different form? Why?

10. Explain the significance of the title, "Up on Fong Mountain."

Respond to Literature

Do you keep a journal? If you do, what do you like most about writing in it? If you do not, why not?

46

WRITE ABOUT THE SELECTION

When Jessie returns to school the following year, her English teacher asks that each student update last year's journal: "Your assignment for this first week of school is to write about what has happened to you since you handed in your journal to Miss Durmacher on June 24. I want you to follow up on something you wrote about in that journal. Write in one entry or several."

Imagine that you are Jessie Granatstein or BD. How would you complete the assignment?

Prewriting: What has happened between you two since June 24? Is the relationship on, off, or over? How did it get that way? Make a brief cluster of what your journal entry or entries will say.

Writing: Use the cluster to write additional entries in your journal. Remember that you may use one or several entries. Write the way a teen would write.

Revising: Look again at Jessie's original journal and study the tone of the entries. Can you do anything to make your entry or entries sound more authentic? Since journals are forms of personal writing, they are written in the first person, using the pronouns *I* and *me*. Did you follow this style?

Proofreading: Reread your journal entry or entries and check for errors. Describing the timing of actions is important in a journal. Make sure you have used the same date form as Jessie and that you have indented the first line of each entry. Check your punctuation throughout.

Unit 1

ANSWERS TO WRITE ABOUT THE SELECTION

Prewriting: Have students work in pairs as boy-girl. Ask students to role play a meeting between Jessie and BD on the first day of the new school year. The exercise should help focus ideas on what's happened to the relationship.

Writing: Circulate as students work individually. Ask to read an entry or two. Check that students are writing "in character," including first-person point of view.

Revising: As a class examine one or several specific entries. Discuss what creates the tone of her journal, and how it can be copied.

Proofreading: Have students regroup in pairs and share their journal entries with their partner. The partner should check for errors while reading the journal update.

LDP Activity: Have LDP students write a few sentences on how they would feel about keeping a journal. Depending on the group, this might be a worthwhile activity. Journal writing builds *fluency* in the writing process.

THINK ABOUT THE SHORT STORY

One of the most important elements of a short story is theme. **Theme** is the main idea behind what the author has written. Sometimes there are several themes in a story, but one main theme always overshadows the others.

1. Think about the theme of "Up on Fong Mountain." Look at the introductory "memo" for hints about the theme. Are there any?

2. Look at the first entry in Jessie's journal. Do you see any other hints about the theme?

3. What do you think is the main theme of "Up on Fong Mountain"?

4. How does the plot relate to the theme?

5. Titles of short stories often relate to the theme. Does the title of "Up on Fong Mountain" relate to the theme? Explain your answer.

DEVELOP YOUR VOCABULARY

A **root word** is a word, or a part of a word, that is used to form other words. Often finding the root word can help you figure out the meaning of the entire word.

An example is *dictatorial*. You might not know what it means, but you might know what the root word, *dictator*, means. A dictator is someone who tells others what to do; dictatorial is an adjective applied to the action of being a dictator, or forcing one's beliefs upon someone else.

Find the root of each of the following words. Check definitions in a dictionary if you are not sure. Then figure out the meaning of the entire word, and use each word in a sentence.

1. relationship
2. gangster
3. froggy
4. disregard
5. slippery
6. picky
7. cooperation
8. sneakers
9. impossible
10. amazement
11. monstrous
12. metallic

1. Yes, the last two paragraphs discuss the purpose of journals.
2. Yes, Jessie says she has nothing to write about—and then goes on, in the next months, to write a lot.
3. Love lost, love gained, we all have feelings to write about.
4. The back-and-forth seesaw elicits all sorts of feelings in Jessie.
5. Yes, it does. For Jessie, being "up on Fong Mountain" is the equivalent of being lonely, having no one who will listen to her, no outlet for expressing her feelings—and that's exactly the role the journal has filled.

ANSWERS TO DEVELOP YOUR VOCABULARY

1. relation; relationship is the connection between two people
2. gang; a gangster is someone who belongs to a gang, usually for criminal purposes
3. frog; froggy refers to a scratchy, hoarse voice
4. regard; disregard is not paying attention to or respecting someone
5. slip; slippery is slick
6. pick; picky means choosey
7. cooperate; cooperation is working with others
8. sneak; sneakers are lightweight shoes, often made of canvas or a synthetic material, worn for playing sports or for casual dress
9. possible; impossible means not capable of being done
10. amaze; amazement is surprise or awe
11. monster; monstrous means big and scary
12. metal; metallic means like metal

Sample sentences:

1. Our relationship ended on Valentine's Day because I forgot to buy a present.
2. That gangster should not be allowed within 100 miles of a bank.
3. After days of tough campaigning, his voice was froggy.
4. Disregard for others has no place at this school.
5. Whoa! This ice is slippery!
6. The young child was a picky eater.
7. Cooperation is necessary for survival.
8. She slid on her sneakers whenever it rained.
9. Completing this assignment is impossible.
10. He gazed in amazement at the scene before him.
11. What a monstrous, hideous thing to do!
12. The water had a metallic taste to it.

More About Figures of Speech: Remind students that figures of speech are words or phrases that say things indirectly. What is meant is *not* exactly what is said. Many figures of speech compare different things by using the words "like" or "as"; for example, "I wandered lonely *as* a cloud." This kind of comparison is called a simile. Another figure of speech which also compares different things but does *not* use "like" or "as" is called a "metaphor"; for example, "I'm a lonely cloud in the sky." Other figures of speech include personification and hyperbole. In order that students won't be overwhelmed by Shakespeare's rich use of language, encourage them to concentrate on just one figure of speech in this selection—the simile. Others will be pointed out, however, and students should be helped in exploring those, as well.

Cooperative/Collaborative Learning Activity: Have students work in groups to brainstorm ideas about similes and metaphors. To begin, they might want to peruse this book for specific examples by modern writers, such as Langston Hughes and Maya Angelou. Next, give each group a different subject—the last day of school, a day at summer camp, a 4th of July picnic. Ask students to write a simile or metaphor about their subject, and share it with the group. Then challenge the groups

Figures of speech are expressions that follow a particular form. Two important figures of speech are similes and metaphors. Similes and metaphors are comparisons. They point out similarities between things that ordinarily do not seem similar. **Similies** use *like* or *as* to point out a comparison—*eyes like stars*—while **metaphors** compare without special words—*her eyes are stars.*

Figures of speech add punch to a poem or literary passage; they make literature more powerful and effective.

William Shakespeare is considered by many the greatest English-language writer who ever lived. What makes him stand out among writers is his creative use of language. Among other things, Shakespeare includes many figures of speech in his plays and poems.

As you read the adaptation of *Romeo and Juliet,* ask yourself:

1. How are similes and metaphors used?
2. How do figures of speech enrich the play?

SKILL BUILDER

Use a simile or metaphor to describe your feelings about reading Shakespeare. Try writing several different ones, and then choose your favorite.

48   Unit 1

to unite their sentences into a single work, prose or poetry, for presentation to the class.

More About Vocabulary: Nearly 200 new words are introduced in this adapted version of "Romeo and Juliet." It is unrealistic to expect students to master them all, and many are archaic words that won't benefit a student's active vocabulary. Perhaps the best procedure is to ask students, as they read the play individually, to study the meaning of new words for better understanding of the passage in which it appears. For an even greater appreciation of its aural beauty, a class reading of the play is suggested.

ROMEO
and
JULIET

ADAPTED   *by William Shakespeare*

*R*omeo and Juliet opens with a chorus providing background that serves as an introduction to the play.

The story takes place in Verona, Italy in the 1500s. Two socially prominent families, the Capulets and the Montagues, have had a long-running feud, and lately new violence has broken out.

The chorus provides some foreshadowing. "A pair of star-crossed lovers," from the opposing families, will lose their lives because of the feud. The only hopeful note is that through their deaths, the families' conflict will end.

The lovers are, of course, Romeo and Juliet. Romeo is the son of Montague; Juliet, the daughter of Capulet. We meet Romeo first—not during the fight that opens the play, but afterwards. He has been off by himself, and he is depressed. He loves a woman, Rosaline, who, unfortunately, does not seem to love him.

A friend, Benvolio, tells him that Rosaline is not so pretty. He promises to show him some much prettier women if he will go to a banquet that evening. He must go in disguise, though, for the banquet is hosted by Capulet.

We meet Juliet as she is preparing for the banquet. Her father is hosting it partly as a way to introduce his daughter to Verona society. She is 14, and her parents think that it is time for her to marry. They hope to match her with Paris, a handsome young

Looking at Love   49

Vocabulary: Preteach the vocabulary words. See the Comprehension Workbook in the TRB.

LDP Activity: Partners: Have LDP students discuss with their partner some of the many movies about young love, e.g. "Sixteen Candles," "Dirty Dancing," etc. Have students list three movies that deal with young love. Note whether they ended happily or unhappily. Can they offer explanations why? Discuss and write.

SELECTION OBJECTIVES

After completing this selection, students will be able to
- identify similes in literary works
- express a feeling through simile
- discuss the ageless appeal of "Romeo and Juliet"
- write a letter of advice on a serious subject
- analyze the effectiveness of a specific simile
- find definitions for archaic words.

Sidelights: Shakespeare did not create the characters and story of Romeo and Juliet. He "borrowed" them from a long narrative poem written by another Englishman, Arthur Broke, who in turn had borrowed them from an Italian writer, Bandello. Such "rewriting" has been quite common throughout history. Shakespeare's version of the "Tragicall Historye" of Romeo and Juliet (as Broke's work was called) differs from previous versions in several respects: in shortening the action from nine months to less than a week; in having Juliet 14 years old rather than 18 (as in Bandello) or 16 (as in Broke); in expanding Mercutio's role; and in developing more fully the character of the Nurse.

Motivation for Reading: One literary critic has noted that the most popular Shakespearean passages among Oxford University students in centuries past have come from "Romeo and Juliet." Ask students if they can repeat any lines from this play. Then use Bartlett's *Familiar Quotations*, or another reference book, to point out some famous lines from "Romeo and Juliet". Perhaps, however, you might simply want to emphasize that, at fourteen, Juliet was just about the same age as the class.

More About the Thematic Idea: While this selection is grouped in the unit Overview under the category "Love Found," there is another theme—and that is where the tragedy lies. Romeo and Juliet do find love, and express it to each other, but hostility between their families prevents them from showing their love publicly, and from marrying. Both die at the end of the play, yet romantics might say their love remains alive in the grave—that it is immortal.

Purpose-Setting Question: Does love conquer all?

T49

Reading Strategy: After students have read the play individually, reread the play aloud as a class. Assign speaking roles for each scene, giving everyone in class a chance to perform. If you have access to any Shakesperean recordings—John Gielgud as "Hamlet," Paul Robeson as "Othello"—you may want students to listen to their interpretations before the class reading.

Critical Thinking: "When good manners shall lie all in one or two hands, and they unwashed too..." seems like the gossip of one servant about another, but the master Shakespeare is actually foreshadowing, in symbolic terms, a main theme of the play: Good manners, or general civility, when defined for generations by a corrupt and powerful handful, will adversely affect a whole city. Verona, the city, suffers from the feud of two leading families—the Capulets and Montagues—and the servant's assertion "tis a foul thing" could portend trouble.

count. Paris has already declared his love for her. Juliet promises to consider him.

We join the action at the banquet, Act I, Scene 5. Use this list of characters to help you identify the players.

CHARACTERS

THREE SERVING MEN	FRIAR LAWRENCE
CAPULET	PARIS
SECOND CAPULET	PARIS' PAGE
ROMEO	BALTHASAR, *Romeo's man*
TYBALT	THREE WATCHMEN
JULIET	A PRINCE, *with* ATTENDANTS
NURSE	LADY CAPULET
BENVOLIO	MONTAGUE
MERCUTIO	

ACT I, SCENE 5
A hall in CAPULET'S *house.*

[Enter CAPULET, *his* WIFE, JULIET, TYBALT, NURSE, *and all the* GUESTS *and* GENTLEWOMEN *to the* MASKERS.*]*

CAPULET: Welcome, gentlemen! Ladies that have their toes
    Unplagued with corns will walk a bout[1] with you.
    Ah, my mistresses, which of you all
    Will now deny to dance? She that makes dainty.[2]
    She I'll swear hath[3] corns. Am I come near ye[4] now?
    Welcome, gentlemen! I have seen the day
    That I have worn a visor and could tell
    A whispering tale in a fair lady's ear.
    Such as would please. 'Tis gone, 'tis gone, 'tis gone.
    You are welcome, gentlemen! Come, musicians, play.

[Music plays, and they dance.]

    A hall,[5] a hall! Give room! And foot it, girls.
    More light, you knaves,[6] and turn the tables up,
    And quench the fire; the room is grown too hot.
    Ah, sirrah, this unlooked-for sport comes well.
    Nay,[7] sit; nay, sit, good cousin Capulet;
    For you and I are past our dancing days.
    How long is't now since last yourself and I
    Were in a mask?
SECOND CAPULET: By'r[8] Lady, thirty years.
CAPULET: What, man? 'Tis not so much, 'tis not so much:
    'Tis since the nuptial of Lucentio.
    Come Pentecost[9] as quickly as it will,
    Some five-and-twenty years, and then we masked.
SECOND CAPULET: 'Tis more, 'tis more. His son is elder, sir;
    His son is thirty.

---

nuptial (NUP shul) wedding
[1]**walk a bout:** dance a turn
[2]**makes dainty:** hesitates
[3]**hath:** *(archaic)* has
[4]**ye:** *(archaic)* you
[5]**a hall:** clear the hall for dancing
[6]**knave:** *(archaic)* serving boy or male servant; also sometimes a
   dishonest, deceitful person; a rogue
[7]**nay:** *(archaic)* no
[8]**by'r:** contraction of "by your"
[9]**Pentecost:** Christian holiday fifty days after Easter, marking the
   descent of the Holy Spirit upon Christ's apostles

Looking at Love   **51**

Clarification: As Capulet and his guests enter, the characters change but not the scene. The setting stays the same. Throughout the play, scene changes are marked with notations at the beginning of each new scene.

Enrichment: On the entrance of Capulet, a scene notation mentions "to the maskers." Masked balls were common entertainments of the time.

Clarification: Remind students that Romeo, a Montague, is not welcome at the party and, therefore, is in disguise. Nor does he know many of the people there.

Literary Focus: Point out the first simile encountered in this adaptation. It occurs when Romeo, in his opening speech, describes Juliet "as a rich jewel in an Ethiop's ear." It is a classic example of "love at first sight."

Clarification: When Capulet says "...gentle coz, let him alone," he is putting Tybalt in his place and telling him that he, Capulet, is the master of his house.

Literary Focus: Tybalt's bitterness at Romeo's presence is a foreshadowing of the trouble that lies ahead.

CAPULET: Will you tell me that?
    His son was but a ward two years ago.
ROMEO [to a SERVINGMAN]: What lady's that which doth
        enrich the hand
    Of yonder knight?
SERVINGMAN: I know not, sir.
ROMEO: O, she doth teach the torches to burn bright!
    It seems she hangs upon the cheek of night
    As a rich jewel in an Ethiop's[10] ear—
    Beauty too rich for use, for earth too dear!
    So shows a snowy dove trooping with crows
    As yonder lady o'er[11] her fellows shows.
    The measure done, I'll watch her place of stand
    And, touching hers, make blessed my rude hand.
    Did my heart love till now? Forswear[12] it, sight!
    For I ne'er[13] saw true beauty till this night.
TYBALT: This, by his voice, should be a Montague.
    Fetch me my rapier, boy. What! Dares the slave
    Come hither, covered with an antic face,[14]
    To fleer[15] and scorn at our solemnity?
    Now, by the stock and honor of my kin,
    To strike him dead I hold it not a sin.
CAPULET: Why, how now, kinsman? Wherefore[16] storm you so?
TYBALT: Uncle, this is a Montague, our foe,
    A villain, that is hither come in spite
    To scorn at our solemnity this night.
CAPULET: Young Romeo is it?
TYBALT: 'Tis he, that villain Romeo.
CAPULET: Content thee, gentle coz,[17] let him alone.

---

ward (WAWRD) a minor, or someone under the age of 18 or 21
rude (ROOD) crude or rough; also, impolite
rapier (RAY pee ur) sword
hither (HITH ur) to, toward, or here
[10]**Ethiop:** old term for a Black person; short for Ethiopian
[11]**o'er:** shortened form of "over"
[12]**forswear:** (archaic) deny
[13]**ne'er:** shortened form of "never"
[14]**antic face:** (archaic) strange or funny; an "antic face" is a mask
[15]**fleer:** (archaic) sneer or mock
[16]**wherefore:** (archaic) why
[17]**coz:** usually "cousin" but used here as a term of address for any relative. Capulet is Tybalt's uncle.

A bears him like a portly gentleman,[18]
And, to say truth, Verona brags of him
To be a virtuous and well-governed youth.
I would not for the wealth of all this town
Here in my house do him disparagement.
Therefore be patient; take no note of him.
It is my will, the which if thou respect,
Show a fair presence and put off these frowns,
An ill-beseeming[19] semblance for a feast.

Meanwhile, Romeo and Juliet meet.

ROMEO: If I profane with my unworthiest hand
   This holy shrine, the gentle sin is this:
My lips, two blushing pilgrims, ready stand
   To smooth that rough touch with a tender kiss.
JULIET: Good pilgrim, you do wrong your hand too much,
   Which mannerly devotion shows in this;
For saints have hands that pilgrims' hands do touch,
   And palm to palm is holy palmers' kiss.
ROMEO: Have not saints lips, and holy palmers too?
JULIET: Ay, pilgrim, lips that they must use in prayer.
ROMEO: O, then, dear saint, let lips do what hands do!
   They pray; grant thou, lest faith turn to despair.
JULIET: Saints do not move,[20] though grant for prayers' sake.
ROMEO: Then move not while my prayer's effect I take.
   Thus from my lips, by thine my sin is purged.   *[Kisses her.]*
JULIET: Then have my lips the sin that they have took.
ROMEO: Sin from my lips? O trespass sweetly urged![21]
   Give me my sin again.   *[Kisses her.]*

---

portly (PAWRT lee) heavy, but dignified
virtuous (VUR choo us) honorable
disparagement (di SPAR ij munt) discredit, insult
semblance (SEM bluns) appearance
profane (proh FAYN) show disrespect for holy things
shrine (SHRYN) place of worship or devotion
palmers (PAHM urz) pilgrims
lest (LEST) for fear that
purge (PURJ) get rid of
[18]**A . . . gentleman:** He behaves like a dignified gentleman.
[19]**ill-beseeming:** *(archaic)* inappropriate
[20]**move:** initiate involvement in earthly affairs
[21]**O . . . urged!:** Romeo is saying, in substance, that he is happy. Juliet
   calls his kiss a sin, for now he can take it back—by another kiss.

Looking at Love   53

Clarification: "A bears him like a portly gentleman" indicates that Romeo, in Capulet's opinion, is behaving with dignity: He will not ask Romeo to leave the party.

Enrichment: Juliet's mention, on first meeting Romeo, of "palm to palm" refers to the pilgrims who carried palms from the Holy land as proof of their journey.

Reading Strategy: On their meeting, Romeo and Juliet engage in repartee of the highest order, witty and spirited, that reveals the playful yet earnest nature of the budding relationship between them.

Literary Focus: When she tells Romeo that pilgrims must use lips "in prayer," Juliet is clarifying her "Good Pilgrim" address for Romeo. In using end rhyme twice in this address, Juliet is following Romeo's lead. You might want to review the scene for other examples of rhyme. When is rhyme used, and what is its effect?

JULIET: You kiss by th' book.

NURSE: Madam, your mother craves a word with you.

ROMEO: What is her mother?

NURSE: Marry, bachelor,
    Her mother is the lady of the house,
    And a good lady, and a wise and virtuous.
    I nursed her daughter that you talked withal[22]
    I tell you, he that can lay hold of her
    Shall have the chinks. [23]

ROMEO: Is she a Capulet?
    O dear account! My life is my foe's debt.[24]

BENVOLIO: Away, be gone; the sport is at the best.

ROMEO: Ay,[25] so I fear; the more is my unrest.

CAPULET: Nay, gentlemen, prepare not to be gone;
    We have a trifling foolish banquet towards.[26]
    Is it e'en[27] so?[28] Why then, I thank you all.

---

[22]**withal:** *(archaic)* with

[23]**chinks:** *(archaic)* money

[24]**My life . . . debt:** Since Juliet is a Capulet, Romeo's life is at the mercy of the enemies of his family

[25]**ay:** *(archaic)* yes

[26]**towards:** being prepared

[27]**e'en:** even

[28]**Is . . . so?:** Is it the case that you really must leave?

Unit 1

I thank you, honest gentlemen. Good night.
More torches here! Come on then; let's to bed.
Ah, sirrah,[29] by my fay,[30] it waxes late:
I'll to my rest.   *[Exit all but* JULIET *and* NURSE.]

JULIET: Come hither, nurse. What is yond[31] gentleman?

NURSE: The son and heir of old Tiberio.

JULIET: What's he that now is going out of door?

NURSE: Marry, that, I think, be young Petruchio.

JULIET: What's he that follows here, that would not dance?

NURSE: I know not.

JULIET: Go ask his name—if he is married,
My grave is like to be my wedding bed.

NURSE: His name is Romeo, and a Montague,
The only son of your great enemy.

JULIET: My only love, sprung from my only hate!
Too early seen unknown, and known too late!
Prodigious birth of love it is to me
That I must love a loathèd enemy.

NURSE: What's this? What's this?

JULIET: A rhyme I learnt even now.
Of one I danced withal.   *[One calls within, "Juliet."]*

NURSE: Anon,[32] anon!
Come, let's away; the strangers all are gone.   *[Exit.]*

ACT II

The second act begins again with the chorus. It tells us that
Romeo has replaced his love for Rosaline with love for Juliet, and
that Juliet is "alike bewitched." It reminds us of the conflict
between the families, but notes that "passion lends them [Romeo
and Juliet] power."

Benvolio and another of Romeo's friends, Mercutio, discuss
Romeo's new state of mind. They, and Romeo, have snuck into
Capulet's orchard. Then comes one of the most famous love
scenes in literature, the "balcony meeting" between Romeo and
Juliet.

---

prodigious (pruh DIJ us) monstrous
loathe (LOH*TH*) detest, hate
[29]**sirrah:** old form of address, usually said to show anger
[30]**fay:** faith
[31]**yond:** yonder; at a distance
[32]**anon:** *(archaic)* immediately, at once; also, very soon

CAPULET'S *orchard.*

ROMEO *[coming forward]:* He jests at scars that never felt a wound.
[Enter JULIET *at a window.]*

But soft! What light through yonder window breaks?
It is the East, and Juliet is the sun!
Arise, fair sun, and kill the envious moon.
Who is already sick and pale with grief
That thou her maid art[33] far more fair than she.
Be not her maid, since she is envious.
Her vestal livery is but sick and green,
And none but fools do wear it. Cast it off.
It is my lady! O, it is my love!
O, that she knew she were!
She speaks, yet she says nothing. What of that?
Her eye discourses; I will answer it.
I am too bold; 'tis not to me she speaks:
Two of the fairest stars in all the heaven,
Having some business, do entreat her eyes
To twinkle in their spheres[34] till they return.
What if her eyes were there, they in her head?
The brightness of her cheek would shame those stars
As daylight doth a lamp; her eyes in heaven
Would through the airy region stream so bright
That birds would sing and think it were not night.
See how she leans her cheek upon that hand,
O, that I were a glove upon that hand,
That I might touch that cheek!

JULIET: Ay me!

ROMEO: She speaks.
O, speak again, bright angel, for thou art
As glorious to this night, being o'er my head,
As is a wingèd messenger of heaven

---

vestal (VES tul) virtuous, pure
livery (LIV ur ee) clothing worn by servants
discourses (dis KAWRS iz) utters, talks, communicates
entreat (en TREET) beg, ask earnestly
[33]**art:** *(archaic)* is
[34]**spheres:** orbits

Literary Focus: The scene begins as Romeo uses metaphor to compare Juliet to the sun; the light at the window comes from the East, where Romeo's "fair sun" stands.

Clarification: Romeo is hiding; Juliet, at the window, is unaware that Romeo is there. The window opens onto a balcony; it is, perhaps, Shakespeare's most famous setting.

Unit 1

Clarification: "O Romeo, Romeo wherefore art thou..." begins a famous passage in which Juliet wishes he would take another name; or, if he won't do that, so great is her love she will deny that she is a Capulet.

Clarification: As she continues, Juliet declares that even if he were not a Montague, Romeo would still be himself. It is the forerunner of one of the most famous passages in world literature: "What's in a name?..."

Clarification: Romeo now speaks to Juliet, revealing his presence and his love.

Unto the white-upturnèd wond'ring eyes
Of mortals that fall back to gaze on him
When he bestrides the lazy puffing clouds
And sails upon the bosom of the air.

JULIET: O Romeo, Romeo! Wherefore art thou Romeo?[35]
Deny thy father and refuse thy name:
Or, if thou wilt[36] not, be but sworn my love,
And I'll no longer be a Capulet.

ROMEO: *[Aside]* Shall I hear more, or shall I speak at this?

JULIET: 'Tis but thy name that is my enemy.
Thou art thyself, though not[37] a Montague.
What's Montague? It is nor hand, nor foot,
Nor arm, nor face. O, be some other name
Belonging to a man.
What's in a name? That which we call a rose
By any other word would smell as sweet.
So Romeo would, were he not Romeo called.
Retain that dear perfection which he owes[38]
Without that title. Romeo, doff thy name:
And for thy name, which is no part of thee,
Take all myself.

ROMEO: I take thee at thy word.
Call me but love, and I'll be new baptized:
Henceforth I never will be Romeo.

JULIET: What man art thou, thus bescreened in night,
So stumblest on my counsel?[39]

ROMEO: By a name
I know not how to tell thee who I am.
My name, dear saint, is hateful to myself
Because it is an enemy to thee.
Had I it written, I would tear the word.

JULIET: My ears have yet not drunk a hundred words

---

bestride (bih STRYD) sit or mount
bosom (BUH zem) breast
retain (rih TAYN) hold or keep
doff (DOF) take off or discard
bescreened (bih SKREEND) hidden
[35]**Wherefore . . . Romeo?:** Why are you Romeo, a Montague?
[36]**wilt:** *(archaic)* will
[37]**though not:** even if you were not
[38]**owes:** owns, possesses
[39]**counsel:** here, secret thoughts or plans

Of thy tongue's uttering, yet I know the sound.
Art thou not Romeo, and a Montague?

ROMEO: Neither, fair maid, if either thee dislike.

JULIET: How camest thou hither, tell me, and wherefore?
The orchard walls are high and hard to climb,
And the place death, considering who thou art,
If any of my kinsmen find thee here.

ROMEO: With love's light wings did I o'erperch[40] these walls;
For stony limits cannot hold love out,
And what love can do, that dares love attempt.
Therefore thy kinsmen are no stop to me.

JULIET: If they do see thee, they will murder thee.

ROMEO: Alack[41] there lies more peril in thine eye
Than twenty of their swords! Look thou but sweet,
And I am proof[42] against their enmity.

JULIET: I would not for the world they saw thee here.

ROMEO: I have night's cloak to hide me from their eyes;
And but[43] thou love me, let them find me here.
My life were better ended by their hate
Than death proroguèd, wanting of thy love.

JULIET: By whose direction found'st thou out this place?

ROMEO: By love, that first did prompt me to inquire.
He lent me counsel, and I lent him eyes.
I am no pilot; yet, wert thou as far
As that vast shore washed with the farthest sea,
I should adventure[44] for such merchandise.

JULIET: Thou knowest the mask of night is on my face;
Else would a maiden blush bepaint my cheek
For that which thou hast heard me speak tonight.
Fain[45] would I dwell on form—fain, fain deny
What I have spoke; but farewell compliment![46]
Dost thou love me? I know thou wilt say "Ay";

---

enmity (EN muh tee) hate
prorogued (proh ROHGD) postponed
[40]o'erperch: shortened form of "overperch," meaning "fly over"
[41]alack: exclamation of surprise or disappointment
[42]proof: here, protected with armor
[43]and but: unless
[44]adventure: here, risk as a voyage
[45]fain: (archaic) with eagerness, gladly
[46]compliment: here, etiquette

Looking at Love

Literary Focus: When Juliet tells Romeo that "my ears have yet not drunk...", it is a good example of the many rhetorical techniques Shakespeare constantly uses; in this instance, it is a *synecdoche*, or using a part to stand for the whole. Thus "ears," represent the whole of Juliet. In the same way, Romeo is represented by his "tongue."

Enrichment: When Romeo says, "With love's light wings...", he is saying, in short, "love conquers all."

Clarification: There's more danger in your eye, to paraphrase Romeo, than in twenty of their swords, for you have only to look sweet and I am protected from their hatred of me.

Clarification: In telling Romeo that "the mask of night is on my face..." Juliet might be paraphrased as saying, It's dark, and the darkness hides my blushing, caused by what you heard. I could do what polite manners tell me to do, which is deny what I said; but I won't! Goodbye to convention!

Literary Focus: When Juliet speaks of "this contract [marriage] tonight...", Shakespeare uses a simile to compare lightning with Romeo's marriage proposal. Then he enlarges on the image by describing Juliet's fear that too quickly love like lightening, "doth cease to be."

And I will take thy word. Yet, if thou swear'st,
Thou mayst prove false. At lovers' perjuries,
They say Jove[47] laughs. O gentle Romeo,
If thou dost love, pronounce it faithfully.
Or if thou thinkest I am too quickly won,
I'll frown and be perverse and say thee nay,
So thou wilt woo; but else, not for the world.
In truth, fair Montague, I am too fond,
And therefore thou mayst think my havior[48] light:
But trust me, gentleman, I'll prove more true
Than those that have more cunning to be strange.[49]
I should have been more strange, I must confess,
But that thou overheard'st, ere[50] I was ware,
My truelove passion. Therefore pardon me,
And not impute this yielding to light love,
Which the dark night hath so discovered.

ROMEO: Lady, by yonder blessed moon I vow,
That tips with silver all these fruit-tree tops—

JULIET: O, swear not by the moon, th' inconstant moon,
That monthly changes in her circle orb,
Lest that thy love prove likewise variable.

ROMEO: What shall I swear by?

JULIET: Do not swear at all;
  Or if thou wilt, swear by thy gracious self,
  Which is the god of my idolatry,
  And I'll believe thee.

ROMEO: If my heart's dear love—

JULIET: Well, do not swear. Although I joy in thee,
I have no joy of this contract[51] tonight.
It is too rash, too unadvised, too sudden;
Too like the lightning, which doth cease to be
Ere one can say it lightens. Sweet, good night!
This bud of love, by summer's ripening breath,

---

perverse (pur VURS) here, stubbornly difficult or contrary
impute (im PYOOT) charge to or blame
[47]**Jove:** supreme god in Roman mythology: also called "Jupiter"
[48]**havior:** behavior
[49]**strange:** distant and cold
[50]**ere:** before
[51]**contract:** betrothal

Unit 1

May prove a beauteous flow'r when next we meet.
Good night, good night! As sweet repose and rest
Come to thy heart as that within my breast!

ROMEO: O, wilt thou leave me so unsatisfied?

JULIET: What satisfaction canst thou have tonight?

ROMEO: Th' exchange of thy love's faithful vow for mine.

JULIET: I gave thee mine before thou didst request it;
And yet I would it were to give again.

ROMEO: Wouldst thou withdraw it? For what purpose, love?

JULIET: But to be frank[52] and give it thee again.
And yet I wish but for the thing I have.
My bounty[53] is as boundless as the sea,
My love as deep; the more I give to thee,
The more I have, for both are infinite,
I hear some noise within. Dear love, adieu!

[NURSE calls within.]

---

repose (rih POHZ) rest, or peace of mind
adieu (uh DYOO) French for "goodbye"
[52]**frank:** here, generous
[53]**bounty:** what I have to give

Looking at Love

61

Enrichment: As Juliet hears a noise, she says "Adieu" to Romeo. Thus begin their efforts to leave one another. Parting is never easy when love is found, so Shakespeare draws the scene out.

Anon, good nurse! Sweet Montague, be true.
Stay but a little, I will come again.   [Exit.]
ROMEO: O blessed, blessed night! I am afeard,
Being in night, all this is but a dream,
Too flattering-sweet to be substantial.

[Enter JULIET again.]

JULIET: Three words, dear Romeo, and good night indeed.
If that thy bent of love be honorable,
Thy purpose marriage, send me word tomorrow,
By one that I'll procure to come to thee,
Where and what time thou wilt perform the rite;
And all my fortunes at thy foot I'll lay
And follow thee my lord throughout the world.
NURSE [within]: Madam!
JULIET: I come anon.—But if thou meanest not well,
I do beseech thee—
NURSE [within]: Madam!
JULIET: By and by[54] I come.—
To cease thy strife[55] and leave me to my grief.
Tomorrow will I send.
ROMEO: So thrive my soul—
JULIET: A thousand times good night!   [Exit.]
ROMEO: A thousand times the worse, to want thy light!
Love goes toward love as schoolboys from their books;
But love from love, toward school with heavy looks.
[Enter JULIET again.]
JULIET: Hist![56] Romeo, hist! O for a falc'ner's[57] voice
To lure this tassel[58] gentle back again!
Bondage[59] is hoarse and may not speak aloud,

---

substantial (sub STAN chul) real
bent (BENT) purpose or inclination
procure (proh KYUUR) obtain, arrange
beseech (bih SEECH) ask earnestly
[54]**By and by:** at once
[55]**strife:** *(archaic)* strong efforts
[56]**hist:** exclamation said to draw attention, like "listen" or "quiet"
[57]**falc'ner:** falconer, or someone who keeps and trains the hawklike
  birds known as falcons
[58]**tassel:** a male falcon, properly called a "tiercel"
[59]**bondage:** slavery, or being subjected to someone else. Juliet means
  the nearness of her family makes it hard to talk

62   **Unit 1**

Else would I tear the cave where Echo[60] lies
And make her airy tongue more hoarse than mine
With repetition of ''My Romeo!''
ROMEO: It is my soul that calls upon my name.
How silver-sweet sound lovers' tongues by night,
Like softest music to attending ears!
JULIET: Romeo!
ROMEO: My sweet?
JULIET: What o'clock tomorrow
Shall I send to thee?
ROMEO: By the hour of nine.
JULIET: I will not fail. 'Tis twenty year till then.
I have forgot why I did call thee back.
ROMEO: Let me stand here till thou remember it.
JULIET: I shall forget, to have thee still stand there,
Rememb'ring how I love thy company.
ROMEO: And I'll stay, to have thee still forget,
Forgetting any other home but this.
JULIET: 'Tis almost morning. I would have thee gone—
And yet no farther than a wanton's bird,
That lets it hop a little from his hand,
Like a poor prisoner in his twisted gyves,[61]
And with a silken thread plucks it back again,
So loving-jealous of his liberty.
ROMEO: I would I were thy bird.
JULIET: Sweet, so would I.
Yet I should kill thee with much cherishing.
Good night, good night! Parting is such sweet sorrow
That I shall say good night till it be morrow.   [Exit.]
ROMEO: Sleep dwell upon thine eyes, peace in thy breast!
Would I were sleep and peace, so sweet to rest!
Hence will I to my ghostly friar's[62] close cell,
His help to crave and my dear hap[63] to tell.   [Exit.]

---

wanton (WAHN tun) spoiled child
cell (SEL) small room
[60]**Echo:** in Greek mythology, a nymph whose love for Narcissus made
her waste away until nothing was left of her but her voice
[61]**gyves:** chains or fetters
[62]**ghostly friar's:** spiritual father's
[63]**dear hap:** good luck or fortune

Romeo goes to see Friar Lawrence, a Catholic priest. The friar, who knows Romeo well, consents to marry Juliet and him. Friar Lawrence hopes the marriage will end the feud between the Capulets and Montagues.

The marriage takes place, secretly, in Friar Lawrence's cell, or room.

ACT III

Act III brings another confrontation between the Capulets and Montagues. Tybalt and Mercutio fight. Romeo tries to stop them, but only hinders Mercutio, his friend. Tybalt stabs Mercutio. He dies. Romeo, distraught that he had not defended his friend, kills Tybalt.

Romeo is banished from the city for the murder. Juliet hears of the fight, and is overcome with grief: Tybalt, a cousin, has been killed by Romeo, her husband. And now Romeo is exiled.

Both Romeo and Juliet feel banishment from each other is the worst of the tragedies, however. With the help of Friar Lawrence, they spend their wedding night together, and plan for Romeo to leave for the city of Mantua. There, he will wait until tempers cool, Friar Lawrence can arrange a pardon, and the wedding is made public.

The situation, however, is complicated by Juliet's father. He announces that she is to marry Paris in three days. Juliet begs her parents to delay the wedding, but they will not. They order her to obey their wishes.

ACT IV

In Act IV Juliet flees to Friar Lawrence for guidance. She sees no way out of the situation.

Friar Lawrence, though, comes up with a plan. Juliet will take a potion that will make her appear dead. Her body will be taken to the Capulet family tomb. Romeo will be summoned from Mantua and will wait at the tomb while the potion wears off. Reunited, the two lovers can then flee together to Mantua.

ACT V

The plan goes awry, however. In Act V, the letter that Friar Lawrence sends to Romeo informing him of the plan does not reach Romeo in Mantua. Instead, Balthasar, Romeo's old servant, arrives hurriedly in Mantua and tells him he has seen Juliet's body being taken to the Capulet vault for burial. Romeo, thinking her dead, leaves immediately for Verona. He takes with him a bottle of poison. If Juliet is dead, he, too, does not wish to live. The stage is set for the dramatic climax.

SCENE 3

A churchyard: in it a monument belonging to the CAPULETS.

[Enter PARIS *and his* PAGE *with flowers and sweet water.]*

PARIS: Give me thy torch, boy. Hence, and stand aloof.
Yet put it out, for I would not be seen.

aloof (uh LOOF) at a distance, apart

Looking at Love   65

Clarification: At the beginning of the scene, the page is to stand guard to make sure no one sees Paris at the churchyard.

T65

Under yond yew trees lay thee all along,[64]
Holding thy ear close to the hollow ground.
So shall no foot upon the churchyard tread
(Being loose, unfirm, with digging up of graves)
But thou shalt hear it. Whistle then to me,
As signal that thou hearest something approach.
Give me those flowers. Do as I bid thee, go.

PAGE *[aside]:* I am almost afraid to stand alone
Here in the churchyard; yet I will adventure.[65]   *[Retires.]*

PARIS: Sweet flower, with flowers thy bridal bed I strew
(O woe! thy canopy is dust and stones)
Which with sweet[66] water nightly I will dew;
Or, wanting that, with tears distilled by moans.
The obsequies that I for thee will keep
Nightly shall be to strew thy grave and weep.

[Whistle BOY.*]*

The boy gives warning something doth approach.
What cursèd foot wanders this way tonight
To cross[67] my obsequies and true love's rite?
What, with a torch? Muffle me, night, awhile.   *[Retires.]*

[Enter ROMEO, *and* BALTHASAR *with a torch, a mattock, and a crow[67] of iron.]*

ROMEO: Give me that mattock and the wrenching iron.
Hold, take this letter. Early in the morning
See thou deliver it to my lord and father.
Give me the light. Upon thy life I charge thee,
Whate'er thou hearest or seest, stand all aloof
And do not interrupt me in my course.
Why I descend into this bed of death
Is partly to behold my lady's face.
But chiefly to take thence[69] from her dead finger

---

yew (YOO) a kind of evergreen shrub or small tree
obsequies (OB sih kweez) funeral rites or ceremonies
mattock (MAT uk) a tool like a pickax for loosening soil
[64]**lay . . . along:** lie down flat
[65]**adventure:** chance it
[66]**sweet:** perfumed
[67]**cross:** interrupt
[68]**crow:** here, crowbar
[69]**thence:** *(archaic)* from that place

A precious ring—a ring that I must use
In dear employment.[70] Therefore hence, be gone.
But if thou, jealous,[71] dost return to pry
In what I farther shall intend to do,
By heaven, I will tear thee joint by joint
And strew this hungry churchyard with thy limbs.
The time and my intents are savage-wild,
More fierce and more inexorable far
Than empty[72] tigers or the roaring sea.

BALTHASAR: I will be gone, sir, and not trouble ye.

ROMEO: So shalt thou show me friendship. Take thou that.
Live, and be prosperous; and farewell, good fellow.

BALTHASAR *[aside]:* For all this same, I'll hide me hereabout.
His looks I fear, and his intents I doubt.   *[Retires.]*

ROMEO: Thou detestable maw, thou womb of death,
Gorged with the dearest morsel of the earth,
Thus I enforce thy rotten jaws to open.
And in despite[73] I'll cram thee with more food.

[ROMEO opens the tomb.]

PARIS: This is that banished haughty Montague
That murd'red my love's cousin—with which grief
It is supposed the fair creature died—
And here is come to do some villainous shame
To the dead bodies. I will apprehend him.
Stop thy unhallowèd toil, vile Montague!
Can vengeance be pursued further than death?
Condemnèd villain, I do apprehend thee.
Obey, and go with me; for thou must die.

---

morsel (MAWR sul) a small piece or bit
haughty (HAWT ee) proud, showing disdain for others
apprehend (ap ree HEND) catch, seize, or arrest
unhallowed (un HAL ohd) unholy
vengeance (VEN juns) revenge
inexorable (in EKS uh ruh bul) unable to change or control
detestable (dih TES tuh bul) hateful
maw (MAW) stomach
womb (WOOM) stomach or uterus; any place that holds or generates
    something else
[70]**dear employment:** important business
[71]**jealous:** here, curious; that is, jealous of one's privacy
[72]**empty:** hungry
[73]**in despite:** to spite

Looking at Love   67

ROMEO: I must indeed: and therefore came I hither.
Good gentle youth, tempt not a desp'rate man.
Fly hence and leave me. Think upon these gone;
Let them affright thee. I beseech thee, youth,
Put not another sin upon my head
By urging me to fury. O, be gone!
By heaven, I love thee better than myself,
For I come hither armed against myself.
Stay not, be gone. Live, and hereafter say
A madman's mercy bid thee run away.
PARIS: I do defy thy conjurations.
And apprehend thee for a felon here.
ROMEO: Wilt thou provoke me? Then have at thee, boy!

[They fight.]

PAGE: O Lord, they fight! I will go call the watch.

[Exit. PARIS *falls.]*

PARIS: O, I am slain! If thou be merciful,
Open the tomb, lay me with Juliet.   *[Dies.]*
ROMEO: In faith, I will. Let me peruse this face.
Mercutio's kinsman, noble County Paris!
What said my man when my betossèd[74] soul
Did not attend[75] him as we rode? I think
He told me Paris should have married Juliet.
Said he not so, or did I dream it so?
Or am I mad, hearing him talk of Juliet.
To think it was so? O, give me thy hand,
One writ[76] with me in sour misfortune's book!
I'll bury thee in a triumphant grave.
A grave? O, no, a lanthorn,[77] slaught'red youth,
For here lies Juliet, and her beauty makes

---

conjuration (kon juu RAY shun) threatening appeal
felon (FEL un) criminal
provoke (pruh VOHK) excite, irritate, or anger to action
slain (SLAYN) from "slay," to kill
peruse (puh ROOZ) look at or read
[74]**betossed:** upset
[75]**attend:** give attention to
[76]**writ:** *(archaic)* wrote or written
[77]**lanthorn:** structure with windows at the top of a room to admit light; sometimes also used instead of "lantern"

Critical Thinking: In Romeo's long soliloquy after the death of Paris, he unknowingly speaks an important truth: Juliet isn't dead. Had he known, what would have been their fate?

This vault a feasting presence[78] full of light.
Death, lie thou there, by a dead man interred.

[Lays him in the tomb.]

How oft when men are at the point of death
Have they been merry! Which their keepers call
A lightning before death. O, how may I
Call this a lightning? O my love, my wife!
Death, that hath sucked the honey of thy breath,
Hath had no power yet upon thy beauty.
Thou art not conquered. Beauty's ensign yet
Is crimson in thy lips and in thy cheeks,
And death's pale flag is not advanced there.
Tybalt, liest thou there in thy bloody sheet?
O, what more favor can I do to thee
Than with that hand that cut thy youth in twain[79]
To sunder his that was thine enemy?

---

keepers (KEE purz) jailers
interred (in TURD) buried
ensign (EN sun) flag or banner
sunder (SUN dur) break apart or split
[78]**feasting presence:** chamber fit for celebration
[79]**twain:** *(archaic)* two

Looking at Love

Forgive me, cousin!. Ah, dear Juliet.
Why art thou yet so fair? Shall I believe
That unsubstantial Death is amorous,
And that the lean abhorrèd monster keeps
Thee here in dark to be his paramour?
For fear of that I still will stay with thee
And never from this pallet of dim night
Depart again. Here, here will I remain
With worms that are thy chambermaids. O, here
Will I set up my everlasting rest
And shake the yoke of inauspicious stars
From this world-wearied flesh. Eyes, look your last!
Arms, take your last embrace! And, lips, O you
The doors of breath, seal with a righteous kiss
A dateless[80] bargain to engrossing death!
Come, bitter conduct;[81] come, unsavory guide!
Thou desperate pilot,[82] now at once run on
The dashing rocks thy seasick weary bark!
Here's to my love! *[Drinks.]* O true apothecary!
Thy drugs are quick. Thus with a kiss I die.   *[Falls.]*

[Enter FRIAR LAWRENCE, *with lanthorn, crow, and spade.]*

FRIAR: Saint Francis be my speed![83] How oft tonight
    Have my old feet stumbled[84] at graves! Who's there?
BALTHASAR: Here's one, a friend, and one that knows you well.
FRIAR: Bliss be upon you! Tell me, good my friend,
    What torch is yond that vainly lends his light

---

amorous (AM uh rus) full of love
abhorred (ab HAWRD) hated, dreaded
paramour (PAR uh muur) lover
pallet (PAL it) bed
inauspicious (in aw SPISH us) unlucky, forecasting misfortune
righteous (RY chus) morally right, virtuous
engrossing (in GROHS ing) taking all one's attention
unsavory (un SAY vuh ree) unpleasant
bark (BAHRK) a small sailing boat
apothecary (uh POTH uh kear ee) someone who prepares and
  dispenses drugs
[80]dateless: eternal
[81]conduct: here, guide (referring to the poison)
[82]pilot: captain (Romeo himself)
[83]speed: help
[84]stumbled: stumbling was thought to be a bad omen

Unit 1

To grubs and eyeless skulls? As I discern,
It burneth in the Capels' monument.
BALTHASAR: It doth so, holy sir; and there's my master,
One that you love.
FRIAR: Who is it?
BALTHASAR: Romeo.
FRIAR: How long hath he been there?
BALTHASAR: Full half an hour.
FRIAR: Go with me to the vault.
BALTHASAR: I dare not, sir.
My master knows not but I am gone hence,
And fearfully did menace me with death
If I did stay to look on his intents.
FRIAR: Stay then; I'll go alone. Fear comes upon me.
O, much I fear some ill unthrifty[85] thing.
BALTHASAR: As I did sleep under this yew tree here.
I dreamt my master and another fought,
And that my master slew him.
FRIAR: Romeo!
Alack, alack, what blood is this which stains
The stony entrance of this sepulcher?
What mean these masterless[86] and gory swords
To lie discolored by this place of peace?   *[Enters the tomb.]*

Romeo! O, pale! Who else? What, Paris too?
And steeped in blood? Ah, what an unkind[87] hour
Is guilty of this lamentable chance!
The lady stirs.   *[JULIET rises.]*

JULIET: O comfortable[88] friar! Where is my lord?
I do remember well where I should be,
And there I am. Where is my Romeo?

---

grubs (GRUBZ) young wormlike stage of some insects
discern (dih SURN) make out or recognize
sepulcher (SEP ul kur) small chamber used as a tomb
gory (GOR ee) bloody
lamentable (LAM en tuh bul) distressing, sorrowful
[85]**unthrifty:** *(archaic)* unfortunate
[86]**masterless:** discarded
[87]**unkind:** unnatural
[88]**comfortable:** *(archaic)* comfort-giving

Looking at Love   71

Literary Focus: When the friar says that "fear comes upon me," he foreshadows the tragedy that is about to be discovered.

FRIAR: I hear some noise. Lady, come from that nest
Of death, contagion, and unnatural sleep.
A greater power than we can contradict
Hath thwarted our intents. Come, come away.
Thy husband in thy bosom there lies dead;
And Paris too. Come, I'll dispose of thee
Among a sisterhood of holy nuns.
Stay not to question, for the watch is coming.
Come, go, good Juliet. I dare no longer stay.
JULIET: Go, get thee hence,[89] for I will not away. *[Exit FRIAR.]*
What's here? A cup, closed in my truelove's hand?
Poison, I see, hath been his timeless[90] end.
O churl! Drunk all, and left no friendly drop
To help me after? I will kiss thy lips.
Haply[91] some poison yet doth hang on them
To make me die with a restorative.   *[Kisses him.]*
Thy lips are warm!
CHIEF WATCHMAN *[within]:* Lead, boy. Which way?
JULIET: Yea, noise? Then I'll be brief. O happy[92] dagger!

[Snatches ROMEO'S dagger.]

This is thy sheath: there rust, and let me die.

[She stabs herself and falls.]

[Enter PARIS' BOY and WATCH.]

BOY: This is the place. There, where the torch doth burn.
CHIEF WATCHMAN: The ground is bloody. Search about the
churchyard.
Go, some of you: whoe'er you find attach.[93]

[Exit some of the WATCH.]

---

contagion (kun TAY jun) spreading disease
thwarted (THWAWRT id) blocked or stopped
churl (CHURL) selfish, mean, rude person
restorative (rih STAWR uh tiv) something that brings back
   consciousness or health generally; a medicine
[89]**hence:** *(archaic)* away from this place
[90]**timeless:** here, too soon
[91]**haply:** perhaps
[92]**happy:** *(archaic)* convenient
[93]**attach:** here, arrest

Unit 1

Pitiful sight! Here lies the County slain:
And Juliet bleeding, warm, and newly dead,
Who here hath lain this two days burièd.
Go, tell the Prince; run to the Capulets;
Raise up the Montagues: some others search.

[Exit others of the WATCH.*]*

We see the ground whereon these woes do lie,
But the true ground[94] of all these piteous woes
We cannot without circumstance[95] descry.

[Enter some of the WATCH, *with* ROMEO'S MAN, BALTHASAR.*]*

SECOND WATCHMAN: Here's Romeo's man. We found him in the
    churchyard.
CHIEF WATCHMAN: Hold him in safety till the Prince come hither.

[Enter FRIAR LAWRENCE *and another* WATCHMAN.*]*

THIRD WATCHMAN: Here is a friar that trembles, sighs, and
    weeps.
    We took this mattock and this spade from him
    As he was coming from this churchyard's side.
CHIEF WATCHMAN: A great suspicion! Stay[96] the friar too.

[Enter the PRINCE *and* ATTENDANTS.*]*

PRINCE: What misadventure is so early up,
    That calls our person from our morning rest?

[Enter CAPULET *and his* WIFE *with others.]*

CAPULET: What should it be, that is so shrieked abroad?
LADY CAPULET: O, the people in the street cry "Romeo,"
    Some "Juliet," and some "Paris": and all run
    With open outcry toward our monument.
PRINCE: What fear is this which startles in your ears?

---

woes (WOHZ) misery, sorrows
 descry (dih SKRY) discover, see clearly
[94]**ground:** cause
[95]**circumstance:** here, details
[96]**stay:** here, keep or hold

Looking at Love   73

Enrichment: Juliet, now conscious, tells the friar she will "not away." She hopes that Romeo has left at least a drop of poison for her—but he has drunk it all. She kisses him, hoping some poison is left on his lips. Then, when she realizes the nightwatch is coming, she takes Romeo's dagger and kills herself—proving her resolve to join her lover in death.

Clarification: Upon his entrance, the chief watchman realizes that something very strange has happened, but he's not sure exactly what. Supposedly, Juliet died two days ago, yet her body is bloody and still warm.

CHIEF WATCHMAN: Sovereign, here lies the County Paris lain;
    And Romeo dead; and Juliet, dead before,
    Warm and new killed.
PRINCE: Search, seek, and know how this foul murder comes.
CHIEF WATCHMAN: Here is a friar, and slaughtered Romeo's man.
    With instruments upon them fit to open
    These dead men's tombs.
CAPULET: O heavens! O wife, look how our daughter bleeds!
    This dagger hath mista'en, for, lo, his house[97]
    Is empty on the back of Montague.
    And it missheathèd in my daughter's bosom!
LADY CAPULET: O me, this sight of death is as a bell
    That warns my old age to a sepulcher.

[Enter MONTAGUE *and others.]*

PRINCE: Come, Montague; for thou art early up
    To see thy son and heir more early down.
MONTAGUE: Alas, my liege, my wife is dead tonight!
    Grief of my son's exile hath stopped her breath.
    What further woe conspires against mine age?
PRINCE: Look, and thou shalt see.
MONTAGUE: O thou untaught! What manners is in this,
    To press before thy father to a grave?
PRINCE: Seal up the mouth of outrage[98] for a while,
    Till we can clear these ambiguities
    And know their spring, their head, their true descent;
    And then will I be general of your woes[99]
    And lead you even to death. Meantime forbear,
    And let mischance be slave to patience.[100]
    Bring forth the parties of suspicion.

Clarification: When Capulet arrives at the death scene, he sees that the dagger isn't in the sheath carried by Romeo, but is plunged into Juliet's breast.

Clarification: That sight leads Lady Capulet to wonder if the horror of it all will, literally, frighten her to death.

liege (LEEJ) lord
conspire (kun SPYR) plan and act together secretly
ambiguities (am buh GYOO uh teez) things that are not clear
forbear (fawr BAIR) keep under control, endure
mischance (mis CHANS) misfortune
[97]**house:** sheath
[98]**mouth of outrage:** violent cries
[99]**general . . . woes:** leader in your sorrowing
[100]**let . . . patience:** be patient in the face of misfortune

Unit 1

FRIAR: I am the greatest, able to do least,
     Yet most suspected, as the time and place
     Doth make against me, of this direful murder;
     And here I stand, both to impeach and purge
     Myself condemnèd and myself excused.
PRINCE: Then say at once what thou dost know in this.
FRIAR: I will be brief, for my short date of breath[101]
     Is not so long as is a tedious tale.
     Romeo, there dead, was husband to that Juliet;
     And she, there dead, that's Romeo's faithful wife.
     I married them; and their stol'n marriage day
     Was Tybalt's doomsday, whose untimely death
     Banished the new-made bridegroom from this city;
     For whom, and not for Tybalt, Juliet pined.
     You, to remove that siege of grief from her,
     Betrothed and would have married her perforce
     To County Paris. Then comes she to me
     And with wild looks bid me devise some mean
     To rid her from this second marriage,
     Or in my cell there would she kill herself.
     Then gave I her (so tutored by my art)
     A sleeping potion: which so took effect
     As I intended, for it wrought on her
     The form of death. Meantime I writ to Romeo
     That he should hither come as[102] this dire night
     To help to take her from her borrowed grave,
     Being the time the potion's force should cease,
     But he which bore my letter, Friar John,
     Was stayed by accident, and yesternight
     Returned my letter back. Then all alone
     At the prefixèd hour of her waking
     Came I to take her from her kindred's vault:

Literary Focus: With the climax past, the resolution now begins. The Prince demands an explanation, and Friar Lawrence explains the whole story.

---

direful (DYR ful) terrible, dreadful
impeach (im PEECH) accuse
bridegroom (BRYD groom) groom
potion (POH shun) a drink with special powers, such as medicine or
     poison
wrought (RAWT) formed or brought about
[101]**date of breath:** term of life
[102]**as:** here, on

Looking at Love

Meaning to keep her closely[103] at my cell
Till I conveniently could send to Romeo.
But when I came, some minute ere the time
Of her awakening, here untimely lay
The noble Paris and true Romeo dead.
She wakes; and I entreated her come forth
And bear this work of heaven with patience;
But then a noise did scare me from the tomb,
And she, too desperate, would not go with me,
But, as it seems, did violence on herself.
All this I know, and to the marriage
Her nurse is privy; and if aught[104] in this
Miscarried by my fault, let my old life
Be sacrificed some hour before his time
Unto the rigor of severest law.

CAPULET: O brother Montague, give me thy hand.
This is my daughter's jointure,[105] for no more
Can I demand.

MONTAGUE: But I can give thee more;
For I will raise her statue in pure gold,
That whiles Verona by that name is known,
There shall no figure at such rate[106] be set
As that of true and faithful Juliet.

CAPULET: As rich shall Romeo's by his lady's lie—
Poor sacrifices of our enmity!

PRINCE: A glooming[107] peace this morning with it brings.
The sun for sorrow will not show his head.
Go hence, to have more talk of these sad things;
Some shall be pardoned, and some punishèd;
For never was a story of more woe
Than this of Juliet and her Romeo.

[Exit all.]

---

untimely (un TYM lee) coming before the expected time
privy (PRIV ee) secretly informed
miscarried (mis KAR eed) went wrong
rigor (RIG ur) strictness
[103]**closely:** here, hidden
[104]**aught:** *(archaic)* anything whatever
[105]**jointure:** marriage gift
[106]**rate:** value
[107]**glooming:** cloudy, gloomy

Discussion: Does the end of the feud signify permanent peace in Verona, or must each generation vow not to be the victims of hatred?

Unit 1

William Shakespeare (1564-1616)

William Shakespeare is considered by many to be the greatest playwright, and perhaps the greatest author, of all time. His works show a talent for characterization and poetic expression that have never been equaled.

Shakespeare was born in Stratford-upon-Avon in 1564. Little is known about his early life, except that he was the son of a businessman and probably attended the local grammar school. In 1582 he married Anne Hathaway, and they had three children.

Shakespeare was an actor as well as a playwright, and was a member of a group of actors called Lord Chamberlain's Men. Shakespeare was part owner of the company's theater, the Globe, and he wrote his plays exclusively for this company at the rate of about two a year.

The characters in Shakespeare's plays are the first "modern" dramatic characters—with both strengths and weaknesses. Shakespeare skillfully conveys a sense of his characters' psychological identities, and this is part of the reason why these characters have endured so vividly for so many years.

In the course of his life, Shakespeare wrote 36 plays, 154 sonnets, and 2 narrative poems. Because Shakespeare wrote his plays for performance, he was indifferent about their publication. Many of the plays that were published shortly after his death were reconstructed from memory by actors.

Looking at Love

MINI QUIZ

Write the following questions on the chalkboard or overhead projector and call on students to fill in the blanks. Discuss the answers with the class.

1. The banquet at which Romeo and Juliet meet is hosted by _____.
2. Juliet's balcony overlooks an _____.
3. In the balcony scene, Romeo and Juliet are interrupted by the _____.
4. Romeo meets _____ at the Capulet grave and kills him.
5. Juliet uses a _____ to kill herself.

Answers to Mini Quiz

1. Juliet's father, Capulet
2. orchard
3. nurse
4. Paris
5. dagger

1. Tybalt
2. in Friar Lawrence's cell
3. Where is Romeo?
4. He is young, impetuous, and in awe of Juliet's beauty.
5. Romeo is still Juliet's handsome lover, regardless of the fact he is a Montague.
6. She has discovered Romeo is dead. Friar Lawrence wants to hide her, and cover up the failed plan.
7. One example: Friar Lawrence's letters don't get through to Romeo.
8. Answers will vary, but could include street gangs and political opponents.
9. Answers will vary. Sample answer: The prince should punish no one, for the people who kept the feud alive must now suffer the loss of their beloved children.
10. The drama tells a classic story: two lovers fated not to find love because of hatred between their families.

Respond to Literature: As hinted in Question 10 above, the theme of Romeo and Juliet is timeless. Anyone who has experienced love can appreciate the tragedy in which the two lovers are caught. A modern film version of the story was "West Side Story." Also the Russian composer Prokoviev set the story to a ballet score.

Prewriting: Review as a class the roles the various characters play in the story. Ask whether students have any special thoughts or ideas they would like to share about any of the characters.

Writing: Circulate as students work individually. A general theme should be identified in the cluster,

UNDERSTAND THE SELECTION

Recall

1. Who threatens Romeo at the banquet?

2. Where are Romeo and Juliet married?

3. What is the first question Juliet asks when she awakes in the tomb?

Infer

4. How could Romeo change his love so quickly from Rosaline to Juliet?

5. Explain "That which we call a rose by any other word would smell as sweet."

6. Why does Friar Lawrence suggest Juliet go to a convent of nuns?

7. Chance plays an important part in this story. Give one example.

Apply

8. The Capulets and Montagues fight not because there is a good reason to fight, but because they are supposed to be enemies. Give a modern-day example of such conflict.

9. Whom should the prince pardon, and whom should he punish? Why?

10. Why is *Romeo and Juliet* the most famous love story in literature?

Respond to Literature

The story of *Romeo and Juliet* has been retold in many ways and sometimes adapted and modernized. Why?

78

WRITE ABOUT THE SELECTION

During Shakespeare's time, educated people wrote many letters. If you could write a letter of advice to any of the characters in *Romeo and Juliet*, to whom would you write—Romeo, Mercutio, or Juliet? How about giving advice to Tybalt, the friar, or Juliet's nurse? Choose one character with which to correspond and compose a letter.

Prewriting: As you choose the character, you will be thinking of things you would like to say to him or her. Write them down in clusters around the character's name. If at first you cannot decide on one character, choose several, make clusters, and then pick the one you think will give you the chance to write the most interesting letter.

Writing: Use the cluster to write your letter. Make sure the comments and help you offer are clear. Since you are writing a letter, you need to use the second-person pronouns—*you, yourself.*

Revising: You may write in poetry or prose. Whichever form you use, have you thought of trying to make the letter sound "old"? That is, can you make it sound as though it were written by a contemporary of the person to whom you are writing?

Proofreading: Reread what you have written and check for mistakes. Pay particular attention to **homophones,** or words that sound alike but are spelled differently. The person reading your letter might think that you are trying to make a joke instead of simply having misspelled something!

Unit 1

and students should organize their letter around it. Discuss this with any students having difficulty.

Revising: Students might like writing a "parallel" letter that "translates" their original letter into an older style. Explore with students what makes Shakespeare's writing different from modern writing. Some of it is due to his superior writing abilities, but much of it comes from the use of archaic words, different verb endings, and a more complicated style generally. Analyze one or two brief passages to pinpoint these qualities.

Proofreading: Write on the chalkboard or overhead projector some examples of homophones. Then suggest that a number can be found among the new vocabulary words. Show how slight spelling changes can create large differences in meaning.

LDP Activity: Have LDP students review their list of movies and choose one. Have students write a few sentences discussing whether the movie was realistic or unrealistic, and why they think so.

THINK ABOUT FIGURES OF SPEECH

Let us examine one specific case of Shakespeare's imaginative use of language—simile, which uses the words *like* or *as* to compare two unlike things. Figures of speech like similes add richness to literature. Shakespeare explains feelings about love by making an interesting comparison. Romeo speaks these lines when he must leave Juliet at the end of the balcony scene:

"Love goes toward love as schoolboys from
their books,
But love from love, toward school with
heavy looks."

1. What figure of speech is used?

2. What is being compared?

3. Explain the meaning of the first part of the comparison.

4. Explain the meaning of the second part of the comparison.

5. What adds to the effectiveness of the comparison?

DEVELOP YOUR VOCABULARY

Shakespeare uses many words that today are uncommon. Sometimes the meaning he intended has dropped out of use, or sometimes the word itself is no longer used.

The words *thou* and *thee* are good examples. They are pronouns, and in Shakespeare's time were used instead of *you* to address friends and other close acquaintances. *Thou* is the nominative case, *thee* the objective case, and *thy* or *thine* the possessive case.

The dictionary can help you learn about old usages. Sometimes it will note that a word, or a particular definition of a word, is **archaic** (abbreviated *arch.*). This means the word, or a definition, is rarely used today.

Look up the following words in a dictionary. Write down the definition that fits with Shakespeare's time, and then use the word in a sentence.

1. knave	**4.** hither
2. sirrah (or "sirah")	**5.** perforce
3. doth	**6.** choler

1. Simile.
2. Love and schoolboys.
3. Meeting up with the person you love is like quitting studying.
4. Leaving someone you love is like having to go to school.
5. The use of rhyme—"books" and "looks."

ANSWERS TO
DEVELOP YOUR
VOCABULARY

1. knave; a serving boy or male servant, also a rascal
2. sirrah; old form of address, often used to show contempt; fellow.
3. doth; do.
4. hither; to, toward, or here.
5. perforce; by force, enforced.
6. choler; anger.

Sample sentences:

1. Remove that knave from this hall!
2. Sirrah, I wish never to see you in my house again!
3. He doth move like a deer chased by dogs.
4. Come hither, boy, and take your punishment.
5. Ambition and greed perforce create trouble.
6. His choler flashed like sparks from a welder's torch.

Imagery and Character

An image is a mental "sensation." You are provided with information that creates a picture that you can see, hear, smell, feel, or taste in your mind. You form this picture with your imagination. The use of language that stimulates these mental pictures is called **imagery.**

Imagery appeals to the senses and helps you experience what a writer is describing. For example, a visual image allows you to "see"; an aural image allows you to "hear." When you read, you are not really seeing or hearing these things, but you can imagine that you are. You experience, in your imagination, what the writer creates.

Poets use all kinds of objects and activities to create images in their poems. In fact, if an image is unexpected or unique, it is usually very effective.

Look for answers to the following questions as you read the poems:
1. Why is imagery a powerful tool?
2. How is imagery used effectively?

SKILL BUILDER

Using imagery, describe something in your classroom. Try to think of an image that gives a vivid sense of what you are describing.

Greyday

by Maya Angelou

The day hangs heavy
loose and grey
when you're away.

A crown of thorns
a shirt of hair
is what I wear.

No one knows
my lonely heart
when we're apart.

Summer Millinery, Charles W. Hawthorne.
Chrysler Museum

Here—Hold My Hand

by Mari Evans

Here
hold my hand
let me touch you
there is
5   nothing
we can
say . . . your
soul
eludes me
10   when I reach
out
your eyes
resent
my need to know
15   you
here
hold my hand
since
there is nothing
20   we can
say

---

eludes (ih LOODS) avoids or escapes
resent (rih ZENT) to feel or show anger

Looking at Love   81

FINIS

by Waring Cuney

Now that our love has drifted
To a quiet close,
Leaving the empty ache
That always follows when beauty goes;
5 Now that you and I,
Who stood tiptoe on earth
To touch our fingers to the sky,

Have turned away
To allow our little love to die—
10 Go, dear, seek again the magic touch.
But if you are wise,
As I shall be wise,
You will not again
Love overmuch.

Maya Angelou (1928-Present)

When the American choreographer Alvin Ailey was a college student at San Francisco State, he took time away from the books to form a nightclub dance act with a young woman named Marguerite Angelos. Little did the two dancers know that in a few decades, both would be famous—Ailey as the founder of the Alvin Ailey Dance Company and Marguerite Angelos as the celebrated author Maya Angelou.

Twelve years after her partnership with Ailey, Angelou was in Cairo, Egypt as associate editor of the Arab Observer. A year later she went to Ghana, where she became a writer for the Ghanaian Times and an assistant administrator at the University of Ghana. In 1966 she returned to the states as a lecturer at the University of California.

Maya Angelou is best known for her autobiography, *I Know Why the Caged Bird Sings*, which was written in 1970. The book tells the moving and often humourous story of her childhood in segregated Arkansas. The book was made into a play for television in 1977.

In addition to her careers as a dancer and a writer, Angelou has worked as a movie and stage actress. She has written plays, books of poetry, and screen plays, and has also composed music.

Sidelights: What makes a poet? Increased sensitivity to everything in the immediate environment is one ingredient. Where does that sensitivity come from? In the case of Maya Angelou, it could be attributed to the broad range of her experiences, some of which were quite oppressive. Angelou, whose real name is Marguerite Angelos, grew up in Arkansas when segregation between black and white was prevalent. Her account of those years in her autobiography *I Know Why the Caged Bird Sings* makes it clear she learned at an early age what pain and survival really mean. Later she lived abroad, in Egypt and Ghana. Adapting to new experiences probably helped her develop a special sensitivity to the world around her.

ANSWERS TO UNDERSTAND THE SELECTION

ANSWERS TO UNDERSTAND THE SELECTION

1. When "you" are away.
2. To touch the person she has loved.
3. It "has drifted to a quiet close."
4. She describes the day as hanging "grey."
5. They are images, religious in nature, suggesting great pain.
6. No; "your eyes resent my need to know you," suggests the speaker's partner has difficulty in communication.
7. Because the "empty ache" is too hard to bear.
8. The love they once shared reached great heights.
9. She feels hurt, alone, and rejected.
10. No. The first-person character of "Finis" is sensitive, realistic, and more mature.

Respond to Literature: It was Tennyson who asserted that "'Tis better to have loved and lost, Than never to have loved at all." Ask students, Do you agree? Should one—like our three poets—bear both the pain and the beauty of love?

ANSWERS TO WRITE ABOUT THE SELECTION

Prewriting: In this assignment students may use any image they want, including metaphor, to describe the feeling they choose. As a warmup, have the class pick a feeling, and do the "Z" mapping suggested in the Student's Book.

Writing: Circulate as students work individually. Encourage students to try writing in poetry; it might be an easier way for them to express feelings.

Revising: On the chalkboard or overhead projector, write the lines from "Finis" that express the desire to reach upward—"Who stood tip-

UNDERSTAND THE SELECTION

Recall

1. When does the day seem grey to the speaker in "Greyday"?
2. Why does the speaker of "Here—Hold My Hand" want to hold hands?
3. How has love ended in "Finis?"

Infer

4. Why did Maya Angelou choose the title "Greyday" for her poem?
5. Explain the images of a "crown of thorns" and "a shirt of hair".
6. Do you think that the two people in "Here—Hold My Hand" can look at each other honestly? Why or why not?
7. Why does the speaker of "Finis" tell his partner not to "love overmuch" again?

Apply

8. What is suggested to you by the lines "Who stood tiptoe on earth to touch our fingers to the sky" in "Finis"?
9. What is the character of "Here—Hold My Hand" feeling?
10. Is the character of "Finis" the same as "Here—Hold My Hand"? Explain.

Respond to Literature

Is it better to love and then lose that love, rather than never to love at all? Why?

WRITE ABOUT THE SELECTION

Maya Angelou loses love only temporarily in "Greyday," while Mari Evans and Waring Cuney lose their loved ones completely in their poems.

All three poets are trying to capture the feeling of losing love, however. Each does it in his or her unique way, based on feelings.

How do you best express your feelings when writing about something? Do you use the first person? Do you think of images that describe your feelings? Express an important feeling with images.

Prewriting: Concentrate on one feeling. Write the feeling at the top left corner of a piece of paper. Now, make a Z from there. Along the line, fill in words or draw pictures that describe your feeling.

Writing: Combine your thoughts into a single paragraph or a few lines of poetry. "Translate" any pictures into words, using imagery if you can. Appeal to several different senses, not just sight. Can you make your readers hear, taste, smell, or feel?

Revising: Are your words communicating your feeling? Think of changing or adding words that "sharpen" your description. Make every word count!

Proofreading: Reread your description and check for unnecessary repetition. Also, check that your punctuation is consistent throughout; for example, Maya Angelou uses only a final period at the end of each verse.

toe on earth To touch our fingers to the sky." Rewrite the phrase using less expressive words—"Who tried reaching as high as we could toward the sky." Discuss with the class how just a few carefully-chosen words can sharpen an image.

Proofreading: Repetition is not necessarily bad: In "Here—Hold My Hand," several lines are re-

peated. Unnecessary repetition, however, can be boring. If you chose to write a paragraph, don't say, for example, "several lines are repeated again"; "again" is redundant. As you read for punctuation and spelling, also concentrate on deleting such unnecessary words.

LDP Activity: Have each LDP student review the large list of words describing "love lost." Have

students write a few sentences or a short poem about lost love. They may wish to work with a partner or alone.

THINK ABOUT IMAGERY

Imagery is one device an author uses to appeal to the senses. Images can be strengthened by appealing to the same sense in different ways or by appealing to a different sense at the same time. Maya Angelou describes "the day" as hanging "heavy loose and grey." "Heavy" and "loose" appeal to touch. "Grey" appeals to sight.

1. Think of an image that describes the "hand" in "Here—Hold My Hand." To which sense will you appeal?

2. Try to add an image to the description you have just thought of. Appeal to the same or a different sense.

3. None of the three poems has imagery appealing to the senses of hearing, smell, or taste. Why is this so?

4. Is any one sense "best" for imagery?

5. Think of an image appealing to the sense of hearing, smell, or taste that describes something mentioned in one of the poems.

DEVELOP YOUR VOCABULARY

Context, or the words surrounding a word, can be an important help in understanding words you do not know. Even when you do know a word, context can help to understand added meaning behind a word.

Look at the word *elude* in "Here—Hold My Hand": "your soul *eludes* me when I reach out." The theme of the poem is falling out of love. The two people cannot communicate anymore. You might guess that *elude* relates to not being able or not wanting to "reach" something. It does. *Elude* means "to avoid or escape."

Use context to help you write the meaning of the *italicized* words in the following lines. When you have finished, use a dictionary to check your meanings.

1. "Your eyes *resent* my need to know you."

2. "The sweetest joy, the wildest *woe* is love."

3. "Many waters cannot *quench* love, neither can the floods drown it."

Answers may vary, samples are given.

1. tired hand, which appeals to the sense of feel
2. cold, tired hand
3. The lack of communication is an important aspect in the poems, so it's logical that hearing is absent. As to smelling and tasting, it's more likely that these senses would be used to portray love more positively—for example, smelling the flower of love, or tasting the sweet cup of love.
4. No. The "best" sense is the one that best communicates the writer's thoughts.
5. An image of love in "Finis" might be "a glass with only a scent of the sweet wine that once filled it."

ANSWERS TO DEVELOP YOUR VOCABULARY

1. to feel angry or bitter at
2. sorrow
3. take away heat or desire

Portrait of Langston Hughes,
Winold Reiss.
National Portrait Gallery, Gift of W. Tjark Reiss

LEARN ABOUT

Tone in Poetry

Writers often have strong opinions about what they are writing. These opinions usually show in the attitude a writer expresses towards his or her subject. This attitude is usually expressed in the **tone** of a selection.

The tone can be light-hearted and mocking. It can be serious and depressing. It can be several things at once.

Poems that have strong tones tell you something about the poet's attitude. The speaker in the poem can say things in a certain way that reveals the poet's opinions about the theme.

Look for answers to the following questions as you read the poems:

1. What is the tone of each of the poems?
2. What creates the tone?

SKILL BUILDER

Think of a recent conversation you have had with somebody. How did you reveal your opinions, other than by direct comments? Did you use certain words that sounded angry, disappointed, proud, or expressed some other feeling? Did you talk about something else in order to describe your thoughts? Write a few lines of what you said. What kind of tone do the lines have? Why?

Housecleaning

by Nikki Giovanni

i always liked housecleaning
even as a child
i dug straightening
the cabinets
5   putting new paper on
the shelves
washing the refrigerator
inside out
and unfortunately this habit has
10   carried over and i find
i must remove you
from my life

Anna Washington Derry, Laura Wheeler Waring. National Museum of American Art, Smithsonian Institution, Gift of the Harmon Foundation

Where have you gone

by Mari Evans

Where have you gone

with your confident
walk with
your crooked smile

5   why did you leave
me
when you took your
laughter
and departed

10   are you aware that
with you
went the sun

all light
and what few stars
there were?

where have you gone
with your confident
walk your
crooked smile the
20   rent money
in one pocket and
my heart
in another . . .

Looking at Love   87

Reading Strategy: How can "housecleaning" possibly have anything to do with love? Ask students to keep this question in mind as they read through the poem.

Discussion: Why "unfortunately"? Giovanni almost seems to regret her housecleaning efficiency.

Literary Focus: The message in "Housecleaning" doesn't become clear until the last lines. End weight is used effectively because the reader doesn't discover until then that housecleaning is a metaphor for ending a relationship.

Critical Thinking: Ask students to contrast the title with "Where Have You Gone" with "Housecleaning." It reveals the theme immediately, while Giovanni kept us guessing about its significance.

Literary Focus: Alliteration connects the key adjectives, "confident" and "crooked" in the last verse of Evans's poem. These words convey the only feeling; remove them, and the lines are "neutral."

Literary Focus: Evans has focused on small attributes to describe the person she loved—his walk, his smile, his laughter.

Enrichment: The third verse is a cry of loneliness. The speaker feels as though she is surrounded by darkness.

Literary Focus: Repetition of the opening lines provides unity to the poem.

Critical Thinking: Worrying about the rent money *and* a broken heart may seem like a strange combination, but isn't the poet revealing her own vulnerability toward being used, both literally and figuratively?

More About Vocabulary: Since there are no new vocabulary words, you could use this time to ask the class for slang words that are currently in vogue. Note to the class that such respected a poet as Giovanni purposefully used slang.

MINI QUIZ

Write the following questions on the chalkboard or overhead projector and call on students to fill in the blanks. Discuss the answers.

1. Both poems are written in _____-person point of view.
2. The speaker in "Housecleaning" dug _____ the cabinets.
3. She also liked putting _____ _____ on the shelves.
4. The speaker in "Where Have You Gone" says her ex-partner has a _____ walk.
5. The rent money and her heart are in her ex-partner's _____.

Answers to Mini Quiz

1. first
2. straightening
3. New paper
4. confident
5. pockets

ANSWERS TO
UNDERSTAND
THE SELECTION

1. When she was a child
2. A habit
3. "Rent money" and "my heart"
4. It means removing the food before cleaning inside and out.
5. The only way she can end a relationship is to stop it and remove the person from her life; that is the only way she knows, "unfortunately."
6. She distrusts him.
7. Her life is generally depressing; her lover brought some of the few rays of happiness she has known.
8. Answers will vary. Students might say they thought the poem was going to be sappily romantic; instead it is both sensitive and realistic.
9. A pocket is an appropriate place for money to be kept; as a location for her heart, it plays on the idea that things or people said to be in someone's pocket imply total domination—which is the relationship the speaker's ex-partner had with her.
10. She must forget about the person entirely.

Respond to Literature: Two very different responses to the break-up of a relationship are suggested by the poems. One response is a practical "let's get on with life," the other is a realistic reflection tinged with depression. Have students "vote" for the poet they'd like to meet. If you can't discern a pattern in their response, poll the students for their reasons.

**ANSWERS TO
WRITE ABOUT
THE SELECTION**

Prewriting: As a class discuss possibilities of why the relationship ended. Try to elicit a broad range of responses.

T88

UNDERSTAND THE SELECTION

Recall

1. When did the housecleaner begin to love cleaning?
2. What does the speaker call housecleaning?
3. What "things" were in the friend's pocket when he left?

Infer

4. The housecleaner uses "inside out" to describe washing the refrigerator. Why?
5. What does "unfortunately" mean in the next line of "Housecleaning"?
6. What does the "crooked smile" tell you about the person who walked out?
7. Why does the speaker of "Where Have You Gone" say "what few stars there were" when she describes life?

Apply

8. What did you think the tone of "Where Have You Gone" was going to be when you read the title? Did your idea change?
9. How does the speaker in "Where Have You Gone" feel after the friend left?
10. Why must the housecleaner remove someone from her life?

Respond to Literature

If you could meet either speaker, which one would you choose to meet. Explain your answer.

88

WRITE ABOUT THE SELECTION

Why do you think the "you" in the poem "Where Have You Gone" left the speaker? Do you think the person is a good-for-nothing who cheated the speaker? Do you think the speaker did not mention something about how the relationship ended, and that the speaker is as much to blame as the partner for their falling out of love?

Write a "reply" to the speaker of the poem. Present your ideas about why the relationship broke up.

Prewriting: What happened to end the relationship? Answer that question and write it in the middle of a piece of paper. Cluster reasons for the ending and the partner's feelings around it in boxes.

Writing: Read over your cluster and add any new ideas. Decide what reasons you will use in your response. Assemble your information into a few lines of poetry. See if you can keep the same style as Mari Evans. Write in the first person.

Revising: Pay attention to tone. Is your attitude toward the ending of the relationship clear? Are you happy, sad, relieved, or happy-go-lucky? Does your poem reflect this?

Proofreading: If you have kept the same style as Mari Evans, you will have no punctuation or capital letters. However, what words would be capitalized and what punctuation would there be in "normal" writing? Make notes in the margin to indicate the correct style.

Unit 1

Writing: Circulate as students work individually. Check to see that students are writing in poetry, and from a first-person point of view.

Revising: Using some of the responses from the "Prewriting" exercise, discuss how tone can be used to convey the partner's feelings. What specific words or figures of speech could be used?

Proofreading: Have students write a "correct" version of their poem, with proper punctuation and capitalization. For students who didn't use Evans's style, encourage them to produce another version that doesn't use punctuation or capitalization.

LDP Activity: Have LDP students review the list of ways to end a relationship. Have students choose the one they think is best. Have them write a few sentences explaining why they think it is a good way to end a relationship: e.g., No one is hurt, everyone will feel okay, etc.

THINK ABOUT TONE

Tone is the overall attitude a writer brings to his or her work. Tone gives you a clue about what a writer feels about the subject and theme.

1. One word can change what you thought were the poet's feelings toward someone. Read the opening of "Where Have You Gone" without "crooked" before "smile." Does the tone seem different?

2. Mentioning two very different things to create one impression can be very effective in setting tone. How do the lines "the rent money in one pocket and my heart in another" make you feel? Do they tell anything about the speaker?

3. "Where Have You Gone" ends with an **ellipsis**, three periods in a row. Does this add to the tone of the poem? How?

4. Tone is often best created when you do not say directly how you feel. Does the speaker in "Housecleaning" say directly how she feels? How do you think she feels?

5. What do you think people mean by the expression "the tone of your voice"?

DEVELOP YOUR VOCABULARY

Words used informally to mean something other than their usual, accepted definitions are called **slang**.

An example is *dug* in "Housecleaning": "I dug straightening the cabinets."

The usual definition of *dug* is "made a hole." This definition does not fit in the context of the poem, however. The poet means the slang definition of *dug*, which is "liked."

Dictionaries usually give definitions for slang. When you look up the word, the slang definition is usually given following the notation "slang." Make sure that you look under root words (under *dig* for *dug*, for example).

What are the slang definitions of the *italicized* words in these sentences? Check them in a dictionary.

1. The lead drummer plays *cool*.

2. She *aced* the test with ease.

3. His one-man show *bombed*.

4. Jimmy *beat* the robbery charge.

5. Hey, let's *rap* about this first.

6. "*Split!* Cat's here!" said the mice.

Write five original sentences with slang. Be sure the context makes the meaning clear.

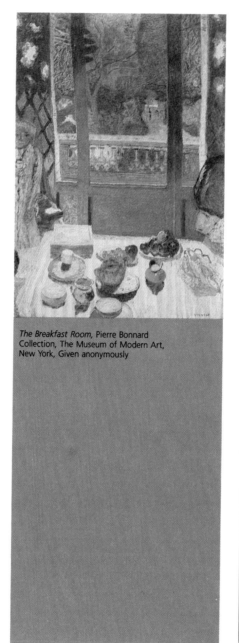

The Breakfast Room, Pierre Bonnard
Collection, The Museum of Modern Art,
New York, Given anonymously

90

LEARN ABOUT

Tone in Nonfiction

Like a poet writing a poem, when a writer tells a story what he or she thinks about the subject is very important. If a writer thinks the subject is funny, his or her attitude will probably be humorous. If a writer thinks the subject is serious, the attitude will be earnest.

A writer often sends "messages" to you, the reader, hinting how he or she feels about the subject. How those messages are expressed is also very important, for it reveals the writer's attitude toward you.

These attitudes—toward the subject and toward you—make up **tone.** Tone is all the unstated understandings between the writer and you about what the writer is trying to do.

As you read "Where Are You Now, William Shakespeare?", ask yourself:

1. What is the author's attitude toward the subject?
2. What is the author's attitude toward the reader?

SKILL BUILDER

Write a short paragraph on something you feel strongly about. Exchange papers with a partner. Read your partner's paragraph, and determine its tone. Discuss with your partner your evaluation.

Unit 1

Where Are You Now, William Shakespeare?

by M. E. Kerr

My very first boyfriend was named William Shakespeare. This was his real name, and he lived over on Highland Hill, about a block from my house.

I often went to his house to get him, or I met him down in the empty lot on Alden Avenue, or over at Hoopes Park, where we caught sunfish and brought them from the pond in bottles of murky water with polliwogs.

Marijane is ten [my father wrote in his journal]. *She plays with boys and looks like one.*

This was true.

My arms and knees were full of scabs from falls out of trees and off my bicycle. I was happiest wearing the pants my brother'd grown out of, the vest to one of my father's business suits over one of my brother's old shirts, Indian moccasins, and a cap. Everything I said came out of the side of my mouth, and I strolled

---

murky (MUR kee) clouded; unclear
journal (JUR nul) daily record; diary
stroll (STROHL) walk in a leisurely way

Looking at Love

91

Sidelights: "Where Are You Now, William Shakespeare?" looks at the same subject as "Up on Fong Mountain": young love. However, M.E. Kerr's approach is different from Norma Fox Mazer's. Both use first-person point of view. However, Mazer creates a fictional character and writes a journal as though she is that person: Kerr writes autobiographically by drawing directly on her past. Hers is the only nonfiction selection in this unit.

Motivation for Reading. Ask students to remember their first "crush." What was it like? Have them share as much as they are willing, especially the humorous side. Then say, Now, meet Marijane. She's only ten, has a boyfriend with an awesome name, and loves to climb trees.

More About the Thematic Idea: The question, "What is love?" has been posed before. Do you call "love" that childish adoration sometimes dubbed "puppy love"? This selection comes under the category "Love for Friends and Family." The main character, Marijane, says she had her "very first boyfriend" at the age of 10. She also has imaginary boyfriends, movie stars such as Clark Gable and Ronald Reagan. How do a 10-year-old's feelings fit into the emotions that are broadly labeled "love"? (Remember, Juliet was only fourteen when she fell for Romeo.)

Purpose-Setting Question: Does love look the same to you now as it did five years ago?

Vocabulary: Preteach the vocabulary words. See the Comprehension Workbook in the TRB.

More About Vocabulary: Have students work in pairs. Tell them that all the new vocabulary words are nouns or verbs—except "murky." Ask one partner to learn all the new nouns, the other partner all the verbs. They then "quiz" each other to see if they've mas-tered pronunciations and definitions.

LDP Activity: Partners: Have LDP students discuss boyfriends and girlfriends first. Then have them consider that Marijane also had crushes on some movie stars. If they were to update the story, who would be the crushes of to-day? Have students make a list of possible crushes. Don't forget those rock stars!

Literary Focus: Good description creates a definite picture in the reader's mind of a "tomboy." (Paragraph 5)

T91

Discussion: Ask, What does it reveal about the writer's and Billy's character to name their future child—when they're only 10 years old! (Paragraphs 6–11)

Enrichment: Parents are usually heroes to ten-year olders, aren't they? Pay attention to the weaving of heroes and presidents (Paragraph 13). The theme will emerge again.

around with my fists inside my trouser pockets.

This did not faze Billy Shakespeare, whose eyes lit up when he saw me coming, and who readily agreed that when we married we'd name our first son Ellis, after my father, and not William after him.

"Because William Shakespeare is a funny name," I'd say.

"It isn't funny. It's just that there's a famous writer with the same name," he'd say.

"Do you agree to Ellis Shakespeare then?"

"Sure, if it's all right with your father."

"He'll be pleased," I'd tell Billy.

Around this time, I was always trying to think of ways to please my father. (The simplest way would have been to wear a dress and a big hair ribbon, stay out of trees, stop talking out of the side of my mouth, and act like a girl . . . but I couldn't have endured such misery even for him.)

Billy Shakespeare accepted the fact early in our relationship, that my father was my hero. He protested only slightly when I insisted that the reason my father wasn't President of the United States was that my father didn't want to be.

That was what my father told me, when I'd ask him why he wasn't President. I'd look at him across the table at dinner, and think, He knows more than anybody knows, he's handsome, and he gets things done—so he ought to be President. If he was, I'd think, there'd be no problems in the world.

Sometimes I'd ask him: "Daddy, why aren't you President of the United States?"

His answer was always the same.

"I wouldn't want that job for anything. We couldn't take a walk without Secret Service men following us. Do you think we could go up to the lake for a swim by ourselves? No. There'd be Secret Service men tagging along. It'd ruin our lives. It'd end our privacy. Would you want that?"

Billy Shakespeare would say, "He's not President because nobody elected him President."

"He won't let anyone elect him," I'd answer. "He doesn't want Secret Service men around all the time."

"I'm not sure he could *get* elected," Billy would venture.

"He could get elected," I'd tell Billy. "He doesn't want to! We like our privacy."

"Okay." Billy'd give in a little. "But he never tried getting elected, so he really doesn't know if he could."

I'd wave that idea away with my dirty hands. "Don't worry. He'd be elected in a minute if he wanted to be. You don't know *him*."

Billy Shakespeare's other rivals for my attention were movie stars. I'd write

---

faze (FAYZ) confuse; weaken
endure (en DUUR) put up with
venture (VEN chur) proceed onward; risk
rival (RY vul) one who wants the same thing as another person

Unit 1

Clark Gable and Henry Fonda and Errol Flynn, and they'd send back glossy photos of themselves and sometimes letters, too.

These photographs and letters were thumbtacked to the fiberboard walls of a playhouse my father had built for me in our backyard.

When I did play with a girl, the game was always the same: getting dinner ready for our husbands. I had an old set of dishes back in the playhouse, and my girl friend and I played setting the table for dinner. During this game, Billy Shakespeare was forgotten. When my husband came through the playhouse door, he would be one of the movie stars pinned to the wall.

I played this game with Dorothy Spencer, who lived behind our house.

She was a tall redhead who looked like a girl, and who always had it in her head to fix meat loaf with mashed potatoes for a movie star named Spencer Tracy.

I changed around a lot—the menu as well as the movie star—but Dorothy stuck to meat loaf with mashed for Spencer.

I'd be saying, "Well, Clark is a little late tonight and the turkey is going to be overdone," or "Gee, Henry isn't here yet and the ham is going to be dried up." But Dorothy would persist with "Spencer's going to love this meat loaf when he gets here. I'll wait until I hear his footsteps to

The Letter, Pierre Bonnard. National Gallery of Art, Washington, D.C., Chester Dale Collection

mash the potatoes."

Billy Shakespeare was jealous of this game and tried his best to ruin it with reality.

He'd say, "What are two famous movie stars doing living in the same house?"

He'd say, "How come famous movie stars only have a one-room house with no kitchen?"

But Dorothy Spencer and I went on happily playing house, until the movie *Brother Rat* came to town.

That was when we both fell in love with the movie star Ronald Reagan.

Suddenly we were both setting the table for the same movie star—different menus, but the same husband.

---

fiberboard (FY bur bawrd) building material made from compressed wood chips
persist (PUR SIST) say over and over; keep on going
reality (ree AL uh tee) actual fact

Looking at Love

93

Literary Focus: A new development is introduced (Paragraph 24). The movie stars mentioned were popular in the 1940s and 1950s.

Discussion: Ask the girls in the class what games they played when they were 10. Ask the same of the boys. Kerr is describing a time when play activities were defined very strictly along gender lines (Paragraph 26). Has that changed?

"You've always stuck to meat loaf and mashed for Spencer!" I said angrily. "Now you want my Ronald!"

"He's not *your* Ronald," she said.

"It's my playhouse, though," I reminded her.

"But I won't play if I can't have Ronald," she said.

"We both can't have Ronald!" I insisted.

We took the argument to her mother, who told us to pretend Ronald Reagan was twins. Then we could both have him.

"He isn't twins, though," Dorothy said.

"And if he is," I put in, "I want the real Ronald, and not his twin."

Our game came to a halt, but our rivalry did not. Both of us had written to Ronald Reagan and were waiting for his reply.

"No matter what he writes her," I told Billy Shakespeare, "my letter from him will be better."

"You might not even get a letter," Billy said. "She might not get one either."

"She might not get one," I said, "but I will."

"You don't know that," Billy said.

"Do you want to know why I know I'll get one?" I asked him.

I made him cross his heart and hope to die if he told anyone what I'd done.

Billy was a skinny little kid with big eyes that always got bigger when I was about to confess to him something I'd done.

"Crossmyheartandhopetodie," he said very fast. "What'd you do?"

"You know that Ronald Reagan isn't like any of the others," I said.

"Because Dorothy Spencer likes him, too."

"That's got nothing to do with it!" I said. "He's just different. I never felt this way about another movie star."

"Why?"

"*Why?*" I don't know why! That's the way love is."

"Love?" Billy said.

"Yes. What did you think made me write him that I was a crippled child, and had to go to see him in a wheelchair?"

"Oh migosh!" Billy exclaimed. "Oh migosh!"

"I had to get his attention somehow."

"Oh migosh!"

"Just shut up about it!" I warned him. "If word gets out I'll know it's you."

Dorothy Spencer was the first to hear from Ronald Reagan. She didn't get a letter, but she got a signed photograph.

"Since I heard from him first," she said, "he's my husband."

"Not in my playhouse!" I said.

"He wrote me back first," she said.

"Just wait," I said.

"I don't have to wait," she said. "I'm setting the table for him in my own house."

"It's not even your house, it's your father's," I said. "At least when he's married to me, we'll have our own house."

---

rivalry (RY vul ree) competition; trying to get the same thing as another

94

"He's married to me now," she said.

"We'll see about that," I said.

I was beginning to get a panicky feeling as time passed and no mail came from Ronald Reagan. You'd think he'd write back to a crippled child first. . . . Meanwhile Dorothy was fixing him meat loaf and mashed at her place.

I had pictures of him cut out of movie magazines scotch-taped to my bedroom walls. I went to sleep thinking about him, wondering why he didn't care enough to answer me.

The letter and photograph from Ronald Reagan arrived on a Saturday.

I saw the Hollywood postmark and let out a whoop, thereby attracting my father's attention.

"What's all the excitement?"

I was getting the photograph out of the envelope. "I got a picture from Ronald Reagan!"

"Who's he?"

"Some movie star," my mother said.

By that time I had the photograph out. My heart began to beat nervously as I read the inscription at the bottom. "To a brave little girl, in admiration, Ronald Reagan."

"What does it say?" my father said.

"Nothing, it's just signed," I said, but he already saw what it said as he stood behind me looking down at it.

"Why are you a brave little girl?" he asked.

"How do I know?" I said.

"There's a letter on the floor," said my mother.

"That's my letter," I said, grabbing it.

"Why are you considered a brave little girl?" my father said again. "Why does *he* admire *you*?"

I held the letter to my chest. "Those are just things they say," I said.

"They say you're *brave*?" my father said.

"Brave or honest or any dumb thing," I said weakly.

"Read the letter, Marijane," said my father.

I read the letter to myself,

Dear Marijane,

Thank you for your letter.

Remember that a handicap can be a challenge.

Always stay as cheerful as you are now.

> Yours truly,
> Ronald Reagan

"What does it say?" my mother asked.

"Just the usual," I said. "They never say much."

"Let me see it, brave little girl," my father said.

"It's to me."

"Marijane . . ." and he had his hand out.

After my father read the letter, and got the truth out of me concerning my correspondence with Ronald Reagan, he told me what I was to do.

What I was to do was to sit down immediately and write Ronald Reagan, telling him I had lied. I was to add that I thanked God for my good health. I was to

---

correspondence (kor uh SPON duns) exchange of letters

return both the letter and the photograph.

No Saturday in my entire life had ever been so dark.

My father stood over me while I wrote the letter in tears, convinced that Ronald Reagan would hate me all his life for my deception. I watched through blurred eyes while my father took my letter, Ronald Reagan's letter, and the signed photograph, put them into a manila envelope, addressed it, sealed it, and put it in his briefcase to take to the post office.

For weeks and weeks after that, I dreaded the arrival of our postman. I was convinced a letter'd come beginning,

Dear Marijane,
How very disappointed I am in you. . . .

"I don't think he'll write back," Billy Shakespeare told me. "I don't think he'll want anything more to do with you."

That ended getting dinner for movie stars in my playhouse.

I told Dorothy Spencer that I'd outgrown all that.

Three years after I wrote Ronald Reagan that letter, I slumped way down in my seat in humiliation as I watched him lose a leg in the movie *King's Row*. . . . I was sure he thought of the little liar from upstate New York who'd pretended she was crippled.

Many, many years later, the man I always thought should be President of the United States was dead, and Ronald Reagan was President of the United States.

I didn't vote for him.
I heard Dorothy Spencer got married, and I envision her making meat loaf and mashed for her husband.

The only remaining question is,
Where are you now,
William Shakespeare?

---

deception (dih SEP shun) trick; act of deceiving

Looking at Love

97

Discussion: (Paragraph 101) Was Marijane's father right in making her apologize and send back the letter and photograph?

Critical Thinking: The presidency may be a strange thread to tie the connection between Ronald Reagan and her father, but it's (Paragraph 110) effective.

Discussion: Had you forgotten about William Shakespeare? Why do you think the author even cares where William Shakespeare is now? In light of never receiving a reply to her second letter, should the author have chosen a different title such as, Why I Didn't Vote for Ronald Reagan?

MINI QUIZ

Write the following questions on the chalkboard or overhead projector and call on students to fill in the blanks. Discuss the answers with the class.

1. Marijane thought her father could easily become _____ .
2. When Marijane played with other girls, they always played the same "game": _____ .
3. Dorothy Spencer's first movie-star love was _____ .
4. Marijane wrote Ronald Reagan and told him she was _____ .
5. Marijane told Dorothy Spencer she stopped hosting dinners for movie stars because, she had _____ all that.

Answers to Mini Quiz

1. president
2. getting dinner ready for their husbands
3. Spencer Tracy
4. crippled
5. outgrown

ANSWERS TO UNDERSTAND THE SELECTION

1. Marijane's father, Ellis
2. Meat loaf with mashed (potatoes)
3. Ronald Reagan lost a leg, and she was sure he'd thought of "the little liar from upstate New York who'd pretended she was crippled."
4. ten years old, looks and plays like a boy, wants to marry William Shakespeare or any of a number of movie actors
5. She thought he would reply faster and that he would express greater love than in his answer to Dorothy.
6. It is what they imagined a wife's main job to be, and the way that women were supposed to show love for their husbands.
7. He was jealous of it; why should he give up his "wife" to some movie actor?
8. Answers will vary. Many students will recognize Marijane's dishonesty and her father's attempt to make her face up to it.
9. Answers will vary. Students should at least recognize that some political experience is a help in becoming president.
10. Answers will vary. Students may see that she still thinks of him as he himself wants to be remembered, as a good actor.

Respond to Literature: What do students think of a 10-year-old falling for Ronald Reagan? Who are some of the current heartthrobs in the public eye? Ask, Why do we often worship from afar?

ANSWERS TO WRITE ABOUT THE SELECTION

Prewriting: As a class, brainstorm ideas about the life William Shakespeare might now be leading. Ask students to imagine where they

UNDERSTAND THE SELECTION

Recall

1. Who did Marijane and Billy plan to name their first child after?
2. What meal did Dorothy Spencer always like to serve Spencer Tracy?
3. Why did Marijane slump in her seat when she saw the film *King's Row?*

Infer

4. Describe Marijane.
5. Why did Marijane write Ronald Reagan that she was crippled?
6. Why do you think Marijane and Dorothy always played the same "game" with their actor husbands?
7. What was Billy Shakespeare's reaction to the dinner game Marijane and Dorothy played?

Apply

8. Would you have reacted in the same way to Marijane's letter to Ronald Reagan as her father did? Explain.
9. Do you think Marijane's father would have made a good president?
10. Why do you think Marijane did not vote for Ronald Reagan as president?

Respond to Literature

Were you in love with anyone when you were ten years old? Who and why?

98

WRITE ABOUT THE SELECTION

Where do you think Marijane's friend, William Shakespeare, is now? Marijane decides to find out. She asks old high school friends what has become of him, she writes some letters to addresses she has been given, and one day a letter with the return address marked "William Shakespeare" arrives. What do you think the letter says?

Imagine that you are William Shakespeare. What would you say to an old friend who wonders what you are doing?

Prewriting: What are you, William Shakespeare, doing now? Are you married? Do you have a family? What is your job? How do you now feel about the "relationship" you and Marijane had many years before? Make some notes, and organize your ideas into paragraphs using an informal outline.

Writing: Write your letter to Marijane, using the informal outline. Write as much as you want. Remember, you have not seen or talked to Marijane in years.

Revising: What is the tone of your letter? Is it consistent with how you imagine William Shakespeare to be now? Make any changes to make clear your attitude toward him and the reader. Remember letters include inside addresses, dates, salutations, and closings. Add them if you do not have them.

Proofreading: Reread your letter and check for errors. Make sure transitions from one paragraph to the next are clear. A good letter is well-organized.

Unit 1

will be, what they will be doing, and with whom they'll be in twenty years.

Writing: Circulate as students work individually. Remind them that this is a letter, and must be written in first-person. Stress that although a letter can be "chatty," it must still be well-organized.

Revising: There are actually three levels of tone at play in the letter.

First, the student's attitude toward William. Second, the student's attitude toward the actual reader. Third, William's attitude toward Marijane. Discuss with students how these tones are expressed in their letters.

Proofreading: Have students exchange letters and check for correct punctuation, paragraphing and spelling.

LDP Activity: Have LDP students review their lists of possible crushes. Have students choose one and write a short paragraph about their choice. Why is the "crushee" worthy of the crusher's affections?

THINK ABOUT TONE

A writer sets the tone of a story in many ways. The tone can be set through the choice of individual words, the use of certain phrases, detailed descriptions, or by including or omitting specific things.

1. The title of this selection sounds like a trick. Yet M.E. Kerr says in the first paragraph no trick is involved. How does she do this? What does this say about her attitude toward the reader?

2. M.E. Kerr offers a detailed description in the fifth paragraph of herself at age ten. What is the tone?

3. M.E. Kerr gives her father's reason why he did not want to be president. What is the effect of this information?

4. The first time Marijane tells about Dorothy's meal she calls it ''meat loaf with mashed potatoes.'' After that she calls it ''meat loaf with mashed.'' How does that change make you feel?

5. How does the use of the phrase ''Crossmyheartandhopetodie'' affect tone?

DEVELOP YOUR VOCABULARY

Homophones are words that sound alike but have different spellings and different meanings.

Examples: son-sun days-daze
flour-flower

In each sentence below is at least one word that has a homophone. Find the word, and give its homophone.

1. We would name our first son Ellis.

2. This did not faze Billy Shakespeare.

3. This was his real name.

4. Is it all right with your father?

5. She wanted to please my father.

6. I wanted a Ronald Reagan photograph.

7. We had been playing house.

8. Dorothy served Spencer meat loaf.

9. She also gave him mashed potatoes.

10. They were in love.

11. We loved these little games.

12. My hair never had a ribbon.

13. He knows more than anybody else.

14. So, he should become president.

15. He would be a good president.

16. We would have no problems.

17. He did not want the job for anything.

Looking at Love

99

LEARN ABOUT

Theme

Did you ever get to the end of a poem and ask, "What does it mean?" You re-read the poem, maybe two or three times. You look up definitions for all the unfamiliar words. You examine each line to understand its meaning, but still you are in doubt.

Now you sit back and try to get the "bigger" picture. You are searching for the "theme" of the poem. The **theme** of a poem is its main idea or meaning.

Perhaps the theme is about the difficulty in expressing love, as in "First Person Demonstrative," or it may be about the ending of a relationship, as in "Finis." Theme can be anything the poet chooses.

The poems you have read so far in this unit have been about love between individual people. The last two poems are a bit different.

As you read them, look for answers to the following questions:
1. How are they different from the other poems in this unit?
2. What is the theme of each of the two poems?

SKILL BUILDER

Songs are often lyric poetry. Write the lyrics of a song you like, then in a sentence or two, explain the theme.

I Dream a World

by Langston Hughes

I dream a world where man
No other man will scorn,
Where love will bless the earth
And peace its paths adorn.
5   I dream a world where all
Will know sweet freedom's way,
Where greed no longer saps the soul
Nor avarice blights our day.
A world I dream where black or white,
10   Whatever race you be,
Will *share* the bounties of the earth
And every man is free,
Where wretchedness will hang its head,
And you, like a pearl,
15   Attends the needs of all mankind.
Of such I dream—
Our world!

Reflections

by Vanessa Howard

If the world looked in a looking glass,
It'd see back hate, it'd see back war and it'd see
    back sorrow,
It'd see back fear.
If the world looked in a looking glass, it'd run
    away with shame, and hide.

---

adorn (uh DAWRN) to beautify or embellish
greed (GREED) a great desire for wealth or material things
avarice (AV uh ris) greed
blights (BLYTS) destroys, disappoints, frustrates

Looking at Love   101

Literary Focus: The shame of wretchedness becomes alive through the use of personification.

Discussion: How does the final line reinforce the optimism of the poem?

Literary Focus: In "Reflections," personification helps form the central image of the poem: the world looking in a mirror.

Enrichment: The opening lines tell what the world would see if it looked in a mirror. Contrast them with the final line in which the poet says what the world would *do* if it looked in a mirror.

Discussion: Look back at the title. What does it mean? (It plays on the idea of "reflections" as both thoughts as well as images in a mirror.)

Literary Focus: In the Hughes poem, inversion of the natural order of words (also called "anastrophe") draws attention to the second line, and emphasizes "scorn." End rhyme is also achieved.

Clarification: "Where love will bless the earth" is the only mention of "love" in the poem, but it's clear Hughes's vision depends on the transforming power of love to make his dream a reality.

Literary Focus: "I dream" is repeated. Point out how repetition of a simple phrase provides unity; Martin Luther King used a nearly identical phrase in his "I Have A Dream" speech.

Enrichment: Almost any line has the feel of a speech by an eloquent politician, such as Jesse Jackson. Hughes never ignored the political realities of his day. Indeed, one of the most important aspects of the Harlem Renaissance was recognition of blacks' oppression in a predominantly white America.

Vocabulary: Preteach the vocabulary words. See the Comprehension Workbook in the TRB.

More About Vocabulary: Have students make flashcards of the new words and their pronunciation. Ask students to use the words in the writing assignment for this selection, or writing assignments in the next unit.

MINI QUIZ

Write the following questions on the chalkboard or overhead projector and call on students to fill in the blanks. Discuss the answers with the class.

1. "I Dream A World" is written in _____-person point of view.
2. Hughes dream _____ will adorn earth's paths.
3. Hughes hopes all races will one day _____ the bounties of the earth.
4. "Reflections" is written in _____-person point of view.
5. Howard writes about the world looking into a _____ _____

Answers to Mini Quiz

1. first
2. peace
3. share
4. third
5. looking glass

ANSWERS TO UNDERSTAND THE SELECTION

1. people of all races
2. a pearl
3. hate, war, sorrow, or fear
4. The other poems were about love between individuals; "you" indicated the two-person relationship. These last two poems are about love—or the lack of love—between groups of people, such as the black and white races.
5. There are problems with the world the way it is, but we can dream of a better world.
6. She wants the world to look in a looking glass to see reality.
7. The world is a place not of love but of hate.
8. They both have as part of their theme the lack of love in the world.
9. "I Dream A World" expresses hope for a better world, "Reflections" expresses no hope.
10. Answers will vary. Sample answers: Both might have had sad lives, but Hughes must have had some experiences that made him feel people have some good in them. Howard seems to be filled only with bitterness.

RESPOND TO LITERATURE

Hughes expresses hope, Howard only anger. Even though someone feels there is little love in the world, can hope create love?

ANSWERS TO WRITE ABOUT THE SELECTION

Prewriting: Use students' answers to "Respond to Literature" as a class brainstorming session.

Writing: Circulate as students work individually. Using Howard's style will make writing easier, but some students may wish to experiment with other styles.

UNDERSTAND THE SELECTION

Recall

1. Who does the speaker of "I Dream A World" hope will one day share the Earth's bounties?

2. The speaker of "I Dream A World" compares the "joy" he is dreaming about to something. What is it?

3. Name at least two things the speaker in "Reflections" feels the world would see in a looking glass.

Infer

4. Speakers in other poems in this unit have addressed a "you." These two poems do not. Why?

5. What is the theme of "I Dream A World"?

6. Why is the title of Vanessa Howard's poem "Reflections"?

7. What is the theme of "Reflections"?

Apply

8. How are the themes similar?

9. How are these themes different?

10. What do you think the poets are like? What kind of lives do they have?

Respond to Literature

Explain which of these poems presents more accurately your view of the world and the love in it.

102

WRITE ABOUT THE SELECTION

Vanessa Howard uses personification when she describes the world looking in a mirror. The world cannot "look" into a mirror. It also cannot "run" or "hide." Only people can do that.

The mirror is a way for the poet to talk about what she feels exists in the world. Since a mirror reflects only what is there, the technique adds a touch of reality to her opinions.

What do you think the world would see if it looked in a mirror? Vanessa Howard thinks it would see hate, war, sorrow, and fear. Do you agree?

Write what you think would be in the mirror if the world looked at itself.

Prewriting: Draw a frame around a blank sheet of paper. Imagine that it is a mirror. Write some words or phrases in the mirror describing what the world would see.

Writing: Turn your words and phrases into a poem. You can use the same style Vanessa Howard did, or you can try something different.

Revising: What is the theme of your poem? Is it clear? Add any words or phrases that will help to make the meaning clear. Eliminate any words or phrases that are confusing.

Proofreading: Have you used any contractions in your poem? Check to make sure that you have spelled them correctly. Be sure to be consistent with your capitalization and punctuation.

Unit 1

Revising: As a class, discuss the "strong" words that Howard uses—"hate," "war," "fear," etc. Point out that these words create sharp pictures in the reader's mind and help to communicate the poem's theme.

Proofreading: Point out that both Hughes and Howard follow capitalization and punctuation rules in their poems. Compare them with previous selections, such as

"Housecleaning" and "Where Have You Gone." Do capitalization and punctuation help or hinder in communicating a poem's theme?

LDP Activity: Have LDP students choose one of the projects from the earlier exercise and write a paragraph discussing: the problem, what changes they would make, and how they would accomplish these changes.

THINK ABOUT THEME

There are many clues you can look for when you are searching for theme.

1. Does the poet use "negative" or "positive" words? **Negative words** make you feel hopeless and sad. **Positive words** make you feel hopeful and happy. Look at "I Dream A World" and "Reflections." Make a list of key words, and mark them with a + or −.

2. What is the tone of each poem? What is each poet's attitude in these two poems toward his and her respective subject?

3. Is there any form of humor (such as hyperbole or irony) in either of the poems? Are the poets speaking "straight," or are they hiding meaning? Examine "I Dream A World" and "Reflections."

4. Look at the titles of the poems. Explain how "I Dream A World" and "Reflections" relate to the themes.

5. Use your feelings as a guide to finding the theme. How do you feel when you read these two poems?

DEVELOP YOUR VOCABULARY

Synonyms are words having the same or nearly the same meaning. Langston Hughes uses *greed* in one line of his poem, and *avarice* in the next. Both mean "a great desire for wealth or material things." They are synonyms.

Synonyms are very useful if you are trying to rhyme. You can choose a synonym that rhymes with another word, rather than one that does not.

Use a dictionary to find synonyms for the following words as they are used in "I Dream A World." Then use each in a sentence.

1. scorn	**5.** blight
2. bless	**6.** bounties
3. adorn	**7.** wretchedness
4. sap	**8.** attend

Note: The Teacher's Resource Book contains worksheets to accompany both writing assignments.

Motivation: Songwriters are poets who draw their lyrics from experiences in their own lives. Everyone has thought about or experienced love. This unit has explored other people's ideas; not it's time for students to express their own.

Prewriting: On the chalkboard or overhead projector, write the titles of the selections. Ask students for short descriptions (a few words or a phrase) of the theme of each. Reviewing the themes will help students choose one selection and focus their thoughts on it. (Save this information for the next writing assignment.)

Writing: Circulate among students as they work individually. You could point out that many songs use an A-A-B-A format: the melody is stated and repeated, then a variation is introduced, and finally the melody is restated. Thinking of the musical organization of a song might help students in writing the lyrics.

Revising: Ask students to write a title for their song. It should reflect the theme.

Proofreading: Have a partner read the song lyrics and tell what he or she thinks the message of the song is. If it isn't clear, have the writer check punctuation.

Motivation: It's the students' turn to be critics. They have a chance to say "thumbs up" or "thumbs down" to what they've read—but they must support their opinions.

Prewriting: Use the information from the "Prewriting" portion of the previous writing assignment to review the various poems. Discuss

---

LITERATURE-BASED WRITING

1. You have just been hired by a record company to write songs. You are given your first assignment: Write a love song.

You panic. What can you write about?

Then you remember that you once read a series of stories and poems on love in English class. Themes come back to you: love lost, love found, love for friends and family, love for the world.

You decide to write a song based on the feelings expressed in one of the stories or poems. You will imagine that you are writing poetry, since song lyrics are like poetry.

You have not been told whether the music has already been written for the song. You decide that you can write the words for a tune you already know, or for a tune not yet composed.

Prewriting: Think back on the stories and poems. Which "message" did you like the best? Choose one poem or story, and think about the feelings presented in it. Write them down, quickly, with some ideas on how to describe the feelings. Decide on point of view for the song.

Writing: Assemble your material as a song. Think about other love songs you know. What makes their lyrics effective? Think of each verse as a paragraph.

Revising: Make sure that your song has stuck to the feeling that you want to describe. The theme should be clear.

Proofreading: Check that you have used commas and semicolons to make your ideas easy to understand.

2. This unit has concentrated on helping you see the elements of poetry, or how a poem is put together. You now should be better able to analyze poetry, to recognize what you like and do not like, and give reasons for your opinion.

Choose two poems in the unit, one that you did like and one that you did not. You will figure out why you formed these opinions by looking at the elements involved in each poem.

Prewriting: Review the work you did for the "Think About . . ." sections in this unit. Then make a chart with the name of the selections you have chosen at the top, and the elements of poetry down the side: character, imagery, theme, tone, rhyme, and figures of speech. Reread each poem. Write down character, theme, and tone. Look for other elements in each poem: imagery, rhyme, and figures of speech. Note if they are present.

Writing: Look at your chart and determine how one element or the other makes you like or dislike a poem. Were you disappointed by the theme? Was there a lot of good imagery? Was the tone appealing? Write why that was important to you.

Revising: Make sure each paragraph has a topic sentence that expresses the paragraph's main idea.

Proofreading: Reread your writing for errors in spelling, punctuation, and mechanics. Neatly insert any changes.

---

as a class what students liked and what they didn't like.

Writing: Circulate as students work individually. Picking the most important factor that influenced their opinion of the poem will give students a focus for their critique. They should include information about other factors, as well.

Revising: Have students write the central idea of each paragraph. Is

there a topic sentence in the paragraph that reflects this idea?

Proofreading: After students have proofread their own papers, have them exchange papers with a partner for a second review. A new draft should be written if the partner finds a number of errors.

BUILDING LANGUAGE SKILLS

Vocabulary

Suffixes are often used to turn nouns into adjectives. Notice in this sentence how the suffix *-ful* is added to the noun *success* to form the adjective *successful:* Henry Curran was big, busy, and successful.

If you know how a particular suffix is used, you can often figure out the meaning of the new word.

-ful	=	having the quality of
-ic	=	characteristic of
-less	=	without
-able	=	able to or having
-ard	=	possessing something to excess
-ish	=	characteristic of or tending toward something

Try to define each *italicized* adjective by examining the root noun and suffix. Remember that spellings sometimes change slightly when a suffix is added. Check your definition in a dictionary. Then write your own sentence using each word.

1. She spoke in an *apologetic* voice.
2. "I do not care if he is *armless*," he said.
3. She had a *sorrowful* look.
4. My time is *valuable*.
5. A *haggard* look was on her face.
6. "He is sixteen, but he is *smallish*," she said.
7. My dog looks *pathetic* after her bath.

Usage and Mechanics

Verbs always must agree with their subjects. Singular subjects take singular verbs, and plural subjects take plural verbs.

You must be careful to match a verb with its subject and not other words in the sentence.

You must remember that "there" is never the subject of a sentence. The verb of a sentence beginning with "there" matches the subject, which comes after the verb.

Here are some examples of correct verb-subject agreement:

Examples: All snowflakes are six-sided. The question on verbs is a good one. There are the buses.

Correct the verb-subject agreement errors in these sentences:

1. It are always one or the other with you innocent victims.
2. Why, I never were in Springfield in my life!
3. Her father own the bank.
4. There is lots of nickel-plated shoehorns in there.
5. Underneath the pigeonholes were a row of three, brass-knobbed little drawers.
6. My hand and shirt cuff was streaked with old dust.

Usage and Mechanics

More About Usage and Mechanics: Here are examples of some difficult verb-subject questions.

1. The car, as well as the truck and the bus, has influenced our lifestyles. (The "as well" phrase doesn't make the subject plural. It remains "car.")
2. My friend and teacher is Miss Durmacher. ("friend" and "teacher" refer to the same person.)
3. Either Bill or I has to go. ("either-or" doesn't make the subject plural.)
4. Either Bill or the boys have to go. (The verb should agree with the nearest subject, in this case "boys.")
5. The number of apples on a single tree is never the same. ("number" is singular here; one definite number is meant.)
6. A number of the apples have to be thrown out because they're spoiled. (Changing from a definite to indefinite article before "number" changes the sense of "number"—it's now plural.)

Additional Examples Cooperative/Collaborative Learning Activity: Have students ever encountered verb-subject problems which they couldn't figure out? Have the class make a list. If you're comfortable with verb-subject agreement rules, ask students to try to "stump" you with their questions.

Answers to exercises in Student's Book:

1. It *is* always one or the other with you innocent victims.
2. Why, I never *was* in Springfield in my life!
3. Her father *owns* the bank.
4. There *are* lots of nickel-plated shoehorns in there.
5. Underneath the pigeonholes *was* a row of three, brass-knobbed little drawers.
6. My hand and shirt cuff *were* streaked with old dust.

ANSWERS TO BUILDING LANGUAGE SKILLS

Vocabulary

More About Word Attack: Here are some general spelling rules students might find helpful.

1. If a suffix begins with a vowel, drop the final "e" of the root word. Example: usable
2. If the suffix begins with a consonant, retain the final "e." Example: useful

Cooperative/Collaborative Learning Activity: Have students work in pairs to look back at the selections and find other adjectives using the suffixes defined in this exercise. Give them 10 minutes and see how many examples each pair can find.

Answers to exercises in Student's Book:

1. sounding like an apology
2. without arms
3. full of sorrow
4. having value
5. gaunt, pale
6. tending toward being small for his age
7. pitiful

Sentences will vary.

ANSWERS TO
SPEAKING AND
LISTENING

Motivation: Prepare a poem that you can recite to the class. It needn't be from this unit, and it needn't be long. Reciting it from memory should allow you to concentrate on dramatic emphasis and eye contact.

Teaching Strategy: With the students, go through the steps of preparing for reading a poem. You could outline the steps on the chalkboard or overhead projector, noting the goal of each practice "read."

Evaluation Criteria: Evaluate the students' readings of the poems they've chosen by marking pluses, minuses, or checks on these points:

1. correct pronunciation of words
2. expressive pronunciation of words or phrases used in alliteration, onomatopoeia, or similar devices
3. attention to punctuation
4. projection, including eye contact with audience
5. proper pacing; speed is appropriate to the poem's theme. You could give this checklist to students and have them evaluate a recording of their reading before they make their class presentation.

SPEAKING AND LISTENING

When you select a poem to read aloud, it should be one that you especially like. If you like it, you will be able to read it in such a way that your audience will like it, too.

Reading poems aloud is much different than reading other types of literature aloud. Most poems have so much emotion that they require certain procedures so the reader and the audience enjoy the poem.

Practice the following steps before you read the poem of your choice.

1. Read the poem to yourself.

2. Read the poem again. Determine the subjects of the verbs and the antecedents of the pronouns. This will help you understand what the poem is about.

3. Pay attention to words that you may not be familiar with. Check their definitions and pronunciations to ensure understanding of the poem.

4. Read the poem aloud softly and slowly so you hear the sounds of the words. This will help the meaning of the poem to set in.

5. Now read the poem once again. This time pay particular attention to the punctuation. Remember, most poetry is written in sentences just as prose is. The way a poem is punctuated tells you how it should be read. Pause when necessary!

6. Practice reading the poem in front of a mirror. Decide when to look at your audience. You want to maintain some eye contact not just out of courtesy, but also because looking forward will help project your voice.

7. Ask a friend or a family member to listen to you read the poem. If someone is not available, use a tape recorder so you can listen to your delivery. Concentrate on reading the poem just loud enough and just slow enough for your audience to enjoy. Think about improvements as you listen to yourself. Then read the poem again if you decide on any changes.

Once you have prepared yourself for this assignment, choose a poem or part of a poem from this unit. Follow the procedures above so you can successfully read your poem to a group or your entire class. Limit your reading to approximately two minutes. There is no need to be nervous if you are prepared adequately. Enjoy yourself!

Critical Thinking: Deductive reasoning (from "The Love Letter"): "When you're twenty-four and a bachelor, you usually figure you'll be married before much longer." The speaker starts with a general principle—that people who are twenty-four and single usually get married—and reasons that he'll be married before too long.

CRITICAL THINKING

Inductive and deductive reasoning are used to make conclusions based on evidence.

In **inductive reasoning,** you begin with evidence and arrive at a conclusion. Here is an example of inductive reasoning: The desk lamp in your room goes out. You replace the bulb with a new one. The lamp still does not work. You try another new bulb. Still no luck. You try a third bulb. No luck. Something is wrong with the lamp, you conclude.

In **deductive reasoning,** you reason the other way: You begin with a conclusion that is generally accepted as true. You consider the evidence of a particular situation, and you make a specific conclusion based on whether the evidence fits the general conclusion with which you started. Here is an example of deductive reasoning: Animals with six legs are insects. You see an animal with six legs. You conclude, therefore, that the animal is an insect.

You must be careful to reason correctly. Incorrect inductive reasoning leads to hasty generalization, and incorrect deductive reasoning leads to unsound conclusions. A hasty generalization is a statement made about a whole group on the basis of a few examples. For example: *teenagers are poor drivers and cause most accidents.* Unsound conclusions result when facts and evidence are not true. For example: *John is qualified to be class president because he has run for other offices.*

Look back at the selections in this unit, and find one example each of inductive and deductive reasoning. Explain the reasoning process.

Looking at Love

EFFECTIVE STUDYING

The exercises at the end of this unit's selections had very specific questions about what you had read.

This was particularly true of the poetry selection exercises. You were asked to study in depth the elements of poetry in order to understand how a poem is constructed and how it "works."

Sometimes, such close study makes it hard to see the whole picture. The expression "You cannot see the forest for the trees" can apply. You are so close to the individual parts of something that you cannot see the whole.

It is sometimes helpful, therefore, to "step back" from what you are reading to get the "bigger picture."

When you study a poem, read it straight through once without stopping. This first quick "read" will give you an idea about character, tone, and theme. It will also put things "in context," which could give you clues to parts of the poem you do not understand.

Then go back and read the poem again. Stop whenever you do not understand a word or phrase, and find its meaning. Look for imagery, figures of speech, and rhyme. Take the poem apart, but think how all the elements fit together.

Then step back and get the bigger picture. Read the poem again, straight through. The poet's message now should be loud and clear.

Choose one poem from this book. Use these techniques and write a paragraph analyzing it.

A Career to Consider

Shakespearean plays are drama at its best. A student who enjoyed "Romeo and Juliet" might want to investigate a career in the theater—not so much, perhaps, as an actor or actress, but as one of the numerous technical people who work behind the scenes to put on the play. An example would be someone involved in lighting. This person should have an artistic sense of emphasizing people's actions through the use of light. He or she must also have technical training in how lights are set up and operated. Direct experience is often just as useful as specialized, advanced education; on-the-job training can easily be gained by volunteering to help with local stage productions. A high school education and a general interest in the theater are necessary.

The Unknown

UNIT ACTIVITY

A Continuing Project: Travel Poster

The theme of this unit is the unknown. Many of the stories and poems describe places, either real or imaginary. All of the selections describe a state of mind or an imagined place. The unit offers an excellent opportunity for students to create travel posters that express the setting, mood, or inner reality of the poems and stories that they read.

Explain to students that they are to imagine being literary travel agents. It is their job to plan and advertise a tour of the Unknown. In order to do this, they must create travel posters that will make people want to "visit" each selection in the unit. The poster can focus on an actual place, such as Baghdad in the first selection. The poster can describe an imaginary place, such as Verna in "Of Missing Persons." The poster can advertise the opportunity to see an unusual character in action, such as the ghosts described in "On the Path of the Poltergeist." Or the poster can entice the traveler to visit the scene of a story or poem while it is taking place; for example, the police station while Mrs. Stevenson is talking to Sergeant Duffy in "Sorry, Wrong Number."

Discuss with students some characteristics of a good travel poster. Obtain from a local travel agent some posters and travel brochures to display to the class. Point out that the most important aspect of a travel poster is an eye-catching picture or photograph. Students who are less artistically inclined can cut pictures from magazines or photocopied pictures from books. Also point out that a travel poster should communicate some information in words. The poster should name the place that is pictured and have a phrase or sentence that will make a person want to go there. (For example, "Visit Exotic Baghdad.") Since these posters will represent literary "places," students should also include a few sentences that give a clue as to what the story or poem is about. (For example, "Listen in on a murder being planned!")

Have students create a travel poster after reading each selection. Some general questions to help them get started include:

What is the setting of this selection? What would it be like to go there?

What parts of the story might be especially exciting for a visitor to experience first-hand?

What places or people exist in the characters' imaginations?

What is the mood of the selection? Can you recreate this mood as if it were an actual place?

What character or characters might a visitor enjoy seeing in action?

If students need more specific guidance, ask questions such as the following for each selection.

"Appointment in Baghdad"
Would you like to be in Baghdad when Death meets the young man?

"Appointment at Noon"
Where do you think Henry Curran's visitor came from?

"Incident in a Rose Garden"
Would you like to visit a rose garden where Death meets the Master?

"Boy in the Shadows"
What story could you unravel if you visited Jayse's grave?

"Sorry, Wrong Number"
How would you like to be on Second Avenue in New York City when Mrs. Stevenson is murdered?

"Thus I Refute Beelzy"
Can you create the place in Small Simon's mind where Mr. Beelzy exists?

"hist, whist"/"Overheard on a Saltmarsh"
Would you enjoy seeing a variety of ghost things?

"Of Missing Persons"
Have you ever dreamed of living in an ideal place where everyone is happy?

"The Listeners"/"Eldorado"
What would it be like to visit Eldorado?

"Loch Ness Monster"
How would you like to spend a few days at Expedition Headquarters?

"On the Path of the Poltergeist"
What would it be like to go to Esther Cox's house and watch "Maggie" and "Bob" in action?

After the travel posters have been completed, display them around the classroom. Discuss with students how various interpretations may have been given to each selection. Also discuss with students how they found this assignment. Were certain selections easier to make posters for than others? For which selection did they most enjoy making a poster? Why? Explain your answer.

"Appointment in Baghdad"
(Traditional Version) (page 113)

SELECTION SYNOPSIS

This very short story takes place in and around the palace of the Sultan in Damascus. One morning, the Sultan's most valued assistant comes in and asks for the Sultan's fastest horse. He says that he must escape to Baghdad. When the Sultan asks the young man why he is in such a rush, he replies that he has just seen Death in the palace garden, and he must escape at once. The Sultan gives the young man the horse, then goes into the garden to ask Death why he frightened his assistant. In a twist of irony, Death informs the Sultan that he was surprised to see the young man in the garden, because he has an appointment to meet him tonight in Baghdad.

SELECTION ACTIVITY

In this activity, students will research the setting of the story, which is Damascus. They will also research the city where Death would meet the young man, which is Baghdad. The purpose of the research will be to locate the cities geographically, to learn something about the history of these cities, and to get a feel for the old Middle East. Students should also be able to give an approximate time period for the story based on the following factors (students should discover these connections for themselves; the information is given here only as a teacher's guide).

1. A main character in the story is the Sultan. A sultan is a ruler of a Muslim state. Rulers in the Ottoman Empire (Turks) were Sultans.

2. The city of Damascus, which was a center of early Christianity, was captured by the Arabs in A.D. 635 and became Islamic. After 750 B.C., it was held by many conquerors; then was seized by the Turks (Ottoman Empire) in 1516. It remained under Turkish rule until 1918, when it came under British control.

3. The city of Baghdad was founded in A.D. 762. It became an Islamic city and was ruled by a monarch, called a caliph. It became part of the Ottoman Empire in 1638 and remained so until the British took control in 1917.

It seems reasonable to assume that this story could have taken place in the Ottoman Empire between the mid-1600s and the end of the nineteenth century. Once students have found this information, have them learn as much as they can about the life and times of the Middle East during this period. (You may find it helpful to agree on a certain period of time to research, perhaps the nineteenth century.) Have students work in groups or pairs to learn about such aspects as trade, dress, life in the city, art, social structures in the family, such as marriage, or political structures. Students should also prepare a map showing the relative location of the two cities. The map should show the geography of the Middle East as it was then rather than as it is today.

After students have completed their research, have each group or pair display their information in the form of a chart or poster. Display the charts and posters, along with the maps, around the classroom.

"Appointment at Noon"
by Eric Frank Russell (page 119)

SELECTION SYNOPSIS

Henry Curran is a ruthless but very successful businessman, who has nothing but contempt for the law and accepted standards of behavior. The story begins when he enters his office at 11:50 A.M. After barking a few commands to his secretary, he learns from her that a visitor is waiting to see him. The visitor claims to have an appointment with Curran at two minutes to twelve. Curran snorts that he has made no appointment, but his curiosity is aroused when he learns that the visitor accurately predicted the time at which he would return to the office. He agrees to see the stranger, who is ushered in at three minutes to twelve. The stranger is Death personified, and a minute later Henry Curran keeps his appointment.

SELECTION ACTIVITY

In this activity, students will write an obituary of Henry Curran as it might appear in a newspaper. Begin the activity by collecting and displaying some well-written obituaries from local and national newspapers. Aim to present obituaries that are full-length articles rather than just listings or short entries in the Obit. column.

Discuss with students the things that are included in an obituary. The most essential and obvious are name, date of death, age at time of death, occupation, cause of death if known, where the person lived, and the names of surviving family members. A more lengthy obituary may include the person's early life, major events in the person's career, what has been said or written about the person, the person's major contribution, some quotations by the person, a discussion of the person's character and personality, or a discussion of any controversy surrounding the person.

Explain to students that, usually, the better known a person is, the more complete the obituary will be. Also point out that an obituary writer may give a "feel for" the person being written about, making that person very vivid and real to the reader. An obituary writer should not express an opinion about the person, but the writer can use facts skillfully to convey a certain impression.

Since Henry Curran is described as "big" and "successful," it is likely that his obituary would be quite substantial. Although certain things about Henry Curran are made clear in the story, much of the information needed for an obituary will have to be composed by the students. Students must also deal with the fact that, according to the story, Curran's death took place in a rather unusual way. Some questions that students might ask themselves as they write their obituaries include:

How would a newspaper describe Henry Curran's "cause of death"?

Would anyone interview his secretary to find out exactly how Curran died?

Who are Curran's survivors? Do you think he had a family? Sisters or brothers? Parents? Do you think he had any friends?

Where do you think Curran lived? In a small town? In the city?

How was Curran known in the area where he lived?

Do you think there would be any controversy surrounding Curran's death? Might some people think that he was "done in" by underworld figures?

When students have completed the assignment, ask for volunteers to read their obituaries aloud. Discuss the similarities and differences in the ways in which students view Henry Curran.

"Incident in A Rose Garden"
by Donald Justice (page 123)

Like the two selections that precede it, the theme of this poem is also death. In this case, a gardener is frightened when he meets Death in the rose garden. The gardener tells his master, who confronts Death for scaring his worker only to learn that the person Death wants is not the gardener, but the master himself.

SELECTION ACTIVITY

Have students work in groups of three to dramatize the text of this selection. Assign one student the role of the Gardener, another the role of the Master, and another the role of Death. Death should be costumed as described in the poem; each group can decide how to costume the other characters. Have each group perform their dramatization for the class.

"Boy in the Shadows"
by Margaret Ronan (page 127)

SELECTION SYNOPSIS

Irene and Ernest Platt retire to a small house in the foothills of the Ozarks. Irene plants a garden, and as she works in it, she notices a thin, hollow-eyed boy watching her. He disappears, only to return a day or so later with his mother, a haggard-looking woman of about forty. She offers Irene the boy's services as a gardener and handyman for $2 a day, to be paid to her. The boy, Jayse, is to live in a small shed near the garden, and his mother is to bring him his meals. Irene is warned not to feed Jayse, who has a "finicky stomach." Jayse is an excellent worker, but he never speaks to the Platts. Time passes, and Jayse begins to look even more emaciated than before. Irene, determined to feed Jayse a decent meal, cooks ham and eggs. When she sets it before the silent boy, he eats a few bites and then strides out of the house and into the woods. The next day, Jayse's mother demands to know what Irene fed Jayse. Irene demands to be taken to Jayse. His mother leads Irene to a half-opened grave near her cabin. There Irene sees Jayse's body. His mother explains that Jayse and his father died of pneumonia two years before. She "wished them back" because she needed their help, but only Jayse returned. She tells Irene that one cannot feed the dead salt because it makes them forget everything except the last place they rested. The salt in the food Irene gave Jayse has caused him to return to his grave, which he will never leave again.

SELECTION ACTIVITY

Jayse's mother takes Irene Platt to see Jayse's body in an open grave. Ask students to imagine that the grave is eventually closed, and that a tombstone is placed over it. What might be written on that tombstone? Might there be a picture or symbol of some kind carved on the stone?

Have each student create a tombstone for Jayse. Students should draw their tombstones on pieces of posterboard. Display the finished tombstones on a bulletin board.

"Sorry, Wrong Number"
by Lucille Fletcher   (page 137)

SELECTION SYNOPSIS

Mrs. Stevenson is a neurotic, bedridden invalid. One day, when she attempts to call her husband's office, she overhears two men on another line plotting a murder. Alarmed and excited, she asks the telephone operator to try to trace the overheard call. When these efforts fail, she calls the police and demands a city-wide search for the killers. As she reports the call to the desk sergeant, Mrs. Stevenson begins to realize that many of the details fit her own situation. A telephone call from Western Union tells her

that the husband, whom she has been expecting home, has gone to Boston on business. His telegram says that he was unable to reach her by telephone because her line was busy. Now quite upset, Mrs. Stevenson calls a nearby hospital in hopes of hiring a practical nurse for the night. During this call, she realizes that it is almost the moment at which the murder is to be committed. She also hears the downstairs phone being lifted. She hangs up and dials the operator again, asking for the police. When the call is put through and the desk sergeant answers again, George, the hired killer, says, "Sorry, wrong number" and hangs up.

SELECTION ACTIVITY

In this activity, students will write a news story about the murder of Mrs. Stevenson as it might appear in a New York City newspaper. An important question for students to consider is, How much information about the murder will be known to the media by the time the story is written?

Point out that, as readers of the play, students have "inside information" about the murder. The writer has allowed them to know exactly what is happening and why. Once the murder is committed, however, the facts may become difficult for the authorities to discover.

Encourage students to recall what they know about the crime from the play. Then ask these questions: Do you think that the police and news media will realize what happened? Do you think that it will be apparent that Mr. Stevenson played an important part in the crime? Do you think that George will get caught, or do you think that the identity of the murderer will remain a mystery? What about Sergeant Duffy? Will he be criticized for not taking Mrs. Stevenson's telephone calls seriously? Will he have learned enough from her calls to help catch the murderer? In the beginning of the story, the men on the telephone say that they want the murder to look like a robbery. Do you think that the police and news media will be deceived?

Students' news stories should include a headline, for example, "Eastside Woman Murdered—Police Suspect Husband Involved in Crime." Give students the option of writing one news story or a series of stories. The series might be very effective if the clues about the murder become evident over a period of time. Students who wish to write a series might enjoy working in pairs or small groups in which members take turns writing articles.

When students have completed their stories, make a bulletin board display in the form of newspaper pages. Title the display "The Murder of Mrs. Stevenson."

"Thus I Refute Beelzy"
by John Collier   (page 155)

SELECTION SYNOPSIS

Small Simon is a young boy who spends all of his time playing alone in a small garden house. Small Simon's mother complains that he always comes inside all tired and nervous. Small Simon's father, who calls himself Big Simon, believes that children should choose for themselves what they want to do. Big Simon becomes upset, however, when Small Simon claims to have a playmate named Mr. Beelzy. Big Simon insists that the playmate is imagined; Small Simon insists that he is real. The conflict escalates, and Small Simon is sent upstairs. Big Simon soon follows with the intention of punishing Small Simon. Small Simon insists that Mr. Beelzy will protect him from harm. Shortly after Big Simon goes upstairs, Small Simon's mother and her guest hear a terrible sound. They rush upstairs, only to find on the stairs a man's shoe with the foot still in it.

SELECTION ACTIVITY

A minor character in this story is Betty, who appears to be a guest of Mrs. Carter. Betty seems quite familiar with the Carter family, yet she does not play a central role in the action.

Ask students to imagine they are Betty and in the Carter home when this story takes place. Then ask them to write a letter to a friend, describing what happened on this particular afternoon. Tell students that, while their descriptions must not contradict anything that is stated in the story, they are free to add to and elaborate on the story in any way that they wish. They should also develop as much as possible the character of Betty, making it clear how she feels about what she is witnessing.

When students have completed the assignment, have them exchange letters with a classmate to read. Then ask for several volunteers to share their letters with the class.

"hist, whist"
by E. E. Cummings   (page 163)

"Overheard on a Saltmarsh"
by Harold Monro   (page 164)

SELECTION SYNOPSES

The subject matter of both poems is the world of supernatural beings. The poem "hist, whist" describes a variety of "ghostthings." "Overheard on a Saltmarsh" describes a squabble between a nymph and a goblin over a set of green glass beads.

SELECTION ACTIVITY

In this activity, students will work in teams to create a play for children based on one or both of the poems in this selection.

Begin by discussing with students how the subject matter and language of these poems might appeal to children. Point out that the poems would be especially appealing around Halloween, when children naturally begin thinking about ghosts and other supernatural creatures.

Give students time to suggest some of the ways these poems might be used to create a play. For example, the encounter between the nymph and the goblin in "Saltmarsh" could be very effectively acted out. The special words and sounds in "hist, whist" could be made into a song, or spoken aloud in choral reading. "Hist, Whist" would also lend itself well to dance, perhaps with some of the words and sounds being spoken or sung as accompaniment. Students might also create dialogue to be spoken by the various creatures in this poem.

Encourage each team to create scenery and costumes for their performances as time permits. Have each team perform their Children's Theater for other members of the class. Then try to arrange for all or some of the teams to perform for children. You might try calling nearby pre-schools and elementary schools, as well as day-care centers and children's hospitals.

"Of Missing Persons"
by Jack Finney   (page 169)

SELECTION SYNOPSIS

Charley Ewell, the narrator of the story, is dissatisfied with his lonely and boring life. At a party, he hears of a travel agency that offers selected applicants passage to a distant, happier world. Charley visits the agency and, after answering some questions, is accepted as an emigrant bound for Verna, the far-off paradise. He travels with other passengers on a rickety bus to an empty barn somewhere on

Long Island. As he awaits transportation to his new life, Charley begins to suspect that he and his companions have been duped. He jumps up, opens the barn door, and steps out, intending to report the whole incident to the police. At that very moment, the inside of the barn lights up and the other emigrants are transported to their new world. Charley makes a futile attempt to obtain another chance, but is coldly turned away from the travel agency. He is doomed to continue living the life he does not like and to recall the chance he had—but lost—to go to Verna.

SELECTION ACTIVITY

In this selection, life in Verna is hinted at, but not fully described. In this activity, students will create detailed models of what they think the land of Verna is really like.

Divide the class into small groups. Give each group time to suggest the kinds of information they want to include in their project. Use questions such as the following to help them get started:

1. Where is Verna geographically located?
2. How big is Verna in area? In population?
3. How old are most of the people? Are most people married or single?
4. Does Verna have laws? If so, what are they?
5. Does Verna have a government? If so, how is it set up?
6. What is the economy of Verna? Are things bought and sold for money?
7. What kinds of things do people do for a living?
8. What forms of entertainment exist? Are there sports and cultural activities?
9. How do people dress?
10. Are there schools? What are they like? What is taught in the schools?
11. Does anyone leave Verna after having lived there awhile?
12. What is the weather and climate like? What is the landscape like?

Point out to students that, while they can get some of this information from the story, most of it will have to be imagined. In addition, each group must decide how they want to present their "model" of Verna. Some suggestions include making a three-dimensional display of a miniature community, drawing pictures, writing a description as it might appear in an encyclopedia, or creating a play with costumes and scenery in which life in Verna is acted out.

Have each group present their completed model of Verna to the class. Then discuss with students the similarities and differences that exist among the various representations of this imaginary place.

"The Listeners"
by Walter de la Mare   (page 181)

"Eldorado"
by Edgar Allen Poe   (page 183)

SELECTION SYNOPSIS

"The Listeners" tells of a traveler on horseback, who comes to a house in the forest at night and knocks on the door. It appears that he has come to keep a promise made long before. No one answers his call, and the house appears to be empty. The poem suggests that it is filled with phantom listeners, who are probably spirits of the people who once lived in the house. After staying a short time, the traveler rides away. The poem "Eldorado" describes an aging knight who has spent his life searching for "Eldorado," a kind of Camelot. For advice, the knight consults a pilgrim shadow, who tells him to continue to ride on in his search for Eldorado.

SELECTION ACTIVITY

The poem "Eldorado" is similar to the novel *Don Quixote* by Cervantes, for both works describe a person's quest for the ideal. Have students read excerpts from this novel and report on what they have read.

Students may also enjoy learning about the popular musical based on *Don Quixote*, called *The Man of La Mancha*. You may wish to obtain a record or cassette tape of the songs from this show to play for the class. You may also be able to obtain a copy of the movie version of this musical.

"The Loch Ness Monster"
by John McPhee   (page 187)

SELECTION SYNOPSIS

In this real-life story, the narrator has joined an expedition formed to sight and positively identify the Loch Ness Monster. This story is primarily expository, with the senior crew-member, Skelton, relating many details about the Monster to the reader. Through the conversations with the narrator, Skelton tells about his experiences at Expedition Headquarters. He relates information about past sightings of the Loch Ness Monster, its physical appearance, and many of its behavioral patterns. The reader is able to get a sense of Skelton's burning desire to one day know exactly what the creature is. The reader, however, can sense that, based on the Monster's long history of elusiveness, Skelton might never really know.

SELECTION ACTIVITY

Reading "The Loch Ness Monster" will probably heighten the students' interest in what the Loch Ness Monster really is. On the chalkboard, develop a list of questions pertaining to the Monster. Allow the students to offer any valid questions they might have. Then, if necessary, suggest a few questions of your own. Some possible questions might be:

Does the Loch Ness Monster really exist?
What does the Monster look like?
Where does the Monster live?
What kind of food does it eat?
Why is it so hard to actually spot the Monster?

After you and the class have developed a list of 8–10 questions, break the students into groups of 5 or 6. Have each group research the questions in the school library. After their research, have a spokesperson from each group lead a discussion about the answers they found.

"On the Path of the Poltergeist"
by Walter Hubbell   **(page 201)**

SELECTION SYNOPSIS

This nonfiction selection describes the strange story of Esther Cox, a young woman who becomes the target of the activities of ghosts, or poltergeists. The reporter who goes to verify the story (he is the author of the selection) claims

not to believe in ghosts, but says afterward that this experience made him a "believer."

SELECTION ACTIVITY

In this activity, students will work in groups to present a television round-table discussion. The topic of the discussion will be "Poltergeists—Are They For Real?"

Have students use the selection by Walter Hubbell as the basis for their discussion. Students may do additional research on the topic, but this need not be mandatory. Encourage each group to use characters from the selection as members of the round table. These could include the reporter Walter Hubbell, Dr. Carritte, Esther's sister Jennie, the Teeds, and Esther Cox herself. The round table should also include one or two other characters that the students create—perhaps a noted psychologist who does not believe in ghosts, or an expert on ESP who definitely does. An interesting twist to the round table would be to have the ghosts "Maggie" and "Bob" appear.

Set a time limit for each group's round table discussion, perhaps about twenty minutes. After each presentation, have the class discuss the effectiveness of the dialogue and any general conclusions reached in the discussion. Also have students evaluate how well their classmates have used the facts and opinions presented in the selection.

STUDENT READING LIST

Poe, Edgar Allan. *The Fall of the House of Usher and Other Tales.* New York: New American Library, 1960.

Spencer, John Wallace. *Limbo of the Lost—Today.* Westfield, Mass.: Phillips, 1969. Paper, Bantam, updated and revised, 1973.

Harding, Lee. *Misplaced Persons.* New York: Harper, 1979. Paper, Bantam.

Molin, Charles, Ed. *Ghosts, Spooks and Spectres.* New York: David White, 1967.

From Globe Classroom Libraries

Science Fiction:
Extraterrestrials by Isaac Asimov, et al.
The Danger Quotient by Annabel and Edgar Johnson

OVERVIEW OF THE UNIT

The theme of this unit is the unknown, that world of the supernatural—ranging from unexplained creatures such as ghosts and poltergeists to mysterious occurences in human experience.

The first selection, "Appointment in Baghdad," presents death as a "real" person.
Literary skill: foreshadowing
Vocabulary: comparison of adjectives
Writing: development of thoughts and actions of main character

The annotated selections are "Appointment at Noon" and "Incident in a Rose Garden." The first is a modern version of "Appointment in Baghdad." The second is a poetic version of the same story.
Literary skill: elements of poetry
Vocabulary: using suffixes
Writing: description

"Boy in the Shadows," set in the Ozarks of Arkansas, is an eerie story about superstitions.
Literary skill: character
Vocabulary: using flashcards to build vocabulary
Writing: epitaphs

The short drama "Sorry, Wrong Number" is a tale of terror about telephone conversation.
Literary skill: conflict
Vocabulary: negative words
Writing: news stories

"Thus I Refute Beelzy" pits a boy's fantasies against a father's reason.
Literary skill: plot
Vocabulary: drawing inferences
Writing: creating a postscript

Two poems, "hist, whist" by E.E. Cummings and "Overheard on a Saltmarsh" by Harold Monro, depict imaginary creatures.
Literary skill: sound segments
Vocabulary: synonyms
Writing: descriptions of settings

In "Of Missing Persons," a young New Yorker imagines how good life might be on another planet.
Literary skill: theme
Vocabulary: allusions

Writing: descriptive text for an advertising brochure

The poems "The Listeners" and "Eldorado" touch on the supernatural as travelers look for the unobtainable.
Literary skill: narrative poetry
Vocabulary: archaic verb forms
Writing: poetry to prose

"The Loch Ness Monster" tells about a famous monster who "lives" in a lake in Scotland, and the people who "hunt" it.
Literary skill: exposition
Vocabulary: American/British English differences
Writing: focused description

"On the Path of the Poltergeist" details one man's search for the "truth" about poltergeists.
Literary skill: persuasion
Vocabulary: borrowed words
Writing: developing a convincing argument

UNIT 2

The Unknown

We are such stuff
As dreams are made on.

—William Shakespeare

The Sleeping Gypsy, 1897, Henri Rousseau. Oil on canvas, 51" x 6'7". Collection, The Museum of Modern Art, New York. Gift of Mrs. Simon Guggenheim.

109

UNIT OBJECTIVES

After completing this unit, students should be able to
- understand the four basic elements of a short story: plot, characters, setting, and theme
- recognize elements in a poem that are similar to elements in a short story
- use a dictionary to understand words based on a foreign language and words that are archaic
- understand the meaning of words having suffixes or prefixes by finding the root word
- write accurate, detailed descriptions
- recognize how good exposition is crafted
- edit their own writing more effectively
- use facts to support opinions

Teaching Strategy: Have students discuss whether the opening quotation—"We are such stuff as dreams are made on"—can be applied to the unknown. (Dreams are not controlled by reason but come into the human mind from an unknown source.) Then, point out examples of the unknown that students will read about in this unit: death; unexplainable sightings of a prehistoric animal; and documented evidence of spirits, such as poltergeists. Next, stress the problem of proving, scientifically, the actual existence of the unknown.

Fine Arts Note

Henry Rousseau (1844–1910) was a French customs collector who began painting in his middle age with no training. He is known as a "primitive" painter because his work is simple, uncluttered by formal artistic conventions. Mystery pervades "The Sleeping Gypsy," as it does in many of his paintings. Is the lion real, or is it what the gypsy is dreaming? Where does the scene take place?

Gypsies symbolize romance and the unknown, and nightime is a time when thoughts about the supernatural become more vivid.

AUDIOVISUAL MATERIALS

"Appointment at Noon" and "Incident in a Rose Garden"—Poetry of Death: Part II (Spectrum Educational Media, Inc.)

"Bond of Reunion" on "A Graveyard of Ghost Tales," stories told by Vincent Price. Record. New York, Caedmon.

"Poetry of Death: Part II," Spectrum Educational Media, Inc.

"The Lavender Evening Dress" on "A Graveyard of Ghost Tales," stories told by Vincent Price. Record. New York, Caedmon.

"Sorry, Wrong Number." Video tape. Hal Wallis Productions, Paramount Home Video, 1948.

"Fancies and Goodnights" by John Collier, performed by Vincent Price. Audio tape. Caedmon.

"Pleasure Dome"; poems read by E.E. Cummings. Audio tape. CBS Records Group/Columbia.

"The Loch Ness Monster," documentary. Video tape. Ted Higgenbotham, TV Sports Scene.

The Unknown.   Have you ever had the feeling there are "things" out there that you know nothing about?

The question is not raised lightly, for many people truly believe that strange creatures—like ghosts, monsters, and poltergeists—really do exist.

The conflict between whether such creatures exist or not, between what is known and what is unknown, is a very old theme in literature. William Shakespeare suggests that you yourself might be nothing more than dreams. Are you then but part of the unknown?

Throughout time, writers everywhere have created stories and poems about the unknown. As you read a few of them in this unit, try to keep an open mind about that other, invisible world.

Matters of Life and Death.   One part of the unknown that you can never know about—despite all our logical thinking—is death. Yet writers have tried for centuries to make death "come alive."

In the first two selections in the unit, "Appointment in Baghdad," a folktale that originated long ago in the Middle East, and "Appointment at

Unit 2

Noon," death is a "real" person who comes to claim victims whose time on earth has run out. The same theme appears in "Incident in a Rose Garden," a poem.

Can people come back from the dead? In the story "Boy in the Shadows," Irene and Ernest Platt wonder about their hired hand; how can his thinness, his listlessness, and his odd manner be explained? You decide for yourself.

Modern city life abounds with all sorts of fears. What if you overhear a very scary phone conversation concerning a murder about to happen where you live? In "Sorry, Wrong Number," a woman is faced with just that situation and she tries to do something to prevent the crime. What steps would you take if you were aware of similar circumstances?

The Supernatural. When you were young, did you have imaginary playmates that you thought were real? What about the present? Now that you've grown up, do you believe intelligent life exists somewhere other than on Earth?

"Small Simon" is sure a companion he calls "Mr. Beelzy" exists in "Thus I Refute Beelzy." His father, "Big Simon," tries to convince him otherwise. Big Simon's logic has no effect on the boy, although Mr. Beelzy does have one remarkable effect on Big Simon.

In one poem E.E. Cummings shows his remarkable skill in using language creatively as he conjures images of ghosts, witches, goblins, and toads. "Overheard on a Saltmarsh" describes a tussle between imaginary creatures over green glass beads stolen from the moon.

In "Of Missing Persons," a young New York man, tired and bored with his life, walks into a travel office looking for a change. An obliging agent is willing to sell him a ticket to a place that seems too good to be true. To buy the ticket, however, he must give up everything. What would you be willing to give to live in a perfect world?

"The Listeners" and "Eldorado" tell of travelers on searches. They seem to be chasing dreams. Yet, if man himself is made of dreams, are the travelers searching for themselves?

Could It Be Real? In a world of computers and hi-tech, you might be inclined to dismiss the supernatural as "bunk"—there are no such things as ghosts or monsters. You might feel that the unknown is not worth thinking about.

Well, what do you do when sincere, trustworthy observers provide evidence that suggests you are wrong?

Read "The Loch Ness Monster" and "On the Path of the Poltergeist" before you close your mind to the unknown. Who knows what is really "out there"?

The Unknown   111

APPOINTMENT IN BAGHDAD

The Race Track, or Death on a Pale Horse, Albert P. Ryder. The Cleveland Museum of Art. Purchased from the J. H. Wade Fund

traditional version
retold by Edith Wharton

One morning the Sultan was resting in his palace in Damascus.[1] Suddenly the door flew open, and in rushed a young man, out of breath and wild with excitement. The Sultan sat up alarmed, for the young man was his most skillful assistant.

"I must have your best horse!" the youth cried out. "There is little time! I must fly at once to Baghdad!"[2]

The Sultan asked why the young man was in such a rush.

"Because," came the hurried reply, "just now, as I was walking in the palace garden, I saw Death standing there. And when Death saw me, he raised his arms in a frightening motion. Oh, it was horrible! I must escape at once!"

The Sultan quickly arranged for the youth to have his fastest horse. And no sooner had the young man thundered out through the palace gate, than the Sultan himself went into the garden. Death was still there.

The Sultan was angry. "What do you mean?" he demanded. "What do you mean by raising your arms and frightening my young friend?"

"Your Majesty," Death said calmly, "I did not mean to frighten him. You see, I raised my arms only in surprise. I was astonished to see him here in your garden, for I have an appointment with him tonight in Baghdad."

---

[1]**Damascus:** an important Middle Eastern city, now capital of Syria
[2]**Baghdad:** an important city in the old Middle East, now capital of Iraq

The Unknown   113

MINI QUIZ

Write the following questions on the chalkboard or overhead projector, and call on students to fill in the blanks. Discuss the answers with the class.

1. The Sultan was _____ when the young man rushed into the palace.
2. The young man had seen Death in the palace _____.
3. Death _____ when he saw the young man.
4. The real reason Death had raised his arms was _____.
5. Death's appointment with the young man was in _____.

Answers to Mini Quiz

1. resting
2. garden
3. raised his arms in a frightening motion
4. in surprise
5. Baghdad

Sidelights: Baghdad sounds like a very romantic and exotic city, and that could be why it has often been mentioned in stories. The "modern" Baghdad dates back to 763. At one point it was one of the most populous and important cities in the world. Important trade routes passed through it, and a university with a large library was located there. It has always been an important Moslem religious and political center; the ruler of the Saracen empire (made up of Middle Eastern Islamic Arabs) was based in Baghdad; he was called "sultan." Today Baghdad, with a population of two million people, is the capital of modern-day Iraq.

Motivation for Reading: Ask students what they would do if they suddenly encountered a figure of death. Would they run from it, talk to it, try to kill it, or what? Students could be encouraged to develop skits about the encounter and to present them to the class.

More About the Thematic Idea: In "Appointment in Baghdad," death is personified, or made to seem to be a real person. Ask students to think of other examples of death personified, such as the grim reaper. Why is death, an abstraction, often portrayed as a real person?

Purpose-Setting Question: Is it natural to want to flee death?

Reading Strategy: Point out to students that no proper names are used in this story—except for Death. Even though "Sultan" is capitalized, it does not refer to a specific Sultan. The focus of the story is to fall on Death.

Literary Focus: Notice how Death is presented as a very gracious figure; he even addresses the Sultan as "Your Majesty." Death goes about his business in a very professional way.

T113

ANSWERS TO UNDERSTAND THE SELECTION

1. The Sultan's palace in Damascus.
2. The Sultan's "most skillful assistant."
3. He raised them in surprise because he was astonished to see the young man in Damascus instead of Baghdad, where he had an appointment with him that night.
4. The young man interpreted Death's raising his arms as a sign that Death had come to claim him.
5. To get to Baghdad, which is fairly far away and, therefore, supposedly safe from Death.
6. He is angry, he confronts Death, Death explains that he had expected to see the young man in Baghdad, not Damascus.
7. It is a reference to an inevitable meeting.
8. Answers will vary. Sample answer: Yes; I would be scared, too, and try to get away.
9. Answers will vary, but the Sultan's actions are not implausible. He is, no doubt, a much older man than the young assistant, and he might think that he and Death are bound to meet soon anyhow.
10. We cannot escape death.

Respond to Literature: The quotation from Shakespeare that opens this unit ("We are such stuff as dreams are made on") is from Act IV, scene i of "The Tempest." The lines are spoken by Prospero. He is explaining that the actors in a play within the play "were all spirits and are melted into air, into thin air." Shakespeare is suggesting that we all might be actors on a stage. If so, we have our parts to play, and then we leave the stage. The script holds our fate, and we can do nothing to change it. Ask students why the notion of "fate" has per-

UNDERSTAND THE SELECTION

Recall

1. Where does the story take place?
2. Who is the young man who rushes in asking to borrow a horse?
3. Why did Death raise his arms when he encountered the young man?

Infer

4. Why did Death's actions frighten the young man so alarmingly?
5. Why did the young man want a horse?
6. Describe what happens when the Sultan goes out to the palace garden.
7. What is the significance of the word "Appointment" in the title?

Apply

8. Imagine that you are the young man and you have seen Death in the palace garden. How would you react?
9. The Sultan seems to be a brave man to go out to the palace garden and confront Death. Is this part of the story hard for you to believe?
10. What is the point of this story?

Respond to Literature

Is there such a thing as fate? Do you believe that all our actions have been predetermined, like "players" on a stage acting out their parts? Explain your ideas.

114

WRITE ABOUT THE SELECTION

What do you think the young man thought when he saw Death in the palace garden? Many thoughts must have raced through his mind when he encountered the figure.

Imagine that you are the young man. Write what happened and what you thought when you were walking in the garden and first saw Death.

Prewriting: Draw a quick sketch of the garden to help you visualize the scene before describing it in words. Place the young man in the scene, and mark where he sees Death. Then write a few words next to the man to describe his thoughts just before he met Death, at the moment he met Death, and immediately after their encounter. Finally, try to draw a picture of Death itself.

Writing: Use your picture and notes to write one or several paragraphs to describe what happened in the garden. Remember to use first-person point of view so that your description fits into the rest of the story.

Revising: Try to write in the same style as Edith Wharton, using short sentences and simple, direct language. Consider adding specific details and vivid words to make your paragraph really come alive.

Proofreading: As you reread what you have written, check carefully that references to the character Death begin with a capital letter. If you have included direct conversation, make sure you have followed the rules of punctuation.

Unit 2

sisted in literature for hundreds, even thousands, of years.

WRITE ABOUT THE SELECTION

Prewriting: Use students' suggestions to create a drawing on the chalkboard or overhead transparency.

Writing: Allow students to work on their descriptions individually.

Circulate, asking about the sketches they have made in order to prompt ideas on things to include.

Revising: Have students revise cooperatively by working in small groups. Each student reads his or her description aloud to the group, and group members offer feedback. Remind students that the description should be written in first person.

Proofreading: Have students continue working in small groups. Ask them to exchange papers for proofreading. Students should ask for explanations from their partner, another student, or the teacher if they do not understand a suggested change.

LDP Activity: Discuss the prefixes "super" and "un." Examples are "superman," "supermarket,"

THINK ABOUT FORESHADOWING

What makes "Appointment in Baghdad" such a good short story? Surely it is short—even for a short story—but that is not all. Let us look again at expectations, what really happens, and foreshadowing. The writer's skillful use of foreshadowing—hints or clues that suggest what might happen—helps you to accept an event that will happen.

1. After the young man rides off on the horse, what do you expect will happen?

2. How do you think that expectation was formed?

3. How does the story actually end?

4. Look back at the story again. Are there hints about what will actually happen?

5. Do you feel the writer has played a trick on you? Explain your answer.

DEVELOP YOUR VOCABULARY

The comparative and superlative forms of almost all one-syllable adjectives are formed by adding *er* and *est*.

Some two-syllable adjectives are formed in the same way, but others are formed, (like all adjectives of more than two syllables) by adding *more* and *most*.

fast	faster	fastest
skillful	more skillful	most skillful

Some adjective forms are irregular:

good	better	best

If you are in doubt about adjective forms, check the dictionary.

Give the forms for these adjectives:

1. eager
2. many
3. plain
4. beautiful
5. dear
6. pretty
7. friendly
8. thin
9. humble
10. contented

"unwanted," and "unhappy."

In your dictionary find three examples of words using the prefixes "super" and "un." Make up sentences using the words. Now explain what you think the prefixes "super" and "un" mean.

Short stories are a very popular form of literature. Why?

You can read them so quickly that, sometimes, you can complete one on a short subway ride. Short stories are so concentrated they can have a lot of impact in a few pages. The conciseness of a short story also provides the chance for a clear examination of the four basic elements of any story. These are plot, characters, setting, and theme.

Plot. Plot is usually the most obvious element of a short story. Many people think of it first when they talk about a "story": the telling of one event after another to form a series of actions leading to a conclusion.

The plot is usually introduced through **exposition,** or written interpretation, by the author. Exposition provides background information for the actions that will take place in the story.

As the action unfolds, a "complication" arises. The **complication** is like a question demanding an answer. It keeps the story moving, as you wonder what will happen next. Sometimes the answer ends the story, or it can lead to another question.

As the plot develops, the action "rises." **Rising action** leads to a crisis with a climax at the end, or near the end, of the story. **Climax** is the peak of the action.

If the story continues beyond the climax, the action "falls." The plot develops further, but only to resolve a final question. The **falling action** ends in **resolution.**

When you read a story quickly, you are probably unaware of all those plot developments. Try to keep them in mind as you read the next selections, especially in "Thus I Refute Beelzy," when you'll be studying plot developments in detail.

Characters. The characters are the people in a short story. They act, or are acted upon, as the plot develops.

You learn about characters in two ways. First, the writer might tell you directly whether a certain character is clever, mean, bold or shy. The writer is creating **traits** that describe the character.

FICTION

Second, the writer can tell you indirectly about a character by describing what the character says, or how the character acts. This information portrays the character, too, but you must use some imagination to fit the pieces into the overall description.

Usually a writer uses both methods. In "Appointment in Baghdad," you learn that one character is a "young" man. That is **direct information.** You also learn that he "rushes" into the Sultan's palace "out of breath and wild with excitement." That is **indirect information,** giving you clues to his general state of mind and how he reacts in certain situations.

Setting. A third element of a short story is "setting." You can probably guess that setting includes where a story takes place; however, it also includes when a story happens. Additionally, it can include natural events, such as a blizzard or a hurricane.

The short stories in this unit have a variety of settings. "Of Missing Persons" takes place in modern-day New York, while "Appointment in Baghdad" takes place in the Middle East in a much earlier period.

Theme. "Theme" is the fourth element of a short story.

A writer usually has a reason for telling us a story. He or she chooses a subject, and then develops plot, setting, and characters. What the writer wants you to learn from the story is the theme. It is the story's idea or message.

"Appointment in Baghdad" has a single, clear theme: Death cannot be avoided.

Sometimes a short story has more than one theme. Sometimes there is no theme of real importance, or it is not clear.

As you read the selections in this unit, look for the elements of the short stories. Ask yourself these questions:

1. Which elements are easiest to identify and understand? Which are hardest?
2. Are elements more important in some stories than in others?

The Unknown 117

After completing the next two selections, students will be able to

- understand the elements of a short story
- relate the theme to their own lives
- use personification in describing death
- see similarities between elements in short stories and poems
- recognize how certain suffixes change adjectives into nouns

More About Elements of the Short Story: For many readers plot is often the element on which they concentrate most of their attention. Suggest to students that in the next selection they try to concentrate on character. Henry Curran is the natural person to focus on in "Appointment at Noon." In the short poem "Incident in a Rose Garden," note to students that the character of the Master, although briefly sketched, contrasts sharply with Curran.

Cooperative/Collaborative Learning Activity: Divide students into groups. Have each student tell a different story than his or her choice in the Elements of the Genre, Practical Application section. This time, to solidify an understanding of inferred elements, ask each student to make a chart listing all the elements of his or her chosen story. Then, as they tell their story to the group, have them point out at least one element that can be deduced from context clues only.

Death on a Pale Horse, J. M. W. Turner. Courtesy of the Tate Gallery

APPOINTMENT AT NOON

by Eric Frank Russell

Henry Curran was big, busy, and successful. He had no patience with people who weren't successful. He had the build of a fighter and the soul of a tiger. His time was worth a thousand bucks an hour. He knew of nobody who was worth more.

And crime did not pay? "Bah!" said Henry Curran.

The law of the jungle paid off. Henry Curran had learned that nice people are soft people, and that smiles are made to be slapped.

Entering his large office with the fast, heavy step of a big man in fighting shape, Henry threw his hat onto a hook. He glanced at the wall clock. He noted that it was ten minutes to twelve.

Seating himself in the large chair behind his desk, he kept his eyes on the door. His wait lasted about ten seconds. Frowning at the thought of it, Curran reached over and pushed a red button on his big desk.

"What's wrong with you?" he snapped when Miss Reed came in. "You get worse every day. Old age creeping over you or something?"

She paused. She was tall, neat, and steady. She faced him across the desk, her eyes showing a touch of fear. Curran hired to work for him only people he knew too much about.

STUDY HINTS

The main character is introduced right away. His traits are described directly as well as indirectly.

Note the writer's statement of the setting. The office's location and the date do not matter. The description of Henry Curran acts as exposition. Now, with background information and setting provided, the plot begins to unfold.

The second character of the story is introduced. Notice how information about Miss Reed tells us more about Curran.

The Unknown

119

Vocabulary: Preteach the vocabulary words. See the Comprehension Workbook in the TRB.

More About Vocabulary: Write on the chalkboard or a transparency the definitions for the footnoted vocabulary in the story. Then, read each new vocabulary word and ask students to choose the definition that seems to be correct. This exercise can be done as an entire class or with students working individually.

Sidelights: Henry Curran is a caricature of the prototypical American businessman: big, busy, successful, impatient, and ruthless. Romanticism has no place in his life. Traditionally, businessmen have been used as central characters in American literature. Sinclair Lewis vilified the small-town businessman in the novel *Babbit,* and Arthur Miller showed the emptiness of a traveling salesman's life in *Death of a Salesman.* Is there something about business that makes businesspeople literary targets?

Motivation for Reading: Ask students what connection there might be, if any, between this story and the previous one. The titles are nearly identical, substituting a time for a place. (Although, you can point out, that both time and place are part of a story's setting.) Whet their appetites further by noting that both stories have three characters.

More About the Thematic Idea: In the previous story, Death was personified as a gracious but sure figure. How might Death be portrayed in a more modern story?

Purpose-Setting Question: How can the passage of time (in "Appointment at Noon," just 8 minutes) be used to help tell a story?

Critical Thinking: Parallelism in structure and phrasing is used to good effect in this sentence describing Henry Curran: "He had the build of a fighter and the soul of a tiger."

Literary Focus: A number of interesting expressions are used in "Appointment at Noon"—His time was worth a thousand bucks an hour, the law of the jungle paid off, smiles are made to be slapped. Make sure that students understand them.

T119

"I'm sorry, Mr. Curran, I was—"

"Never mind the excuse. Be faster—or else! Speed's what I like. SPEED—SEE?"

"Yes, Mr. Curran."

"Has Lolordo phoned in yet?"

"No, Mr. Curran."

"He should be through by now if everything went all right." He looked at the clock again, tapping angrily on his desk. "If he's made a mess of it and the mouthpiece comes on, tell him to forget about Lolordo. He's in no position to talk, anyway. A little time in jail will teach him not to be stupid."

"Yes, Mr. Curran. There's an old—"

This is the plot complication.

"Shut up till I've finished. If Michaelson calls up and says the *Firefly* got through, phone Voss and tell him without delay! And I mean without delay! That's important!" He thought for a moment. Then he finished, "There's that meeting downtown at twelve-twenty. God knows how long it will go on. If they want trouble, they can have it! If anyone asks, you don't know where I am. You don't expect me back before four."

"But, Mr. Curran—"

"You heard what I said. Nobody sees me before four."

"There's a man already here," she got out in an apologetic voice. "He said you have an appointment with him at two minutes to twelve."

The third character, the uninvited guest, is described indirectly. Despite this description, he is pretty mysterious. This mystery creates tension. Further hints about him heighten the mystery.

"And you fell for a joke like that?" He studied her with a cutting smile.

"I can only repeat what he said. He seemed quite sincere."

"That's a change," snapped Curran. "Sincerity in *my* office? He's got the wrong address. Go tell him to spread himself across the tracks."

"I said you were out and didn't know when you would return. He took a seat and said he'd wait because you would be back at ten to twelve."

Without knowing it, both suddenly stared at the clock. Curran lifted an arm and looked at his wristwatch to check the instrument on the wall.

---

mouthpiece (MOUTH pees) slang for criminal lawyer
apologetic (uh POL uh JET ik) filled with apology; suggesting that one is sorry
sincerity (sin SER uh tee) honesty; quality of being sincere

Literary Focus: Again, informal language helps build Curran's character. Make sure that students understand what the expression "spread himself across the tracks" means.

Unit 2

"That's what the scientific bigbrains would call precognition. I call it a lucky guess. One minute either way would have made him wrong. That guy ought to bet money on the horses." He made a gesture of dismissal. "Push him out—or do I have to get the boys to do it for you?"

"That wouldn't be necessary. He is old and blind."

"I don't care if he's armless and legless—that's *his* tough luck. Give him the rush."

Obediently she left. A few moments later she was back. She had the sorrowful look of a person whose job forced her to face Curran's anger.

The action continues to rise. Note how time has become very important to the story.

"I'm terribly sorry, Mr. Curran. He insists that he has a date with you for two minutes to twelve. He is to see you about a personal matter of great importance."

Curran scowled at the wall. The clock said four minutes to twelve. He spoke with purpose.

"I know no blind man and I don't forget appointments. Throw him down the stairs."

She hesitated, standing there wide-eyed. "I'm wondering whether—"

"Out with it!"

"Whether he's been sent to you by someone else, someone who'd rather he couldn't tell who you were by sight."

He thought it over and said, "Could be. You use your brains once in a while. What's his name?"

"He won't say."

"Nor state his business?"

"No."

"H'm! I'll give him two minutes. If he's trying to get money for some church or something he'll go out through the window. Tell him my time is valuable and show him in."

The visitor now confronts Henry Curran. What can you infer about the old man from the description?

She went away and brought back the visitor. She gave him a chair. The door closed quietly behind her. The clock said three minutes before the hour.

Curran sat back and looked at his guest, finding him tall, thin, and white-haired. The old man's clothes were black, a deep,

---

precognition (pree kog NISH un) knowledge of future events
scowl (SKOUL) frown and look angry

The Unknown   121

Enrichment: Juxtapose on the chalkboard or overhead transparency the words **precognition** and **recognition**. Then point out the difference between the meaning of the prefixes, **pre-** for **before**, and **re-** for **again**. Show how the prefixes create two different words from the same root, "cognition."

Clarification: Do students understand Miss Reed's reasoning here? It is a clever thought. You could return to it at the end of the story and discuss Death's blindness. Why is death blind? Is it a hindrance or a help?

Critical Thinking: The description of Death's voice in the story is rich in images. Analyze it by beginning with the simile and, then, discuss how a voice can be compared to an organ.

Discussion: You could ask students to compare the character of Death in this story with Death in "Appointment in Baghdad." This Death seems cold and frightening—possibly because that is the only kind of person people such as Henry Curran take seriously.

somber black. They set off the bright, blue, unseeing eyes staring from his colorless face.

Those strange eyes were the old man's most noticeable feature. They were odd, as if somehow they could look *into* the things they could not look at. And they were sorry—sorry for what they saw.

For the first time in his life, Henry Curran felt a little alarmed. He said, "What can I do for you?"

"Nothing," replied the other. "Nothing at all."

His voice was like an organ. It was low, no more than a whisper, and with its sounding a queer coldness came over the room. He sat there unmoving and staring at whatever a blind man can see. The coldness increased, became bitter. Curran shivered despite himself. He frowned and got a hold on himself.

The theme emerges in the visitor's rejoinder to Henry Curran's sharp comment.

"Don't take up my time," advised Curran. "State your business or get out."

"People don't take up time. Time takes up people."

"Just what do you mean? Who are you?"

This is the climax. Henry Curran even asks the two questions we want answered.

"You know who I am. Every man is a shining sun to himself, until he is dimmed by his dark companion."

"You're not funny," said Curran, freezing.

"I am never funny."

The tiger light blazed in Curran's eyes as he stood up. He placed a thick, firm finger near his desk button.

"Enough of this nonsense! What d'you want?"

Suddenly holding out a lengthless, dimensionless arm, the man whispered sadly, "You!"

And Death took him.

At exactly two minutes to twelve.

---

somber (SOM bur) gloomy and dark; very sad
dimensionless (duh MEN shun les) without dimensions, or size that can be measured in length, height, or width

Unit 2

INCIDENT IN A ROSE GARDEN

by Donald Justice

GARDENER: Sir, I encountered Death
Just now among our roses.
Thin as a scythe he stood there.

> Notice how this poem shares elements with the short story. The title and the first two lines establish the setting.

5   I knew him by his pictures.
He had his black coat on,
Black gloves, a broad black hat.

> The poem has characters, like a short story.

I think he would have spoken,
Seeing his mouth stood open.
Big it was, with white teeth.

10   As soon as he beckoned, I ran.
I ran until I found you.
Sir, I am quitting my job.

> The plot has developed from the very first line of the poem. Now the plot complication appears.

15   I want to see my sons
Once more before I die.
I want to see California.

MASTER: Sir, you must be that stranger
Who threatened my gardener.
This is my property, sir.
I welcome only friends here.

20   DEATH: Sir, I knew your father.
And we were friends at the end.

As for your gardener,
I did not threaten him.
Old men mistake my gestures.

25   I only meant to ask him
To show me to his master.
I take it you are he?

> The theme emerges in the climax. What is the theme?

---

scythe (SYTH) a long, curved blade fixed at an angle to a long, bent handle and used to cut down grass or grain

The Unknown   123

ANSWERS TO
UNDERSTAND
THE SELECTION

1. ten minutes to twelve
2. a contribution to "some church or something"
3. black
4. He was a businessssman of some sort, because he is so preoccupied with money and time. We do not know exactly what kind of business, though. The writer seems to want to leave this deliberately vague.
5. "Tall, neat, and steady." A bit fearful of Curran, but persistent because she insists on making Curran see the visitor in the waiting room. Clever, because she thinks that maybe a blind man had been sent to Curran by somebody who did not want the man to recognize Curran.
6. "Old" represents the passing of time, "blind" represents a lack of prejudice as to who dies when—everybody's time comes up at some point. The old, blind man is a perfect personification of Death.
7. The gardener ran away too quickly; anyway, it is the gardener's master that Death is after, not the gardener. There is no real need for Death to speak to the gardener.
8. One talks about an "appointment" at a place, the other an "appointment" at a time. Both involve the setting, but different parts. Time and place do not matter when it comes to Death's arrival.
9. Answers will vary on the first part of the question. As to the second, there is some foreshadowing: the title itself, for instance, but also the continual emphasis on time, and Curran's nervousness about time. And when Death walks into Curran's office, he is described as very odd. Even Henry Curran "felt a little alarmed" then.

T124

UNDERSTAND THE SELECTION

Recall

1. When did Henry Curran enter his office?

2. Before the visitor enters Curran's office, what does Curran think about him?

3. What color were Death's clothes?

Infer

4. What was Curran's profession?

5. Describe Miss Reed.

6. For what purpose is the visitor in "Appointment at Noon" old and blind?

7. Why did Death not speak to the gardener in "Incident in a Rose Garden"?

Apply

8. Discuss the difference in titles between "Appointment in Baghdad" and "Appointment at Noon."

9. Did "Appointment at Noon" turn out the way you expected? Was there any foreshadowing to help you?

10. Why do you think both "Appointment in Baghdad" and "Incident in a Rose Garden" include gardens for settings?

Respond to Literature

"Appointment in Baghdad," "Appointment at Noon," and "Incident in a Rose Garden" show Death as being uninterested in the ages of his "victims." Why?

124

WRITE ABOUT THE SELECTION

If you had to describe Death as a person, what would you say? Is Death a man or a woman? Does it look like a person? Do only certain parts look like a person? Can Death talk? Can it hear, feel, smell, and touch? What does it wear? Does it carry anything?

Imagine that you are writing a story and death is a character. Write a description of death.

Prewriting: Using clusters, answer the questions above. Add any other information that helps to provide an accurate description of what you think Death looks like. Make a sketch or illustration of the character Death if that will stimulate your imagination.

Writing: Use the information in the clusters and your drawing to write your description. You may introduce another character if you want to use conversation to build the description, but Death must remain the central figure.

Revising: You want your readers to have as clear a picture as possible of how you imagine Death to be. Can you add any similes to make the description more vivid? Think about using sensory details; description that appeals to the senses of sight, sound, smell, feeling, or taste.

Proofreading: Reread what you have written and check that all sentences end with a punctuation mark. Check also that Death as a character should always begin with a capital D.

Unit 2

10. Gardens are symbols of life and cultivated security. That Death encounters his victims in gardens underlines the theme that Death takes us all, no matter who or where we are.

Respond to Literature: You probably will want to treat this question with sensitivity. Young people who have experienced the death of a close friend or relative— or heard on TV the mounting number of very young victims—may not want to share their feelings. Some students, on the other hand, may see themselves as immortal, and answer the question with a sincere, but too brief conviction. Small groups could be used to prompt discussion before opening the topic for general class consideration.

WRITE ABOUT
THE SELECTION

Prewriting: Make a cluster on the chalkboard or overhead transparency of the characteristics of Death in any of the last three selections. Where given, include all their physical traits, to show exactly how death is personified.

Writing: Circulate among students as they work individually on

THINK ABOUT FICTION

Were you surprised that the poem "Incident in a Rose Garden" was similar to "Appointment at Baghdad"? Were you also surprised that a poem could seem like a short story by sharing the same elements?

1. Point to all the similarities between "Incident in a Rose Garden" and "Appointment at Baghdad."

2. Now point to the differences between the two.

3. "Appointment at Noon" is much longer than "Incident in a Rose Garden." Yet the elements of a short story are in each. Point them out.

4. Now, point to things that are lacking in the poem compared to the story.

5. Which of these three selections is your favorite? Why?

DEVELOP YOUR VOCABULARY

Many times suffixes are added to adjectives to make them nouns:

patient + **-ence** = **patience**

If you know the suffix and the root word you can figure out the meaning.

-ence	=	act, quality, or result of
-ity	=	state, character, condition of
-ness	=	state or quality of being
-tude	=	state or quality of being

Define each *italicized* noun by determining the root adjective and suffix. Check your definition in a dictionary. Then write your own sentence using each word.

1. "*Sincerity* in my office?" he snapped.

2. Did he state his *business?*

3. A queer *coldness* came over the room.

4. Her *certitude* was a real advantage.

5. "*Capability* is the thing!" he said.

The Unknown

125

Stories are about characters who may not be real but are probably drawn from real life. A character is a reasonable copy of a real human being with all the good and bad traits that people can have. A story revolves around the problems the main character or characters have.

Writers can develop characters directly by telling you what they look like or what characters are thinking. Characters also can be developed indirectly through their actions or their speech. Good characters make you care about their problems.

As you read "Boy in the Shadows," ask yourself these questions:

1. How might dialogue between characters reveal their traits?
2. Where do actions reveal character?

SKILL BUILDER

Imagine that you are on vacation. You meet someone who is interesting, and you want to write about him or her in a letter to a friend. Describe the person through an event in which the character traits of that person are revealed.

126

Unit 2

BOY IN THE SHADOWS

by Margaret Ronan

Is it true that love is stronger than death? That the human spirit can survive the grave? Perhaps the answer can be found in the strange experience of Irene and Ernest Platt.

The Platts had always lived in cities, but when Ernest retired, they decided they wanted to spend the rest of their lives in the country. They bought a small house tucked away on the lower slopes of the Ozarks.[1] Irene at once planted a vegetable garden. With what she could grow, and a trip once a week to the supermarket in the nearest town, they should have all the food they needed.

Food was the first thing she thought of when she saw the boy. She had been working in the garden when she became aware that someone was watching her. She raised her eyes, and there, standing at the edge of the field, was the boy—a thin, hollow-eyed boy wearing faded jeans and no shoes.

Irene raised her hand and waved, but the boy did not wave back. Perhaps he doesn't have the strength to wave, she thought to herself. He was very thin, and his ribs showed plainly.

The boy stood there a few more minutes. Then, as if he had seen all he wanted to, he turned and slipped away—vanishing among the thicket of trees at the edge of the field.

Two days later he was back. With him was a haggard-looking woman of about 40. When she saw Irene, she came straight up to the fence. The boy lagged slightly behind, head hanging listlessly.

"Are you the lady who bought this place?" the woman asked.

"I'm Mrs. Platt," replied Irene. "What can I do for you?"

"I've come about what we can do for you, Ma'am," replied the woman firmly. "This here's my son, Jayse. He's a good worker and a lot stronger than he looks. He'll work for you, do your garden and your chores, for two dollars a day."

---

thicket (THIK it) bushes or small trees growing close together
haggard (HAG urd) thin and worn from too much worry or pain
listlessly (LIST lis lee) in a tired, inactive way
[1]**Ozarks:** mountains that run through Arkansas and Missouri, Oklahoma, and Illinois

The Unknown   127

Vocabulary: Preteach the vocabulary words. See the Comprehension Worksheet in the TRB.

More About Vocabulary: Almost all of the footnoted vocabulary in this selection can be applied to people. Go over each footnote with students, illustrating the words in sentences; then call for volunteers to give other examples.

Sidelights: The Ozarks, also called the Ozark Mountains or the Ozark Plateau, cover an area of 60,000 square miles in southwestern Missouri, northwestern Arkansas, and eastern Oklahoma. The mountains are low—1,500 to 2,500 feet—but the area remained isolated and remote for many years. Even today it is considered very rural. In his book, *Blue Highways*, William Least Heat Moon writes about an interesting experience he had in the Ozarks.

Motivation for Reading. On a relief map of the United States, point out to students where the Ozarks are. Discuss what it would be like to move to a rural, mountainous area, such as the Ozarks, after spending one's life in cities (as the Platt couple have in this selection). Elicit ideas on what "country folks" might be like, and how they might differ from "city folks."

More About the Thematic Idea: This selection presents the belief that someone can return from the dead. The story is written in such a matter-of-fact way that belief can be accepted as fact and as part of rural folklore. Ask students whether they can think of other examples in literature in which people have returned from the dead. There are numerous well-known ones, such as the return of Christopher Marley in Charles Dickens's *A Christmas Carol*.

Purpose-Setting Question: If someone related a strange incident by referring to the unknown or to supernatural events, what would be your reaction?

Literary Focus: Point out that the introductory physical description of Jayse, that he is a mysterious figure. Contrast the way the Platts were introduced.

Reading Strategy: Point out the use of colloquial language in the text; for example, "You won't have no cause for complaint." The sentence contains a double negative. Previous sentences used other informal (sometimes incorrect) constructions; "This here's my son", for example. You could discuss how the use of colloquial language helps build character.

Discussion: Why does Jayse not talk? Why does his mother insist on setting the conditions by which he will work and live at the Platts? How are the characters of both Jayse and his mother being developed?

Reading Strategy: Ask students what happens every time Mrs. Platt decides to draw the line and help Jayse. Jayse's mother comes up with a logical excuse for her not to. The story seems realistic until the woman tells Mrs. Platt, "Yes Ma'am, I'll take you to him." Then, it enters into fantasy or the unknown.

Irene was about to say that she didn't need any help, that she enjoyed doing her own chores. But the sight of Jayse's thin, dangling arms and hollow-cheeked face stopped her.

"He's very young—and he doesn't look strong," she began, but the woman held up a work-scarred hand to stop her.

"He's 16," she said, "but he's smallish and looks younger. And he's a lot stronger than he looks, like I said. You won't have no cause for complaint. Jayse's a good worker."

"All right," said Irene. Two dollars a day wasn't much, and having Jayse on her own ground would give her a chance to feed him properly. "All right. That will be fine. Jayse can come at ten every morning and go home at five. I'll give him his dinner at noon." She turned to the boy. "Will that be all right with you, Jayse?"

Jayse didn't answer. Irene wondered if he had even heard her, for he kept his head down, never raising his eyes. His mother beckoned Irene to one side and spoke in a low voice. "No, Ma'am. I don't want Jayse traveling back and forth. We live a fair distance from here. He can sleep in that little shed there. And don't you be worrying about feeding him. I'll come every day and bring his food. He's got a finicky stomach. I know just what he can eat and I'll fix it for him. When I come, you can give me his two dollars."

"But what about Jayse?" Irene asked. "If he's working for the money, shouldn't I pay it to him?"

The woman shook her head. "You don't understand. I need that money to feed my other children. Jayse's pa is dead, and now the boy is the only one who can go out to work. He wants to do it to help us out. You won't be sorry you took him on. He's a good worker, is Jayse. He never gets tired, never complains. You'll see."

"Well, all right, but I don't think he should sleep in the shed. I could fix up a room in the house."

"No, Ma'am. Jayse wouldn't care for that. He's a poor sleeper and he wouldn't want to think he might disturb you. The shed will be fine."

So Jayse came to work for the Platts. Irene soon found that the claims his mother had made were true. Jayse never complained and never seemed to get tired. No matter how early Irene and Ernest got up in the morning, the boy was already at work, feeding the chickens, tending the garden. Gradually, Irene let him take over some of the cleaning chores in the house, and once she showed him what she wanted done, she never had to remind him to do it.

"He's a wonder," she told Ernest, "but he's not like a boy at all. He's like . . . like a machine. Do you know he's never said a word to me. He never even looks at me, only at the ground."

Ernest grunted. "All I know is that the kid gives me the creeps. Maybe he can't talk. And if you ask me, he's not all there mentally."

Irene shook her head. "No, he isn't

---

finicky (FIN ik ee) fussy; very hard to please
creeps (KREEPS) feeling of fear or horror

stupid. It's more as though he's walking around in his sleep."

"Well, the price is right," said Ernest. "In fact, it's wrong—two dollars a day is ridiculous for the work he's doing. Let's raise it to four. I'm not crazy about having Jayse around, but let's see if a raise gets some reaction from him."

Why should it? Irene wondered. Jayse never touched the money he earned. Every day, shortly before noon, he would stop what he was doing. Then he would stand, eyes lowered, head turned slightly to one side as though listening. A few minutes later his mother would appear from the wooded thicket, carrying his dinner in a covered tin plate. She would wait until Irene handed her Jayse's daily wages, then lead him to the shed and sit with him while he ate.

"Why won't she let me feed him?" Irene asked furiously. "I've seen the stuff she brings him—it's some kind of mush. That's not decent food for a boy who works as hard as he does. I think he's even thinner than he was when he first came here."

Ernest had to agree. The bones of Jayse's face were more prominent. When the boy bent over the hoe in the garden, his knobby spine was plainly outlined under his thin T-shirt.

Irene decided to try again. "I want to give Jayse a hot meal every day," she told his mother. "Otherwise I can't let him go on working here the way he does. He's getting thinner all the time. I'm afraid he'll get sick."

There was a frightened glitter in the woman's eyes. "You don't understand, Mrs. Platt. Jayse's like his father. He can't eat the food you and I can eat. He can't take salt—his system can't handle it. Please, Ma'am, let things be. Don't say you won't let him stay. He's the only one the kids and I can depend on. Without what he earns here, his brothers and sisters will starve."

Irene gave in. "All right, he can stay. I must admit he's a wonderful worker— but he doesn't seem happy about being with us. He never smiles or laughs. And he's never said a word to either my husband or myself."

The woman shrugged. "It don't mean anything, Ma'am. Jayse's different. He don't feel things the way most kids do. All he cares about is helping me and the other kids. Don't worry about him. He's doing what he wants to do."

But *is* it what he wants? Irene wondered. She stood at her bedroom window later. She could see the shed where Jayse slept—but he wasn't asleep. He was sitting in the doorway, arms resting slackly on his knees, staring unmovingly into the moonlit night.

"Something's wrong," she said aloud.

"What are you talking about?" her husband asked sleepily.

"Jayse. I've been watching him for half an hour. He's never moved so much as a muscle. With the day he's put in, you'd think he'd have gone to sleep

---

prominent (PROM uh nunt) easy to see; standing out
knobby (NOB ee) lumpy
slackly (SLAK lee) loosely

The Unknown

hours ago. But no—he's just sitting there."

Ernest got up and came to stand at her side. "I could have told you that. He always sits there at night. As far as I know, he never sleeps. I'll admit he's one spooky kid—but he's not really bothering anyone, is he?"

No one but me, Irene thought. As the days wore on, the sight of the boy wrung her heart. His skin, which had been pale, was now yellow and shiny. There were discolored patches on his forehead, cheekbones, and along the ridge of his nose. Even more disquieting, his movements seemed to be slower and more labored.

"Aren't you feeling well, Jayse?" she asked. But the boy only ducked his head and brushed past her. Uneasily, she went to her husband. "Look at Jayse. I think he's sick. He's moving around like an old man."

Ernest peered at Jayse, who was slowly cutting grass. "You're right. What are those dark patches on his skin?"

"I don't know, but I'm sure of one thing. He's going under from malnutrition. I don't care what his mother says—I'm going to get some decent food into him. Tomorrow you can drive him into town to see the doctor."

Protein! Irene thought. Jayse needed some high-grade protein, and fast. She went into the kitchen and began to pre-pare a hearty meal of ham and eggs. That, plus plenty of milk and apple pie, should help.

When it was ready she called Jayse and brought him into the kitchen. "Sit down at the table," she told him. "I've made you a special dinner because you've been here three months today. That's cause for celebration."

Jayse took one bite of the food, then another. He chewed the ham slowly, and swallowed. Then he put down his fork and rose from the table.

"What's the matter?" Irene asked anxiously. "Where are you going?"

But he had already gone. The kitchen door closed behind him. Irene ran to the door and flung it open. The boy had already reached the line of trees that bordered the property. He was moving with long, steady strides. She called his name, but he never looked back.

"Leave him alone," said Ernest, who had just come into the kitchen. "He's going home. His mother was probably right. You shouldn't have given him that food."

Irene slept badly that night. She was up before dawn, walking about the garden. As she feared, Jayse had not come back. But shortly before noon, his mother appeared.

She walked straight up to Irene, her mouth fixed in a hard line. "You did it,

---

disquieting (dis KWY ut ing) disturbing; worrisome
labored (LAY burd) not easy; done with effort
malnutrition (mal noo TRISH un) poor health condition caused by not having enough of the right kinds of food
stride (STRYD) long step

Unit 2

Albert's Son, Andrew Wyeth. Nasjonalgalleriet, Oslo

Journey, Morris Graves. Collection of The Whitney Museum of American Art

didn't you? You fed my boy after I told you not to. What did you give him to eat?"

"Ham and eggs," replied Irene. "Good food, the kind he needed."

"Ham . . ." the woman whispered, "so salty. . . ." Then her voice rose to a shriek. "You're a fool, a meddling fool! Why couldn't you leave well enough alone?"

"I'm sorry if my cooking made Jayse sick," Irene retorted angrily, "but he was starving to death in front of me. I couldn't let it go on. My husband and I will pay any medical bills and see that a doctor takes care of him. Now I want you to take me to him or we will have to notify the authorities."

For a moment the woman was silent, then she began to laugh mirthlessly.

---

authorities (uh THAWR uh teez) people with official power
mirthlessly (MURTH lis lee) without humor

Unit 2

"Yes, Ma'am. I'll take you to him. You come with me and see what you've done."

She turned and Irene followed her through the stretch of woods. For half an hour they climbed through the scraggy foothills. Finally they came to a shabby house where three young children sat listlessly on the stoop. But when Irene stopped, the woman took her arm and pulled her on.

"Isn't that your home?" asked Irene. "Isn't Jayse there?"

The woman shook her head and went on. Presently they came to another stand of trees. Beyond lay an open space with grass-covered mounds. Some of the mounds had wooden markers; others had none.

"What is this place?" Irene cried frantically.

"Old graveyard," replied the woman. "Nobody—hardly nobody uses it anymore. Over here, Ma'am." She pointed to one mound. Irene saw with horror that great tufts of grass had been torn from it, and that someone had tried to scoop a hollow in the dry dirt underneath.

Nothing could have made her go close to the mound. But from where she stood she could see what lay in it—a shriveled, withered something dressed in worn jeans and a stained T-shirt.

"There's Jayse," said the woman. "There's where you sent him. He and his pa died two years ago, that bad winter, of pneumonia. I wished them back, but only Jayse came. He knew I needed him, you see. He wanted to take care of me. He was a good boy, always."

"I don't understand," Irene said.

But the woman wasn't listening. She talked on, as if to herself. "I had to take special care of him. You can't feed the dead salt, you know. It makes them forget everything but the last place they rested. That's why Jayse had to come here. Now he won't leave it again, ever."

---

scraggy (SKRAG ee) rough and uneven
tufts (TUFTS) bunches of grass or hair
shriveled (SHRIV uld) dried up
pneumonia (noo MOHN yuh) disease of the lungs

The Unknown
133

MINI QUIZ

Write on the chalkboard or overhead projector the following questions and call on students to fill in the blanks. Discuss the answers with the class.

1. One of the first things Irene Platt did when they moved to the Ozarks was to plant a _____.

2. Jayse was _____ years old.

3. Mrs. Platt paid Jayse _____ a day.

4. Jayse had worked at the Platts for _____ before Mrs. Platt gave him a meal.

5. Some graves in the cemetery by Jayse's family's house were identified with _____.

Answers to Mini Quiz

1. vegetable garden
2. 16
3. two dollars
4. three months
5. wooden markers

ANSWERS TO UNDERSTAND THE SELECTION

1. the Ozarks
2. "food without salt"
3. Ham and eggs, milk, and apple pie.
4. The Ozarks still contain remote areas, providing a good setting for strange happenings.
5. The plot question must be answered: Who is Jayse and why does he act so strangely?
6. She laughed "mirthlessly," meaning without humor; she was laughing from crazed grief.
7. Jayse, his mother claims, had come back from the dead. The dead can't eat salt, she says, because they forget everything except the last place they rested—which for Jayse was the grave he had been buried in when he "died."
8. Answers will vary. Sample answer: Yes, he needed to work to help his family.
9. Answers will vary. Some students might reject the idea, although others might see Jayse as an opportunity to "enter" the supernatural world.
10. Answers will vary. On the literal or actual level, the story of a return from the dead is so hard to believe that it borders on being a gloomy folk tale. On the symbolic level, however, belief is not important. On this level the story could be interpreted as one of devotion to family.

Respond to Literature. Answers will vary. Students might think that Jayse's mother was evil, but she kept him "alive." Irene Platt appears to be good, but, inadvertently, caused Jayse's death.

UNDERSTAND THE SELECTION

Recall

1. Where did the Platts retire?

2. What kind of food did Jayse's mother insist that Jayse eat?

3. What food did Irene Platt prepare for Jayse?

Infer

4. How does the setting contribute to the story?

5. What is the "complication" to the plot that keeps the story going?

6. Why do you think Jayse's mother began to laugh when Irene Platt asked to be taken to see the sick Jayse?

7. Explain the significance of Jayse eating the salty food.

Apply

8. Would you have hired Jayse if you had been Irene Platt? Explain your answer.

9. Would you have liked to have had Jayse for a friend? Think before you answer!

10. What is your opinion of the story? Is it believable literally? Symbolically?

Respond to Literature

Does this story have any evil characters or does each character show both good and evil traits? Explain your answer.

WRITE ABOUT THE SELECTION

Years ago, interesting information about a person and his or her life was inscribed often on a headstone marking his or her grave. It could be written in poetry or prose. Imagine Jayse's mother and the Platts have decided to mark Jayse's grave with a headstone, and inscribe something on it. What should be written on it?

Prewriting: Draw a headstone. Next to the headstone, write a list of what you would like to mention about Jayse. Decide if you will write in poetry or prose. Remember that tombstones are not very big, so you cannot write much.

Writing: Use your list to write the inscription. Try several versions of your message and decide which you like the best. Write it in the headstone you have drawn. You must keep your "message" short and to the point.

Revising: If you wrote in verse, would rhyming help improve the inscription? Synonyms can be used to make rhymes. If you wrote in prose, would a simile or metaphor help? They were commonly used in inscriptions on old headstones.

Proofreading: Reread what you have written and check to make sure all words are spelled correctly. Your inscription will be chiseled into stone, and there must be no mistakes. Use a dictionary to check any words you are not sure of. Because of limited space, delete all unnecessary words.

ANSWERS TO WRITE ABOUT THE SELECTION

Prewriting: Here is an opportunity for a cooperative learning activity that begins outside the class. Have students work in pairs or groups to find an interesting epitaph on a tombstone. They can visit a cemetery, or research the subject in the school library. At this step, have them list only the main points of the epitaph for background for their own writing. Suggest that they avoid, "Here lies. . . ." Perhaps Jayce's youth would make a good opening.

Writing: You could allow students to work in the same pairs or groups to examine how the epitaph they found was written. Is it poetry or prose? Are any figurative expressions used, or other literary devices? Then students can work individually on their descriptions.

Revising: Remind students that epitaphs should be short and to the point. Suggest that they read the epitaphs, specifically, to delete all unnecessary words.

Proofreading: Ask volunteers to proofread each other's work before the class.

THINK ABOUT CHARACTER

Margaret Ronan tells us about Jayse directly by describing traits and indirectly by telling how he acted in situations. Each bit adds to the mystery surrounding him.

1. In the third paragraph, how is Jayse described? What is your impression of him?

2. In the fourth and fifth paragraphs, what do we learn about Jayse?

3. What do we learn about Jayse from his mother's introduction?

4. When Jayse arrives for work at the Platts, more description is given. Which impression of Jayse seems correct, Mrs. Platt's initial impression or the one given by Jayse's mother?

5. Action tells us more about Jayse after he eats Mrs. Platt's dinner. Explain.

DEVELOP YOUR VOCABULARY

A good way to learn and to remember vocabulary words is to use flashcards. Write the words below on a card. On the back of the card, write the definition and an original sentence.

Use the cards to exercise your vocabulary skills. If you are working alone, shuffle the cards, choose one, and give the definition. Go through all the cards, putting aside those in which you need more practice.

You can also practice your vocabulary skills by first looking at the definitions and then giving the correct words. If working with a partner, you can use the same methods.

1. listless
2. work-scarred
3. hollow-eyed
4. hollow-cheeked
5. haggard-looking
6. disquieting
7. finicky
8. creepy
9. knobby
10. spooky

The Unknown

135

LDP Activity: On page 128, paragraph 10, which begins "So Jayse...," is written in the past tense. Change the verbs from past tense to present tense.

After completing this selection, students will be able to
- understand conflict
- describe a conflict in a story they have already read
- write a news story about a murder
- understand minor conflicts in stories
- form negative words

More About Conflict: Literature reflects real conflicts in everyday life. They may be the grand conflicts of superpowers and political leaders, or the personal conflicts of a parent and child. Ask students for real-life examples of different kinds of conflict: between people, within a single person, between people and things, and between people and nature. Write them on the chalkboard or an overhead transparency.

Cooperative/Collaborative Learning Activity: Have students work in groups of three. First, ask them to do the skill builder by themselves, and then report to their group. Group members should be asked for feedback on each conflict description, as well as its resolution. Encourage students to consult the texts of each selection, especially if disagreement arises over the interpretation of a particular selection.

LEARN ABOUT
Conflict

The plot in literature often focuses on **conflict,** or the meeting of opposing forces. The conflict can be between people, within a single person, between people and things, or between people and nature. A work of literature may contain more than one kind of conflict, but usually only one is the main conflict.

In drama the conflict can also be physical, psychological, or, most often, a combination. Usually, conflict in a play is easier to identify than in fiction because you can actually see the clash of personalities on stage or imagine it from dialogue on the page.

As you read "Sorry, Wrong Number," ask yourself these questions:
1. What conflicts are in the play?
2. What is the main conflict?

SKILL BUILDER

Think back on the selections you have read in this unit or the previous unit. Describe a main conflict in one of the selections and tell how it is resolved. If there were other lesser conflicts in the same selection, write them down in a sentence or two.

Sorry, Wrong Number

ADAPTED

by Lucille Fletcher

CHARACTERS

MRS. STEVENSON	SERGEANT DUFFY
OPERATOR	THIRD OPERATOR
FIRST MAN	WESTERN UNION
SECOND MAN (GEORGE)	INFORMATION
CHIEF OPERATOR	WOMAN
SECOND OPERATOR	

ACT I

(SOUND: *Number being dialed on phone; busy signal.*)

MRS. STEVENSON (*a complaining, self-centered person*)**:** Oh—dear! (*Slams down receiver. Dials* OPERATOR.)

OPERATOR: Your call, please?

MRS. STEVENSON: Operator? I've been dialing Murray Hill 4–0098 now for the last three quarters of an hour, and the line is always busy. But I don't see how it *could* be busy that long. Will you try it for me, please?

OPERATOR: Murray Hill 4–0098? One moment, please.

MRS. STEVENSON: I don't see how it could be busy all this time. It's my husband's office. He's working late tonight, and I'm all alone here in the house. My health is very poor—and I've been feeling so nervous all day—

OPERATOR: Ringing Murray Hill 4–0098.

---

self-centered (SELF SENT urd) selfish; concerned with oneself

The Unknown

137

Sidelights: "Sorry, Wrong Number" was written for radio. Today, radio dramas are a dying genre, but once they were a staple of family entertainment. People would gather around a big "wireless" to hear renditions of well-known plays, new plays, and serials. Perhaps the most famous radio adaptation was Orson Welles's production of "War of the Worlds"—the story of a Martian invasion of Earth. So realistic was the broadcast, it drew national headlines the next day. Some of the better known serials were "The Shadow" and "I Love a Mystery." Television spelled the doom of radio drama. Some shows, such as "The Lone Ranger," were turned into TV programs.

Motivation for Reading. Point out that the theme of "Sorry, Wrong Number" is as current as the day it was written: an invalid at the mercy of circumstances beyond her control. Tell students the setting of the story: a Manhattan apartment building, in which, apparently, she has no friends. Her only connection to the outside world is a telephone. As the phone starts ringing, her disability makes her all the more helpless, dependent, and vulnerable.

More About the Thematic Idea: Suspense is built into any situation when the reader thinks something is going to happen but is not sure exactly what. When a person's life is at stake (as it may be in this play), the suspense takes on a special importance. Ask students if they have ever been in a dangerous situation, and, if so, to describe the suspense.

Purpose-Setting Question: How might your outlook on the world be different if you were bed-ridden in a big-city apartment building, and left alone?

Vocabulary: Preteach the vocabulary words. See the Comprehension Workbook in the TRB.

More About Vocabulary: Divide students into small groups. Ask them to review, as a group, the footnoted vocabulary. Then, ask them to use—in no more than 10 sentences—all twenty-two footnotes. Suggest that they work together to write the sentences, then read them aloud to the class. As an added challenge, you may want to set a time limit.

Clarification: Point out the stage directions in italics within the parentheses. Explain that these are directions to the actors, as well as extra information for the reader.

Critical Thinking: From the stage directions and her telephone dialogues, the reader can generalize about the kind of person Mrs. Stevenson is. Ask students if her plight is believable; that is, can they imagine a person—at home in bed alone and ill—speaking as she does?

Reading Strategies: You may want to hint to students that a murder has been planned. If so, subtly suggest that the two men talk as if they were professional "hit men."

Enrichment: You could suggest that a student research how crossed telephone connections occur. Why, for example, is a background conversation sometimes heard when you are making a call?

(SOUND: *Phone buzz. It rings three times. Receiver is picked up at other end.*)

MAN: Hello.

MRS. STEVENSON: Hello? (*A little puzzled.*) Hello. Is Mr. Stevenson there?

MAN (*into phone, as though he had not heard*): Hello. (*Louder.*) Hello.

SECOND MAN (*slow, heavy voice, faintly foreign accent*): Hello.

FIRST MAN: Hello, George?

GEORGE: Yes, sir.

MRS. STEVENSON (*louder and more commanding, to phone*): Hello. Who's this? What number am I calling, please?

FIRST MAN: We have heard from our client. He says the coast is clear for tonight.

GEORGE: Yes, sir.

FIRST MAN: Where are you now?

GEORGE: In a phone booth.

FIRST MAN: Okay. You know the address. At eleven o'clock the private patrolman goes around to a place on Second Avenue for a break. Be sure that all the lights downstairs are out. There should be only one light visible from the street. At eleven fifteen a subway train crosses the bridge. It makes a noise in case her window is open and she should scream.

MRS. STEVENSON (*shocked*): Oh—hello! What number is this, please?

GEORGE: Okay. I understand.

FIRST MAN: Make it quick. As little blood as possible. Our client does not wish to make her suffer long.

GEORGE: A knife okay, sir?

FIRST MAN: Yes. A knife will be okay. And remember—remove the rings and bracelets, and the jewelry in the bureau drawer. Our client wishes it to look like simple robbery.

GEORGE: Okay. I get—

(SOUND: *A soft buzzing signal.*)

MRS. STEVENSON (*clicking phone*): Oh! (*Soft buzzing signal continues. She hangs up.*) How awful! How unspeakably—

---

client (KLY unt) person who pays for a duty performed
unspeakably (un SPEEK uh blee) horribly; not to be spoken of

(SOUND: *Dialing. Phone buzz.*)

OPERATOR: Your call, please?

MRS. STEVENSON (*uptight and breathless, into phone*)**:** Operator, I—I've just been cut off.

OPERATOR: I'm sorry, madam. What number were you calling?

MRS. STEVENSON: Why—it was supposed to be Murray Hill 4–0098, but it wasn't. Some wires must have crossed—I was cut into a wrong number—and—I've just heard the most dreadful thing—a—a murder—and—(*As an order*) Operator, you'll simply have to retrace that call at once.

OPERATOR: I beg your pardon, madam—I don't quite—

MRS. STEVENSON: Oh—I know it was a wrong number, and I had no business listening—but these two men—they were cold-blooded fiends—and they were going to murder somebody —some poor innocent woman—who was all alone—in a house near a bridge. We've got to stop them—we've got to—

OPERATOR (*patiently*)**:** What number were you calling, madam?

MRS. STEVENSON: That doesn't matter. This was a *wrong* number. And *you* dialed it. And we've got to find out what it was—immediately!

OPERATOR: But—madam—

MRS. STEVENSON: Oh, why are you so stupid? Look, it was obviously a case of some little slip of the finger. I told you to try Murray Hill 4–0098 for me—you dialed it—but your finger must have slipped—and I was connected with some other number—and I could hear them, but they couldn't hear me. Now, I simply fail to see why you couldn't make that same mistake again—on purpose—why you couldn't *try* to dial Murray Hill 4–0098 in the same careless sort of way—

OPERATOR (*quickly*)**:** Murray Hill 4–0098? I will try to get it for you, madam.

MRS. STEVENSON: *Thank* you.

(*Sound of ringing; busy signal.*)

OPERATOR: I am sorry. Murray Hill 4–0098 is busy.

MRS. STEVENSON (*madly clicking receiver*)**:** Operator. Operator.

OPERATOR: Yes, madam.

---

cold-blooded fiends (KOHLD blud id FEENDZ) very wicked people without mercy

The Unknown

139

Literary Focus: When Mrs. Stevenson tells the operator that she overheard two men plan a murder, could this possibly be foreshadowing? Point out to students the stress revealed in her broken sentences to the operator. Suggest, without revealing the plot, that it could be important.

MRS. STEVENSON *(angrily)*: You *didn't* try to get that wrong number at all. I asked explicitly. And all you did was dial correctly.

OPERATOR: I am sorry. What number were you calling?

MRS. STEVENSON: Can't you, for once, forget what number I was calling, and do something specific? Now I want to trace that call. It's my civic duty—it's *your* civic duty—to trace that call—and to apprehend those dangerous killers—and if *you* won't—

OPERATOR: I will connect you with the Chief Operator.

MRS. STEVENSON: *Please!*

(Sound of ringing.)

CHIEF OPERATOR *(a cool pro)*: This is the Chief Operator.

MRS. STEVENSON: Chief Operator? I want you to trace a call. A telephone call. Immediately. I don't know where it came from, or who was making it, but it's absolutely necessary that it be tracked down. Because it was about a murder. Yes, a terrible, cold-blooded murder of a poor innocent woman—tonight—at eleven fifteen.

CHIEF OPERATOR: I see.

MRS. STEVENSON *(high-strung, demanding)*: Can you trace it for me? Can you track down those men?

CHIEF OPERATOR: It depends, madam.

MRS. STEVENSON: Depends on what?

CHIEF OPERATOR: It depends on whether the call is still going on. If it's a live call, we can trace it on the equipment. If it's been disconnected, we can't.

MRS. STEVENSON: Disconnected?

CHIEF OPERATOR: If the parties have stopped talking to each other.

MRS. STEVENSON: Oh—but—but of course they must have stopped talking to each other by *now*. That was at least five minutes ago—and they didn't sound like the type who would make a long call.

CHIEF OPERATOR: Well, I can try tracing it. Now—what is your name, madam?

---

explicitly (eks PLIS it lee) very clearly
specific (spuh SIF ik) definite; exact
civic (SIV ik) having to do with good citizenship
apprehend (ap rih HEND) seize; arrest

Unit 2

Telephone Booths, Richard Estes. Thyssen-Bornemisza Foundation

MRS. STEVENSON: Mrs. Stevenson. Mrs. Elbert Stevenson. But—listen—

CHIEF OPERATOR *(writing it down)*: And your telephone number?

MRS. STEVENSON *(more bothered)*: Plaza 4–2295. But if you go on wasting all this time—

CHIEF OPERATOR: And what is your reason for wanting this call traced?

MRS. STEVENSON: My reason? Well—for heaven's sake—isn't it obvious? I overhear two men—they're killers—they're planning to murder this woman—it's a matter for the police.

CHIEF OPERATOR: Have you told the police?

MRS. STEVENSON: No. How could I?

CHIEF OPERATOR: You're making this check into a private call purely as a private individual?

MRS. STEVENSON: Yes. But meanwhile—

CHIEF OPERATOR: Well, Mrs. Stevenson—I seriously doubt whether we could make this check for you at this time just on your say-so as a private individual. We'd have to have something more official.

The Unknown 141

Critical Thinking: Have students evaluate the chief operator's approach to the problem as opposed to Mrs. Stevenson's. Is the operator's behavior a reflection of her personal character or the duties of her job?

MRS. STEVENSON: Oh, for heaven's sake! You mean to tell me I can't report a murder without getting tied up in all this red tape? Why, it's perfectly idiotic. All right, then. I *will* call the police. (*She slams down receiver.*) Ridiculous!

(*Sound of dialing.*)

SECOND OPERATOR: Your call, please?

MRS. STEVENSON (*very annoyed*)**:** The Police Department—*please.*

SECOND OPERATOR: Ringing the police department.

(*Rings twice. Phone is picked up.*)

SERGEANT DUFFY: Police department. Precinct 43. Duffy speaking.

MRS. STEVENSON: Police department? Oh. This is Mrs. Stevenson —Mrs. Elbert Smythe Stevenson of 53 North Sutton Place. I'm calling to report a murder.

DUFFY: Eh?

MRS. STEVENSON: I mean—the murder hasn't been committed yet. I just overheard plans for it over the telephone . . . over a wrong number that the operator gave me. I've been trying to trace down the call myself, but everybody is so stupid—and I guess in the end you're the only people who could *do* anything.

Duffy (*not too impressed*)**:** Yes, ma'am.

MRS. STEVENSON (*trying to impress him*)**:** It was a perfectly *definite* murder. I heard their plans distinctly. Two men were talking, and they were going to murder some woman at eleven fifteen tonight—she lived in a house near a bridge.

DUFFY: Yes, ma'am.

MRS. STEVENSON: And there was a private patrolman on the street. He was going to go around for a break on Second Avenue. And there was some third man—a client—who was paying to have this poor woman murdered—They were going to take her rings and bracelets—and use a knife—Well, it's unnerved me dreadfully—and I'm not well—

DUFFY: I see. When was all this, ma'am?

---

red tape (RED TAYP) needless complications of official rules
precinct (PREE singkt) division of a city for police control
unnerved (un NURVD) took away courage; terrified

MRS. STEVENSON: About eight minutes ago. Oh . . . *(relieved)* then you *can* do something? You *do* understand—

DUFFY: And what is your name, ma'am?

MRS. STEVENSON *(losing patience)*: Mrs. Stevenson. Mrs. Elbert Stevenson.

DUFFY: And your address?

MRS. STEVENSON: 53 North Sutton Place. *That's* near a bridge, the Queensborough Bridge, you know—and *we* have a private patrolman on *our* street—and Second Avenue—

DUFFY: And what was that number you were calling?

MRS. STEVENSON: Murray Hill 4–0098. But—that wasn't the number I overheard. I mean Murray Hill 4–0098 is my husband's office. He's working late tonight, and I was trying to reach him to ask him to come home. I'm an invalid, you know—and it's the maid's night off—and I *hate* to be alone—even though he says I'm perfectly safe as long as I have the telephone beside my bed.

DUFFY *(trying to end it)*: Well, we'll look into it, Mrs. Stevenson, and see if we can check it with the telephone company.

MRS. STEVENSON *(using more patience)*: But the telephone company said they couldn't check the call if the parties had stopped talking. I've already taken care of *that*.

DUFFY: Oh, yes?

MRS. STEVENSON *(getting bossy)*: Personally I feel you ought to do something far more immediate and drastic than just check the call. What good does checking the call do, if they've stopped talking? By the time you track it down, they'll already have committed the murder.

DUFFY: Well, we'll take care of it, lady. Don't worry.

MRS. STEVENSON: The whole thing calls for a search—a complete and thorough search of the whole city. I'm very near a bridge, and I'm not far from Second Avenue. And I know *I'd* feel a whole lot better if you sent around a radio car to *this* neighborhood at once.

DUFFY: And what makes you think the murder's going to be committed in your neighborhood, ma'am?

---

invalid (IN vuh lid) sick person
drastic (DRAS tik) forceful; severe

The Unknown   143

MRS. STEVENSON: Oh, I don't know. The coincidence is so horrible. Second Avenue—the patrolman—the bridge—

DUFFY: Second Avenue is a very long street, ma'am. And do you happen to know how many bridges there are in the city of New York alone? Not to mention Brooklyn, Staten Island, Queens, and the Bronx? And how do you know there isn't some little house out on Staten Island—on some little Second Avenue you've never heard about? How do you know they were even talking about New York at all?

MRS. STEVENSON: But I heard the call on the New York dialing system.

DUFFY: How do you know it wasn't a long-distance call you

---

coincidence (koh IN suh duns) two or more related events accidentally happening at the same time

Unit 2

overheard? Telephones are funny things. Look, lady, why don't you look at it this way? Supposing you hadn't broken in on that telephone call? Supposing you'd got your husband the way you always do? Would this murder have made any difference to you then?

MRS. STEVENSON: I suppose not. But it's so inhuman—so cold-blooded—

DUFFY: A lot of murders are committed in this city every day, ma'am. If we could do something to stop 'em, we would. But a clue of this kind that's so vague isn't much more use to us than no clue at all.

MRS. STEVENSON: But surely—

DUFFY: Unless, of course, you have some reason for thinking this call is phony—and that someone may be planning to murder *you?*

MRS. STEVENSON: *Me?* Oh, no, I hardly think so. I—I mean—why should anybody? I'm alone all day and night—I see nobody except my maid Eloise—she's a big two-hundred-pounder—she's too lazy to bring up my breakfast tray—and the only other person is my husband Elbert—he's crazy about me—adores me—waits on me hand and foot—he's scarcely left my side since I took sick twelve years ago—

DUFFY: Well, then, there's nothing for you to worry about, is there? And now, if you'll just leave the rest of this to us—

MRS. STEVENSON: But what will you *do?* It's so late—it's nearly eleven o'clock.

DUFFY (*firmly*): We'll take care of it, lady.

MRS. STEVENSON: Will you broadcast it all over the city? And send out squads? And warn your radio cars to watch out—especially in suspicious neighborhoods like mine?

DUFFY (*more firmly*): Lady, I *said* we'd take care of it. Just now I've got a couple of other matters here on my desk that require my immediate—

MRS. STEVENSON: Oh! (*She slams down receiver hard.*) Idiot. (*Looking at phone nervously.*) Now, why did I do that? Now he'll think I *am* a fool. Oh, why doesn't Elbert come home? *Why* doesn't he?

(*Sound of dialing operator.*)

---

vague (VAYG) unclear

The Unknown

145

Discussion: Is Sgt. Duffy doing his job properly? His comments may be reasurring, but is his callous manner appropriate?

(Sound of dialing operator).

OPERATOR: Your call, please?

MRS. STEVENSON: Operator, for heaven's sake, will you ring that Murray Hill 4–0098 number again? I can't think what's keeping him so long.

OPERATOR: Ringing Murray Hill 4–0098. *(Rings. Busy signal.)* The line is busy. Shall I—

MRS. STEVENSON *(nastily)*: I can hear it. You don't have to tell me. I know it's busy. *(Slams down receiver.)* If I could only get out of this bed for a little while. If I could get a breath of fresh air—or just lean out the window—and see the street—*(The phone rings. She answers it instantly.)* Hello. Elbert? Hello. Hello. Hello. Oh, what's the *matter* with this phone? *Hello? Hello?* *(Slams down receiver. The phone rings again, once. She picks it up.)* Hello? Hello—Oh, for heaven's sake, who is this? Hello, Hello, *Hello.* *(Slams down receiver. Dials operator.)*

THIRD OPERATOR: Your call, please?

MRS. STEVENSON *(very annoyed and commanding)*: Hello, operator. I don't know what's the matter with this telephone tonight, but it's positively driving me crazy. I've never seen such inefficient, miserable service. Now, look. I'm an invalid, and I'm very nervous, and I'm *not* supposed to be annoyed. But if this keeps on much longer—

THIRD OPERATOR *(a young, sweet type)*: What seems to be the trouble, madam?

MRS. STEVENSON: Well, everything's wrong. The whole world could be murdered, for all you people care. And now, my phone keeps ringing—

OPERATOR: Yes, madam?

MRS. STEVENSON: Ringing and ringing and ringing every five seconds or so, and when I pick it up, there's no one there.

OPERATOR: I am sorry, madam. If you will hang up, I will test it for you.

MRS. STEVENSON: I don't want you to test it for me. I want you to put through that call—whatever it is—at once.

OPERATOR *(gently)*: I am afraid that is not possible, madam.

---

inefficient (in ih FISH unt) wasteful of time or energy; poorly run

---

MRS. STEVENSON (*storming*): Not possible? And why may I ask?

OPERATOR: The system is automatic, madam. If someone is trying to dial your number, there is no way to check whether the call is coming through the system or not—unless the person who is trying to reach you complains to the particular operator—

MRS. STEVENSON: Well, of all the stupid, complicated—! And meanwhile *I've* got to sit here in my bed, *suffering* every time that phone rings, imagining everything—

OPERATOR: I will try to check it for you, madam.

MRS. STEVENSON: Check it! Check it! That's all anybody can do. Of all the stupid, idiotic . . . ! (*She hangs up.*) Oh—what's the use . . . (*Instantly* MRS. STEVENSON'S *phone rings again. She picks up the receiver. Wildly.*) Hello. HELLO. Stop ringing, do you hear me? Answer me? What do you want? Do you realize you're driving me crazy? Stark, staring—

MAN (*dull, flat voice*): Hello. Is this Plaza 4–2295?

MRS. STEVENSON (*catching her breath*): Yes. Yes. This is Plaza 4–2295.

MAN: This is Western Union. I have a telegram here for Mrs. Elbert Stevenson. Is there anyone there to receive the message?

MRS. STEVENSON (*trying to calm herself*): I am Mrs. Stevenson.

WESTERN UNION (*reading flatly*): The telegram is as follows: "Mrs. Elbert Stevenson. 53 North Sutton Place, New York, New York. Darling. Terribly sorry. Tried to get you for last hour, but line busy. Leaving for Boston 11 P.M. tonight on urgent business. Back tomorrow afternoon. Keep happy. Love. Signed. Elbert."

MRS. STEVENSON (*shocked, to herself*): Oh—no—

WESTERN UNION: That is all, madam. Do you wish us to deliver a copy of the message?

MRS. STEVENSON No—no, thank you.

WESTERN UNION: Thank you, madam. Good night. (*He hangs up phone.*)

MRS. STEVENSON (*softly, to phone*): Good night. (*She hangs up slowly, suddenly bursting into tears.*) No—no—it isn't true! He couldn't do it. Not when he knows I'll be all alone. It's some trick—some fiendish—(*She dials operator.*)

---

stark (STAHRK) absolutely; totally
fiendish (FEEN dish) savagely cruel

The Unknown 147

Clarification: Make sure students understand that telegrams are "delivered" via the telephone; if desired, a printed copy of the message can be requested.

OPERATOR *(coolly)*: Your call, please?

MRS. STEVENSON: Operator—try that Murray Hill 4–0098 number for me just once more, please.

OPERATOR: Ringing Murray Hill 4–0098. *(Call goes through. We hear ringing at other end. Ring after ring.)*

MRS. STEVENSON: He's gone. Oh, Elbert, how could you? How could you—? *(She hangs up phone, sobbing with pity to herself, turning nervously.)* But I can't be alone tonight. I can't. If I'm alone one more second—I don't care what he says—or what the expense is—I'm a sick woman—I'm entitled—*(She dials Information.)*

INFORMATION: This is Information.

MRS. STEVENSON: I want the telephone number of Henchley Hospital.

INFORMATION: Henchley Hospital? Do you have the address, madam?

MRS. STEVENSON: No. It's somewhere in the seventies, though. It's a very small, private, and exclusive hospital where I had my appendix out two years ago. Henchley. H-E-N-C—

INFORMATION: One moment, please.

MRS. STEVENSON: Please—hurry. And please—what *is* the time?

INFORMATION: I do not know, madam. You may find out the time by dialing Meridian 7–1212.

MRS. STEVENSON *(angered)*: Oh, for heaven's sake! Couldn't you—?

INFORMATION: The number of Henchley Hospital is Butterfield 7–0105, madam.

MRS. STEVENSON: Butterfield 7–0105. *(She hangs up before she finishes speaking, and immediately dials number.)*

(Phone rings.)

WOMAN *(middle-aged, solid, firm, practical)*: Henchley Hospital, good evening.

MRS. STEVENSON: Nurses' Registry.

WOMAN: Who was it you wished to speak to, please?

MRS. STEVENSON *(bossy)*: I want the Nurses' Registry at once. I

---

entitled (en TYT uld) have as a claim or right; empowered
exclusive (eks KLOO siv) private and expensive
registry (REJ is tree) department where registers, or lists, are kept

148

Unit 2

want a trained nurse. I want to hire her immediately. For the night.

WOMAN: I see. And what is the nature of the case, madam?

MRS. STEVENSON: Nerves. I'm very nervous. I need soothing—and companionship. My husband is away—and I'm—

WOMAN: Have you been recommended to us by any doctor in particular, madam?

MRS. STEVENSON: No. But I really don't see why all this catechizing is necessary. I want a trained nurse. I was a patient in your hospital two years ago. And after all, I *do* expect to *pay* this person—

WOMAN: We quite understand that, madam. But registered nurses are very scarce just now—and our superintendent has asked us to send people out only on cases where the physician in charge feels it is absolutely necessary.

MRS. STEVENSON (*growing very upset*): Well, it *is* absolutely necessary. I'm a sick woman. I—I'm very upset. Very. I'm alone in this house—and I'm an invalid—and tonight I overheard a telephone conversation that upset me dreadfully. About a murder—a poor woman who was going to be murdered at eleven fifteen tonight—in fact, if someone doesn't come at once—I'm afraid I'll go out of my mind—(*Almost off handle by now.*)

---

catechizing (KAT uh kyz ing) asking many questions

The Unknown

149

T149

Discussion: Is hiring a private nurse a reasonable solution to Mrs. Stevenson's problem? Ask students what they would do in her situation.

Literary Focus: The action rises quickly at the climactic moment—Mrs. Stevenson calls the hospital. Suspense builds: Will all the previous clues be realized?

WOMAN (calmly): I see. Well, I'll speak to Miss Phillips as soon as she comes in. And what is your name, madam?

MRS. STEVENSON: Miss Phillips. And when do you expect her in?

WOMAN: I really don't know, madam. She went out to supper at eleven o'clock.

MRS. STEVENSON: Eleven o'clock. But it's not eleven yet. (She cries out.) Oh, my clock has stopped. I thought it was running down. What time is it?

WOMAN: Just fourteen minutes past eleven.

(Sound of phone receiver being lifted on same line as MRS. STEVENSON'S. A click.)

MRS. STEVENSON (crying out): What's that?

WOMAN: What was what, madam?

MRS. STEVENSON: That—that click just now—in my own telephone? As though someone had lifted the receiver off the hook of the extension phone downstairs—

WOMAN: I didn't hear it, madam. Now—about this—

MRS. STEVENSON (scared): But I did. There's someone in this house. Someone downstairs in the kitchen. And they're listening to me now. They're—(Hangs up phone. In a hushed voice.) I won't pick it up. I won't let them hear me. I'll be quiet—and they'll think—(with growing terror) But if I don't call someone now—while they're still down there—there'll be no time. (She picks up receiver. Soft buzzing signal. She dials operator. Ring twice)

OPERATOR (a slow, lazy voice): Your call, please?

MRS. STEVENSON (a desperate whisper): Operator, I—I'm in desperate trouble—I—

OPERATOR: I cannot hear you, madam. Please speak louder.

MRS. STEVENSON (still whispering): I don't dare. I—there's someone listening. Can you hear me now?

OPERATOR: Your call, please? What number are you calling, madam?

MRS. STEVENSON (desperately): You've got to hear me. Oh, please. You've got to help me. There's someone in this house. Someone who's going to murder me. And you've got to get in touch with the—(Click of receiver being put down in MRS. STEVENSON'S home. Bursting out wildly.) Oh, there it is—he's put it down—he's put down the extension—he's coming—

(*She screams.*) He's coming up the stairs—(*Wildly.*) Give me the police department—(*Screaming.*) The police!

OPERATOR: Ringing the police department.

(*Phone is rung. We hear sound of a subway train coming nearer. On second ring, MRS. STEVENSON screams again, but roaring of train drowns out her voice. For a few seconds we hear nothing but roaring of train, then dying away, phone at police headquarters ringing.*)

DUFFY: Police department. Precinct 43. Duffy speaking. (*Pause.*) Police department. Duffy speaking.

GEORGE: Sorry. Wrong number. (*Hangs up.*)

Lucille Fletcher (1912–Present)

If you look in the mystery section of your local library, you are bound to find at least one book by Lucille Fletcher. Noted as a writer of plays, screenplays, and novels, Fletcher is most famous for her suspense classic, "Sorry, Wrong Number." This work was originally written as a radio play, then later adapted as a novel, TV play, and motion picture.

Born in Brooklyn, New York, Lucille Fletcher attended the public schools there, then later received her bachelor of arts degree from Vassar College in Poughkeepsie. She is married to the novelist Douglass Wallop, who is best known for his book, *The Year the Yankees Lost the Pennant.* Speaking of her life at the time her two daughters were growing up, Ms. Fletcher referred to her writing as a "hobby"—then admitted that "the major part of my life is spent in housekeeping and cooking meals."

The Unknown 151

Reading Strategy: Point out the significance of the "roaring" subway.

Discussion: What a cool criminal George is! He even has the presence of mind to make up an excuse to the police department about the telephone call. What do you think the police will do next? Anything?

1. Her husband is working late at his office.
2. The operator's finger "slipped" when she dialed her husband's office number, and she was connected with another number.
3. The operator says she can not do a trace at the request of a private individual—"we'd have to have something more official."
4. The operator has a social responsibility to try to prevent someone's being harmed.
5. Names used to be used to identify telephone "exchanges." The first two letters of the words refer to numbers on the telephone.
6. He reminds her that the location the men described could have been any one of a number of places in and even beyond New York. He points out that if her phone call had gone through, she would not have overheard anything, and what difference would the murder have made to her then?
7. First, Mr. Stevenson's message that he will not be home is a signal to us of her increasing vulnerability. Second, once we realize who is to be murdered, we begin to think that Mr. Stevenson is the "client" who has ordered the murder.
8. Answers will vary. Students will know that precinct stations in New York receive many frantic calls every night, and that they all can not be taken seriously. On the other hand, his rationale for Mrs. Stevenson's not worrying about the murder because it apparently does not involve her is a good example of look-the-other-way cynicism.

UNDERSTAND THE SELECTION

Recall

1. Why is Mrs. Stevenson home alone?
2. How did she get the wrong number?
3. Why is the chief operator unwilling to trace the call?

Infer

4. Why is it the operator's "civic duty" to trace the wrong-number call?
5. What do the words "Murray," "Plaza," and "Butterfield" mean?
6. How does the policeman try to reassure Mrs. Stevenson?
7. What complications are added to the plot by the telegram?

Apply

8. Do you think Sgt. Duffy handled Mrs. Stevenson's call responsibly?
9. Why is this radio drama heard rather than seen on stage?
10. Have you ever overheard a private conversation? What was it like to be an eavesdropper?

Respond to Literature

How would you feel if your only way of communicating with the outside world was with a telephone?

WRITE ABOUT THE SELECTION

Newspapers almost always report murders. Sometimes the report is long, sometimes short. However, a good reporter will try to learn from everyone who might know something about what happened.

Imagine that you are a reporter. Mrs. Stevenson is murdered, and you must write a story about the murder. You learn that a Sgt. Duffy took a call from Mrs. Stevenson shortly before the killing. You talk with him, and his information forms the basis of your story.

Prewriting: Look at a newspaper story reporting a crime. Notice how it is constructed, with the important facts first. Make an informal outline of your story about Mrs. Stevenson's murder.

Writing: Use your informal outline to write the news story. Make sure you include comments from Sgt. Duffy.

Revising: Is your story written in the third person? Is it objective? Make sure that your own opinion is not in the story. Rely instead on the people you interviewed to develop the theme of your story.

Proofreading: Reread what you have written and check for errors. If you have quoted Sgt. Duffy, make sure punctuation and capitalization for the quotations are correct. Also be sure that all your sentences end with periods, quotation marks or exclamation marks. Check interior punctuation as well.

9. Answers will vary. One advantage is that noises, such as dial tones, ringings, and subway train rumbles, heighten the tension of the story. A disadvantage could be that we can not see Mrs. Stevenson's reactions.
10. Answers will vary.

Respond to Literature: Answers will vary. Older people are likely to be cited as examples of home-bound invalids dependent on telephones. Some students might be familiar with publicly-supported "lifeline" programs that provide free, or reduced-cost, telephone service to invalids. Students might point out that in earlier generations extended families did not need a phone.

Prewriting: Obtain a newspaper story about a murder. Make an overhead transparency of it, or make photocopies for students. Have students work cooperatively in groups outlining it. Then, ask

THINK ABOUT CONFLICT

Conflict results from opposing forces—interpersonal, environmental, social, or internal—that drive the plot in many kinds of literature. "Sorry, Wrong Number" contains a number of examples of conflict.

1. What is the main conflict of the story? Who is the conflict between?

2. Conflicts can also be implied, rather than directly stated or described. Do you think there is an implied conflict between Mr. and Mrs. Stevenson?

3. What are some examples of conflict between people in this drama?

4. Is there an example of conflict between people and nature?

5. The final conflict in this story acts as the resolution of the plot. It is the main force behind the story. What is this conflict?

DEVELOP YOUR VOCABULARY

Some words are formed by adding prefixes that reverse the meaning. Some common negative prefixes are: *un-, in-, im-, dis-, non-.*

Find one word in the sentence that you can make into a negative. Then use the "new" negative word in a sentence.

1. Thank you for your efficient service.

2. I appreciate your courteous behavior.

3. "It's possible," she said, "that I made a mistake."

4. The plane became visible as it emerged from the clouds.

5. A little nonsense now and then is relished by the wisest men.

6. I'm glad I can count on you to be reliable.

7. I need someone to give me attention.

The Unknown

153

ANSWERS TO THINK ABOUT CONFLICT

1. The conflict is between Mrs. Stevenson's thinking something horrible might happen, but not being able to do anything to change her circumstances.
2. Definitely, at least from Mr. Stevenson's side. He wants his wife killed.
3. Mrs. Stevenson came in conflict with every character to whom she spoke on the phone and, finally, with George.
4. Yes, Mrs. Stevenson vs. her illness.
5. The meeting between Mrs. Stevenson and George. It is left to our imaginations to provide the details of the murder.

ANSWERS TO DEVELOP YOUR VOCABULARY

1. inefficient—The shipping company is very inefficient.
2. discourteous—His behavior was very discourteous.
3. impossible—Reaching the top of the mountain is impossible without better equipment.
4. invisible—If I were invisible, I would love to play pro football.
5. unwisest—This was the unwisest thing that the court could do.
6. unreliable—Not only is the shipping company inefficient, it is also unreliable.
7. inattention—Her creativity dried up from inattention.

one group to present to the class its outline.

Writing: Circulate as students work individually. Suggest that direct quotations from officials or witnesses add credibility to a story.

Revising: Refer students back to the murder story you found. Discuss the point of view, third person, and how it differs from first-person point of view in establishing credibility.

Proofreading: Use the same murder story for an illustration of correct punctuation of quotations.

LDP Activity: Delete the last line of the play. End the story differently.

After completing this selection, students will be able to
- understand plot
- outline the plot of a personal story
- discuss imaginary characters
- create a postscript to the story
- understand the role of rising action in a plot
- infer meaning from a verb that describes a direct response

More About Plot: Write on the chalkboard or overhead projector the words: "exposition," "complication," "crisis," "climax," and "resolution." Using a story the class has read recently, outline the plot according to these five major developments.

Cooperative/Collaborative Learning Activity: After students have told their partners their stories, have them continue working together in pairs to draw a "road map" of their stories. You could have the listener make the map and the narrator check for accuracy.

The Sphinx and the Milky Way, Charles Burchfield.
Munson-Williams-Proctor Institute Museum of Art

LEARN ABOUT
Plot

The events in a short story are called the plot. A story's plot is its skeleton—the framework that holds it together. It consists of exposition, complication, rising action, climax, and usually resolution. Try to think of a plot as a series of problems that the main character has to overcome. For instance, at the beginning of "The Love Letter," (Unit 1) Jake Belknap has a big decision to make: Should he or should he not try to contact Helen Elizabeth Worley?

Here are two other plot questions Jake meets in "The Love Letter."
1. How can Jake contact her and how can Helen reply?
2. What are the implications of these letters in the lives of Helen and Jake?

As you read "Thus I Refute Beelzy," think about these questions.
1. What are the plot questions?
2. How do they correspond to the stages of the plot?

SKILL BUILDER
Review a favorite story you have read in this book. List the plot questions. Which one leads to the climax?

Unit 2

Thus I Refute Beelzy

by John Collier

"There goes the tea bell," said Mrs. Carter. "I hope Simon hears it."

They looked out from the window of the drawing room. The long yard, agreeably neglected, ended in a waste plot. Here a little summer house was passing close by beauty on its way to complete decay. This was Simon's retreat: it was almost completely screened by the tangled branches of the apple tree and the pear tree, planted too close together, as they always are in suburban yards. They caught a glimpse of him now and then, as he strutted up and down, mouthing and gesticulating, performing all the solemn mumbo jumbo of small boys who spend long afternoons at the forgotten ends of long gardens.

"There he is, bless him," said Betty.

"Playing his game," said Mrs. Carter. "He won't play with the other children any more. And if I go down there—the temper! He comes in tired out."

"He doesn't have his sleep in the afternoons?" asked Betty.

"You know what Big Simon's ideas are," said Mrs. Carter. "'Let him choose for himself,' he says. That's what he chooses, and he comes in as white as a sheet."

"Look. He's heard the bell," said Betty. The expression was justified, though the bell had ceased ringing a full minute ago. Small Simon stopped in his parade exactly as if its tinny ring had at that moment reached his ear. They watched him perform certain ritual sweeps and scratchings with his little stick, and come lagging over the hot and flaggy grass toward the house.

Mrs. Carter led the way down to the playroom or garden room, which was

---

gesticulating (jes TIK yoo layt ing) making motions, as in attracting attention or speaking

ritual (RICH uu ul) a set pattern.

The Unknown 155

Vocabulary: Preteach the vocabulary words. See the Comprehension Workbook in the TRB.

More About Vocabulary: Write on separate cards each of the ten vocabulary footnotes. Also, write on another card the definition for each new word. Divide students into groups, and give each group a card. Arrange the definition cards on a table. Ask the groups to come to the table and choose what they think is the correct definition for their word. (They will have to negotiate with one another if they think a group has chosen incorrectly.) Then, have the groups use their word in an original sentence.

LDP Activity: The following words are part of the British vocabulary. Explain the meanings of these words. "tea bell"; "drawing room"; "garden room"; "biscuits"; "trifle"; "crumpets"; "sullery"; "old chap." ("the loo")

Motivation for Reading: Children's fantasies are always dismissed as just that: fantasies. Adult discovery of the fantasies as real often makes for a good story.

More About the Thematic Idea: In this selection a child comes in touch with the unknown and accepts it. His father, on the other hand, refutes it.

Purpose-Setting Question: Is there reality behind fantasies?

Sidelights: "Thus I Refute Beelzy" was written by a Briton. There are British word usages, such as "chap" for "friend," and the names "Big Simon" and "Small Simon," an example of condescending, pseudo-aristocratic irony: The similar names are supposed to show a bond between father and son, yet they seem to live in different worlds.

Enrichment: "Tea" is a famous British custom of the late afternoon. It usually consists of a light dessert and hot tea, but it can also be sandwiches and other light food. The term "mumbo jumbo" is of West African origin. It originally referred to an idol or god believed to protect people from evil and terrorize women into subjection. Here, it refers to "meaningless ritual."

LDP Activity: In which other cultures does tea play a significant role? Discuss.

Clarification: A "drawing room" is a British term for "living room." Living rooms were once the formal rooms to which people "withdrew" after a meal.

Literary Focus: The selection opens with a good example of British irony: "a little summer house was passing close by beauty on its way to complete decay". Students might miss the juxtaposition of "beauty" and "decay."

also the tearoom for hot days. It had been the huge scullery of this tall Georgian house. Now the walls were cream-washed, there was coarse blue net in the windows, canvas-covered armchairs on the stone floor, and a reproduction of Van Gogh's "Sunflowers" over the mantle-piece.

Small Simon came drifting in, and gave Betty a routine greeting. His face was an almost perfect triangle, pointed at the chin, and he was paler than he should have been. "The little elf child!" cried Betty.

Simon looked at her. "No," said he.

At that moment the door opened, and Mr. Carter came in, rubbing his hands. He was a dentist, and washed them before and after everything he did. "You!" said his wife. "Home already!"

"Not unwelcome, I hope," said Mr. Carter, nodding to Betty. "Two people cancelled their appointments: I decided to come home. I said, I hope I am not unwelcome."

"Silly!" said his wife. "Of course not."

"Small Simon seems doubtful," continued Mr. Carter. "Small Simon, are you sorry to see me at tea with you?"

"No, Daddy."

"No what?"

"No, Big Simon."

"That's right. Big Simon and Small Simon. That sounds more like friends, doesn't it? At one time little boys had to call their father 'sir.' If they forgot—a good spanking. On the bottom, Small Simon! On the bottom!" said Mr. Carter,

washing his hands once more with his invisible soap and water.

The little boy turned crimson with shame or rage.

"But now, you see," said Betty, to help, "you can call your father whatever you like."

"And what," asked Mr. Carter, "has Small Simon been doing this afternoon, while Big Simon has been at work?"

"Nothing," muttered his son.

"Then you have been bored," said Mr. Carter. "Learn from experience, Small Simon. Tomorrow, do something amusing, and you will not be bored. I want him to learn from experience, Betty. That is my way, the new way."

"I have learned," said the boy, speaking like an old tired man, as little boys so often do.

"It would hardly seem so," said Mr. Carter. "If you sit on your behind all the afternoon, doing nothing. Had *my* father caught me doing nothing, I would not have sat very comfortably."

"He played," said Mrs. Carter.

"A bit," said the boy, shifting on his chair.

"Too much," said Mrs. Carter. "He comes in all nervy and dazed. He ought to have his rest."

"He is six," said her husband. "He is a reasonable being. He must choose for himself. But what game is this, Small Simon, that is worth getting nervy and dazed over? There are very few games as good as all that."

"It's nothing," said the boy.

---

scullery (SKUL er ee) a room for cleaning and storing dishes and pots.

156   Unit 2

Allegory, Ben Shahn. Collection of the Modern Art Museum of Fort Worth.

"Oh, come," said his father. "We are friends, are we not? You can tell me. I was a Small Simon once, just like you, and played the same games you play. Of course there were no airplanes in those days. With whom do you play this fine game? Come on, we must all answer civil questions, or the world would never go round. With whom do you play?"

"Mr. Beelzy," said the boy, unable to resist.

"Mr. Beelzy?" said his father, raising his eyebrows inquiringly at his wife.

"It's a game he makes up," said she.

"Not makes up," cried the boy. "Fool!"

"That is telling stories," said his mother. "And rude as well. We had better talk of something different."

"No wonder he is rude," said Mr. Carter. "If you say he tells lies, and then insist on changing the subject. He tells you his fantasy: you create a guilt feeling. What can you expect? A defense mechanism. Then you get a real lie."

---

civil (SIV ul) here, polite.
fantasy (FAN tuh see) something imagined.
mechanism (MEK uh niz um) a system whose parts work together like a machine. Here, a psychological system of defense.

The Unknown   157

Literary Focus: Until Small Simon mentioned "Mr. Beelzy" to his father, the plot was mostly exposition. Now a complication arises.

Enrichment: The name "Beelzy" is odd and obviously suggestive of "Beelzebub." "Beelzebub" has Hebrew roots and means "god of flies." In the Bible, Beelzebub is the chief devil, or Satan.

Reading Strategy: When Mr. Carter speaks of "guilt-feeling" and "defense mechanism," he is playing amateur psychologist. Students might want to reread the passage to understand his reasoning.

"Like in *These Three*," said Betty. "Only different, of course. *She* was an unblushing little liar."

"I would have made her blush," said Mr. Carter, "in the proper part of her anatomy. But Small Simon is in the fantasy stage. Are you not, Small Simon? You must make things up."

"No I don't," said the boy.

"You do," said his father. "And because you do, it is not too late to reason with you. There is no harm in a fantasy, old chap. There is no harm in a bit of make-believe. Only you have to know the difference between daydreams and real things, or your brain will never grow. It will never be the brain of a Big Simon. So come on. Let us hear about this Mr. Beelzy of yours. Come on. What is he like?"

"He isn't like any thing," said the boy.

"Like nothing on earth," said his father. "That's a terrible fellow."

"I'm not frightened of him," said the child, smiling. "Not a bit."

"I should hope not," said his father. "If you were, you would be frightening yourself. I am always telling people, older people than you are, that they are just frightening themselves. Is he a funny man? Is he a giant?"

"Sometimes he is," said the little boy.

"Sometimes one thing, sometimes another," said his father. "Sounds pretty vague. Why can't you tell us just what he's like?"

"I love him," said the small boy. "He loves me."

"That's a big word," said Mr. Carter. "That might be better kept for real things, like Big Simon and Small Simon."

"He is real," said the boy, passionately. "He's not a fool. He's real."

"Listen," said his father. "When you go down to the yard there's nobody there. Is there?"

"No," said the boy.

"Then you think of him inside your head, and he comes."

"No," said Small Simon. "I have to do something with my stick."

"That doesn't matter."

"Yes, it does."

"Small Simon, you are being obstinate," said Mr. Carter. "I am trying to explain something to you. I have been longer in the world than you have, so naturally I am older and wiser. I am explaining that Mr. Beelzy is a fantasy of yours. Do you hear? Do you understand?"

"Yes, Daddy."

"He is a game. He is a 'let's-pretend.'"

The little boy looked down at his plate, smiling resignedly.

"I hope you are listening to me," said his father. "All you have to do is say, 'I have been playing a game of let's-pretend. With someone I make up, called Mr. Beelzy.' Then no one will say you tell lies, and you will know the difference

---

anatomy (uh NAT uh mee) here, body.

between dreams and reality. Mr. Beelzy is a daydream."

The little boy still stared at his plate.

"He is sometimes there and sometimes not there," pursued Mr. Carter. "Sometimes he's like one thing, sometimes another. You can't really see him. Not as you see me. I am real. You can't touch him. You can touch me. I can touch you." Mr. Carter stretched out his big, white, dentist's hand, and took his little son by the shoulder. He stopped speaking for a moment and tightened his hand. The little boy sank his head still lower.

"Now you know the difference," said Mr. Carter, "between a pretend and a real thing. You and I are one thing; he is another. Which is the pretend? Come on. Answer me. Which is the pretend?"

"Big Simon and Small Simon," said the little boy.

"Don't!" cried Betty, and at once put her hand over her mouth, for why should a visitor cry "don't" when a father is explaining things in a scientific and modern way?

"Well, my boy," said Mr. Carter, "I have said you must be allowed to learn from experience. Go upstairs. Right up to your room. You shall learn whether it is better to reason, or to be perverse and obstinate. Go up. I shall follow you."

"You are not going to beat the child?" cried Mrs. Carter.

"No," said the little boy. "Mr. Beelzy won't let him."

"Go on up with you," shouted his father.

Small Simon stopped at the door. "He said he wouldn't let anyone hurt me," he whimpered. "He said he'd come like a lion, with wings on, and eat them up."

"You'll learn how real he is," shouted his father at him. "If you can't learn it at one end, you shall learn it at the other. I'll have your breeches down. I shall finish my cup of tea first, however," said he to the two women.

Neither of them spoke. Mr. Carter finished his tea, and unhurriedly left the room, washing his hands with his invisible soap and water.

Mrs. Carter said nothing. Betty could think of nothing to say. She wanted to be talking: she was afraid of what they might hear.

Suddenly it came. It seemed to tear the air apart. "Good God!" she cried. "What was that? He's hurt him." She sprang out of her chair, her silly eyes flashing behind her glasses. "I'm going up there," she cried, trembling.

"Yes, let us go up," said Mrs. Carter. "Let us go up. That was not Small Simon."

It was on the second-floor landing that they found the shoe, with the man's foot still in it, like that morsel of a mouse which sometimes falls unnoticed from the side of the jaws of the cat.

---

obstinate (OB stuh nut) stubborn.
perverse (pur VURS) wrong, improper.
morsel (MAWR sul) small piece.

The Unknown

159

Discussion: What are the students' reactions to Small Simon's assertion that Mr. Beelzy will not let Small Simon be beaten? Does it seem completely ridiculous? But Small Simon says it with such conviction. If taken seriously, the comment is foreshadowing.

Enrichment: When Small Simon speaks of a "lion, with wings on," it suggests that Collier might have visited Venice shortly before writing the story. St. Mark is its patron saint and protector, based on the assertion that Venetians recovered and took back to Venice the bones of this biblical evangelist. The attribute, or symbol, for St. Mark is a winged lion, and the image appears all around the city—most conspicuously on an obelisk, brought from the Orient, at the main entrance to St. Mark's Plaza by the Doges' Palace.

Clarification: "I'll have your breeches down" is of British construction, meaning, "You shall take down your pants." (Notice how Mr. Carter insists on finishing his tea before beating his son, however. Things must be done properly.)

Discussion: The ending is somewhat vague. The author does not say directly that Mr. Carter was eaten by Mr. Beelzy, but that is obviously what he implies. Where is Small Simon, though?

MINI QUIZ

Write on the chalkboard or overhead projector the following questions and call on students to fill in the blanks. Discuss the answers with the class.

1. Small Simon's retreat was hidden by the tangled branches of a _____ and an _____ tree.
2. The playroom or garden room doubled as a _____ in hot weather.
3. Mr. Carter works as a _____.
4. At first, Mr. Carter thinks Small Simon has been _____ all day.
5. Small Simon calls Mr. Beelzy with a _____.

3. dentist
4. bored
5. stick

Answers to Mini Quiz

1. pear, apple
2. tearoom

ANSWERS TO UNDERSTAND THE SELECTION

1. In a little summer house at the end of the Carters' long yard.
2. He is a dentist and must have clean hands.
3. He wants him to "learn" by "experience" that it is better to reason than to be stubborn and to insist on something that can not be true.
4. It gives background and sets the stage for the story.
5. No; in the beginning of the story Mrs. Carter expresses worry that Simon chooses to play alone, and that he seems scared and tired—"white as a sheet"—after he has been playing at his retreat.
6. His father wants to know more about what he is doing at the retreat.
7. His father thinks Simon is "making things up" and is in a "fantasy stage," while Simon insists his "game" is real.
8. Answers will vary. Sample answer: No; families should talk about rules together so that everyone understands what the rules are.
9. Answers will vary. Students should recognize the crisis must come to climax, but physical violence is not the only alternative.
10. Answers will vary. Some students may wish the story continued in order to provide a clearer resolution.

Respond to Literature: Students should see the roles that imagination and belief play in our lives, from childhood fantasies to adult faiths.

ANSWERS TO WRITE ABOUT THE SELECTION

Prewriting: Draw on the chalkboard or overhead projector a plot development "map," with a points

---

UNDERSTAND THE SELECTION

Recall

1. Where did Simon play?
2. Why is Mr. Carter always washing his hands?
3. What does Mr. Carter hope to accomplish by punishing Simon?

Infer

4. What do you think is the purpose of all the description in the beginning?
5. Do you think Mrs. Carter agrees with her husband's idea of letting Simon "choose for himself"? Explain.
6. What complicates the plot question: What is Simon doing at his retreat?
7. What is the main conflict?

Apply

8. Mrs. Carter seems to allow her husband to determine what Simon can and cannot do. Do you think that is good?
9. Imagine that you are Mr. Carter. Would you treat Simon the way he does?
10. Do you like the way the story ends? Would you have ended it differently?

Respond to Literature

Explain why Simon's invention of Mr. Beelzy is unusual.

160

WRITE ABOUT THE SELECTION

What do you think happened on the second floor when Mr. Carter went to punish Simon? Do you think Mr. Beelzy actually existed and devoured Mr. Carter, or do you think there is a more rational explanation?

Write a postscript to the story, describing what happened. Think of the postscript as continuing the resolution of the story. It can be like a short, short story.

Then consider the plot question: What has happened to Mr. Carter? You might want to start with some exposition, perhaps just a sentence or two describing the second floor of the house. Next, begin your answer to the plot question. Present a brief complication that is followed quickly by crisis, climax, and a final resolution.

Prewriting: Map your short, short story. Show all the plot development points, and make notes on how you will reach each one.

Writing: Use the map to write your postscript. Make sure the plot question is answered.

Revising: The author uses vivid language. Can you add a simile or metaphor to add color to your postscript? Check also for redundancy. Your postscript should be tightly written.

Proofreading: If you used dialogue in the resolution, be sure each speaker's lines are a separate paragraph. Also check for errors in spelling, usage, and mechanics.

Unit 2

"exposition," "complication," "crisis," "climax," and "final resolution." Connect each point with a line to indicate flow.

Writing: Circulate as students work individually. Check plot maps and determine if students are using them as rough outlines.

Revising: Divide students into groups and have them look for similes and metaphors in the story.

Proofreading: Have students work in pairs. The writer starts reading his or her postscript aloud, noting a new paragraph to the partner. The partner then checks for a paragraph mark and returns the paper for final copying.

T160

THINK ABOUT PLOT

"Rising action" builds excitement in a story. The events of a story are called the plot. Plot begins with exposition; then moves to complications where rising action builds excitement. The action reaches a crisis, and then something does give, in the climax.

1. What is the first sign of resistance from Simon to his father's questions about the game he plays?

2. Simon gives in by answering his father's question about whom he plays with. What is Simon's answer, and why is it important?

3. How does the crisis build?

4. How do you learn that the climax has been reached?

5. In one short paragraph after the *climax*, there is the "falling" action of the *resolution*. What happens in the resolution?

DEVELOP YOUR VOCABULARY

John Collier sometimes uses different verbs when he tells who says something. Instead of simply saying, "he said," for example, he sometimes says, "he cried." These different verbs give us clues about the state of mind of the person talking. For example:
"I'm going up there," she said.
"I'm going up there," she cried.

The first sentence is "neutral." The second sentence tells us the speaker is upset.

Look at the following sentences. Make sure you understand what the italicized verb means, and explain, in a sentence, how it tells us something about the speaker:

1. "Nothing," *muttered* his son.
2. "He is sometimes there and sometimes not there," *pursued* Mr. Carter.
3. "He said he wouldn't let anyone hurt me," he *whimpered*.
4. "Go on up with you," *shouted* his father.

The Unknown   161

T161

The Three Witches, Henri Fuseli.
The Granger Collection.

162

LEARN ABOUT
Sound Segments

Poets use segments—vowel sounds and consonant sounds—in pattern: to link sounds with meanings or ideas. In descriptive poetry, segments may even combine with rhythm to imitate something being described. The most common ways poets use sound segments are alliteration, onomatopoeia, and assonance.

The repetition of the initial sound of words; for example, *great grow* the *grizzlies.* This technique is called **alliteration**, and its usage is standard in poetry. Also a word, when pronounced, can sound like the sound it is describing; for example, the *splashing* water. This technique is called **onomatopoeia**, and it, too, is a poetic standard. When a poet repeats a vowel sound in a line of poetry, he or she is using **assonance**. "T*is* h*a*rd to s*ay* *if* gr*ea*ter want of sk*i*ll."

As you read the two poems, ask yourself these questions:
1. Where is alliteration and assonance used?
2. Where is onomatopoeia used?

SKILL BUILDER

Use alliteration or assonance in a sentence describing something you have done recently. Write a follow-up sentence using onomatopoeia.

Unit 2

Mist Fantasy, J. E. H. MacDonald. Art Gallery of Ontario.

HIST, WHIST

E. E. Cummings

hist   whist
little ghostthings
tip-toe
twinkle-toe   20
5 little twitchy
witches and tingling
goblins
hob-a-nob   hob-a-nob

little hoppy happy   25
10 toad in tweeds
tweeds
little itchy mousies
with scuttling
eyes   rustle and run   and
15 hidehidehide
whisk

whisk   look out for the old woman
with the wart on her nose
what she'll do to yer
nobody knows

for she knows the devil   ooch
the devil   ouch
the devil
ach   the great

green
dancing
devil
devil

devil
30 devil
wheeEEE

---

scuttling (SKUT ling) moving quickly.
nymph (NIMF) a minor nature goddess in Greek and Roman myths.
lagoon (luh GOON) a shallow body of water, usually connected to a
  larger one.

The Unknown   163

by Harold Monro

Nymph, nymph, what are your beads?
Green glass, goblin. Why do you stare at them?
Give them me.

       No.

5   Give them me. Give them me.

       No.

Then I will howl all night in the reeds,
Lie in the mud and howl for them.

Goblin, why do you love them so?

10   They are better than stars or water,
Better than voices of winds that sing,
Better than any man's fair daughter,
Your green glass beads on a silver ring.

Hush, I stole them out of the moon.
15   Give me your beads, I desire them.

       No.

I will howl in a deep lagoon
For your green glass beads, I love them so.
Give them me. Give them.

20   No.

164

E. E. Cummings (1894–1962)

Edward Estlin Cummings was born in Cambridge, Massachusetts, on October 14, 1894. He graduated from Harvard University with a major in English and classics, and spent a part of his life as a volunteer in the army. Cumming's name often appears with lower case spelling—the result of a printer's error in *Eight Harvard Poets,* published in 1917. From that time on, Cummings always signed his name "e. e. cummings."

The unusual capitalization of his name is extremely appropriate, for Cummings is noted for his unique use of punctuation, word forms, and topography.

Words such as "puddle-wonderful" and "mud-luscious" roll from his pen like little jewels. Phrases such as "nonsufficiently inunderstood" seem to sum up feelings more accurately than ordinary language ever could. And his unusual arrangement of words on a page gives Cummings' poetry a visual, as well as a verbal, meaning.

In addition to being a poet, Cummings was a painter, novelist, and playwright. In all of his works, Cummings reveals his disillusionment with "mostpeople" and celebrates the value of the individual.

The Unknown

165

ANSWERS TO
UNDERSTAND
THE SELECTION

1. toads
2. a wart on her nose
3. from "out of the moon"
4. He wants to include all sorts of mysterious, supernatural things in his poem, not just ghosts.
5. We should avoid her because, as is the case with witches, she "knows the devil" and might even do devilish things herself.
6. He will howl from positions close to the ground.
7. Simple greed: They both want the same thing.
8. Answers will vary. Sample answer: the old woman with the wart on her nose; she sounds ugly and unpredictable.
9. Answers will vary, but students should recognize that throughout history many women have been branded unfairly as witches, which is the clear allusion here.
10. Yes. The moon represents mystery, and so, therefore, do the beads.

Respond to Literature:
Witches, goblins, and nymphs are mysterious, unprovable, formless. Writing about them allows free use of the imagination. Ask students if they can think of other examples from poems.

ANSWERS TO
WRITE ABOUT
THE SELECTION

Prewriting: Explore with the class what a saltmarsh is. Find its dictionary definition, and contrast it with the definition for a "marsh." Look for a picture of a saltmarsh in an encyclopedia or biology book.

Writing: As you circulate among the students working individually, reinforce the idea of appealing to one of the senses for description.

UNDERSTAND THE SELECTION

Recall

1. What wears tweeds in "hist whist"?

2. What distinctive feature does the old woman have in the same poem?

3. Where did the nymph's green glass beads come from in Monro's poem?

Infer

4. Why does Cummings use the word "ghostthings" rather than just "ghosts"?

5. Why does Cummings tells the reader to "look out for the old woman with the wart on her nose"?

6. What do the places where the goblin will howl have in common?

7. What causes the conflict between the nymph and the goblin?

Apply

8. Explain which character in "hist, whist" is least appealing to you.

9. Do you think the stereotype of the old woman with the wart is fair?

10. What is significant about the fact that the nymph's green glass beads came from the moon?

Respond to Literature

Why do you think poets like to write about supernatural things?

166

WRITE ABOUT THE SELECTION

You have been asked by poet Harold Monro to provide an introduction to his poem "Overheard on a Saltmarsh." The introduction does not have to be long. You just need to describe the setting of the poem.

Prewriting: You first need to make sure you understand what a saltmarsh is. Consult a dictionary if you are not sure. Then imagine standing in a saltmarsh. What would it feel like, smell like, and look like? What sounds would you hear? Write on your paper the four senses "touch," "smell," "sight," and "hearing." Under each, list several sensations.

Writing: Choose from your list of sensations the best ones that provide a vivid description of a saltmarsh. Keep in mind the content and theme of the poem. You may write in poetry or prose. Make sure your thoughts are well-organized.

Revising: Can you use alliteration or onomatopoeia anywhere in your description? Remember that these techniques are not limited to poetry. Add more sensory details and vivid words to make your introduction come alive. And eliminate any dead words or phrases that could make your description seem boring.

Proofreading: Reread your description to check for errors. Make sure there are no misspellings. Alliteration, onomatopoeia, and other techniques require that you spell correctly. Otherwise the reader is confused and the effect you want to create is lost.

Unit 2

Help them imagine smelling salt air or touching a reed.

Revising: Caution students that alliteration must not be take too far (for example, too many repetitions of the same sound), and onomatopoeia must be accurate.

Proofreading: Have students make flashcards of any words they misspell so they can review them.

THINK ABOUT SOUND SEGMENTS

Poets use sound segments to link vowel and consonant sounds with ideas. Alliteration repeats consonant sounds while assonance is repetition of vowel sounds. Onomatopoetic words imitate real sounds.

1. Look at the description in "hist, whist" of how "little ghostthings" walk. What technique is this?

2. Identify the onomatopoeia in "Overheard on a Saltmarsh."

3. Cummings likes to "play" with words. The very first line of the poem is a good example. What is going on here?

4. Find a good example of assonance.

5. How do sound segments help make these poems more interesting?

DEVELOP YOUR VOCABULARY

There are so many supernatural creatures that it is tempting to lump them all together. Is there any real difference, for example, between a "ghost" and a "goblin"? Here are shortened definitions for each:

ghost: the spirit of a dead person
goblin: an evil or mischievous spirit.

Thus, there *is* a difference between a ghost and a goblin—even though the words are often used as synonyms.

Below are more names for supernatural creatures. Consult your dictionary for their precise definitions. Then write a paragraph in which you tell the specific distinction of each.

1. witch	6. elf
2. wizard	7. gnome
3. nymph	8. ghoul
4. warlock	9. sorceress
5. sorcerer	10. zombie

LEARN ABOUT

Theme

Why do we tell stories?

Usually, it is because we have something to say—a message, actually—to our listeners or readers; that "something" is the theme.

When there is more than one theme in a story, the writer should include enough information, both in the plot and in descriptions of characters and settings, to show the various themes clearly.

Only rarely does a story have no real theme. In such a story, another element can become so important that an implied theme emerges during the writing. For example, detailed descriptions of a story's characters often reflect the complexity of people and the world in which we live. The complications of life itself become the theme.

As you read the next selection, ask yourself these questions:

1. What is the theme?
2. How is the theme presented in the story?

SKILL BUILDER

At sometime in your life, you have been asked to tell a story of some kind. Think about one of the stories. What was your purpose in telling it? What is its message?

OF MISSING PERSONS

by Jack Finney

Walk in as though it were an ordinary travel agency. That's what the stranger I'd met at a party told me. *Ask a few ordinary questions about a vacation or something. Then hint about The Folder. But whatever you do, don't mention it straight out. Wait till he brings it up. If he doesn't, you might as well forget it. If you can. Because you'll never see it. You're not the type, that's all. He'll just look at you as though he doesn't know what you're talking about.*

I went over it all in my mind, again and again. But what seems possible at midnight at a party isn't easy to believe on a raw, rainy day. I felt like a fool, searching the store fronts for the street number. It was noon, West 42nd Street, New York. I walked with my head bent into the slanting rain. This was hopeless.

Anyway, I thought, who am I to see The Folder, even if there is one? Charley Ewell, a young guy who works in a bank. A teller. I don't like the job. I don't make much money, and I never will. I've lived here for over three years and haven't many friends. I see too many movies, and I'm sick of meals alone in diners. I have

ordinary abilities, looks, and thoughts. Do I qualify?

Now I saw it, the address in the 200 block, an old office building. I pushed into the dirty lobby. The name was second on the list. "Acme Travel Agency" between "A-1 Copy Shop" and "Ajax Magic Supplies." I pressed the bell for the rickety elevator. I almost turned and left—this was crazy.

But upstairs, the Acme office was bright and clean. Behind a counter stood a tall man with a dignified look. He nodded at me to come in. My heart was pumping—he fitted the description exactly.

"Yes, United Air Lines," he was saying into the phone. "Flight"—he glanced at a paper—"seven-oh-three. I suggest you get there forty minutes early."

I waited, leaning on the counter, looking around. He was the man, all right. Yet this was just an ordinary travel agency. Big bright posters on the walls. Racks full of folders. Again I felt like a fool.

"Can I help you?" he said.

"Yes." Suddenly I was terribly nerv-

---

rickety (RIK it ee) feeble; shaky

The Unknown   169

Vocabulary: Preteach the vocabulary words. See the Comprehension Workbook in the TRB.

More About Vocabulary: Group the new vocabulary words by part of speech: nouns, verbs, adjectives, and adverbs. Divide the class into four groups and assign a list to each group to report on the words, giving the correct pronunci-ation and definition, and using the word in a sentence.

Sidelights: Loneliness is often associated with cities, even in the midst of millions of people. Why is this so? Are people too close to each other in cities, and, therefore, cut themselves off from others in an attempt to achieve privacy? Do people live in cities partly because of the anonymity that cities promise? Finney has written other stories that touch on this same theme; point out "The Love Letter" from Unit 1.

Motivation for Reading: Simon and Garfunkel's "Sounds of Silence" strikes a chord, even today, among young people. The lyrics touch on the loneliness and anonymity in modern life. Play the song and ask students to analyze it as a historical document shedding light on a previous generation's frustrations and fears.

More About the Thematic Idea: "Thus I Refute Beelzy" dealt with a child's fantasy. This selection deals with an adult's fantasy. Can you compare the two fantasies?

Purpose-Setting Question: What do you think lies behind your own fantasies?

Clarification: Italics are used at the beginning and end of the story. The technique emphasizes the internal thoughts of the narrator.

Reading Strategy: Point out that "The Folder" is capitalized. It must be important. Suggest that students keep it in mind as a hint to the theme of the story.

Literary Focus: Note the point of view, first person. Other selections in this unit have been third person. Also point out the establishment of setting.

Literary Focus: Charley Ewell himself describes his character. Does auto-description seem more or less accurate then third-person description?

Literary Focus: There is more information on Charley's character: He is a desperate man, looking for a big change. Could "The Folder" help?

Critical Thinking: Do students know anyone like Charley? Have them apply Charley's desire for "escape" to their own lives, or to the lives of people they know.

ous. "I'd like to—get away," I said. You fool, that's too fast, I told myself. Don't rush it! I watched in a kind of panic, but he didn't flick an eyelash.

"Well, there are a lot of places to go," he said politely. He brought out a folder: "Fly to Buenos Aires[1]—Another World!"

I looked at it long enough to be polite. Then I just shook my head. I was afraid to talk, afraid I'd say the wrong thing.

"Something quieter, maybe?" He brought out another folder: "The Unspoiled Forests of Maine." "Or"—he laid a third folder on the counter— "Bermuda[2] is nice just now."

I decided to risk it. "No," I said. "What I'm really looking for is a new place to live." I stared right into his eyes. "For the rest of my life." Then my nerve failed me, and I tried to think of a way to get out of it.

But he only smiled and said, "I don't know why we can't advise you on that." He leaned forward. "What are you looking for? What do you want?"

I held my breath, then said it. "Escape."

"From what?"

"Well—" Now I wasn't sure. I'd never put it into words before. "From New York, I'd say. And all cities. From worry. And fear. And the things I read in my newspapers. From loneliness." And then I couldn't stop, though I knew I was

---

[1]**Buenos Aires:** capital city of Argentina in South America
[2]**Bermuda:** islands in the Atlantic Ocean, east of South Carolina, popular with tourists

170　　　　　　　　　　　　　　　　　　　　　　　　　　**Unit 2**

talking too much. "From never doing what I really want to do or having much fun. From selling my days just to stay alive." I looked straight at him and said softly. "From the world."

Now he was studying my face, staring at me. I knew that in a moment he'd shake his head. "Mister," he'd say, "you better get to a doctor." But he didn't. He kept staring. He was a big man, his lined face very intelligent, very kind. He looked the way ministers should look. He looked the way all fathers should look.

He lowered his gaze. I had the sudden idea that he was learning a great deal about me. More than I knew myself. Suddenly he smiled. "Do you like people?" he asked. "Tell the truth. I'll know if you aren't."

"Yes. It isn't easy for me to relax, though, and be myself, and make friends."

He nodded. "Would you say you're a pretty decent kind of man?"

"I guess so. I think so." I shrugged. "Why?"

This was hard to answer. "Well—at least when I'm not, I'm usually sorry about it."

He grinned. "You know," he said casually, "we sometimes get people in here who seem to be looking for pretty much what you are. So just as a sort of little joke—"

I couldn't breathe. This was what I'd been told he would say if he thought I might do.

"—we've had a little folder printed.

Simply for our own amusement, you understand. And for a few customers like you. So I'll have to ask you to look at it here, if you're interested."

I could barely whisper, "I'm interested."

He brought out a long, thin folder, the same size and shape as the others. He slid it over the counter toward me.

I looked at it, pulling it closer with a fingertip—I was almost afraid to touch it. The cover was dark blue, the shade of a night sky. Across the top in white letters it said, "Visit Enchanting Verna!" The cover was sprinkled with stars. In the lower left was a globe, the world, with clouds around it. At the upper right, just under the word "Verna" was a star larger and brighter than the others. Across the bottom it said, "Romantic Verna, where life is the way it *should* be."

Inside were pictures, so beautiful they looked real. In one picture you could see dew shining on the grass, and it looked wet. In another, a tree trunk seemed to curve out of the page. It was a shock to touch it and feel paper instead of bark. Tiny human faces, in a third picture, seemed about to speak.

I studied a large picture taken from the top of a hill. The valley was covered with forest. Curving through it, far below, ran a stream, blue as the sky with spots of foaming white. It seemed that if you'd only look closely, you'd be sure to see that stream move. In clearings beside the stream were rough cabins. Under the picture were the words, "The Colony."

casually (KAZH oo uh lee) in an off-hand or indifferent way

The Unknown

Critical Thinking: "He looked the way ministers should look." Why might this allusion create a clear picture of character?

Reading Strategy: The opening paragraph of the story served as an outline of what had to happen if Charley Ewell were "the type." The reference—"we've had a little folder printed—is a marker noting that things are going according to plan.

Discussion: What would *your* reaction be if a travel agent handed a folder like this to you?

"Fun fooling around with a thing like that," the man said. "Eases the boredom. Nice-looking place, isn't it?"

I could only nod, staring at that forest-covered valley. This was how America must have looked when it was new. And you knew this was only a part of a whole land of unspoiled forests, where every stream ran pure.

Under that picture was another, of six or eight people on a beach. They were sitting, kneeling, or squatting in an easy way. It was morning, just after breakfast. They were smiling, one woman talking, the others listening. One man had half risen to skip a stone out onto the surface of the water.

You knew this: that they were spending twenty minutes or so down on that beach after breakfast before going to work. You knew they were friends, and that they did this every day. You knew—I tell you, you *knew*—that they liked their work, all of them, whatever it was. I'd never seen anything like their faces before. They were ordinary enough in looks. But these people were *happy*. Even more, you knew they'd *been* happy, day after day, for a long time. And that

they always would be, and they knew it.

I wanted to join them. I *longed* to. And I could hardly stand it. I looked up at the man, and tried to smile. "This is—very interesting," I said.

"Yes." He smiled back. "We've had people so interested, so carried away, that they didn't want to talk about anything else." He laughed. "They actually wanted to know prices, details, everything."

I nodded. "And I suppose you've worked out a whole story to go with the folder?" I said.

"Oh, yes. What would you like to know?"

"These people," I said softly, touching the picture of the group on the beach. "What do they do?"

"They work. Everyone does." He took a pipe from his pocket. "Some study. Some of our people farm, some write, some make things with their hands. Most of them raise children, and—well, they work at whatever it is they really want to do."

"And if there isn't anything they really want to do?"

He shook his head. "There's always

something for everyone. It's just that here, we so rarely have time to find out what it is." He looked at me gravely. "Life is simple there, and it's serene. In some ways, the good ways, it's like the life of early American pioneers. But without the drudgery that killed people young. We have electricity, washing machines, vacuum cleaners, modern bathrooms, and modern medicine.

"But there are no radios, televisions, telephones, or cars. People live and work in small villages. They raise or make most of the things they use. They build their own houses, with all the help they need from their neighbors. They have a lot of fun, but there's nothing you buy a ticket to. They have dances, card parties, weddings, birthdays, harvest parties, swimming, and sports of all kinds. People talk with each other a lot, and visit, and share meals. There are no pressures. Life holds few threats. Everyone is happy." After a moment, he smiled. "That's how the story goes in our little joke," he said, nodding at the folder.

"Who are you?" I lifted my eyes from the folder to look at him.

"It's in the folder," he said. "The people of Verna—the original ones—are just like you. Verna is a planet of air, sun, land, and sea, like Earth. The weather's about the same. There are a few small bodily differences between you and us—but nothing important. We read and en-joy your books. We like your chocolate, which we didn't have, and your music. But our thoughts, and aims, and history—those have been very different from Earth's." He smiled. "Amusing fantasy, isn't it?"

"Yes." I knew I sounded abrupt. "And where is Verna?"

"Light years away, by your measurements."

I was suddenly annoyed. I didn't know why. "A little hard to get to then, wouldn't it be?"

He turned to the window beside him. "Come here," he said, and I walked around the counter to stand beside him. "There, off to the left, are two apartment buildings, built back to back. See them?"

I nodded, and he said, "A man and his wife live on the fourteenth floor of one of those buildings. A wall of their living room is the back wall of the building. They have friends on the fourteenth floor of the other building. A wall of *their* living room is the back wall of *their* building. In other words, these two couples live within two feet of one another.

"But when the Robinsons want to visit the Braedens, they walk from their living room to the front door. Then they walk down a long hall to the elevators. They ride fourteen floors down. Then, in the street, they must walk around to the next block. And the city blocks there are long. In bad weather, they've sometimes

---

gravely (GRAYV lee) in a serious way
serene (suh REEN) calm; peaceful
drudgery (DRUJ uh ree) dull, tiring work; boring labor
fantasy (FAN tuh see) daydream; idea created by the imagination
abrupt (uh BRUPT) sudden; a little rude
light years (LYT YIRZ) huge distances in space

The Unknown   173

Reading Strategy: The two paragraphs describing life on Verna could be a commentary on what life on Earth *should* be like. Is that the author's message?

Enrichment: A light year is the distance light—in a vacuum—can travel in one year, that is, about 5,880,000,000,000 (5 trillion, 880 billion) miles.

Discussion: Would *you* make the same choice as Charley? Take a vote in class to see how many people would like to go to Verna—permanently.

actually taken a cab. They walk into the other building, then go on through the lobby. They ride up fourteen floors, walk down a hall, ring a bell, and finally go into their friends' living room—only two feet from their own.''

He turned back to the counter, and I walked around to the other side again. "All I can tell you," he said, "is that the way the Robinsons travel is like space travel. But if they could only step through those two feet of wall—well, that's how we travel. We don't cross space, we avoid it." He smiled. "Draw a breath here—and exhale it on Verna."

I said softly, "That's how they arrived, isn't it? The people in the picture. You took them there." He nodded, and I said, "Why?"

He shrugged. "If you saw a neighbor's house on fire, would you rescue his family if you could?"

"Yes."

"Well—so would we."

"You think it's that bad, then? With us?"

"How does it look to you?"

I thought about the headlines every morning. "Not so good."

He just nodded and said, "We can't take you all. We can't even take very many. So we've been choosing a few."

"For how long?"

"A long time." He smiled. "One of us was a member of Lincoln's cabinet."

I leaned across the counter toward him. "I like your little joke," I said. "I like it very much. When does it stop being a joke?"

depot (DEE poh) station

For a moment, he studied me. Then he spoke. "Now, if you want it to."

You've got to decide on the spot, the man at the party had told me. *Because you'll never get another chance. I know. I've tried.*

Now I stood there thinking. There were people I'd hate never to see again, and a girl I was just getting to know. This was the world I'd been born in. Then I thought about going back to my job, back to my room at night. And finally I thought of the deep-green valley in the picture, and the beach.

"I'll go," I whispered. "If you'll have me."

He studied my face. "Be sure," he said sharply. "Be certain. We want no one there who won't be happy. If you have any least doubt, we'd prefer that—"

"I haven't."

After a moment, he slid open a drawer under the counter and brought out what looked like a railroad ticket. The printing said, "Good for ONE TRIP TO VERNA. Not transferable. One-way only."

"Ah—how much?" I said, reaching for my wallet.

"All you've got. Including your small change." He smiled.

"I don't have much."

"That doesn't matter. We once sold a ticket for $3,700. And we sold another just like it for six cents." He handed the ticket to me. On the back were the words, "Good this day only" and the date. I put $11.17 on the counter. "Take the ticket to the Acme Depot," he said. Leaning

across the counter, he gave me directions.

It's a tiny hole-in-the-wall, the Acme Depot. You may have seen it. It's just a little store front on one of the narrow streets west of Broadway. Inside, there's a worn wooden counter and a few battered, chrome-and-plastic chairs. The man at the counter glanced up as I stepped in. He looked for my ticket. When I showed it, he nodded at the last empty chair. I sat down.

There was a girl beside me, hands folded on her purse. Rather pretty, she looked like a secretary. Across the way sat a young man in work clothes. His wife, beside him, was holding their little girl in her lap. And there was a man of around fifty. He was expensively dressed. He looked like the vice-president of a bank, I thought. I wondered what his ticket had cost.

Maybe twenty minutes passed. Then a small, battered old bus pulled up at the curb outside. The bus had dented fenders and tires with worn tread. It was just the sort of little bus you see around, ridden always by shabby, tired, silent people, going no one knows where.

It took nearly two hours for the little bus to work south through the traffic. We all sat, each wrapped in thought. We stared out the rain-spattered windows. I watched wet people huddled at city bus stops. I saw them rap angrily on the closed doors of full buses. At 14th Street I saw a speeding cab splash dirty water on a man at the curb. I saw the man's mouth twist as he cursed. I saw hundreds of faces, and not once did I see anyone smile.

The Unknown

175

Discussion: What might the people going to Verna have in common? They seem like a varied group.

I dozed. Then we were on a shiny black highway somewhere on Long Island. I slept again and woke up in darkness. I caught a glimpse of a farmhouse. Then the bus slowed, lurched once, and stopped. We were parked beside what looked like a barn.

It *was* a barn. The driver walked up to it. He pulled the big sliding door open and stood holding it as we filed in. Then he let it go, stepping inside with us. The big door slid closed of its own weight.

The barn smelled of cattle. There was nothing inside on the dirt floor but a bench of unpainted pine. The driver pointed to it with the beam of his flashlight. "Sit here, please," he said quietly. "Get your tickets ready." Then he moved down the line, punching tickets. His beam of light moved along the floor. I caught a glimpse of tiny piles of round bits of cardboard, like confetti. Then he was at the door again. He slid it open just enough to pass through. For a moment, we saw his outline against the night sky.

"Good luck," he said. "Just wait where you are." He let go of the door. It slid closed, snipping off the beam of his flashlight. A moment later, we heard the motor start and the bus lumber away.

The dark barn was silent now, except for our breathing. Time ticked away. I felt an urge to speak. But I didn't quite know what to say. I began to feel embarrassed, a little foolish. I was very aware that I was simply sitting in an old barn. The sec-onds passed. I moved my feet restlessly. Soon I was getting cold.

Then suddenly I knew! My face blushed in violent anger and shame. We'd been tricked! We'd been swindled out of our money. How? By our pitiful desire to believe an absurd fairy tale. Now we were left to sit there as long as we pleased. Finally, we'd come to our senses. Then we'd make our way home, like others before us, as best we could.

It was suddenly impossible to understand how I could have been so stupid. I was on my feet, stumbling in the dark across the uneven floor. I had some idea of getting to a phone and the police. The big barn door was heavier than I'd thought. But I slid it back and stepped through. Then I turned to shout back to the others to come along.

As I turned, the inside of that barn came alight. Through every wide crack of its walls and ceiling and windows streamed light. It was the light of a brilliantly blue sky. I opened my mouth to shout. Suddenly, the air was sweeter than any I had ever tasted. Then dimly, through a dusty window of that barn, I saw it. For less than the blink of an eye. I saw a deep, forest-covered valley, a blue stream winding through it, and a sunny beach. That picture was imprinted in my mind forever.

Then the heavy door slid shut. My fingernails scraped along the wood in a desperate effort to stop it. I failed. I was

lurched (LURCHT) tipped to one side suddenly
lumber (LUM bur) move heavily
absurd (ab SURD) silly; making no sense
imprinted (im PRINT id) printed on; impressed deeply, as on the mind

Discussion: Would you have done the same if you had been sitting in the barn? Would you have felt tricked? How far can faith carry one through what seems like an irrational situation?

Unit 2

standing alone in a cold, rainy night.

It took four or five seconds, no longer, to get the door open again. But it was four or five seconds too long. The barn was empty, dark. There was nothing inside but a worn pine bench. By the light of a match, I saw tiny drifts of what looked like confetti on the floor. I knew where everyone was. They were laughing out loud in that forest-green valley, and walking toward home.

I work in a bank, in a job I don't like. I ride to and from it in the subway, reading the daily news. I live in a rented room. In my battered dresser, under a pile of handkerchiefs, is a little square of yellow cardboard. Printed on its face are the words, "Good for ONE TRIP TO VERNA." Stamped on the back is a date. But the date is gone, long since.

I've been back to the Acme Travel Bureau. The tall man walked up to me and laid $11.17 on the counter. "You left this the last time you were here," he said. He looked me right in the eyes and added blankly. "I don't know why." Then some customers came in. He turned to greet them, and there was nothing for me to do but leave.

Walk in as though it were an ordinary travel bureau. You can find it, somewhere, in any city you try! Ask a few ordinary questions about a vacation, anything. Then hint about The Folder. But whatever you do, don't mention it straight out. Give him time to size you up and offer it. And if he does, if you can believe—then make up your mind and stick to it! Because you won't ever get a second chance. I know, because I've tried. And tried. And tried.

Clarification: The light years of travel to Verna have been compressed to an instant—just as the travel agent said they would be.

Reading Strategy: The resolution of the story is abrupt, just as Charley's return to the real world was.

Reading Strategy: Ending a story with the repetition of the initial paragraph is not always a good idea, but here it is effective: The reader is reminded of the opportunity Charley Ewell had and let slip away.

MINI QUIZ

Write on the chalkboard or overhead projector the following questions and call on students to fill in the blanks. Discuss the answers with the class.

1. Charley Ewell lives and works in _____.

2. The first destination the Acme travel agent suggested Charley consider was _____.

3. After looking at the folder about Verna, Charley knew the people there were _____.

4. The agent says that one traveler to Verna was _____ _____.

5. The Acme Depot bus took Charley and the others to a _____ on Long Island.

Answers to Mini Quiz

1. New York
2. Buenos Aires
3. happy
4. a member of Abraham Lincoln's cabinet
5. barn

ANSWERS TO UNDERSTAND THE SELECTION

1. bank teller
2. ministers and fathers
3. He is trying to rescue them from a world where things look pretty bad.
4. He wants to get away from all cities, from worry, fear, bad news, and loneliness—and from not doing what he wants or not really having fun. In short, he wants to escape "from the world."
5. This was a signal that Charley was being considered for the trip to Verna. The agent was perhaps testing him further, seeing what his reaction to the folder would be so he could determine if Charley really was suitable for the trip.
6. The agent tells the story in response to Charley's comment that Verna must be hard to get to because it is so far away. He is telling Charley that long travel can be made short by avoiding rather than crossing space.
7. First theme: We all get discouraged with our lives and hope there is a better world out there someplace. Second theme: The opportunity to find a better life might knock only once.
8. Answers will vary. Sample answer: Yes; although I have not had a job, I still often have felt bored with life. When I get bored, I buy a pint of ice cream and eat it.
9. Answers will vary. Certainly people in urban areas are subjected to more obvious forms of stress, such as noise, traffic, dirty air, and general crowdedness.
10. Answers will vary. A common similar situation is a surprise birthday party.

Respond to Literature: Verna represents a Garden of Eden, a

T178

UNDERSTAND THE SELECTION

Recall

1. What was Charley Ewell's job?

2. To what type of people did Charley compare the agent?

3. Why does the agent arrange for people to go to Verna?

Infer

4. Why does Charley want to "escape"?

5. Why did the travel agent tell Charley at first that the folder about Verna was "a sort of little joke"?

6. Explain the significance of the story the travel agent tells about the couples who live in nearby apartment buildings.

7. What is the theme or themes of the story?

Apply

8. Have you ever felt like Charley does at the beginning of the story? Did you do anything about your feelings?

9. Are Charley's complaints about city life valid? Explain your answer.

10. Describe a time when you, like Charley, thought someone had played a trick and was making fun of you?.

Respond to Literature

Do you think a place such as Verna could or even might exist? Explain your answer.

178

WRITE ABOUT THE SELECTION

The brochure that the travel agent hands Charley Ewell has very little written description about Verna. The travel agency has decided to add more advertising copy.

You have been hired to write some text for the brochure. What will you write?

Prewriting: Reread the part of the story where Charley looks at the brochure. What do the photos "say"? What is Charley's reaction? List the main points about Verna that you want to describe in your text. How do your want your potential clients to feel?

Writing: Use your list of main points to write the text. A good copywriter reinforces the ideas suggested by photos or other visual material (such as big headlines). Think back to Charley's reaction to the brochure. Try to capture those thoughts in the text so that the next "traveler" to Verna will have more information.

Revising: Advertising brochures use positive words, so make your text as upbeat as possible. Tell what Verna *is,* rather than what it *is not.* Smart readers will know at once what they will be escaping by going to Verna. Eliminate any dead words or dull phrases. Add details to create excitement.

Proofreading: It is fine to use contractions in informal writing such as advertising brochures. Make sure, however, that you use them correctly. Check their spelling and the correct placing of the apostrophe. Be sure your sentences end with periods, question marks or exclamation marks. Check interior punctuation as well.

Unit 2

land where life is perfect. People have searched for such a place for centuries. It might not exist, but places where people can lead slower, more human, and perhaps more meaningful lives do exist here on Earth.

ANSWERS TO WRITE ABOUT THE SELECTION

Prewriting: Work cooperatively as a class to get a good "feel" for the brochure. Reread the section in the story when Charley first sees the brochure. What does the cover look like? Ask for a volunteer to make a "mock-up" on the board

or overhead projector of the brochure.

Writing: As students work individually, circulate among them and check their lists of points. Suggest ways that the points can be incorporated into the text.

Revising: Ask students to reread their text and circle any negative words. Suggest they change them to positive words or expressions.

THINK ABOUT THEME

Theme is the main idea or message in a story or play. The theme in "No Missing Persons" is developed in a number of ways.

1. One way the theme in "No Missing Persons" is developed is through the negative description of characters; for example, the writer tells us why Charley Ewell is *not* happy. Point to another example.

2. The theme is also developed through positive description of setting (or imagined settings). Point to an example.

3. Conversation is also used to develop the theme. Point to an example.

4. Plot is also used to develop the theme. Explain how.

5. The final three paragraphs are the resolution of the story, coming after the climax. What is their purpose?

DEVELOP YOUR VOCABULARY

Proper nouns often have "hidden meanings." "Acme," the name of the travel agency Charley Ewell visits, is a good example. If you look in a dictionary, you will find that its common noun root means "the highest point" or "peak." The name "Acme Travel Agency" suggests this particular travel agency is the best.

When you are searching for hidden meanings, do not stop your search at the definitions. Look also at the information provided between brackets [ ] before the definitions. In the case of foreign words, consult a foreign-language dictionary or ask a friend who speaks the language.

Below are several words with "hidden meanings." Can you find the meanings?

1. Verna
2. *Ajax* Magic Supplies
3. *A-1* Copy Shop
4. Buenos Aires
5. Bermuda

The Unknown 179

T179

After completing this selection, students will be able to

- understand the elements of narrative poetry
- recognize many nursery rhymes as narrative poems
- examine the quests of other literary figures
- rewrite a narrative poem as a short story
- see the advantages of using poetry in narratives
- recognize and define archaic verb forms

More About Narrative Poetry: The two selections here are short narrative poems. Many narrative poems are much longer. In the 19th century in America, narrative poems were very popular, and some told long, involved stories. Longfellow's "The Midnight Ride of Paul Revere," for example, describes many aspects of the Boston patriot's famous trip to warn colonists of British soldiers on the march.

Cooperative/Collaborative Learning Activity: Almost everyone can remember a nursery rhyme, although memories may have to be jogged a bit. Have students work in groups. They can ask group members for help in remembering the rhyme. Then, have them tell the rhyme to the group. Ask them to discuss how certain poetry techniques, such as rhyme, help in remembering the poem.

LEARN ABOUT
Narrative Poetry

Many poems are written simply to give you an impression or feeling about the subject. They have no real story to tell. Other poems, however, do tell a story. They are like short, short stories written in verse.

Poems that tell a story are called **narrative poems.** They have the elements of a short story—setting, characters, plot, and theme. These elements may not be as well developed as in a short story, however, since a poem is usually shorter.

Why do authors tell stories in poetry rather than prose? That is a question to keep in mind as you read the next two selections. Remember that techniques such as imagery, rhyme, personification, and metaphor can often be used to best advantage in poetry.

As you read "The Listeners" and "Eldorado," ask yourself:

1. What are the poems' elements?
2. What would the story be like if it were in prose rather than poetry?

SKILL BUILDER

Nursery rhymes, which are poems, are usually a form of narrative poetry. Think of a nursery rhyme. Tell its plot in a paragraph or two.

THE LISTENERS

by Walter de la Mare

"Is there anybody there?" said the Traveller,
  Knocking on the moonlit door;
And his horse in the silence champed the grasses
  Of the forest's ferny floor:
5 And a bird flew up out of the turret,
  Above the Traveller's head:
And he smote upon the door again a second time;
  "Is there anybody there?" he said.
But no one descended to the Traveller;
10   No head from the leaf-fringed sill
Leaned over and looked into his grey eyes,
  Where he stood perplexed and still.
But only a host of phantom listeners
  That dwelt in the lone house then
15 Stood listening in the quiet of the moonlight
  To that voice from the world of men:
Stood thronging the faint moonbeams on the dark stair,
  That goes down to the empty hall,
Hearkening in an air stirred and shaken
20   By the lonely Traveller's call.
And he felt in his heart their strangeness,
  Their stillness answering his cry,
While his horse moved, cropping the dark turf,
  'Neath the starred and leafy sky;
25 For he suddenly smote on the door, even
  Louder, and lifted his head:—
"Tell them I came, and no one answered,
  That I kept my word," he said.
Never the least stir made the listeners,

---

champed (CHAMPT) bit or chewed, usually impatiently
turret (TUR it) small tower on top of a building
smote (SMOHT) pounded; struck
perplexed (pur PLEKST) confused; puzzled
host (HOHST) large group
thronging (THRAWNG ing) crowding; jostling
cropping (KROP ing) biting off the tops
turf (TURF) short grass

The Unknown 181

Motivation for Reading: Read aloud to the class another de la Mare or Poe poem. A good choice would be Poe's "Annabel Lee." It is straightforward and talks of young love. Point out that Poe's wife, Virginia, was 14 when they married.

More About the Thematic Idea: De la Mare's poem has remained a mystery to readers over the years. That is part of its appeal. The Traveller's question, "Is there anybody there?", is an effort to discover who the listeners are. Poe's poem is more straightforward. It is reminiscent of medieval tales of the search for the Holy Grail.

Purpose-Setting Question: Have you ever been sure that something was there, searched and searched for it, but never found it?

Reading Strategy: Stress the need to pay attention to punctuation in this poem. Pause or stop only when indicated by punctuation.

Clarification: "Hearken," used often in poetry, means "to listen attentively."

Critical Thinking: This might be a good place to make sure that students understand who is "real" and who is a "phantom." How can the Traveller feel in his heart the phantoms' "strangeness"?

Discussion: Who is "them"? The poet never reveals to whom he is referring. Do students have any ideas?

Reading Strategy: Ask a group of volunteers to reread the poem aloud as a chorus.

Vocabulary: Preteach the vocabulary words. See the Comprehension Workbook in the TRB.

More About Vocabulary: Ask students to make flashcards of the new vocabulary words, and to use each word in a sentence.

The Battle of Life (Golden Knight), Gustav Klimt, Galerie St. Etienne, New York

30   Though every word he spake
      Fell echoing through the shadowiness of the still house
         From the one man left awake:
      Ay, they heard his foot upon the stirrup,
      And the sound of iron on stone,
35   And how the silence surged softly backward,
      When the plunging hoofs were gone.

---

surged (SURJD) rolled; swelled up

ELDORADO

by Edgar Allan Poe

Gaily bedight,
A gallant knight,
In sunshine and in shadow,
Had journeyed long,
5 Singing a song,
In search of Eldorado.

But he grew old—
This knight so bold—
And o'er his heart a shadow
10 Fell as he found
No spot of ground
That looked like Eldorado.

And, as his strength
Failed him at length,
15 He met a pilgrim shadow—
"Shadow," said he,
"Where can it be—
This land of Eldorado?"

"Over the Mountains
20 Of the Moon,
Down the Valley of the Shadow,
Ride, boldly ride,"
The shade replied—
"If you seek for Eldorado."

bedight (bih DYT) adorned.
El Dorado (el duh RAH doh) a fabled place full of money-making
opportunities

The Unknown   183

1. somewhere in the forest (because his horse eats grass from "the forest's ferny floor")
2. rides away
3. from "a pilgrim shadow"
4. spirits, because the traveler is described as having a voice "from the world of men," which implies they are not of this world. Also, they are described as "phantom" listeners.
5. because he felt "their stillness answering his cry"; somebody or something was inside the house.
6. when he was young, because he had "journeyed long."
7. He became discouraged and depressed.
8. Answers will vary. Sample answer: It was frightening. I felt like somebody was watching me, but I could not see them.
9. Knights are symbols of gallant, idealistic searches for things that probably do not exist.
10. Answers will vary, but students should see the theme of searching for a dream.

Respond to Literature: Suggest to students that other characters in literature are similar to the knight: They range from cowboys to spacemen or to Charley Ewell in the previous selection. The point is that the knight is a symbol of a restless quest for some perfect thing or place. Ask students to name specific examples.

Prewriting: Divide the class into four groups. Assign a verse to each. Ask them to "translate" troublesome words or phrases; for example, "gaily bedight" in verse

UNDERSTAND THE SELECTION

Recall

1. Where is the house the traveler stopped at in "The Listeners"?

2. What does the traveler do at the end of the poem?

3. From whom did the knight in "Eldorado" ask directions?

Infer

4. Who do you think the listeners are?

5. Why did the traveler knock on the door a third time?

6. When do you think the knight in "Eldorado" began his search?

7. What does Poe mean by the lines "And o'er his heart a shadow fell"?

Apply

8. Have you ever been in an empty building but felt as if someone else were there? Explain.

9. Why do you think a knight is used as the character in "Eldorado"?

10. Will the knight ever find Eldorado?

Respond to Literature

Can you think of other characters in books you have read who are like the knight in "Eldorado"? What are they looking for?

WRITE ABOUT THE SELECTION

Let us go back to a question asked in the opening: Why do authors sometimes tell stories in poetry when they could write in prose? Maybe you can find an answer by experimenting with the Edgar Allan Poe poem. Like every narrative poem, it has all the elements of a short story. So why not change it into a short story?

Prewriting: Make sure you understand all the words and phrases in the poem. Use a dictionary if you are not sure of any meanings. Then freewrite about the events in the poem to flesh out the narrative with details.

Writing: The poem is a natural outline for your story. Use it and your freewriting to write your version, changing the poetry to prose. Do a stanza at a time. Each stanza could be one paragraph. You will probably need to add details and even events to make your tale logical and enjoyable.

Revising: Read your story through without stopping to make any changes or corrections. Does it read smoothly? Is the theme as clear as in the original poem? Check the transitions between paragraphs. Then go back and make any changes you think are needed.

Proofreading: Reread your story and check for errors. Make sure you use correct punctuation, particularly at the ends of sentences. The poem uses many dashes, which you should not use for end punctuation in your prose story.

1, or "as his strength failed him at length" in verse 3. Then have the group turn its verse into prose.

Writing: Students should work individually. They already have one verse converted to prose. Circulate among students as they work, offering additional help.

Revising: It might help students if they think "each verse converts to one paragraph." The transitions

then should be smooth, for Poe's verses link together nicely.

Proofreading: Discuss as a class the use of punctuation in poems as compared to prose. Remind students of the extreme liberties taken by e.e. cummings. Point out that poetry usually allows freer expression, and that includes less stringent punctuation rules.

THINK ABOUT NARRATIVE POETRY

A narrative poem tells a story. The poem will have elements similar to a short story—plot, setting, characters, and theme. In addition, narrative poems can have other poetic elements. The structures of "Eldorado" and "The Listeners" show one of the strengths of using poetry to tell a story.

1. What is the plot of the two poems?

2. Describe the main characters in "The Listeners" and "Eldorado." How are they similar?

3. What is the setting of "The Listeners"? Of "El Dorado"? What do the settings have in common?

4. Explain the themes of both poems in your own words.

5. Rhythm and rhyme together can give a poem a distinctive feeling. What feeling do they create in these poems?

DEVELOP YOUR VOCABULARY

You often find odd verbs and verb forms in poems. This might be because the poet is trying to find one word to rhyme with another. Perhaps, as in the case of "The Listeners," it might be because the poem was written a long time ago when different verbs and verb forms were used commonly.

An example of an old verb is the word *smote*, which appears twice in the poem. A dictionary can help you understand both its meaning and whether it still is used.

Here is the entry:

smote (smot) v., past tense of *smite*.

If you look up smite, you will find all the forms of the verb. You will find also that smite as a verb meaning "to hit or strike hard" is "Now Rare."

Choose five old verbs from the poems. Then use them in original sentences. Use a dictionary to find the present/past tenses and definitions of these "old" verbs.

1. They tell about a traveller and a knight who encounter spirits on their journeys through life.
2. The Traveller is a lonely man of unspecified age who remains faithful to a promise he made. The knight is a gaily dressed old man who remained true to his quest for Eldorado. Both are travellers who remain faithful to their quest; both come across spirits.
3. The setting of "The Listener" is outside a lone house in a forest. "Eldorado" takes place on an unspecified road. Both are mysterious, unknown settings.
4. Answers will vary. Students may identify loneliness, fulfillment, or death.
5. A feeling of endless searching because of the regular repetition of stress and sound.

**ANSWERS TO
DEVELOP YOUR
VOCABULARY**

Student sentences will vary.

LEARN ABOUT

Exposition

Exposition is one of the four types of nonfiction composition. Often when you are asked to write an essay in science or history about types of animals or the causes of World War I, you are writing exposition. The purpose of **exposition** is to explain something to your readers.

While exposition can exist in a form of its own, it is often combined with other types of writing. Exposition can be used to support arguments in persuasive writing, and descriptive writing can blend with exposition to offer examples that explain an important point.

As you read the next selection, ask yourself these questions:

1. What is John McPhee explaining to his readers?
2. What other types of writing does the author use in this essay?

SKILL BUILDER

Think about something you really enjoy or something that you are good at doing. Use exposition to explain about your "something" to a reader who knows very little about your subject. What do your readers really need to understand?

186

Unit 2

T186

THE LOCH NESS MONSTER

ADAPTED

by John McPhee

The road—the A-82—stayed close to the lake, often on ledges that had been blasted into the mountainsides. The steep forests continued, broken now and a-gain, on one shore or the other, by fields of fern, clumps of bright-yellow shrubs and isolated stands of cedar. Along the far shore were widely separated houses and farms, which to the eyes of a traveller appeared almost unbelievably green and fertile after the spare desolation of some of the higher glens. We came to the top of the rise and suddenly saw, on the right-hand side of the road, on the edge of a

---

glens (GLENZ) narrow, secluded valleys.

The Unknown 187

Sidelights: John McPhee has a special connection with England: His ancestors were from the Heb-rides, the islands north of Scot-land, and he studied at Cambridge University. He calls himself "funda-mentally... a working journalist," a profession in which he received rigorous training while working for *Time* magazine.

Motivation for Reading. Find a copy of a purported photo-graph of the Loch Ness Monster. Discuss with students the prob-lems of verifying the existence of something many people doubt.

More About the Thematic Idea: McPhee's skill is in writing description. Students should not expect a fast-paced suspense story.

Purpose-Setting Question: Does on-the-spot reporting prove that a phenomenon such as the Loch Ness Monster really exists?

Enrichment: "Loch" is a Scot-tish word for "lake." Loch Ness, about 25 miles long but very nar-row, is in the northern third of Scotland, about 100 miles due north of Glasgow.

LDP Activity: Point to it on a map. Are there other Lochs in this part of Great Britain?

Clarification: Major highways in Britain use the prefixes "M" or "A." "M" stands for "motorway," a four-lane road (called a "dual car-riageway" in Britain). "A" roads are other major roads (Usually two lanes), and "B" roads are minor roads (two lanes).

Reading Strategy: The open-ing paragraph offers a good intro-duction to McPhee's style: It is long and detailed. Ask students to pause in their reading and describe what the scene looks like, and what more they might like to know about it.

Vocabulary: Preteach the vo-cabulary words. See the Compre-hension Workbook in the TRB.

More About Vocabulary: McPhee does not write simply, and even though this story has been adapted students should expect challenging vocabulary. Introduce the new words in a "vocabulary bee." Divide the class into two teams, and, as in a spelling bee, ask students in turn for the correct definition of the word. Have stu-dents write on the chalkboard or overhead projector the new words and their definitions.

high meadow that sloped sharply a considerable distance to the lake, a cluster of caravans and other vehicles, arranged in the shape of a C, with an opening toward the road—much like a circle of covered wagons formed for protection against savage attack. All but one or two of the vehicles were painted bright lily-pad green. The compound, in its compact half acre, was surrounded by a fence, to keep out, among other things, sheep, which were grazing all over the slope in deep-green turf among buttercups, daisies, and thistles. Gulls above beat hard into the wind, then turned and planed toward the south. Gulls are inland birds in Scotland, there being so little distance from anywhere to the sea. A big fireplace had been made from rocks of the sort that were scattered all over the meadow. And on the lakeward side a platform had been built, its level high position emphasizing the slope of the hill, which dropped away below it. Mounted on the platform was a thirty-five-millimeter motion-picture camera with an enormous telephoto lens. From its point of view, sticking out at two hundred feet above the lake, the camera could take in a dazzling scene that covered thousands of acres of water.

This was Expedition Headquarters, the principal field station of the Loch Ness Phenomena Investigation Bureau —dues five pounds per annum,[1] life membership one hundred pounds, tax on donations recoverable under covenant.[2] Those who join the bureau receive newsletters and annual reports, and are allowed to participate in the fieldwork if they so desire. I turned into the compound and parked between two bright-green reconditioned old London taxis. The central area had long since been worn grassless, and was covered at this moment with fine-grain dust. People were coming and going. The place seemed rather public, as if it were a depot. No one even halfway interested in the natural history of the Great Glen would think of driving up the A-82 without stopping in there. Since the A-82 is the principal route between Glasgow and Inverness,[3] it is not surprising that the apparently amphibious creature as yet unnamed, the so-called Loch Ness Monster, has been seen not only from the highway but on it.

The atmosphere around the headquarters suggested a scientific frontier and also a boom town, much as Cape Canaveral and Cocoa Beach do. There were, as well, hints of show business and fine arts. Probably the one word that

---

caravans (KAR uh vanz) in Great Britain, camping trailers.
telephoto (TEL uh foht oh) a camera lens that is able to make faraway things appear large.
amphibious (am FIB ee us) able to live on land and in water.
[1] **dues five pounds per annum:** amount of British money per year that it costs to belong.
[2] **tax on donations recoverable by covenant:** Taxes paid on donations will be refunded.
[3] **Glasgow** and **Inverness:** cities in southern and northern Scotland.

Unit 2

might have been applied to everyone present was adventurer. There was, at any rate, nothing really laboratorial about the place, although the prevailing mood seemed to be one not of holiday but of matter-of-fact application and patient dedication. A telephone call came in that day, to the caravan that served as an office, from a woman who owned an inn south of Inverarigaig, on the other side of the lake. She said that she had seen the creature that morning just forty yards offshore—three humps, nothing else to report, and being very busy just now, thank you very much, good day. This was recorded, with no particular display of excitement, by an extremely attractive young woman who appeared to be in her late twenties, an artist from London who had missed but one summer at Loch Ness in seven years. She wore sandals, dungarees, a black pullover, and gold earrings. Her name was Mary Piercy, and her toes were painted pink. The bulletin board where she recorded the sighting resembled the kind used in railway stations for the listing of incoming trains.

The office walls were decorated with photographs of the monster in various postures—basking, cruising, diving, splashing, looking up questioningly. A counter was covered with some of the essential publications: the bureau's annual report (twenty-nine sightings the previous year), J. A. Carruth's *Loch Ness and Its Monster* (The Abbey Press, Fort Augustus), Tim Dinsdale's *Loch Ness Monster* (Routledge and Kegan Paul, London), and a report by the Joint Air Reconnaissance Center of the Royal Air Force on a motion picture of the monster swimming about half a mile on the lake's surface. These books and documents could, in turn, lead the interested reader to less available but nonetheless highly important works such as R. T. Gould's *The Loch Ness Monster and Others* and Constance Whyte's *More Than a Legend*.

My children looked over the photographs with absorption but not a great deal of awe, and they bought about a dozen postcards with glossy prints of a picture of the monster—three humps showing, much the same sight that the innkeeper had described—that had been taken by a man named Stuart, directly across the lake from Urquhart Castle. The three younger girls then ran out into the meadow and began to pick daisies and buttercups. Their mother and sister sat down in the sun to read about the creature in the lake, and to write postcards. We were on our way to Inverness, but with no need to hurry. "Dear Grammy, we came to see the monster today."

From the office to the camera-observation platform to the caravan that served as a pocket cafeteria, I wandered around among the crew, was offered and accepted tea, and squinted with imaginary experience up and down the lake, where the water had grown even rougher. Among the crew at the time were two

---

basking (BASK ing) warming oneself pleasantly, as in sunlight.
reconnaissance (rih KON uh sens) quick survey of information.

The Unknown 189

Critical Thinking: Point out the use of a specific example to illustrate a point McPhee wants to make, that the "prevailing mood" was not one "of holiday" but of "application" and "patient dedication." For example, he mentions a counter covered with "essential bibliography."

Discussion: Talk about the way McPhee goes about gathering information: He writes down practically everything he sees, down to the titles, authors, and publishers of books on display. The recording of these titles was probably also self-serving; the books are references which he can consult later if he wants more information on the monster.

Clarification: McPhee is always the reporter. He can not accept silence about people's professional lives because he is trying to understand what makes them "tick."

Reading Strategy: Direct speech is used in sustained fashion in the text. Ask students if they find information presented in this style as helpful as direct description. Does it add authenticity?

Literary Focus: Rich, perceptive description of a single person, such as Clem Lister Skelton, adds to the overall impression of the scene. Point out that McPhee is like a literary camera.

Canadians, a Swede, an Australian, three Americans, two Englishmen, a Welshman, and one Scot. Two were women. When I asked one of the crew members if he knew what jobs some of the others had when they were not at Loch Ness, he said, "I'm not sure what they are. We don't go into that." This was obviously a place where now was all that mattered, and in such surroundings it is distinctly pleasant to accept that approach to things. Nonetheless, I found that I couldn't stick completely to this principle, and I did find out that one man was a medical doctor, another a farmer, another a retired naval officer, and that several were students, as might be expected. The daily watch begins at four in the morning and goes on, as one fellow put it, "as long as we can stand up." It has been the pattern among the hundreds of sightings reported that the early-morning hours are the most promising ones. Camera stations are manned until ten at night, dawn and sunset being so close to midnight at that latitude in summer, but the sentries tend to thin out with the lengthening of the day. During the autumn, the size of the crew reduces almost to one.

One man lives at the headquarters all year long. His name is Clem Lister Skelton. "I've been staring at that piece of water since five o'clock," he said, while he drank tea in the mess caravan.

"Is there a technique?" I asked him.

"Just look," he said. "Look. run your eye over the water in one quick skim. What we're looking for is not hard to see. You just sit and sort of gaze at the loch, that's all. Mutter a few incantations. That's all there is to do. In wintertime, very often, it's just myself. And of course one keeps a very much more perfunctory watch in the winter. I saw it once in a snowstorm, though, and that was the only time I've had a clear view of the head and neck. The neck is obviously very mobile. The creature was quite big, but it wasn't as big as a seventy-foot MFV. Motor fishing vessel. I'd been closer to it, but I hadn't seen as much of it before. I've seen it eight times. The last time was in September. Only the back. Just the sort of upturned boat, which is the classic view of it."

Skelton drank some more tea, and refilled a cup he had given me. "I must know what it is," he went on. "I shall never rest peacefully until I know what it is. Some of the largest creatures in the world are out there, and we can't name them. It may take ten years, but we're going to identify the genus. Most people are not as fanatical as I, but I would like to see this through to the end, if I don't get too broke first."

Skelton is a tall, informed man, English, with reddish hair that is uncombed in long strings from the thinning crown of his head. In outline, Skelton's life

---

technique (tek NEEK) method of doing something.
incantations (in kan TAY shunz) magical words used in enchantment.
perfunctory (pur FUNK tuh ree) routine; superficial.
genus (JEE nus) main subdivision of a family of closely related species.
fanatical (fuh NAT ih kul) incredibly devoted, to the point of being unreasonable.

there in the caravan on the edge of the high meadow over the lake, in a place that must be uncorrectably gloomy during the wet rains of winter, seemed cage-like and hopeless to me—unacceptably lonely. The impression he gave was of a man who had drawn a circle around himself many hundreds of miles from the rest of his life. But how could I know? He was saying that he had flown Supermarine Spitfires[4] for the R.A.F. during the Second World War. His father had been a soldier, and when Skelton was a boy, he lived, as he put it, "all over the place." As an adult, he became first an actor, later a writer and director of films. He acted in London in plays like *March Hare* and *Saraband for Dead Lovers*. One film he directed was, in his words, "a dreadful thing called *Saul and David*." These appearances on the surface apparently did not occur so frequently that he needed to do nothing else for a livelihood. He also directed, in the course of many years, several hundred educational films. The publisher who distributed some of these films was David James, a friend of Skelton's, and at that time a Member of Parliament.[5] James happened to be, as well, the founder of the Loch Ness Phenomena Investigation Bureau—phenomena, because, for breeding purposes, there would have to be at least two monsters living in the lake at any one time, probably more, and in fact two had

on occasion been sighted at the same time. James asked Skelton if he would go up to the lake and give the bureau the benefit of his technical knowledge of movie cameras. "Anything for a laugh," Skelton had said to James. This was in the early nineteen-sixties. "I came for a fortnight," Skelton said now, in the caravan. "And I saw it. I wanted to know what it was, and I've wanted to know what it was ever since. I thought I'd have time to write up here, but I haven't. I don't do anything now except hunt this beast."

Skelton talked on about what the monster might be—a magnified newt, a long-necked variety of giant seal, still existing *Elasmosaurus*. Visitors wandered by in groups outside the caravan, and unexplained strangers kept coming in for tea. In the air was a feeling, utterly hidden by the relative permanence of the place, of a country carnival on a two-night stand. The caravans themselves, in their placement, suggested a section of a carnival. I remembered a woman shouting to attract people to a big caravan on a carnival midway one night in May in New Jersey. That was some time ago. I must have been nineteen. The woman, who was standing on a small platform, was fifty or sixty, and she was trying to get people to go into the caravan to see big jungle cats, I suppose, and brown bears—"Ferocious Beasts," at any rate,

---

fortnight (FAWRT nyt) two weeks.
newt (NOOT) small salamander found in damp places.
[4]**Supermarine Spitfires** for the **R.A.F.:** Fighter planes for the British Royal Air Force.
[5]**Parliament:** The national legislative body of Great Britain.

Literary Focus: The long passage about Skelton is an example of rich, perceptive description. The reader gains insights into what motivates the people who run the Loch Ness Phenomena Investigation Bureau.

Clarification: "Phenomena" is plural, "phenomenon" is singular.

Clarification: Fish of the "elasmobranch" include the shark, skate, and ray. Their skeletons are cartilage, and their scales are sometimes shed and replaced by new ones.

Reading Strategy: McPhee uses the placement of the caravans as the link to a description of a New Jersey carnival midway. Ask students to look for a broader meaning: McPhee suggests that the Loch Ness monster is like the carnival bear kept in a cage only for the enjoyment of spectators.

according to block lettering on the side of the caravan. A steel cage containing a small black bear had been set up on two sawhorses outside the caravan—a fragment to suggest what might be found on a large scale inside.

So young that it was no more than two feet from nose to tail, the bear was engaged in desperate motion, racing along one side of the cage from corner to corner, striking the steel bars bluntly with its nose. Whirling then tossing its head over its shoulder like a racing swimmer, it turned and bolted crazily for the opposite end. Its eyes were deep red and shining in a kind of full-sighted blindness. It had gone mad there in the cage and its motion, rhythmic and tortured, never stopped, back and forth, back and forth, the head tossing with each jarring turn. The animal skinned its sides on the steel bars as it ran. Hair and skin had scraped from its sides so that pink flesh showed in the downpour of the carnival arc lights. Blood drained freely through the thinned hair of its belly and dropped onto the floor of the cage. What had a paralyzing effect on me was the animal's almost perfect and now involuntary rhythm—the wild toss of the head after the crash into the corner, the turn, the scraping run, the crash again at the other end, never stopping, regular—the exposed interior of some brutal and living time piece.

Beside the cage, the plump, critical woman, red-faced, red-nosed, kept shouting to the crowds, but she said to me, leaning down with her eyes bloodshot, "Why don't you move on, sonny, if you ain't going to buy a ticket? Beat it. Come on, now. Move on,"

"I argue about what it is," Skelton said. "I'm inclined to think it's a giant slug, but there is an amazingly impressive theory for its being a worm. You can't rule out that it's one of the big dinosaurs, but I think this is more wishful thinking than anything else." In the late nineteen-thirties, a large and strange-looking footprint was found along the shore of Loch Ness. It was carefully studied by various people and was assumed, for a time, to be an impression from a foot or flipper of the monster. Eventually, the print was identified. Someone who owned the preserved foot of a hippopotamus had successfully brought off a trick that put layers of mockery and incredibility over the creature in the lake for many years. The Second World War further turned aside any serious interest that amateurs or naturalists might have taken. Sightings continued, however, in a regular pattern, and finally, in the early nineteen-sixties, the Loch Ness Phenomena Investigation Bureau was established. "I have no plans whatever for leaving," Skelton said. "I am prepared to stay here ad infinitum. All my worldly goods are here."

A dark-haired young woman had stepped into the caravan and poured herself a cup of tea. Skelton, introduc-

---

slug (SLUG) a small animal like a snail, but without such a hard, outer shell.
ad infinitum (ad in fuh NYT um) Latin phrase meaning forever.

The Unknown   193

ing her to me, said, "If the beast has done nothing else, it has brought me a wife. She was studying Gaelic and Scottish history at Edinburgh University, and she walked into the glen one day, and I said, 'That is the girl I am going to marry.'" He gestured toward a window of the caravan, which framed a view of the hills and the lake. "The Great Glen is one of the most beautiful places in the world," he continued. "It is peaceful here. I'd be happy here all my life, even if there were nothing in the loch. I've even committed the unforgivable sin of going to sleep in the sun during a flat calm. With enough time, we could shoot the beast with a crossbow, and a line, and get a bit of skin. We could also shoot a small transmitter into its hide and learn more than we know now about its habits and characteristics."

The creature swims with remarkable speed, as much as 12 to 18 mph when it is really moving. It makes no noise other than sudden splashes, but it is apparently responsive in a highly sensitive way to sound. A shout, an approaching engine, any loud report, will send it into an immediate dive, and this shyness is in large part the cause of why it can't be found, and therefore of its mystery. Curiously, though, the echoing sound was what apparently brought the creature wide attention, for the first series of frequent sightings occurred in 1933, when A-82 was blasted into the cliffsides of the western shore of the lake. Immense boulders kept falling into the depths, and shock waves from dynamite repeatedly ran through the water, causing the creature to lose confidence in its environment and to alter, at least temporarily, its shy and preferred nightlife. In that year it was first observed on land, perhaps attempting to seek a way out forever from the blasts that had alarmed it. A couple named Spicer saw it, near Inverarigiag, and later described its long, serpent-like neck, followed by an awkward hulk of a body, lurching toward the lake and disappearing into high undergrowth as they approached.

With the exception of one report recorded in the sixth century, which said that a monster (fitting the description of the current creatures in the lake) had killed a man with a single bite, there have been no other examples of savagery on its part. To the contrary, its sensitivity to people seems to be sharp, and it keeps a wide margin between itself and mankind. In all likelihood, it feeds on fish and particularly on eels, of which there are millions in the lake. Loch Ness is unparalleled in eel-fishing circles, and has drawn commercial eel fishermen from all over the United Kingdom. The monster has been observed with its neck bent down in the water, like a swan feeding. When the creatures die, they apparently settle into the seven-hundred-foot floor of the lake, where the temperature is always forty-two degrees Fahrenheit—so cold that the lake is known for never

Gaelic (GAYL ik) A Celtic language spoken in Scotland and Ireland.
crossbow (KRAWS boh) a kind of bow that is set flat for firing.
transmitter (trans MIT ur) radio device that sends out signals.

giving up its dead. Loch Ness never freezes, despite its high latitude, so if the creature breathes air, as has seemed apparent from the reports of observers who have watched its mouth rhythmically opening and closing, it does not lose access to the surface in winter. It clearly prefers the smooth, sunbaked waters of summer, however, as it seems to love to bask in the sun, like an upturned boat, slowly rolling, plunging, squirming around with what can only be taken as pleasure. By observers' reports, the creature has two pairs of side flippers, and when it swims off, tail thrashing, it leaves behind it a trail of water as impressive as the track of a small warship. When it dives from a still position, it unexplainably goes down without leaving a bubble. When it dives as it swims, it leaves on the surface a churning signature of foam.

Skelton leaned back against the wall of the caravan in a lazy and calm posture. He was wearing a dark blue tie that was monogrammed in small block letter sewn with white thread—L.N.I. (Loch Ness Investigation). Above the monogram and embroidered also in white thread was a small picture of the monster—humps rising regularly, head high, tail extending in back. Skelton gave the tie a tap with one hand. "You get this with a five-pound membership," he said.

The sea-serpent effect given by the white thread on the tie was less a cartoon-like drawing than an attempt toward a naturalistic sketch. As I studied it there, framed on Skelton's chest, the thought occurred to me that there was something inconvenient about the monster's actual appearance. In every sense except possibly the sense that involves cruelty, the creature in Loch Ness is indeed a monster. An average taken from many films and sightings gives its mature length at about forty feet. Its general appearance is very unattractive, in the sense in which reptiles are repulsive to many human beings, and any number of people might find difficulty in accepting a creature that looks like the one that was slain by St. George.[6] Its neck, about six feet long, column-like, powerfully muscled, is the neck of a serpent. Its head, scarcely broader than the neck, is a serpent's head, with uncompromising, lens-shaped eyes. Sometimes as it swims it holds its head and neck erect. The creature's mouth is at least a foot wide. Its body rises and falls with the waves. Its skin glistens when wet and appears coarse, spotted, gray, and elephant-like when exposed to the air long enough to become dry. The tail, long and column-like, stretches back to something of a point. It seemed to me, sitting there at Headquarters, that the classical, mythical, dragon likeness of this living thing—the modified dinosaur, the fantastically exaggerated newt—was an obstacle to the work of the investigation bureau. The bureau has no real interest in what the monster resembles or calls to mind but a great deal in what it actually is. Their goal is a final and positive identification of the genus.

[6]**St. George:** Christian saint who supposedly killed a large dragon.

"What we need is a good, lengthy, basking sighting," Skelton said. "We've had one long surfacing—twenty-five minutes. I saw it. Opposite Urquhart Castle. We only had a twelve-inch lens then, at four and a half miles. We have thirty-six-inch lenses now. We need a long, clear, close-up—in color."

My children had watched, some months earlier, the killing of a small snake on a lawn in Maryland. About eighteen inches long, it came out from a basement-window well, through a covering screen of redwood, and was noticed with shouts and shrieks by the children and a young retriever that barked at the snake and leaped about it in a circle. We were the weekend guests of another family, and eight children in all crowded around the snake, which had been gliding slowly across the lawn during the moments after it had been seen, but had now stopped and was turning its head from side to side in apparent indecision. Our host hurried into his garage and came running back to the lawn with a long shovel. Before he killed the snake, his wife urged him not to. She said the snake could not possibly be poisonous. He said, "How do you know?" The children, mine and theirs, looked back and forth from him to her. The dog began to bark more rapidly and at a higher pitch.

"It has none of the markings. There is nothing triangular about its head," she told him.

"That may very well be," he said. "But you can't be sure."

"It is *not* poisonous. Leave it alone. Look at all these children."

"I can't help that."

"It is *not* poisonous."

"How do you know?"

"I know."

He hit the snake with the flat of the shovel, and it twisted. He hit it again. It kept moving. He hit it a third time, and it stopped. Its underside, whitish green, turned up. The children moved in for a closer look.

Discussion: The ending is not about the Loch Ness Monster, but about the killing of a snake in Maryland. What is the purpose of the anecdote? Direct students towards the realization that the unknown, particularly when it involves a weird or frightening animal, troubles us.

MINI QUIZ

Write on the chalkboard or overhead projector the following questions and call on students to fill in the blanks. Discuss the answers with the class.

1. The A-82 highway runs between _____ and _____.
2. The one sighting of the monster that occurred the day McPhee visited came from a woman who owned an _____.
3. The crew of observers starts looking for the monster at _____.
4. The only clear view Clem Lister Skelton had of the monster's head and neck was during a _____.
5. The footprint found in the 1930s was not of the monster but of a _____.

Answers to Mini Quiz

1. Glasgow, Inverness
2. inn
3. 4 a.m.
4. snowstorm
5. hippopotamus

ANSWERS TO UNDERSTAND THE SELECTION

1. like covered wagons circled to guard against attack
2. Cape Canaveral and Cocoa Beach.
3. a sixth-century report, when the monster supposedly "killed a man with a single bite"
4. He wants to convey the impression of his being an actual observer with a camera recording everything he sees.
5. to make the essay more interesting, and believable, and give the work of the Loch Ness Expedition more validity
6. The children's lackadaisical attitude is not unlike the mood of methodical curiosity of the "members" of the Loch Ness Phenomena Investigation Bureau.
7. The Expedition Headquarters area reminds McPhee of "a country carnival on a two-night stand." The bear show is described because of the manner in which the barker tried to get people interested in seeing the show. Pay up (meaning get interested) or get out is the message at both Loch Ness and New Jersey.
8. Answers will vary. Sample answer: Send in teams of divers to look for the monster.
9. He writes in a neutral tone.
10. Answers will vary. Sample answer: There have been many sightings, and McPhee shows that the people hunting the monster are not crazy but sincere and dedicated.

Respond to Literature: Lake monster sightings also have been reported in North America: in Lake Champlain between Vermont and New York and in Lake Mephremagog between Vermont and Quebec province in Canada. This could corroborate the existence of lake monsters, or simply be the result of the power of suggestion.

T198

UNDERSTAND THE SELECTION

Recall

1. Describe the cluster of trailers.

2. What two places does Expedition Headquarters remind McPhee of?

3. What is the only report of the monster's hurting people?

Infer

4. Why do you think McPhee writes in first-person point of view?

5. Why does McPhee include so many details in his story?

6. Why do you think McPhee describes what his children did when they looked at the Expedition exhibits?

7. Explain the significance of the story about the New Jersey carnival show.

Apply

8. Standing all day next to a camera seems an inefficient way to "track" the monster. Do you have any better ideas?

9. Do you think John McPhee believes the Loch Ness Monster exists? Explain.

10. Do you believe the Loch Ness Monster exists? Give some reasons.

Respond to Literature

Why do some people believe creatures like Nessie and Bigfoot exist?

WRITE ABOUT THE SELECTION

John McPhee is an expert nonfiction writer. No one can expect you to write like him; however, you can learn from the way he writes, particularly his use of exposition.

In the selection opening, you were asked to explain about something you enjoyed or are good at. Look again at what you wrote. Do you have any ideas for improving it?

Prewriting: Think of a reason or purpose for telling about your hobby or talent. McPhee always has a purpose for his writing. What is the purpose of yours? Will you entertain, inform, persuade? Write that purpose at the top of your paper. Then freewrite for five minutes on your topic.

Writing: Keeping the purpose in mind, use any parts of what you have written already to write a new explanation. Add new details, or focus in on one or two important features about the building.

Revising: Look at a single descriptive paragraph in McPhee's story. Then read your paragraph. Can you borrow any of McPhee's techniques to improve your writing? Make sure you vary sentence structures. Too many sentences constructed in the same way can bore readers.

Proofreading: Reread your description and check that you have used initial capital letters for all proper nouns; the name of your school, football team, school newspaper, and so forth. Check the spelling of each proper noun you include.

ANSWERS TO WRITE ABOUT THE SELECTION

Prewriting: Encourage students to think of a specific feeling they have when they see the school building. How can their descriptions relay this feeling?

Writing: As students work individually, circulate and ask to see their first draft (from the selection opening). Ask how they are improving on it.

Revising: Work cooperatively as a class to review a paragraph in McPhee's story. The annotations point out two particularly well-done descriptive paragraphs.

Proofreading: Review basic capitalization rules with the class. Ask for examples from students' descriptions to illustrate the rules.

LDP Activity: (Cooperative Learning Structures-Brainstorming) How many different names for money can you think of? Find the name of Peru's, Britain's, Japan's, Italy's, France's and Switzerland's money.

THINK ABOUT EXPOSITION

This selection uses more description and exposition than any other selection you've read so far. The purpose of exposition is to explain something. While it can be used by itself, it is often combined with other types of composition. McPhee combines exposition and description but other writers blend persuasion or narration with exposition.

1. How does the story begin? What feeling do you have after reading the first paragraph?

2. Look at the third paragraph about the atmosphere of the headquarters. How does McPhee describe it? What does he explain with his description?

3. Why do you think McPhee provides names of books about the monster in the next paragraph?

4. Why is it important for McPhee to try to report about the "adventurers'" jobs?

5. What is John McPhee explaining to his readers?

DEVELOP YOUR VOCABULARY

People in Britain sometimes use different words for things than people in the United States. For example, the *hood* of a car is called a *bonnet* in Britain and what Americans call the *trunk* is the *boot* to the British. Some words commonly used in Britain are not used in the United States. *Fortnight,* for example, means two weeks. People in the United States do not usually use this word.

You can check for alternative or new meanings of words in the dictionary. If a word is used mainly in Britain rather than the U.S., the note [Chiefly Brit.] will come before the definition. Knowing about the background of a new word can help you understand a selection.

Use a dictionary to help you find definitions people in Britain might have for these words. Then use the words in sentences.

1. caravan
2. chips
3. crisp
4. boot
5. nappy
6. hoover
7. goods
8. lorry
9. petrol
10. holiday

The Unknown   199

After completing this selection, students will be able to

- understand the nuances of persuasion
- make a convincing argument
- evaluate reports of supernatural creatures
- write a persuasive text
- understand why opinions need supporting facts
- recognize the foreign roots of words.

More About Persuasion: Did John McPhee's story convince students that the Loch Ness Monster exists? If it did, that was not really the author's intention: He did not set out to **persuade** the reader but rather, simply, to inform. A **persuasive** story, on the other hand, uses exposition as evidence to convince readers to accept a stated point of view: its purpose *is* intentional.

Cooperative/Collaborative Learning Activity: Divide the class into groups of four or five. Ask each group to think of something—a TV program, the dentist's office, a particular neighborhood—that nearly everyone **does not** like. Then ask them to build a case **for** it. Suggest that they turn resistance to their advantage by mounting a persuasive presentation of facts that are favorable. After each group presents its case to the class, take a poll to find out who was the most persuasive, and why. You may also, at this time, ask volunteers to present their individual arguments on food, which were developed in the Skill Builder activity.

LEARN ABOUT
Persuasion

Is it possible that monsters, ghosts, and spirits really exist? In this selection, the author tells us about "poltergeists," or ghosts that create noisy disturbances. He did not believe in ghosts until he did some investigative work of his own. Now, he is a believer. He has been persuaded that poltergeists are real. He says he has seen what they can do.

"On the Path of the Poltergeist" was written to persuade you, too. **Persuasion** is writing or speech that attempts to convince the reader or listener to adopt an opinion or course of action. The author tries to establish the truth of a proposition by presenting facts, testimony of reliable witnesses, and other evidence. He also uses other types of composition such as exposition, description, and narration. He wants to convince you to believe ghosts might exist.

As you read the next selection, ask yourself these questions:

1. How does the author try to persuade us that poltergeists exist?
2. Are the author's points convincing?

SKILL BUILDER

Try to persuade a friend to eat a certain kind of food he or she does not like. Write one paragraph arguing your case.

THE PATH OF THE POLTERGEIST

by Walter Hubbell

It's a strange world, this one we live in. I don't believe in ghosts. That is, I didn't believe in ghosts before I investigated the mystery of Esther Cox. Now the only question is what to call them— ghosts, spirits, poltergeists, or what?

My name is Walter Hubbell. By vocation, I'm an actor. By avocation, I'm an investigator of the "supernatural." During the past few years, I've investigated many people who claimed they could talk to the spirits of the dead. They were all fakes, and I exposed them. As an actor, I know all the tricks that we use on the stage. I also know most of the tricks that magicians use to fool the public. I am, beyond doubt, able to judge whether or not deception was used in the case of Esther Cox. And it was not.

Truth is often stranger than fiction. What I have written here is truth—not fiction—and it is *very strange.*

I was acting in Canada when I first heard of Esther Cox. She was 19 years old at the time. She and her sister Jennie, age 22, lived in the home of an older married sister, Olive Teed. Daniel Teed, Olive's husband, was a foreman in a shoe factory. The Teeds had two small boys. Before the trouble started, all lived together in a big old house in the town of Amherst.

Then things started to happen. One night Esther thought she heard a mouse somewhere in her bed. She awakened her sister

---

poltergeist (POHL tur gyst) a noisy ghost
vocation (voh KAY shun) profession; career
avocation (av uh KAY shun) hobby
deception (dih SEP shun) trickery; action intended to fool another person

The Unknown   201

Sidelights: Unlike most of the authors in this unit, Walter Hubbell is not a professional writer; he notes he is an actor "by vocation," and "by avocation an investigator of the 'supernatural.'" His style is straightforward, with few literary embellishments. Such a style can often be a real advantage: Candiness indicates the writer is sincere, and sincerity goes a long way in winning people to your point of view.

Motivation for Reading: Ask students, "How do you feel when you walk into a deserted old house? Even if you do not believe in ghosts or other spirits, do you not feel like an intruder? Do you wonder, Will something bad happen because I do not belong here?

More About the Thematic Idea: Have students recall the poem, "hist, whist," in which supernatural beings were treated lightheartedly. "Is that," you might ask, "what most people think of spirits from the unknown? Or, do they shudder just a little?"

Purpose-Setting Question: Has the writer persuaded you that poltergeists exist?

Critical Thinking: The first paragraph in the story hints at the thesis, or argument, Hubbell wants to "prove." The second paragraph states the thesis directly: Deception was not used in the case of Esther Cox; her poltergeists are real.

Discussion: Ask students what they think about the setting of the story Hubbell is about to tell. Could the circumstances of so many closely related people living in the same house influence events at the house?

Vocabulary: Preteach the vocabulary words. See the Comprehension Workbook in the TRB.

More About Vocabulary: Almost all the new vocabulary words end in suffixes, and four of them share the same suffix: -tion. Write on the chalkboard or overhead projector the new words. Point out the suffixes and their meanings. Have students identify the root of each word and determine its meaning.

Jennie, who slept in the same room. They listened in silence, and soon went back to sleep. But the next night, both sisters heard the noise again, louder than ever. "It's in that box, under my bed," declared Esther. Together the two sisters pulled the green cardboard box out from under the bed. It jumped, and both girls screamed. Jennie slowly took hold of the box and placed it in the middle of the room. It jumped again, rising a foot in the air and falling back on its side. The girls' screams brought Daniel Teed hurrying into the room. He listened to their story. "You're both crazy," he announced, shaking his head as he kicked the box back under the bed. "Now go to sleep and don't disturb me again!"

This was just the beginning. A few nights later, another scream echoed through the house. It was Esther: "What's happening to me? I'm swelling up! I'm going to burst!" This time the whole family ran to the bedroom, and there was Esther, confused and worried, her whole body swollen beyond belief. What had happened? What could they do? Daniel Teed was about to call a doctor, when, quite suddenly, came a loud rapping noise, as if someone were pounding with a heavy hammer on the floor under Esther's bed. The swelling started to go down. The rapping continued, and Esther looked more comfortable. Soon she fell into a tired, troubled sleep.

The next morning Daniel Teed hurried to the family doctor. Dr. Thomas W. Carritte listened patiently, but he didn't believe a word. "I'll come this evening, and I'll stay through the night if I have to," he told Daniel. "But I guarantee you, none of this nonsense is going to happen while *I'm* in the house."

The doctor couldn't have been more wrong. After supper that evening, as he sat in Esther's room, he watched in wonder as an unseen hand seemed to slide the pillow out from under her head. A sheet and a light blanket were pulled from her bed. She began to swell up. Now the doctor had a job to do—but it was not he who cured Esther. It was, again, the loud rapping noises.

Dr. Carritte was as puzzled as everyone else. He knew the family, and he felt sure that no one was trying to fool him. As the rapping went on, he walked outside the house to see if he could discover what caused the noise. From outside the rapping sounded louder, like someone pounding on the roof. But there was no one—on the roof, in the yard, or anywhere.

Not long after, my acting job in Canada having ended, I arrived at the troubled house myself. At the time, I did not believe in ghosts, poltergeists, or spirits of any kind. I did believe that everything that happens has an explanation. From what I'd heard about Esther Cox, it didn't seem likely that she was playing tricks on people. But still, there had to be an explanation. Fortunately, I was able to rent a room from the Teeds, to be nearer the mystery I had come to investigate.

Esther Cox was a short, stout girl who could only be described as plain (her sister Jennie was the pretty one). Though far from dumb, she was not overly intelligent. She certainly didn't understand what was going on. Neither, I was soon persuaded, could she have planned it.

After I'd rented the room, I hadn't been in the house five minutes when my umbrella suddenly seemed to come to life. It flew across the living room. Soon after, Esther appeared in the kitchen doorway, carrying a plate. From behind her, something came flashing through the air—a large knife. It narrowly missed me. I rushed into the kitchen to see who had thrown it. That was my first introduction to ghosts. There was no one there.

"It looks like they don't like you," said Esther.

By "they," it turned out, Esther meant two poltergeists (or *ghosts*, as she called them). One she called "Maggie," the other "Bob." She claimed sometimes that she could see them. Once, as Olive Teed and I looked on in amazement, Esther stared at the thin air in the middle of the living room and told us that Maggie was standing there. Even more strange, the girl swore that Maggie was wearing a pair of black and white socks that belonged to Esther. Feeling a little foolish, I shouted, "Now Maggie, take off Esther's socks—and be quick about it!" A minute later, a pair of black and white socks appeared from out of nowhere. They dropped from the air in front of us to the floor.

After that I stopped looking for explanations. The only explanation was . . . the supernatural.

Whoever—or whatever—"Maggie" and "Bob" were, they seemed to be always in action. With my own eyes, I saw a heavy ashtray leave its place on a table and come whizzing at me, crashing into the wall as I ducked. Furniture constantly slid around the floors. As I entered the dining room one time, every chair fell over with a crash. Another time, needing a light for my pipe, I remarked, "Bob, give me a few matches, if you please." Immediately, a lighted match fell out of the air.

But the poltergeists were not always so helpful. As the weeks passed, Esther's spells continued, and even grew worse. Sometimes she would lie on her bed as if dead, her body swelling up like a balloon, and then collapsing, over and over. Also, the poltergeists were ruining the furniture and damaging the walls. When they started lighting small fires, the Teeds were asked to move. The owner of the house had risked enough. The Teeds were good people, but they would have to go.

As an experiment, the Teeds decided to see what would happen if only Esther left. She was sent to live with a family named Van Amburgh on a farm in the country. And here the affair came to an end with the biggest mystery of all. With Esther out of the house, everything returned to normal. The rappings, the flying objects, the sliding furniture, the fires—all stopped at once.

And perhaps even more strangely, Esther's life in her new home was completely untroubled. Like all poltergeists, "Maggie" and "Bob" had departed as mysteriously as they had come.

It must be stated that the Teeds made no attempt to keep the strange events secret. Dr. Carritte and others were constantly in and out of the house. I have a statement signed by 16 persons who witnessed at least some of the happenings I've described. I have a letter from Olive Teed declaring that *all* I've written here is true. And Dr. Carritte writes:

"I take pen in hand to say that what Mr. Walter Hubbell has written about the mysterious Esther Cox is entirely correct. The young lady was a patient of mine both previous to and during those wonderful demonstrations. I tried various experiments, but with no satisfactory results. Honestly doubtful persons were on all occasions soon convinced that there was no fraud or deception in the case. Were I to publish the case in medical journals, as you suggest, I doubt it would be believed by doctors generally. I am certain I could not have believed such miracles had I not witnessed them."

---

wonderful (WUN dur ful) curious; strange
demonstration (dem un STRAY shun) any happening that can be observed

The Unknown   205

Literary Focus: The penultimate paragraph tries to establish solid credibility for what Hubbell has witnessed with the testimony of others, much as a courtroom lawyer might do.

Literary Focus: The last paragraph relies on the respect given medical doctors to establish credibility further. The letter is effective, for it sums up Hubbell's basic argument and restates his thesis: Poltergeists exist.

MINI QUIZ

Write on the chalkboard or overhead projector the following questions and call on students to fill in the blanks. Discuss the answers with the class.

1. Walter Hubbell's profession is _____.

2. The first time Esther Cox heard a noise under her bed she thought it was a _____.

3. When Hubbell went to investigate the strange events, he rented a room from the _____.

4. Esther called the poltergeists _____ and _____.

5. The strange events in the house stopped when _____ left.

Answers to Mini Quiz

1. acting
2. mouse
3. Teeds
4. Maggie and Bob
5. Esther

ANSWERS TO UNDERSTAND THE SELECTION

1. Esther thought that she heard a noise in a box under her bed; the next night, she and her sister Jennie heard the noise again, pulled a box out from under the bed, and watched as the box jumped.

2. Esther had swollen up terribly the night before and then fallen into a deep sleep. She seemed sick and the Teeds logically thought a doctor was needed.

3. The sock incident: Hubbell tells the poltergeist "Maggie" to take off Esther's socks, and they appear "out of nowhere."

4. As an actor, he knows how people can fake supernatural events; he knows what is real and what is not; he knows the tricks of stage magicians. These theatrical insights add credibility to his views.

5. The doctor's professional status lends more credibility to the claims that poltergeists exist.

6. "Bob" provides a match for Hubbell when he wants to light his pipe.

7. The poltergeists were active only when Esther was present in the Teeds' house. Students might wish to consider the question, What would have happened had Esther moved back into the house?

8. Answers will vary. Sample answer: Esther Cox should have moved back into the Amherst house, if only briefly, just to see what might have happened.

9. Facts. Students might conclude, however, that Hubbell's opinions are usually backed up by facts, which make the opinions seem particularly strong.

10. Answers will vary. Sample answer: Esther's swelling could

---

UNDERSTAND THE SELECTION

Recall

1. How did poltergeists first appear?

2. Why is Dr. Carritte called to the house?

3. What incident convinces Hubbell supernatural forces must be at work?

Infer

4. Why is it important that we know Hubbell's profession?

5. What effect does the doctor's presence in the story have?

6. Give an example of the poltergeists' being helpful.

7. Explain the significance of Esther's departure from the house to live in the country.

Apply

8. Would you have conducted the poltergeist investigation any differently?

9. Hubbell gives both opinions and facts. Which are more convincing?

10. Can you think of a rational, natural explanation for one of the incidents involving a poltergeist? Explain your answer.

Respond to Literature

Have you ever had any experiences involving supernatural forces? What happened? Where and when?

206

WRITE ABOUT THE SELECTION

Have you ever tried something you did not want to do at first, and ended up really liking it? Did you then try to convince others they should try it because they, too, might like it?

You were persuaded by that experience to change your mind. You now want to try to persuade others by relating your experience in writing.

Prewriting: You need a topic. Brainstorm for a few minutes to come up with some ideas. You could write about an experience involving food, music, a sport—anything. Once you have chosen a topic, make notes about what happened.

Writing: Refer to your notes when writing your story. Keep in mind your purpose, which is to persuade the reader to try what you are describing or to accept an opinion that you hold. Facts are needed to support your opinion that your experience is worthwhile.

Revising: Use specific language in your description. If a new kind of music sounded nice to you, for example, tell why. Did it have a driving beat? Which instruments were particularly good? Tell your reactions, but try to combine them with facts.

Proofreading: Reread your paper to check for errors in verb forms, particularly irregular verbs. Check also that you use the correct tense throughout the story. Use a dictionary to check any tense forms you are not sure of.

Unit 2

---

have been caused by an allergic reaction to food.

Respond to Literature: Begin a general discussion of personal experiences that students found mysterious. Because the mere mention of "poltergeists" or "supernatural forces" might discourage students, you could start off with an analysis by the class of a current movie with supernatural undertones.

ANSWERS TO WRITE ABOUT THE SELECTION

Prewriting: Students could brainstorm cooperatively in groups. Then, discussion might help them focus their ideas.

Writing: As you circulate among students, stress the need for facts to support opinion. Suggest that they avoid cliches, such as "Try it, you'll like it." The reader should be told *why* he or she will like it.

Revising: Have students exchange papers. Partners can provide feedback on whether the text is convic-

THINK ABOUT PERSUASION

The purpose of Hubbell's story is to persuade us that supernatural forces might exist. The author uses a large amount of exposition and description of events, to provide evidence supporting his view.

In the previous selection, John McPhee was like a detective collecting facts. In this selection, Hubbell is like a detective and prosecutor together. He gathers facts and from them argues his case.

1. Is the first paragraph of the story fact or opinion?

2. Is the second paragraph fact or opinion?

3. The story "shifts gears" after the third paragraph. What happens?

4. What is the effect of the doctor's statement?

5. Read the first paragraph of the story again. Do you think a reader is more likely to accept Hubbell's statements after reading the whole story?

DEVELOP YOUR VOCABULARY

Many words that we use in English are actually "borrowed" from foreign languages. "Poltergeist" is a good example. It comes from these German words:

poltern: to make noise, rumble
geist: ghost

You can find information on the foreign roots of words in the dictionary. The information is given in brackets [ ] following the part-of-speech designation.

Find the foreign word in the following sentences. Use a dictionary to explain its roots.

1. The tall buildings shoot into the air like walls of a canyon.

2. My baby brother goes to kindergarten.

3. He likes buffet dinners because he can take exactly what he wants.

4. No anchovies on my pizza, please.

5. Old Faithful is a famous geyser out west.

6. Is her attitude a bit naive for her age?

The Unknown

ANSWERS TO THINK ABOUT PERSUASION

1. Opinion.
2. Both. Students should see that Hubbell now starts to present factual background to back up his opinions. Credibility is starting to be built.
3. Hubbell begins to describe specific incidents showing the presence of the poltergeists.
4. It gives credibility, both to the events Hubbell has described and to Hubbell himself.
5. Yes. Facts and quoted testimony (from an "expert" such as the doctor) support Hubbell.

ANSWERS TO DEVELOP YOUR VOCABULARY

1. canyon: from the Spanish *canon*; a pipe, tube, or deep gorge.
2. kindergarten: from the German *kinder* and *garten*; a children's garden.
3. buffet: from the French *buffet*; a sideboard or bench.
4. pizza: from the Italian *pizza*, which means the same in English.
5. geyser: from the Icelandic *Geysir*; the name of a specific hot spring in Iceland.
6. naive: from the French *naif*; simple, natural, lacking skill or training.

ing. Remind students, however, that they are free to accept or reject suggestions. As writers, decision making is their privilege!

Proofreading: Ask students to check that all verbs are in the correct form and tense.

Note: The Teacher's Resource Book contains worksheets to accompany both writing assignments.

Motivation 1: Explain to students that this is their chance to imagine what it would be like to enter the supernatural world. A recording of the theme music for "The Twilight Zone" would help set the mood.

Prewriting: How many different kinds of supernatural beings can students think of? As a class, make a list on the board. Note any special characteristics that might affect a dialogue with them; for example, poltergeists usually do not talk.

Writing: Circulate among students as they work individually. Comment on questions that seem particularly perceptive and on answers that seem particularly imaginative.

Revising: Have students choose a partner to read their dialogue to them. If the partner stumbles or hesitates between speakers, it is an indication that the dialogue does not flow smoothly. Students should note these points.

Proofreading: Have the same partner read the dialogue for correct punctuation. Ask that readers pay close attention to all punctuation marks and that they do exactly what the marks indicate. The writer should listen for the appropriateness of the punctuation.

Motivation 2: Relate the four elements of a short story to points on a compass. Draw a horizontal and vertical axis, and at each of the four points write one of the following: "plot," "characters," "setting," and "theme." Discuss how all four work together.

LITERATURE-BASED WRITING

1. One summer day you are sitting in a park or in your backyard, and a strange-looking creature walks up to you.

"Hello," it says.

You realize you are facing a supernatural or extraterrestrial being. You, for some unexplained reason, have been chosen to have the first human contact with this creature.

Write a dialogue of your encounter with this strange-looking creature. What will you learn about the unknown?

Prewriting: Decide first what the creature will be: a supernatural being such as a ghost, or an extraterrestrial being such as "E.T." For five minutes freewrite questions you would like to ask the creature. Then take another five minutes to freewrite possible answers.

Writing: Put your questions in a logical order, and fill in the answers. Use this form for writing:

Me:

Creature:

Revising: The best dialogues are those that flow logically from one question-and-answer to the next. This may be hard when you are talking with a strange being but consider revising any sections that seem to "jump around" too much. Be sure you have the creature explain elements of the unknown with sharp detail.

Proofreading: Although you have written a dialogue, you still need to punctuate correctly. Carefully use special punctuation marks, such as exclamations, for emphasis.

208

2. You have learned in this unit that all short stories have four basic elements: plot, characters, setting, and theme. It helps in analyzing stories if you look very closely at these elements.

Choose one selection you particularly liked. Think why, and then analyze how plot, characters, setting, and theme add to the story.

Prewriting: Review any work you did for the "Think About . . . " sections that discuss the elements. How does the author of the story you have chosen develop a particular element? On the other hand, maybe he or she does not develop another element, and that interests you. Write the elements in the middle of a piece of paper, and make a cluster of your ideas around it.

Writing: Use the cluster to write your analysis. Make sure you have a clear thesis statement, such as "Although all elements are present, plot is not important in John McPhee's nonfiction narrative 'The Loch Ness Monster.'" Develop your analysis from there.

Revising: An analysis is similar to persuasion. You want to convince the reader that what you say is correct. Readers are more convinced by facts than opinions. Can you add more facts, or evidence, from the story to support your opinions?

Proofreading: Reread your analysis carefully. Do you need new paragraphs when you discuss each element?

Unit 2

Prewriting: Divide the class into groups, and have each group review one of the "Think About" sections. Then, ask each group to present a report to the whole class, giving examples.

Writing: Circulate among students as they work individually. Offer help to students having difficulty; use their clusters to prompt ideas.

Revising: Have students make a quick outline of the major points in their analysis. Under each point they must list the facts supporting that point. Any point that does not include at least one fact should be revised.

Proofreading: Point out that having a separate paragraph for each element discussed is a logical way to organize the analysis. If students have focused on just one element, suggest that they break the text according to major points.

BUILDING LANGUAGE SKILLS

Vocabulary

Idioms are groups of words that have a special meaning all their own. You cannot "add up" the meanings of the individual words. You must simply know the "new" meaning of the entire group. An example is "over one's head." The literal meaning is that something is positioned right over your head.

However, look at the phrase's meaning in this sentence: *Trigonometry is simply over my head.* Here, "over my head" means "too difficult."

Each sentence below contains a figurative expression. Find it, and explain its meaning.

1. Please, put your best foot forward this time.

2. The forty-year-old man was getting gray above the ears.

3. The boy lit up when the teacher asked the question about computers.

4. I got a load of their shoulder holsters when they leaned over.

5. We rested on the stoop for awhile, getting our nerves back in shape.

6. "This particular problem," he said, "is only the tip of the iceberg."

7. The red leather basketball shoes in the wind caught Sam's eye.

8. Peggy's new haircut was cuter than a bug's ear.

Usage and Mechanics

Three or more words linked in a series by the conjunctions *and* or *or* must be correctly punctuated as follows: I have ordinary abilities, looks, and thoughts. Note that a comma is used after all the words in a series except the last. One easy way to remember how many commas you need is to count the items in a series and then use one less comma. However, if there is a conjunction between every word in the series, you need no commas.

Correct the punctuation errors in the following sentences:

1. They were sitting kneeling or squatting in an easy way.

2. We have electricity washing machines vacuum cleaners modern bathrooms and modern medicine.

3. But there are no radios televisions telephones or cars.

4. They have dances card parties weddings birthdays block parties swimming and sports of all kinds.

5. Verna is a planet of air sun land and sea, like Earth.

6. Now the only question is what to call them—ghosts spirits poltergeists or what?

7. John McPhee used photographs and testimony and legends as support for Nessie's existence.

More About Usage and Mechanics: Some usage experts argue that a comma is unnecessary after the penultimate item in a series. Newspapers often use this style. Not inserting a comma could cause confusion, however, if the last two items in a series could be considered in apposition to the first item:

Example: With me on the trip were my sisters, Judy and Gaye. Are Judy and Gaye my sisters, or are they two friends who went with me in addition to my sisters? We can not tell. A comma would clear things up:

Example: With me on the trip were my sisters, Judy, and Gaye.

1. They were sitting, kneeling, or squatting in an easy way.
2. We have electricity, washing machines, vacuum cleaners, modern bathrooms, and modern medicine.
3. But there are no radios, televisions, telephones, or cars.
4. They have dances, card parties, weddings, birthdays, harvest parties, swimming, and sports of all kinds.
5. Verna is a planet of air, sun, land, and sea, like Earth.
6. Now the only question is what to call them—ghosts, spirits, poltergeists, or what?
7. John McPhee used photographs, testimony, and legends as support for Nessie's existence.

Cooperative/Collaborative Learning Activity 2: Have students make up their own exercises, and then give them to others as a "test." Working in pairs, students look through the unit selections for five other examples of items in a series. They then write down the sentences, omitting the commas. Pairs exchange papers, and insert correct punctuation.

Vocabulary

More About Word Attack: Figurative expressions (sometimes called "idioms" because of their peculiar meanings) are a kind of language code. They often have interesting stories behind them.

Cooperative/Collaborative Learning Activity: Have students work in pairs, in groups, or as an entire class to think of as many figurative expressions as they can.

1. best foot forward: do the best you can; show off your strong points
2. getting gray above the ears: getting old because hair is turning gray
3. lit up: got excited
4. got a load: saw, noticed
5. getting our nerves back in shape: calming down
6. tip of the iceberg: a small problem that is part of a much bigger one
7. caught Sam's eye: appealed to Sam
8. cuter than a bug's ear: very becoming

Motivation: Relate an incident from your own experience to the class. As you speak, make sure you do not use slang, but do try to use at least one quotation, and do explain why the incident is memorable.

Teaching Strategy: Go through the directions with the students. Make sure that they understand all the steps. As homework, assign steps 2 and 3. In class have them work with a partner in organizing their paraphrase (step 4). Then suggest a practice run with their partner, followed by an evaluation to ensure that steps 5, 6, and 7 were covered. Students are then ready for the class presentations.

Evaluation Criteria: Have students first do a self-evaluation, using the seven steps and the final suggestion (on telling the title of the selection) as checkpoints. They can then go over the self-evaluation with their partners. Partners should be encouraged to provide additional feedback.

SPEAKING AND LISTENING

It is human nature to want to share experiences with others. If you see a movie, you may want to talk about a scene that you particularly liked. If you hear a new song, you often want to tap the melody out for friends so they can get a feel for it, too. For this activity, you will be telling an incident you remember from a selection in this unit.

Before you share an incident from one of the selections in this unit, read over the following directions. They will help make your assignment clear.

1. You will have about two minutes to share your choice with the class. Remember to focus on one incident. Also, try to get to the point and keep to it.

2. In this assignment, the selection itself is not as important as the incident that you choose. Therefore, instead of thinking about a certain story, think about a single incident. It can be frightening, exciting, suspenseful, or just your favorite.

3. Go back to the selection, skim through it, find the incident, and reread it.

4. Now, paraphrase the incident in your mind. Think about how you would relate this incident to a friend. If necessary, take a few notes to help you focus on what you will say.

5. It is easy to get personally involved when you are talking about an incident that was your favorite. It is also easy to get caught using slang expressions. For this assignment, try to use vocabulary and expressions that are suitable for a literary discussion.

6. Do not be afraid to quote. Perhaps there was a particular way a character said something that added to the sheer excitement of this incident. Let the class in on it by sharing the exact words.

7. Be sure to tell why the incident was memorable to you. Think about the feelings you had after you read it, and express them to your audience.

By following the hints given above, you will find it easy to relate your favorite incident from this unit to your classmates. One last suggestion: Before you begin to talk about the incident, tell the title of the selection it came from; others might be interested in reading the entire story.

CRITICAL THINKING

This unit has contained selections about the unknown. It is a tricky subject to write about. The very word "unknown" presents a challenge. How can anyone write something about which he or she does not know much?

The writers of the nonfiction selections in this unit solved the problem through investigation. They went to the places where monsters or ghosts had supposedly been seen or felt, and gathered facts.

In the case of "On the Path of the Poltergeist," the writer then used the facts to back up an opinion. Walter Hubbell said he believes that poltergeists and other such supernatural beings really do exist. If there had been no facts to back up his opinion, Hubbell would have looked very funny. However, he had fact after fact, supported by a number of people and their testimonies, to give his opinion "credibility." It was far easier to accept his ideas on poltergeists after the facts had been presented.

When you write, support your opinions with facts. They are the things that convince readers. Remember Mr. Gradgrind's comment in Charles Dickens's *Hard Times*: "Now, what I want is, Facts . . . Facts alone are wanted in life."

Choose either "On the Path of the Poltergeist" or "The Loch Ness Monster." List ten facts that the author used to tell his story.

EFFECTIVE STUDYING

Good study habits can help you not only when you are studying literature, but also when you are working in any subject.

It helps to choose a study setting, one place you go regularly for studying. If you associate that place just with studying, it is easier to work there. You do not think that you *could* be doing something else. Ideally, the place would be quiet and away from distractions.

Along with choosing a study setting, you should develop a study schedule. When will you do your work? Consider two things here. First, when *can* you study? If you play sports, obviously you cannot study after school. You need to find another time. Second, what times of day are you at your best? Some people cannot function after 8 o'clock at night. Others are just getting going then. When you have a choice of study times, pick the time you are at peak power. Your work will go easier and faster.

A third tip is to keep an assignment book. Professional workers have appointment books just so they know what must be done by when. Their schedules are organized so time is used efficiently. You should keep an assignment book for the same reason. It will also help you turn work in on time!

Where and when do you study? Describe your special space, and develop your study schedule.

A Career to Consider

This unit focuses on the unknown, and how we can learn more about it. The role of investigator is key to many of the stories. A writer is an investigator, and the best examples are reporters at newspapers. Becoming an investigative reporter requires many years of work and a desire to find information and make it both accessible and intelligible. Newspapers employ many kinds of reporters, many of whom start out as "stringers" or "freelancers"; that is they accept specific assignments from an editor rather than work full-time. Writing for a high school newspaper provides a taste of a reporter's work.

SUGGESTIONS FOR EFFECTIVE STUDYING

Discuss with students where and when they study, and if they keep an assignment book. Show them an appointment book or class outline schedule you might have.

MINI QUIZ

1. Which is likely to be the best study place?
   a. in front of the television
   b. the kitchen table
   c. a desk in your bedroom
2. What two things determine when you should study?
   a.
   b.
3. Name two advantages of keeping an assignment book.
   a.
   b.

Answers to Mini Quiz

1. c.
2. a. when it is possible for you to study
   b. when you are at your "peak"
3. a. you are organized
   b. you remember to turn assignments in on time

ANSWERS TO CRITICAL THINKING

The question in this section is, How does an author write about something he or she does not know much about, particularly when the subject is as challenging as the "unknown"?

The answer is that an author first investigates, gathers facts, and then uses the facts to back up opinions. The good nonfiction writer is a scientist. He or she starts with a hypothesis and then investigates to see whether the hypothesis is correct. The hypothesis can be based on anecdotal evidence or on vague personal feelings, but if the writer stops there and does not investigate any further, the narrative will be unconvincing. Everybody has an opinion, but the skilled investigator has an informed opinion. Writers must, too. They must have information to support their points.

UNIT 3: Suspense

A Continuing Unit Project: Writing Newspaper Articles

Several of the stories in this unit involve the committing of a crime. Nearly all of the selections involve newsworthy events. Some of the stories would make front page headlines; others might show up on features pages, or in the obituary column.

Have students write a newspaper story about each selection they read. Let students decide what the focus of each story will be. Students can create additional details when they need to, but this information must always be in keeping with the selection.

Point out to students that a news story must always answer five basic questions: What happened? When did it happen? Where did it happen? Why did it happen? Who was involved? Ideally, these questions should be answered briefly within the first paragraph or two; the rest of the story should add supporting details.

A feature article may have a freer format, since features do not always focus on a specific event. Sometimes, for example, a feature will explore a certain subject, such as a science article about whales. Or a feature may consist of an interview with a famous person. A good feature will contain background information about the topic as well as any current developments in the field.

Another type of newspaper story that students might enjoy writing is the editorial or editorial column. In this type of article, the writer is free to express an opinion about an event or situation. Remind students that opinions should always be presented logically and supported by facts.

Here are some general questions to help students get started as they write their newspaper articles:

What is the major event described in the selection?
What are the circumstances surrounding this event?
Who is the most important character in the selection?
What happens to this character?

How would you sum up in one sentence what the selection is about?

If students need more specific guidance, ask questions such as these about each selection.

"The Getaway"
How might a news story portray the counterman in the restaurant as a hero?

"Sherlock Holmes and the Speckled Band"
How would a newspaper reporter write about Dr. Roylott's death?

"Trifles"
How would a newspaper story describe Mrs. Wright?

"The Rattlesnake Hunt"
How might this selection form the basis for a science feature in the newspaper?

"Earth"/"Earth"
What might a newspaper editor on another planet write about the destruction of Earth?

"The Lady, Or the Tiger?"
How would a newspaper describe the marriage of the young man to the lady behind the door? How would it describe the death of the young man when he is killed by a tiger?

"The Bat"/"The Bird of Night"
How would a science writer describe one or both of these birds?

"A Secret for Two"
How might Pierre's death be written up in a local newspaper?

Have students suggest photos, maps, or charts that might accompany their articles. When the articles are finished, create a booklet in which all the stories can be "published" for students to read on their own.

"The Getaway"
by John Savage   (page 217)

SELECTION SYNOPSIS

While driving through western Texas, the narrator stops for coffee at an isolated diner. Soon two men appear, order coffee, and ask to see a map. The men are looking for a short way across the Rio Grande to Mexico. The counterman suggests that they head for a bridge at Hackett, a bridge too new to be shown on the map they are consulting. The men start to leave, then turn and pull guns on the counterman and the narrator. They disconnect the phone and empty the till. As they drive off, one of them deflates a tire on the narrator's car with a gun.

The counterman repairs the telephone quickly and calls the police. He learns that the holdup men have robbed a supermarket in nearby Wichita Falls. He informs the police that the men are headed for Hackett. When he hangs up, the narrator observes regretfully that the criminals will be across the border before the police can overtake them. The counterman smiles a knowing smile and says that the fugitives will not escape, for there is no bridge at Hackett.

SELECTION ACTIVITY

Have students write a play to dramatize the story, "The Getaway." Students can work in small groups to create their plays, or you can work with the class as a whole by using transparencies and an overhead projector.

Begin by discussing with students how to go about changing a story into a play. Point out some of the things they must do: choose a cast of characters, divide the story into scenes, decide on the setting for each scene, establish the plot, and write a script.

First, have students make a list of the characters in the story. The obvious and essential characters are the narrator, the counterman, and the two outlaws. The story could

be dramatized effectively using just these people. Characters who are not essential but who could be added to the play include the policeman who answers the phone and the policemen who go after the outlaws. Another character who could be added to the play is a narrator who stands outside the story—perhaps as the actual narrator who is now much older and telling this story as a flashback. If this technique is used, another character might be added to the play, a person to whom the narrator is speaking. For example, the narrator might be sitting in this very same restaurant 20 years later, reminiscing as he talks to a friend. He might start out by saying, "It was just about 20 years ago that I had a most incredible experience in this very restaurant. Let me tell you how it happened."

Next, have students decide how to divide the story into scenes. Usually in a play, a new scene indicates a change in location or a change in time, or both. If the action of a story is continuous in the same location, and if the story is short, it may be necessary to have only one scene unless a narrative technique such as the one described above is used. If this is the case, then the scene would shift back and forth between the conversation going on in the present and the narrator's memory of the events that happened in the restaurant many years ago.

Once the play has been divided (or not divided) into scenes, have students decide on the setting. In this story, the entire play could be set in the restaurant. Some additional settings that might be included are the highway before the narrator pulls into the restaurant, the police station when the counterman's phone call is received, and the interior of one of the patrol cars chasing the outlaws.

Tell students that their next task is to establish the plot. Have each student write a brief description of the plot of the short story. Have several students read their summaries aloud. Correct any misconceptions students might have. Then ask students if they wish to alter or extend the plot in any way. (Since this story is so well crafted, you will probably want to encourage students to keep the plot as it is.)

Finally, have students write a script. Most of the script for this play can be taken from the dialogue used in the story. Simply assign each quotation to the proper character. Have students add dialogue where they feel it is necessary or appropriate.

Once the play is complete, type it, or have it typed, and distribute copies to each student.

Discuss ways in which scenery, costumes, and props might enhance a performance of the play.

"Sherlock Holmes and the Speckled Band"
by Arthur Conan Doyle and
Alice Delman   (page 225)

SELECTION SYNOPSIS

Sherlock Holmes and Dr. John Watson enter Holmes's Baker Street sitting room to find a frightened woman waiting for them. She says that she fears for her life, and Holmes promises to help her. The woman, whose name is Helen Stoner, tells Holmes that she and her twin sister Julia went to live in her stepfather's manor house upon the accidental death of their mother eight years before. The stepfather has little money, but the thousand pounds from the estate of his wife (Helen and Julia's mother) enabled the three to live comfortably. Helen explains that a substantial amount of the mother's estate was willed to each daughter when she marries. Helen goes on to say that a few years earlier, Julia became engaged. Then, two weeks before the wedding, Julia died mysteriously.

Through a flashback, the reader learns more details. On the night of Julia's death, Helen is awakened by a woman's scream. She also hears a low whistle and a clanging sound. She runs to the hallway, where she finds Julia about to collapse. All Julia can say before she dies is "It was the band! The speckled band."

Under Holmes's questioning, it is revealed that Julia managed to point toward her stepfather's room before dying, that Julia's room was locked and could not have been entered, and that the coroner was unable to determine the cause of death.

Helen reveals that she is now engaged. She has been obliged to move into Julia's room because of some repairs being done on the manor house. Holmes tells Helen that he must inspect Julia's room and the surrounding area and arranges to visit the manor house that afternoon, while Dr. Roylott, the stepfather, is away.

Helen has barely left the apartment when Dr. Roylott bursts in and angrily threatens Holmes for interfering in his affairs. Holmes remains unruffled during the encounter, and after a short time, Roylott leaves.

After doing some research, which reveals that Dr. Roylott would lose a great deal of income if a daughter marries, Holmes and Watson go to Stoke Moran, Dr. Roylott's manor.

Holmes, accompanied by Watson, visits Stoke Moran and inspects the murder scene. He notes especially a recently installed bellrope, which turns out to be a dummy, and nearby, a small, high vent, connecting Julia's room to her stepfather's. Holmes looks into Dr. Roylott's room, where he is interested to find a large iron safe, a saucer of milk, and a small dog leash.

Holmes tells Helen that he and Watson will stay at the nearby inn until Roylott goes to bed. When Helen hears him retire, she is to signal Holmes and Watson, leave her window unlocked, and move into her old room for the night. Holmes and Watson will spend the night in Julia's room.

Holmes and Watson await Helen's signal at the inn and then hurry back to the manor. After waiting several hours, they hear a gentle hissing sound. Holmes strikes a match and then begins lashing at the bellrope with his cane. A low, clear whistle is heard. Then, a moment later, a horrible cry is heard in the next room.

Holmes and Watson hurry to Roylott's room, where they find his lifeless body slumped in a chair. A deadly swamp adder—the speckled band—is wound tightly around his brow. Holmes puts the snake back into the safe and locks the door. They leave the room to take Helen away from the house and get the police.

Back at the Baker Street apartment, Holmes sums up the mystery for Watson. Dr. Roylott, who made a hobby of keeping animals from India, used a deadly Indian snake to kill Julia, and then intended the same fate for Helen. When Holmes attacked the snake, the snake was driven back through the ventilator and turned on its master. Thus Roylott was destroyed by his own evil design.

SELECTION ACTIVITY

Have students do research to learn about Arthur Conan Doyle and his famous Sherlock Holmes stories. Then have students present their information in written or oral reports. Some of the information students can include in their reports is summarized below.

Doyle originally studied to be a doctor, but his practice was unsuccessful. He turned to writing as a means of supplementing his income. The character of Sherlock Holmes was patterned after one of Doyle's medical school professors, a man named Dr. Bell. Bell was noted for his uncanny reasoning ability and his habit of diagnosing his patients' characters, along with their ailments.

Sherlock Holmes is one of the more famous fictional characters. The first Holmes story was *Study in Scarlet*, written in 1887. Other books followed: *The Memoirs of*

Sherlock Holmes, The Hound of the Baskervilles, The Return of Sherlock Holmes, The Valley of Fear, His Last Bow, and *The Case Book of Sherlock Holmes.*

"Trifles"
by Susan Glaspell   (page 252)

SELECTION SYNOPSIS

Lewis Hale stopped by John Wright's farm to ask if his neighbor would be interested in joining him in a party telephone. At first no one answered the door; then a voice told him to come in. Hale found Mrs. Wright sitting in a rocking chair. When Hale asked to speak to John, Mrs. Wright told him that her husband was dead, that he died of a rope around his neck while he slept. Mrs. Wright claimed that she did not know who committed the crime.

When the play opens, Hale, Mrs. Hale, the county attorney, the sheriff, and the sheriff's wife have come to the Wright farmhouse to inspect the scene of the crime. Mrs. Wright has been taken to jail, for she is the prime suspect in the murder.

As the farmhouse is inspected for clues, it becomes apparent to the two women that Mrs. Wright has had a hard and unhappy life with her husband. These feelings are augmented when the women discover a strangled pet canary in Mrs. Wright's sewing box.

As the play progresses, the two women struggle with their feelings that perhaps the murder was justified—at least, they are in sympathy with Mrs. Wright. The play ends with no hint given about the outcome of Mrs. Wright's trial.

SELECTION ACTIVITY

Have students work in small groups to present the trial of Mrs. Wright. Discuss with students who the characters in the trial would be: Mrs. Wright and her lawyer, the prosecutor for the state, and witnesses such as Mr. and Mrs. Hale and Mrs. Peters. Instead of including a jury in each trial, have members of the class who view each group's trial act as a jury.

"The Rattlesnake Hunt"
by Marjorie Kinnan Rawlings   (page 273)

SELECTION SYNOPSIS

In this true story, the writer is invited to go on a rattlesnake hunt with a young herpetologist from Florida. At first, fear is the writer's dominant emotion, but as she learns more about the snakes, she becomes more courageous. By the end of the hunt, the writer joyfully states that she has won a victory over a great fear.

SELECTION ACTIVITY

Many facts about rattlesnakes can be learned from this selection. Some misconceptions about rattlesnakes are also discussed. In this activity, students will verify facts and gain additional information about rattlesnakes.

Have students begin by listing facts about rattlesnakes found in the article. Also have them list some of the misconceptions the writer had about snakes before she went on this trip. Students should verify all of the facts stated or implied in the story by checking encyclopedias and other reference books.

Then have students make a list of additional facts that they would like to know about rattlesnakes. Some possible questions include:

1. Where else besides the Everglades do rattlesnakes live?
2. Do rattlesnakes vary in size?
3. What should a person do if bitten by a rattlesnake?
4. What is a rattlesnake's main habitat?
5. What are the rattlesnake's sources of food?

Have students make notes of the information they gather. Have them prepare their notes in legible form to be handed in and graded. Then have students use their notes to participate in a class discussion about the characteristics of rattlesnakes.

"Earth"
by John Hall Wheelock   (page 281)

"Earth"
by Oliver Herford   (page 281)

SELECTION SYNOPSIS

The subject matter of both poems is the end of the planet Earth. The poem by Wheelock implies that the earth is destroyed by human beings. In the poem by Herford, the earth burns up like a meteoroid and is seen from a distant planet as a shooting star.

Two issues very much on the minds of concerned citizens today are the threat of nuclear war and the destruction of the earth's environment. Groups concerned about both of these causes might choose to use Wheelock's poem as part of a propaganda campaign.

Have students work in small groups. Ask each group to choose one of these issues to represent. Then challenge them to use Wheelock's poem in a creative way to further their cause. For example, the poem might be printed on fliers the group could hand out. Also included on the fliers might be a commentary on the relevance of the poem and information about what concerned citizens can do. Another possibility would be to reproduce the poem on a poster. Yet a third possibility would be for a student to give an impassioned speech about the cause chosen, effectively using the poem and through well-placed quotations.

As students work on their projects, remind them of the irony expressed in this poem; the Martian decides that Earth creatures must have been intelligent in order to find a way to destroy themselves.

"The Lady, Or the Tiger?"
by Frank Stockton   (page 285)

SELECTION SYNOPSIS

This is a famous story, and one of the elements that makes it famous is that it has no ending. The story tells the tale of a semibarbaric king, who lived in olden times. When someone was accused of a crime that reached the king's attention, the accused person was thrown into an arena. There he had the choice of opening one of two doors. Behind one door was a tiger which would devour him. Behind the other door was a beautiful lady who would marry him. The king reasoned that if the person were guilty, the Law of Chance would have him open the door with the tiger. If he were innocent, he would open the door with the lady.

This king had a beautiful daughter. A young man, a commoner, fell in love with her. The king was outraged, for the young man had no right to love his daughter. The young man was to be thrown into the arena to decide his fate. The king's daughter, who loved the young man, learned the secret of which door had the tiger and which had the lady. When the young man stepped into the arena, she signaled to him which door to open. Yet she knew that she would lose him either way; for if he lived, he would marry the lady behind the door. What happened when the young man opened the door? The writer never tells. He says that he will leave it up to the reader to decide which came out of the door: the lady, or the tiger?

SELECTION ACTIVITY

Have students work in small groups to dramatize a possible ending to the story. Students can choose various ways to present their endings. One possibility would be to write a monologue about the thoughts of the princess before she goes to the arena. The decision she makes, and the reasons for it, can infer the ending of the story. Another method would be to dramatize the actual opening of the door, and the young man's reaction.

"The Bat"
by Ruth Hershberger   (page 295)

"The Bird of Night"
by Randall Jarrell   (page 297)

SELECTION SYNOPSIS

The first poem describes a bat, as told from the bat's point of view. The second poem is a third-person description of the owl.

SELECTION ACTIVITY

Have students choose one of the two animals, the bat or the owl, to research. Have students correlate their research with the poem and verify or refute any ideas about the animals that are presented. For example, they should verify facts about the bat presented in the first poem. Students who choose to research the owl should see if pictures of an owl match the description given in "The Bird of Night."

"A Secret for Two"
by Quentin Reynolds   (page 301)

SELECTION SYNOPSIS

For half of the 30 years he has delivered milk, Pierre has been helped by his faithful horse, Joseph. The two have so much rapport that they appear to share a secret. Joseph pulls the wagon from the dairy to Pierre's route without direction and stops by habit at each customer's house. Pierre cannot read or write, so customers call out any change in their regular orders when they hear his wagon. The dairy manager offers to let Pierre retire on full salary, but he declines.

One cold morning, Pierre comes to work to be told that Joseph is dead. He stumbles off down the street, tears streaming from his eyes. He is struck and killed instantly by a large truck. The ambulance doctor observes that the old man has been blind for years. With Joseph's help, Pierre has been able to keep his blindness a secret.

SELECTION ACTIVITY

Have students find out about the life and work of the author of this story, Quentin Reynolds. One fact that students might uncover is that Reynolds, who lived from 1902 to 1965, was best known as a war correspondent during World War II.

STUDENT READING LIST

Bethancourt, T. Ernesto. *Dr. Doom: Superstar.* New York: Holiday House, 1978. Paper, Bantam.

Doyle, Arthur Conan. *The Adventures of Sherlock Holmes, Book One.* adapted for young people by Catherine Edwards Adler. New York: Avon, 1981.

Yep, Lawrence. *The Mark Twain Murders.* New York: Four Winds, 1982.

Kahn, Joan, ed. *Some Things Dark and Dangerous.* New York: Harper, 1970.

Newman, Robert. *The Case of the Baker Street Irregulars.* New York: Atheneum, 1978. Paper, Bantam.

From Globe Classroom Libraries

The Teen Years
   The Talking Earth by Joan Craighead George

The theme of this unit is suspense. The selections range from crime stories to stories with surprise endings. Also included are several poems having animals or extraterrestrial beings as characters.

"The Getaway" is a crime story told from an observer's unique perspective, although the observer is not as perceptive as he thinks.
Literary skill: setting
Vocabulary: compound words
Writing: adding a postscript

One of the world's most famous fictional detectives solves a murder at an English manor in "Sherlock Holmes and the Speckled Band." The story is presented as a drama.
Literary skill: characters
Vocabulary: crime story vocabulary
Writing: short television script

"Trifles" is also a drama. Its suspense lies partly in solving a murder but mainly in understanding the motive of the murderer. It is the annotated text of the unit.
Literary skill: elements of drama
Vocabulary: precise definitions
Writing: a murder confession

"The Rattlesnake Hunt" is a nonfiction narrative by a woman who accompanies a scientist as he gathers rattlesnakes in the Florida Everglades.
Literary skill: narration
Vocabulary: formation of nouns describing scientists
Writing: explaining of process

Two poems, both entitled "Earth," raise suspense beyond human comprehension by offering extraterrestrials' explanations of what happens when life on earth ends.
Literary skill: tone
Vocabulary: using a thesaurus
Writing: news story

"The Lady, or the Tiger?" challenges readers to finish where the author leaves off—which is by no means at the end of the story.
Literary skill: irony
Vocabulary: identifying root words

Writing: developing a conclusion

Birds to which some mystery and suspense are attached are described in the poems "The Bat" and "The Bird of Night."
Literary skill: connotation and denotation
Vocabulary: shades of meaning in synonyms
Writing: first person point of view

The unit ends with "Secret for Two," a story of affection between a man and his horse. Mystery and suspense are built into their relationship.
Literary skill: plot
Vocabulary: using context clues
Writing: eulogy

Suspense

I tell you a tale tonight
    Which a seaman told to me
With eyes that gleam in the lanthorn light
    And a voice as low as the sea

—Alfred Noyes

The Whale Ship, Joseph Mallord William Turner. The Metropolitan Museum of Art, Wolfe Fund, 1896. Catharine Lorillard Wolfe Collection.

213

Fine Arts Notes

Joseph Mallord William Turner (1775–1851) painted many sea scenes. He was part of the Romantic movement that dominated European art in the late 18th, early 19th centuries. As with other Romantics, nature figures prominently in his works. His style was described by his famous contemporary John Constable as "airy visions, painted with tinted steam." Turner strived to convey emotion in his paintings. A sense of the vastness of the sea, and the suspense of man's striving against the sea, are evident in "The Whale Ship."

Teaching Strategy: When are the best time and place to tell a suspense story? Ask students to examine the Alfred Noyes poem to determine setting. As a class, discuss this setting. Why does it seem particularly suited for telling tales of suspense? What would it be like to sit on the deck of a sailing vessel at sea and have "an old salt" "spin yarns" in the darkness? Ask students when they like to tell or read suspense stories. Make a list of the settings, and determine common features.

UNIT OBJECTIVES

After completing this unit, students should be able to

- understand the basic elements of a drama: plot, characters, setting, theme, and conflict
- recognize aspects of a drama that distinguish it from a short story
- use a thesaurus to find synonyms
- use a dictionary to distinguish shades of meaning in synonyms
- recognize and understand vocabulary specific to professions or lifestyles
- anaylzye plot and write a conclusion or postscript to a story
- distinguish differences between first-person and third-person point of view presentations

Suspense. Everyone loves the excitement of not knowing what is going to happen next. You think, you feel, you imagine a dozen different possibilities. Your heart beats faster, your hands get somewhat clammy.

Suspense means waiting. In literature, a good author knows how to use that waiting period to get you more and more interested in the story. You see the setting and characters in your mind. You feel the plot and theme taking you on a roller coaster ride. A part of you seems to be with the characters as the suspense builds.

"You could almost hear the stars twinkling up in the sky," the poet Alfred Noyes said when a seaman was about to tell a story of suspense. Explore the world of suspense in this unit.

Crimes. Crimes always make good suspense stories. The perpetrators must be found, and their motives explained. Detectives get on the case. They piece together clues. They begin making sense out of what seems nonsense. A theory emerges, and it is proven true. The guilty are revealed!

Within this simple framework of the crime story, a writer can add twists and turns that are guaranteed to keep you guessing or to surprise you.

That is what John Savage does in "The Getaway." The story seems rather simple at first, but look for clues that will prepare you for the ending.

The master crime storyteller of all time is probably Arthur Conan

Unit 3

Doyle. He created that detective of detectives, Sherlock Holmes, and his sidekick, Dr. Watson. Holmes and Watson try to solve a very strange murder in a dramatized version of "Sherlock Holmes and the Speckled Band."

"Trifles" is a crime story that goes beyond the usual "whodunit" tale. It is important to know who killed John Wright, but this time understanding the reasons is essential to feeling the real suspense.

Happy and Not So Happy Endings.   Suspense cannot go on forever. It must end sometime. How it ends in a story can make you feel happy or sad.

"The Rattlesnake Hunt" presents a different kind of suspense. Instead of people trying to outwit one another, a "herpetologist" teaches a writer how to outwit rattlesnakes.

Two poems, both titled "Earth," present not-so-happy endings to human existence on this planet. Even so, suspense is built into each through their clever final lines.

Puzzles.   "The Lady, or the Tiger?" is one of the most interesting suspense stories ever written. It ends in a rather puzzling fashion, and you will have to use all your skills and abilities to figure out the conclusion.

Think whether you could have named the flying animal described in "The Bat" if the poem had a different title. Even though "The Bird of Night" has no such giveaway in its title, you should be able to guess what the poet is describing before you reach the end.

Make doubly sure that you keep the title in mind when you read the last short story in the unit, "A Secret for Two." This story about a Montreal milk wagon driver is innocent enough, but there is real mystery behind it.

Now, explore the world of suspense—and hold your breath as the writers tell their tales!

After completing this selection, students will be able to
- understand setting
- explain the importance of a story's setting
- analyze the believability of a story
- write a postscript to a story's conclusion
- consider specific aspects of setting
- identify the root words that make up a compound word

More About Setting: The where of setting can be, but is not usually, more important than the "when." Point out to students that all great novelists—Flaubert, Tolstoy, Thomas Mann, Joyce, and, more recently, Toni Morrison—reflect the times, or the *when*, of their own lives.

Then, ask students, why do you think great novels live from generation to generation? Lead students to understand that from their keen observations of the world around them, great writers draw universal truths. Ask students to name their favorite great novel, epic poem, or drama; suggest that they specify the setting—and its importance.

Cooperative/Collaborative Learning Activity: Divide students into groups of four or five. Have them each relate an international border incident—from TV or their own reading—and then choose one that the group can make into a skit for class presentation.

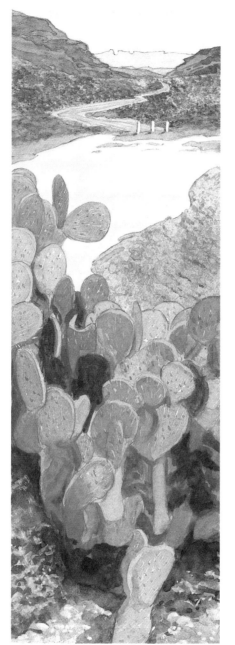

216

LEARN ABOUT

Setting

Setting is the "where" and "when" of a story. It includes the place and the time the story unfolds. Setting is always important to a story, but sometimes it is so important that you cannot imagine the story happening in any other place at any other time. The story requires that the action happen in this specific setting.

When that is the case, setting plays an important part in the story's plot. Somehow, where or when the story takes place will have a big impact on the action. In suspense stories, the answer to "when?" can keep you on the edge of your seat. The answer to "where" can spell life or death for the characters.

As you read the next selection, ask yourself these questions:

1. Why is the "where" of the setting so important to this story?
2. Is the "when" of the setting also important to this story?

SKILL BUILDER

Exotic foreign locales, are sometimes the setting for stories or parts of stories. Think of a written story or a film where such a scene is important. In two or three sentences, explain why you think so.

Unit 3

THE GETAWAY

by John Savage

Whenever I get sleepy at the wheel, I always stop for coffee. This time, I was going along in western Texas and I got sleepy. I saw a sign that said GAS EAT, so I pulled off. It was long after midnight. What I expected was a place like a bunch of others, where the coffee tastes like copper and the flies never sleep.

What I found was something else. The tables were painted wood, and they looked as if nobody ever spilled the ketchup. The counter was spick-and-span. Even the smell was OK, I swear it.

Nobody was there, as far as customers. There was just this one old boy—really only about forty, getting gray above the ears—behind the counter. I sat down at the counter and ordered coffee and apple pie. Right away he got me started feeling sad.

I have a habit: I divide people up. Winners and losers. This old boy behind the counter was the kind that they *mean* well. They can't do enough for you, but their eyes have this gentle, faraway look, and they can't win. You know? With their clean shirt and the little bow tie? It makes you feel sad just to look at them. Only take my tip: Don't feel too sad.

He brought the coffee steaming hot, and it tasted like coffee. "Care for cream and sugar?" he asked. I said, "Please," and the cream was fresh and cold and thick. The pie was good, too.

A car pulled up outside. The old boy glanced out to see if they wanted gas, but they didn't. They came right in. The tall one said, "Two coffees. Do you have a road map we could look at?"

"I think so," the old boy said. He got their coffee first, and then started rooting through a pile of papers by the telephone, looking for a map. It was easy to see he was the type nothing's too much trouble for. Tickled to be of service.

---

root (ROOT) dig or search around

Suspense

217

I'm the same type myself, if you want to know. I watched the old boy hunting for his map, and I felt like I was looking in a mirror.

After a minute or two, he came up with the map. "This one's a little out of date, but . . ." He put it on the counter, beside their coffee.

The two men spread out the map and leaned over it. They were well dressed, like a couple of feed merchants. The tall one ran his finger along the Rio Grande and shook his head. "I guess there's no place to get across, this side of El Paso."

He said it to his pal, but the old boy behind the counter heard him and lit up like a light bulb. "You trying to find the best way south? I might be able to help you with that."

"How?"

"Just a minute." He spent a lot of time going through the papers by the telephone again. "Thought I might have a newer map," he said. "Anything recent would show the Hackett Bridge. Anyway, I can tell you how to find it."

"Here's a town called Hackett," the tall one said, still looking at the map. "It's on the river, just at the end of a road. Looks like a pretty small place."

"Not any more. It's just about doubled since they built the bridge."

"What happens on the other side?" The short one asked the question, but both of the feed-merchant types were paying close attention.

"Pretty fair road, clear to Chihuahua. It joins up there with the highway out of El Paso and Juarez."

The tall man finished his coffee, folded the map, put it in his pocket, and stood up. "We'll take your map with us," he said.

The old boy seemed startled, like a new kid at school when somebody pokes him in the nose to show him who's boss. However, he just shrugged and said, "Glad to let you have it."

---

feed merchant (FEED MUR chunt) person who buys and sells food for animals
Rio Grande (ree oh GRAND) river that separates the state of Texas from Mexico
El Paso (el PAS oh) a city in western Texas, near the border of Mexico
Chihuahua (chi WAH wah) city in northern Mexico
Juarez (HWAH res) Mexican city across the Rio Grande from El Paso

Unit 3

Chateau Diner, John Baeder. O.K. Harris Works of Art, New York

The feed merchants had a little conference on the way out, talking in whispers. Then they stopped in the middle of the floor, turned around, reached inside their jackets, and pulled guns on us. Automatic pistols, I think they were. "You sit where you are and don't move," the tall one said to me. "And *you*, get against the wall."

Both of us did exactly what they wanted. I told you we were a lot alike.

The short man walked over and pushed one of the keys of the cash register. "Every little bit helps," he said, and he scooped the money out of the drawer. The tall man set the telephone on the floor, put his foot on it, and jerked the wires out. Then they ran to their car and got in. The short man leaned out the window and shot out one of my tires. Then they took off fast.

I looked at the old boy behind the counter. He seemed a little pale, but he didn't waste any time. He took a screwdriver out of a drawer and squatted down beside the telephone. I said, "It doesn't always pay to be nice to people."

Suspense 219

He laughed and said, "Well, it doesn't usually cost anything," and went on taking the base plate off the telephone. He was a fast worker, actually. His tongue was sticking out of the corner of his mouth. In about five minutes he had a dial tone coming out of the receiver. He dialed a number and told the rangers about the men and their car. "They did?" he said. "Well, well, well. . . . No, not El Paso. They took the Hackett turnoff." After he hung up, he said, "It turns out those guys robbed a supermarket in Wichita Falls."

I shook my head. "They sure had me fooled. I thought they looked perfectly all right."

The old boy got me another cup of coffee, and opened himself a bottle of pop. "They fooled me, too, at first." He wiped his mouth. "Then I got a load of their shoulder holsters when they leaned on the counter to look at the map. Anyway, they had mean eyes, I thought. Didn't you?"

"Well, I didn't at the time."

We drank without talking for a while, getting our nerves back in shape. A pair of patrol cars went roaring by outside and squealed their tires around the Hackett turnoff.

I got to thinking, and I thought of the saddest thing yet. "You *knew* there was something wrong with those guys, but you still couldn't keep from helping them on their way."

He laughed. "Well, the world's a tough sort of place at best, is how I look at it."

"I can understand showing them the map," I said, "but I'd never have told about the bridge. Now there's not a chance of catching them. If you'd kept your mouth shut, there'd at least be some hope."

"There isn't any—"

"Not a shred," I went on. "Not with a car as fast as they've got."

The way the old boy smiled made me feel better about him and me. "I don't mean there isn't any hope," he said. "I mean there isn't any bridge."

Enrichment: Witchita Falls is in north central Texas, about 500 miles from El Paso.

Literary Focus: Suspense holds to the very end, as the narrator interrupts the counterman. Only then is the full import of what really happened revealed.

MINI QUIZ

Write the following questions on the chalkboard or overhead projector and call on students to fill in the blanks. Discuss the answers with the class.

1. The narrator stopped for coffee because he _____ .
2. When they came into the restaurant, the two men asked to look at a _____ .
3. They were trying to get to _____ .
4. The first thing the counterman did after the robbery was _____ .
5. the two men carried their guns in _____ .

Answers to Mini Quiz

1. became tired while driving
2. road map
3. Mexico
4. fix the telephone
5. shoulder holsters

ANSWERS TO UNDERSTAND THE SELECTION

1. in west Texas, near the Mexican border
2. feed merchants
3. when he saw their shoulder holsters, as they leaned on the counter to look at the map
4. a winner (The narrator's first impression that he is a "loser" was wrong.)
5. Probably, but he didn't want to give them anything that might have made them suspicious about the nonexistent Hackett Bridge.
6. To prevent the counterman and narrator from calling the police or pursuing them.
7. It's an excellent example of "end weight," or keeping the most important information in a sentence until the end. In this sentence, nothing makes sense until we read the very last word. And then not only the sentence, but the whole story, takes on a new meaning.
8. Probably a good idea, since it's used so well. We are quickly drawn into the story because the narrator is part of it. Also, he can use colloquial language, which adds a sense of realistic immediacy to the story.
9. Yes. In the fourth paragraph of the story, the narrator tells us not to feel "too sad" for the "losers" of the world. It's a hint the counterman is not a loser. However, the character of the counterman is so finely crafted that we have few hints from his actions that he knows exactly what he is doing when the criminals are planning their getaway.
10. Answers will vary.

Respond to Literature: One weakness in the story that could be pointed out is that it's hard to

believe that criminals—on the run in unfamiliar territory— don't have a decent road map.

LDP Activity: Discuss in small groups or as a class. Is it important to judge a person on his/her personal appearance? Is it possible to make a valid judgment about a person when you first meet him/her? Have students come to a consensus through their discussion.

UNDERSTAND THE SELECTION

Recall

1. Where does the story take place?

2. At first, who did the narrator think the two men were?

3. When did the counterman say he first thought that the men were criminals?

Infer

4. At the end of the story, is the counterman a "winner" or a "loser"?

5. Do you think the counterman had a newer map than the one he gave the men?

6. Why did the two men cut the telephone line?

7. How does the last sentence helps maintain the story's suspense?

Apply

8. Does first-person point of view work well in this story?

9. Are there any hints about the surprise ending earlier in the story?

10. How might you have reacted if you had been the counterman?

Respond to Literature

Do you think that there are any weak points in this story? Is anything not believable?

WRITE ABOUT THE SELECTION

What did the narrator of the story think when the counterman told him that there was no Hackett Bridge? Imagine that you are the narrator. How would this affect your opinion of the counterman? Imagine that you want to add a postscript describing what you felt and did after you learned that the bridge did not exist.

Prewriting: Do a little reviewing before you begin writing. Reread the paragraphs that describe the narrator's feelings about the counterman, especially the third and fourth paragraphs at the beginning and the six paragraphs at the end of the story. How do you feel about those observations now that you know the ending of the story? Make a cluster of your feelings. Then imagine how each of those feelings might make you act. Add a phrase about each of those possible actions on your cluster.

Writing: Use your cluster to write your postscript. Try to make a smooth transition from the story's current ending to your addition. Remember that you are telling the story from the narrator's point of view.

Revising: Try to imitate the author's writing style. He uses short sentences, informal language, and figures of speech. Add some of these characteristics to your writing.

Proofreading: Reread your description to check for errors. Authors often use incomplete sentences. You may, too, but make sure you know how to rewrite them so that they are complete sentences.

ANSWERS TO WRITE ABOUT THE SELECTION

Prewriting: Have students read the relevant section aloud. Ask for volunteers to be the narrator and the counterman and to "perform" the sections before the class.

Writing: As students work on their postscripts individually, circulate among them to observe their use of the clusters. If any student seems to be having difficulty, you might prompt some cluster additions.

Revising: Ask the class for a particularly distinctive passage from the story. Then write it on the chalkboard or overhead projector. Analyze what makes it distinctive by rewriting it in a neutral style, and then compare the passages.

THINK ABOUT SETTING

John Savage, the author of "The Getaway," blends the setting so skillfully into the plot of the story that it is easy to overlook the setting's importance. Consider both general and specific time and place when you think about setting.

For example, a story can take place in Los Angeles sometime in the 1980s: Those would be the general "where" and "when." The specific setting might be in a house after dinnertime.

1. When do we learn the setting of "The Getaway"?

2. Why is the geographic location of the restaurant important?

3. Why is the restaurant itself important as a setting for the story?

4. Why is setting an important part of the plot of this story?

5. Is the time this story takes place important? Think both about the specific time and the general time.

DEVELOP YOUR VOCABULARY

Compound words are made up of two or more root words. Sometimes they are hyphenated.

Often compound words are so common that you do not realize they are made from other words. A good example is the noun in the title of this selection: **getaway** = get + away.

Knowing the root words in a compound word can often help you find its meaning.

There are few strict rules on when a compound word is hyphenated. Check a dictionary if you are unsure which form is correct.

Tell the root words of the following compound words:

1. faraway   4. mother-in-law
2. zigzag   5. turnoff
3. screwdriver   6. newspaper

What compound words are made up of the following root words? Make sure you spell them correctly.

1. law, father, in   3. way, rail
2. noble, man   4. smith, black

Use all compound words from this exercise in an original sentence.

Part I

1. far + away 2. zig + zag 3. screw + driver 4. mother + in + law 5. turn + off 6. news + paper

Part 2

1. father-in-law 2. nobleman 3. railway 4. blacksmith

Sample sentences:

1. He had a faraway look in his eyes.
2. The screwdriver fell into the hole.
3. The highway turnoff isn't hard to find.
4. The road zigzags over the mountain pass.
5. My mother-in-law recently retired as school principal.
6. The newspaper's slogan is, News you can use.
7. My father-in-law still works the nightshift at the ice cream factory.
8. It was important to her mother that she marry a nobleman.
9. Railway lines are often in disrepair.
10. A blacksmith is as rare today as a buffalo nickel.

Proofreading: Ask students to exchange papers and check that the postscripts have the same point of view as the story. Have them correct any errors in pencil before returning the paper.

ANSWERS TO THINK ABOUT SETTING

1. in the first paragraph of the story
2. It's close to the Mexican border.
3. The author is able to make it seem a very lonely an desolate place. It's deserted except for the counterman, and that's important as the story unfolds.
4. The counterman uses his familiarity with the area to outsmart the criminals. The criminals, who are not familiar with the area, must rely on him for knowledge on how to reach Mexico.
5. The specific time is "long after midnight," which is important in creating a sense of emptiness and in making the timing of the getaway seem plausible. The general time is sometime in the automobile era. While it's possible to imagine the story set at another time of day, it's hard to imagine it set in another century, when there were no automobiles or highway bridges.

SELECTION OBJECTIVES

After completing this selection, students will be able to
- understand the development of characters in a story
- recognize the protaganist and antagonist in a conflict
- analyze the appeal of certain characters
- write a short television script
- describe the conflict of a drama
- understand the special vocabulary in crime stories

More About Characters:

Characters are often called either "flat" or "rounded." Flat characters are somewhat like the supporting players in a theatrical stock company, necessary to advance the plot but never in the lead. Rounded characters are distinct individuals whom the writer describes in detailed complexity. Because their actions are not predictable, they, like Hamlet, intrigue us: They are stars. So once was Sherlock Holmes. If Holmes has become a flat character it is only because of the great popularity of the Conan Doyle stories; We tend now to see only the hat, the tweeds, the magnifying glass—not the man. Yet students should understand that Sherlock Holmes is the original "master detective," the prototype of all the know-it-all sleuths who would follow.

Cooperative/Collaborative Learning Activity:

Have students organize, direct, and stage a one-act drama. They may write it themselves or adapt an old-time two-reeler (now available for VCRs) that clearly portrays both protaganist and antagonist. The first step would be to organize the class into groups of four or five and, then, assign each a task. Possible audiences: school assembly, another class, their parents.

T224

224

LEARN ABOUT
Characters

Stories can have many characters. Some of them may not be human.

Usually, however, there is a main character. Likewise, there is usually a character who comes in conflict with the main character. The main character is called the **protagonist.** The character who comes in conflict with him or her is called the **antagonist.**

The conflict between the two characters is very important to the story. Usually, it must be resolved before the story concludes. How it is resolved often determines the ending. A skillful writer can use the conflict between the protagonist and antagonist to develop the story's characters and make them come alive.

As you read the next selection, ask yourself these questions:

1. Who are the protagonist and antagonist?
2. What is the conflict between them?

SKILL BUILDER

"Antagonize" is a verb which means "to oppose" or "to provoke to action." A noun with the same root is *antagonist,* one who comes in conflict with or opposes the protagonist. Think of someone or something that antagonizes you. Write a paragraph or two about this.

Unit 3

SHERLOCK HOLMES AND THE SPECKLED BAND

by Arthur Conan Doyle
dramatized by Alice Delman

CHARACTERS

SHERLOCK HOLMES, *the famous detective*
DR. WATSON, *his friend*
HELEN STONER, *the lady in danger*

JULIA STONER, *her sister*
DR. GRIMESBY ROYLOTT, *her stepfather*

SCENE 1

TIME: About 1900.

SETTING: The parlor in HOLMES'S *apartment on Baker Street, London, England.*

AT RISE[1]: A woman dressed in black and wearing a veil is seated on the window seat in the parlor. The room is comfortably filled with sofas, chairs, old furniture, and the usual belongings of the bachelor detective: books, newspapers, slippers, magnifying glass, pipe rack, various hats, and a violin among them. HOLMES *and* DR. WATSON *enter. The lady rises to greet them.*

HOLMES: Good morning, Madam. I'm Sherlock Holmes. *(Nodding toward* Watson*)* My close friend, Dr. Watson. You can speak freely in front of him. Please sit down by the fire. I'll order coffee, since I see that you're shivering.

HELEN *(changing her seat)*: Not from cold.

HOLMES: What then?

HELEN: Fear, Mr. Holmes. Terror.

She raises her veil to reveal a face tired and gray. She looks about 30, but her hair already shows traces of gray. Her eyes are restless and frightened. She looks like a hunted animal. HOLMES *studies her face.)*

---

[1] **at rise:** at the start of the scene; when the curtain rises

Suspense
225

Sidelights: If Sherlock Holmes seems to approach a case like a scientist, it's no wonder: His creator, Sir Arthur Conan Doyle, was himself trained as a scientist—a doctor, to be exact. He was born in 1859 in Edinburgh, Scotland and practiced medicine for about eight years before becoming a full-time writer.

Motivation for Reading: What does Holmes look like? Most people have a definite image of him—tall, with a cape; smoking a pipe; wearing a characteristic hat; and often holding a manifying glass. His friend Dr. Watson doesn't seem quite up to the mark, but is still a worthy foil as, together, they track a murder case.

More About the Thematic Idea: Suspense is built into all murder cases. Holmes solves his cases intellectually, through "deduction." He's always at least one step ahead of Watson and sometimes even farther ahead of his readers. Other, more recent sleuths approach a case doggedly, tracking down clues almost from door to door. With all, however, suspense is the key ingredient.

Purpose-Setting Question: How can you use deduction to solve a crime?

Enrichment: The setting of the opening scene is a Victorian parlor. Explain to students that England's Queen Victoria reigned from 1837–1901 and that her name has defined an era—in architecture, manners, dress, even world politics.

Critical Thinking: When Helen Stoner shivers, Holmes deduces she is cold and orders coffee. Interestingly, the master detective deduces incorrectly in this instance: Helen Stoner claims she is shivering not from the cold, but from fear. The claim provides the lead into a description of the case.

Vocabulary: Preteach the vocabulary words. See the Comprehension Workbook in the TRB.

More About Vocabulary: Write the new vocabulary words on separate cards, and place face down. Divide the class into groups. Have each group choose one card. Give them two minutes to discuss their word and write a definition on the board. Repeat until all the cards have been used. Groups are given one point for each correct definition.

LDP Activity: Class discussion of a television show. (example, "Murder She Wrote") or a film where the plot is similar. Talk about suspense. What makes a story have suspense?

Clarification: Make sure students understand the meaning of a "stepfather" and that Dr. Grimesby Roylott is the stepfather of Helen and Julia Stoner.

Reading Strategies: There are fourteen scenes in this drama. You may want to review with students the main points of each scene as you finish it.

HOLMES: Don't be afraid. Just leave everything to me. Now . . . what sent you all this way by train? And so early in the morning, too.

HELEN: How did you know I . . .?

HOLMES *(breaking in)*: There's the second half of a return ticket in the palm of your left glove. Plain as day. Please relax. That drive in the dogcart must have been difficult.

(HELEN *gives a start of surprise. She stares at* HOLMES.)

HOLMES: It's no mystery, my dear madam. The left arm of your jacket has mud spots in seven places. The marks are fresh. Only a dogcart splashes mud in that way.

HELEN: Well, whatever your reasons, you're right. Mr. Holmes, I can't stand this strain any longer! I'll go mad. I have no one else to turn to, except . . . well, someone who cares for me, but can't help. I've heard of you, Mr. Holmes. Can you help me? I . . . right now, I can't pay you. But in a month or so, I'll be married, and then . . .

HOLMES *(breaking in)*: Madam, my work is its own reward. I'll be happy to help you. Now, tell us everything. Everything.

HELEN: I'm afraid that . . . that's the horror of it. It's . . . so vague. My fears—they come from small things that might seem like nothing to you. Even my fiancé thinks it's all just nerves.

HOLMES: He says so?

HELEN: No, but it's in his soothing answers. And the way he turns his eyes from me. But you, Mr. Holmes—I've heard you can see all the evils that lie in the human heart. I'm surrounded by danger. Can you help me?

WATSON: Yes!

HOLMES: Thank you, Watson. Now, Madam—start with your name.

HELEN: It's Helen Stoner.

HOLMES: And you live . . . ?

HELEN: With my stepfather. He's the last member of one of the oldest families in England, the Roylotts of Stoke Moran.

---

vague (VAYG) not clear; hazy
fiance (fee ahn SAY) husband-to-be
soothing (SOOTH ing) calming

Unit 3

HOLMES: Yes, I've heard the name.

HELEN: The family was once very rich. But they were ruined in the last century. Nothing's left but a few acres and the ancient house. And that's crushed under a mortgage. The last Roylott lived out his life there—a horrible life as a penniless nobleman. But his only son—that's my stepfather—he saw that things had to change. He borrowed some money. He got a medical degree and went out to India. He built a large practice there.

---

mortgage (MAWR gij) loan given to purchase a house
practice (PRAK tis) the business of a doctor or lawyer

Suspense 227

HOLMES: But he came back to England? Why?

HELEN: A string of robberies in his house in India. He got into a fit of anger about them and beat his native butler to death. They almost hanged him. He spent a long term in prison. Then he came back to England. A sad man. A very disappointed man.

HOLMES: And your mother, his wife?

HELEN: He married my mother in India. She was the widow of a Major-General Stoner. My sister Julia and I were twins. We were only two years old when my mother remarried.

HOLMES: Hm. Was she well-off at the time?

HELEN: Well, yes. She had quite a bit of money—at least £1000 a year. And she gave it all to Dr. Roylott while we lived with him. Julia and I were to each get a certain amount a year when we married.

HOLMES: Is your mother still living?

HELEN: She died soon after we came to England—eight years ago. A railway accident.

HOLMES: And you went on living with your stepfather?

HELEN: Yes, he gave up trying to practice medicine. He took us to live in the family house at Stoke Moran. The money my mother left was more than enough. We had all we needed to be happy.

HOLMES: But?

HELEN: It was my stepfather. A terrible change came over him. At first, the neighbors were so happy to see a Roylott back in the old family home. But instead of making friends, he shut himself up in the house. He hardly ever came out, except to get into fights with anyone who crossed his path. He has a terrible temper. As a matter of fact, some of his ancestors showed traces of . . . well, madness. In his case, it got worse because of those years in India.

HOLMES: What happened?

HELEN: A series of brawls. Two ended in the police court. He became the terror of the village. People would run when they saw him coming.

HOLMES: Is he dangerous?

HELEN: Well, he's a man of huge strength. And when he's angry, he's just out of control. Last week he threw the blacksmith

---

brawl (BRAWL) noisy fight

over a bridge into a stream. I had to pay all the money I could get in a hurry to keep it quiet.

HOLMES: He has no friends, then?

HELEN: Only the gypsies. He lets them camp on his land. And they give him the hospitality of their tents. Sometimes for weeks on end. Oh, and he also has animals—Indian animals.

HOLMES: Really?

HELEN: Yes. They're sent over to him by a man in India. He's got a cheetah and a baboon. They just wander loose on the grounds. They scare people almost as much as he does! You can imagine what our life was like, Julia's and mine. No great pleasure. Julia was only 30 when she died, but her hair had already started to turn white. Like mine.

HOLMES: Your sister is dead, then?

HELEN: She died just two years ago. It's her death that I came to see you about.

HOLMES: Go on.

HELEN: Well, living the life we did, Julia and I met very few people our own age. But we had an Aunt Honoria, who lives near Harrow. We went to visit her sometimes. Julia was there at Christmas two years ago, and she met a major of the marines. They got engaged.

HOLMES: What did your stepfather think of that?

HELEN: He didn't object. But within two weeks of the date set for the wedding . . . *(She is very upset.)*

HOLMES: Please go on.

HELEN: The terrible event that . . .

HOLMES *(breaking in)*: Please be precise. Details! I must have details.

HELEN: That's easy. It's all burned in my memory.
(She appears about to cry.)

HOLMES: Take it easy. Go ahead.

HELEN: The house, as I said, is very old. We use only one wing. The bedrooms are on the ground floor. The first is Dr. Roylott's, the second my sister's, and the third is mine. No connecting doors. But all three rooms open into the same hallway. Is that clear?

---

cheetah (CHEET uh) wild cat with a spotted coat
precise (pri SYS) very exact

Suspense 229

HOLMES: Perfectly.

HELEN: The windows of the three rooms open out on the lawn. That night—the night she died—Dr. Roylott had gone to his room early. But we knew he hadn't gone to bed.

HOLMES: How?

HELEN: Because my sister smelled the strong Indian cigars he smokes. So she left her room and came into mine. We sat for a while, talking about the wedding. Then we said goodnight. I remember it all so vividly. She got up to go. . . .

SCENE 2

SETTING: Helen's bedroom in the Roylott mansion.

AT RISE: JULIA *and* HELEN STONER *are seated on the bed. They kiss each other goodnight.* JULIA *walks to the door, then pauses, turning to look back at* HELEN.

JULIA: Helen, have you ever heard anyone whistle in the dead of the night?

HELEN: No! Why?

JULIA: You couldn't be whistling in your sleep, could you?

HELEN: No! What are you talking about?

JULIA: It's just that the last few nights, I've heard a strange

---

vividly (VIV id lee) very clearly; as if lifelike

whistling. At about three o'clock in the morning! A low, clear whistle. I'm a light sleeper, and it wakes me up. I can't tell where the sound comes from—the next room, the lawn, I don't know.

HELEN: It must be the gypsies.

JULIA: I guess so. But if it's on the lawn, I wonder why you didn't hear it too.

HELEN: Oh, I sleep like a log.

JULIA: Well, it doesn't matter, anyway. Good night.

SCENE 3

SETTING: The parlor in HOLMES'S *apartment.*

AT RISE: HOLMES, WATSON *and* HELEN STONER *are sitting as before.* HELEN *goes on with her story.*

HELEN: She smiled at me and closed my door. I heard her key turn in the lock.

HOLMES: Her key? Did you usually lock yourselves in at night?

HELEN: Always.

HOLMES: Why?

HELEN: Remember—the cheetah and the baboon! We didn't feel safe unless our doors were locked at night.

HOLMES: Right. Go on.

HELEN: I couldn't sleep that night. It was wild weather, howling wind. The rain beat against the windows. Suddenly I heard a scream—a woman's scream. I knew it was my sister's voice. I rushed into the hall. Then I seemed to hear a low whistle— just as my sister had described it. Then there was a clanging sound, like metal falling. My sister's door was unlocked— and it started to open slowly. I stared at it. I didn't know what would come out! It was Julia. Her face was white with terror. Her hands were groping for help. She swayed as if she was drunk. I ran to her and threw my arms around her, but her knees gave way and she fell to the ground. She was twisting in terrible pain. I bent over her. Then suddenly, she shrieked —I'll never forget her voice! "Oh! Helen! It was the band! The speckled band!"

HOLMES: That's all? She didn't explain?

---

grope (GROHP) feel about blindly

Suspense

231

Reading Strategy: Scene 3 brings the reader back to the present. Now might be the time for students to summarize what Holmes knows so far.

Literary Focus: You might want to point out to students that the flashback in Scene 2 allowed the story to be told in the present tense—even though it was a past event.

Critical Thinking: In Scene 3, Helen tells Holmes what happened during a night of "howling wind." Her description is a good example of the importance of sequential order in telling about an event.

Discussion: What do students think? Do they have any theories as to what happened?

HELEN: She tried to say more. She stabbed her finger in the air towards the doctor's room. But then she choked and couldn't get the words out. I called out for my stepfather. But when he got to my sister's side, she was unconscious.

HOLMES: Didn't he do anything to bring her around?

HELEN: He sent for medical help from the village. But it was useless. She died without speaking again.

HOLMES: One moment. Are you sure about this whistle and this metallic sound? Could you swear to it?

HELEN: I don't know. I felt strongly that I heard it. But with the wind crashing, and the creaking of an old house—I don't know.

HOLMES: Was your sister dressed?

HELEN: No, she was in her nightgown. And she had a burnt match in one hand and a matchbox in the other.

HOLMES: So she struck a match and looked about her when it happened. That's important. And what did the coroner find was the cause of death?

HELEN: He was very careful because Dr. Roylott had caused so much trouble in the neighborhood. But he couldn't find the cause of death.

HOLMES: Could anyone have entered her room?

HELEN: The door was locked on the inside. The windows have old-fashioned shutters with broad iron bars, and they were locked every night. The walls are solid all around. So is the floor. The chimney's wide, but it's barred. My sister had to be alone when it happened. Besides, there were no marks of violence on her.

HOLMES: Poison?

HELEN: The doctors examined her for it. There wasn't any.

HOLMES: What do *you* think your sister died of, then?

HELEN: I think she died of pure fear and nervous shock. But what could have frightened her? I can't imagine.

HOLMES: The gypsies—were they on the grounds that night?

HELEN: Yes, there are nearly always some there.

HOLMES: Ah. And what did you think she meant by her last words about a band—a speckled band?

---

coroner (CAWR uh nur) public officer who investigates deaths that may not be due to natural causes

Unit 3

HELEN: I don't know. Sometimes I've thought it was just wild talk—she was dying. Or maybe it meant . . . some band of people. Perhaps the gypsies. Because of the spotted handkerchiefs they wear—she might have called them "the speckled band."

(HOLMES *shakes his head. Clearly, he is far from satisfied.*)

HOLMES: We're in deep waters here. Please tell us the rest.

HELEN: That was two years ago. My life became lonelier than ever—until lately. About a month ago, a friend—a dear friend I've known for years—asked me to marry him. My stepfather hasn't objected. So we're going to be married in the spring.

HOLMES: Then what brings you here?

HELEN: Two days ago, some repairs were started in the west wing of the house. My bedroom wall has been ripped up. So I've had to move into the room where my sister died. And sleep in the bed she slept in. It was terrifying. Last night, I lay awake thinking about her. Her terrible death. I suddenly heard—it was very quiet—I heard the low whistle. Just like the whistle on the night she died. I jumped up and lit the lamp. But there was nothing in the room. I was too shaken to go to bed again. So I got dressed. As soon as it was daylight, I came here.

HOLMES: Very wise. But have you told me everything?

HELEN: Yes. Everything.

HOLMES: You have not, Miss Roylott. You're protecting your stepfather.

HELEN: Why, what do you mean?

(HOLMES *leans toward* HELEN *and pushes back the bit of lace that covers her hand.*)

HOLMES: Ah. Five little black-and-blue spots. Just the sort of spots made by four fingers and a thumb. You've been treated cruelly.

HELEN (*embarrassed*): He's a hard man. Perhaps he doesn't really know his own strength.

(*A silence.* HOLMES *leans his chin on his hands and stares into the fire.*)

---

treat (TREET) deal with

Suspense

233

Discussion: What clues to Dr. Roylott's personality make him a suspect? Point out such things as his violent, and intimidating behavior to his stepdaughter and others.

Discussion: What is Holmes's hurry in Scene 3? Why must he and Watson go to Stoke Moran immediately? And why do they want to look over the rooms without Dr. Roylott's knowing about it? Ask students for their ideas.

Critical Thinking: In the same scene, Holmes "put a few things together" into a theory. Both Watson and he know it's got some "holes", though. Only at Stoke Moran can they test and refine the theory.

HOLMES: This is a very deep business. I have to know a thousand details before I decide what to do. But we haven't a moment to lose. If we come today to Stoke Moran, will we be able to look over these rooms? Without your stepfather knowing?

HELEN: Well, yes. As a matter of fact, he said he'd be going into town today. He'll probably be away all day.

HOLMES: Good. You wouldn't mind the trip, Watson?

WATSON: I'd love it.

HOLMES: Then we'll both come.

HELEN: Thank you. I feel better already. I'll be waiting for you this afternoon, then.

(HELEN *drops her veil back over her face and exits.*)

HOLMES: Well, what do you think of it all, Watson?

WATSON: Hm. Seems to be a dark, evil business.

HOLMES: Yes, it does.

WATSON: But the floor and the walls were all solid. The door, the windows, and the chimney were all blocked. If she's right about that, then her sister must have been alone when she fell ill.

HOLMES: Then what about those whistles? And what about the "speckled band"?

WATSON: I really couldn't say.

HOLMES: Well, let's put a few things together. First, the whistles at night. Second, the band of gypsies—very friendly with the old doctor. Third, the fact that the doctor has an interest in stopping his stepdaughter's marriage. And finally, the metallic clang. A sound that *might* have been caused by one of the metal bars on the shutters falling into place. I think we can wrap things up along those lines.

WATSON: But how could the gypsies have done it?

HOLMES: I haven't the faintest idea.

WATSON: Holmes, I can think of quite a few objections to this theory.

HOLMES: So can I. That's why we're going to Stoke Moran today. We'll see if the objections make sense. Or if they can be explained away.

---

deep (DEEP) hard to understand
theory (THEE uh ree) guess based on reasoning

(The door has burst open. A huge man stands in the doorway. He wears a black top hat. He has on a long coat and carries a riding whip. He has a wrinkled, sun-burned face, which looks angrily at HOLMES *and* WATSON *in turn.)*

ROYLOTT: Holmes?

HOLMES: Here. And you?

ROYLOTT: Dr. Grimesby Roylott, of Stoke Moran.

HOLMES *(very pleasant):* Have a seat, doctor.

ROYLOTT: I won't. My stepdaughter's been here. I've traced her. What's she been saying to you?

HOLMES: It's a little cold for this time of year, isn't it?

ROYLOTT *(yelling):* What has she been saying to you?

HOLMES *(still pleasant):* But I've heard the crocuses are doing well.

ROYLOTT: Hah! You put me off, do you? *(He takes a step forward and shakes his riding whip at* Holmes.*) I know you, you dog! I've heard of you before. Holmes, the meddler.*

*(*HOLMES *smiles.)*

ROYLOTT: Holmes, the busybody!

*(*HOLMES *smiles even more broadly.)*

ROYLOTT: Holmes, the Scotland Yard² puppet!

HOLMES: Talking with you is very entertaining. When you go out, please close the door. There's a draft.

ROYLOTT: I'll go when I've had my say. Don't you *dare* meddle

---

crocus (KROH kus) spring flower
meddler (MED lur) one who butts in to other people's business
²**Scotland Yard:** detective department of the London police

Suspense   235

Clarification: "Busybody" is a synonym for "meddler."

Literary Focus: The interchange between Holmes and Roylott at the end of Scene 3 is a good example of indirect character description. Holmes is cool under fire, Roylott agressive and violent.

Clarification: A poker is used to stir the coals of a fire. It must be strong to withstand heat.

Discussion: Ask students, Were you surprised in Scene 3 that Holmes was able to straighten an iron poker? Do we tend to think that intelligence and strength don't go together?

with my business. I know she's been here. I traced her! I'm a dangerous man to go up against!

(So saying, ROYLOTT picks up an iron poker and bends it over double.)

ROYLOTT: See that you keep out of my grip.

(ROYLOTT hurls the poker into the fireplace and stomps out.)

HOLMES *(laughing):* He seems friendly. Larger than I am, of course. But still, too bad he didn't hang around. We could have matched grips.

(So saying, HOLMES picks up the poker and straightens it out again.)

HOLMES: He's rude, though. Imagine thinking I'm—*I*—a puppet of the police! But this little visit makes the job more interesting, though, doesn't it? I only hope Miss Stoner won't be hurt by her carelessness—letting this brute trace her here. Now, Watson, let's have some breakfast. Then I'll do a little detecting.

SCENE 4

SETTING: HOLMES'S *parlor, later that day.*

AT RISE: WATSON *is studying a medical book as* HOLMES *returns.*

HOLMES *holds in his hand a sheet of blue paper. On it are written a bunch of notes and numbers.*

WATSON: Find anything?
HOLMES: I've seen the will of the dead wife, Miss Stoner's mother.
WATSON: And?
HOLMES: Not an easy job! I had to work out the present prices of all these investments. But the result is—at the time she died, the total income was almost £1100 a year. Now, with the fall in farm prices, it's only about £750. Each daughter was to get about £250 if she married.
WATSON: What does that mean for Roylott?
HOLMES: It means that if both girls had married, the old hulk would have had very little for himself. Even one marriage would be a serious blow for him.

WATSON: So he has a strong motive for standing in the way of their marriages.

HOLMES: Right.

WATSON: What now?

HOLMES: Get your revolver. An Eley's Number 2[3] is an excellent argument with gentlemen who can twist steel pokers into knots. That and a toothbrush should be all you need. Then—let's go!

---

motive (MOHT iv) reason to act
[3]Eley's Number 2: old make of pistol

Suspense   237

Literary Focus: At the end of Scene 4, Holmes uses irony to provide a bit of comic relief: Who would expect a detective to carry the odd combination of a pistol and a toothbrush?

SETTING: A hallway in the mansion at Stoke Moran.

AT RISE: HOLMES *and* WATSON *are received by* HELEN STONER.

HELEN: I've been waiting. It's turned out very well. He's gone to town. And he's not likely to be back before dark.

HOLMES: Yes, we had the pleasure of meeting the doctor. He followed you to my office. Demanded to know what your business was. Then he threatened us with a poker.

HELEN: Good heavens! You weren't hurt?

HOLMES: Certainly not.

HELEN: He's so tricky. I never know when I'm safe from him. What will we do when he gets back?

HOLMES: Better ask what *he'll* do. He'll have to be on guard. Because now he's got someone more cunning than he is on his track. *You* must lock yourself in tonight. If he's violent, we'll take you to your aunt's at Harrow. Now, let's examine the outside and then the rooms.

SCENE 6

SETTING: Outside the house.

AT RISE: HOLMES *is walking slowly. He examines the outsides of the windows.*

HOLMES: This window belongs to the room where you used to sleep. The center one is your sister's room, and the one next to the main building is Dr. Roylott's. Correct?

HELEN: Exactly. But now I'm sleeping in the middle room.

HOLMES: Ah, the alterations. I notice there doesn't seem to be any urgent need for repairs there.

HELEN: There isn't. I think it was an excuse to move me from my room.

HOLMES: That's important. Now, on the other side of this narrow wing is the hallway. All three rooms open off it. There are windows in the hallway, of course?

HELEN: Yes, but very small ones. Too narrow for anyone to get through.

---

alteration (awl tuh RAY shun) change made to a building

Clarification: At the end of Scene 5, when Holmes refers to "someone more cunning" than Roylott, he is speaking of himself, of course.

Literary Focus: The opening of Scene 6 might be a good place to point out to students that a scene change is often a writer's device to change the setting. Now, the actors are outside rather than inside the house.

HOLMES: Anyway, you both locked your doors at night. So your rooms couldn't have been entered from that side. Now, you've bolted these shutters?

HELEN: Yes, they're locked from the inside.

(HOLMES *examines the shutters very closely, trying every way to open them. He tests the hinges with a magnifying glass.*)

HOLMES: No one could pass these shutters—if they were bolted. Hm. This brings up a few problems with my theory.

SCENE 7

SETTING: *A bedroom in the mansion.*

AT RISE: *The bedroom is furnished with fireplace, bed, chest of drawers, dresser, and two chairs.* HOLMES *sits in one of them. He looks over every detail of the room.* HELEN *and* WATSON *stand watching him.*

WATSON: This is the room where your sister died?

HELEN: Yes. And where I'm sleeping now.

(HOLMES *points to a thick bell-rope that hangs down beside the bed. The end of the rope lies on the pillow.*)

HOLMES: This bell-rope[4]—where does the bell ring?

HELEN: In the housekeeper's room.

HOLMES: This rope looks newer than the other things.

HELEN: Yes, it was put there only a couple of years ago.

HOLMES: Your sister asked for it, I suppose.

HELEN: No, I never heard of her using it. We always used to get what we wanted ourselves.

HOLMES: Hm. Then why was such a nice bell-rope put in? Excuse me while I satisfy myself about this floor.

(HOLMES *throws himself face down on the floor. He has his magnifying glass in his hand. He crawls swiftly backward and forward. He examines the cracks between the boards. Then he jumps up and examines the woodwork on the walls. Then he stares at the bed closely. Finally, he takes the bell-rope and yanks it.*)

---

[4]**bell-rope:** rope that is attached to a bell that is used to call a servant

Suspense   239

Critical Thinking: At the end of Scene 6, when Holmes can't open the shutters from the outside, it upsets his working hypothesis. If the killer could not have broken in from outside, must Holmes now redirect his theory?

Reading Strategy: You might take five minutes at the end of Scene 6 to have students summarize the new bits of information. What can they mean?

HOLMES: It's a dummy!

WATSON: Won't it ring?

HOLMES: No. It's not even attached to a wire. Interesting. It's tied to a hook just above the little opening for the ventilator.

HELEN: How absurd! I never noticed that before.

HOLMES (*pulling the rope*): Very strange. There are one or two odd points about this room.

WATSON: What are they? I don't see anything odd.

HOLMES: Well, the builder must be a fool to open a vent into another room. With the same trouble, he could have opened it to the outside.

HELEN: The ventilator's quite recent, too.

HOLMES: Done about the same time as the bell-rope?

HELEN: Yes.

HOLMES: *Very* interesting. Dummy bell-ropes. Ventilators that don't ventilate.

WATSON: What does it mean?

HOLMES: Let's carry on in Dr. Roylott's room, please.

SCENE 8

SETTING: A slightly larger bedroom.

AT RISE: The room is plainly furnished. A cot, a shelf of books, an armchair beside the bed, a plain wooden chair, and a round table are the main pieces. There is also a large iron safe. HOLMES *walks slowly around the room. He examines everything.* HELEN *and* WATSON *look on.*

---

ventilator (VEN tul ay tur) opening to allow fresh air into and stale air out of a room

HOLMES (*tapping the safe*): What's in here?

HELEN: My stepfather's business papers.

HOLMES: Oh. You've seen inside, then?

HELEN: Only once. Years ago. I remember a lot of papers in it.

HOLMES: There isn't a cat inside, for example?

HELEN: No! What a strange idea!

HOLMES: Well, look at this.

(HOLMES *lifts up a saucer of milk that stands on top of the safe.*)

HELEN: We don't keep a cat. But there's the cheetah. And the baboon.

HOLMES: Ah, yes, of course. Well, a cheetah is just a big cat. But a saucer of milk won't do much to satisfy its appetite. There's one thing. . . .

(HOLMES *squats down in front of the wooden chair and examines the seat.*)

HOLMES: Good. That's settled.

WATSON: What's settled? Holmes, what have you . . .?

HOLMES (*breaking in*): Hello! Here's something interesting.

(HOLMES *picks up a small dog leash hanging on one corner of the bedpost. The leash is curled to make a loop, and tied.*)

HOLMES: What do you make of that, Watson?

WATSON: It's a common enough leash. But I don't know why it's tied that way.

HOLMES: That's not so common, is it? Oh, it's a wicked world. When a clever man turns his brains to crime, it's the worst of all. I think I've seen enough. (Holmes's *face is stern.*) Miss Stoner, you *must* follow my advice. In every way.

HELEN: Of course I will.

HOLMES: This is too serious for dilly-dallying. Your life may depend on it.

HELEN: Believe me—I'm in your hands.

HOLMES: Good. In the first place, both my friend and I must spend the night in Julia's room.

(WATSON *and* HELEN *look at* HOLMES *in amazement.*)

HOLMES: I'll explain. (*looking out the window*) Is that the village inn over there?

HELEN: Yes, the Crown.

Clarification: At the opening of Scene 8, when Holmes says, "That's settled," he has found proof for part of his theory, and that is, an animal is involved.

Enrichment: In Scene 8, after Holmes declares he's going to spend the night in Julia's room, Watson and Helen "look at Holmes in amazement." Understandably, they want to know what Holmes has deduced from the things they, too, have seen—but haven't been able to explain.

HOLMES: Good. Your windows could be seen from there?

HELEN: Yes.

HOLMES: All right, here's what you do. Stay in your room. When your stepfather comes back, say you've got a headache. Then when you hear him go to bed, open the shutters of your window. Undo the lock. Put your lamp there as a signal to us. Then take everything you need, and go back to your old room. Even with the repairs, you can manage there for one night, can't you?

HELEN: Oh, yes, easily.

HOLMES: Leave the rest to us.

HELEN: But what will you do?

WATSON: Yes, what *will* we do?

HOLMES: We'll spend the night in that room and find out what caused this whistling noise.

HELEN: I think you already know, Mr. Holmes.

HOLMES: Perhaps.

HELEN: Then please tell me. What caused my sister's death?

HOLMES: I'd rather have proof before I answer that.

HELEN: At least tell me if I'm right—did she die from some sudden shock?

HOLMES: No, I don't think so. I think there was something else. Something more . . . some *thing.* Now, Miss Stoner, we must leave. If Dr. Roylott came back and found us, our trip would have been useless. Be brave. If you do as I've said, we'll soon solve everything.

SCENE 9

SETTING: A room at the Crown.

AT RISE: HOLMES *is looking out a dark window.* WATSON *sits nervously.*

HOLMES: Here comes Roylott. Huge monster, isn't he? He's roaring at the poor driver. Look at him shaking his fists! *(turning to* Watson) You know, Watson, I don't know if I ought to take you tonight. It could be dangerous.

WATSON: Will I be any help?

HOLMES: Possibly a great deal.

WATSON: Then I'll come.

HOLMES: Very kind of you.

WATSON: You say danger. You must have seen more in those rooms than I did.

HOLMES: I didn't *see* more. I *deduced* more. I imagine you saw everything I did.

WATSON: I didn't see anything unusual. Except the bell-rope. And what could that be for? I can't imagine.

HOLMES: What about the ventilator?

WATSON: Well, yes, but I don't think that's so unusual—a small opening between two rooms. It was so small, a rat could hardly get through it.

HOLMES: Even before we got here, I knew there'd be a ventilator.

WATSON: What!

HOLMES: Oh, yes. Remember what she told us? Her sister could smell Dr. Roylott's cigar? So there had to be an opening between the two rooms. Nothing was said about it at the coroner's inquest. So it had to be small. Therefore—a ventilator.

WATSON: But what harm could that do?

HOLMES: Well, at the very least, it's an odd coincidence. A ventilator is made. A cord is hung. And a lady who sleeps in the bed dies. Doesn't that strike you?

WATSON: What's the connection? I can't see any.

HOLMES: Notice anything odd about that bed?

WATSON: No.

HOLMES: It was clamped to the floor. Ever see a bed bolted down like that before?

WATSON: Can't say I have.

HOLMES: She couldn't move her bed. It had to stay there right under the ventilator and the rope. We might as well call it a rope, since it was never meant to be used as a bell-rope.

WATSON: Holmes! I'm beginning to guess. If that's it, then . . . Why, we're just in time to prevent a horrible crime. A clever, horrible crime.

HOLMES: Clever enough. And horrible enough. Watson, when a doctor goes wrong, he makes a first-rate criminal. He has

---

deduce (dih DOOS) figure out by reasoning
inquest (IN kwest) legal investigation into the cause of death
coincidence (koh IN suh duns) two related events accidentally happening at the same time

Suspense

243

Critical Thinking: At the end of Scene 9, Holmes strongly suspects the killer's identity.

Discussion: At the end of Scene 9, Holmes says "We'll have plenty of horror." Does Holmes mean this figuratively or literally? Ask students, Are Watson and Holmes really in great danger?

Discussion: What special expertise might a doctor have that would help in committing the crime?

nerve, and he has knowledge. Don't *you* ever turn your mind to crime!

WATSON: Never! What a horrible idea!

HOLMES: Believe me, we'll have plenty of horror before the night is over. Would you hand me my pipe, please? Might as well have a few cheerful hours first.

SCENE 10

SETTING: *The same, later.*

AT RISE: HOLMES, *looking out the window, sees a single light appear across the way.*

HOLMES: That's our signal!

(*The two hurry out.*)

SCENE 11

SETTING: JULIA'S *bedroom.*
AT RISE: *The room is dark.* HOLMES *and* WATSON, *their shoes off, enter.* HOLMES *carries a candle and a cane.*

HOLMES (*whispering*)**:** The least sound would be fatal to the plan.

(WATSON *nods.*)

HOLMES (*whispering*)**:** We have to sit without light. He'd see it through the ventilator.

(WATSON *nods again.* HOLMES *blows out the candle. Darkness.*)

HOLMES (*whispering*)**:** Don't go to sleep. Your *life* may depend on it. Have your pistol ready.

(HOLMES *motions to* WATSON *to sit in the chair.* HOLMES *sits on the edge of the bed.* WATSON *takes out his pistol.* HOLMES *places his cane on the side of the bed. They wait. Total silence. Then a bird cries suddenly outside, and the two jump. Then they go back to waiting. A clock strikes twelve.*)

SCENE 12

SETTING: *The same.*

AT RISE: HOLMES *and* WATSON *are sitting in the same places.*

They are slumped over, showing signs of tiredness. WATSON *shakes his head to keep his eyes open. A clock strikes three. Suddenly, there is the sound of something moving. Then comes a gentle, soothing sound—like the sound of steam coming out of a kettle.* HOLMES *strikes a match. He springs from the bed. Then he begins lashing the bell-rope with his cane.*

HOLMES *(yelling)*: You see it, Watson? You see it?
WATSON: What? What?

(There is the sound of a low, clear whistle. HOLMES *stops striking the bell-rope. He watches it closely. After a moment, a horrible cry is heard off-stage. It becomes louder and louder. It is a hoarse yell of pain and fear and anger.* WATSON *and* HOLMES *look at each other. The scream finally dies away.)*

WATSON: What does it mean?
HOLMES: It means it's all over. Probably for the best, too. Take your pistol, Watson. We'll go into Dr. Roylott's room.

SCENE 13

SETTING: DR. ROYLOTT'S *bedroom.*

AT RISE: HOLMES *and* WATSON, *with his pistol ready, enter the room. They see the iron safe, with its door ajar. Next to it, on a chair, sits* DR. ROYLOTT, *in his bathrobe. The dog leash is across his lap. Rigid, he stares at the ceiling. Around his brow is a yellow band, with brownish speckles. It seems to be bound tightly around his head.*

HOLMES: There's the speckled band!

*(*WATSON *takes a step forward. The speckled band begins to move! It lifts up a diamond-shaped head. It reveals the puffed neck of a deadly snake.)*

HOLMES: A swamp adder! The deadliest snake in India. Ten seconds after he was bitten—he died! It was obvious. The rope had to be there as a bridge for something passing through the hole and coming to the bed.
WATSON: But who'd think of a snake?
HOLMES: I thought of it right away. Remember, the doctor had pets from India. We knew that. A snake seemed just the sort

Suspense   245

Discussion: At the end of Scene 12, when the screaming stops, what has happened? Why does Holmes say. " . . . it's all over"? Does he know what has happened? He certainly seems to.

Enrichment: The term "adder" in North America usually applies to nonpoisonous snakes; in Europe and India, an adder is a poisonous snake.

Discussion: How was the crime committted? Ask students to reconstruct Julia Stoner's death. Then point out—if students haven't—that Roylott was killed the same way. Ask, in literature, what is this called? (irony)

of weapon he'd choose. A kind of poison no test could discover. Then, too, it would take effect so quickly. A big advantage from his point of view.

WATSON: A wicked point of view, you mean.

HOLMES: Wickedly clever. Only a sharp-eyed coroner would find the two little punctures left by the fangs. Of course, there was also the whistle. That was a clue.

WATSON: I've been wondering about that. Snakes don't whistle, do they?

HOLMES: Don't be silly, Watson. The *doctor* whistled. The point is, he had to call back the snake before morning. He must have trained it—probably with milk—to return to him when he whistled. He'd put it through the ventilator. He knew it would crawl down the rope and land on the bed.

WATSON: But how could he be sure the snake would bite?

HOLMES: It might or it might not. She might escape every night for a week. But sooner or later . . .

WATSON: Horrible. Yes, I can see now how he must have done it.

HOLMES: Oh, I figured that out before I even went into his room. Then looking at his chair—that settled it.

WATSON: The chair?

HOLMES: Scuff marks. He'd been in the habit of standing on it. He'd have to in order to reach the ventilator. Then there was the speckled band. Let's put this thing back in its den. Then

we can get Miss Stoner out of here and get the police in.

(HOLMES *picks up the dog leash and throws it around the snake's neck. He carries the deadly reptile at arm's length, throws it into the safe, and locks the door.*)

SCENE 14

SETTING: The parlor in HOLMES'S *apartment. The next day.*
AT RISE: HOLMES *and* WATSON *sit, having tea.*

HOLMES: I'm afraid I'd had the wrong idea about the case all along, Watson.

WATSON: You too?

HOLMES: That shows you how dangerous it is to reason without having *all* the facts.

WATSON: A natural mistake. After all, the gypsies, the word "band"—it was logical to suspect them.

HOLMES: Not at all. Sloppy thinking. There's only one thing *I* can say in my defense. That is, I instantly changed my mind when I saw the room couldn't be gotten at from outside.

WATSON: You were very clever to notice the ventilator and the bell-rope. I didn't. But even when you pointed them out, I was at sea.

HOLMES: Surely, Watson, after I showed you that the bell-rope was a dummy, you must have guessed . . . safe, the saucer of milk, the loop of cord for a leash. Elementary, my dear Watson.

WATSON: Wait a second. What about that metallic clang heard by Miss Stoner? What was that?

HOLMES: Her stepfather closing the safe, of course. And don't forget the softer noise—that was the snake's hiss. As soon as I heard it, I attacked the thing with my cane.

WATSON: To drive it back through the ventilator.

HOLMES: Exactly. And also, frankly, I had another purpose. My attack roused the snake's temper. Made it fly at the first person it saw.

WATSON: Dr. Grimesby Roylott!

HOLMES: Mmm. You might even say I sort of indirectly caused his death. Can't say it's likely to weigh very heavily on my mind. Will you pass me some toast, please, Watson?

Suspense 247

1. Nothing; "Madam, my work is its own reward."
2. It was Dr. Roylott calling the snake back.
3. It was clamped to the floor so it couldn't be moved.
4. Very upset. She said she was "surrounded by danger." She was afraid some "evil" existed that might cause her harm.
5. This is the only direct confrontation between protagonist and antagonist in the play. Roylott comes across as brutish, fearsome, and evil; Holmes comes across as cool, sophisticated, and unflappable.
6. To force her to move into Julia's room. (which was next to the doctor's and had the vent through which the snake could crawl.)
7. It is through the process of deduction, Holmes is arrogantly implying to Watson, that crimes can be solved easily.
8. He is her stepfather, and she is dependent on him.
9. A good example, in Scene 9, is Holmes's observation that there must be a ventilator shaft between the doctor's and Julia's room because Julia and Helen had smelled the doctor's cigars before they went to bed the night of Julia's death.
10. Some students might notice a contradiction in Holmes himself, between his urge for quick justice and his denial of due process entitled any person suspected of a crime.

Respond to Literature: The Holmes mysteries present problem-solving conflicts that allow the reader to play detective along with Holmes.

FOCUS ON THE SELECTION

UNDERSTAND THE SELECTION

Recall

1. How much does Holmes charge Helen Stoner for his work?
2. What is the significance of the whistling that Helen's sister heard?
3. What was odd about Julia's bed?

Infer

4. Describe Helen Stoner's state of mind when she came to see Holmes.
5. The first meeting between Holmes and Dr. Roylott was stormy. How do you know that?
6. What was the real reason for the renovation in Helen's room?
7. Explain the meaning of, "Elementary, my dear Watson."

Apply

8. Why do you think Helen protects Dr. Roylott?
9. Give an example of "deduction," the type of reasoning for which Sherlock Holmes is famous.
10. Did Holmes have the right to cause the death of Dr. Roylott? Explain.

Respond to Literature

Why do you think the Holmes mysteries have been popular for a century?

WRITE ABOUT THE SELECTION

Can you write the script for a 60-second television crime show? Imagine the television producer has agreed to pick the best script submitted and produce it. The show will be used as a "filler." You must follow the basic rule in crime stories: enough information must be given to allow the viewer to solve the crime himself or herself. However, you must not make it too easy.

Prewriting: First, think of a crime story. You can make up one, or use one you already know. Make a flow chart that shows the action of the story. Next to each box write the dialogue that will be needed for each character.

Writing: Use the flow chart to help you write your script. You may use characters and stage directions; you may use a first-person narrator; or, you may use third-person point of view. Indicate all stage directions and sound effects.

Revising: Can the crime be solved with the information you have given? Check to make sure it can. Can the script be "performed" in 60 seconds? It will not be accepted for judging unless it can. Finally, make sure transitions between speakers or between thoughts is clear. The script must make sense to the reader.

Proofreading: Reread your script and check that the dialogue of each speaker is marked as a new paragraph. Did you use correct punctuation? The script must be tight, with no loose ends.

Prewriting: You may want to have students work in pairs for this entire assignment. If so, have them first brainstorm ideas, then write a sequential flow chart of the action.

Writing: Circulate as students work in pairs, giving help where needed. Make sure that point of view is consistent, and that students divide the flow chart into separate writing assignments.

Revising: Have pairs exchange scripts. The script should be checked to make sure enough information is given to solve the crime. Then, have the partners combine their writing into a single script. Finally have them time the script.

Proofreading: Ask students whether cuts must be made because of a time overrun. If so, advise them to go over the script together, deleting all unnecessary adjectives and adverbs.

THINK ABOUT CHARACTERS

Holmes notes at one point in the story, "We're in deep waters here." Indeed, in this episode of Holmes's adventures, he is pitted against an adversary he himself calls "cunning" and "clever." Do you agree? Explain the reasons for your answer.

1. Who is the protagonist and who is the antagonist in the story? Are they equally matched? Explain your answer.

2. Describe the conflict between them. What does each want to accomplish?

3. Do the protagonist and antagonist respect each other? What makes you think so?

4. The one direct confrontation between the protagonist and antagonist ends in a show of physical strength. Who won the confrontation?

5. How does the conflict between the protagonist and antagonist end?

DEVELOP YOUR VOCABULARY

Writing crime stories requires a special vocabulary. You must know terms associated with police work and the legal system.

An example is the word *coroner*. It means a "public officer who investigates deaths that may not be due to natural causes." A coroner can play a very important part in a murder mystery, so you should know the meaning of the word.

Below are some more words associated with crime stories. Make sure that you know how each one is pronounced and what it means. Use a dictionary if you are unsure. Then use each word in a sentence.

1. deduce
2. felony
3. autopsy
4. will
5. inquest
6. homicide
7. arrest
8. plea
9. trial
10. verdict
11. sentence
12. forensic
13. robbery
14. assault
15. defendant
16. perpetrator

Suspense

249

T249

MORE ABOUT ELEMENTS OF THE DRAMA

MORE ABOUT ELEMENTS OF THE DRAMA

Begin a class discussion on drama by first reviewing its main elements: setting, characters, plot, theme, conflict. You may want to write the elements on the chalkboard as a checklist. Next, ask students to specify those elements in both *Romeo and Juliet* (Unit 1) and *Sorry, Wrong Number* (Unit 2). Then, call on volunteers to outline the elements of a favorite stage play, movie or TV drama. Encourage students to choose a drama of superior quality, such as Lorraine Hansbury's "A Raisin in the Sun."

Suggested Questions

Use *Sherlock Holmes and the Speckled Band* to strengthen students' grasp of the elements of drama. You may want a volunteer to write these questions on the board. A suggested procedure appears in parenthesis:

- What is the plot? As students provide answers, map out the plot on the board.
- Who are the characters? (Students may turn to the list at the beginning of the play, if necessary.)
- What is the setting? (Students should check in their books to see that the setting changes in almost every scene, either to indicate change of time or of place.)
- What is the theme? (Students might find more than one theme; each should be listed.)
- What is the major conflict in the plot? (Refer students, also, to the other dramas they have read: *Romeo and Juliet* and *Sorry Wrong Number*. Ask the conflict in each.)

You might want to note, if students disagree with one another, that literature is not set fast in right or wrong answers, but remains open to personal interpretation.

A drama is a play that tells a story that revolves around a conflict. Drama is made up of dialogue and action. When you go to the theater to see a play, you are not only hearing what the characters say, you are also seeing what they do.

When you read a drama, you are reading what the characters say, but you obviously do not see what they are doing. You must imagine this. Often notes called **stage directions,** in parentheses or brackets, indicate actions.

Since a drama tells a story, it shares the elements of all stories: plot, characters, setting, and theme. A part of the plot often stressed in drama is conflict. Conflict, usually between human characters, creates the action that keeps the play moving.

Plot. Since you have already studied the short story, you know that plot is the series of events, or actions, in a story. The plot of a story often begins with **exposition,** or background information. Then a *complication* develops. The action *rises,* leading to a *climax.* Resolution of any unanswered questions comes about after the climax, in *falling action.*

You should pay particular attention to plot clues when reading a drama because the events of the plot are presented differently than in a short story. Plot develops solely through the conversation of the characters. There is often no narrator so you must interpret the information the characters provide and piece it together.

Characters. It is the presentation of information through conversation that makes the characters an important element in any drama. You read exactly what the characters say, not what someone else reports them to have said.

The characters in a drama are, of course, the people in the story. You are introduced to them at the very beginning of the play, in the list of characters. This introduction is just that—a list. Unless you are already familiar with the drama, you have no idea which characters are the main ones and how they interact. You learn this through the dialogue.

D RAMA

To help your imagination, stage directions are sometimes given to describe character's actions. Besides what we learn through these actions, any ideas or descriptions about the characters come indirectly, from what other characters say about them.

Setting. The setting of a drama is stated usually at the beginning of the play. If the setting changes during the play, the new setting is given at the opening of a scene or act.

When you see a drama performed on stage, you learn the "where" of the setting by looking at the stage set. You learn the "when" of the setting also by looking at the stage set and by seeing how the characters are dressed. The objects, or props used in the setting, as well as the clothes, or costumes, of the characters, provide clues to the time that the drama takes place.

Theme. Theme is the message of the drama. It is the central idea behind the drama. As in short stories, there might be more than one theme in a drama. Sometimes there is no theme of real importance. Usually, however, from studying the conflict, a single, clear theme will emerge.

Conflict. Conflict is what keeps a drama moving. The need to resolve the conflict creates dramatic action that drives the plot to a climax. Conflict usually develops between characters, because characters and their actions are the basis of any play. In "Sherlock Holmes and the Speckled Band," the conflict is between a protagonist and antagonist.

Conflict can also be within a character. If a character struggles to perform a difficult physical feat, for example, the conflict is between the character and his or her own fear.

As you read the next selection in this unit, look for the elements of drama. Ask yourself these questions:

1. How are the literally elements presented differently in a drama than they are in a short story?
2. What is the conflict in the drama?

Suspense 251

Practical Application

Many television shows are dramas. Ask students for examples; remind them that dramas tell a serious story (often with humor) and, therefore, "sitcoms" aren't appropriate. Then ask them, "Has television in general increased your awareness of good drama?" Since TV has become such a dominant influence in the lives of everyone, you might want to have a formal, classroom debate on the question.

by Susan Glaspell

CHARACTERS

GEORGE HENDERSON, *county attorney*	MRS. PETERS
HENRY PETERS, *sheriff*	MRS. HALE
LEWIS HALE, *a neighboring farmer*	

Scene: *The kitchen in the now abandoned farmhouse of* JOHN WRIGHT, *a gloomy kitchen, and left without having been put in order—unwashed pans under the sink, a loaf of bread outside the breadbox, a dish towel on the table—other signs of incompleted work. At the rear the outer door opens and the* SHERIFF *comes in followed by the* COUNTY ATTORNEY *and* HALE. *The* SHERIFF *and* HALE *are men in middle life, the* COUNTY ATTORNEY *is a young man; all are much bundled up and go at once to the stove. They are followed by the two women—the* SHERIFF'S *wife first; she is a slight wiry woman, a thin nervous face.* MRS. HALE *is larger and would ordinarily be called more comfortable looking, but she is disturbed now and looks fearfully about as she enters. The women have come in slowly, and stand close together near the door.*

COUNTY ATTORNEY (*rubbing his hands*)**:** This feels good. Come up to the fire, ladies.

MRS. PETERS (*after taking a step forward*)**:** I'm not—cold.

SHERIFF (*unbuttoning his overcoat and stepping away from the stove as if to mark the beginning of official business*)**:** Now, Mr. Hale, before we move things about, you explain to Mr. Henderson just what you saw when you came here yesterday morning.

COUNTY ATTORNEY: By the way, has anything been moved? Are things just as you left them yesterday?

---

attorney (uh TUR nee) lawyer. A county attorney is a lawyer responsible for bringing criminal charges against someone.
wiry (WYR ee) lean and strong

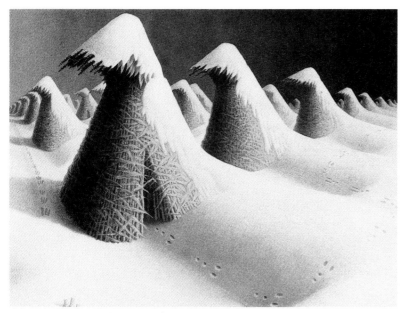

January, 1940, Grant Wood. Collection of King W. Vidor Trust

SHERIFF (*looking about*)**:** It's just the same. When it dropped below zero last night I thought I'd better send Frank out this morning to make a fire for us—no use getting pneumonia with a big case on, but I told him not to touch anything except the stove—and you know Frank.

COUNTY ATTORNEY: Somebody should have been left here yesterday.

SHERIFF: Oh—yesterday. When I had to send Frank to Morris Center for that man who went crazy—I want you to know I had my hands full yesterday. I knew you could get back from Omaha by today and as long as I went over everything here myself—

COUNTY ATTORNEY: Well, Mr. Hale, tell just what happened when you came here yesterday morning.

HALE: Harry and I had started to town with a load of potatoes. We came along the road from my place and as I got here I said, "I'm going to see if I can't get John Wright to go in with me on

Notice how the characters of the sheriff and the county attorney are developed through dialogue. The county attorney seems businesslike and thorough. The sheriff seems to be confronted with a great many problems. Still, he worries about things such as heat in the old farmhouse.

Here is the main question of the plot: "What happened at the Wright farmhouse yesterday morning?" The plot develops as the characters search for an answer.

pneumonia (noo-MOHN-yuh) disease of the lungs; caused by an
  infection, and results in swelling and soreness

Suspense 253

a party telephone." I spoke to Wright about it once before and he put me off, saying folks talked too much anyway, and all he asked was peace and quiet—I guess you know about how much he talked himself; but I thought maybe if I went to the house and talked about it before his wife, though I said to Harry that I didn't know as what his wife wanted made much difference to John—

COUNTY ATTORNEY: Let's talk about that later, Mr. Hale. I do want to talk about that, but tell now just what happened when you got to the house.

HALE: I didn't hear or see anything; I knocked at the door, and still it was all quiet inside. I knew they must be up, it was past eight o'clock. So I knocked again, and I thought I heard somebody say, "Come in." I wasn't sure, I'm not sure yet, but I opened the door—this door *(indicating the door by which the two men are still standing)* and there in that rocker—*(pointing to it)* sat Mrs. Wright.

(They all look at the rocker.)

COUNTY ATTORNEY: What—was she doing?

HALE: She was rockin' back and forth. She had her apron in her hand and was kind of—pleating it.

COUNTY ATTORNEY: And how did she—look?

HALE: Well, she looked queer.

COUNTY ATTORNEY: How do you mean—queer?

HALE: Well, as if she didn't know what she was going to do next. And kind of done up.

COUNTY ATTORNEY: How did she seem to feel about your coming?

HALE: Why, I don't think she minded—one way or other. She didn't pay much attention. I said, "How do, Mrs. Wright, it's cold, ain't it?" And she said, "Is it?"—and went on kind of pleating at her apron. Well, I was surprised; she didn't ask me to come up to the stove, or to sit down, but just sat there, not even looking at me, so I said, "I want to see John." And then she—laughed. I guess you would call it a laugh. I thought of Harry and the team outside, so I said a little sharp: "Can't I see John?" "No," she says, kind of dull like. "Ain't he home?"

These notes in parentheses are stage directions. An actor would use them in playing the part of Hale on the stage. However, they also help us to "see" the action and to understand what is happening.

This is a story within a story. It is a way for more background information to be introduced, even though the people mentioned are not characters in the play.

---

pleating (PLEET-ing) pressing cloth together

says I. "Yes," says she, "he's home." "Then why can't I see him?" I asked her, out of patience. "'Cause he's dead," says she. *"Dead?"* says I. She just nodded her head, not getting a bit excited, but rockin' back and forth. "Why—where is he?" says I, not knowing what to say. She just pointed upstairs— like that *(himself pointing to the room above).* I got up, with the idea of going up there. I walked from there to here—then I says, "Why, what did he die of?" "He died of a rope around his neck," says she, and just went on pleatin' at her apron. Well, I went out and called Harry. I thought I might—need help. We went upstairs and there he was lyin'—

COUNTY ATTORNEY: I think I'd rather have you go into that upstairs, where you can point it all out. Just go on now with the rest of the story.

HALE: Well, my first thought was to get that rope off. It looked . . . *(stops, his face twitches)* . . . but Harry, he went up to him, and he said, "No, he's dead all right, and we'd better not touch anything." So we went back downstairs. She was still sitting that same way. "Has anybody been notified?" I asked. "No," says she, unconcerned. "Who did this, Mrs. Wright?" said Harry. He said it businesslike—and she stopped pleatin' her apron. "I don't know," she says. "You don't *know?*" says Harry. "No," says she. "Weren't you sleeping in the bed with him?" says Harry. "Yes," says she, "but I was on the inside." "Somebody slipped a rope round his neck and strangled him and you didn't wake up?" says Harry. "I didn't wake up," she said after him. We must have looked as if we didn't see how that could be, for after a minute she said, "I sleep sound." Harry was going to ask her more questions but I said maybe we ought to let her tell her story first to the coroner, or the sheriff, so Harry went fast as he could to Rivers' place, where there's a telephone.

COUNTY ATTORNEY: And what did Mrs. Wright do when she knew that you had gone for the coroner?

HALE: She moved from that chair to this one over here *(pointing to a small chair in the corner)* and just sat there with her hands held together and looking down. I got a feeling that I ought to

Here is the plot complication: Did Mrs. Wright kill her husband? A few lines further on the county attorney is already trying to determine a motive for the killing.

---

twitches (TWICH iz) pulls with a sudden jerk
notified (NOHT uh fyd) advised; informed
strangled (STRANG guld) choked; killed by squeezing

Suspense   255

Discussion: The county attorney gathers information as Holmes did in *Sherlock Holmes and the Speckled Band.* Ask students to compare their styles.

Critical Thinking: The important aspect of Hale's long answers, in response to the County Attorney, is the picture that emerges of Mrs. Wright.

The Judges c. 1907, Georges Rouault.
The Portland Museum of Art

make some conversation, so I said I had come in to see if John wanted to put in a telephone, and at that she started to laugh, and then she stopped and looked at me—scared. *(The COUNTY ATTORNEY, who has had his notebook out, makes a note.)* I dunno, maybe it wasn't scared. I wouldn't like to say it was. Soon Harry got back, and then Dr. Lloyd came, and you, Mr. Peters, and so I guess that's all I know that you don't.

COUNTY ATTORNEY *(looking around)*: I guess we'll go upstairs first—and then out to the barn and around there. *(To the SHERIFF)* You're convinced that there was nothing important here—nothing that would point to any motive?

SHERIFF: Nothing here but kitchen things.

(The COUNTY ATTORNEY, after again looking around the kitchen, opens the door of a cupboard closet. He gets up on a chair and looks on a shelf. Pulls his hand away, sticky.)

---

cupboard (KUB urd) a closet fitted with shelves for holding cups

Unit 3

Literary Focus: More foreshadowing: The sheriff says there is nothing of any importance downstairs in the house, just "kitchen things." But it is from close examination of small, domestic objects that the women of the play will begin to understand what happened.

COUNTY ATTORNEY: Here's a nice mess.

(The women draw nearer.)

MRS. PETERS *(to the other woman)***:** Oh, her fruit; it did freeze. *(To the* LAWYER.*)* She worried about that when it turned so cold. She said the fire'd go out and her jars would break.

SHERIFF: Well, can you beat the women! Held for murder and worryin' about her preserves.

COUNTY ATTORNEY: I guess before we're through she may have something more serious than preserves to worry about.

HALE: Well, women are used to worrying over trifles.

(The two women move a little closer together.)

COUNTY ATTORNEY *(With the gallantry of a young politician)***:** And yet, for all their worries, what would we do without the ladies? *(The women do not unbend. He goes to the sink, takes a dipperful of water from the pail and pouring it into a basin, washes his hands. Starts to wipe them on the roller-towel, turns it for a cleaner place)* Dirty towels! *(Kicks his foot against the pans under the sink)* Not much of a housekeeper, would you say, ladies?

MRS. HALE *(stiffly)***:** There's a great deal of work to be done on a farm.

COUNTY ATTORNEY: To be sure. And yet *(with a little bow to her)* I know there are some Dickson county farmhouses which do not have such roller towels.

(He gives it a pull to expose its full length again.)

MRS. HALE: Those towels get dirty awful quick. Men's hands aren't always as clean as they might be.

COUNTY ATTORNEY: Ah, loyal to your sex, I see. But you and Mrs. Wright were neighbors. I suppose you were friends, too.

MRS. HALE *(shaking her head)***:** I've not seen much of her of late years. I've not been in this house—it's more than a year.

COUNTY ATTORNEY: And why was that? You didn't like her?

MRS. HALE: I liked her all well enough. Farmers' wives have their hands full, Mr. Henderson. And then—

---

preserves (pri ZURVZ) fruit kept from spoiling by special treatment
trifles (TRY fulz) anything of little value or importance
gallantry (GAL un tree) heroic courage; elaborate politeness to women
expose (ik SPOHZ) to lay open; uncover

Suspense

257

Critical Thinking: A small clue about Mrs. Wright's state of mind: "Well, women," says Hale, "are used to worrying over trifles." The use of the word "trifles" (the title of the play) is a signal that this is an important statement.

Clarification: "Roller towels" refer to a piece of cloth whose ends are sewn together and then attached to a roller. The user turns to a clean place on the towel to dry his or hands. The system works only as long as the towel is washed periodically.

Reading Strategy: The county attorney pursues a new line of inquiry: questioning Mrs. Hale and Mrs. Peters. What does he learn from them? Does it seem important?

Critical Thinking: In blaming the deputy sheriff—not Mrs. Wright's cleaning habits—for a "filthy" roller towel, is Mrs. Hale starting to defend Mrs. Wright?

COUNTY ATTORNEY: Yes—?

MRS. HALE (*looking about*): It never seemed a very cheerful place.

COUNTY ATTORNEY: No—it's not cheerful. I shouldn't say she had the homemaking instinct.

MRS. HALE: Well, I don't know as Wright had, either.

COUNTY ATTORNEY: You mean that they didn't get on very well?

MRS. HALE: No, I don't mean anything. But I don't think a place'd be any cheerfuller for John Wright's being in it.

COUNTY ATTORNEY: I'd like to talk more of that a little later. I want to get the lay of things upstairs now.

(*He goes to the left, where three steps lead to a stair door.*)

SHERIFF: I suppose anything Mrs. Peters does'll be all right. She was to take in some clothes for her, you know, and a few little things. We left in such a hurry yesterday.

COUNTY ATTORNEY: Yes, but I would like to see what you take, Mrs. Peters, and keep an eye out for anything that might be of use to us.

MRS. PETERS: Yes, Mr. Henderson.

The action shifts gears right here. The sheriff and county attorney leave the kitchen and go upstairs to continue their investigation. The women remain downstairs.

(*The women listen to the men's steps on the stairs, then look about the kitchen.*)

This is an important comment, for it indicates a general conflict between men and women.

MRS. HALE: I'd hate to have men coming into my kitchen, snooping around and criticizing.

(*She arranges the pans under the sink which the* LAWYER *had shoved out of place.*)

MRS. PETERS: Of course it's no more than their duty.

MRS. HALE: Duty's all right, but I guess that deputy sheriff that came out to make the fire might have got a little of this on. (*Gives the roller towel a pull*) Wish I'd thought of that sooner. Seems mean to talk about her for not having things slicked up when she had to come away in such a hurry.

MRS. PETERS (*who has gone to a small table in the left rear corner of the room, and lifted one end of a towel that covers a pan*): She had bread set.

---

instinct (IN stingkt) a natural tendency; unconscious skill

snooping (SNOOPing) searching or looking into other people's property or affairs without permission

(Stands still)

MRS. HALE *(Eyes fixed on a loaf of bread beside the breadbox, which is on a low shelf at the other side of the room. Moves slowly toward it.)*: She was going to put this in there. *(Picks up loaf, then abruptly drops it, as though returning to familiar things.)* It's a shame about her fruit. I wonder if it's all gone. *(Gets up on the chair and looks)* I think there's some here that's all right, Mrs. Peters. Yes—here; *(holding it toward the window)* this is cherries, too. *(Looking again)* I declare I believe that's the only one. *(Gets down, bottle in her hand. Goes to the sink and wipes it off on the outside.)* She'll feel awful bad after all her hard work in the hot weather. I remember the afternoon I put up my cherries last summer.

(She puts the bottle on the big kitchen table, center of the room. With a sigh, is about to sit down in the rocking-chair. Before she is seated realizes what chair it is; with a slow look at it, steps back. The chair which she has touched rocks back and forth.)

MRS. PETERS: Well, I must get those things from the front room closet. *(She goes to the door at the right, but after looking into the other room, steps back.)* You coming with me, Mrs. Hale? You could help me carry them.

(They go in the other room; reappear, MRS. PETERS *carrying a dress and a skirt,* MRS. HALE *following with a pair of shoes.)*

MRS. PETERS: My, it's cold in there.

(She puts the clothes on the big table and hurries to the stove.)

MRS. HALE *(examining the skirt)*: Wright was close. I think maybe that's why she kept so much to herself. She didn't even belong to the Ladies Aid. I suppose she felt she couldn't do her part, and then you don't enjoy things when you feel shabby. She used to wear pretty clothes and be lively, when she was Minnie Foster, one of the town girls singing in the choir. But that—oh, that was thirty years ago. This all you were to take in?

MRS. PETERS: She said she wanted an apron. Funny thing to want,

---

shabby (SHAB ee) seedy; poorly dressed

Suspense 259

Clarification: When Mrs. Hale says that she "put up my cherries," she is referring to canning, or preserving, fruits and vegetables for winter use.

Clarification: Ladies Aid is one of several organizations common in rural areas. It serves a charitable as well as social function.

for there isn't much to get you dirty in jail, goodness knows. But I suppose just to make her feel more natural. She said they were in the top drawer in this cupboard. Yes, here. And then her little shawl that always hung behind the door.

(Opens stair door and looks) Yes, here it is.

(Quickly shuts door leading upstairs)

MRS. HALE *(abruptly moving toward her)*: Mrs. Peters?

MRS. PETERS: Yes, Mrs. Hale?

MRS. HALE: Do you think she did it?

MRS. PETERS *(in a frightened voice)*: Oh, I don't know.

MRS. HALE: Well, I don't think she did. Asking for an apron and her little shawl. Worrying about her fruit.

MRS. PETERS *(Starts to speak, glances up, where footsteps are heard in the room above. In a low voice)*: Mr. Peters says it looks bad for her. Mr. Henderson is awful sarcastic and he'll make fun of her sayin' she didn't wake up.

MRS. HALE: Well, I guess John Wright didn't wake when they were slipping that rope under his neck.

MRS. PETERS: No, it's strange. It must have been done awful crafty and still. They say it was such a—funny way to kill a man, rigging it all up like that.

MRS. HALE: That's just what Mr. Hale said. There was a gun in the house. He says that's what he can't understand.

MRS. PETERS: Mr. Henderson said coming out that what was needed for the case was a motive; something to show anger, or—sudden feeling.

MRS. HALE *(who is standing by the table)*: Well, I don't see any signs of anger around here. *(She puts her hand on the dish towel which lies on the table, stands looking down at the table, one half of which is clean, the other half messy.)* It's wiped to here. *(Makes a move as if to finish the work, then turns and looks at loaf of bread outside the breadbox. Drops towel. Speaks in that voice of coming back to familiar things.)* Wonder how they are finding things upstairs. I hope she had it a little more ready up there. You know, it

The question the drama must answer is repeated. The dramatic action begins to rise, ever so slowly.

---

shawl (SHAWL) a loose scarf used by women to cover the shoulders
abruptly (uh BRUPT lee) suddenly
sarcastic (sah KAS tik) sneering or ironic, and meant to hurt feelings
crafty (KRAFT i) shrewd; tricky
rigging (RIG ing) any gear or tackle

Unit 3

Reading Strategy: Make sure students understand what is meant when Mrs. Hale says, "I don't see any signs of anger around here." It is a small but important aspect of the conflict that is unfolding between the women and the county attorney, who needs to find a motive.

Ground Hog Day, Andrew Wyeth. Philadelphia Museum of Art

seems kind of *sneaking*. Locking her up in town and then coming out here and trying to get her own house to turn against her!

MRS. PETERS: But Mrs. Hale, the law is the law.

MRS. HALE: I s'pose 'tis. *(unbuttoning her coat)* Better loosen up your things, Mrs. Peters. You won't feel them when you go out.

(MRS. PETERS *takes off her fur tippet, goes to hang it on hook at back of room, stands looking at the under part of the small corner table.)*

MRS. PETERS: She was piecing a quilt.

Here sympathy is created for Mrs. Wright and the situation she is in. Mrs. Hale feels a kind of common bond with Mrs. Wright. Do you think so?

---

tippet (TIP it) garment like a scarf that covers the neck and shoulders
quilt (KWILT) a bed cover made by stitching a layer of cotton between
 two layers of fabric

Suspense

(She brings the large sewing basket and they look at the bright pieces.)

MRS. HALE: It's log cabin pattern. Pretty, isn't it? I wonder if she was goin' to quilt it or just knot it?

(Footsteps have been heard coming down the stairs. The SHERIFF enters followed by HALE and the COUNTY ATTORNEY.)

SHERIFF: They wonder if she was going to quilt it or just knot it?

(The men laugh, the women look abashed.)

COUNTY ATTORNEY *(rubbing his hands over the stove)*: Frank's fire didn't do much up there, did it? Well, let's go out to the barn and get that cleared up.

(The men go outside.)

MRS. HALE *(resentfully)*: I don't know as there's anything so strange, our takin' up our time with little things while we're waiting for them to get the evidence. *(She sits down at the big table smoothing out a block with decision.)* I don't see as it's anything to laugh about.

MRS. PETERS *(apologetically)*: Of course they've got awful important things on their minds.

(Pulls up a chair and joins MRS. HALE at the table.)

MRS. HALE *(examining another block)*: Mrs. Peters, look at this one. Here, this is the one she was working on, and look at the sewing! All the rest of it has been so nice, and even. And look at this! It's all over the place! Why, it looks as if she didn't know what she was about!

(After she has said this they look at each other, then start to glance back at the door. After an instant MRS. HALE has pulled at a knot and ripped the sewing.)

MRS. PETERS: Oh, what are you doing, Mrs. Hale?

MRS. HALE *(mildly)*: Just pulling out a stitch or two that's not sewed very good. *(Threading a needle)* Bad sewing always

knot (NOT) tie a knoblike lacing
abashed (uh BASHT) embarrassed
resentfully (rih ZENT ful ee) angrily
apologetically (uh pol uh JET ik lee) defensively; spoken with excuses

made me fidgety.

MRS. PETERS (*nervously*): I don't think we ought to touch things.

MRS. HALE: I'll just finish up this end. (*Suddenly stopping and leaning forward*) Mrs. Peters?

MRS. PETERS: Yes, Mrs. Hale?

MRS. HALE: What do you suppose she was so nervous about?

MRS. PETERS: Oh—I don't know. I don't know as she was nervous. I sometimes sew awful queer when I'm just tired. (MRS. HALE *starts to say something, looks at* MRS. PETERS, *then goes on sewing.*) Well I must get these things wrapped up. They may be through sooner than we think. (*Putting apron and other things together.*) I wonder where I can find a piece of paper, and string.

MRS. HALE: In that cupboard, maybe.

MRS. PETERS (*looking in cupboard*): Why, here's a bird-cage. (*Holds it up.*) Did she have a bird, Mrs. Hale?

MRS. HALE: Why, I don't know whether she did or not—I've not been here for so long. There was a man around last year selling canaries cheap, but I don't know as she took one; maybe she did. She used to sing real pretty herself.

MRS. PETERS (*glancing around*): Seems funny to think of a bird here. But she must have had one, or why would she have a cage? I wonder what happened to it.

MRS. HALE: I s'pose maybe the cat got it.

MRS. PETERS: No, she didn't have a cat. She's got that feeling some people have about cats—being afraid of them. My cat got in her room and she was real upset and asked me to take it out.

MRS. HALE: My sister Bessie was like that. Queer, ain't it?

MRS. PETERS (*examining the cage*): Why, look at this door. It's broke. One hinge is pulled apart.

MRS. HALE (*looking, too*): Looks as if someone must have been rough with it.

MRS. PETERS: Why, yes.

(*She brings the cage forward and puts it on the table.*)

MRS. HALE: I wish if they're going to find any evidence they'd be about it. I don't like this place.

It is Mrs. Peters's turn to "play" detective, although she might not be doing it consciously.

---

fidgety (FIJ it ee) nervous or uneasy

Enrichment: In legal terms, Mrs. Hale is tampering with evidence by pulling out a knot and resewing part of the quilt. The bad sewing reflects on Mrs. Wright's state of mind, which could be an important aspect of the case against her. Mrs. Peters, the wife of the sheriff, recognizes this and is nervous about what Mrs. Hale is doing.

Clarification: Consciously or unconsciously, Mrs. Hale refers to Mrs. Wright by her maiden name, Minnie Foster. Is she saying she lost touch with Minnie Foster once Minnie married John Wright?

Literary Focus: Passing time with John Wright, says Mrs. Hale, was "like a raw wind that gets to the bone." Slowly but surely the depth of the conflict between the Wrights is emerging.

Here is some information about the setting tucked into the dialogue.

MRS. PETERS: But I'm awful glad you came with me, Mrs. Hale. It would be lonesome for me sitting here alone.

MRS. HALE: It would, wouldn't it? *(Dropping her sewing)* But I tell you what I do wish, Mrs. Peters. I wish I had come over sometimes when *she* was here. I—*(looking around the room)*—wish I had.

MRS. PETERS: But of course you were awful busy, Mrs. Hale—your house and your children.

MRS. HALE: I could've come. I stayed away because it wasn't cheerful—and that's why I ought to have come. I—I've never liked this place. Maybe because it's down in a hollow and you don't see the road. I dunno what it is, but it's a lonesome place and always was. I wish I had come over to see Minnie Foster sometimes. I can see now—

(Shakes her head.)

MRS. PETERS: Well, you mustn't reproach yourself, Mrs. Hale. Somehow we just don't see how it is with other folks until—something comes up.

MRS. HALE: Not having children makes less work—but it makes a quiet house, and Wright out to work all day, and no company when he did come in. Did you know John Wright, Mrs. Peters?

MRS. PETERS: Not to know him; I've seen him in town. They say he was a good man.

MRS. HALE: Yes—good; he didn't drink, and kept his word as well as most, I guess, and paid his debts. But he was a hard man, Mrs. Peters. Just to pass the time of day with him—*(shivers)* Like a raw wind that gets to the bone. *(Pauses, her eye falling on the cage)* I should think she would 'a wanted a bird. But what do you suppose happened to it?

MRS. PETERS: I don't know, unless it got sick and died.

(She reaches over and swings the broken door, swings it again, both women watch it.)

MRS. HALE: You weren't raised round here, were you? (MRS. PETERS *shakes her head.)* You didn't know—her?

MRS. PETERS: Not until they brought her yesterday.

---

reproach (rih PROHCH) accuse and blame for a fault

Christina's World, Andrew Wyeth, 1948. Tempera on gesso panel 32¼" × 47¾". Collection, The Museum of Modern Art, New York. Purchase.

MRS. HALE: She—come to think of it, she was kind of like a bird herself—real sweet and pretty, but kind of timid and—fluttery. How—she—did—change. *(Silence; then as if struck by a happy thought and relieved to get back to everyday things.)* Tell you what, Mrs. Peters, why don't you take the quilt in with you? It might take up her mind.

MRS. PETERS: Why, I think that's a real nice idea, Mrs. Hale. There couldn't possibly be any objection to it, could there? Now, just what would I take? I wonder if her patches are in here—and her things.

(They look in the sewing basket.)

MRS. HALE: Here's some red. I expect this has got sewing things in it. *(Brings out a fancy box)* What a pretty box. Looks like

Mrs. Hale gives us another glimpse of Mrs. Wright's character. Note the simile comparing her to the now-dead caged bird.

Literary Focus: The playwright is very skillful in advancing the plot. A generous thought of Mrs. Hale's—taking the quilt to Mrs. Wright—leads to finding more crucial evidence: a pretty box.

---

timid (TIM id) shy
fluttery (FLUT ur ee) moving rapidly and with uncertainly

something somebody would give you. Maybe her scissors are in here. *(Opens box. Suddenly puts her hand to her nose.)* Why— *(*MRS. PETERS *bends nearer, then turns her face away)* There's something wrapped up in this piece of silk.

MRS. PETERS: Why, this isn't her scissors.

MRS. HALE *(lifting the silk):* Oh, Mrs. Peters-s-its—

A desire to give Mrs. Wright some "women's" work to pass the time in jail turns up what surely must be important evidence.

*(*MRS. PETERS *bends closer.)*

MRS. PETERS: It's the bird.

MRS. HALE *(jumping up):* But, Mrs. Peters—look at it! Its neck! Look at its neck! It's all—other side *to.*

MRS. PETERS: Somebody—wrung—its—neck.

The women are hiding something from the men. Why? Is everyone trying to solve the crime?

(Their eyes meet. A look of growing comprehension, of horror. Steps are heard outside. MRS. HALE *slips box under quilt pieces, and sinks into her chair. Enter* SHERIFF *and* COUNTY ATTORNEY. MRS. PETERS *rises.)*

COUNTY ATTORNEY *(as one turning from serious things to little pleasantries):* Well, ladies, have you decided whether she was going to quilt it or knot it?

MRS. PETERS: We think she was going to—knot it.

COUNTY ATTORNEY: Well, that's interesting, I'm sure. *(Seeing the birdcage)* Has the bird flown?

MRS. HALE *(putting more quilt pieces over the box):* We think the—cat got it.

COUNTY ATTORNEY *(preoccupied):* Is there a cat?

*(*MRS. HALE *glances in a quick, covert way at* MRS. PETERS.)*

MRS. PETERS: Well, not *now.* They're superstitious, you know. They leave.

We learn through dialogue that the men are looking for clues telling who could have entered the house to commit the murder. The women, suggest the stage directions, have a much greater understanding of what happened.

COUNTY ATTORNEY *(to* SHERIFF PETERS, *continuing an interrupted conversation):* No sign at all of anyone having come from the outside. Their own rope. Now let's go up again and go over it piece by piece. *(They start upstairs.)* It would have to have been

---

comprehension (kom-pree-HEN-shun) understanding or knowledge of something
pleasantries (PLEZ un treez) lively, agreeable talks
preoccupied (pree OK yuh pyd) thinking of something else
covert (KOH vert) hidden or disguised
superstitious (soo pur STISH us) too much fear of the unknown

Enrichment: The women don't miss a step. They have shared an important discovery the conents of the pretty box—but they aren't going to let the men in on it. They pretend nothing significant has happened.

someone who knew just the—

(MRS. PETERS sits down. The two women sit there not looking at one another, but as if peering into something and at the same time holding back. When they talk now it is in the manner of feeling their way over strange ground, as if afraid of what they are saying, but as if they cannot help saying it.)

MRS. HALE: She liked the bird. She was going to bury it in that pretty box.

MRS. PETERS *(in a whisper)*: When I was a girl—my kitten—there was a boy took a hatchet, and before my eyes—and before I could get there—*(covers her face an instant)* If they hadn't held me back I would have—*(catches herself, looks upstairs where steps are heard, falters weakly)*—hurt him.

MRS. HALE *(with a slow look around her)*: I wonder how it would seem never to have had any children around. *(Pause)* No, Wright wouldn't like the bird—a thing that sang. She used to sing. He killed that, too.

MRS. PETERS *(moving uneasily)*: We don't know who killed the bird.

MRS. HALE: I knew John Wright.

MRS. PETERS: It was an awful thing was done in this house that night, Mrs. Hale. Killing a man while he slept, slipping a rope around his neck that choked the life out of him.

MRS. HALE: His neck. Choked the life out of him.

(Her hand goes out and rests on the bird cage.)

MRS. PETERS *(with rising voice)*: We don't know who killed him. We don't *know*.

MRS. HALE *(her own feeling not interrupted)*: If there'd been years and years of nothing, then a bird to sing to you, it would be awful—still, after the bird was still.

MRS. PETERS *(something within her speaking)*: I know what stillness is. When we homesteaded in Dakota, and my first baby died—after he was two years old, and me with no other then—

---

peering (PIR ing) looking closely
hatchet (HACH it) a tool for chopping; like an ax
falters (FAWL terz) walks unsteadily; stumbles
homesteaded (HOHM sted id) occupied land as a home

Suspense

267

The note, "with rising voice," suggests the action is rising faster and we are heading for the climax. The women seem to have a theory about what happened. What is their theory?

Literary Focus: The anecdote of Mrs. Peters about her kitten is a subtle way for the playwright to suggest what might have happened. A direct question—"Do you think she killed Mr. Wright because he killed her little bird?"—wouldn't have been nearly as effective.

Mrs. Peters, the wife of the sheriff, sees the conflict clearly—crimes must be punished, but what if the crime is justifiable?

Here is the theme that has been hinted at before—life for farmers' wives is hard, and the suffering creates a common bond among women.

MRS. HALE (*moving*): How soon do you suppose they'll be through, looking for the evidence?

MRS. PETERS: I know what stillness is. (*Pulling herself back*) The law has got to punish crime, Mrs. Hale.

MRS. HALE (*not as if answering that*): I wish you'd seen Minnie Foster when she wore a white dress with blue ribbons and stood up there in the choir and sang. (*A look around the room*) Oh, I *wish* I'd come over here once in a while! That was a crime! That was a crime! Who's going to punish that?

MRS. PETERS (*looking upstairs*): We mustn't—take on.

MRS. HALE: I might have known she needed help! I know how things can be—for women. I tell you, it's queer, Mrs. Peters. We live close together and we live far apart. We all go through the same things—it's all just a different kind of the same thing. (*Brushes her eyes, noticing the bottle of fruit, reaches out for it*) If I were you I wouldn't tell her her fruit was gone. Tell her it *ain't*. Tell her it's all right. Take this in to prove it to her. She—she may never know whether it was broke or not.

MRS. PETERS (*Takes the bottle, looks about for something to wrap it in; takes petticoat from the clothes brought from the other room, very nervously begins winding this around the bottle. In a false voice.*): My, it's a good thing the men couldn't hear us. Wouldn't they just laugh! Getting all stirred up over a little thing like a—dead canary. As if that could have anything to do with—with—wouldn't they *laugh!*

(*The men are heard coming down stairs.*)

MRS. HALE (*under her breath*): Maybe they would—maybe they wouldn't.

COUNTY ATTORNEY: No, Peters, it's all perfectly clear except a reason for doing it. But you know juries when it comes to women. If there was some definite thing. Something to show—something to make a story about—a thing that would connect up with this strange way of doing it—

(*The women's eyes meet for an instant. Enter* HALE *from outer door.*)

HALE: Well, I've got the team around. Pretty cold out there.

---

petticoat (PET ee koht) a loose underskirt

Unit 3

COUNTY ATTORNEY: I'm going to stay here a while by myself. *(To the* SHERIFF.*) You can send Frank out for me, can't you? I want to go over everything. I'm not satisfied that we can't do better.*

SHERIFF: Do you want to see what Mrs. Peters is going to take in?

(The LAWYER *goes to the table, picks up the apron, laughs.)*

COUNTY ATTORNEY: Oh, I guess they're not very dangerous things the ladies have picked out. *(Moves a few things about, disturbing the quilt pieces which cover the box. Steps back.)* No, Mrs. Peters doesn't need supervising. For that matter, a sheriff's wife is married to the law. Ever think of it that way, Mrs. Peters?

MRS. PETERS: Not—just that way.

SHERIFF *(chuckling)*: Married to the law. *(Moves toward the other room.)* I just want you to come in here a minute, George. We ought to take a look at these windows.

COUNTY ATTORNEY *(scoffingly)*: Oh, windows!

SHERIFF: We'll be right out, Mr. Hale.

*(*HALE *goes outside. The* SHERIFF *follows the* COUNTY ATTORNEY *into the other room. Then* MRS. HALE *rises, hands tight together, looking intensely at* MRS. PETERS, *whose eyes make a slow turn, finally meeting* MRS. HALE'S. *For a moment* MRS. HALE *holds her, then her own eyes point the way to where the box is concealed. Suddenly* MRS. PETERS *throws back quilt pieces and tries to put the box in the bag she is wearing. It is too big. She opens box, starts to take bird out, cannot touch it, goes to pieces, stands there helpless. Sound of a knob turning in the other room.* MRS. HALE *snatches the box and puts it in the pocket of her big coat. Enter* COUNTY ATTORNEY *and* SHERIFF.*)*

The bond among women will prevent Mrs. Peters and Mrs. Hale from telling the men what they know about John Wright's death.

COUNTY ATTORNEY *(facetiously)*: Well, Henry, at least we found out that she was not going to quilt it. She was going to—what is it you call it, ladies?

MRS. HALE *(her hand against her pocket)*: We call it—knot it, Mr. Henderson.

---

supervising (soo pur VYZ ing) inspecting with authority
scoffingly (SKOF ing lee) spoken with scorn or contempt
snatches (SNACH iz) grabs suddenly, rudely, or eagerly
facetiously (fuh-SEE-shus-lee) jokingly, especially at an inappropriate time

Suspense

Literary Focus: An ironic ending. The county attorney refers jokingly to quilting. His attitude, no doubt, steels the will of Mrs. Peters to withhold evidence. His little joke has quietly—and significantly—backfired.

Literary Focus: Mrs. Hale has the last word. The play ends with a remark about a supposed trifle—which, in reality, led the women to solve the crime.

Discussion: Ask students, why do you suppose the entire play takes place in only one place and in one scene?

MINI QUIZ

Write the following questions on the chalkboard or overhead projector and call on students to fill in the blanks. Discuss the answers with the class.

1. The county attorney wasn't immediately available because he was on a trip to _____.
2. The weather at the time the crime took place was _____.
3. The only jar of preserves left was a jar of _____.
4. Mrs. Wright's pet was a _____.
5. The article of clothing Mrs. Wright had asked to be brought to the jail was _____.

Answers to Mini Quiz

1. Omaha
2. cold
3. cherries
4. canary
5. an apron

ANSWERS TO UNDERSTAND THE SELECTION

ANSWERS TO UNDERSTAND THE SELECTION

1. to ask if John Wright would be interested in getting a party telephone line
2. because that's where the body of John Wright had been found
3. a quilt
4. once a very pretty, outgoing woman, now grown old, lonely, and sad with no life outside of her farmhouse. She's married to a hard, humorless man.
5. He was a loner who didn't want much to do with anyone.
6. She wanted to "hurt" the boy who killed the kitten—exactly what Mrs. Wright probably wanted to do to Mr. Wright after he had killed the bird.
7. Even though inaction can't be punished, the things people neglect to do can perhaps cause as much suffering as a crime that is actually commited.
8. Answers will vary. Possible answer: He should have paid more attention to the information that the women had about Mrs. Wright.
9. Answers will vary. What will come out at the tiral? How sympathetic will the jury be? Will a motive ever be proved? How will Mrs. Wright defend herself?
10. the desire to find out who killed John Wright, and why

Respond to Literature: In the example given, answers will vary: Yes, you should go to jail—a crime is a crime; no, you should not go to jail—human life is more important than property rights. Encourage students to give different reasons for a *yes* or *no* answer.

UNDERSTAND THE SELECTION

Recall

1. Why had Lewis Hale stopped at the Wright farmhouse?
2. Why did the sheriff and county attorney go upstairs in the farmhouse?
3. What was Mrs. Wright sewing, at about the time of John Wright's death?

Infer

4. Mrs. Wright is an "absent" character we learn much about. Describe her.
5. What does John Wright's resistance to getting a telephone tell you about him?
6. Why does Mrs. Peters tell about the kitten she had as a little girl?
7. Why does Mrs. Hale consider it a "crime" not to have visited at the Wrights?

Apply

8. How would you investigate John Wright's death if you were county attorney?
9. If Mrs. Wright is put on trial for murder, do you think she will be found guilty?
10. What keeps the story moving?

Respond to Literature

Can any crimes ever be justified? What if your sister is deathly sick, your family has no money to buy the medicine she needs to get well, and you break into a drugstore to steal the medicine? Should you be sentenced to jail if you are caught?

270

WRITE ABOUT THE SELECTION

Pretend that Mrs. Hale did make a neighborly visit to the Wright Farm. Write an imaginary conversation that happens between Mrs. Hale and Mrs. Wright before the murder takes place. Include Mrs. Wright's confession.

Prewriting: Make a list of topics Mrs. Hale might talk about. Next to each topic on the list, jot down Mrs. Wright's response. Then make another list of things Mrs. Wright might want to discuss. Next to each item, jot down Mrs. Hale's response.

Writing: Use your list of topics and responses to create an imaginary two-character scene for the play "Trifles." Your scene should take place before the murder actually happens. Use the play as a model to write the dialogue between Mrs. Hale and Mrs. Wright. Then add whatever stage directions you think are necessary.

Revising: Read your scene aloud. Does your dialogue sound as if two women who are neighbors are actually talking to one another? Change any lines that do not sound real.

Proofreading: Do not use quotation marks for dialogue in a play; instead, make sure each speech is preceded by the correct character's name followed by a colon. Also, check to see that you have inserted a parenthesis at the beginning and ending of all stage directions.

Unit 3

ANSWERS TO WRITE ABOUT THE SELECTION

Prewriting: Go over the relevant sections as a class. Encourage students to make notes as you review the sections; these might help later when they freewrite the points they'll cover.

Writing: Circulate as students work individually. Check for effective openings and conclusions, and remind students that the most convincing arguments are those supported by evidence.

Revising: Have students work in pairs as they read their confessions aloud, asking partners for feedback on ways to improve their draft.

Proofreading: Review as a class what a run-on sentence is. You might also suggest that varying sentence length is important, especially when something is to be spoken. Sentences of similar length tend to bore listeners.

LDP Activity: Brainstorm possible reasons for committing a justifiable crime. (Ex. Stealing food for a poor family.) Use the sentence pattern: It might be okay to _____ if you are.

THINK ABOUT DRAMA

"Trifles" is much more than a simple "who-dunit." In it, the elements of drama: plot, characters, setting, and theme combine to make a suspenseful and meaningful play. The author has something important to tell us. She suggests her message through the play's conflicts. Who murdered John Wright quickly becomes secondary to why he was murdered.

1. The theme is closely related to the conflict presented in the play. What conflict exists between the five characters who actually appear in this play?

2. A second important conflict involves the play's "absent" characters. Explain this conflict.

3. Both of the conflicts involve a lack of understanding. Explain who is involved and what he or she did not understand.

4. How do the characters resolve the conflicts by the end of the play?

5. What do you think is the author's message, the theme of the play?

DEVELOP YOUR VOCABULARY

Using specific words or phrases appropriate to a certain lifestyle makes a story seem more real. You must know exactly what the words mean, however, to understand fully what the author is talking about.

In "Trifles" many words associated with country or farm life are used. For example, at one point Hale mentions "Harry and the team outside." Harry is his companion outside, and the "team" is the horses they are using to haul potatoes to town. The dictionary gives this as a second definition for "team": "two or more horses or oxen harnessed to the same vehicle."

Make sure you know the precise definitions of the following words as they are used in "Trifles." Consult a dictionary if you need help.

1. party telephone	6. dipperful
2. stove	7. roller-towel
3. pleating	8. quilt
4. load of potatoes	9. preserves
5. put up food	10. a hollow

Choose five of the above words and use them in an original paragraph.

ANSWERS TO
THINK ABOUT DRAMA

1. men vs. women, as they try to find out who killed John Wright and why

2. the conflict between Mr. and Mrs. Wright, which must have been simmering for years and finally boiled over when she killed him

3. men in the general case, John Wright in the specific case

4. No. The men will probably try Mrs. Wright in court, but there has been no increase in understanding about the hard life of a farm woman.

5. The author wants us to realize the hard conditions and unjust life that many women have been subjected to by the men they've married.

ANSWERS TO
DEVELOP YOUR
VOCABULARY
Student paragraphs will vary.

1. party telephone, two or more telephones connected to the same line.

2. stove, a wood or coal stove used for heating and, possibly, baking (although it would then be called a "cookstove").

3. pleating; to press cloth together.

4. load of potatoes; an imprecise amount of potatoes.

5. preserves; fruit preseved whole or in large pieces by cooking with sugar.

6. dipper; pumps often had dippers hanging next to them so people could use the dipper as a glass to drink water.

7. roller-towel; circular cloth towel on a roller that can be rotated to find a clean section.

8. quilt; a bedcover made by stitching a layer of soft cotton or wool between two layers of fabric.

9. to put up food; to preserve or can fruits and vegetables.

10. hollow; a depression below the surrounding ground level.

T271

After completing this selection, students will be able to
- understand narration
- describe the difficulties in telling a story
- discuss the symbolism of snakes
- explain a process
- analyze non-fiction narration
- define words used to describe different kinds of scientists

More About Narration: The ordering of events in a story is the most important part of narration, yet it is just the foundation for the story. A good storyteller, whether telling the story verbally or in writing, knows how to develop other aspects of the story. Try telling a story by simply listing the major points of the plot; it's not very appealing.

Cooperative/Collaborative Learning Activity: What makes a good storyteller? Divide the class into groups of four or five. Have each student in the group tell a favorite story. Then, ask the groups to choose one story to tell the whole class. Reassemble the class, and have the person in each group whose story was chosen tell it. Ater each story is told, the group members must tell the class why they chose that particular story. What did they find appealing about it?

More About Vocabulary: First, have students make flashcards of the new vocabulary; perhaps each student could make one card. Next, circulate the flashcards by having students pass theirs to a neighbor. They should then pronounce the new word and read the definition, asking their neighbor for help, if needed. Finally, they should use the word in a sentence.

272

LEARN ABOUT

Narration

The ability to tell a story has played an important part in human life as long as man has been able to communicate.

At first, stories were told orally. Then with the development of alphabets, stories began to be written down. Even today, however, the oral tradition remains strong in some cultures.

Whether stories are told orally or in writing, narration is the most common form of presenting them. **Narration** is simply the orderly telling of events.

The person doing the telling is the **narrator.** The narrator may be a character within the story. Sometimes the narrator does not take part in the events of the story but reports them from outside. Whether the narrator is inside or outside the action determines the point of view of the story.

As you read the next selection, ask yourself these questions:
1. Who is the narrator?
2. How does narration help organize the telling of the story?

SKILL BUILDER

Did your parents tell stories to you when you were younger? Do you tell stories to a brother or sister? What is hard about telling a story? Write down three or four things.

Unit 3

Rattlesnake Hunt

ADAPTED

by Marjorie Kinnan Rawlings

Sidelights: Marjorie Kinnan Rawlings was born in Washington, D.C., but spent much of her adult life in Florida. She first moved there in 1928, when she and her first husband, Charles Rawlings, bought an orange grove in the back country of north central Florida. It was after the move to Florida that the budding writer began to have luck selling her stories to New York publishers. Rawlings found much material for her stories in the people, places, animals, and plants of her adopted state. Her husband didn't share her love for her adopted state, however, and they divorced in 1933. She married again eight years later. Her second husband was a businessman from St. Augustine, Fla., and except for summers in an old farmhouse in New York state, she continued to live in Florida. She is buried near Cross Creek, Fla., not far from the orange grove she had owned with her first husband.

Ross Allen, a young Florida herpetologist, invited me to join him on a hunt in the upper Everglades—for rattlesnakes. Ross and I drove to Arcadia in his coupe on a warm January day.

I said, "How will you bring back the rattlesnakes?"

"In the back of my car."

My courage was not sufficient to inquire whether they were thrown in loose and might be expected to appear between our feet. Actually, a large portable box of heavy-meshed wire made a safe cage. Ross wanted me to write an article about his work, so on our way to the unhappy hunting grounds I took notes on the mass of data he had gathered in his years of herpetological research. The scientific and calm tone of the material made it easier to go into rattlesnake territory. As I had discovered with insects and varmints, it is difficult to be afraid of anything when enough facts are known, and Ross' facts were fresh from the laboratory.

The hunting ground was Big Prairie, south of Arcadia and west of the northern tip of Lake Okeechobee. Big Prairie is a desolate cattle country, half marsh, half pasture, with islands of palm trees and cypress and oaks. At that time of year cattlemen and Indians were burning the country, on the theory that the young fresh wire grass that springs up from the

Motivation for Reading: Ask students, How do you handle a snake? If possible, have them visit a pet shop or zoo and interview personnel about dealing with snakes. They can also consult reference books. Set aside time for reports on their research. Then ask, Now that you know all about snakes, would you be willing to hunt them?

More About the Thematic Idea: Remind students that it's only natural to become tense when threatened—and most people look upon snakes as a threat; some even have difficulty watching them in zoos. Ask students how they feel about rattlesnakes, or other poisonous snakes. Say, In your research, could you find any ecological good derived from the snake?

Purpose-Setting Question: Is there any way to overcome a specific fear?

---

herpetologist (hur puh TOL uh jist) someone who studies reptiles and amphibians
everglade (EV ur glayd) a large region of swampland; the Everglades a region of such land in southern Florida, about 100 miles long and 50 to 75 miles wide
coupe (KOOP) a small, two-door automobile
portable (PAWRT uh bul) capable of being easily carried
meshed (MESHT) made into a net
data (DAYT uh) collected facts
varmints (VAHR munts) animals regarded as troublesome
desolate (DES uh lit) having no people; in a state of ruin
cypress (SY prus) a cone-bearing tree of the pine family

Suspense

273

Clarification: Arcadia, Fla., is about 30 miles east of Sarasota, Fla. It is in the northwest corner of the Everglades. It would be useful to have a map of Florida available to pinpoint the location of the hunt.

Reading Stategy: The opening sounds more like a news story than a suspense story, perhaps because Rawlings worked as a news reporter for several years. Usually, however, a news story leads with the most important item; a nonfiction narrative sticks to a straight time sequence.

Enrichment: Rawlings wrote many stories about Florida, and spent a lot of time learning about the animals and plants that lived and grew there.

roots after a fire is the best cattle food. Ross planned to hunt his rattlers in front of the fires. They lived in winter, he said, in gopher holes, coming out in the midday warmth to feed, and would move ahead of the flames and be easily taken. We joined forces with a big man named Will, his snake-hunting companion of the territory, and set out in early morning, after a long rough drive over deep-rutted roads into the open wilds.

I hope never in my life to be so frightened as I was in those first few hours. I kept on Ross' footsteps, I moved when he moved, sometimes jolting into him when I thought he might leave me behind. He does not use the usual snake-hunting forked stick but a steel prong, shaped like an L, at the end of a long stout stick. He hunted casually, calling my attention to the varying vegetation, to hawks overhead, to a pair of the rare whooping cranes that flapped over us. In mid-morning he stopped short, dropped his stick, and brought up a five-foot rattlesnake draped limply over the steel L. It seemed to me that I should drop in my tracks.

"They're not active at this season," he said quietly. "A snake takes on the temperature of its surroundings. They can't stand too much heat for that reason, and when the weather is cool, as now, they're sluggish."

The sun was bright overhead, the sky a hazy blue, and it seemed to me that it was warm enough for any snake to do as it willed. The sweat poured down my back. Ross dropped the rattler in a crocus sack and Will carried it. By noon, he had caught four. I felt faint and ill. We stopped by a pond and went swimming. The region was flat, the horizon limitless, and as I came out of the cool blue water, I expected to find myself surrounded by a ring of rattlers. There were only Ross and Will, opening the lunch basket. I could not eat. Will went back and drove his truck closer, for Ross expected the hunting to be better in the afternoon. The hunting was much better. When we went back to the truck to deposit two more rattlers in the wire cage, there was a rattlesnake lying under the truck.

Ross said, "Whenever I leave my car or truck with snakes already in it, other rattlers always appear. I don't know whether this is because they scent or sense the presence of other snakes, or whether in this dry area they come to the car for shade in the heat of the day."

The problem was scientific, but I had no interest.

That night Ross and Will and I

---

gopher (GOH fur) a rodent that digs into the ground
companion (kum PAN yun) a friend
jolting (JOHLT ing) shaking from sudden jerks
prong (PRAUNG) a sharp-pointed instrument
vegetation (vej uh TAY shun) plant life
sluggish (SLUG ish) lacking energy; slow, inactive
crocus sack (KROH kus SAK) a term used in the southern United States for a burlap bag

Literary Focus: Rawlings uses few embellishments in her narrative; when she does, they almost seem out of place, as in the repetition of the verb "drop" for effect.

Critical Thinking: When Rawlings writes "The problem was scientific but I had no interest," she sums up the thrust of the previous paragaph and contrasts it with her own feelings. The direct, concise style effectively conveys her point.

camped out in the vast spaces of the Everglades prairies. We got water from an abandoned well and cooked supper under buttonwood bushes by a flowing stream. The camp fire blazed cheerfully under the stars and a new moon lifted in the sky. Will told tall tales of the cattlemen and the Indians, and we were at peace.

Ross said, "We couldn't have a better night for catching water snakes."

After the rattlers, water snakes seemed harmless enough. We worked along the edge of the stream and here Ross did not use his L-shaped prong. He reached under rocks and along the edge of the water and brought out harmless reptiles with his hands. I had said nothing to him of my fears, but he understood them. He brought a small dark snake from under a willow root.

"Wouldn't you like to hold it?" he asked. "People think snakes are cold and clammy, but they aren't. Take it in your hands. You'll see that it is warm."

Again, because I was ashamed, I took the snake in my hands. It was not cold, it was not clammy, and it lay trustingly in my hands, a thing that lived and breathed like the rest of us. I felt a lifting of spirit.

The next day was magnificent. The air was crystal, the sky was blue-green, and the far horizon of palms and oaks lay against the sky. I felt a new boldness and followed Ross bravely. He was making the rounds of the gopher holes. The rattlers came out in the mid-morning warmth and were never far away. He could tell by their trails whether one had come out or was still in the hole. Sometimes the two men dug the snake out. At times it was down so long and winding a tunnel that the digging was hopeless. Then they blocked the entrance and went on to other holes. In an hour or so they made the original rounds, unblocking the holes. The rattler in every case came out hurriedly, as though anything were preferable to being shut in. All the time Ross talked to me, telling me the scientific facts he had discovered about the habits of the rattlers.

"They pay no attention to a man standing perfectly still," he said, and proved it by letting Will unblock a hole while he stood at the entrance as the snake came out. It was exciting to watch the snake crawl slowly beside and past the man's legs. When it was at a safe distance he walked within its range of vision, which he had proved to be no higher than a man's knee, and the snake whirled and drew back in an attitude of fighting defense. The rattler strikes only for paralyzing and killing its food, and for defense.

"It is a slow and heavy snake," Ross said. "It lies in wait on a small game trail and strikes the rat or rabbit passing by. It waits a few minutes, then follows along the trail, coming to the small animal, now dead or dying. It noses it from all

---

buttonwood (BUT un wuud) a small sycamore tree
attitude (AT uh tood) in this case, a position or posture of the body
paralyzing (PAR uh lyz ing) losing of power or movement

Suspense   275

Reading Strategy: When Ross gives Rawlings a snake to hold, it is the beginning of his lesson on how to overcome a fear of snakes. Have students pay attention to his methods; He is a good teacher.

Critical Thinking: "The next day was magnificent" is the opening sentence in a long, descriptive paragraph. How does this description show Ross and his friend to be accomplished snake hunters?

sides, making sure that it is dead and ready for swallowing."

A rattler will lie quietly without revealing itself if a man passes by and it thinks it is not seen. It slips away without fighting if given the chance. Only Ross' sharp eyes sometimes picked out the gray and yellow diamond pattern, hidden among the grasses. In the cool of the morning, chilled by the January air, the snakes showed no fight. They could be looped up limply over the L-shaped prong and dropped in a sack or up into the wire cage on the back of Will's truck. As the sun mounted in the sky and warmed the moist Everglades earth, the snakes were warmed too, and Ross warned that it was time to go more cautiously. By now I had learned many things: that it was we who were the aggressors; being quiet and still meant complete safety; that the snakes, for all their lightning flash in striking, were inaccurate in their aim because of limited vision. Having watched again and again the liquid grace of their movement and the beauty of pattern, suddenly I understood: I had no fear of what might be under my feet. I went off hunting by myself, and though I found no snakes, I should have known what to do.

The sun was dropping low in the

---

aggressors (uh GRES urz) those who make the first move in a quarrel

276   Unit 3

west. Masses of white cloud hung above the flat marshy plain and seemed to be tangled in the tops of distant palms and cypresses. The sky turned orange, then saffron. I walked leisurely back toward the truck. In the distance I could see Ross and Will making their way in, too. The season was more advanced than at the Creek, two hundred miles to the north, and I noticed that spring flowers were blooming among the lumpy hummocks. I leaned over to pick a white violet. There was a rattlesnake under the violet.

If this had happened the week before —if it had happened the *day* before—I think I would have lain down and died on top of the rattlesnake. The snake did not coil, but lifted its head and shook its rattles lightly. I stepped back slowly and put the violet in a buttonhole. I reached forward and laid the prong across the snake's neck, just back of the blunt head. I called to Ross:

"I've got one."

He walked toward me.

"Well, pick it up," he said.

I released it and slipped the prong under the middle of the thick body.

"Go put it in the box."

He went ahead of me and lifted the top of the wire cage. I made the truck with the rattler, but when I reached up the six feet to drop it in the cage, it slipped off the stick and dropped on Ross's feet. It made no effort to strike.

"Pick it up again," he said. "If you'll pin it down lightly and reach just back of its head with your hand, as you've seen me do, you can drop it in more easily."

I pinned it and leaned over.

"I'm awfully sorry," I said, "but you're pushing me a little too fast."

He grinned. I lifted the snake on the stick and again, just when as I had it at head height, it slipped off, down Ross's boots and on top of his feet. He stood as still as a stump. I dropped the snake on his feet for the third time. It seemed to me that the most patient of rattlers might in time resent being hauled up and down, and—for all Ross's quiet certainty that in standing motionless there was no danger—it would strike at whatever was nearest, and that would be Ross.

I said, "I'm just not man enough to keep this up any longer," and he laughed and reached down with his smooth quickness and lifted the snake's back of the head and dropped it in the cage. It slid in among its mates and settled in a corner. The hunt was over and we drove back over the uneven trail to Will's village and left him and went on to Arcadia and home. Our catch for the two days was thirty-two rattlers.

I said to Ross, "I believe that tomorrow I could have picked up that snake."

Back at the Creek, I felt a new lightness. I had done battle with a great fear, and the victory was mine.

---

saffron (SAF run) orange-yellow in color
hummocks (HUM uks) areas of fertile, wooded land, higher than the surrounding swamp
blunt (BLUNT) having a rounded point
resent (rih ZENT) to consider as an insult

Suspense 277

1. the upper Everglades, at a place called Big Prairie
2. an L-shaped steel prong attached to a long stick
3. For "paralyzing and killing its food, and for defense."
4. The cooler temperatures mean the snakes will be lethargic, especially early in the day, and easier to catch. Also, cattlemen and Indians are burning fires at this time of year; the snakes will be moving ahead of the fires, making their capture easier.
5. She was terrified. She couldn't even eat lunch.
6. He wanted to show Rawlings that snakes are not cold and clammy, but are warm, living, breathing animals. He succeeded in making her begin to overcome her fears of snakes.
7. The narrator, who is not a man, is hiding behind the false stereotype that women are weaker in strength and courage than men.
8. Answers will vary. Sample answer: I almost stepped on a snake on a Civil War battlefield in Virginia. I was so surprised I wasn't even frightened—until a park ranger said it probably was a poisonous copperhead!
9. Answers will vary. Possible answer: Yes, if for no other reason than all the information I learned about rattlesnakes.
10. Answers will vary. Sample answer: No. I'm still scared of a tall building, even though I know it won't fall over.

Respond to Literature: Examples: The American Revolutionary War flag of a coiled snake with the legend, "Don't tread on me"; the story in Genesis that the fall of man was caused by the devil disguised as a snake.

UNDERSTAND THE SELECTION

Recall

1. In what general area of Florida did the rattlesnake hunt take place?

2. What sort of tool does Ross use?

3. Why does a rattler strike?

Infer

4. Why does Ross hunt in January?

5. Describe the narrator's feelings the first few hours of the hunt.

6. What motive does Ross have for hunting water snakes the first night?

7. Why does Ross laugh when, the narrator says, "I'm just not man enough to keep this up any longer"?

Apply

8. How might you react to seeing a snake?

9. The narrator was planning to write an article about Ross Allen's work. Do you think she succeeded in writing an interesting article? Why or why not?

10. The narrator says "it is difficult to be afraid of anything about which enough is known." Do you agree or disagree?

Respond to Literature

Snakes have been symbols of danger and evil for centuries. Give some examples.

WRITE ABOUT THE SELECTION

One of the best ways to practice clear, precise writing is to explain a process to someone. When the process is how to catch a snake, the danger of not explaining things well is real!

Since you are now an authority on rattlesnakes, you have been asked to explain to a scout troop how to catch a rattlesnake.

Prewriting: Identify each step for catching a rattlesnake by scanning "Rattlesnake Hunt" for information the author provides. Note the steps explained in the story. As an example, you might write: Step 1, gather equipment and supplies, including a strong cage. Include all steps necessary for success and safety.

Writing: Begin by making a general statement about the process you will describe. Then use your list of steps to write a detailed description of each step in the process.

Revising: Review the information the author gives for hunting snakes, and check to be sure you have not omitted any of her steps. Read your description to someone else. Ask that person to comment about parts that seem unclear. Then, revise those parts.

Proofreading: Reread your description to check for errors. Make sure that you have used words correctly and precisely. Change any words that might confuse a reader who lives in the city.

Prewriting: To accelerate this stage, students could work together in pairs. While one student reads the steps in catching a rattlesnake, the other jots them down in simple terms. Together they then map out the process.

Writing: The students could continue working together as a team, with each describing a different part of the process. Circulate as students work, offering assistance.

Revising: When their explanation is finished, have one student read it aloud while the other checks for accuracy against the map they laid out.

Proofreading: Remind students of their reading audience: a scout troop. Clear communication rather than a wordy, academic style is the keynote. Advise students, therefore, to delete all pretentious words and phrases.

THINK ABOUT NARRATION

You have been reading mostly mysteries and detective stories in this unit. "Rattlesnake Hunt" is a little different. It is a nonfiction narration—reporting true events in their natural order.

1. Who is the narrator? For what purpose did he or she go on the rattlesnake hunt?

2. In what ways does the narrator help to organize the events of the story?

3. Since Ross Allen and his partner are old hands at catching rattlesnakes, the only suspense is created by the narrator's experiences. Which of her experiences provide suspense?

4. Does the narrator take part in the events of the story or report them from outside the action of the story?

5. How might the stories have changed if another character had been the narrator?

DEVELOP YOUR VOCABULARY

Ross Allen, the snake hunter in the story, is a herpotologist, a person who studies reptiles and amphibians. The word *herpotologist* includes the suffix *-ist*. A suffix is an addition to the end of a word that forms another related word. The suffix *-ist* means "a person who studies, seeks, makes, or does." For example, an adventurist is a person who seeks adventure. Each word below includes the suffix *-ist*. Tell what each word means. Use a dictionary as needed.

1. scientist
2. geologist
3. phrenologist
4. botanist
5. chemist
6. alchemist
7. journalist
8. physicist
9. philatelist
10. numismatist
11. artist
12. opthalmologist
13. dentist

Now, use the words in original sentences.

Suspense   279

After completing these selections, students will be able to
- understand the element of tone
- analyze the relationship between tone and theme
- exercise the mental skill of speculation
- write a TV news account of a developing event
- analyze how tone deepens the meaning of a poem
- use a thesaurus to find synonyms

More About Tone: Begin by emphasizing that Tone exists in all writing. Next, ask students to think back on a previous selection, such as Rattlesnake Hunt. What was the tone? Compare its tone to that of Trifles. Then, point out that all literature—that is, the body of writing notable for beauty and force—has a distinctive, often subtle tone. It informs the reader of the writer's attitude toward his or her subject. Suggest that students consider carefully the tone in each of the next selections—two poems about the Earth.

Cooperative/Collaborative Learning Activity: Have students share their findings with the class. You could write the slogans on the chalkboard or a transparency, and then have students vote for which sloan they think is the most clever. Does tone have anything to do with a slogan's appeal?

More About Vocabulary: Ask students what these words tell about the tone of Oliver Herford's poem: shriveling, lice, cockroaches, mice, and maggots. After discussion, continue with, Why are they interspersed between such words as philosophers, kings, millionaires?

When people talk, you often can determine how they really feel by listening to their tones. How a person's voice sounds —angry, excited, bored, tired—is sometimes as important as what the person says. What happens when you cannot listen to the person, but instead must read what he or she writes? Does tone still exist? It certainly does. However, you must pay closer attention to discover the tone.

Tone is the writer's attitude toward his or her subject as well as toward the reader. It is expressed indirectly, through the choice of words or the combining of words. Even the construction of a sentence, or punctuation, might hint at how the writer feels.

Look for answers to the following questions as you read the poems:
1. How is tone created?
2. What is the relationship between tone and the theme of the poem?

SKILL BUILDER

Look in a newspaper or magazine for an advertisement with a catchy slogan. What is the tone of the slogan? How does it fit with the visual message? Report your findings in a paragraph.

MINI QUIZ

Write on the chalkboard or overhead projector the following questions and call on students to fill in the blanks. Discuss the answers with the class.

1. Both poems are titled _____ .
2. The Martian astronomer thinks that _____ must have been living on earth.
3. Oliver Herford suggests the world might fall _____ .
4. Herford calls all animal life on earth _____ .
5. The observer in Herford's poem is watching from _____ .

4. little crawling things
5. some planet far

Reading Strategy: Read the Wheelock poem through once for effect; then, on a second reading, ask students to listen for the apparent paradox that intelligence is the source of destruction.

Answers to Mini Quiz

1. "Earth"
2. highly intelligent beings
3. through space (into the sun)

EARTH

"A planet doesn't explode of itself," said drily
The Martian astronomer, gazing off into the air—
"That they were able to do it is proof that highly
Intelligent beings must have been living there."

by John Hall Wheelock

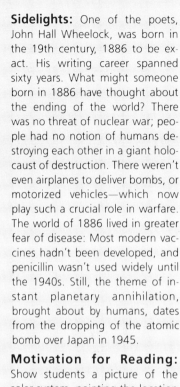

EARTH

If this little world tonight
    Suddenly should fall through space
In a hissing, headlong flight,
    Shrivelling from off its face,
5   As it falls into the sun,
    In an instant every trace
Of the little crawling things—
    Ants, philosophers, and lice,
Cattle, cockroaches, and kings,
10   Beggars, millionaires, and mice,
Men and maggots all as one
As it falls into the sun. . . .
Who can say but at the same
    Instant from some planet far
15 A child may watch us and exclaim:
    "See the pretty shooting star!"

by Oliver Herford

Martian (MAHR shun) inhabitant of the planet Mars.
shrivelling (SHRIV ul ing) shrinking; drying up.
lice (LYS) plural of louse, a small insect that lives in the skin and hair
  of people.
cockroaches (KOK rohch is) large black or brown insects that live
  everywhere.
maggots (MAG uts) small wormlike animals that are the young form
  of flies or other insects.

Suspense   **281**

ANSWERS TO UNDERSTAND THE SELECTION

1. a Martian astronomer
2. It falls into the sun.
3. The child thinks the earth is actually a meteor, or shooting star.
4. The Martian astronomer thinks it destroyed itself.
5. Cold, scientific—"he said drily."
6. When the end comes, we shall all be equals, the smallest maggots and the richest millionaires.
7. That life on this earth might seem important to us, but might be inconsequential in terms of the entire universe.
8. End weight—we don't know the "explanation" of the earth's ending until the last line of each poem.
9. Answers will vary. Sample answer: I think about someone on another planet peering through a telescope and looking at me.
10. Answers will vary. Sample answer: Probably nuclear war.

Respond to Literature: Do students believe that UFOs exist? Has the Earth already had visitors from other planets? There are some very persuasive accounts documenting UFOs. If they do exist, doesn't that mean there is intelligent life on other planets?

ANSWERS TO WRITE ABOUT THE SELECTION

Prewriting: Discuss as a class how news reporters decide on whom to call when they're covering a story. What gives a story credibility? and what makes it complete? How can an in-depth story about a mysterious explosion in the sky be written in time for the next edition?

Writing: Have students listen to and analyze a news broadcast before they begin their writing. You could assign this as homework, or bring a tape of a broadcast to class. As they write, remind them of the "inverted pyramid" style of news stories: the most important news first, followed by more detailed information, such as eyewitness accounts.

Revising: Have students work in pairs, reading their news stories aloud to each other. How do the stories sound? Reading a story can help pinpoint transition problems.

Proofreading: Review with the class the correct way of writing a person's title. Rules on capitalization can be found in a style book.

UNDERSTAND THE SELECTION

Recall

1. Who observes the explosion of Earth in John Hall Wheelock's poem?

2. How is Earth destroyed in Oliver Herford's "Earth" poem?

3. What does a child on a distant planet think as Earth is being destroyed?

Infer

4. How is Earth destroyed in John Hall Wheelock's "Earth" poem?

5. Explain the astronomer's attitude as he watches Earth explode.

6. Explain "Men and maggots all as one."

7. What is the theme of the Herford poem?

Apply

8. How is suspense achieved in each poem?

9. What do you think about when you see a shooting star?

10. Have you ever imagined how life on Earth could end? What do you think could be the most likely cause?

Respond to Literature

Both poems suggest that there is intelligent life on other planets. Do you think there is? Why do you think as you do?

282

WRITE ABOUT THE SELECTION

You are a television news reporter on a distant planet working the night news desk. Suddenly, there is a big explosion in the sky. How would you describe the explosion to your audience? How would you explain what caused it?

Prewriting: You have no film footage, so you must do some quick interviews for your story. Make a list of people you might call for information, such as an astronomer, a military official or an astronaut. Also, you want to locate some eyewitnesses. Imagine what each of these people might tell you. List the information, keeping what each person says separate so you know what information came from what source.

Writing: Organize your information into a news story. Remember, the most important information comes first in a news story, and you should answer the questions: who, what, where, when, and how. You may quote the people you interviewed.

Revising: Since this is a broadcast news story, read your story aloud. Make sure all your information is stated clearly. Ask yourself which parts of your story will create pictures in the listeners' minds. Revise those parts that do not create word pictures. Think of a snappy way to end your story.

Proofreading: Make sure that you pronounce the names and titles of the people you interviewed correctly.

Unit 3

THINK ABOUT TONE

Tone is the way a poet reveals attitudes and feelings. Literally, everything in a poem helps to create tone. You must be a literally detective to discover clues to the way tone is created in a written work.

1. In the first line of Herford's poem, how does the poet indicate his attitude about the importance of the world?

2. How does Herford show his attitude toward living things, including people?

3. Alliteration is often a key to tone. It can be used to show humor, anger, or other feelings. Find an example of alliteration. Identify a feeling the poet is communicating.

4. The attitude of the Martian astronomer in Wheelock's poem very well could be the poet's attitude, too. What is the attitude about life on the planet in the poem.

5. What is the theme of Wheelock's poem? Does the tone reflect this?

DEVELOP YOUR VOCABULARY

A thesaurus can be a useful reference book. If you want to use alliteration, you will find many words with similar initial sound. You will also find synonyms; words that have meanings similar to the original word.

In some thesauruses, you look up the word for which you want a synonym, and the synonyms are listed. In other thesauruses, you look for the word in the index. Following the word is a page number. You then turn to that page to find the word and list of synonyms.

Now that you know how to use a thesaurus, find some synonyms for the word *beggar*. Choose the synonym beginning with *m*. Then find synonyms for the other words listed. For each numbered word, choose a synonym that starts with the letter indicated.

1. beggar (m)   4. millionaire (p)
2. philosopher (i) 5. crawling (c)
3. proof (v)   6. exclaim (s)

Use the synonyms in an original sentence.

SELECTION OBJECTIVES

After completing this selection, students will be able to
- understand irony in literature
- recognize how irony is used to create humor
- analyze alternative endings to a story
- develop a conclusion to a story
- explain examples of irony
- identify root words

Discussion: Does the accused person *really* have any rights? Is there any hope for justice in his situation?

More About Irony: Situational irony occurs when what a character expects to happen doesn't. Dramatic irony occurs when the reader knows something a character doesn't know. "The Lady, or the Tiger?" turns dramatic irony around: A character knows something the reader doesn't know, and doesn't find out. The unexpected reversal makes Stockton's story one of the best-known "trick" stories ever written.

Cooperative/Collaborative Learning Activity: Ask the class to think of a joke or epigram and analyze its humor. More often than not, the humor lies in irony. Example: It's so exhausting not to talk. Oscar Wilde, a famous wit and satirist, has turned the table with the word *not*; It's a reversal of the idea that listening is a bore.

LEARN ABOUT
Irony

In Wheelock's poem about Earth exploding, he says, "Intelligent beings must have been living there." It seems like he is complimenting humans, but this is not so. He is really questioning how intelligent a species could be if it blows itself up.

When a writer means the opposite of what he or she actually says, the writer is using irony. Irony is a way to call attention to an idea by deliberately saying the opposite.

In literature, characters, settings, and plots can all have ironic features. The farmhouse setting in "Trifles" is in some ways ironic. Rural settings are usually considered peaceful. Farms are places for nurturing plant and animal life. That farmhouse setting is instead a place of death.

As you read further ask yourself:
1. What is ironic about the king?
2. What is ironic about his justice?

SKILL BUILDER

Irony is often used in jokes. What we expect to happen does not. Think of examples. Write them down. Then you and a partner Create a short routine of ironic comedy to present to the class.

284

Unit 3

T284

THE LADY, OR THE TIGER?

by Frank R. Stockton

In the very olden time, there once lived a semi-barbaric king. His ideas, though somewhat polished and sharpened by the more civilized ways of distant neighbors, were still raw, savage and reckless, as became the half of him that was still barbaric. He was a man of wild imagination, and his word was law. Whenever he wished, his varied fancies became facts. He was greatly given to self-questioning, and when he and himself agreed upon anything, that thing was done. When everything in his kingdom moved smoothly, his manner was happy and genial; but whenever there was a little trouble, he was happier and more genial still. For nothing pleased him so much as to make the crooked straight, and crush down uneven places.

Among the borrowed ideas by which his barbarism had become softened was that of the public arena. In his arena, both men and beasts displayed their courage. These displays, the king thought, uplifted the minds of his people.

But even here the wild imagination expressed itself. The arena of the king was not built to let his people watch men fight each other with sword and shield. It was not built to settle arguments between religious opinions and hungry jaws. No, its purpose was far better fitted to uplifting the minds of the people. The huge arena, with its many rows of seats, its unseen passages, was a hall of justice. There crime was punished. There goodness was rewarded. There justice was decided by the completely fair and unprejudiced Law of Chance.

The system was simple. First a person had to be accused of a crime of enough importance to interest the king. Then public notice was given that on a certain day the accused man would appear in the king's arena. When the people of the city

---

semi- (SEM ih *or* SEM ee) prefix meaning half.
barbaric (bahr BAR ik) wild and cruel; not yet civilized.
fancies (FAN seez) notions or ideas, usually pleasant.
genial (JEEN yul) pleasant; good-natured.

Suspense

285

Sidelights:
Imagine starting life as a wood engraver and ending it as a well-known writer and editor. That's what Frank Stockton did. His early stories were written for children's magazines, and then he turned to writing for adults. He never lost his sense of whimsy and imagaination, though. "The Lady, or the Tiger?" is perhaps his best-known work, and his later works were all compared to it—usually unfavorably.

Motivation for Reading:
Read a short suspense story to the class, but stop before the ending. Ask students, Can you guess how the story ends? Then suggest that the Stockton story ends with a puzzle.

More About the Thematic Idea:
Why is Irony so effective? Suggest to students that the humor of almost all successful comedians is rooted in irony. Then, ask students to watch their favorite TV comic and note a few jokes on paper. During a class review of their jokes, point out the surprise reversal behind every good joke.

Purpose-Setting Question:
Does a good story always conclude with a decisive resolution?

Vocabulary:
Preteach the vocabulary words. See the Comprehension Workbook in the TRB.

Literary Focus:
What is the tone of this story? Stockton has a very distinctive style.

Literary Focus:
The third paragraph in the story ends with irony. How can the Law of Chance be used to dispense justice?

Enrichment:
Stockton was well-known for his ability to create absurd scenes and situations. Skillfully woven into the general theme is a deadpan absurdity that doesn't seem ridiculous.

More About Vocabulary:
Write the new vocabulary one one part of a chalkboard or transparency, and the definitions in a different order. Ask students to match them, and then to use each new word in a sentence.

had gathered, the king entered. Surrounded by his family and servants, he sat on a throne high up on one side of the arena. Suddenly he gave a signal. A door far beneath him opened, and the accused person stepped out.

Right across from the man on trial were two doors, exactly alike and side by side. It was the duty and the privilege of the person on trial to walk straight to the doors and open one of them. He could open either door he pleased. He was given no help but that of the Law of Chance. If he opened the one, there came out of it a hungry tiger, the wildest and most cruel that could be found. The tiger immediately sprang upon him and tore him to pieces, as punishment for his guilt. The moment that the case of the criminal was so decided, doleful iron bells were rung. Great sighs went up, and the people left the arena with bowed heads and broken hearts. Why did one so young and handsome, or so old and well known, deserve so horrible an end?

But if the accused person opened the other door, there came out of it a lady, always well fitted to the man's age and place in life. In fact, she was always the most perfect wife that his majesty's servants could find among his fair subjects. And to this lady the man was immediately married, as a reward for his innocence. It mattered not that he might already have a wife and family, nor that he might be engaged to a woman of his own choice. The king allowed no such details

to interfere with his grand ideas about punishment and reward. The wedding took place right away, and in the arena. Another door opened beneath the king, and a priest, followed by dancing maidens and a group of singers, advanced to where the pair stood side by side. The wedding was short and joyful. Then the happy brass bells rang out, the people cheered and cheered, and the innocent man, following children throwing flowers in his path, led his bride to his home.

This was the king's semi-barbaric method of handing out justice. Its perfect fairness is clear. The criminal could not know out of which doorway would come the lady. He opened either door he pleased. He had not the slightest idea whether, in the next instant, he was to be devoured or married. Sometimes the tiger came out of one door, sometimes out of the other. The king's justice was not only fair, but also fast. The accused person was instantly punished if he found himself guilty. And if innocent, he was rewarded on the spot, whether he liked it or not. There was no escape from the judgments of the king's arena.

The system was a very popular one. The people never knew whether they were to witness a bloody slaughter or a joyous wedding. There was just no way they could know. This gave an interest to the event which it could not otherwise have had. Thus the masses were entertained and pleased. And even the thinking persons in the community could find

---

doleful (DOHL ful) sorrowful.
fair (FAIR) nice looking.
subject (SUB jikt) person under authority of a king or government.

Unit 3

Reading Strategy: Point out to students that the repetition of words "fair," "perfect fairness" and "justice." Stress the irony of an obviously unjust situation.

Tiger, Edward J. Detmold. The Metropolitan Museum of Art, The Elisha Whittelsey Collection.

Suspense

Critical Thinking: Note that starting with Paragraph 7, the interpretive part of the story shifts effortlessly to the specific situation with the alternating transitional words, "this" and "the."

Critical Thinking: In the brief description of the young man (Paragraph 10), Stockton seems to be pooking fun at stock characters, but hasn't he created one?

Clarification: The "king's duty" is to prevent the marriage of his daughter (a noble woman) to a commoner.

no reason to say that the plan was unfair. For did not the accused person have the whole matter in his own hands?

This semi-barbaric king had a daughter as blooming as his own lively imagination and with a soul as fiery and as proud as his own. As is usual in such cases, she was the apple of his eye, and was loved by him above all others. And her love? Well . . . among the king's servants was a handsome young man of that fineness of blood and lowness of station common to story-book heroes who love royal maidens.

This royal maiden was well satisfied with her lover. He was better looking and braver than anyone else in all the kingdom, and her love for him had enough of barbarism in it to make it very warm, and very, very strong. The love affair moved on happily for many months, until, one day, the king happened to learn of it. He did not waste an instant! He knew his duty in the matter at once. The youth was immediately put into prison, and a day was set for his trial in the king's arena.

This, of course, was an especially important happening in the kingdom. His majesty, as well as all the people, was greatly interested in the preparation for the trial. Never before had such a case occurred—never before had a subject dared to love the daughter of the king!

The tiger cages of the kingdom were searched for the most savage and relentless of beasts, from which the fiercest monster was to be chosen for the arena. And a search was also made among the ranks of maiden youth and beauty throughout the land. The young man was to have a fitting bride, if bride it was to be. Of course, everyone knew that the act of the accused man had, in fact, been done. He had loved the princess, and neither he, she, nor anyone in the kingdom thought of saying anything else. But the king would not think of letting any fact of this kind interfere with the tribunal, in which he took such great delight and satisfaction. No matter how it turned out, the youth's future would be decided. The king was especially interested in finding out whether the young man had done wrong in allowing himself to love the princess.

The day arrived. From far and near the people gathered, and they soon filled the great arena. Outside, more huge crowds, unable to get in, stood against the walls. The king was in his place, opposite the twin portals—sc horrible in their likeness to each other!

All was ready. The signal was given. A door beneath the king opened, and the lover of the princess walked into the arena. Tall and handsome, he was greeted with a low hum of wonder and worry. Half the people had not known that such a youth had lived among them. No wonder the princess loved him! What a terrible thing for him to be there!

station (STAY shun) place in life.
relentless (rih LENT lis) without pity; harsh and cruel.
tribunal (try BYOO nul) court of justice.
portals (PAWRT ulz) doors; entrances.

As the youth advanced into the arena, he stopped to turn, as the custom was, and bow to the king. But he did not think at all of that royal person. His eyes were fixed on the princess, who sat to the right of her father. Had it not been for the barbaric half of her soul, the lady probably would not have been there. But her strong spirit would not allow her to be absent from an event in which she was terribly interested. From the very moment of the king's order, she had thought of nothing else, night or day. She knew only that her lover's future was to be decided in the king's arena. Having more power and determination than anyone who had ever before been interested in such a case, she had done what no other person had done. She had learned the secret of the doors. She knew about the two little rooms across the arena from them. She knew in which stood the tiger, and in which waited the lady. Gold and power had brought that secret to the princess.

Not only did she know in which room stood the lady, ready to come out, all blushing and radiant, should her door be opened, but she also knew who the lady was. It was one of the most beautiful and lively maidens of the palace—and the princess hated her. Often she had seen, or imagined she had seen, things she didn't like. The lovely girl would throw glances of delight upon her lover, and sometimes, she thought, they had even been returned. Now and then she had seen them talking together. It was only for a moment or two, but much can be said in a brief time. And what had they talked about? Something unimportant, probably. But how could she know that? The girl was lovely, but she had dared to raise her eyes to the loved one of the princess. With all the strength of the savage blood of her barbaric ancestors, the princess hated the woman who blushed and trembled behind that silent door.

And now, the man in the arena had turned to look at her. She sat there paler and whiter than anyone else in the sea of worried faces around her. His eye met hers. At once he saw, by that power of quick perception given only to those whose souls are one, that she knew! She knew behind which door waited the tiger, and behind which stood the lady. He had expected her to know it. He understood her perfectly. He knew that she would never rest until she had discovered this secret, hidden to all others, even to the king. The only sure hope for the youth was the success the princess had in solving this mystery, and the moment he looked upon her, he knew she had succeeded.

Then it was that his quick and anxious glance asked the question, "Which?" It was as plain to her as if he shouted it from where he stood. There was not an instant to be lost. The question was asked in a flash; it must be answered in another.

Her right arm lay on the cushioned wall before her. She raised her hand, and

---

perception (pur SEP shun) awareness; understanding

Suspense

Literary Focus: This is where the story "shifts gears." All of a sudden, the writer asks the reader to explore the situation with him, as though he doesn't know what will happen either. Notice his shift in point of view, from third person to the first person "we."

made a slight, quick movement to the right. No one but her lover saw it. Every eye but his was fixed on the man in the arena.

He turned, and with a rapid step he walked across the empty space. Every heart stopped beating. Every breath was held. Every eye was fixed as if frozen upon that man. Without the slightest pause, he went to the door on the right, and opened it.

Now, the point of the story is this: Did the tiger come out of that door, or did the lady?

The more we reflect upon that question, the harder it is to answer. It involves a study of the human heart. It leads us into a wild jungle of love and hate, out of which it is difficult to find our way. Think of it, fair reader, not as a question that you yourself had to answer. No, the answer involves that hot-blooded, semi-barbaric princess. Think of her soul, at white heat in the combined fires of despair and jealousy. She had lost him, but who should have him?

How often, in her daylight hours and in her dreams, had she thought of her lover opening the door to find the cruel teeth of the tiger? How often had that thought made her tremble in horror and cover her face with her hands?

But how much oftener had she seen him at the other door! To think of his surprised delight as he opened the door of the lady! How her soul had burned! How she had torn her hair when she had seen him rush to meet that woman, with

her flashing cheek and sparkling eye! When she had seen him lead her from the door! When she had heard the glad shouts from the crowd! When she had seen the priest, with his happy followers, advance to make them husband and wife! When she had seen them walk away upon their path of flowers, followed by the tremendous cheers of the people, in

---

reflect (rih FLEKT) think.

The Colosseum, Rome, Joseph Mallord William Turner. Courtesy of the Trustees of the British Museum

Discussion: Do students feel cheated? Does a writer have a responsibility to tell the *whole* story?

which her own shriek of despair was lost and drowned!

Would it not be better for him to die at once? Would it not be better to think of him waiting for her in some semi-barbaric heaven?

And yet, that awful tiger! Those shrieks! That blood!

The slight wave of her right hand had taken just an instant. But the motion had been made after days and nights of ago-nizing thought. She had known she would be asked, she had decided what she would answer, and without the slightest pause, she had moved her hand to the right.

The question of her decision is not one to be taken lightly, and it is not for me to set myself up as the one person who can answer it. So I leave it with all of you: Which came out of the opened door—the lady, or the tiger?

Suspense   291

ANSWERS TO UNDERSTAND THE SELECTION

1. the Law of Chance
2. The lady emerged, and the couple was married immediately.
3. the one on the right, as the princess had indicated
4. If a person were guilty, he would—because of the Law of Chance—choose the door where the tiger lay in wait. If he were innocent, he would choose the door where a beautiful woman awaited him.
5. The young man was of "low" station; also, the king was presumably jealous that anyone might take his daughter away from him.
6. No. He has made an informed choice based on the princess's inside information.
7. This is the question posed to the reader by the author at the end of the story. The reader must decide whether a lady or a tiger has been chosen.
8. No. The Law of Chance does not assure justice.
9. Answers will vary, but students should be able to explain their answers. Sample answer: The tiger. The daughter has too much of the barbarian in her.
10. If the accused is a woman instead of a man, the reward doesn't seem very appropriate.

Respond to Literature: The king wins in both cases. He breaks up his daughter's relationship with the young man no matter who or what is behind the right door.

ANSWERS TO WRITE ABOUT THE SELECTION

Prewriting: Refer to discussion of Question 9 in the "Understand the

UNDERSTAND THE SELECTION

Recall

1. What law governed the proceedings in the arena?

2. What happened to a person who chose the door that revealed a lady?

3. Which door did the daughter's lover choose?

Infer

4. Explain how the king achieved justice.

5. Why did the king disapprove of the young man chosen by his daughter?

6. Is the Law of Chance being observed in the case of the daughter's lover?

7. Explain the significance of the title.

Apply

8. Is justice really being done in the king's "hall of justice"? Explain your answer.

9. Was the lady or the tiger behind the right door? Why do you think so?

10. What is a basic flaw with the king's system of justice?

Respond to Literature

Think about whether the king will achieve his goal in this story. What will happen if the open door reveals the tiger? What will happen if the open door reveals the lady?

WRITE ABOUT THE SELECTION

Well, which will it be: the lady or the tiger? Frank Stockton has given you a rather unusual opportunity. He has provided the setting, theme, and characters of a story, and most of the plot. He has left you hanging right before the climax. Now it is up to you to provide an ending.

Prewriting: The last section of "The Lady, or the Tiger?" has questions to help you decide what will be revealed behind the right door. Reread it. Then choose the lady or the tiger as the basis for an ending. Make an informal plot outline including what happens, as well as the reactions of the princess, the lover, the king, and the crowd.

Writing: Use your informal outline to write a conclusion for the story. The length is up to you, but there must be resolution of the questions raised by the story. Imitate Frank Stockton's style as you write your narration.

Revising: Reread parts of the story, and analyze what makes Frank Stockton's style distinctive. Revise or make additions to your conclusion to make your writing sound as though Stockton himself has written it. Use questions, as he does, for suspense.

Proofreading: Reread your conclusion to check for errors. Pay close attention to end punctuation. Stockton uses many question marks and exclamation points, as well as periods. Make sure you know when to use each.

Selection." Students could even debate informally which ending seems more appropriate. Points contradicting their view should be rebutted in their ending.

Writing: Circulate as students work individually. help students to use their outline as they write.

Revising: As a class, reread a section of Stockton's story and analyze what makes the style distinctive. Ask students—perhaps working in groups—to look at specific points such as vocabulary, sentence length and construction, use of figurative expressions. Have them report back to the class.

Proofreading: Review end punctuation rules with students. Illustrate your review with examples from Stockton's story.

THINK ABOUT IRONY

"The Lady, or the Tiger?" is filled with irony.

1. What is ironic about this description of the king: ". . . his manner was happy and genial; but whenever there was a little trouble, he was happier and more genial still." Why did the author include this irony?

2. Stockton describes the king's system of justice and says, "Its perfect fairness is clear." What is ironic about this statement?

3. "The king was especially interested in finding out whether the young man had done wrong in allowing himself to love the princess." Explain the irony in this statement.

4. Stockton writes, "The king's justice was not only fair, but also fast." Given the way the story ends, what is ironic about this?

5. The young man is quite likely in a very ironic situation. Explain this statement.

6. There is a reversal in the structure of the story, too. Often, the reader knows something the characters do not. Is this true for "The Lady or the Tiger"? Explain how this feature of the story is an example of irony.

DEVELOP YOUR VOCABULARY

Prefixes and suffixes allow you to make additions to a root word to create new words with related meanings. Frank Stockton uses three related words from one base:

semi-barbaric   barbaric   barbarism

If you are familiar with the meaning of the base word and can identify and define the prefixes and suffixes, you can figure out the meaning of each of the following words.

Identify the bases and suffixes or prefixes of the following *italicized* words. Explain the meaning of the bases and the suffixes or prefixes. Use a dictionary as needed.

1. *Doleful* iron bells were rung.

2. The king was in his place, opposite the twin *portals*.

3. Gold and power had brought that secret to the *princess*.

4. The power of quick *perception* is only given to those whose souls are one.

5. Without the *slightest* pause, she moved her hand to the right.

LEARN ABOUT
Word Meaning

When you look for a word in a dictionary you find a specific meaning. Words communicate feelings and attitudes as well as specific meanings. For example, you might describe something as *cheap*, meaning that it is low in price. However, some people have an attitude of contempt about things that are cheap. They look down upon them. Therefore, the word *cheap* also carries a feeling of contempt, or scorn with its meaning.

The actual meaning of a word is called **denotation**. The feeling or attitude associated with a word is **connotation**.

Poets choose their words carefully. They use connotation as well as denotation to create tone and emotional impact.

Look for answers to the following questions as you read the poems:

1. What words suggest to you meanings in addition to their literal definitions?
2. What feelings do you associate with each word you identified?

SKILL BUILDER

Think of a word that provokes a strong feeling or attitude. Use a dictionary to find its specific meaning. Then write two sentences showing the denotation and connotation of the same word.

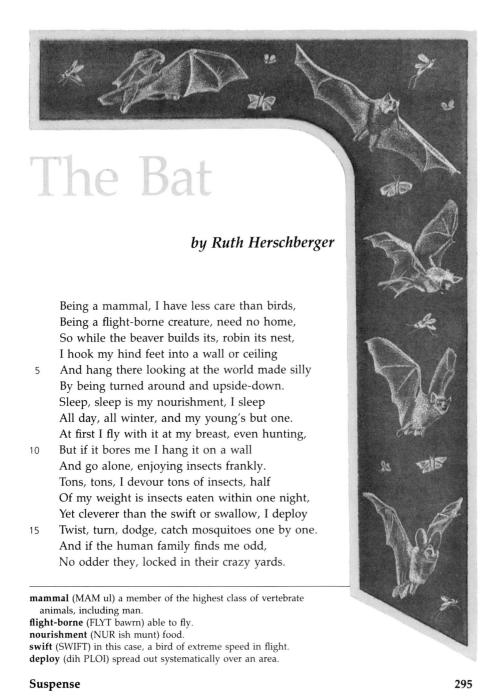

The Bat

by Ruth Herschberger

Being a mammal, I have less care than birds,
Being a flight-borne creature, need no home,
So while the beaver builds its, robin its nest,
I hook my hind feet into a wall or ceiling
5   And hang there looking at the world made silly
By being turned around and upside-down.
Sleep, sleep is my nourishment, I sleep
All day, all winter, and my young's but one.
At first I fly with it at my breast, even hunting,
10 But if it bores me I hang it on a wall
And go alone, enjoying insects frankly.
Tons, tons, I devour tons of insects, half
Of my weight is insects eaten within one night,
Yet cleverer than the swift or swallow, I deploy
15 Twist, turn, dodge, catch mosquitoes one by one.
And if the human family finds me odd,
No odder they, locked in their crazy yards.

---

mammal (MAM ul) a member of the highest class of vertebrate
  animals, including man.
flight-borne (FLYT bawrn) able to fly.
nourishment (NUR ish munt) food.
swift (SWIFT) in this case, a bird of extreme speed in flight.
deploy (dih PLOI) spread out systematically over an area.

Suspense   295

Los Caprichos: El Sueño de la Razon Produce Monstruos (The Sleep of Reason Produces Monsters), Francisco de Goya. National Gallery of Art

Unit 3

The Bird of Night

by Randall Jarrell

A shadow is floating through the moonlight,
Its wings don't make a sound.
Its claws are long, its beak is bright.
Its eyes try all the corners of the night.

5   It calls and calls: all the air swells and heaves
And washes up and down like water.
The ear that listens to the owl believes
In death. The bat beneath the eaves,

10   The mouse beside the stone are still as death—
The owl's air washes them like water.
The owl goes back and forth inside the night,
And the night holds its breath.

---

swells (SWELZ) increases in size, volume, or force.
heaves (HEEVZ) lifts up with effort.
eaves (EEVZ) lower edges of a roof, especially that part sticking out
over the walls of the building.

Suspense   297

Critical Thinking: In "The Bird of Night," the word "shadow" could mean a shadow of an owl, or maybe an owl itself. Shadows and figures tend to become indistinguishable in moonlight.

Literary Focus: "Its" is used in the first verse to tie the verse together. End rhyme is used, too, giving this poem a different feeling than "The Bat."

Literary Focus: The theme of this poem is fear, not strange habits as in "The Bat." Fear intensifies in mysterious images, such as moonlight and water.

Discussion: Ask students to contrast their feelings about this poem with those they felt in "The Bat."

MINI QUIZ

Write the following questions on the chalkboard or overhead projector and call on students to fill in the blanks. Discuss the answers with the class.

1. The bat says that because it's a mammal it has less care than _____ .

2. The world looks silly to the bat when _____ .

3. Bats eat _____ .
4. Owls eat _____ .
5. The owl hunts at _____ .

Answers to Mini Quiz

1. birds
2. it's hanging upside down
3. insects
4. bats and mice
5. night

ANSWERS TO UNDERSTAND THE SELECTION

1. a mammal
2. on a wall, hanging
3. fear of death
4. It's a "flight-borne" creature; when it needs rest, it hangs itself from a wall or ceiling.
5. It would fly quickly and erratically.
6. very quiet, with eyes roving from right to left in search of prey
7. the bat, the mouse
8. Answers will vary. Possibilities are that it isn't a bird, that it eats a lot of insects, that it carries its young on its breast.
9. two pounds
10. It is most likely because of their eyes, which are often fixed in what seems a vacant stare but is really keen vision.

Respond to Literature: Answers to the question will vary, but many might choose owls. Bats are made out to be rather interesting, useful creatures in the poem while owls appear bloodthirsty and terrifying in "The Bird of Night."

ANSWERS TO WRITE ABOUT THE SELECTION

Prewriting: Remind students that writing in first person point of view means all information must come through *you*, the speaker. *You* must cause any action to happen. Point to "The Bat" to illustrate this.

Writing: Circulate as students work individually. Suggest specific reference books (for example, Peterson's *Field Guide to Birds*) for more information on owls.

Revising: Before having to consult a thesaurus, students might be able to help each other find words with appropriate connotations. Ask students for words for which they would like to find a more

---

UNDERSTAND THE SELECTION

Recall

1. What kind of an animal is a bat?

2. Where does a mother bat put its baby if it wants to go hunting alone?

3. What fear do animals listening have to the owl?

Infer

4. Why does the bat say it needs no home?

5. Describe what a bat hunting mosquitoes looks like.

6. Describe an owl flying.

7. What are some of the animals an owl preys upon?

Apply

8. "The Bat" contains a lot of information about this much-despised animal. What new things did you learn about bats?

9. If a bat weighs about 4 pounds, how many pounds of insects would it eat in one night?

10. Why do you think owls are thought to be wise?

Respond to Literature

In what ways do bats and owls help create suspense? Give examples.

298

WRITE ABOUT THE SELECTION

"The Bat" is written in a first-person point of view, but "The Bird of Night" is written in a third-person point of view.

The tone of each poem is very different. Could that be because of the different point of view in which each is written.

See if you can find out by writing in the first person about owls. Plan to write poetry. You may either adapt "The Bird of Night" to a poem written in the first person, or you may write a new poem.

Prewriting: Decide if you will adapt Jarrell's poem, or write your own. If you are adapting, circle all the words in Jarrell's poem you will have to change. If you are writing your own poem, make a cluster of words about the owl that you may want to use.

Writing: Use either the circled poem or your cluster to write a first-person poem on owls. Remember that information must be presented from the owl's point of view. You may want to consult a reference book to learn more about the owl's habitat.

Revising: When you revise your poem, think about adding words with connotations that fit the meaning and feeling you want. Use a thesaurus as needed.

Proofreading: Reread your poem to check for errors. Decide where to break lines, what indentions you want, and whether you want to use end-of-line punctuation. Mark your copy accordingly.

Unit 3

---

appropriate synonym, and solicit suggestions from the class.

Proofreading: Review as a class the structure of "The Bird of Night." What is the rhyme pattern, where do lines break, and what punctuation is used?

LDP Activity: Have the LDP students brainstorm in small groups what they learned about how a bat lives. They should take notes on what they learned.

THINK ABOUT WORD MEANING

Poets rely on connotations of words when they use figurative langugage in their poems. Below are examples from the previous poems.

1. In "The Bird of Night," a simile is used in the second stanza. What is being compared to water? How is the word *swells* connected to water? What feeling or image does the word *swells* connote?

2. What other words in the poem also have a connection to or a connotation involving water?

3. Another simile is used to describe the bat and mouse as the owl floats through the night. What is it?

4. Hyperbole is used in "The Bat." Where? What feelings or connotations are associated with this exaggeration?

5. What word fits particularly well with the hyperbole?

6. List five other words with connotations that really add to both poems' effectiveness.

DEVELOP YOUR VOCABULARY

Knowing the connotation of a certain word requires that you know the denotations of the word as well.

Examine the word *swells*, for example, from "The Bird of Night." Why did the poet use *swells* instead of *expands*? They both mean "to increase in size."

Swell is often used to describe waves at sea. The connotation of *swell* is therefore, appropriate for comparing air to water.

Below are other words used in the two poems. Each is paired with a synonym the way *swells* was paired with expands. Decide why the poet chose to use the word he did. Write the denotation for each. Then identify the connotation of each word. Be ready to explain why the connotation is appropriate for the poem in which the word is used.

1. floating/flying
2. bright/colorful
3. heaves/moves
4. hook/attach
5. devour/eat
6. deploy/move

6. deploy—to spread out systematically over an area; associated especially with armies
move—to go from one place to another
"Deploy" connotes a plan of action and an organized attack.

LEARN ABOUT

Plot

The most important element of many stories, dramas included, is plot. Such stories depend upon action for their developments. Characters and settings are important, and so are the themes, but the "energy" of the plot moves the story forward.

You should be familiar with the basic pattern of plots. First, there is **exposition**, or background information. Then, a **complication** develops, raising a question or several questions that must be answered during the remainder of the story. The **action rises**, and the **climax** is reached. The **action falls**, and any questions not answered in the climax are answered in the **resolution**.

As you read the selection, ask yourself these questions:

1. What are the main complications or questions involved in the plot?
2. How is each complication resolved or question answered?

SKILL BUILDER

In a few sentences explain the plot of any story you have read in this unit. Describe the major points of the plot identifying necessary background information, all important complications, the climax, and the resolution.

300

Unit 3

A SECRET FOR TWO

by Quentin Reynolds

Montreal is a very large city. But, like all large cities, it has some very small streets. Streets, for instance, like Prince Edward Street, which is only four blocks long. No one knew Prince Edward Street as well as did Pierre Dupin. For Pierre had delivered milk to the families on the street for thirty years now.

During the past fifteen years, the horse that drew the milk wagon used by Pierre was a large white horse named Joseph. In Montreal, especially in that part of Montreal that is very French, the animals, like children, are often given the names of saints. When the big white horse first came to the Provincale Milk Company, he didn't have a name. They told Pierre that he could use the white horse. Pierre stroked the softness of the horse's neck. He stroked the sheen of its splendid belly, and he looked into the eyes of the horse.

"This is a kind horse, a gentle and faithful horse," Pierre said. "I can see a beautiful spirit shining out of the eyes of the horse. I will name him after good St. Joseph, who was also kind and gentle and faithful and a beautiful spirit."

Within a year, Joseph knew the milk route as well as Pierre. Pierre used to boast that he didn't need reins—he never touched them. Each morning Pierre arrived at the stables of the Provincale Milk Company at five o'clock. The wagon would be loaded and Joseph hitched to it. Pierre would call, *"Bonjour, vieil ami,"* as he climbed into his seat. Joseph would turn his head, and the other drivers would smile and say that the horse would smile at Pierre. Then Jacques, the foreman, would say, "All right, Pierre, go on." Pierre would call softly to Joseph, *"Avance, mon*

Montreal (mon tree AWL) city in eastern Canada that has French as its official language.
sheen (SHEEN) brightness; shininess

Suspense   301

Enrichment: Montreal's mix of English and French cultures is evident in the opening paragraph. Pierre Dupin, of French origin, has a milk route on Prince Edward Street, named for a member of the British royal family.

Clarification: (Paragraph 3) Joseph was husband to Mary, mother of Jesus. He was a carpenter. Little is known about him from the Bible; the impression created there is he was a kind and faithful husband and father.

Clarification: The French words and expressions in the story are examined in the "Develop Your Vocabulary" section of the Student's Book on page ____ .

Literary Focus: Specific description allows the reader to "see" exactly how Pierre and Joseph work together.

Sidelights: Montreal—named for "Mount Royal," an 800-foot-high hill that rises above the city—is the largest city in Canada; it maintains the air of a European city with many distinctive neighborhoods. It was originally an Indian settlement called "Hochelaga," but the French took it over and made it the center of their fur-trading industry. The British gained possession of it and all of Canada during the French and Indian War (1756–1763); tension between English- and French-speaking residents persists to this day. Montreal's strategic location on the St. Lawrence River has assured it an economic importance that has made it the artistic and cultural center of the country as well. Although it was once also the political capital of Canada, the city of Ottawa, 130 miles to the west, is Canada's seat of government. Montreal is about 400 miles north of New York City.

Motivation for Reading: Deliverymen were once common fixtures in American cities and towns, but they are fast disappearing. Do you have any personal anecdotes concerning deliverymen that you can tell the class? If not, ask older teachers or local residents. Talk with students about the various roles of the deliveryman (food seller, bearer of gossip, dispenser of treats to children), and how shopping patterns have changed.

More About the Thematic Idea: Attachments between people, or between people and their pets, are often puzzles. Others can't understand what they see in each other. Mystery seems to surround the bond between them; the chance to penetrate the mystery provides suspense.

Purpose-Setting Question: Can a person become dependant on an animal?

ami." And this splendid combination would stalk proudly down the street.

The wagon, without any direction from Pierre, would roll three blocks down St. Catherine Street, then turn right two blocks along Roslyn Avenue; then left, for that was Prince Edward Street. The horse would stop at the first house, allow Pierre perhaps thirty seconds to get down from his seat and put a

---

stalk (STAWK) walk in a stiff, proud way.

Unit 3

bottle of milk at the front door, and would then go on, skipping two houses and stopping at the third. So down the length of the street. Then Joseph, still without any direction from Pierre, would turn round and come back along the other side. Yes, Joseph was a smart horse.

Pierre would boast, at the stable, of Joseph's skill. "I never touch the reins. He knows just where to stop. Why, a blind man could handle my route with Joseph pulling the wagon."

So it went on for years—always the same. Pierre and Joseph both grew old together, but gradually, not suddenly. Pierre's huge walrus mustache was pure white now. Joseph didn't lift his knees so high, or raise his head quite as much. Jacques, the foreman of the stables, never noticed that they were both getting old until Pierre appeared one morning carrying a heavy walking stick.

"Hey, Pierre," Jacques laughed. "Maybe you got the gout, hey?"

"*Mais oui, Jacques*," Pierre said a bit uncertainly. "One grows old. One's legs get tired."

"You should teach that horse to carry the milk to the front door for you," Jacques told him. "He does everything else."

He knew every one of the forty families he served on Prince Edward Street. The cooks knew that Pierre could neither read nor write. So instead of following the usual custom of leaving a note in an empty bottle if an additional quart of milk was needed, they would sing out when they heard the rumble of his wagon wheels over the cobbled street, "Bring an extra quart this morning, Pierre."

"So you have company for dinner tonight," he would call back gaily.

Pierre had a remarkable memory. When he arrived at the stable, he'd always remember to tell Jacques, "The Paquins took an extra quart this morning. The Lemoines bought a pint of cream."

Jacques would note these things in a little black book he always carried. Most of the drivers had to make out the weekly

---

gout (GOUT) painful disease of the joints, usually of the feet and the hands

cobbled (KOB uld) paved with stones, usually refering to a street (when used as an adjective).

Enrichment: A "walrus mustache" is a bushy, drooping mustache.

Reading Strategy: Important little details about Pierre are sprinkled throughout the story. Remind students that this story is a puzzle, and that they should be on the lookout for important bits of information, such as Pierre's inability to read.

bills and collect the money. But Jacques, liking Pierre, had always excused him from this task. All Pierre had to do was to arrive at five in the morning, walk to his wagon, which was always in the same spot at the curb, and deliver his milk. He returned some two hours later, got down stiffly from his seat, called a cheery "Au'voir" to Jacques, and then limped slowly down the street.

One morning the president of the Provincale Milk Company came to inspect the early morning deliveries. Jacques pointed Pierre out to him and said, "Watch how he talks to that horse. See how the horse listens and how he turns his head toward Pierre? See the look in that horse's eyes? You know, I think those two share a secret. I have often noticed it. It is as though they both sometimes chuckle at us as they go off on their route. Pierre is a good man, Monsieur Président, but he gets old. Would it be too bold of me to suggest that he be retired and be given perhaps a small pension?" he added anxiously.

"But of course," the president laughed. "I know his record. He has been on this route now for thirty years and never once has there been a complaint. Tell him it is time he rested. His salary will go on just the same."

But Pierre refused to retire. He was panic-stricken at the thought of not driving Joseph every day. "We are two old men," he said to Jacques. "Let us wear out together. When Joseph is ready to retire—then I, too, will quit."

Jacques, who was a kind man, understood. There was something about Pierre and Joseph that made a man smile tenderly. It was as though each drew some hidden strength from the other. When Pierre was sitting in his seat, and when Joseph was hitched to the wagon, neither seemed old. But when they finished their work, then Pierre would limp down the street slowly, seeming very old indeed. The horse's head would drop, and he would walk very wearily to his stall.

Then one morning Jacques had dreadful news for Pierre when he arrived. It was a cold morning and still pitch-dark. The air was iced that morning. And the snow that had fallen during the night glistened like a million diamonds piled together.

Jacques said, "Pierre, your horse, Joseph, did not wake up this

---

Monsieur (muh SYUR) French for Mister.
pension (PEN shun) retirement pay.

Unit 3

Critical Thinking: "You know I think those share a secret." This comment must be important: The title of the story derives from it. What secret might Pierre and Joseph share? Can students deduce anything from the clues they've been gathering?

Clarification: "...he gets old", rather than the grammatically correct "he's getting old" is used to remind us that Jacques is a native French speaker.

Literary Focus: The action of the plot begins to rise when Jacques tells Pierre the "dreadful news." A complication has developed.

morning. He was very old, Pierre. He was twenty-five, and that is like being seventy-five for a man."

"Yes," Pierre said, slowly. "Yes. I am seventy-five. And I cannot see Joseph again."

"Of course you can," Jacques soothed. "He is over in his stall, looking very peaceful. Go over and see him."

Pierre took one step forward, then turned. "No . . . no . . . you don't understand, Jacques."

Jacques clapped him on the shoulder. "We'll find another horse just as good as Joseph. Why, in a month you'll teach him to know your route as well as Joseph did. We'll . . ."

The look in Pierre's eyes stopped him. For years Pierre had worn a heavy cap. The peak came low over his eyes, keeping the bitter morning wind out of them. Now Jacques looked into Pierre's eyes, and saw something that startled him. He saw a dead, lifeless look in them. The eyes were mirroring the grief that was in Pierre's heart and his soul. It was as though his heart and soul had died.

"Take today off, Pierre," Jacques said. But already Pierre was hobbling off down the street; and had one been near, one would have seen tears streaming down his cheeks and have heard half-smothered sobs. There was a warning yell from the driver of a huge truck that was coming fast. There was the scream of brakes. But Pierre apparently heard neither.

Five minutes later an ambulance driver said, "He's dead. Was killed instantly."

"I couldn't help it," the driver of the truck protested. "He walked right into my truck. He never saw it, I guess. Why, he walked into it as though he were blind."

The ambulance doctor bent down. "Blind? Of course the man was blind. See those cataracts? This man has been blind for five years." He turned to Jacques. "You say he worked for you? Didn't you know he was blind?"

"No . . . no . . . ," Jacques said softly. "None of us knew. Only one knew—a friend of his named Joseph. . . . It was a secret, I think, just between those two."

---

peak (PEEK) front part of a cap.
cataract (KAT uh rakt) clouding of the eye's lens that can cause blindness.

Suspense

305

Critical Thinking: An important clue to their secret (Paragraph 21). Pierre says he can't "see" Joseph again. The "see" theme is developed further in the next few paragraphs.

Critical Thinking: Jacques deduces that the dead, lifeless look in Pierre's eyes is caused by grief. Is the deduction sound?

Literary Focus: Here is the climax of the story: Pierre is killed.

Literary Focus: And now the resolution. The reader learns, in the last two paragraphs, the secret Pierre and Joseph shared.

Discussion: What details of the story make sense now that the reader knows Pierre was blind? Ask students to think back and piece the puzzle together.

MINI QUIZ

Write the following questions on the chalkboard or overhead projector and call on students to fill in the blanks. Discuss the answers with the class.

1. Pierre's milk route was along _____ Street.
2. Pierre's horse was named for _____.
3. The president, of the milk company offered Pierre a _____, but he refused it.
4. The season during which Joseph died was _____.
5. _____ caused Pierre's blindness.

3. pension
4. winter
5. cataracts

Answers to Mini Quiz

1. Prince Edward
2. St. Joseph

ANSWERS TO UNDERSTAND THE SELECTION

ANSWERS TO UNDERSTAND THE SELECTION

1. Montreal, in Canada
2. They sing out when they hear his wagon coming.
3. 30 years
4. He is able to look at Joseph, his new horse, and "see a beautiful spirit shining out of the eyes of the horse."
5. Jacques doesn't make Pierre write out weekly bills and collect money, as the other drivers must do. Also, Jacques asks the milk company president for a pension for Pierre.
6. Pierre says that "a blind man could handle my route with Joseph pulling the wagon." Later, Jacques tells the milk company president, "You know, I think those two share a secret." And a bit later, the author notes, "It was as though each [Joseph and Pierre] drew some hidden strength from the other." Actually, the title itself—"A Secret for Two"—is foreshadowing.
7. It's not shame, but understanding—an understanding of the secret he had felt that Joseph and Pierre had shared.
8. Probably so; he seemed to enjoy his work. He certainly stayed with it long enough, without complaining.
9. Answers will vary. It's possible, but highly unlikely in this day and age. We depend on eyesight for too many things.
10. "Suspense" is the growing interest or excitement felt as you read a story. This story gives you that feeling, but it's subtle; it really doesn't hit home until the end. The reader is given enough clues throughout the story, however, to indicate that there is something magical about the relationship between Pierre and Joseph. Determining

UNDERSTAND THE SELECTION

Recall

1. In what city is "A Secret for Two" set?

2. How do Pierre's customers order extra milk?

3. How long had Pierre worked for the Provincale Milk Company?

Infer

4. How do you know that Pierre is not blind at the beginning of the story?

5. Give an example showing that Pierre has a good relationship with his boss.

6. Find an example of foreshadowing.

7. What was Jacques's reaction when he learned that Pierre had been blind for five years?

Apply

8. Do you think Pierre was happy with his life? Why or why not?

9. Do you think it is possible for someone to be blind without others' knowing about it?

10. This unit has as its theme "suspense." Is "A Secret for Two" a suspense story? Explain your answer.

Respond to Literature

Why do foreign cities make especially good settings for stories?

306

WRITE ABOUT THE SELECTION

A **eulogy** is a speech or piece of writing praising someone who has died. What might be said to eulogize Pierre Dupin? On the surface, he was a simple man. He even could not read or write. However, inside, he must have been very strong to endure the life that he led.

Imagine you are speaking at Pierre Dupin's funeral delivering the eulogy.

Prewriting: Start by thinking of an epitaph you could write for Pierre's tombstone. (An epitaph is an inscription on a headstone in memory of the person buried there.) The epitaph will serve as an outline for writing a longer, more complete eulogy. List these qualities that you admire exhibited by Pierre Dupin in the story.

Writing: Write the eulogy based on the epitaph you wrote and the list of qualities you compiled. Expand on any ideas you have mentioned, and add new ones.

Revising: As you revise the eulogy, think back on the information about Pierre given in the story. Are there any traits or characteristics you have neglected to mention? Add them. Make sure you have provided examples from the story for each of the traits mentioned.

Proofreading: Reread your eulogy and check for errors. Make sure that all verbs agree with their subjects. Check to see that verb tenses are consistent. If you begin speaking of Pierre in past tense, make sure all verbs are past tense.

Unit 3

what it is is the mystery of the story, and creates suspense.

Respond to Literature: Answers will vary. Students should see, however, that the romance associated with anything foreign presents an opportunity that a good writer can explore in depth.

ANSWERS TO WRITE ABOUT THE SELECTION

ANSWERS TO WRITE ABOUT THE SELECTION

Prewriting: Have the class work cooperatively to collect a sample of epitaphs. Ask students to visit a cemetery and copy some from headstones, or do research in the library. Point out that some epitaphs are autobiographical; that is, the person wrote his or her own

epitaph before he died. An interesting example of one such epitaph is Benjamin Franklin's, which is sometimes found in appendices to his *Autobiography*.

Writing: Circulate as students work individually. Check their epitaphs to see if enough information is provided to make a brief outline for the eulogy.

THINK ABOUT PLOT

The **plot**, the action of a story, is based on conflicting human motivations and responses. To develop a plot successfully, the sequence of events must include human motivations. For instance, some motivations in "The Lady, or the Tiger" are jealousy, protectiveness, and love. In the story "A Secret for Two," human motivations are a major element of the plot. However, the other literary elements also affect the plot.

1. The plot of this story requires a certain kind of character. What kind of person is Pierre? What does he value? What motivates his behavior?

2. The plot also requires a certain kind of setting. What characteristics of the neighborhood in Montreal where Pierre works are important to the plot?

3. What complications of questions develop in the story?

4. What is the climax of the story?

5. How do the human motivations of Pierre's boss, Jacques, affect the plot of "A Secret for Two"?

6. What is the conflict in the story? How does this conflict affect the plot?

DEVELOP YOUR VOCABULARY

Using context clues can sometimes help in understanding the meaning of foreign words and expressions. Follow these steps to use context clues:

a. Reread the sentence in which the foreign word or phrase appears, and also the sentences before and after.

b. Substitute words that you think are similar to the English words.

c. If the English words make sense, your choice of meaning is probably accurate.

Use context clues to discover the meaning of the French phrases from "A Secret for Two." Copy the sentences substituting an English meaning for each French phrase.

1. Pierre would call, *"Bonjour, vieil ami,"* as he climbed into his seat.

2. Pierre would call softly to Joseph, *"Avance, mon ami."*

3. *"Mais oui, Jacques,"* Pierre said a bit uncertainly.

4. He returned some two hours later, got down stiffly from his seat, and called a cheery *"Au'voir"* to Jacques.

5. Pierre is a good man, *Monsieur* President, but he gets old.

ANSWERS TO THINK ABOUT PLOT

1. Kind, uncomplaining, and willing to work hard for many years.

2. Unchanging, which makes it possible for Joseph to memorize the route. The same families seem to stay in the same houses, and there don't seem to be any high-rise buildings of any sort. High-rises would certainly have given Pierre problems when he became blind.

3. Pierre and Joseph become dependent on each other, partly through love—if that's possible for an animal—and partly through necessity.

4. The accident in which Pierre dies.

5. Jacques was a kind man who let Pierre work and not retire. He also excused Pierre from the regular duties of filling out receipts or using another horse. Jacques, therefore, never noticed that Pierre was going blind.

6. Pierre's devotion and dependence on his horse keep him working long beyond his retirement years. This conflict keeps Pierre inseparable from Joseph. When Joseph dies, Pierre has no one "to see" for him, and, thus, Pierre is killed.

ANSWERS TO DEVELOP YOUR VOCABULARY

1. Bonjour, vieil ami—Good day, old friend.
2. Avance, mon ami—Forward, my friend.
3. Mais oui, Jacques—Of course, Jacques.
4. au'voir—shortened form of "au revoir," meaning goodbye
5. monsieur—mister

ANSWERS TO
LITERATURE-BASED
WRITING

Note: The Teacher's Resource Book contains worksheets to accompany both writing assignments.

Motivation 1: Divide students into groups. Ask each group to choose a section from one of the stories they've read that they think would make an interesting "playlet." Only dialogue can be used, so they might have to adapt the section. The sections don't have to be long. Ask the groups to perform their playlets.

Prewriting: The peformances of the playlets should refresh students' memories of the selections in this unit, and the characters and plot in each. If any selections haven't been represented, remind students of them and review the characters and plot.

Writing: Circulate among students as they work individually. Make sure they have a list of characters, and that they have mapped a plot. Remind them they can change scenes if they want different settings.

Revising: Have students work in pairs. The writer reads his or her drama aloud, while the partner listens. After the reading, the listener "critiques" the drama, paying particular attention to plot development.

Proofreading: Have students choose new partners. The partner reads over the drama, checking for errors. The partner also provides general feedback and offers suggestions for improvements.

Motivation 2: Remind the students that in the last unit the elements of a short story were shown as points on a compass. Draw the four-pointed compass again, with "plot," "characters," "setting," and "theme" labeled. Add a fifth line

LITERATURE-BASED WRITING

1. In this unit, you have been introduced to some interesting characters who have been involved in some exciting situations. Two stories were dramas, so you have studied the elements of drama. Why not put your knowledge of drama to work?

Write an original play, using any of the characters from any of the selections in this unit. Make the play suspenseful. After all, suspense is what these characters are accustomed to!

Prewriting: Choose the characters you would like to use in your play. List them. Then think of a plot. Map the plot, with each major development in a box. Write some ideas on the map about how the dialogue or the stage directions will advance the plot.

Writing: Use the plot map, your list of characters, and your notes about the dialogue and stage directions to write the play.

Revising: Make sure you have "paced" the action of the play. Review the steps in plot development, and check to see that you have followed them.

Proofreading: Reread your play to check for errors. When writing a play, you need not worry about punctuation of quotations, unless someone quotes someone else. Then standard punctuation rules apply. Make any changes you feel are necessary.

2. The elements of drama are the same as those for all stories, with added emphasis on the conflict. Conflicts in dramas are usually between human characters. The conflict is caused by a clash between their personalities, traits, or beliefs. How the characters struggle with one another is a very important part of the drama.

Take a closer look at the conflict in one of the dramas you have read.

Prewriting: Review the work you did for the "Thinking About" sections. Then choose the drama that most interests you. Make a chart, listing the conflict and the characters involved. Under each character's name, write all of the traits important to the conflict.

Writing: Use the chart to write a description of the conflict. Then analyze the role of the conflict in the drama. How does it relate to other elements, particularly theme?

Revising: When you are revising, think of ways to use material from the drama itself to illustrate what you are saying. For example, can you quote something a character says to illustrate a point?

Proofreading: Reread what you have written as a check for errors. Try to vary the structure of sentences. If too many sentences are constructed in the same way, the reader could become bored.

and label it "conflict." Ask, In what genre of literature is conflict the central element? (drama)

Prewriting: Have students work in pairs or groups to discuss the dramas they've read, and the conflicts in each.

Writing: Circulate among students as they work individually. Check the charts they've made for accuracy and completeness.

Revising: Have students work again in pairs or groups. They might want to reread portions of the dramas together in order to find material, particularly quotations, to illustrate a point.

Proofreading: Ask students to analyze the structure of their sentences. Is a similar pattern used in many of them? Show how sentences can be rewritten to vary

structure.

BUILDING LANGUAGE SKILLS

Vocabulary

Characters are developed through description. The words the author chooses for the description are important. Pay attention not only to the **denotations,** or "dictionary definitions," of the words, but also to their **connotations,** or "emotional meanings."

Many words used to describe people have negative or positive connotations. These connotations help the reader form an impression of the character.

Below are some words used in the selections in this unit to describe characters. Make a "+" after positive words, and a "−" after negative words. Then use each in a sentence.

1. kind	**12.** blooming
2. gentle	**13.** fiery
3. faithful	**14.** proud
4. beautiful	**15.** brave
5. smart	**16.** cunning
6. semi-barbaric	**17.** clever
7. reckless	**18.** rude
8. raw	**19.** spare
9. wildly imaginative	**20.** honest
10. happy	**21.** gentle
11. genial	**22.** odd

Usage and Mechanics

Verbs must agree with their subjects. If the subject is singular, the verb must be singular. If the subject is plural, the verb must be plural. Make sure you match the verb with the subject, not another word.

In the sentences below, what is the correct form of the verbs in parentheses? Write the verb, and tell whether it is singular or plural.

1. This old boy behind the counter was the kind that (mean) well.

2. Both of the feed-merchant types (were) paying close attention.

3. It (lead) us into a wild jungle of love and hate.

4. (Do) the tiger come out of the door, or (do) the lady?

5. There (was) only Ross and Will, opening the lunch basket.

More About Usage and Mechanics: Usually the key to solving subject-verb agreement problems is finding the subject. And usually the number of the subject is clear (singular or plural), but not always. Encourage students to underline the subject of each sentence before they determine verb number.

Cooperative/Collaborative Learning Activity: Divide the class into two teams. Give the teams 20 minutes to come up with 20 sentences testing subject-verb agreement. Verbs should be in present tense. Gather their sentences and have the two teams sit on opposite sides of the room. Read one of Team A's sentences to Team B, leaving out the verb as they read the sentence; supply the infinitive form at the end. Correct responses receive 1 point. The team with the highest point total wins.

Answers to Mechanics Exercises

1. means; singular **2.** were; plural **3.** leads; singular **4.** Does, does; singular **5.** were; plural

---

ANSWERS TO BUILDING LANGUAGE SKILLS

Vocabulary

More About Word Attack: Most words in the list that follows have definite positive or negative connotations. Some, however, tend either way. In such cases, context within a sentence determines which connotation is meant.

Cooperative/Collaborative Learning Activity: Students could do the exercise individually, and then compare answers with a partner. Where there are disagreements, students should look for the word in one of the selections, and base their answer on the context.

Answers to Vocabulary Exercises:

1. kind +
2. gentle +
3. faithful +
4. beautiful +
5. smart +
6. semi-barbaric −
7. reckless −
8. raw −
9. wildly imaginative −
10. happy +
11. genial +
12. blooming +
13. fiery − or +
14. proud +
15. brave +
16. cunning −
17. clever − or +
18. rude −
19. spare −
20. honest +
21. odd −

T309

Motivation: A theme song is a song written for a movie or TV show. Play a well-known theme song for the class, and ask them to identify it. Why is it called a "theme" song?

Teaching Strategy: Plot and theme can be related to travel. The plot is the places you go and the stops you make; the theme is the purpose of your trip. The people who travel with you are like the characters in a story; why they are with you, and what they are like, are usually closely related to the purpose of your trip. Just as with the theme of a story, the purpose of a trip may be unstated; for example, every day you might ride a subway, bus, train to school, yet how often do you say directly, "The purpose of my trip on the subway is to go to school"? Instead, the theme becomes obvious from your route and the people you are with.

Evaluation Criteria: Use the chart below to evaluate students' discussion. A plus (+) represents outstanding work, check (✓) adequate work, and a dash (—) a need for further discussion.
   Analysis of plot:
   Analysis of characters:
   Description and interpretation of theme:

SPEAKING AND LISTENING

A theme is the meaning or message of a piece of literature. Some stories and poems have more than one theme, and others have a theme of only minor importance.

Sometimes plot and theme are confused. A plot is the "what happens" in a poem or story. For example, the plot of a story might concern a young soldier during his first battle. The events of the plot might include the man's thoughts, the battle itself, and the outcome of the battle. However, the theme of the story might be the idea that fighting solves nothing.

Understanding the plot and theme of a story is sometimes easier if you share your ideas with classmates and talk about how the events of a story help illustrate the theme.

Before you begin a discussion of the plot and theme of a selection in this unit, consider the following:

1. Read the selection carefully. Try to identify the author's message. Since a story or play can contain more than one idea, it is possible to have several themes. Be aware that although there may be several, only one is the main theme.

2. Think about the events in the story. As you become familiar with what happens, you will be able to see how these events point toward a theme.

3. Study the characters until you know them well and understand their outlooks on life. Notice what any personal-

ity traits of important characteristics they have make a particular statement about life.

4. Consider the different points of view of the characters. Decide whether others share their outlooks. Think about general ideas the different characters might represent.

5. Remember that an author may or may not state his theme somewhere in the story. He or she may merely suggest a theme through the events of the plot and the attitudes of the characters. If this is the case in the selection you choose to discuss, be sure to examine the events in the plot, the dialogue of the characters, and the setting for clues to the theme of the story.

Now, as a class or in small groups, choose a poem, play, or story from this unit that you believe has a strong theme: one that seems to be written to get a certain idea across to the reader. First, discuss what you believe the main theme to be. Then talk about how the events and characters in the selection illustrate the theme. Discuss elements of the setting that contribute to the theme. Keep the steps and suggestions above in mind as you and your classmates discuss the selection.

A Careeer to Consider: A number of the stories in this unit involve police officers and detectives. Students might like to know more about work in the law enforcement field. Police officers are usually required to have a high school education, and many departments—such as the state police—give preference to college graduates. Police officers work hard and are often in dangerous situations. A concern for people is necessary, as well as a sense of fairness and justice. Most departments offer on-the-job training. Promotions are made "up through the ranks," as in the military. Police officers who show a special interest and skill in investigating and solving crimes can be assigned to a department's investigation unit.

CRITICAL THINKING

Sherlock Holmes's detecting skills are based on deduction. "You must have seen more in those rooms than I did," states Watson in the "Speckled Band" case. The master detective replies, "I didn't *see* more. I *deduced* more. I imagine you saw everything I did."

Actually, Holmes's first deductions about who killed Julia Stoner were wrong. He had reached an "unsound conclusion." Why? Holmes himself explains: It is dangerous "to reason without having *all* the facts."

There are three parts to deductive reasoning. They are called a **syllogism**: a major premise, a minor premise, and a conclusion. You must be sure the two premises are correct before making a deduction. If any facts are missing or incorrect, your conclusion will be wrong, or "unsound."

Example:
Policemen wear blue uniforms.
Mr. Kahil wears a blue uniform.
Mr. Kahil is, therefore, a policeman.

Sound logical? Well, maybe. However, what if you find out that Mr. Kahil is a bus driver? The deduction does not seem very sound, does it? The problem with this syllogism is that the premises may be true, but other important facts are ignored. Many people besides policemen wear blue uniforms.

Rewrite the examples. Make a correct deduction.

EFFECTIVE STUDYING

Reading and writing are not always easy. You might not know the definition of a words. You might want to use a certain synonym that you are sure exists, but you just cannot think of it. What if you encounter a foreign word or phrase? There are many sources you can turn to for help.

A **dictionary** lists words alphabetically. It also provides information about definitions of words, pronunciations of words, origins of words, and different forms of words, such as noun, verb, adjective and adverb forms. A "pocket" dictionary gives less information than a "desk" edition, but a pocket dictionary is much handier.

Two-language dictionaries "translate" foreign words into English. They are useful if you read stories with foreign phrases.

A **thesaurus** lists synonyms for words, and sometimes antonyms as well. Some thesauruses list words alphabetically, as in a dictionary. Others have indexes that refer you to numbered sections.

If you use a computer for writing, you should know that many word-processing programs include **spell-checkers** and thesauruses. These features can be a great help, although a "spell-checker" is certainly no substitute for a dictionary.

What reference books would you use to find the meaning of *adios,* find a substitute for the word *afraid,* and check the spelling of a difficult word?

Effective Studying: Have a desk-size dictionary, a pocket-size dictionary, a two-language dictionary, and a thesaurus on hand to show the class. Compare entires for the same word in a desk-size and pocket-size dictionary, and show students how to use the thesaurus. Explain that a two-language dictionary translates words in both directions, not just into English.

Answers to Questions in Effective Studying:

1. Meaning of "adios"; Spanish/ English dictionary.
2. A substitute for the word "afraid"; a thesaurus.
3. check the spelling of a difficult word; a dictionary.

ANSWERS TO CRITICAL THINKING

The syllogism would be correct if rewritten this way:
  Terrorists believe in carrying guns.
  John Doe carries a gun.
  John Doe might be a terrorist.
Here's a variation that produces a more definite premise:
  Plastic explosives are illegal and anyone carrying them is considered a terrorist.
  John Doe is carrying plastic explosives.
  John Doe is therefore a terrorist.

UNIT 4: Discoveries

A Continuing Unit Project: Literary Magazines

The theme of this unit is discoveries. The word "discoveries" might also be an appropriate title for a series of literary reviews.

Tell students that, during their study of this unit, they are to imagine they are writers for a literary magazine. The magazine, a quarterly, is about to publish its winter (or spring, or summer) edition. The title of this edition is to be "Discoveries." Students will write for the magazine a review of each selection they read in this unit.

Take a few minutes to discuss with students the elements a literary review might include. One obvious item would be a discussion of the particular genre that a selection represents: fiction, nonfiction, drama, poetry. Another important item would be an analysis of how the writer handles certain elements of storytelling: theme, setting, plot, character, use of sound, imagery, symbolism, tone, or point of view. In some cases, for example, a writer will be very masterful in developing the psychology and personality of a particular character. In other cases, a writer may paint a vivid picture of a particular setting. Or, a writer may make a unique and powerful statement about a particular theme.

Students may find it helpful to read excerpts from literary magazines, such as the *Saturday Review* or the literary reviews published by major universities. Some general questions to help students get started include:

What is the genre of this selection?

How does this particular genre work well for the subject matter?

What literary element in this selection especially stands out? Why?

What is your overall impression of the selection? Did you find it interesting or moving? Did you feel that you could not put it down? Or did you find yourself becoming bored or confused as you read?

Would you recommend the selection to a friend? Why or why not?

If your class needs more structure, try creating questions for each selection such as these listed below.

"Chee's Daughter"/"Navaho Chant"
How does the writer use symbolism to make this story more meaningful?

"The Gold Medal"
How does the writer create a contrast between flat and rounded characters?

"Conversation with Myself"/"Happy Thought"
How do these poets make effective use of points-of-view?

"Ta-Na-E-Ka"
How is the autobiographical aspect of this story effective?

"Dead at Seventeen"
What unusual literary techniques are used in this selection?

"Thank You, M'am"
How does the writer create the characters of Luella Bates Washington Jones and the boy?

"Four Haiku"/"A Bee Thumps"
Why is the form of haiku especially suited to the subject matter of these poems?

"Starvation Wilderness"
Do you feel that the writer's narrative of this real-life adventure story is effective?

"Dreams"/"Untitled"/"Sympathy"
Which poet, Hughes or Dunbar, comes across as more optimistic and hopeful about life? Why?

Have students place their finished reviews in a looseleaf binder or folder. Then have students exchange reviews with a partner to read and evaluate.

"Chee's Daughter"
by Juanita Platero and Siyowin Miller   (page 317)

"Navaho Chant"
(Traditional Navaho Song)   (page 333)

SELECTION SYNOPSIS

A young Navaho named Chee loses his wife in a battle against tuberculosis. When Chee returns home to the family compound, he discovers that his precious little daughter is gone. Chee's parents tell him that his in-laws, with whom he has never gotten along, have taken his daughter to live with them. They have done this according to the Navaho custom where a dead woman's children go to live with her parents.

The loss of the little girl is more than Chee can bear. He goes to talk to his father-in-law, Old Man Fat. Old Man Fat is not willing to part with the child, however. Chee does not know what to do. At first he thinks he might escape his grief by leaving the area and getting a job in a distant place. Then he hears news of a new road that might take a lot of business away from Old Man Fat's trading post. In Chee's mind, a plan forms. Chee works night and day for many months, farming his land; only he knows why.

Finally, the day comes when Chee has an abundance of food from his land. He rides out to see Old Man Fat and Fat's wife. Much as Chee suspected, his in-laws have become impoverished. The little girl has become a burden, another mouth to feed. Chee dumps the food that he has brought at their feet. They see that it is just enough food for two people to get through the winter. They keep the food and hand Chee his little girl.

SELECTION ACTIVITY

Have students research various aspects of Navaho history and culture. Students may wish to research in depth one topic that particularly interests them, such as Navaho art or the history of the Navahos in the United States.

"The Gold Medal"
by Nan Gilbert   (page 337)

SELECTION SYNOPSIS

Amanda, a young black girl, is tired of being seen as a "type" by everyone around her. Her mother is concerned that she be a "good example" in the mainly white community into which they have just moved. A neighbor lady and the candy store owner see her, and all teenagers, as potential troublemakers. Even her sympathetic and friendly science teacher seems to "type" her as a black student whom he wants to help integrate.

One day, Amanda becomes upset during science class and runs far from the school. Her awkwardness and unhappiness disappear as she runs. By accident, she runs across a pasture and falls into a huge hole. An old man comes over to see if she is hurt. It turns out that the man has dug the hole as a grave for his dying dog, Chief. The man invites Amanda to meet his dog. He also compliments Amanda by calling her a "runner." The old man shows Amanda medals the dog has won. He also shows her a gold medal that he bought for the dog himself, because he believed the dog would be a true winner. At the end of the story, the man gives Amanda the gold medal to keep. He expresses his belief in her and encourages her to believe in herself.

SELECTION ACTIVITY

A person who would have had something in common with Amanda is Jessie Owens (1913–1981), the black American track star who won four Olympic gold medals. Owen's achievement was especially significant in that he won several of his medals in the 1936 Olympics in Berlin, Germany. At that time, Hitler was in power, and he was declaring that blacks and other races were physically and mentally inferior to Arians. Owens clearly disproved Hitler's theories.

Have students go the library and gather information about Jessie Owens's life and accomplishments. Have them write short biographies of Owens. Then encourage students to learn about other black Americans who have been outstanding in sports.

"Conversation with Myself"
by Eve Merriam   (page 349)

"Happy Thought"
by Jesus Melendez   (page 349)

Both of these short poems are about aspects of privacy. The first poem is clearly introspective; the second talks about experiencing private time in the midst of a crowd.

A very moving and powerful introspective poem is "Who Am I?" by Dietrich Bonhoeffer. Bonhoeffer was a German theologian who was imprisoned and later hanged for his part in a plot to overthrow Hitler. His writings were published posthumously.

Make copies of the poem to pass out to each student. Since the poem may be difficult for some students to read, read the poem along with the students and encourage them to ask questions about parts they do not understand.

Discuss with students how this poem, though very different in tone, has certain things in common with "Conversation with Myself." A theme of both poems is the unknown part of one's self, and how this can cause, at least at times, a lack of self-confidence.

"Ta-Na-E-Ka"
by Mary Whitebird   (page 353)

SELECTION SYNOPSIS

Mary Whitebird and her cousin Roger are nearly eleven years old, the age at which Kaw Indians must undergo an initiation into adulthood, called Ta-Na-E-Ka. In this ritual, Kaw boys and girls are sent into the woods for five days to survive on their own. During this time, they must sleep outdoors and eat insects and anything else they can find.

Mary and Roger both dread the ordeal, but Mary comes up with a plan. Secretly, she borrows five dollars from her teacher, Mrs. Richardson. It is Mary's intention to buy food at a restaurant near the edge of the woods. Ernie, the kind restaurant owner, befriends Mary and lets her sleep as well as eat at the restaurant. Mary helps Ernie cook and set tables, and picks wildflowers in the woods. When Mary returns home after the "ordeal," Roger is bruised and exhausted, but Mary is obviously rested and well fed. Mary confesses her "survival tactics" to her grandfather, who trained her and Roger for the Ta-Na-E-Ka. Her traditional yet understanding grandfather admits that she was clever and courageous in her own way—and did indeed prove that she is a survivor.

SELECTION ACTIVITY

In this activity, students will gather information and write reports about coming-of-age rituals that take place in various cultures. Students can choose to write about familiar rituals, such as the Bar-Mitzvah and Confirmation ceremonies that are probably common among them and their friends; or students can find out about rituals that take place in specific cultures within the Native American, Asian, Indian, and African nations. Students can research a ritual that is still practiced today, or they can learn about one that has been practiced in the past.

Tell students to include in their papers a description of the ritual and its purpose. Also ask them to compare the ritual to the Ta-Na-E-Ka.

"Dead at Seventeen"
by Paul "Bear" Bryant   (page 364)

SELECTION SYNOPSIS

This "Ann Landers" column contains a message that Bear Bryant, the famous football coach, used to read regularly to freshmen at the University of Alabama. The message is in the form of an imaginary plea, written in the first person. It expresses the feelings of a seventeen-year-old boy who has just been killed in an auto accident as a result of his careless driving. The boy bemoans the fact that he is a "traffic fatality." Consequently, his life has been cut short, and he has brought grief to his parents and friends. The teenager asks for "just one more chance" and promises, all too late, to be "the most careful driver in the world."

SELECTION ACTIVITY

Two organizations that have been formed recently for the purpose of reducing traffic fatalities are MADD (Mothers Against Drunk Driving) and SADD (Students Against Driving Drunk). Although both organizations focus on the consequences of reckless driving related to the use of alcohol, they still have much in common with the message of "Dead at Seventeen."

Have students learn about these organizations and what they do. Also ask them to find out if either organization has a chapter in their city or town. If so, you may want to arrange for a member of the organization to come and speak to your class.

"Thank You, M'am"
by Langston Hughes   (page 369)

Roger, a teenage boy, fails in an attempt to snatch the purse of a Mrs. Jones. She refuses to release the boy and drags him to her apartment. She orders him to wash up and later makes a meal for both of them. Roger tells Mrs. Jones that he wanted money to buy a pair of blue suede shoes. After they eat, she gives him ten dollars to buy the shoes and tells him to behave himself from now on. Roger is at a loss for words. He manages to say, "Thank you, M'am." He never sees Mrs. Jones again.

SELECTION ACTIVITY

Arrange for students to read the short story "Where Love Is, There God Is Also" by Tolstoy (available in Globe *World Anthology*). In this story, an incident is described in which the old cobbler, Martin, catches a boy stealing an apple from a woman's basket. The way he handles the incident is similar in certain ways to the way Mrs. Jones treats Roger in "Thank You, M'am." Have students write short papers in which they compare and contrast the two stories.

"Four Haiku"
by Buson, Anonymous, Richard Wright, Issa **(page 377)**

"A Bee Thumps"
by Richard Sund **(page 377)**

The four haikus paint images from nature that have parallels in human life. The short poem about the bee is in a style similar to that of the haiku.

SELECTION ACTIVITY

Japanese art has much in common with Japanese haiku, particularly in its use of nature as subject. Have students go to the library or a museum and find examples of Japanese painting. Have them describe in their own words the characteristics of pictures they find. Then challenge them to find a picture that could be used to illustrate or compliment one of the poems in this selection.

"Starvation Wilderness"
by Olive A. Frederickson **(page 381)**

SELECTION SYNOPSIS

At the beginning of this true adventure, the narrator, her husband, Walter, and their six-month-old daughter, Olive,

set out to trap muskrats and other animals in Canada's Far North. The area in which they camp is rich in fur-bearing animals but lacking in game. Their food supply dwindles dangerously low; thus, they call the area Starvation Wilderness. They set out in bitterly cold weather to find more supplies, and after a difficult journey—made more so by the fact that the narrator is pregnant—they come upon Bennett, another trapper, who sells them food.

They return to their original camp, but find game and animals for trapping scarce. They travel further west, camping in a tent. Trapping is better there, but many hardships follow, not the least being a disastrous fire in their tent. Finally the ice goes out of the river, and the small family makes a difficult journey back to Bennett's cabin. The riverboat picks them up there, and the narrator returns to civilization in time to have her baby, another daughter, named Vala. Walter resumes trapping in the fall, but the narrator has had enough of the Far North. She resolves to remain behind with her children.

SELECTION ACTIVITY

Have students use encyclopedias and other reference books to learn about the fur-trapping industry in North America. Have them relate the information that they find to the story "Starvation Wilderness."

"Dreams"
by Langston Hughes **(page 395)**

"Untitled"
(Anonymous) **(page 396)**

"Sympathy"
by Paul Laurence Dunbar **(page 396)**

The theme of the first poem is the importance of having dreams and goals in one's life. The theme of the second poem is the many "selves" that may exist in one person. The theme of the last poem is the parallel that exists between a caged bird and a person who yearns to be free.

SELECTION ACTIVITY

The message of the Untitled poem in this selection is both humorous and profound. Have students work in small groups to create skits that dramatize the poem. Students can act out the poem in silence, using only pantomime; they can act out the poem as it is read or recited; or they can extend the poem by creating dialogue and/or a more definite plot.

STUDENT READING LIST

Dunbar, Paul Laurence. *I Greet the Dawn.* Poems selected and illustrated, with an introduction by Ashley Bryan. New York: Atheneum, 1978.

Gold, Robert S. *Point of Departure.* New York: Dell, 1967.

Hamilton, Virginia. *Arilla Sun Down.* New York: Morrow, 1976.

Peck, Richard, ed. *Pictures That Storm Inside My Head.* New York: Avon, 1976.

Platt, Kin. *Run for Your Life.* Photos by Chuck Freedman. New York: Franklin-Watts, 1977.

From Globe Classroom Libraries

The Black Experience
   Sister by Eloise Greenfield
   The Contender by Robert Lipsyte

The theme of the unit is discoveries: learning new things about oneself, others, the world, life itself.

In the first selection, "Chee's Daughter," the main character discovers that his values and choices in life have been right, after all.
Literary skill: symbols/symbolism
Vocabulary: adjectives and adverbs
Writing: write about the characters

The second selection, "Navajo Chant," emphasizes the discovery of beauty in a symbol of nature.
Literary skill: symbols/symbolism
Vocabulary: using prepositions
Writing: writing from a different point of view

The third selection, "The Gold Medal," illustrates how others can help a person discover him- or herself.
Literary skill: character traits
Vocabulary: adverbs that end in -ly
Writing: story extension

The next selection includes two poems: "Conversation With Myself" and "Happy Thought." Both poems emphasize self-discovery.
Literary skill: choosing the speaker/first, second, or third person
Vocabulary: pronunciation
Writing: about personal experiences

The fifth selection, "Ta-Na-E-Ka," describes the author's discoveries as she undergoes a traditional ritual of the Kaw Indians.
Literary skill: autobiography
Vocabulary: using contractions
Writing: story extension

The annotated selection, "Dead at Seventeen," tells the poignant story of a discovery made too late.
Literary skill: elements of nonfiction
Vocabulary: understanding slang
Writing: expressing a personal reaction

The seventh selection is entitled "Thank You, M'am." In the story a young boy and an older woman

whom he tries to rob make important discoveries about each other.
Literary skill: theme
Vocabulary: synonyms
Writing: story extension

The next selection, "Chair," is a play about a group of high school students who discover how a physically handicapped person wishes to be treated.
Literary skill: plot
Vocabulary: antonyms

Writing: expressing an opinion

The ninth selection is a group of Haiku. These short poems emphasize discoveries about nature that relate to human experience.
Literary skill: Haiku
Vocabulary: using a thesaurus
Writing: create a Haiku poem

In the next selection, "Starvation Wilderness," the author discovers important things about herself during a life-or-death struggle.

Literary skill: conflict
Vocabulary: using a dictionary
Writing: record a personal plan

The last selection is a group of poems that emphasize discoveries about life.
Literary skill: rhyme
Vocabulary: words with multiple meanings
Writing: record a personal experience

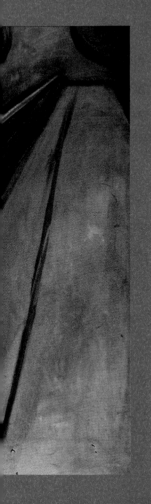

Discoveries

It is well to observe the force and
virtue and consequence of discoveries . . .

—Francis Bacon

Girl on the Bridge, Edward Munch. Three Lions.

313

UNIT OBJECTIVES

After completing this unit, students should be able to

- understand the four basic elements of nonfiction: plot, point of view, tone, and theme
- distinguish between fact and opinion
- use the skill of note-taking effectively
- build on knowledge of literary elements in order to write both creatively and analytically
- use context clues to determine meanings of words
- use new words in sentences.

AUDIOVISUAL MATERIALS

Indian America (Available through the East Orange Public Library, East Orange, N.J.), color; 50 min. Documentary about the problems and broken dreams of the Native Americans.

Great Short Stories (Caedmon). Performed by Edward Woodward and others; videocassette or audiocassette.

Reading Stories—Plots and Themes. (Coronet), 14 mins; 16mm film or videocassette. Visual images that show the relationship between a story's plot and its theme.

A Gathering of Great Poetry for Children Second Grade & Up (Caedmon), audiocassette. Read by Julie Harris and others; includes Eve Merriam's "Metaphor."

Thank You M'am (Phoenix/BFA Films and Video), 12 mins; 16mm film or videocassette. Adaptation of the story by Langston Hughes.

Langston Hughes (Carousel Film and Video), color; 24 mins.; videocassette.

Making Haiku (Encyclopedia Britannica Educational Corporation), 8 mins.; 16mm film or videocassette. Introduces and explains haiku; presents nature scenes to inspire haiku; encourages students to compose their own haiku.

Fine Arts Note

Edvard Munch (1863–1944) was a Norwegian painter and graphic artist. His emotionally-charged paintings often express themes of isolation, fear, death, and anxiety.

Teaching Strategy: Arrange a display of some of these items: a light bulb; empty containers of antibiotics; a computer; a telephone; a piece of synthetic fabric; a radio or TV; a camera. Ask students to imagine life without each of the items; then ask how the item has changed our lives. Encourage students to include broad economic and social changes in their discussion. Point out that each item represents a *discovery* and that discoveries bring about changes, both good and bad.

Discoveries.

What do you think of when you hear the word *discovery*? Perhaps you think of a great scientific discovery, like the automobile engine. Perhaps you think of discovering something valuable, such as diamonds or gold. You may even think of discovering something new, like a cheap source of energy.

Francis Bacon, the English essayist, wrote about the importance of looking at the effects, or consequences, of discoveries. Think of the changes television, frozen food, and computers have made in the twentieth century. Discoveries have the power to shape and change the world, either for better or for worse. Do you see the discovery of nuclear energy as beneficial or destructive? This idea of change also applies to your own personal discoveries. Once you make a discovery, the world in which you live—and your own inner reality—are forever changed. Life is never quite the same again.

The selections in this unit will focus on discoveries that people make about themselves, others, the world around them, and life. The selections will help you think about the discoveries that you have made.

Discoveries About Yourself. In the short story "Chee's Daughter," a Navaho man doubts the wisdom of his own values when his wife dies and he loses his daughter. A bold plan to win back his daughter finally succeeds, and Chee discovers that his values were right for him after all. Have you ever experienced self-doubt when faced with difficult circumstances? What did you discover about yourself and your values? Two poems tell about discoveries that you yourself may have experienced. "Conversations with Myself" explores the question, "Who am I?" while "Happy Thought" discovers reasons for both laughter and embarrassment.

Sometimes a person needs the help of another person to find out who he or she really is. In the short story "The Gold Medal," a young black girl discovers an aspect of her true self through a chance encounter with a wise and kindly old man.

Have you ever taken part in a ritual that is part of your religion or community, such as a bar mitzvah, baptism, or initiation? What did you

314

Unit 4

discover about yourself as a result of this experience? In the true story "Ta-Na-E-Ka," a young Native American girl describes her participation in the coming-of-age ritual that is part of the tradition of the Kaw Indians. Sent out to spend five days and nights alone in the wilderness, the girl comes up with a clever plan. She discovers that she can survive and thrive in the most unusual circumstances.

About Others. People discover things about themselves and one another in relationships. What things have you discovered recently about the people in your life? Did some of these things surprise you? In the short story "Thank You, M'am," a boy is *very* surprised by some things he discovers about a woman whom he meets in a most unusual way. "Navaho Chant" helps you recognize how some Native Americans view nature, the earth, and growing things. Nature is beautiful and the crops think like human beings. Why do you think the Navahos see nature in such a positive way?

About the World. City streets can be very dangerous places, but you can make discoveries—good and bad—there. Is nature dangerous, too? Sometimes, nature can be a harsh teacher. In the true story "Starvation Wilderness," a young couple learns that the far north country is no place for two people and a small baby to survive in winter. Yet the story has a positive side, too, as the hero and heroine discover their own courage and endurance. Like nonfiction and fiction, poems can help you make discoveries about the world. The haiku offers insights into nature and human nature, too. Discover what "Sympathy," "Dreams," and an untitled poem have to say about how people see themselves, the importance of freedom, and keeping dreams alive. These poems offer discoveries about a world inside everyone.

Discoveries are a part of everyday living. Most discoveries come about as a result of analysis, disclosure, and exploration. Sometimes, however, discoveries are made purely by accident. What important discoveries have you made about yourself and others? What changes have these discoveries made in your life?

Discoveries 315

After completing this selection, students will be able to

- understand symbols and symbolism
- identify some common symbols
- identify characters' discoveries
- respond to characters
- identify specific symbols in the story
- use adjectives and adverbs

More About Symbols/Symbolism: Have students think of other examples of common symbols. You might start them off by suggesting that they think of symbols connected with certain holidays: Valentine hearts, St. Patrick's Day shamrocks, Halloween pumpkins, Christmas trees. Write student responses on the chalkboard. Then have them discuss the meaning and significance of each symbol.

Cooperative/Collaborative Learning Activity: Have students work in pairs. Ask each student to draw and color a picture of a symbol—a car, a tree, a catcher's mitt, a castle—that tells something important about him- or herself. Next, have students exchange papers. Ask each student to decide what the symbol tells about his or her partner. Then have the student who originated the symbol reveal his or her reasons for choosing it.

Learn About
Symbolism in Fiction

A **symbol** is something that stands for something else. For example, a red, white, and blue flag is a symbol of the United States.

Literature is full of symbolism, or the use of symbols. Often in a story, a symbol stands for an idea, a feeling, or a quality. Sometimes a certain symbol is used several times throughout a story. When a symbol is used in this way, you know that it emphasizes an important idea. This type of symbol may appear at the beginning or end of a story, as well as at critical points in the plot.

In the story "Chee's Daughter," symbols convey important ideas about Chee and his values. As you read "Chee's Daughter," ask yourself:

1. What symbol in the story represents Chee's faith in the land?
2. At what points in the story is this symbol used?

SKILL BUILDER

Writers use symbols to convey important ideas about characters. Think of something you own that is especially important to you. Then write a paragraph explaining how this object could be used as a symbol to describe the kind of person you are.

Chee's Daughter

by Juanita Platero and Siyowin Miller

The hat told the story, the big, black, drooping Stetson. It was not at the proper angle, the proper rakish angle for so young a Navaho. There was no song, and that was not in keeping either. There should have been at least a humming, a faint, all-to-himself "he he he heya," for it was a good horse he was riding, a slender-legged, high-stepping buckskin that would race the wind with light knee-urging. This was a day for singing, a warm winter day, when the touch of the sun upon the back belied the snow on distant mountains.

Wind warmed by the sun touched his high-boned cheeks like flicker feathers, and still he rode on silently, deeper into Little Canyon, until the red rock walls rose straight upward from the stream-bed and only a narrow piece of blue sky hung above. Abruptly the sky widened where the canyon walls were pushed back to make a wide place, as though in ancient times an angry stream had tried to go all ways at once.

This was home—this wide place in the canyon—levels of jagged rock and levels of rich red earth. This was home to Chee, the rider of the buckskin, as it had been to many generations before him.

He stopped his horse at the stream and sat looking across the narrow ribbon of water to the bare-branched peach trees. He was seeing them each spring-time with their age-gnarled limbs transfigured beneath veils of blossom pink; he was seeing them in autumn laden with their yellow fruit, small and sweet. Then his eyes searched out the indistinct furrows of the fields beside the stream, where each year the corn and beans and squash drank thirstily of the overflow from summer rains. Chee was trying to outweigh today's bitter betrayal of hope by gathering to himself these reminders of the integrity of the land. Land did not cheat! His mind lingered deliberately on all the days spent here in the sun caring for the young plants, his songs to the earth and to the life springing from it: ". . . In the middle of the wide field . . . Yellow Corn Boy . . . He has started both ways . . .," then the harvest and repayment in full measure. Here was the old

rakish (RAYK ish) stylish
transfigured (trans FIG yurd) changed in form or appearance

Discoveries   317

Sidelights: The Navajos constitute the largest Native American tribe in the United States. In 1981 the U.S. Navajo population was estimated to be about 160,000.

Motivation for Reading: Ask students to think of something that represents security to them. It may be a person, place, object, or idea. Encourage them to share their thoughts, then relate what they have chosen to Chee's attachment to the land.

More About the Thematic Idea: In this selection the main character discovers that his choices and values in life still work for him. The plot is set in motion by the death of the main character's wife and, in accordance with Navajo custom, the subsequent claiming of his daughter by his wife's parents. The story ends with the main character winning back his daughter.

Critical Thinking: Chee faced an important point of decision when he could have chosen either of two different paths. What was that point? What choice did Chee make? (The decision whether or not to leave Little Canyon and take a job with his cousins: He chose to stay in Little Canyon.)

Literary Focus: In what way was his daughter an important symbol to Chee? (Suggested answer: She represented his marriage and his hope for the future.)

Purpose-Setting Question: How would you go about trying to reclaim something valuable that had been taken from you?

LDP Activity: Predict after reading to the end of page 311, what Chee will do in the future.

Vocabulary: Preteach the vocabulary words. See the Comprehension Workbook in the TRB.

More About Vocabulary: Familiarize students with the vocabulary words footnoted in the story by writing each word on the chalkboard. Then have students offer suggestions as to what each word means.

feeling of wholeness and of oneness with the sun and earth and growing things.

Chee urged the buckskin toward the family compound where, secure in a recess of overhanging rock, was his mother's dome-shaped hogan, red rock and red adobe like the ground on which it nestled. Not far from the hogan was the half-circle of brush like a dark shadow against the canyon wall—corral for sheep and goats. Farther from the hogan, in full circle, stood the horse corral made of heavy cedar branches sternly interlocked. Chee's long thin lips curved into a smile as he passed his daughter's tiny hogan squatted like a round Pueblo oven beside the corral. He remembered the summer day when together they sat back on their heels and plastered wet adobe all about the circling wall of rock and the woven dome of piñon twigs. How his family laughed when the Little One herded the bewildered chickens into her hogan as the first snow fell.

Then the smile faded from Chee's lips and his eyes darkened as he tied his horse to a corral post and turned to the strangely empty compound. "Someone has told them," he thought, "and they are inside weeping." He passed his mother's deserted loom on the south side of the hogan and pulled the rude wooden door toward him, bowing his head, hunching his shoulders to get inside.

His mother sat sideways by the center fire, her feet drawn up under her full skirts. Her hands were busy kneading dough in the chipped white basin. With her head down, her voice was muffled when she said, "The meal will soon be ready, son."

Chee passed his father sitting against the wall, hat over his eyes as though asleep. He passed his older sister who sat turning mutton ribs on a crude wire grill over the coals, noticed tears dropping on her hands. "She cared more for my wife than I realized," he thought.

Then, because something must be said sometime, he tossed the black Stetson upon a bulging sack of wool and said, "You have heard, then." He could not shut from his mind how confidently he had set the handsome new hat on his head that very morning, slanting the wide brim over one eye: he was going to see his wife and today he would ask the doctors about bringing her home; last week she had looked so much better.

His sister nodded but did not speak. His mother sniffled and passed her velveteen sleeve beneath her nose. Chee sat down, leaning against the wall. "I suppose I was a fool for hoping all the time. I should have expected this. Few of our people get well from the coughing sickness. But *she* seemed to be getting better."

His mother was crying aloud now and blowing her nose noisily on her skirt. His father sat up, speaking gently to her.

Chee shifted his position and started a cigarette. His mind turned back to the Little One. At least she was too small to understand what had happened, the Little One who had been born three years

---

compound (COM pound) group of buildings

Passing By, E. Martin Hennings. The Museum of Fine Arts, Houston

Classification: Chee's wife was being treated for TB in the sanitarium. Tuberculosis was the "coughing sickness" from which he died.

before in the sanitarium where his wife was being treated for the coughing sickness, the Little One he had brought home to his mother's hogan to be nursed by his sister whose baby was a few months older. As she grew fat-cheeked and sturdy-legged, she followed him about like a shadow. Somehow her baby mind had grasped that of all those at the hogan who cared for her and played with her,

he—Chee—belonged most to her. She sat cross-legged at his elbow when he worked silver at the forge; she rode before him in the saddle when he drove the horses to water; often she lay wakeful on her sheep pelts until he stretched out for the night in the darkened hogan and she could snuggle warm against him.

Chee blew smoke slowly and some of the sadness left his dark eyes as he said,

Discoveries

319

"It is not as bad as it might be. It is not as though we are left with nothing."

Chee's sister arose, sobs catching in her throat, and rushed past him out the doorway. Chee sat upright, a terrible fear possessing him. For a moment his mouth could make no sound. Then: "The Little One! Mother, where is she?"

His mother turned her stricken face to him. "Your wife's people came after her this morning. They heard yesterday of their daughter's death through the trader at Red Sands."

Chee started to protest but his mother shook her head slowly. "I didn't expect they would want the Little One either. But there is nothing you can do. She is a girl child and belongs to her mother's people; it is custom."

Frowning, Chee got to his feet, grinding his cigarette into the dirt floor. "Custom! When did my wife's parents begin thinking about custom? Why, the hogan where they live doesn't even face the East!" He started toward the door. "Perhaps I can overtake them. Perhaps they don't realize how much we want her here with us. I'll ask them to give my daughter back to me. Surely, they won't refuse."

His mother stopped him gently with her outstretched hand. "You couldn't overtake them now. They were in the trader's car. Eat and rest, and think more about this."

"Have you forgotten how things have always been between you and your wife's people?" his father said.

That night, Chee's thoughts were troubled—half-forgotten incidents became disturbingly vivid—but early the next morning, he saddled the buckskin and set out for the settlement of Red Sands. Even though his father-in-law, Old Man Fat, might laugh, Chee knew that he must talk to him. There were some things to which Old Man Fat might listen.

Chee rode the first part of the fifteen miles to Red Sands expectantly. The sight of sandstone buttes near Cottonwood Spring reddening in the early sun brought a song almost to his lips. He twirled his reins in salute to the small boy herding sheep toward many-colored Butterfly Mountain, watched with pleasure the feathers of smoke rising high against tree-darkened western mesas from hogans sheltered there. But as he approached the familiar settlement sprawled in mushroom growth along the highway, he began to feel as though a scene from a bad dream was becoming real.

Several cars were parked around the trading store which was built like two log hogans side by side, with red gas pumps in front and a sign across the tarpaper roofs: *Red Sands Trading Post—Groceries · Gasoline · Cold Drinks · Sandwiches · Indian Curios.* Back of the trading post, an unpainted frame house and outbuildings squatted on the drab, treeless land. Chee and the Little One's mother had lived there when they stayed with his wife's people. That was according to custom—living with one's wife's people—but

---

buttes (BYOOTS) small mountains with steep sides

Chee had never been convinced that it was custom alone which prompted Old Man Fat and his wife to insist that their daughter bring her husband to live at the trading post.

Beside the Post was a large hogan of logs, with brightly painted pseudo-Navaho designs on the roof—a hogan with smoke-smudged windows and a garish blue door which faced north to the highway. Old Man Fat had offered Chee a hogan like this one. The trader would build it if he and his wife would live there and Chee would work at his forge making silver jewelry where tourists could watch him. But Chee had asked instead for a piece of land for a cornfield and help in building a hogan far back from the highway and a corral for the sheep he had brought to this marriage.

A cold wind blowing down from the mountains began to whistle about Chee's ears. It flapped the gaudy Navaho rugs which were hung in one long bright line to attract tourists. It swayed the sign *Navaho Weaver at Work* beside the loom where Old Man Fat's wife sat hunched in her striped blanket patting the colored thread of a design into place with a wooden comb. Tourists stood watching the weaver. More tourists stood in a knot before the hogan where the sign said: *See Inside a Real Navaho Home 25¢*.

Then the knot seemed to unravel as a few people returned to their cars: some had cameras; and there against the blue door Chee saw the Little One standing uncertainly. The wind was plucking at her new purple blouse and wide green skirt; it freed truant strands of soft dark hair from the meager queue into which it had been tied with white yarn.

"Isn't she cunning!" one of the women tourists was saying as she turned away.

Chee's lips tightened as he began to look around for Old Man Fat. Finally he saw him passing among the tourists collecting coins.

Then the Little One saw Chee. The uncertainty left her face and she darted through the crowd as her father swung down from his horse. Chee lifted her in his arms, hugging her tight. While he listened to her breathless chatter, he watched Old Man Fat bearing down on them, scowling.

As his father-in-law walked heavily across the graveled lot, Chee was reminded of a statement his mother sometimes made: "When you see a fat Navaho, you see one who hasn't worked for what he has."

Old Man Fat was fattest in the middle. There was indolence in his walk even though he seemed to hurry, indolence in his cheeks so plump they made his eyes squint, eyes now smoldering with anger.

Some of the tourists were getting into their cars and driving away. The old man said belligerently to Chee, "Why do you come here? To spoil our business? To

gaudy (GAWD ee) showy; bright-colored
queue (KYOO) a braid of hair worn at the back of the neck
cunning (KUN ing) cute
indolence (IN duh lens) laziness

Discoveries

321

Discussion: Ask students why they think Chee refused the offer to live in the trading post compound. Suggest to the students to think about how they would feel being made into a tourist attraction.

drive people away?"

"I came to talk with you," Chee answered, trying to keep his voice steady as he faced the old man.

"We have nothing to talk about," Old Man Fat blustered and did not offer to touch Chee's extended hand.

"It's about the Little One." Chee settled his daughter more comfortably against his hip as he weighed carefully all the words he had planned to say. "We are going to miss her very much. It wouldn't be so bad if we knew that *part* of each year she could be with us. That might help you too. You and your wife are no longer young people and you have no young ones here to depend upon." Chee chose his next words remembering the thriftlessness of his wife's parents, and their greed. "Perhaps we could share the care of this little one. Things are good with us. So much snow this year will make lots of grass for the sheep. We have good land for corn and melons."

Chee's words did not have the expected effect. Old Man Fat was enraged. "Farmers, all of you! Longhaired farmers! Do you think everyone must bend his back over the short-handled hoe in order to have food to eat?" His tone changed as

Familia India, Amado M. Pena, Jr. El Taller, Inc.

Unit 4

he began to brag a little. "We not only have all the things from cans at the trader's, but when the Pueblos come past here on their way to town we buy their salty jerked mutton, young corn for roasting, dried sweet peaches."

Chee's dark eyes surveyed the land along the highway as the old man continued to brag about being "progressive." *He* no longer was tied to the land. He and his wife made money easily and could *buy* all the things they wanted. Chee realized too late that he had stumbled into the old argument between himself and his wife's parents. They had never understood his feeling about the land—that a man took care of his land and it in turn took care of him. Old Man Fat and his wife scoffed at him, called him a Pueblo farmer, all during that summer when he planted and weeded and harvested. Yet they ate the green corn in their mutton stews, and the chili paste from the fresh ripe chilis, and the tortillas from the cornmeal his wife ground. None of this working and sweating in the sun for Old Man Fat, who talked proudly of his easy way of living—collecting money from the trader who rented this strip of land beside the highway, collecting money from the tourists.

Yet Chee had once won that argument. His wife had shared his belief in the integrity of the earth, that jobs and people might fail one but the earth never would. After that first year she had turned from her own people and gone with Chee to Little Canyon.

Old Man Fat was reaching for the Little One. "Don't be coming here with plans for my daughter's daughter," he warned. "If you try to make trouble, I'll take the case to the government man in town."

The impulse was strong in Chee to turn and ride off while he still had the Little One in his arms. But he knew his time of victory would be short. His own family would uphold the old custom of children, especially girl children, belonging to the mother's people. He would have to give his daughter up if the case were brought before the Headman of Little Canyon, and certainly he would have no better chance before a strange white man in town.

He handed the bewildered Little One to her grandfather who stood watching every movement suspiciously. Chee asked, "If I brought you a few things for the Little One, would that be making trouble? Some velvet for a blouse, or some of the jerky she likes . . . this summer's melon?"

Old Man Fat backed away from him. "Well," he hesitated, as some of the anger disappeared from his face and beads of greed shone in his eyes. "Well," he said again. Then as the Little One began to squirm in his arms and cry, he said, "No! No! Stay away from here, you and all your family."

The sense of his failure deepened as Chee rode back to Little Canyon. But it was not until he sat with his family that evening in the hogan, while the familiar

---

jerky (JUR kee) beef strips that have been dried in the sun

Discoveries

323

bustle of meal preparing went on about him, that he began to doubt the wisdom of the things he'd always believed. He smelled the coffee boiling and the oily fragrance of chili powder dusted into the bubbling pot of stew; he watched his mother turning round crusty fried bread in the small black skillet. All around him was plenty—a half of mutton hanging near the door, bright strings of chili drying, corn hanging by the braided husks, cloth bags of dried peaches. Yet in his heart was nothing.

He heard the familiar sounds of the sheep outside the hogan, the splash of water as his father filled the long drinking trough from the water barrel. When his father came in, Chee could not bring himself to tell a second time of the day's happenings. He watched his wiry, soft-spoken father while his mother told the story, saw his father's queue of graying hair quiver as he nodded his head with sympathetic exclamations.

Chee's doubting, acrid thoughts kept forming: Was it wisdom his father had passed on to him or was his inheritance only the stubbornness of a longhaired Navaho resisting change? Take care of the land and it will take care of you. True, the land had always given him food, but now food was not enough. Perhaps if he had gone to school he would have learned a different kind of wisdom, something to help him now. A schoolboy might even be able to speak convincingly to this government man whom Old Man

Fat threatened to call, instead of sitting here like a clod of earth itself—Pueblo farmer indeed. What had the land to give that would restore his daughter?

In the days that followed, Chee herded sheep. He got up in the half light, drank the hot coffee his mother had ready, then started the flock moving. It was necessary to drive the sheep a long way from the hogan to find good winter forage. Sometimes Chee met friends or relatives who were on their way to town or to the road camp where they hoped to get work; then there was friendly banter and an exchange of news. But most of the days seemed endless; he could not walk far enough or fast enough from his memories of the Little One or from his bitter thoughts. Sometimes it seemed his daughter trudged beside him, so real he could almost hear her footsteps—the muffled pad-pad of little feet clad in deerhide. In the glare of a snow bank he would see her face, brown eyes sparkling. Mingling with the tinkle of sheep bells he heard her laughter.

When, weary of following the small sharp hoof marks that crossed and re-crossed in the snow, he sat down in the shelter of a rock, it was only to be reminded that in his thoughts he had forsaken his brotherhood with the earth and sun and growing things. If he remembered times when he had flung himself against the earth to rest, to lie there in the sun until he could no longer feel where he left off and the earth began, it was to

acrid (AK rid) bitter to the tongue
forage (FAWR ij) food for animals
banter (BAN tur) good-natured teasing

324

remember also that now he sat like an alien against the same earth; the belonging-together was gone. The earth was one thing and he was another.

It was during the days when he herded sheep that Chee decided he must leave Little Canyon. Perhaps he would take a job silversmithing for one of the traders in town. Perhaps, even though he spoke little English, he could get a job at the road camp with his cousins: he would ask them about it.

Springtime transformed the mesas. The peach trees in the canyon were shedding fragrance and pink blossoms on the gentled wind. The sheep no longer foraged for the yellow seeds of chamiso but ranged near the hogan with the long-legged new lambs, eating tender young grass.

Chee was near the hogan on the day his cousins rode up with the message for which he waited. He had been watching with mixed emotions while his father and his sister's husband cleared the fields beside the stream.

"The boss at the camp says he needs an extra hand, but he wants to know if you'll be willing to go with the camp when they move it to the other side of the town." The tall cousin shifted his weight in the saddle.

The other cousin took up the explanation. "The work near here will last only until the new cutoff beyond Red Sands is finished. After that, the work will be too far away for you to get back here often."

That was what Chee had wanted—to get away from Little Canyon—yet he found himself not so interested in the job beyond town as in this new cutoff which was almost finished. He pulled a blade of grass, split it thoughtfully down the center as he asked questions of his cousins. Finally he said: "I need to think more about this. If I decide on this job, I'll ride over."

Before his cousins were out of sight down the canyon Chee was walking toward the fields, a bold plan shaping in his mind. As the plan began to flourish, wild and hardy as young tumbleweed, Chee added his own voice softly to the song his father was singing: ". . . In the middle of the wide field . . . Yellow Corn Boy . . . I wish to put in."

Chee walked slowly around the field, the rich red earth yielding to his footsteps. His plan depended upon this land and upon the things he remembered most about his wife's people.

Through planting time Chee worked zealously and tirelessly. He spoke little of the large new field he was planting because he felt so strongly that just now this was something between himself and the land. The first days he was ever stooping, piercing the ground with the pointed stick, placing the corn kernels there, walking around the field and through it, singing, ". . . His track leads into the ground . . . Yellow Corn Boy . . . his track leads into the ground." After that,

---

alien (AYL yun) foreigner; stranger
zealously (ZEL us lee) eagerly; fanatically

Discoveries

325

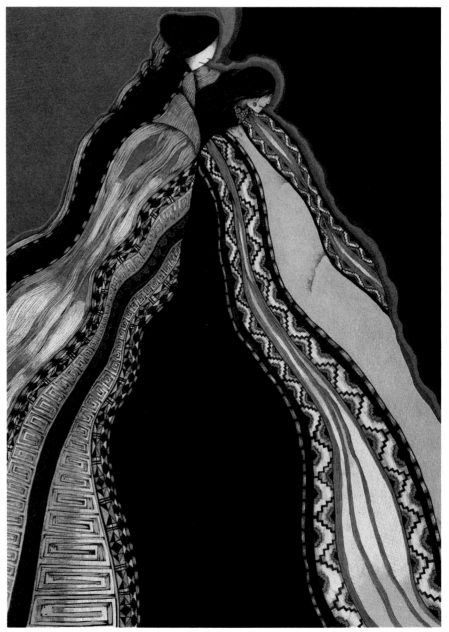

El Mercado, Amado M. Pena, Jr. El Taller, Inc.

each day Chee walked through his field watching for the tips of green to break through; first a few spikes in the center and then more and more until the corn in all parts of the field was above ground. Surely, Chee thought, if he sang the proper songs, if he cared for this land faithfully, it would not forsake him now, even though through the lonely days of winter he had betrayed the goodness of the earth in his thoughts.

Through the summer Chee worked long days, the sun hot upon his back, pulling weeds from around young corn plants; he planted squash and pumpkin; he terraced a small piece of land near his mother's hogan and planted carrots and onions and the moisture-loving chili. He was increasingly restless. Finally he told his family what he hoped the harvest from this land would bring him. Then the whole family waited with him, watching the corn: the slender graceful plants that waved green arms and bent to embrace each other as young winds wandered through the field, the maturing plants flaunting their pollen-laden tassels in the sun, the tall and sturdy parent corn with new-formed ears and a froth of purple, red, and yellow cornbeards against the dusty emerald of leaves.

Summer was almost over when Chee slung the bulging packs across two pack ponies. His mother helped him tie the heavy rolled pack behind the saddle of the buckskin. Chee knotted the new yellow kerchief about his neck a little tighter, gave the broad black hat brim an extra

tug, but these were only gestures of assurance and he knew it. The land had not failed him. That part was done. But this he was riding into? Who could tell?

When Chee arrived at Red Sands, it was as he had expected to find it—no cars on the highway. His cousins had told him that even the Pueblo farmers were using the new cutoff to town. The barren gravel around the Red Sands Trading Post was deserted. A sign banged against the gas pumps: *Closed until further notice.*

Old Man Fat came from the crude summer shelter built beside the log hogan from a few branches of scrub cedar and the sides of wooden crates. He seemed almost friendly when he saw Chee.

"Get down, my son," he said, eyeing the bulging packs. There was no bluster in his voice today and his face sagged, looking somewhat saddened; perhaps because his cheeks were no longer quite full enough to push his eyes upward at the corners. "You are going on a journey?"

Chee shook his head. "Our fields gave us so much this year, I thought to sell or trade this to the trader. I didn't know he was no longer here."

Old Man Fat sighed, his voice dropping to an injured tone. "He says he and his wife are going to rest this winter; then he'll build a place up on the new highway."

Chee moved as though to be traveling on, then jerked his head toward the pack ponies. "Anything you need?"

---

flaunting (FLAWNT ing) showing off

Discussion: Why does Chee pretend not to know that the trader is gone when he has been planning all summer to give supplies to his in-laws in exchange for his daughter?

"I'll ask my wife," Old Man Fat said as he led the way to the shelter. "Maybe she has a little money. Things have not been too good with us since the trader closed. Only a few tourists come this way." He shrugged his shoulders. "And with the trader gone—no credit."

Chee was not deceived by his father-in-law's unexpected confidences. He recognized them as a hopeful bid for sympathy and, if possible, something for nothing. Chee made no answer. He was thinking that so far he had been right about his wife's parents: their thriftlessness had left them with no resources to last until Old Man Fat found another easy way of making a living.

Old Man Fat's wife was in the shelter working at her loom. She turned rather wearily when her husband asked with a noticeable deference if she would give him money to buy supplies. Chee surmised that the only income here was from his mother-in-law's weaving.

She peered around the corner of the shelter at the laden ponies, and then she looked at Chee. "What do you have there, my son?"

Chee smiled to himself as he turned to pull the pack from one of the ponies, dragged it to the shelter where he untied the ropes. Pumpkins and hardshelled squash tumbled out, and the ears of corn—pale yellow husks fitting firmly over plump ripe kernels, blue corn, red corn, yellow corn, many-colored corn, ears and ears of it—tumbled into every corner of the shelter.

"Yooooh," Old Man Fat's wife exclaimed as she took some of the ears in her hands. Then she glanced up at her son-in-law. "But we have no money for all this. We have sold almost everything we own—even the brass bed."

Old Man Fat's brass bed. Chee concealed his amusement as he started back for another pack. That must have been a hard parting. Then he stopped, for coming from the cool darkness of the hogan was the Little One, rubbing her eyes as though she had been asleep. She stood for a moment in the doorway and Chee saw that she was dirty, barefoot, her hair uncombed, her little blouse shorn of all its silver buttons. Then she ran toward Chee, her arms outstretched. Heedless of Old Man Fat and his wife, her father caught her in his arms, her hair falling in a dark cloud across his face, the sweetness of her laughter warm against his shoulder.

It was the haste within him to get this slow waiting game played through to the finish that made Chee speak unwisely. It was the desire to swing her before him in the saddle and ride fast to Little Canyon that prompted his words. "The money doesn't matter. You still have something."

Chee knew immediately that he had overspoken. The old woman looked from him to the corn spread before her. Unfriendliness began to harden in his father-in-law's face. All the old arguments between himself and his wife's people came pushing and crowding in between them.

---

surmised (sur MYZD) supposed; made a guess
straggly (STRAG lee) wandering off course

Unit 4

Old Man Fat began kicking the ears of corn back onto the canvas as he eyed Chee angrily. "And you rode all the way over here thinking that for a little food we would give up our daughter's daughter?"

Chee did not wait for the old man to take the Little One. He walked dazedly to the shelter, rubbing his cheek against her soft dark hair and put her gently into her grandmother's lap. Then he turned back to the horses. He had failed. By his own haste he had failed. He swung into the saddle, his hand touching the roll behind it. Should he ride on into town?

Then he dismounted, scarcely glancing at Old Man Fat, who stood uncertainly at the corner of the shelter, listening to his wife. "Give me a hand with this other pack of corn, Grandfather," Chee said, carefully keeping the small bit of hope from his voice.

Puzzled, but willing, Old Man Fat helped carry the other pack to the shelter, opening it to find more corn as well as carrots and round, pale yellow onions. Chee went back for the roll behind the buckskin's saddle and carried it to the entrance of the shelter where he cut the ropes and gave the canvas a nudge with his toe. Tins of coffee rolled out, small plump cloth bags; jerked meat from several butcherings spilled from a flour sack, and bright red chilis splashed like flames against the dust.

"I will leave all this anyhow," Chee told them. "I would not want my daughter nor you old people to go hungry."

Old Man Fat picked up a shiny tin of coffee, then put it down. With trembling hands he began to untie one of the cloth bags—dried sweet peaches.

The Little One had wriggled from her grandmother's lap, unheeded, and was on her knees, digging her hands into the jerked meat.

"There is almost enough food here to last all winter," Old Man Fat's wife said as she sought the eyes of her husband.

Chee said, "I meant it to be enough. But that was when I thought you might send the Little One back with me." He looked down at his daughter noisily sucking jerky. Her mouth and both fists were full of it. "I am sorry that you feel you cannot bear to part with her."

Old Man Fat's wife brushed a straggly wisp of gray hair from her forehead as she turned to look at the Little One. Old Man Fat was looking too. And it was not a thing to see. For in that moment the Little One ceased to be their daughter's daughter and became just another mouth to feed.

"And why not?" the old man asked wearily.

Chee was settled in the saddle, the barefooted Little One before him. He urged the buckskin faster, and his daughter clutched his shirtfront. The purpling mesas flung back the echo: ". . . My corn embrace each other. In the middle of the wide field . . . Yellow Corn Boy embrace each other."

ANSWERS TO UNDERSTAND THE SELECTION

1. death of his wife
2. that his wife's parents have taken his daughter
3. He goes to see his father-in-law and tries to talk to him.
4. He thought he was "progressive" because he did not have to work the land for a living the way Chee did.
5. his greed
6. The new road cut-off would mean that people would not stop off at his father-in-law's trading post.
7. He hoped that they would see that without the Little One, they would have enough food for the winter.
8. Prosperity: Many tourists and cars are around the trading post; Little One is wearing a new blouse and skirt; Old Man Fat brags about all they have. Poverty: The trading post is deserted; a sign says "Closed Until Further Notice; Old Man Fat is less arrogant; Little One is barefoot and in rags; they have sold the brass bed.
9. Answers may vary. Some students may agree; some may cite examples such as drought or floods that can make the earth fail.
10. Answers may vary. Possible answer: He might never have seen his daughter again.

Respond to Literature: Have students make a list of the discoveries Chee made when he arrived home after his wife's death. Guide students to recognize the following discoveries as central to the plot of the story: Chee's discovery that his daughter is gone; his discovery that a new road cut-off has been built that might alter his father-in-law's prosperity; and his discovery that his in-laws indeed have become poor.

T330

UNDERSTAND THE SELECTION

Recall

1. What event has just taken place in Chee's life?
2. What does Chee find at home?
3. What does Chee decide to do about it?

Infer

4. Why did Old Man Fat think he was superior to Chee?
5. What trait in his father-in-law did Chee hope would work to his advantage?
6. Why did Chee suspect that his father-in-law's fortunes would worsen?
7. Why did Chee empty all the bundles of food on the floor before he left?

Apply

8. Select details in the story that show how Chee's in-laws have gone from prosperity to poverty.
9. Do you agree with Chee that "jobs and people might fail one, but the earth never would"?
10. What might have happened if Chee had taken the job offered by his cousins.

Respond to Literature

What did Chee discover about his values and the choices that he had made?

330

WRITE ABOUT THE SELECTION

In the short story "Chee's Daughter," several characters are important to the story's development. There is Chee himself, the Little One, Old Man Fat, and Old Man Fat's wife. How do you feel about each of these characters? Do you admire Chee? Do you agree with Old Man Fat's values and actions? Do you feel sorry for the Little One? Do you like or dislike Old Man Fat's wife? Explain why.

Prewriting: Make a chart of the four characters. List your feelings about each character, both positive and negative. Then, decide which character you feel about most strongly. That will be the subject of your paragraph.

Writing: Use the ideas in your list to write a paragraph that describes your reaction to a character in "Chee's Daughter."

Revising: To revise your paragraph, think of adding a sentence that reflects an opinion different from yours. For example, if you disliked Old Man Fat, you might add the sentence: "I did not like Old Man Fat, but some people might admire him because he did what was most practical in the situation." Be sure to use evidence from the story to support your opinion and the opposing one.

Proofreading: Check your paper for mistakes in spelling, usage, and mechanics. Be sure you have used commas before the conjunctions in compound sentences.

Unit 4

WRITE ABOUT THE SELECTION

Prewriting: Have students assist you in making the chart, either on a chalkboard or on an overhead transparency.

Writing: Have students work on this section individually. Help any students who are having trouble. As students begin to write, ask them to consider this question:

"How do you think the author feels about the character you have chosen to write about?"

Revising: Have pairs of students read each other's papers. Then tell their partners whether they agree or disagree with the opinions about the character. If students disagree, have them refer to the story and find together those passages in which the author delineates the character. Students then can use their findings as a basis for revision.

Proofreading: Ask for several volunteers to have their paragraphs displayed on an overhead projector. Then involve the class in correcting errors and suggesting improvements.

THINK ABOUT SYMBOLISM

A symbol pulls together a specific thing with ideas, values, people, or ways of life in a way that you would not ordinarily think of. What is important is to see is that the symbol points to something beyond itself, to a greater meaning.

1. What object is used as a symbol at the opening of "Chee's Daughter"?

2. What does this symbol tell you about Chee's mood?

3. What symbol do the authors use to represent the land?

4. In what way is this symbol woven into the story?

5. Explain why the authors end the story with this symbol.

DEVELOP YOUR VOCABULARY

An **adjective** is a word that modifies or describes a noun. For example, the word *fat* is an adjective because it can describe nouns such as man, dog, baby, or face: fat man, fat dog, fat baby, fat face.

An **adverb** is a word that modifies or describes a verb. An adverb tells how an action takes place. For example, the word *fast* is an adverb. Fast can be used to describe the way a person runs (He runs fast.), thinks (She thinks fast.), or talks (The teacher talks fast.).

Review the meaning of each of these words from "Chee's Daughter." Decide whether each word is an adjective or an adverb. Then use each word in an original sentence. In your sentences, underline the noun or verb that the adjective or adverb modifies.

1. rakish
2. zealously
3. straggly
4. compound
5. gaudy
6. acrid

Discoveries

After completing this selection, students will be able to
- understand the use of symbolism
- create symbols from nature
- relate the theme of the poem to discoveries
- write from a different point of view
- analyze the use of figurative language
- use prepositions

More About Symbolism: Although a symbol is usually a tangible object, it can be something less concrete, such as a song, a color, or lines from a story or poem. It also can be something quite vast, such as the land, the sky, the earth, space. Have a student read the lines about the Corn Boy that appear in the story "Chee's Daughter." Guide students to recognize the connection between these lines and "Navaho Chant."

Cooperative/Collaborative Learning Activity: Have students work in pairs. Ask each pair to create a single poem in which something from nature is used as a symbol of a larger idea. Have students read the poem aloud together.

Enrichment: Have interested students create a way to dramatize the poem. Students can make use of both the imagery and the chanting word patterns in the poem.

Literary Focus: Guide students to recognize the use of repetition which is often an important literary device.

332

LEARN ABOUT

Symbolism in Poetry

A **symbol** is an object that represents a larger idea. Symbolism is often used in poetry because it can express a great deal of meaning in the space of a few words.

In the story "Chee's Daughter," the land is very important to Chee. Throughout the story, fragments of a Navaho song about the Corn Boy run through Chee's mind. This song—and the corn itself—are symbols of Chee's deep connection to the land. The Navaho Chant that you are about to read is part of the song that Chee sings.

In the poem "Navaho Chant," there are many symbols. As you read the poem, ask yourself:

1. Who is speaking in the poem?
2. What does the symbol "home" represent?

SKILL BUILDER

Native American writers and others often use objects from nature as symbols. Think of something in nature that is meaningful to you. For example, perhaps you find special meaning in sunsets, the ocean, clouds, snow, or a certain kind of tree. Write a short poem or paragraph in which this object from nature is used as a symbol of a larger idea.

Unit 4

Vocabulary: Preteach the vocabulary words. See the Comprehension Workbook in the TRB.

More About Vocabulary: The vocabulary in this selection is relatively simple. You may wish to point out to students that the word "goods" means fabric or material, and that "pollen" is the powdery substance that is transferred in plant reproduction.

LDP Activity: Recall the two or three most important things to a Navajo Indian.

NAVAHO CHANT

Corn Ceremony, Narciso Abeyta (Ha-So-De), Navaho, Courtesy, Alice G. Howland

I am the White Corn Boy.
I walk in sight of my home.
I walk in plain sight of my home.
I walk on the straight path which is towards my home.
5   I walk to the entrance of my home.
I arrive at the beautiful goods curtain which hangs at the doorway.
I arrive at the entrance of my home.
I am in the middle of my home.
I am at the back of my home.
10 I am on top of the pollen seed footprint.
I am like the Most High Power Whose Ways Are Beautiful.
Before me it is beautiful,
Behind me it is beautiful,
Under me it is beautiful,
15 Above me it is beautiful,
All around me it is beautiful.

Discoveries   333

Sidelights: It is a tradition of the Navajo culture to hang a colorful rug in the doorway of a home. The image in the poem, "beautiful goods curtain which hangs at the doorway" is drawn from this tradition.

Motivation for Reading: Create a classroom display of objects mentioned in the poem. The most obvious objects to include are ears of corn; it would also be effective to include seeds and samples of pollen. Ask students to talk about what these objects make them think of. After they have ready the selection, have students compare their ideas with the way these symbols are used in the poem.

More About the Thematic Idea: This poem is tied in directly with Chee's rediscovery of the faithfulness of the land. The last lines, which celebrate beauty, really could be sung at the end of Chee's story. He has indeed discovered, as he returns home with his daughter, that "all around me it is beautiful."

Purpose-Setting Question: To certain people, how might corn be a symbol of life itself?

Clarification: It is essential that sutdents understand the relationship of this poem to the previous story, "Chee's Daughter." The poem is an expression of faith in the land—and this is what Chee rediscovered.

ANSWERS TO
UNDERSTAND
THE SELECTION

1. the White Corn Boy
2. home
3. the Great High Power Whose Ways are Beautiful
4. Home is the land or the earth.
5. It is a Navajo custom to have a colorful rug hanging in the doorway of a home.
6. the pollen that falls onto the earth from the seeds of a plant
7. one of great beauty, peace, and fulfillment
8. similar in that a great journey has successfully ended and a feeling of beauty and fulfillment is the result
9. Answers may vary. An example: Home. The word is repeated to emphasize the continual movement toward that goal; home is the destination, the place of fulfillment.
10. Suggested answer: Movement of the growing corn plant upward toward and through the surface of the earth, then taller and taller.

Respond to Literature: Have students drawn diagrams to represent a journey in their own lives or in the lives of one of the characters in this unit. Emphasize that a journey need not be a physical one; it can also be a journey toward a personal goal, or an inward journey of changing thoughts, ideas, and feelings.

LDP Activity: Discuss the words that are meaningful in the poem: home, beautiful. Write home and beautiful on the board before discussion begins. Make semantic maps for the two words.

WRITE ABOUT
THE SELECTION

Prewriting: Make a list on the chalkboard or on an overhead transparency of possible points of

UNDERSTAND THE SELECTION

Recall

1. Who is speaking in the poem?
2. Where is the speaker going?
3. To what does the speaker liken himself?

Infer

4. What is the meaning of the word "home" in the poem?
5. What is the significance of the curtain hanging at the doorway?
6. What is the "pollen seed footprint"?
7. What is the speaker's feeling at the end of the poem?

Apply

8. Compare the feeling of the poem to Chee's feeling at the end of "Chee's Daughter."
9. Select a word that is used repeatedly throughout the poem. Explain the importance of the word.
10. Explain how this poem might be dramatized in movement.

Respond to Literature

The speaker in the poem completes a kind of journey and, as a result, discovers certain feelings. What feelings have you discovered in yourself after completing a journey or reaching a goal?

WRITE ABOUT THE SELECTION

The poem "Navaho Chant" is written from the corn's point of view. How might the same poem be written from another point of view? Your task is to write a paragraph in which a person, animal, or object in nature views the Corn Boy.

Prewriting: Make a list of possible points of view. For example, the corn could be seen by a bird, an old person, a child, an insect, or the earth itself. Decide which viewpoint you find most interesting, then let this be the point of view of your paragraph. Jot down as many ideas as you can think of about how the corn would look from the viewpoint you have chosen.

Writing: Use the ideas from your notes to write a paragraph that describes the corn from another point of view. Your paragraph should make it clear who or what is viewing the corn. Do you want to use first—I—or third—he, she, it, they—person point of view?

Revising: Try writing all or part of your paragraph in a chant style similar to the poem itself. It is often helpful to read aloud what you have written to see if it really has the sound of a chant or song.

Consider adding or eliminating details to make your paragraph more descriptive.

Proofreading: Check for errors in spelling, usage, and mechanics. Remember to capitalize the first word in each line if you wrote your paragraph as a chant.

view. Have students discuss the various aspects of each one.

Writing: Have students work on this section individually. Go around the classroom, helping any student who is having difficulty. Ask students to consider the vantage point of the viewer: Is the viewer above the corn, below it, or around it? Is the viewer larger, smaller, shorter, taller, or about the same size as the corn?

THINK ABOUT SYMBOLISM

Symbolism is a form of figurative language. **Figurative language** expresses meaning that is more than just the "dictionary definition" of the words themselves. A symbol is something that has meaning in itself but also stands for something else. The special meaning of a symbol depends on the poem or story in which it appears.

1. What is the special meaning of the word *home* in "Navaho Chant"?

2. Why do you think the author of the poem chose to use this word?

3. What choice of words describes the movement of the corn as it grows?

4. How does the poem make the corn seem like a person?

5. What is the Most High Power Whose Ways Are Beautiful?

DEVELOP YOUR VOCABULARY

A **preposition** can be used to describe the relationship between two words or phrases. For example, in the sentence, "The ground is under the corn," the preposition *under* describes the relationship between the corn and the ground.

In "Navaho Chant," prepositions are important to the meaning of the poem. Explain how each of the prepositions listed below is used in the poem to describe a relationship. Then use each preposition in an original sentence.

1. on
2. to
3. at
4. before
5. behind
6. under
7. above
8. around

1. It means the earth, the land itself.
2. The earth is where the corn lives.
3. The idea of "walking to my home."
4. The corn has a name—White Corn Boy; it speaks; it walks; it lives in a home.
5. The Navajo concept of God; perhaps the earth itself since tribal cultures often worship nature.

After completing this selection, students will be able to
- identify character traits
- write a description of a character
- identify the main character's self-discovery
- create a new episode for a story
- identify flat and rounded characters
- use adverbs ending in -ly

More About Character Traits: Have students recall the story "Chee's Daughter." Ask "Is Chee a flat or rounded character?" Also ask about the other characters in the story. (Chee is a rounded character; the others also are rounded, although they have much less dimension than Chee.) Point out that rounded characters are much more interesting to read about than flat characters. They are easier to identify with because they are three dimensional and, therefore, fuller representations of real people.

Cooperative/Collaborative Learning Activity: Have students work in groups of three or four. Ask students to jot down at least one trait or characteristic of each member of their group; for example, Jeff has red hair; Alicia is a good dancer. Then have students pool their notes and work together to write a brief character sketch of each group member. Ask the students to evaluate among themselves which sketch had the most rounded character; then have the groups present that sketch to the rest of the class.

LEARN ABOUT
Character Traits

In literature, a character is a person whom the author invents through words. An author creates a character by describing the character and by having the character say and do certain things. An author also creates a character by commenting on the character's thoughts and feelings.

Characters in stories can usually be classified as either flat or rounded. **Flat characters** are stereotypes: the crazy teenager, the greedy businessman, the crabby old lady. **Rounded characters** come across as real people. They have many facets, or parts, to their personalities.

The story "The Gold Medal" contains both flat and rounded characters. As you read the story, ask yourself:

1. Is Amanda a flat or a rounded character? What type of character is Amanda?
2. What stereotypes exist among the other characters?

SKILL BUILDER

Think of a person you meet almost every day. If you were writing a story about yourself, would this person appear as a flat or a rounded character? Write a paragraph in which you describe this person.

336

Unit 4

THE GOLD MEDAL

by Nan Gilbert

Sidelights: Amanda, the main character in "The Gold Medal," may have admired a person like Jesse Owens. Owens was an African-American athlete, who won four gold medals in the Olympics and broke many world records for running and broad jump. Owens competed in the 1936 Olympics in Berlin, Germany, and his performance upset Hitler's racist theories.

Motivation for Reading: Ask students to think about how others in their lives see them. Do they feel "typecast" by some people? Do they feel that most people see them as they *really* are? Relate the class discussion to Amanda's feeling that she is not seen as she really is.

More About the Thematic Idea: In this selection the main character discovers an important aspect of herself in a chance encounter with an old man. As the story unfolds it becomes obvious that most people in the main character's life see her as a type, or as filling a certain role. The old man is perhaps the first person who sees her as she really is, at least for a short time.

Purpose-Setting Question: Why do people tend to see others as "types," rather than as the persons they really are?

The day had been too much for Amanda. It had started out bad and got no better, one thing piling on another all day long.

"That skirt is too short," her mother had frowned during this morning's last-minute inspection. "Did you scrub your teeth? Are your fingernails clean?"

"Mom, I'm not a *baby!*" Amanda had let out a hopeless squawk and fled. It was no use. When her mother looked at her, she didn't see Amanda—not really. She saw an Example to help show their new neighbors that the Dawsons were as clean and quiet and well-mannered as any family on the block.

"I'm not an Example!" grumbled Amanda rebelliously. "I'm *me!*"

Amanda Dawson—tall for her years, a little thin, leggy as a newborn colt. Flopping short black ponytail, jutting elbows, springy knees. Long feet that could trip her up—and frequently did. Face plain and unremarkable except for large, liquid, chocolate-brown eyes, just one shade darker than her scrubbed, shining skin.

What did her mother see, if she didn't see Amanda? Amanda's quick imagination leaped to present her with the picture of a Proper Example: a spotlessly clean, tidy creature who kept her elbows in and her knees hidden . . . whose hair never worked loose from its tight rubberband . . . who didn't run or shout or use slang . . . whose name was always on the honor roll. . . .

"You there—shoo! Don't trespass! Keep to the sidewalk!"

Absorbed in her picture-making, Amanda had unthinkingly taken the shortcut across Mrs. Hawthorne's corner

---

rebelliously (rih BEL yus lee) resisting authority
jutting (JUT ing) sticking out sharply
absorbed (ab SAWRBD) deeply interested

Discoveries

337

Vocabulary: Preteach the vocabulary words. See the Comprehension Workbook in the TRB.

More About Vocabulary: Since this selection contains many difficult words, it would be advisable to preteach the meanings of as many of these words as possible. Assign each student one of the words footnoted in the story. Have students look up in the dictionary the meanings of their words, then share their findings with the class. Continue to preteach the words by discussing the meanings and having students use the words in original sentences.

LDP Activity: In paragraph 3, page 41 Amanda's mother is concerned about conforming to the ways of her new neighbors. Do you feel pressure to conform in school? Why? Why not? Discuss in small groups.

lot. Now the old lady had popped from her house like a cuckoo from a clock.

"Oh, woe!" muttered Amanda, retreating quickly. "Here we go again!"

The first time this had happened, Amanda had felt bewildered. The shortcut was worn bare by years of schoolchildren's feet, and others seemed to be using it freely.

"I'm not hurting anything," she had said.

Her protest roused the old lady to a flurry of shrill bird-like cries. "This is private property—I have my rights!"

Now, loping back to the sidewalk, pursued by indignant chirps, Amanda told herself resignedly, "Mrs. Hawthorne doesn't see me either." When the old lady looked at Amanda, it was as though she saw not just one girl, but a whole regiment of Amandas, marching across her lot, crushing flowers and shrubs!

Amanda sighed. How did you make someone really *see* you? So they'd know you were *you?* Not a Regiment. Not an Example.

Not a Gang of Hoodlums, either! That's what Mr. Grogan always saw when he looked at her, Amanda decided. By the time Amanda entered Mr. Grogan's store to buy a candy bar, her imagination was growing livelier by the minute.

Mr. Grogan was all smiles and jokes —"Well, well, what's it going to be this time? A nice big box of chocolates, maybe?" he asked.

But he watched Amanda carefully as she lingered over the candy display. When she brought her purchase to the counter, he made an excuse to peek into her lunch sack—"My, my, won't get any fatter on a diet like that!"

No need to look—I didn't steal anything! For a second, Amanda was afraid she had said the words out loud. Mom would split a seam if she even suspected Amanda of speaking up like that, pert and sassy! Hastily, Amanda grabbed her sack and ducked out of the store. Until she had her imagination under control, she'd better keep a close guard on her tongue!

Head down, Amanda scuffed slowly toward school. The day had hardly begun and already it rested heavily on her shoulders. Nor did she expect anything inside the walls of Jefferson School to lighten the load.

School was Amanda's greatest trial this fall. Instead of a familiar building filled with old friends, her family's move to a new home had made Amanda a stranger among strangers. As yet she had made no real friends to replace those she

Discussion: How does Amanda's imagination make people and places seem worse than they really are? Ask students if they feel like they are being picked on.

---

bewildered (bih WIL durd) confused; puzzled
flurry (FLUR ee) noisy confusion
indignant (in DIG nunt) angry
resignedly (rih ZY nid lee) without a struggle
regiment (REJ uh munt) a military unit
pert (PERT) bold speech or behavior

Discoveries

had lost. Though some of the girls were cordial and kind, nobody asked her home after school or stopped at Amanda's house for cookies and pop. And she knew there were others—or maybe it was their parents—who didn't like her being at Jefferson at all. This thought added to the day's accumulating weight of gloom.

During the noon break, Amanda avoided the lunchroom. She took her sack-lunch outside to a sheltered corner of the building. For some reason, today the sunny nook seemed lonely. Each bite Amanda swallowed had to fight its way past a great lump that unexpectedly blocked her throat.

When the bell summoned her back to class, Amanda reluctantly joined the hurrying, chattering crowds in the hall. Her next class was science, taught by Mr. Moore. Amanda thought Mr. Moore the nicest of all the teachers; for him she tried extra hard to do good work. Her first lonely, awkward day in Jefferson, Mr. Moore had welcomed her with genuine warmth. And he was always generous with his after-school time, ready to help her if there was something she didn't understand.

But now, slumped low in her backrow seat, with the lump still big in her throat and a growing heaviness in her heart,

Amanda thought, "He doesn't see me either. He'd treat *any* black kid the same way." Because he's kindhearted. Because he truly wants to help a black child fit into a white world. For him, she was the symbol of a cause he believed in. She wasn't herself at all.

Mr. Moore had to call her name twice before she realized he had asked her a question. Amanda stared at him somberly.

"I don't know," she said.

"Oh, come now, Amanda, of course you do. Remember, it's what we talked about yesterday—"

"I don't know!" The lump in Amanda's throat broke suddenly into a loud, dismaying sob. "Why is it so awful if *I* don't know? Lots of times *they* don't know, and you never look so—so—" It was Mr. Moore's look of hurt surprise that sent her dashing out of the room, that and the new and louder sob rising in her throat.

From the doorway she turned to face him. "I don't care—it's true!—I've got as much right to be st-stupid as anybody!" The second sob got away from her before she could slam the door. Humiliated, she pelted down the hall and out of the building.

The day was too lovely for gloom— an Indian summer afternoon, with rich

---

cordial (KAWR jul) warm, friendly
reluctantly (ri LUK tunt lee) unwillingly; slowly
genuine (JEN yoo in) real, authentic
somberly (SOM bur lee) sadly; unhappily
dismaying (dis MAY ing) losing courage or confidence
pelt (PELT) to hurry or rush

340

Unit 4

golden warmth spread over the fields and hills like an eiderdown quilt. In spite of herself, her bowed shoulders lifted, her heart lightened. . . .

And she began to run. Running, to Amanda, was like flying. There was special joy in the clean rush of air against her upraised face, the pounding blood in her veins. When Amanda ran, she left all her coltish awkwardness behind. Her stride lengthened; her arms pumped; her long feet—that could trip her up when she walked—barely skimmed the ground.

Down the road she flew, and across a pasture where horses pricked their ears at her in mild amazement. She had to stop for breath—panting, laughing, giddy with this supercharge of oxygen—then she was off again. Up and over a gentle slope where a giant cottonwood offered an oasis of cool green shade she flew.

Too late Amanda saw the high heap of overturned earth below the tree. The springs in her tiring legs coiled and propelled her upward. Arms and legs stretched wide in a split. Thin body bent flat over her forward knee, Amanda cleared the pile of dirt—

But not the excavation behind it. Arms flailing, legs treading the air, she lunged for the far side, then fell back

ingloriously into the hole.

"You hurt?" a voice asked with quavery concern.

Amanda sat up, dazed, and brushed dirt from her hands and skirt. Her startled brown eyes, almost level with the rim of hollowed-out earth, saw for the first time the bent figure of an old man under the tree.

"N-no," she said.

"That was mighty pretty running," the old man said with approval, "and as nice a hurdle as ever I've seen. I'm glad you didn't hurt yourself." After a moment, he added, "That's a grave you're settin' in."

Amanda squeaked and scrambled out onto the grass. "A—a *grave?*"

"Yep, for Chief. Chief's my dog."

"Oh—" Amanda cast about for words. "I—I'm sorry he's dead."

"He isn't. Not yet anyway." The old man struggled to his feet. He leaned heavily on his spade as he surveyed his handiwork. "Just about ready. Yep, a few more days and it'll be done. Wouldn't want anyone else to dig it—not for Chief. But if I was to do it, I figured I'd better get started. Can't turn more'n a few spadefuls a day."

Amanda looked at the excavation

---

eiderdown quilt (EYE dur doun KWILT) a comforter filled with soft duck feathers
giddy (GID ee) dizzy, lightheaded
cottonwood (KOT un wuud) kind of wide-spreading tree
propel (pruh PEL) to drive forward
excavation (eks kuh VAY shun) hole made by digging
flailing (FLAYL ing) waving wildly
treading (TRED ing) stepping on
ingloriously (in GLAWR ee us lee) disgracefully
quavery (KWAY vur ee) trembling; shaking

Critical Thinking: Amanda feels free and totally herself when running. Ask students what activities make them feel really natural and happy? Are they the things in which they excel?

over which the old man was now pulling a piece of tarpaulin. "He—must be a big dog."

"He's that, all right. Used to be, anyway." The old man weighted the tarpaulin with a rock at each corner, then straightened slowly. "Kinda thin now, poor old boy. You want to come meet him? Chief was a runner, too, in his day—and his day lasted a lot longer than most."

Taking her consent for granted, he started down the other side of the slope toward a small house almost hidden behind a tangle of vines and shrubbery. Amanda looked a little wildly toward town, but an emotion much stronger than her alarm tugged her in the opposite direction. A runner, the old man had said—just like that. Here was someone who had looked at her and seen—not a Black Child or an Example or a Black Regiment, but Amanda herself—a runner. Wordless with upswelling gratitude, she followed the old man through a door. When Amanda's eyes adjusted to the dim light inside, she made out the form of a big black dog sprawled near the window in a dappling of green-filtered sunlight. Except for a single thump of tail, he didn't move. The old man stooped low, patted the black head and scratched gently behind long velvety ears.

Cautiously, Amanda went nearer. She didn't know much about dogs; she was uncertain how to treat one that seemed so barely alive. "Is he—uh—pretty old?"

"Sixteen," the old man said. "Yep, that's pretty old for a dog. 'Specially a hunter like Chief . . . we've had some high times together, haven't we, old boy?"

The tail thumped once again. Amanda knelt gingerly and stroked the black coat; it was silky soft, but there seemed nothing between it and the bones beneath. To cover her dismay, she said hurriedly, "I guess a dog is a pretty good friend, isn't he?"

"The right kind of dog—yep, no better."

"You mean, like a hunter maybe?"

The old man snorted. "Breed's the least of it! Line up a hundred Labradors and, chances are, you wouldn't find another like Chief. Wasn't another in his own litter like him. I know—I had the pick of the litter."

Grunting a little with the effort, he straightened and moved to a chair by an ancient roll-top desk. "My friend couldn't figure why I took the pup I did. 'Sam,' he says, 'that's the runt of the lot! Look here—see how lively this one is!' But I held to my choice—yes siree, I knew I had a winner."

"How?" asked Amanda, fascinated.

---

tarpaulin (tahr PAW lin) a waterproof sheet used to protect
dappling (DAP ling) group, or bunch of spots
gingerly (JIN jur lee) very carefully
Labradors (LAB ruh dawrz) breed of big dogs
litter (LIT ur) young animals born at one time

Discoveries

343

"By the look in his eyes. There he sat, all paws and floppy head, as forlorn a pup as you'd see by any ash can, but those eyes were watching me. 'Believe in me,' they said, 'and I can do anything.'" The old man laughed. "Guess you think I'm a little foolish—well, maybe so. But I wasn't wrong about Chief, no sir! This proves it."

The old desk creaked as he rolled up the cover. In every pigeonhole within there was a ribbon—red ribbons, blue ribbons, purple ribbons, and a single gold medal. "Won 'em all, Chief did," the old man said proudly. He touched one after another. "Best working dog . . . best in class . . . best of show . . ."

Out of curiosity, Amanda reached for the gold medal. "Why, it's a *runner's* medal!" she cried.

The old man took the medal from her and studied it fondly. "Yep, this was his first—bought it myself. Chief cried his heart out that day, wanted to do miracles for me but he just didn't have the know-how yet. 'Never you mind,' I told him. 'I know you're a champion.' Next time I went to town, I bought him a medal to wear till he'd proved himself to everyone else."

As if he had followed their conversation, the black dog thumped his tail once more, and fleetingly raised his head. The old man nodded. "Yep, you're right, Chief. You showed 'em. Don't need this one anymore."

Unexpectedly, he extended it to Amanda. "*You* wear it, Sis. You got the look—just like Chief had. Wear it till you win your own."

Amanda gulped. She sniffed back tears and had to rub her nose childishly. "They look at me—" she sobbed, "but they don't *see* me!"

"You see yourself, don't you?" the old man asked mildly. "Well, then, what more do you need? A dream, and the ambition to work for it—enough for anybody." Gently he closed her fingers over the medal.

---

forlorn (fawr LAWRN) miserable
pigeonhole (PIJ un hohl) small compartment in a desk

Discoveries

345

MINI QUIZ

Write on the chalkboard or overhead projector the following questions and call on students to fill in the blanks. Discuss the answers with the class.

1. Amanda's day begins when her mother comments on _____.

2. Mrs. Hawthorne yells at her for _____.

3. The grocer is afraid that Amanda and other teenagers will _____.

4. Amanda runs out of _____.

5. Amanda meets _____, who tells her about his dog.

Answers to Mini Quiz

1. her short skirt
2. cutting across her yard
3. steal things from his store
4. Mr. Moore's science class
5. an old man

T345

ANSWERS TO
UNDERSTAND
THE SELECTION

ANSWERS TO UNDERSTAND THE SELECTION

1. Frustrated; nothing has gone right.
2. She runs out of the class because she is so frustrated at not being seen as herself.
3. She begins to run.
4. She wants to prove that her family is as good as any other family on the block.
5. He believes in helping black people.
6. mostly white
7. Both are runners, and both have the ability to do great things, even though others may not see it.
8. Answers will vary. Possible answer: Amanda will feel better about herself and not mind so much the way she is treated by her mother and others.
9. Answers will vary. Suggested answer: She would have felt guilty about leaving school and more upset with herself than ever.
10. Answers may vary. Possible answer: Hurt that she did not appreciate all that he had done for her.

Respond to Literature: Have students work in small groups. Challenge each group to create a skit that includes several flat characters. Encourage students to make their skits clever, entertaining, and humorous. After each group presents its skit, have the class discuss how the various flat characters represent stereotypes; also have them note the character traits of each.

Write About the Selection

Prewriting: Show students how to make a diagram to help them in brainstorming ideas for their paragraphs. Draw a circle on the chalkboard or overhead transparency. Then write in a word or phrase that describes the topic of the par-

---

UNDERSTAND THE SELECTION

Recall

1. What is Amanda's mood at first?

2. What happens to Amanda in class?

3. What does Amanda do after she leaves school?

Infer

4. Why is Amanda's mother so anxious for her to be an example?

5. According to Amanda, why is Mr. Moore always nice to her?

6. Would you guess that Amanda's school and neighborhood are racially mixed, mostly black, or mostly white?

7. In what ways does the old man think that Amanda and Chief are alike?

Apply

8. How do you think receiving the gold medal will affect Amanda?

9. What do you think would have happened to Amanda that day if she had not met the old man?

10. Imagine you are Mr. Moore. How would you have felt when Amanda left class?

Respond to Literature

How did the old man help Amanda discover herself? Has someone ever helped you discover something about yourself?

WRITE ABOUT THE SELECTION

At the end of the story, Amanda is still with the old man. What do you think will happen to Amanda when she reenters her everyday world of home and school? Write a paragraph that describes something that happens to Amanda within the next 24 hours after the story ends.

Prewriting: Make a list of the situations that Amanda will probably have to face. For example, how will Amanda explain her muddy clothes to her mother? Will she get in trouble for leaving school early? What will she say to Mr. Moore? Choose the situation that most interests you and let this be the subject of your paragraph. Then jot down some of the details that you wish to include.

Writing: As you write your paragraph, ask yourself these questions: Which characters are involved in this situation? What do they say and do? How does Amanda feel about this situation? Has her experience with the gold medal changed her feelings and attitudes? What is the outcome of the situation?

Revising: Rewrite your paragraph so that it flows easily after the last paragraph of the story. See if you can make the tone and style of your paragraph similar to that of the author.

Proofreading: Check your paragraph for mistakes in spelling, usage, and mechanics. Be sure to use question marks if you use questions in your paper.

---

agraph; for example, "next day at school." Next, draw lines around the circle, like the spokes of a wheel. On each line write a phrase or sentence that describes something that could happen the next day; for example, Amanda calls the principal's office; Amanda apologizes to Mr. Moore; other students ask Amanda where she went.

Writing: As students work on this section individually, circulate to

help those who are having difficulty. As students develop their episodes, encourage them to keep asking themselves questions such as "What might happen next?" or "What if . . ."

Revising: Have students work in small groups. Encourage them to read their paragraphs aloud to each other and to consider the comments of the group before they revise.

Proofreading: Have students trade papers with a partner. Then have the pair check each other's papers for errors.

LDP Activity: Cluster words on board that talk about the reasons for conforming in society. In school, in the neighborhood, etc.

THINK ABOUT CHARACTER

Rounded characters tend to develop and change as a story progresses. Flat characters, on the other hand, tend to stay the same. Often the flat characters form a kind of "background" for main characters's stories.

1. Explain why you think Amanda is a flat or a rounded character.

2. How do other characters in the story see Amanda—as flat or rounded?

3. Identify three flat characters in the story and their stereotypes.

4. Based on what you know about Amanda's mother, how do you think she would react if Amanda were to pursue running as a sport or career?

5. Would you say that the animal character in the story is flat or rounded?

DEVELOP YOUR VOCABULARY

Many adverbs are formed by adding -ly to an adjective. For example, the adverb *quickly* is formed by adding *-ly* to the adjective *quick*. If you are not sure of the meaning of an adverb that ends in *-ly*, try to figure out the meaning of the adjective from which it has been formed. The adverb should have a similar meaning. For example, a quick (adjective) runner will run quickly (adverb).

Review the meanings of these adverbs from "The Gold Medal." Underline the adjective from which each is formed. Then use each adverb in an original sentence.

1. rebelliously
2. frequently
3. unthinkingly
4. resignedly
5. reluctantly
6. unexpectedly
7. somberly
8. childishly
9. mildly
10. fleetingly

Discoveries

347

After completing this selection, students will be able to
- identify the speaker in a poem
- choose a speaker to express an idea
- identify aspects of self-discovery
- write about a private thought
- analyze the speaker in a poem
- use a dictionary to determine pronunciation.

More About the Speaker: Have students create statements that might—if they could talk—be made by objects in the classroom. For example, the chalkboard might say "I am a chalkboard. Many teachers have written on me." Encourage students to use the statements as ideas for writing their own paragraphs, using an inanimate speaker.

Cooperative/Collaborative Learning Activity: Have students work in pairs. Challenge each pair to create a poem or paragraph in which two objects in the classroom voice their thoughts or ideas. For example, the clock and the door might tell how students watch the clock and cannot wait to rush out the door.

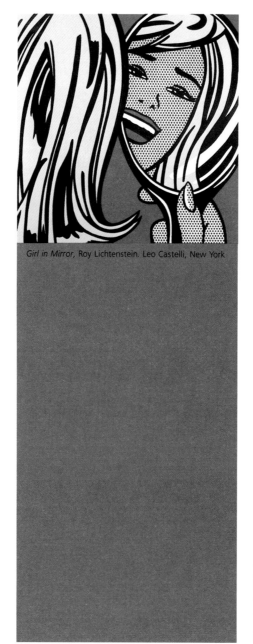

Girl in Mirror, Roy Lichtenstein. Leo Castelli, New York

LEARN ABOUT
Speaker

A poem can be written in the first, second, or third person. A poem written in the **first person** uses the pronouns *I* and *me*. A poem written in the **second person** speaks directly to the reader or to some real or imaginary person or object. This type of poem uses the pronoun *you*. A poem written in the **third person** uses the pronouns *he, she,* or *it*.

The *I* in a poem may not always be the poet. Sometimes a poet creates a speaker to voice his or her ideas. For example, in "Navaho Chant," you may remember that the speaker is the corn. A speaker may also voice the poet's ideas in the second person.

As you read these poems, ask yourself:

1. Who are the speakers in each poem?
2. Why did the poets choose to use these speakers?

SKILL BUILDER

Think of an idea or feeling about a day's event that you would like to communicate. For example, you may be unhappy because it is raining, or glad that a friend is back after being sick. Write a short poem or paragraph in which you create a speaker who is not you to voice your idea.

348

Unit 4

Vocabulary: Preteach the vocabulary words. See the Comprehension Workbook in the TRB.

More About Vocabulary: Familiarize the students with the vocabulary words footnoted in the first poem. Identify the part of speech of each. Then use each word in an original sentence.

CONVERSATION WITH MYSELF

by Eve Merriam

This face in the mirror
stares at me
demanding *Who are you? What will you become?*
and taunting, *You don't even know.*
Chastened, I cringe and agree
and then
because I'm still young,
I stick out my tongue.

HAPPY THOUGHT

by Jesús Papoleto Meléndez

have you ever been in a
crowded train
& thought
a happy thought
& it's slipped
from thought
to smile
& from smile
to giggle? /people stare.

taunting (TAWN ting) jeering at, mocking
chastened (CHAYS end) subdued
cringe (KRINJ) to shrink back from something

Discoveries   349

Sidelights: There is another well-known poem entitled "Happy Thought" with a somewhat different theme. It is a children's poem by Robert Louis Stevenson from the collection "A Child's Garden of Verses:"

> Happy Thought
> The world is so full
> Of a number of things
> That we should all
> be happy as kings!

Motivation for Reading: Ask students to think about how they see themselves when they look in the mirror. Are they pleased with what they see? Do they wish they were someone else? Do they see only the flaws? Relate the discussion to "Conversation With Myself."

More About the Thematic Idea: Both poems deal with self-discovery. In the first poem self-discovery is accomplished in dialogue with oneself. In the second poem the speaker discovers himself in the midst of, yet apart from, other people.

Purpose-Setting Question: How can a young person best discover his or her true self?

Critical Thinking: Ask students how they think the speaker in "Conversation With Myself" feels about what the face in the mirror says. (Possible answer: The speaker realizes that the face in the mirror is right, but there is rebelliousness, as is evident from the tongue being stuck out.)

LDP Activity: What is the common theme of all three poems? Discuss as a class group or in small groups.

MINI QUIZ

Write on the chalkboard or overhead projector the following questions and call on students to fill in the blanks. Discuss the answers with the class.

1. The speaker in "Conversation With Myself" looks in the _____.
2. At the end of the poem, the speaker _____.
3. The speaker in "Happy Thought" talks about being on _____.
4. The thought makes the speaker _____, then _____.
5. The other people around the speaker _____.

Answers to Mini Quiz

1. mirror
2. sticks out her tongue
3. a crowded train
4. smile, giggle
5. stare

Discussion: Pause after each poem for class discussion. Have students identify the speaker and theme for each poem, as well as the way each poem relates to the unit theme of discoveries.

ANSWERS TO UNDERSTAND THE SELECTION

1. looking in the mirror
2. sticks out her tongue at the face in the mirror
3. a crowded train
4. that she really does not know who she is or what she will become
5. somewhat ashamed
6. having a thought that makes you smile or laugh, causing other people to stare
7. separation, since the people on the train do not share the thought
8. Answers will vary. The mirror might say, "Go away! I do not want to see you anymore!"
9. Answers will vary. Possible answers: Waiting for a bus, on an airplane, walking down a crowded street.
10. Answers will vary. Students should have the face in the mirror make some comment that indicates how they feel about themselves, such as "You are a real handsome guy!"

Respond to Literature: Discuss with students how the face in the mirror, in "Conversation With Myself," represents an aspect of the speaker's self. Point out that we all have within us many voices and alternate "selves" that assert themselves at different times. Have students further explore this idea by working in pairs. Challenge each pair to create a dialogue in which one student is the speaker and the other is the "face in the mirror." For example, the speaker may be thinking of dropping out of high school; the voice in the mirror may then reprimand him or her, saying how he or she has little chance of getting a good job without a high school diploma.

LDP Activity: In these poems the concern is with yourself. What did the narrators in each of the poems discover about themselves?

T350

UNDERSTAND THE SELECTION

Recall

1. In "Conversation with Myself," what is the poet doing?

2. What does the poet do at the end?

3. What is the setting of the poem, "Happy Thought"?

Infer

4. In "Conversation with Myself," what does the poet realize about herself?

5. This discovery creates what feelings?

6. What kind of experience is described in "Happy Thought"?

7. What is the relationship between the person thinking the thought and the other people on the train?

Apply

8. In "Conversation with Myself," predict what the mirror might say next if the poem were to continue.

9. Apply the main idea of "Happy Thought" to another setting in which you might have a similar experience.

10. What do you think the face in your mirror would say to you?

Respond to Literature

How do each of these poems comment on the theme of self-discovery?

350

WRITE ABOUT THE SELECTION

Have you ever experienced something similar to what Jesús Papoleto Meléndez describes in "Happy Thought"? What were you thinking about at the time? Write a paragraph or short poem in which you describe a happy or amusing thought that made you smile or laugh out loud.

Prewriting: Take a few minutes to remember some times when a private thought made you smile or laugh out loud. (If you cannot think of such a time, perhaps you can recall an experience of a friend, family member, or character in a story.) List as many details as you can about each situation.

Writing: Decide which incident you recall most vividly, then let this be the subject of your writing. Be sure to include in your poem or paragraph a description of the place in which you were and the reactions, if any, of people around you.

Revising: See what happens if you change the point of view of your poem or paragraph. For example, if you have written in the first person, you might try rewriting in the third person. Then decide which version is most effective.

Proofreading: Check for errors in spelling, usage, and mechanics. Only use a comma if you know the rule for it. Remove any commas that are unnecessary. Also check your interior punctuation and make sure that all your sentences end with a period, question mark or exclamation mark.

Unit 4

WRITE ABOUT THE SELECTION

Prewriting: To help the class get started in planning their paragraphs, have several volunteers share with the class the incident that about which they plan to write. You may wish to have an incident of your own to share, if needed, to start off the discussion.

Writing: Help students think of details to include in their paragraphs by asking them to answer questions such as, Where were you? Who was with you? What was the time of day? The season of the year? How did the other people react? How did your thoughts make you feel? How did others' reactions make you feel?

Revising: Ask students to exchange papers with a partner. Have students make suggestions for changing the point of view of their partner's paper. Point out, however, that each writer may reject the suggestion if not convinced of a partner's argument.

Proofreading: Create a proofreading team of 3–5 students in which one student checks a paper for spelling, another for correct grammar, another for complete sentences, and so on. Ask for several volunteers to submit their pa-

THINK ABOUT THE SPEAKER

The speaker in a poem is like the narrator in a story. You can think of the speaker as a role the poet adopts in a poem. The speaker in a poem can be a real or imaginary person, animal, or object. Sometimes a poem will have more than one speaker, although the entire poem is usually told from one main point of view.

1. Who is the main speaker in "Conversation with Myself"?

2. Who else speaks in the poem? Are there really two speakers, or only one? Explain your answer.

3. Who is the speaker in the poem "Happy Thought"?

4. In what person is "Happy Thought" written?

5. Why do you think the author chose this point of view for the poem?

DEVELOP YOUR VOCABULARY

In English, many words do not sound the way they are spelled. For example, in the word *often*, the *t* is silent.

You can find out how to pronounce a word by looking it up in the dictionary. Following the entry word, you will find the pronunciation of the word in parenthesis. The symbols and letters that tell you how to pronounce the word are called **diacritical** marks. For example, the diacritical marks that show the pronunciation for the word *often* are: ('ȯ-fən). The key to these marks can be found at the bottom of the dictionary page.

Look up in the dictionary each of these words from "Conversation with Myself." Write the diacritical marks for each word and practice saying the word aloud. Then read aloud the entire poem.

1. taunting
2. chastened
3. cringe
4. tongue

THINK ABOUT THE SPEAKER

1. the poet
2. The face in the mirror also speaks, but, of course, this is really the poet. Using the face in the mirror is her way of illustrating that she is talking to herself and thinking about herself.
3. all of us
4. second
5. Answers may vary. Suggestion: He wanted to bring the poem more directly into the reader's own experience.

Develop Your Vocabulary:
After students have completed the vocabulary exercise, have volunteers write on the chalkboard the diacritical marks for each word. Then have the class practice saying the words aloud. Finish the activity by having students use each word orally in an original sentence.

pers for checking by the team. Suggestion: Advise the volunteers that the original creative writer may exercise the ultimate right of overruling the team.

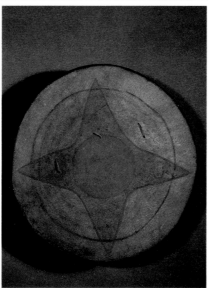

Painted Buffalo Hide Shield, Jemez, NM. Museum of the American Indian, Heye Foundation, NY

LEARN ABOUT
Autobiography

An **autobiography** is the story of a person's life written by that person. Because the author is writing about himself or herself, an autobiography is usually written in the first person.

An autobiography may tell about a person's entire life, or it may focus on just a part of it. Short stories that are autobiographical usually tell about a particular event or incident in the author's life.

From an autobiography you learn about the author as a person. You also learn about the circumstances of the author's life. As you read "Ta-Na-E-Ka," ask yourself:

1. What situation in Mary Whitebird's life is described in the story?
2. What do you learn about the author from the way she handles the situation?

SKILL BUILDER

Choose an interesting or amusing incident that has happened to you during the past several weeks. Write a paragraph in which you recount the incident as if you were writing your autobiography. Be sure to include not only "the facts," but also your feelings about the incident.

TA-NA-E-KA

by Mary Whitebird

As my birthday drew closer, I had awful nightmares about it. I was reaching the age at which all Kaw Indians had to take part in Ta-Na-E-Ka. Well, not all Kaws. Many of the younger families on the reservation were beginning to give up the old customs. But my grandfather, Amos Deer Leg, stood by the old traditions. He still wore handmade beaded moccasins instead of shoes. He kept his iron-gray hair in tight braids. He could speak English, but he spoke it only with white men. With his family he used a Sioux dialect.

Grandfather was one of the last living Indians who actually fought against the U.S. Cavalry. Not only did he fight, he was wounded in a skirmish at Rose Creek. This was the famous battle in which the well-known Kaw chief Flat Nose lost his life. At the time, my grandfather was only eleven years old.

Eleven was a magic word among the Kaws. It was the time of Ta-Na-E-Ka, which means "flowering of adulthood."

My grandfather had told us about it hundreds of times. It was the age, he said, "when a boy could prove himself to be a warrior. And a girl can take the first steps to womanhood."

"I don't want to be a warrior," my cousin, Roger Deer Leg, confided to me. "I'm going to become an accountant."

"None of the other tribes make girls go through the survival ritual," I complained to my mother.

"It won't be as bad as you think, Mary," my mother said. "Once you've gone through it, you'll never forget it. You'll be proud."

I even complained to my teacher, Mrs. Richardson. I felt that, as a white woman, she would side with me.

She didn't. "All of us have rituals of one kind or another," Mrs. Richardson said. "And look at it this way: How many girls have the chance to compete on equal terms with boys? Don't look down on your heritage."

Heritage, indeed! I didn't plan to live

---

dialect (DY uh lekt) local manner of speaking
skirmish (SKUR mish) minor battle in a war
confide (kun FYD) tell as a secret
ritual (RICH uu ul) ceremony; tradition
heritage (HER ih tij) what is handed down to a person from ancestors

Discoveries   353

Sidelights: The Kaw is one of the seven Sioux Native American tribes of North America, who lived in eastern Kansas. The tribe sold their Kansas lands to the government. Diseases such as small pox took a heavy toll, and few Kaw remain today.

Motivation for Reading: Ask students what they think they might do if they had to survive in the woods alone for five days. Relate their responses to the survival ritual that the author undergoes in "Ta-Na-E-Ka."

More About the Thematic Idea: In this story Mary Whitebird makes some important discoveries about herself and the world outside her reservation. Other people in the story also make discoveries about Mary. Some of these people include her grandfather and other family members, her teacher, and Ernie.

Purpose-Setting Question: Why would someone send an eleven-year-old child into the woods alone for five days?

Vocabulary: Preteach the vocabulary words. See the Comprehension Workbook in the TRB.

More About Vocabulary: Familiarize students with the vocabulary words footnoted in the story. Use each word in an original sentence and ask for volunteers to do the same.

on a reservation for the rest of my life. I was a good student. I loved school. My favorite stories were about knights in armor and fair ladies and dragons. I had never once thought that being Indian was exciting.

But I've always thought that equal rights for women started with the Kaw. No other Indian tribe treated women more "equally" than the Kaw. Unlike most other Sioux tribes, the Kaw allowed men and women to eat together. And hundreds of years ago, a Kaw woman had the right to reject a man chosen for her—even if her father had arranged a marriage.

The wisest women (usually the old ones) often sat in tribal councils. Furthermore, most Kaw legends are about "Good Woman," a kind of super person. Good Woman led Kaw warriors into battle after battle, which they always seemed to win.

And girls as well as boys were required to go through Ta-Na-E-Ka.

The actual ceremony varied from tribe to tribe. But since the Indians' life on the plains depended on survival, Ta-Na-E-Ka was a test of survival.

"Endurance is the highest virtue of the Indian," my grandfather explained. "To survive, we must endure. When I was a boy, Ta-Na-E-Ka was more than just the symbol it is now. We were painted white with the juice of a sacred herb. Then we were sent naked into the wilderness, without so much as a knife. We couldn't return until the white had worn off. It wouldn't wash off. It took almost eighteen days.

"During that time," he went on, "we had to stay alive. We did it by trapping food, eating insects and roots and berries, and watching out for enemies. And we did have enemies—both the white soldiers and the Omaha warriors. They were always trying to capture Kaw boys and girls going through their endurance tests. It was an exciting time."

"What happened if you couldn't make it?" Roger asked. He was born only three days after I was, and we were being trained for Ta-Na-E-Ka together. I was happy to know he was frightened, too.

"Many didn't return," Grandfather said. "Only the strongest and shrewdest. Mothers were not allowed to weep over those who didn't return. If a Kaw couldn't survive, he or she wasn't worth weeping over. It was our way."

"What a lot of hooey," Roger whispered. "I'd give anything to get out of it."

"I don't see how we have any choice," I replied.

Roger gave my arm a little squeeze. "Well, it's only five days."

Five days! Maybe it was better than being painted white and sent out naked for eighteen days. But not much better.

We were to be sent, barefoot and in bathing suits, into the woods. Even our very traditional parents put their foot

---

endurance (en DUUR uns) ability to withstand hardship; survival
virtue (VUR choo) good quality
shrewdest (SHROOD ist) cleverest
traditional (truh DISH uh nul) following old customs

Enrichment: Have students discuss the hardships that Native Americans would have to endure before modern conveniences. Why is physical endurance less important than it used to be?

T.C. and Me: Revisited, Amado M. Pena, Jr. El Taller, Inc.

down when Grandfather suggested we go naked. For five days we'd have to live off the land. We'd have to keep warm as best we could and get food where we could. It was May. But on the northernmost shores of the Missouri River, the days were still chilly and the nights fiercely cold.

Grandfather was in charge of the month's training for Ta-Na-E-Ka. One day he caught a grasshopper. Then he showed us how to pull its legs and wings

off in one flick of the fingers. And how to swallow it.

I felt sick, and Roger turned green. "It's a darn good thing it's 1947," I told Roger teasingly. "You'd make a terrible warrior." Roger just made a face.

I knew one thing. This was one Kaw Indian girl who wasn't going to swallow a grasshopper—no matter how hungry she got. And then I had an idea. Why hadn't I thought of it before? It would have saved nights of bad dreams about

Discoveries

355

Discussion: After students have read through the section in which Mary borrows the five dollars from Mrs. Richardson, pause for discussion. Ask students to speculate as to why Mary has borrowed the money and how they think she will use it.

squooshy grasshoppers.

I headed straight for my teacher's house. "Mrs. Richardson," I said, "would you lend me five dollars?"

"Five dollars!" she exclaimed. "What for?"

"You remember the ceremony I talked about?"

"Ta-Na-E-Ka. Of course. Your parents have written and asked me to excuse you from school so you can take part in it."

"Well, I need some things for the ceremony," I said, in a half-truth. "I don't want to ask my parents for the money."

"It's not a crime to borrow money, Mary. But how can you pay it back?"

"I'll baby-sit for you ten times."

"That's more than fair," she said. She went to her purse and handed me a crisp, new five-dollar bill. I'd never had that much money at once.

"I'm happy to know the money's going to be put to a good use," Mrs. Richardson said.

A few days later, Ta-Na-E-Ka began. First came a long speech from my grandfather. It was all about how we had reached the age of decision, how we now had to take care of ourselves. We had to prove that we could survive the most horrendous of ordeals.

All the friends and relatives gathered at our house for dinner and made jokes about their own Ta-Na-E-Kas. They all

advised us to fill up now, since for the next five days we'd be eating crickets. Neither Roger nor I was very hungry.

"I'll probably laugh about this when I'm an accountant," Roger said, trembling.

"Are you trembling?" I asked.

"What do you think?"

"I'm happy to know boys tremble, too," I said.

At six the next morning, we kissed our parents and went off to the woods. "Which side do you want?" Roger asked. According to the rules, Roger and I would stake out "territories" in separate areas of the woods. We weren't to communicate during the whole ordeal.

"I'll go toward the river, if it's okay with you," I said.

"Sure," Roger answered. "What difference does it make?"

To me, it made a lot of difference. There was a marina a few miles up the river, and there were boats anchored there. At least I hoped so. I figured that a boat was a better place to sleep than under a pile of leaves.

"Why do you keep holding your head?" Roger asked.

"Oh, nothing. Just nervous," I told him. Actually, I was afraid I'd lose the five-dollar bill, which I had tucked into my hair with a bobby pin. As we came to a fork in the trail, Roger shook my hand. "Good luck, Mary."

---

horrendous (haw REN dus) horrible; awful
ordeal (awr DEEL) severe test; harsh experience
stake out (STAYK out) mark the limits of
marina (muh REE nuh) large area set up for docking boats

"N'ko-n'ta," I said. It was the Kaw word for *courage*.

The sun was shining and it was warm. But my bare feet began to hurt right away. I saw one of the berry bushes Grandfather had told us about. "You're lucky," he had said. "The berries are ripe in the spring, and they are delicious and nourishing." They were orange and fat and I popped one into my mouth.

Argh! I spat it out. It was awful and bitter. Even grasshoppers were probably better tasting. However, I never intended to find out.

I sat down to rest my feet. A rabbit hopped out from under the berry bush. He nuzzled the berry I'd spat out and ate it. He picked another one and ate that, too. He liked them. He looked at me, twitching his nose. Then I watched a redheaded woodpecker tap on an elm tree. I caught a glimpse of a skunk waddling through some twigs. All of a sudden, I realized I was no longer frightened. Ta-Na-E-Ka might be more fun than I'd expected. I got up and headed toward the marina.

"Not one boat," I said to myself, depressed. But the restaurant on the shore, "Ernie's Riverside," was open. I walked in, feeling silly in my bathing suit. The man at the counter was big and tough-looking. He wore a sweatshirt with the words "Fort Sheridan, 1944," and he had only three fingers on one of his hands. He asked me what I wanted.

"A hamburger and a milk shake," I said. I held the five-dollar bill in my hand so he'd know I had money.

"That's a pretty heavy breakfast, honey," he said.

"That's what I always have for breakfast," I lied.

"Forty-five cents," he said, bringing me the food. (Back in 1947, hamburgers were twenty-five cents and milk shakes were twenty cents.) "Delicious," I thought. "Better'n grasshoppers. And Grandfather never once said that I couldn't eat hamburgers."

While I was eating, I had a grand idea. Why not sleep in the restaurant? I went to the ladies' room and made sure the window was unlocked. Then I went back outside and played along the riverbank. I watched the water birds, trying to identify each one. I planned to look for a beaver dam the next day.

The restaurant closed at sunset, and I watched the three-fingered man drive away. Then I climbed in the unlocked window. There was a night light on, so I didn't turn on any lights. But there was a radio on the counter. I turned it on to a music program.

It was warm in the restaurant, and I was hungry. I helped myself to a glass of milk and a piece of pie. But I meant to keep a list of what I'd eaten, so I could leave money. I also meant to get up early. Then I could sneak out through the window and head for the woods before the three-fingered man returned. I turned off the radio. I wrapped myself in the man's apron. And, in spite of the hardness of the floor, I fell asleep.

---

nuzzle (NUZ ul) nudge with the nose

Discoveries   357

Reading Strategy: Have students compare and contrast the Ta-Na-E-Ka experiences of Mary and Roger. Encourage students to reflect on the differences in personality revealed by the experiences. For example, Mary proves herself to be more creative than Roger, and in a certain sense, more daring.

MINI QUIZ

Write on the chalkboard or overhead projector the following questions and call on students to fill in the blanks. Discuss the answers with the class.

1. The Ta-Na-E-Ka is a _____.
2. Ta-Na-E-Ka takes place when a person is _____ years old.
3. During Ta-Na-E-Ka a person has to spend _____ days in _____.
4. Mary spent her Ta-Na-E-Ka in _____.
5. Robert spent his Ta-Na-E-Ka in _____.

Answers to Mini Quiz

1. survival ritual
2. eleven
3. five, the woods
4. Ernie's Restaurant
5. the woods

"What the heck are you doing here, kid?"

It was the man's voice.

It was morning. I'd overslept. I was scared.

"Hold it, kid. I just wanna know what you're doing here. You lost? You must be from the reservation. Your folks must be worried sick about you. Do they have a phone?"

"Yes, yes," I answered. "But don't call them."

I was shivering. The man, who told me his name was Ernie, made me a cup of hot chocolate. Meanwhile, I explained about Ta-Na-E-Ka.

"Darndest thing I ever heard," he said, when I was through. "Lived next to the reservation all my life, and this is the first I've heard of Ta-Na whatever-you-call-it." He looked at me, all goose bumps in my bathing suit. "Pretty silly thing to do to a kid," he muttered.

That was just what I'd been thinking for months. But when Ernie said it, I became angry. "No, it isn't silly. It's a custom of the Kaw. We've been doing this for hundreds of years. My mother and my grandfather and everybody in my family went through this ceremony. It's why the Kaw are great warriors."

"Okay, great warrior," Ernie chuckled, "suit yourself. And if you want to stick around, it's okay with me." Ernie went to the broom closet and tossed me a bundle. "That's the lost-and-found closet," he said. "Stuff people left on boats. Maybe there's something to keep you warm."

The sweater fitted loosely, but it felt good. I felt good. And I'd found a new friend. Most important, I was surviving Ta-Na-E-Ka.

My grandfather had said Ta-Na-E-Ka would be filled with adventure. I was certainly having my fill. And Grandfather has never said we couldn't accept hospitality.

I stayed at Ernie's Riverside for the whole five days. In the mornings, I went into the woods. There I watched the animals and picked flowers for each of the tables in Ernie's. I had never felt better. I was up early enough to watch the sun rise on the Missouri, and I went to bed after it set. I ate everything I wanted—insisting that Ernie take all my money for the food.

"I'll keep this in trust for you, Mary," Ernie promised. "In case you are ever desperate for five dollars."

I was sorry when the five days were over. I'd enjoyed every minute with Ernie. He taught me how to make western omelets and Chili Ernie Style. (That's still one of my favorite dishes.) And I told Ernie all about the legends of the Kaw. I hadn't realized I knew so much about my people.

But Ta-Na-E-Ka was over. As I neared my house, at about nine-thirty in the evening, I became nervous all over again. What if Grandfather asked me about the berries and the grasshoppers? And my feet were hardly cut. I hadn't lost a pound, and my hair was combed.

---

omelet (OM lit) eggs beaten up, fried, and folded in half when done

Discussion: Ask students why they think Ernie's statement about Ta-Na-E-Ka's being silly helps Mary become aware of how really important it is to her.

"They'll be so happy to see me," I told myself hopefully, "that they won't ask too many questions."

I opened the door. My grandfather was in the front room. He was wearing the ceremonial beaded deerskin shirt which had belonged to *his* grandfather.

"N'g'da'ma," he said. "Welcome back."

I hugged my parents warmly. Then I let go when I saw my cousin Roger sprawled on the couch. His eyes were red and swollen. He'd lost weight. His feet were an unsightly mass of blood and blisters. And he was moaning: "I made it, see. I made it. I'm a warrior. A warrior."

My grandfather looked at me strangely. I looked clean, well fed, and radiantly healthy. My parents got the message. My uncle and aunt gazed at me with hostility.

Finally my grandfather asked, "What did you eat to keep you so well?"

I sucked in my breath and blurted out the truth: "Hamburgers and milk shakes."

"Hamburgers!" my grandfather growled.

"Milk shakes!" Roger moaned.

"You didn't say we *had* to eat grasshoppers," I said meekly.

"Tell us about your Ta-Na-E-Ka," my grandfather commanded.

I told them everything, from borrowing the five dollars, to Ernie's kindness, to watching the beaver.

"That's not what I trained you for," my grandfather said sadly.

I stood up. "Grandfather, I learned that Ta-Na-E-Ka *is* important. I didn't think so during training. I was scared stiff of it. I handled it my way. And I learned I had nothing to be afraid of. There's no reason in 1947 to eat grasshoppers when you can eat a hamburger."

Inside, I was shocked at my own boldness. But I liked it. "Grandfather, I'll bet you never ate one of those rotten berries yourself."

Grandfather laughed! He laughed aloud! My mother and father and aunt and uncle were all dumbfounded. Grandfather never laughed. Never.

"Those berries—they are terrible," Grandfather admitted. "I could never swallow them. On the first day of my Ta-Na-E-Ka, I found a dead deer—shot by a soldier, probably. It kept my belly full for the entire period of the test!"

Grandfather stopped laughing. "We should send you out again," he said.

I looked at Roger. "You're pretty smart, Mary," Roger groaned. "I'd never have thought of what you did."

"Accountants just have to be good at arithmetic," I said comfortingly. "I'm terrible at arithmetic."

Roger tried to smile, but couldn't. My grandfather called me to him. "You should have done what your cousin did. But I think you are more aware of what is happening to our people today than we are. I think you would have passed the test under any circumstances, in any time. Somehow, you know how to live in a world that wasn't made for Indians. I don't think you're going to have any trouble surviving."

Grandfather wasn't entirely right. But I'll tell about that another time.

ANSWERS TO UNDERSTAND THE SELECTION

1. Kaw survival ritual that symbolizes the passage of eleven-year-olds into adulthood
2. her cousin Roger
3. in Ernie's Restaurant by the lake
4. Many Kaws are giving up the old customs to live like modern Americans rather than traditional Native Americans.
5. Because he plans to be an accountant, he does not think that the Kaw traditions are going to help him much in life.
6. They treated them as equals, even in tests of physical endurance such as the Ta-Na-E-Ka.
7. Answers may vary. Suggested answer: They realized that she had had a much easier time of it than their son.
8. Answers may vary. Possible answers: She felt sorry for him but not unhappy about what she had done; she felt a little ashamed of what she had done; she admired Roger for doing what was expected of him; she thought Roger was a little foolish for doing things the "old" way.
9. Answers will vary. Some may think she would have succeeded, others may think she would have had a lot of problems.
10. In today's world, the author's grandfather sees that Ta-Na-E-Ka is not necessary for survival; he understands his granddaughter's adaptability, just as he understands, and is saddened by, the relegation of Ta-Na-E-Ka to mere symbol.

Respond to Literature: Ask students what they think Mary might have discovered if, like Roger, she had stayed in the woods. Encourage students to speculate as to whether she would have been resourceful in this environment, and why.

T360

UNDERSTAND THE SELECTION

Recall

1. What is Ta-Na-E-Ka?
2. Who else goes through Ta-Na-E-Ka?
3. Where does Mary spend Ta-Na-E-Ka?

Infer

4. What can you infer about what is happening in the Kaw culture?
5. Why does Roger object to Ta-Na-E-Ka?
6. What was unusual about the way Kaws treated women?
7. Why were relatives hostile toward the author when she returned?

Apply

8. How do you think Mary Whitebird felt when she saw Roger after Ta-Na-E-Ka?
9. Predict what would have happened if Mary Whitebird had stayed in the woods the way her cousin did.
10. Why does Grandfather say that Ta-Na-E-Ka is just a symbol today?

Respond to Literature

Do you agree or disagree with the following statement? Why?
"Mary Whitebird made some important discoveries during the Ta-Na-E-Ka, but not the ones her grandfather expected her to make."

360

WRITE ABOUT THE SELECTION

At the conclusion of the story, Mary Whitebird's grandfather says, "Somehow, you know how to live in a world that wasn't made for Indians. I don't think you're going to have any trouble surviving." Then the author comments, "Grandfather wasn't entirely right. But I'll tell about that another time."

What do you think may have happened to Mary later in life to cause her to make this comment? Write a paragraph in which you describe an event in Mary's life that happens after Ta-Na-E-Ka.

Prewriting: Make a list of possible situations that could challenge Mary's ability to survive. Write what the outcome might be?

Writing: Choose a situation from your list and let this be the subject of your paragraph. Make it clear in your paragraph how much time has elapsed since the end of Ta-Na-E-Ka. For example, you might be writing about the day that Mary Whitebird enters college. This event would take place about nine years after the Ta-Na-E-Ka ritual.

Revising: Read your paragraph and note any sentences that seem too long or too choppy. Make run-ons into separate sentences. Combine short sentences to make more sophisticated compound or complex ones. Rewrite these sentences.

Proofreading: Check your paper for errors in spelling, usage, and mechanics. Be sure you have used abbreviations correctly.

Unit 4

WRITE ABOUT THE SELECTION

Prewriting Using students' suggestions, create a list of events, on the chalkboard or overhead transparency, that might have challenged Mary's survival in later life.

Writing: Have students work on this section individually. As students write remind them to consider the character and personality of Mary Whitebird as it is revealed in "Ta-Na-E-Ka." Point out that their paragraphs should be consistent with what they already know about Mary.

Revising: Have students work in small groups to revise their paragraphs. Ask the members of each group to think of themselves as literary critics or book editors who must decide if a particular sample would fit in with the original story.

Proofreading: Ask for volunteers to have their papers displayed on an overhead projector. Proofread these papers as a class exercise.

LDP Activity: Make a list of things you would need to survive if you were left in the woods for five days. Use food, clothing, and incidentals as categories.

THINK ABOUT AUTOBIOGRAPHY

When you read an autobiography, you see the author's world through his or her eyes. You learn how the author views the times, the social conditions, and the geographic location in which he or she lives, so, autobiographies provide valuable information.

1. What is the setting for "Ta-Na-E-Ka"?

2. How old is Mary when "Ta-Na-E-Ka" takes place? Why is this age important?

3. If Mary Whitebird's autobiography were cataloged in the library as a social studies book, under what subject might it be classified?

4. Why is Grandfather a significant character in this story?

5. What do Mrs. Richardson's comments about Ta-Na-E-Ka add to the story?

DEVELOP YOUR VOCABULARY

A **contraction** is a shortened form of two words. The two words are joined together by leaving out one or more letters. An apostrophe takes the place of the missing letter or letters. For example, the contraction *isn't* is a combination of the words *is not*. In the story "Ta-Na-E-Ka," the author uses many contractions. She does this in order to give the story a natural, informal tone.

Write the two words that have been combined to form each contraction.

1. I don't want to be a warrior.
2. Once you've gone through it, you'll never forget it.
3. Many didn't return.
4. We couldn't return until the white had worn off.
5. You'd make a terrible warrior.

MORE ABOUT NONFICTION

Nonfiction literature can include biographies, autobiographies, articles and essays, and diaries. A biography is an account of a person's life; an autobiography is an account written about one's own life; an article or essay is a short piece about a specific topic; and a diary is a daily record of a writer's experiences, observations, or feelings. Some types of nonfiction writing usually are not considered literature. These include, among others, straight news reporting, instruction manuals, and recipes.

Suggested Questions

Have students tell the plot of "Ta-Na-E-Ka." Ask them to cite the conflict; that is, what major problem must the main character overcome? (How to survive the Ta-Na-E-Ka). From that starting point find out from students what other lesser problems did she have to face? (Answers will vary.)

Have students relate the idea of plot and conflict to the events of "Chee's Daughter." Ask them to state in the form of a question the problem that faces Chee. (How can Chee get his daughter back?)

Ask students to compare the points of view of the stories they have read so far in this unit. Elicit that "Chee's Daughter" is told in the third person, but "The Gold Medal" and "Ta-Na-E-Ka" are told in the first person. Encourage students to comment on whether they feel these points of view are effective, or whether they would like to read any of the stories told from a different point of view.

Ask students what similarity in tone exists in "The Gold Medal" and "Ta-Na-E-Ka." Guide them to recognize that the similarity is due in part to the similar ages of the storytellers.

Nonfiction is literature that tells about real life, people, and events that actually happened. Autobiographies, biographies, and essays are all types of nonfiction. Autobiographies and biographies tell true stories often narratives about real people. Essays express writers' thoughts and opinions on a topic. You can better understand narratives by thinking about the four main parts, or elements, of nonfiction: plot and story, point of view, tone, and theme.

Plot and Story. The plot is a series of events that make up a narrative, a nonfictional story. In a true story, the plot describes both the things that happen to the characters and the things that the characters do. As the plot unfolds, you learn what happens and why it happens. An important part of the plot is **conflict.** Usually the central character in the story is presented with a set of problems that he or she must overcome. These problems will force the main character to struggle with another character or group of characters, an object, or nature. Sometimes the struggle is within the main character's own self, a psychological conflict.

As you read a piece of nonfiction, you can identify three main parts: introduction, body, conclusion. The **introduction** "sets the stage" for the story and draws you into the world of the characters. A good introduction will spark your curiosity and make you ask questions such as: "What is this story about? Who is this person speaking? What has happened? What is going to happen?" It is in the **body** of the story that the plot unfolds. You follow the main character's struggles and conflicts until you reach the outcome or climax of the story. When the entire story has been told, the author brings the piece of nonfiction to a **conclusion.** The conclusion may sum up the story or it may offer a comment on the story's value or importance. In some cases, the author may hint at what happens next in the characters' lives. For example, in "Ta-Na-E-Ka," Mary Whitebird indicates that, later in life, she did not always cope so well with the world as she did during Ta-Na-E-Ka.

NONFICTION

Point of View.. Every story must be written from a certain point of view. That is, someone must tell what is happening in the story. Usually a story is told from either a first-person or a third-person point of view.

When a story is told in the **first person,** the storyteller is a character in the story. You can tell when a story is told in the first person because the character refers to himself or herself as *I* and *me*. A first-person narrator can be a major character or a minor character. An important point to remember in first-person narration is that everything in the story is limited to what the narrator can see, hear, think, know, and feel. Most autobiographies are written in the first person.

A **third-person** storyteller stands outside the story. The storyteller refers to each character as *he* or *she*. A third-person narrator is not limited by what one person can see, hear, or know, but is free to comment on any aspect of the story. Biographies usually have a third-person point of view.

Tone. The tone communicates the author's feelings about the subject of his or her story. The tone of a story can be serious or humorous, personal or detached, lighthearted or somber, casual, formal, or a combination. For example, in "Ta-Na-E-Ka," Mary Whitebird's narration is serious but also somewhat lighthearted, reflecting an eleven-year-old girl's thinking.

Theme. A person writes a nonfiction story because he or she has something important to say. The message the writer wants to send is the theme, or main idea of the story. Some nonfiction states the theme clearly, while others ask you to figure it out for yourself.

As you read "Starvation Wilderness," examine the story to discover the elements of nonfiction that are present. Ask yourself these questions:

1. What is the story's point of view?
2. How is this point of view unusual?

Discoveries

363

After completing this selection, students will be able to
- identify elements of nonfiction
- write a personal response
- understand a discovery made too late
- understand the use of slang in literature

Literary Focus: Discuss the literary device of simulating an actual happening. Clearly the speaker in "Dead at Seventeen" is dead but his realistic, terse dialogue almost convinces the reader that the story is true. Point out that such a device gives a unique vantage point—omniscient and removed, like a third-person narrator but also totally involved as a first-person storyteller.

Tombstones, Jacob Lawrence. Collection of the Whitney Museum of American Art

Dead at Seventeen

by Ann Landers

Dear Readers: Today's column is dedicated to that beautiful guy. Paul "Bear" Bryant, the "winningest coach" from the University of Alabama. The Bear, who died last Jan. 26, used to read this column to every freshman class on opening day.

It would be lovely if Ray Perkins, the Bear's successor, carried on the tradition. Bryant loved his kids and he wanted them to stay alive.

Agony claws my mind. I am a statistic. When I first got here I felt very much alone. I was overwhelmed with grief, and I expected to find sympathy.

I found no sympathy. I saw only thousands of others whose bodies were as badly mangled as mine. I was given a number and

STUDY HINTS
The introduction sets the tone for the selection. How does the introduction draw you into the story?

364

Unit 4

Vocabulary: Preteach the vocabulary words. See the Comprehension Workbook in the TRB.

More About Vocabulary: Begin by noting that some of the words in the selection are slang, either because they are standard words that have assumed a new meaning—as in *cool, dense, ripped*—or are newly coined. As an oral exercise ask students for other examples of words that are currently "in" with the young. Have students use the words in sentences that show their meanings.

LDP Activity: Slang is often used in writing. Discuss in class or small groups "cool" and "wheedled." Have LDP students illustrate the two words.

placed in a category. The category was called "Traffic Fatalities."

The day I died was an ordinary school day. How I wish I had taken the bus! But I was too cool for the bus. I remember how I wheedled the car out of Mom. "Special favor," I pleaded. "All kids drive." When the 2:50 bell rang, I threw my books in the locker . . . free until tomorrow morning! I ran to the parking lot, excited at the thought of driving a car and being my own boss.

It doesn't matter how the accident happened. I was goofing off—going to fast, taking crazy chances. But I was enjoying my freedom and having fun. The last thing I remember was passing an old lady who seemed to be going awfully slow. I heard a crash and felt a terrific jolt. Glass and steel flew everywhere. My whole body seemed to be turning inside out. I heard myself scream.

Suddenly, I awakened. It was very quiet. A police officer was standing over me. I saw a doctor. My body was mangled. I was saturated with blood. Pieces of jagged glass were sticking out all over. Strange that I couldn't feel anything. Hey, don't pull that sheet over my head. I can't be dead. I'm only 17. I've got a date tonight. I'm supposed to have a wonderful life ahead of me. I haven't lived yet. I can't be dead.

Later I was placed in a drawer. My folks came to identify me. Why did they have to see me like this? Why did I have to look at Mom's eyes when she faced the most terrible ordeal of her life? Dad suddenly looked very old. He told the man in charge, "Yes—he is our son."

The funeral was weird. I saw all my relatives and friends walk toward the casket. They looked at me with the saddest eyes I've ever seen. Some of my buddies were crying. A few of the girls touched my hand and sobbed as they walked by.

Please—somebody—wake me up! Get me out of here. I can't bear to see Mom and Dad in such pain. My grandparents are so weak from grief they can barely walk. My brother and sister are like zombies. They move like robots. In a daze. Everybody. No one can believe this. I can't believe it, either.

Please, don't bury me! I'm not dead! I have a lot of living to do! I want to laugh and run again. I want to sing and dance. Please don't put me in the ground! I promise if you give me just one more chance, God, I'll be the most careful driver in the whole world. All I want is one more chance. Please, God, I'm only 17.

Paul "Bear" Bryant

Discoveries

Notice the point of view. How is this point of view effective?

The body text in the next five paragraphs contains the action of the story. You learn what happened to the storyteller and how he felt.

As the conclusion begins, notice that you are back to where the storyteller is now.

The author's purpose for writing the story is clear. What is the theme of the story?

UNDERSTAND THE SELECTION

Recall

1. Who is telling this story?

2. Where is this person?

3. What has happened to him?

Infer

4. Describe the storyteller's mood as he leaves school at the end of the day.

5. In what state was the storyteller when he "awakened"?

6. Explain the meaning of the phrase "placed in a drawer."

7. How does the storyteller feel about his parents, relatives, and friends?

Apply

8. What kind of "bargain" does the storyteller wish to make with God?

9. How do you think this boy's mother felt after loaning him the car?

10. Imagine if you had been a passenger in the storyteller's car. How would you feel if you had lived?

Respond to Literature

How is this boy's discovery different from other discoveries you have read about so far in this unit? What is your feeling about Bear Bryant's message?

WRITE ABOUT THE SELECTION

The selection "Dead at Seventeen" originally appeared in a column by Ann Landers. Landers wrote that there was a coach at the University of Alabama who used to read this story to every freshman class on opening day. She said that he loved his kids and wanted them to stay alive.

Write a paragraph in which you express your reaction to this selection. Is it one that you will remember? How might it influence you in the future?

Prewriting: Read the selection again and write down any thoughts and feelings that come to mind. Try to relate the selection to your own life and experience. Have you ever been involved in a car accident? Have you ever known anyone who was killed in an accident? Have you ever ridden with someone who was driving carelessly? How did you feel?

Writing: Use your notes to write a response to the story "Dead at Seventeen." Include in your paragraph your overall feeling about the selection.

Revising: Imagine that you are writing this paragraph in a letter to a friend. Add a sentence about why you think your friend should read the selection.

Proofreading: Check your paragraph for errors in spelling, usage, and mechanics. Correct any sentence fragments by making them into complete sentences.

THINK ABOUT NONFICTION

A narrative tells about real people and events. The four main parts of a narrative are plot and story, point of view, tone, and theme. A narrative also has a recognizable introduction, body, and conclusion.

1. What is the tone of "Dead at Seventeen"?

2. What is the story's point of view? Is the storyteller the person to whom the story actually happened? Why or why not?

3. How does the introduction draw you into the story?

4. Briefly summarize the series of events that take place in the story.

5. What is the message of the story? Why do you think the author wrote it?

DEVELOP YOUR VOCABULARY

Slang is nonstandard language that is used in casual speech. Slang expressions are especially popular with teenagers. For example, the author of "Dead at Seventeen" uses slang expressions in order to make the voice of the seventeen-year-old storyteller seem more real and believable.

Slang tends to change with time. For example, teenagers in the 1950s referred to something really great as "keen." When slang expressions are used over a period of time by a large number of people, they often become entry words in the dictionary.

Identify the slang expression in each of the following sentences. Then rewrite each sentence using standard language to express the same idea.

1. I was too cool to take the bus.
2. That's a sharp dress you have on.
3. You're so dense.
4. I blew it.
5. Somebody ripped off my pen.

Discoveries

After completing this selection, students will be able to

- understand the theme
- write about a theme of personal importance
- identify characters' discoveries
- write a story extension
- analyze theme in fiction
- use synonyms

More About Theme: One of the themes in "Thank You, M'am" is that important discoveries can be made when two persons, who do not know each other, meet. Ask students what other story in this unit also has this as one of its themes. ("The Gold Medal")

Cooperative/Collaborative Learning Activity: Divide students into groups of four or five. Ask each group to choose a theme about which they wish to write; the theme should be on an issue that is important to them. Next, have each group member contribute one or two sentences about the theme. Then have the groups use the sentences to write a single paragraph that they can share with the class.

LEARN ABOUT
Theme

A **theme** is an idea or message in a story, play, or poem. It is possible for a piece of literature to have several themes. Only one of these, however, will be the main theme. For example, in the story "The Gold Medal," the main theme is Amanda's discovery of her true self apart from the roles people tried to impose on her. A less important theme, or **subtheme,** is the dilemma of a black girl in a society that is made up mostly of white people.

You can often recognize the theme of a story by thinking, "Why did the author write this story, play, or poem? As you read "Thank You, M'am," ask yourself:

1. What message does Langston Hughes wish to convey?
2. How does the story communicate this message?

SKILL BUILDER

Imagine that you are a short-story writer. What kind of a theme might you choose? Write a paragraph in which you describe a theme that is meaningful to you. (For example, you might want to write about standing up for someone who is being teased.) Discuss how you would handle the theme and the message you would communicate.

THANK YOU, M'AM

by Langston Hughes

Sidelights: The principal theme of Langston Hughes's work is the common man, or, more specifically, the ordinary black person—his pleasures, joys, and sorrows. Hughes has written in almost every literary form: poems, novels, plays, songs, biographies, histories, and essays.

Motivation for Reading: Ask students if they have ever had a chance encounter with a stranger that proved to be unusual. Relate their responses to the encounter between the boy and Luella Bates Washington Jones.

More About the Thematic Idea: In this selection a boy and a woman he tries to rob make interesting discoveries about each other. Central to the meaning of the story is the boy's reason for taking the woman's purse and her unexpected response.

Purpose-Setting Question: How would you react if someone younger than you tried to take your purse or wallet?

She was a large woman with a large purse that had everything in it but hammer and nails. It had a long strap and she carried it slung across her shoulder. It was about eleven o'clock at night, and she was walking alone, when a boy ran up behind her and tried to snatch her purse. The strap broke with the single tug the boy gave it from behind. But the boy's weight, and the weight of the purse combined caused him to lose his balance so, instead of

---

slung (SLUNG) hung; made to swing loosely

Discoveries
369

Vocabulary: Preteach the vocabulary words. See Comprehension Workbook in the TRB.

More About Vocabulary: Write on the chalkboard sentences that use the vocabulary words footnoted in the story. Ask students to determine from the context what they think each word means. Discuss the meanings of the words in preparation for the students' reading of the seleciton.

LDP Activity: Recall in small groups or in class discussion the three main events in sequence. Discuss a possible topic sentence for the three events.

taking off full blast as he had hoped, the boy fell on his back on the sidewalk, and his legs flew up. The large woman simply turned around and kicked him right square in his blue-jeaned sitter. Then she reached down, picked the boy up by his shirt front, and shook him until his teeth rattled.

After that the woman said, "Pick up my pocketbook, boy, and give it here."

She still held him. But she bent down enough to permit him to stoop and pick up her purse. Then she said, "Now ain't you ashamed of yourself?"

Firmly gripped by his shirt front, the boy said, "Yes'm."

The woman said, "What did you want to do it for?"

The boy said, "I didn't aim to."

She said, "You a lie!"

By that time two or three people passed, stopped, turned to look, and some stood watching.

"If I turn you loose, will you run?" asked the woman.

"Yes'm," said the boy.

"Then I won't turn you loose," said the woman. She did not release him.

"I'm very sorry, lady, I'm sorry," whispered the boy.

"Um-hum! And your face is dirty. I got a great mind to wash your face for you. Ain't you got nobody home to tell you to wash your face?"

"No'm," said the boy.

"Then it will get washed this evening," said the large woman starting up the street, dragging the frightened boy behind her.

He looked as if he were fourteen or fifteen, frail and willow-wild, in tennis shoes and blue jeans.

The woman said, "You ought to be my son. I would teach you right from wrong. Least I can do right now is to wash your face. Are you hungry?"

"No'm," said the being-dragged boy. "I just want you to turn me loose."

"Was I bothering *you* when I turned that corner?" asked the woman.

"No'm."

"But you put yourself in contact with *me*," said the woman.

---

frail (FRAYL) weak

Unit 4

"If you think that that contact is not going to last awhile, you got another thought coming. When I get through with you, sir, you are going to remember Mrs. Luella Bates Washington Jones."

Sweat popped out on the boy's face and he began to struggle. Mrs. Jones stopped, jerked him around in front of her, put a half nelson about his neck, and continued to drag him up the street. When she got to her door, she dragged the boy inside, down a hall, and into a large kitchenette-furnished room at the rear of the house. She switched on the light and left the door open. The boy could hear other roomers laughing and talking in the large house. Some of their doors were open, too, so he knew he and the woman were not alone. The woman still had him by the neck in the middle of her room.

She said, "What is your name?"

"Roger," answered the boy.

"Then, Roger, you go to that sink and wash your face," said the woman, whereupon she turned him loose—at last. Roger looked at the door—looked at the woman—looked at the door—*and went to the sink.*

"Let the water run until it gets warm," she said. "Here's a clean towel."

"You gonna take me to jail?" asked the boy, bending over the sink.

"Not with that face, I would not take you nowhere," said the woman. "Here I am trying to get home to cook me a bite to eat and you snatch my pocketbook! Maybe you ain't been to your supper either, late as it be. Have you?"

"There's nobody home at my house," said the boy.

"Then we'll eat," said the woman. "I believe you're hungry—or been hungry—to try to snatch my pocketbook."

"I wanted a pair of blue suede shoes," said the boy.

"Well, you didn't have to snatch *my* pocketbook to get some suede shoes," said Mrs. Luella Bates Washington Jones. "You could of asked me."

"M'am?"

The water dripping from his face, the boy looked at her. There

---

half nelson (HAF NEL sun) wrestling hold on back of neck
whereupon (hwair uh PON) after which
suede (SWAYD) soft leather with a velvet-like surface

Rodger doesn't try to escape when Mrs. Jones releases her grip. Why not? Is he beginning to trust her? Is he just afraid? Ask students if they would try to escape if they were in a similar circumstance.

was a long pause. A very long pause. After he had dried his face and not knowing what else to do dried it again, the boy turned around, wondering what next. The door was open. He could make a dash for it down the hall. He could run, run, run, run, *run!*

The woman was sitting on the daybed. After a while she said, "I were young once and I wanted things I could not get."

There was another long pause. The boy's mouth opened. Then he frowned, but not knowing he frowned.

The woman said, "Um-hum! You thought I was going to say *but,* didn't you? You thought I was going to say, *but I didn't snatch people's pocketbooks.* Well, I wasn't going to say that." Pause. Silence. "I have done things, too, which I would not tell you, son—neither tell God, if He didn't already know. So you set down while I fix us something to eat. You might run that comb through your hair so you will look presentable."

In another corner of the room behind a screen was a gas plate and an icebox. Mrs. Jones got up and went behind the screen. The woman did not watch the boy to see if he was going to run now, nor did she watch her purse which she left behind her on the daybed. But the boy took care to sit on the far side of the room where he thought she could easily see him out of the corner of her eye, if she wanted to. He did not trust the woman *not* to trust him. And he did not want to be mistrusted now.

"Do you need somebody to go to the store," asked the boy, "maybe to get some milk or something?"

"Don't believe I do," said the woman, "unless you just want sweet milk yourself. I was going to make cocoa out of this canned milk I got here."

"That will be fine," said the boy.

She heated some lima beans and ham she had in the icebox, made the cocoa, and set the table. The woman did not ask the boy anything about where he lived, or his folks, or anything else that would embarrass him. Instead, as they ate, she told him about her job in a hotel beauty shop that stayed open late, what the work was like, and how all kinds of women came in and out, blondes, redheads, and Spanish. Then she cut him a half of her ten-cent cake.

"Eat some more, son," she said.

---

plate (PLAYT) small burner for cooking

Critical Thinking: Ask students how they think the boy feels about the woman by the end of the story. (Answers may vary. Suggestion: He is probably awed by her and what she has done; he may very well feel cared for and understood.)

Literary Focus: Have students discuss how the author creates the character of Luella Bates Washington Jones. Begin by asking students to consider what the character says, what she does, and how she reacts. Also guide students to recognize that she is definitely a rounded character, as is the boy.

When they were finished eating she got up and said, "Now, here, take this ten dollars and buy yourself some blue suede shoes. And next time, do not make the mistake of latching onto *my* pocketbook *nor nobody else's*—because shoes come by devilish like that will burn your feet. I got to get my rest now. But I wish you would behave yourself, son, from here on in."

She led him down the hall to the front door and opened it. "Goodnight! Behave yourself, boy!" she said, looking out into the street.

The boy wanted to say something else other than, "Thank you, m'am," to Mrs. Luella Bates Washington Jones, but he couldn't do so as he turned at the barren stoop and looked back at the large woman in the door. He barely managed to say, "Thank you," before she shut the door. And he never saw her again.

---

barren (BAR un) dull; uninteresting
stoop (STOOP) front step

Discoveries   373

**ANSWERS TO
UNDERSTAND THE
SELECTION**

1. A boy snatches Mrs. Washington's purse.
2. to her home
3. ten dollars
4. He either has no parents or they do not spend much time at home.
5. She reminds him that it was he who put himself in contact with her, not the other way around.
6. a rooming house
7. She says that she did things about which she would not tell.
8. Answers may vary. Suggestion: He is curious about what is going to happen next.
9. Answers will vary. Some may think he buys the suede shoes, some may have other ideas.
10. Answers will vary. Encourage students to explain why they think he will or will not behave from now on.

Respond to Literature Point out to students that although certain things about Luella Jones and the boy are revealed in the story, much about them remains a mystery. Have students make a chart of what is known about each character. Then have students discuss things they do not know but, if they had the opportunity, would like to discover about each character. Students may enjoy speculating about some of these, based on their interpretations of the story.

**WRITE ABOUT
THE SELECTION**

Prewriting: On the chalkboard or overhead transparency, create some sample brainstorming notes based on students' suggestions. An outline such as the following may be helpful:

UNDERSTAND THE SELECTION

Recall

1. What is the opening incident?
2. Where does Mrs. Jones take the boy?
3. What does Mrs. Jones give the boy at the end of the story?

Infer

4. What can you infer about the boy's parents?
5. What argument does Mrs. Jones use when the boy begs her to turn him loose?
6. In what kind of house does Mrs. Jones live?
7. What hint in the story tells you that Mrs. Jones did not always behave herself when she was young?

Apply

8. Why do you think the boy does not run from Mrs. Jones's house when he has the chance?
9. What will the boy do with the money?
10. Predict whether or not you think the boy will behave himself from now on.

Respond to Literature

What do Mrs. Jones and the boy discover about each other? Do you think discoveries like this can happen in real life?

374

WRITE ABOUT THE SELECTION

Imagine that many years have passed and that the boy in "Thank You, M'am" is an adult. How do you think he would remember his encounter with Luella Bates Washington Jones? Write a paragraph in which the boy (now grown up) tells about Mrs. Jones.

Prewriting: Take a few minutes to brainstorm about the details you want to include in your paragraph. Decide how old you want the "boy" to be and what the circumstances of his life are (rich, poor, successful, in jail, etc.).

Writing: Use the ideas from your brainstorming session to write a paragraph from the adult "boy's" point of view. Be sure to make clear the boy's feelings about Mrs. Jones and the incident with the purse. Also, make clear what effect, if any, the incident had on the boy as he grew older. Base your paragraph on Langston Hughes's message to the readers in the story.

Revising: You can make your paragraph more effective by adding specific details from the story as seen from the boy's point of view. Rearrange phrases and eliminate boring words to make your story come alive.

Proofreading: Check your paragraph for errors in spelling, usage, and mechanics. Add periods or other end marks to correct run on sentences. Make sure that every sentence ends with a period, question mark or exclamation mark.

Unit 4

"boy's" age: 14
occupation: petty criminal
where he is: jail
why: caught shoplifting
memories: does not remember Luella Jones

Writing: As students write their paragraphs, ask them to think about how they might feel if they had been the boy in the story, and are now grown up.

Revising: Have students work in pairs. Students should suggest to each other ways to make their paragraphs more effective.

Proofreading: Have students proofread their own papers as you proofread a sample paper on an overhead projector.

LDP Activity: In the story "Thank You Ma'm" The boy could't say more than Thank you Ma'am. What other words could he have used to show his feelings? Discuss in small groups or with class the possibilities and then write them. Is thank you expressed in the same manner for all cultures? Discuss.

THINK ABOUT THEME

When thinking about the theme of a story, it is important not to confuse theme with plot. The **plot** of a story is what happens in the story, while the **theme** is the message or main idea of the story. Stories with different plots might have the same theme.

1. What is the theme of "Thank You, M'am"?

2. Do you agree with the message?

3. Why do you think Mrs. Jones treated the boy the way she did?

4. What did Mrs. Jones hope her encounter with the boy would accomplish?

5. In general, do you think that people like Mrs. Jones tend to make other people better, or that others just take advantage of them?

DEVELOP YOUR VOCABULARY

A **synonym** is a word that has the same or almost the same meaning as another word. For example, the boy in "Thank You, M'am" tries to *snatch* Mrs. Jones's purse. Two words that are synonyms for *snatch* are the words *take* and *grab*.

Review these words from "Thank You, M'am" and other stories in this unit. Write at least one synonym for each word. Then write an original paragraph that uses the words from the list.

1. slung
2. frail
3. barren
4. gingerly
5. quaver
6. zealously
7. surmised
8. acrid
9. shrewdest
10. horrendous

After completing this selection, students will be able to
- understand haiku
- create their own haikus
- discover relationships between images from nature and life
- analyze the imagery in haiku
- use a thesaurus to locate new words

More About Haiku: A haiku usually communicates a single image. Students may enjoy creating drawings or other visual representations of the images presented by the haikus they read.

Cooperative/Collaborative Learning Activity: In ancient Japan the haiku was originally a long poem, with 5-7-5 patterns alternating with 7-7 patterns. Have students work in pairs. Challenge each pair to create a haiku in which they take turns writing: The first student will write a 5-7-5 verse, the second student will write a 7-7 verse. The first student will then write another 5-7-5 verse, and so on, until they finish their haiku. Suggest to students that they can make the poem as long as they like—the ancient Japanese poems sometimes consisted of as many as 100 verses!

LEARN ABOUT
Haiku

Haiku is a form of poetry that has been popular in Japan for over 300 years. A **haiku** consists of three lines; it has no title. Haiku often has a 5-7-5 pattern of syllables (the first line has five syllables, the second line has seven, and the third line has five). Sometimes, when haiku are translated into English, they do not follow this pattern. Like all haiku, however, the poems paint a picture in as *few* words as possible.

Usually a haiku refers to or describes something in nature. A haiku may also have some symbolic meaning. You will also notice that the last selection about a bee is too long to be a haiku. But, like haiku, it uses the world of nature as a symbol for something else.

As you read the four haiku that follow, ask yourself:
1. What do these poems say about the objects they are describing?
2. What do these poems say about people and life?

SKILL BUILDER

Think of an object in nature that interests you; perhaps an animal, insect, flower, or tree. Write a description of the object in haiku form, using three lines in a 5-7-5 pattern of syllables.

376

Unit 4

HAIKU

1

Here . . . there . . .
the sound of waterfall is heard—
young leaves, everywhere.   —*Buson*

2

Friend, that open mouth
reveals your whole interior . . .
Silly hollow frog!   —*Anonymous*

3

Make up your mind snail!
You are half inside your house
and halfway out!   —*Richard Wright*

4

Insects, why cry?
We all go
that way.   —*Issa*

A BEE THUMPS

5

A bee thumps against the dusty window,
falls to the sill,
climbs back up, buzzing;
falls again;

and does this over and over.
If only he would climb higher!
The top half of the window is
open.

—*Robert Sund*

Shadows of Evening, Rockwell Kent. Collection of the Whitney Museum of American Art

Discoveries   377

ANSWERS TO UNDERSTAND THE SELECTION

1. outdoors, with trees and a waterfall
2. frog
3. trying to get out of a window
4. spring
5. someone who talks too much
6. It describes something in nature and can be used to symbolize an aspect of human life.
7. A person who keeps trying the same thing over and over again, only to fail again and again.
8. The snail looks as if he does not know whether he wants to be in or out of his shell.
9. Possible answer: We all die eventually.
10. House refers to the snail's shell.

Respond to Literature: As a class project have students create a mural of the images presented by the five haiku. Students can choose to recreate the images from nature, or they can create images that reflect the "human" meaning of each poem—for example, an indecisive person who cannot decide between two paths would be a perfect representation of the snail.

WRITE ABOUT THE SELECTION

Prewriting: Use the chalkboard or an overhead transparency to create a list of possible titles based on suggestions from the class.

Writing: For students who have chosen to write a haiku, provide guidance where needed on how to use the 5-7-5 syllable form.

Revising: Have students read their poems out loud to a partner. Ask the partners to comment on whether the image produced is clear and vivid. Have students suggest adjectives that would improve their partners' poems.

UNDERSTAND THE SELECTION

Recall

1. What is the setting for the first haiku?
2. What animal is described in the second haiku?
3. What is the bee doing in the last poem?

Infer

4. What time of year does the first haiku describe?
5. What human quality might be symbolized by the animal in the second haiku?
6. In what ways is the last poem similar to a haiku.
7. What human predicament might the bee symbolize?

Apply

8. How might the title "Indecision" apply to the haiku about the snail?
9. What is the meaning of the haiku about insects?
10. What is the meaning of the word "house" in the poem about the snail?

Respond to Literature

How do these five poems illustrate discoveries made by the poets?

WRITE ABOUT THE SELECTION

Several of the poems in this selection symbolize human qualities that are represented by animals. Think of a person you know (It might be you!) who has a characteristic that might be presented in a haiku about an animal. Then write a haiku or poem describing this person.

Prewriting: Make a chart of several animals that lend themselves to this assignment. (For convenience, you can use the animals in the haiku you studied, such as "Frog" or "Snail.") Under each title you list, write down the human characteristic that is symbolized. Then write down the names of people you know who have this characteristic.

Writing: Decide which name on your list would make the best subject for your haiku or poem. Then describe this person with words that you could use in the poem. Try to include a specific incident involving the person that illustrates the characteristic you are writing about.

Revising: The use of adjectives is important in a description. Reread your poem and add or substitute at least three adjectives that make the picture of the person you are writing about more vivid.

Proofreading: Check for mistakes in spelling, usage, and mechanics. Be sure to use apostrophes to make nouns possessive.

Proofreading: Punctuation in poetry can be tricky because there are no hard-and-fast rules. Display several students' poems on an overhead projector and ask the class if they agree with the punctuation.

LDP Activity: Illustrate one of the Haiku poems. Then write the poem below the picture.

THINK ABOUT HAIKU

A **haiku** paints a picture in words. The subject of the picture is usually an object in nature. Very often, the meaning of a haiku goes beyond its subject. The subject becomes a symbol of a human characteristic or an aspect of human life.

1. In the second poem, how is the interior of the frog described?

2. How does this description comment on a person who is like the frog?

3. In the poem about the bee, what does the bee not realize?

4. How does this poem apply to someone who keeps making the same mistake over and over?

5. Describe the picture that is painted in the first haiku.

DEVELOP YOUR VOCABULARY

A **thesaurus** is a dictionary of synonyms. When you look up a word in a thesaurus, you will find a list of words that have meanings that are similar to the meaning of that word.

The words in a thesaurus can be very helpful when writing a poem, story, or essay. Suppose you are writing a haiku and you need a one-syllable word that means ocean. If you look up the word *ocean* in a thesaurus, you will find the word *sea*— which is exactly the word that you need.

Look up the following words in a thesaurus, and find at least two synonyms for each word. Then use each word in an original sentence.

1. interior
2. hollow
3. house
4. sound
5. fall
6. window

After completing this selection, students will be able to
- understand the use of conflict
- describe a conflict
- evaluate characters' discoveries
- apply the theme of a story
- analyze conflict in a story
- use a dictionary to find additional information about words

More About Conflict: The conflict in a story sets up the problem or series of problems that the main character will have to overcome. The unknown outcome of the conflict provides suspense—will the character succeed or fail?

Cooperative/Collaborative Learning Activity: Have students work in small groups. Challenge each group to dramatize a conflict. It may be a conflict between persons, within a family, between a person and nature, or a conflict within a person's mind. Each dramatization should show clearly both the conflict and the outcome of the conflict. Have groups share their dramatizations with the class.

Gilded Snow, Ozlas Leduc. The National Gallery of Canada Ottawa

LEARN ABOUT

Conflict

An important ingredient in the plot of a story is **conflict**. A conflict is a meeting of two opposing forces. Often the central character in a story is involved in a struggle with another character. In some stories, however, the struggle is between the main character and nature, or between the main character and things. It is also possible for the conflict to be within a single person.

A story begins to develop once a conflict is established. As you read "Starvation Wilderness," ask yourself:
1. What is the conflict in this story?
2. What is the outcome of the conflict?

SKILL BUILDER

Think of a conflict that you have been involved in recently. It may have been a confrontation with another person, or it may have been a difficult set of circumstances or a conflict within your own mind. Write a short paragraph in which you describe the nature of the conflict and the way it was handled. Also, indicate the outcome of the conflict.

STARVATION WILDERNESS

by Olive A. Fredrickson

Our scow was heavy. It was an old 30-footer that we had bought at Fort Fitzgerald. But with only two grown-ups, a baby, and a pair of sled dogs on board, it rode high. The steady current of the Slave River pushed us north far faster than anyone could have walked on shore.

We had oars, and now and then my young husband, Walter, used them for a short distance. But there was no need for it. Mostly he just steered. We watched the early-fall scenery slip past or played with our six-month-old daughter, Olive. When we weren't cuddling her, she slept as contented as a kitten in the small cardboard box that was her crib.

Muskrat sign was plentiful along the river. Wherever there was green grass along the shore, snow geese pastured by the hundreds. We were rarely out of hearing of their wild voices. We had come to a land of plenty, Walter and I agreed. It was a dream country for a young trapper and his wife.

The time was late August of 1922. The trip had come about when Walter met two trappers, Nels Nelson and Pete Anderson, at Fort Fitzgerald. They had trapped the fall before down the Slave in Northwest Territories. They had come out before Christmas, they said, with 1,600 muskrat skins that brought $1.50 apiece. There were lakes all over the country, they told Walter, and every one of those lakes crawled with marsh rats.

My husband was a trapper at heart, above everything else. For him stories of that kind were like wild tales of gold to other men. He gave up then and there all thought of going to Fort McMurray, where I had been looking forward to the presence of other women, a few comforts, and a doctor in case the baby or I needed one. The three of us, Walter decided, would spend the winter trapping on those rich fur grounds.

We bought the scow and 34 single-spring traps. We also bought 400 pounds of flour, 50 pounds of white sugar, and four 50-pound sacks of potatoes. I remember that we paid $12 for each of those sacks. Coal oil[1] was $2 a gallon at Fitzgerald. We completed our grub list with beans, rice, salt pork, oatmeal, bak-

---

muskrat (MUSK rat) brown animal that lives in and near water, about
   two feet long; also called *marsh rat* and *rat* in the selection
scow (SKOU) barge; tub-like boat for carrying cargo
[1]coal oil: kerosene, sometimes made from coal
cuddling (KUD ling) holding and petting
presence (PREZ uns) nearness; being there

Discoveries   381

Sidelights: Olive A. Frederickson's husband Walter died five years after they returned from the wilderness. He lost his life when a canoe he was paddling alone tipped over a windy lake.

Motivation for Reading: Ask students to think about what they would do if they were stranded in the wilderness during a winter blizzard. Relate the discussion to the situation faced by the couple in "Starvation Wilderness."

More About the Thematic Idea: The hero and heroine in the selection are somewhat naive about what life will be like in Northern Canada in winter. As the plot unfolds the couple find themselves in increasingly precarious circumstances, and they make many harsh discoveries about the realities of nature in the far North.

Purpose-Setting Question: Why would a young man and his pregnant wife, with a little baby, choose to spend a winter in a tent in northern Canada?

Vocabulary: Preteach the vocabulary words. See the Comprehension Workbook in the TRB.

More About Vocabulary: Introduce the words footnoted in the story. Use each word in an original sentence and have student volunteers do the same, orally.

LDP Activity: Discuss in small groups or in class discussion the conflict between man and the wilderness. Discuss Survival. Finish the sentence: Survival is . . .

Discussion: At various points in the story, pause and ask students to discuss alternatives to the plight of the characters. Probably, most students will agree that the author and her husband did not always make the wisest choices. Perhaps there were times when they should have turned back, or sought help; certainly, they might have learned more, beforehand, about where they were going.

ing powder, salt, and tea—and cornmeal for the dogs.

We loaded the scow and shoved off on August 23 for the trip down the Slave to our trapping grounds. We were in completely unfamiliar country. It was the first time either of us had been that far north. We were on our way into what Walter had been told was good fur country. He was completely happy. I'll confess that I wasn't quite so cheerful as he was about wintering with a child not yet a year old hundreds of miles from the nearest doctor.

Nels and Pete had told us to look for an old sawdust pile on the west shore of the river. We should settle down around there, they had said. We passed the sawdust pile on our fourth day of floating. We tied up the scow, let our two dogs loose for a run, got the tent up, and carried our supplies up the bank. It was close to midnight when we finished. We tied the dogs to trees and turned in.

After we had gotten to sleep, I was awakened by some animal gnawing on the salt pork[2] we had brought into the tent. At first I thought one of the dogs had gotten loose. But as my eyes grew accustomed to the dim light in the tent I made out a large skunk.

The tent was only 9 × 12 feet. That skunk was working on the pork within three feet of my face. I shook Walter awake. We tried to drive the skunk off, but it wouldn't budge.

"I'll have to shoot it or we won't have any pork," Walter finally said. We knew it wasn't a very good idea, but we had no choice.

Shooting a skunk inside a tent is a big mistake. Whoever invented tear gas[3] simply copied something that skunks have used for thousands of years. It wouldn't be truthful to say the air turned blue, but it certainly turned something. Our eyes started to water. We were almost blinded. We began to gag. I grabbed the baby and fumbled my way outside. After a minute or so, Walter stumbled out behind me, dragging the dead skunk. He threw it over the riverbank. We hauled our bedding outside and spent the rest of the night in the open. We were tired enough to sleep anywhere. The next morning I told Walter that his way of saving our salt pork was no good. The pork smelled almost as bad as the tent.

Next we started work on a cabin for our winter home. We planned to live in it only until November, when the lakes would freeze and we'd have to quit trapping. So we threw it up hurriedly. It was built of small green logs. It was soon finished, and about October 1 we put our traps out.

As it happened, we stayed on in that rough cabin until spring. For one thing, there was a lot of fur, mink as well as muskrat. There was also firewood handy. The cabin stood in a thick grove of spruces, where it was sheltered from the wind.

---

gag (GAG) cough with a sick feeling

[2]**salt pork:** fat pork cured with salt to keep fresh

[3]**tear gas:** kind of gas that burns the eyes, sometimes used to control riots

We had torn our scow apart to make doors and windows. I suggested to Walter that he build a boat. It was a clumsy boat, for we had no way to bend the heavy boards of the scow.

The trapping looked good, but now we faced another problem. Wild meat was so scarce that we got worried. There wasn't a moose or deer track anywhere. Before winter closed in on us, we had named that belt of timber and swampy lakes Starvation Wilderness. Snow came to stay on October 10. After that the whole country was white and lifeless.

Trapping was good. We were looking at our traps twice a day. We'd hike out to the lakes together. Then I'd take Olive and the dog team with a small toboggan and cover half the line. Walter would go over the other half. We'd meet at midday. On the way back to camp, he covered my end of the line and I took his.

We both trapped until the first of November. Then the lakes were frozen. The temperature had dropped too low for us to be out in the wind and cold. From December until the end of March, the temperature rarely climbed as high as 10° below zero. There were days when it went to 65° below. The wind cut like a knife. We huddled in our shack and tried to keep warm.

Spruce pitch dripped from the roof poles and matted my long curls that Walter liked so much. In desperation I finally took the scissors one day when he was out looking at fox traps and cut my hair as short as I could. He was so upset when he came home that his face turned gray.

We got through that bitter winter until February. By then we knew we'd run out of food long before June, when we had planned to catch the first steamboat coming up the Slave. We had known since October that I was pregnant. Our second baby would be born in July. We didn't dare to wait for the boat, knowing that before the end of winter we'd have nothing to eat.

We were in no shape for the 60-mile trip out to Fort Smith. Our two dogs were old and not strong enough to pull Olive and me on the sled. The baby could ride, but I'd have to walk. We didn't have suitable clothing for cold of 40° and 50° below zero. What we lacked were fur parkas and fur-lined moccasins. But as our food dwindled, we made ready for the trip. Walter would leave Olive and me at Fort Smith and come back in time to trap again as soon as the lakes opened.

We put hot water in the water bottle, and we heated stones. We wrapped the baby in our whole bedroll of four blankets with the stones and water bottle beside her, and struck out up the Slave. The empty toboggan with Olive aboard was all our dogs could pull.

It was bitterly cold, probably around

---

belt (BELT) area; region
toboggan (tuh BOG un) large, flat sled
parka (PAHR kuh) fur jacket with a hood
dwindle (DWIN dul) become less and less
bedroll (BED rohl) roll of blankets or other bedding

Discoveries

40° below. The going was hard. We made poor time. The dogs pulled willingly enough for a while. But the heavy going was too much for them. We had traveled about 15 miles when they began to give out. They stopped frequently. More than once they lay down in the snow. Walter urged them on and pushed all he could on the toboggan handles to help them.

But we both knew we weren't going to go much farther.

The winter days are very short there in the North. By 3:30 in the afternoon, dusk was beginning to come down. Across the river there was a little cabin with smoke curling out of the chimney. I can't remember that I was ever gladder to see a human habitation.

Winter, George Gardner Symons. Scripps College, Claremont

habitation (hab ih TAY shun) a building to live in

Unit 4

The cabin belonged to two young trappers. We pulled in thinking we could stay the night. But there wasn't room to walk between the stove, beds, and table. It was plain that they couldn't put us up. They told us that four miles farther up the Slave another trapper, Bert Bennett, had a comfortable cabin. We rested a little while, and started for Bennett's place with the early dark thickening over the frozen snowy wilderness. I didn't feel as if I could go 500 feet, much less four miles.

That was one of the worst hikes I've ever had. Each mile of the four seemed like 10. The dogs stopped every few yards to lie down. Walter went ahead to break trail and pull them along with a short length of rope. I pushed on the toboggan handles for a change. It was too dark for Walter to see where he was putting his snowshoes, and he must have fallen 100 times. I had pain in every inch of the legs, my back, and all through my body. I finally realized I was leaning on the toboggan handles more than I was pushing. It seemed to me that the easiest thing to do would be to walk off into the snow and lie down and sleep forever.

But there was Olive to think of, I reminded myself. I could hear her whimper now and then, and wondered if she was freezing. There was nothing I could do about it if she was. I didn't dare open the bedroll she was wrapped in to look at her. I just kept putting one foot ahead of the other, stumbling and staggering along, terribly cold, until I lost all track of time and place.

A shout from Walter brought me out of my stupor. "Hello, there!" he yelled. I looked ahead and could see a square of light shining out of a window. Oh, what a welcome sight!

I don't remember Bennett opening the door, or Olive and me being carried into the warmth of the cabin. The first thing I recall was Walter pulling off my coat. Then somebody set a bowl of hot soup in front of me and shook me and told me to eat.

In a daze I watched Bennett take off Olive's rabbit-skin coat and start to feed her. They told me afterward that I cried out, "No, don't take her coat off. She'll freeze!" But I have no memory of that. I did not even realize that we were safe and warm inside four walls. The next thing I remember, Walter was telling me to get up for breakfast.

I was too stiff and sore to make it. But he pulled me out of bed and made me move my legs and body. It's surprising how much power of recovery you have at 21. I was four months pregnant, and I had run and walked 23 miles the day before in deep snow. When Bennett looked at his thermometer that morning it was 61° below. The wonder was that the three of us had not frozen to death on the trail.

We realized then that we could not make it to Fort Smith. It was dangerous and foolhardy to try. Luckily, Bennett

---

stupor (STOO pur) dazed or dull state; loss of feeling
foolhardy (FOOL hahr dee) foolishly risky; much too bold

had extra supplies that he could spare. He sold us flour and beans enough to see us through, and even lent Walter 24 good muskrat traps.

We stayed three days with Bennett. I regained my strength. At the end of the three days I was as good as new. The dogs were in better shape than when we'd begun our terrible trip up-river. We were ready to go back to our cabin and see the winter out. With muskrat at $1.50 each, there was more good money to be made as soon as the lakes started to open. When the first boat came up the Slave, we would be waiting for it.

We started out on a clear morning with the sun shining. Wind had drifted and packed the snow solidly enough that we seldom broke through. The dogs and Walter and I all had easy going. We pulled up in front of our lonely little cabin just as it was coming full dark.

We did not see or hear a living thing except each other, the dogs, and three foxes that Walter trapped, until the end of March. It seemed as if all the game, even rabbits, had died off or left the country. Neither of us had ever seen a winter wilderness so lifeless and still.

We fed the three fox carcasses to the dogs. They were starved enough to gulp them down. The beans and flour Bert Bennett had sold us were running low, and we were eating less than half of what we wanted.

Toward the first of April, we decided to start our mink and muskrat trapping, even though the lakes were still covered with three feet of ice. It wasn't so much that we wanted fur. We needed the muskrats as food for ourselves and the dogs. Things had reached a point where I hated to eat because we had almost nothing for the dogs. None of us would last much longer without meat.

We made a trip to the nearest lake where we had trapped before freeze-up. We found the shallow lake frozen solid. Not a muskrat was left. When we turned the dogs back toward camp that afternoon, Walter and I were about as worried as two people could get.

A few days after that we packed up the little food we had left. We took our tent, bedding, and traps, and went eight miles west to some bigger lakes that Walter had found earlier.

We put up the tent at the first lake. We found water under the ice, cut into muskrat houses, and caught a few muskrat. They eased the pinch of our hunger, but we were not taking enough for ourselves and the dogs.

At last Walter made the unhappy announcement that the dogs would have to be destroyed. I realized that was kinder than letting them starve. But the idea of it almost broke my heart. It had to be done, but I cried until I was sick.

Less than a week after that the weather broke in our favor. The sun came out warm and bright. The snow started to melt, and the lakes opened up around the shores. We began trapping muskrats by

---

carcass (KAHR kus) body of dead animal

Unit 4

Discussion: Ask students how they would feel if they would have to destroy their pets.

Trapper in the Wilderness, Sydney Laurence. Shelburne Museum, Shelburne, Vt.

the dozens. If the night was cold and ice formed, our luck fell off. Some days we took only five or six pelts, but one day we took 70. We were living on muskrat meat, and for the first time that winter we had enough to eat. I boiled it and gave Olive the broth in her bottle. She thrived on it.

When spring comes to the North it comes with a rush. Suddenly it is sunny day after day. The days are long and warm. But the short dark hours of the spring nights are often cold. It was hard to keep warm in our tent, even with a fire in the tiny stove. That stove was to cause the worst disaster of all.

We continued trapping while the snow melted and the creeks rose and became little rivers. Walter and I agreed that we'd stay camped at the lake until May 10. Then we'd hike back to our cabin. We'd go up the Slave to Bert Bennett's place in our rowboat, and there

---

thrive (THRYV) grow healthy and strong

Discoveries

387

catch the first steamer of the season to Forth Smith. But things don't always go as people plan them.

On the morning of May 2, I was in the tent baking bannock in the little stove-pipe oven. I stepped outside to look for Walter and saw him coming a quarter-mile up the lake. I took Olive by the hand and walked to meet him. She was toddling all over by then. When we met, I took part of his load of fresh pelts and the three of us started back.

All of a sudden we heard ammunition exploding at a terrible rate. Then smoke and flames rolled up around the tent. Walter dropped his sack of fur and ran. I grabbed Olive and hurried after him as fast as I could. When I got to the tent my husband was dragging out charred food and burning pieces of blankets. I grabbed the things as he pulled them out and doused them in the lake.

It was all over in 10 minutes. A tent burns fast.

What we had saved would have made a very small bundle. There were two or three half-burned pieces of blanket. There were the few matches in our pockets and in a waterproof container. Walter's .22 was safe. There were four shells in it, and Walter had a box in his pocket. The rest of our ammunition was gone. Most of the rat pelts had been hanging in a tree outside the tent and were safe.

Of our food, we had about four cups of flour, wet and mixed with cinders, and a pound or so of beans. For Olive, luckily, there were a few undamaged cans of milk.

With muskrat meat, that handful of supplies would have to see us through until we could reach Bennett's cabin. That meant a hard hike of 8 or 10 miles through difficult country, and then 23 miles by rowboat against the spring current of the mighty Slave. Worst of all, we knew we could not make the trip up-river until the Slave broke up. We had no idea when that would happen.

Things looked pretty grim. I was expecting a second baby in less than two months, and we knew we had a very rough time ahead. But there was no use sitting beside the ruins of our tent and worrying. The thing was to get started.

We hung our traps in trees where we would be able to find them the following fall. We ate our bannock and a good meal of muskrat we had roasted earlier, rolled Olive in the patches of bedding, and lay down under a tree to rest for a few hours. We did not dare to use a match for a fire. We had to hoard them for times of need.

When we awoke we made up our loads and were ready to start. I wrapped Olive in the blanket pieces. I'd carry her on my back. She was so thin she wasn't very heavy. I rolled one cooking pot, knives, forks, spoons, a cup, and the baby bottle in a scrap of blanket and tied it all on my back behind her. Walter's load consisted of the dry muskrat pelts,

---

bannock (BAN uk) kind of flat bread
charred (CHAHRD) partly burned
douse (DOUS) soak with water
hoard (HAWRD) store away; save

Unit 4

about 250 in all, our stove—it weighed only about 10 pounds—and three lengths of stovepipe.

We left the burned-out camp with me carrying all I could handle and Walter packing a load of about 110 pounds. Every creek was roaring full and was two or three times as wide as usual. Many times Walter had to make three trips through the swollen and icy creeks, one with his pack, one with Olive and my load, and a third to help me across.

It took two days of the hardest kind of travel to get back to our cabin. At the end of the first day we stopped and made a camp under a clump of spruces. We roasted a muskrat we had brought along. We went without breakfast and our noon meal the second day. But in the middle of the afternoon, I shot a small muskrat. It wasn't big enough to make a good meal for one hungry person, let alone three. But we stopped and cooked it on the spot and divided it up.

It was midnight when we trudged up to our cabin. We were tired, discouraged, and hungry. But at least we had a roof over our heads again and four walls to keep out the cold at night. We didn't mind too much going to bed without supper.

When daylight came, I got up and scraped each empty flour sack for the little flour that remained in it. One look at the Slave that morning confirmed our worst fears. Water was running between the ice and shore. We couldn't get out on the river. We wouldn't have dared. There was no hope of following the shore up to Bennett's place either, because of the many large creeks that flowed into the river. We had no choice but to wait for the ice to go out.

The 11 days between May 10 and the time when the ice finally went out of the Slave were a nightmare of hunger and worry—mostly hunger.

Because we were so short of matches, we kept plenty of wood on hand and fed the fire. We never let it go out.

I found a roll of wire and set snares for ducks, rabbits, muskrats—anything. In all, I snared two red squirrels and a blackbird. We pulled up dead grass along the edge of the water and ate the tender yellow shoots below. One day I saw a fool hen—a spruce grouse—perched on a low branch of a tree. I hurried to rig a snare on a pole. I reached up and dropped it over her head and jerked her to the ground. That was the best meal we had all that time. For once poor little Olive got all the broth she wanted.

Hunger cramps kept us awake at night, and when we slept we dreamed troubled dreams of food. In my own case, being seven months pregnant didn't make things any better. Right then I needed to eat for two. Each night we slept less. Each day we got weaker. The

---

confirm (kun FURM) prove true
snare (SNAIR) loop or noose for catching small animals or birds
shoot (SHOOT) first part of growing plant to appear
grouse (GROUS) kind of wild bird, a little smaller than a chicken

Discoveries

389

Discussion: Ask students to imagine how hungry they would get living on grass and bark. What is the longest time a person could live without food?

baby's whimpering for food tore us apart. Walter cursed himself over and over for bringing Olive and me down the Slave.

If we had brought a few traps back from our tent camp, we could have caught muskrats or ducks. But we'd left all the traps behind. For three days our only food was what we called spruce tea. I stripped green needles off and boiled them. We drank a few spoonfuls every couple of hours. It eased the hunger cramps and seemed to give us some strength.

Olive was no longer running around the cabin. She sat quiet and played with whatever was at hand. There was no color in her lips and cheeks. Her eyes looked hollow and dull. I can't put into words how worried and afraid Walter and I were.

We made crude hooks by bending safety pins and tried fishing in the open water along the shore of the river, using pieces of red yarn for bait. Our catch totaled one very small jackfish. I tapped a small birch tree (they were few and far between in that area) for sap. It tasted good, but we had only half a cup to divide among the three of us.

At last, at 10 o'clock on the morning of May 21, the ice in the Slave began to move. By midnight it was gone, and the water was rolling past our door. At 3:00 in the morning of the 22nd we shoved our little boat into the river and were on our way to Bennett's.

It was dangerous to try traveling so soon after the ice went out. Chunks of ice weighing many tons kept sliding off the banks and drifting down with the current, but we had no choice.

Walter rowed, and I sat in the stern and paddled and steered us away from floating ice. It was killing work. Our closest call came that first day. Rowing close to shore, we saw a huge block of ice come sliding off a pile 40 feet high. It crashed into the water almost alongside us. The force of it lifted our rowboat into the air and sent it flying. We wound up 150 feet out in the swiftest part of the current, right side up only because we had happened to be pointed in the right direction when the ice thundered down.

Walter and I drank spruce tea and gathered and ate grass roots. We also drank water often because it seemed to ease our hunger. We just kept rowing until we gave out. Then we'd rest, and then we'd row some more.

It took us six days to make the 23-mile trip up the Slave to Bert Bennett's cabin. They were as dreadful as any days I can remember. We pulled up to shore at his place at midnight on May 27—dirty, ragged, starving, and so burned by wind and sun that we hardly knew our own reflections when we looked in a mirror. In those six days we had eaten nothing but spruce tea, grass roots, and the inner bark of trees.

A Mr. and Mrs. King from Fort Smith were at Bennett's. They had come down on the ice in March. She gave us each half a biscuit and a couple of spoonfuls of stewed apricots, but the food was too much for our stomachs. We awakened three hours later with dreadful cramps and were miserably sick for the next 12

390

hours. It was four days before I was well enough to be out of bed. Mrs. King fed me a few spoonfuls of canned soup and cream every hour, and at the end of that time I felt fine. By then Walter and Olive had bounced back too.

Bennett and the Kings fixed us up with some clothing. We waited out a comfortable and happy month until the *Miss Mackenzie* came up the Slave on her first trip of the year. We boarded her near the end of June, and the trip to Fort Smith was lovely.

We sold our furs in Fort Smith. We had 560 muskrat pelts, 27 mink, three red foxes, four skunks, and a few weasels. The fox pelts brought $25 each, the mink $10. We paid off our debts and had $1,060 left in cash. We had never had money that came harder.

Our second daughter, Vala, was born on July 18. Vala was a scrawny, blue-gray baby, weighing only 3½ pounds. For three weeks my doctor did not think either she or her mother would live. But we made it, and Vala grew to be a healthy, pretty girl.

Walter went back to his trapline in the fall, but I'd had enough of the North. It's a place of great beauty, and the winter stillness is spellbinding, but it can also be terribly cruel. I knew I would never winter in a trapper's shack with my two little girls if I could help it. I stayed behind.

Reading Strategy: Ask students to list the pros and cons of a wilderness experience such as that of the author and her husband. The hardships are fairly obvious, considering the intense cold, lack of food, and lack of medical care. There are positive aspects, however: The thrill of surviving such an experience; learning first-hand about the outdoors; getting to know people like the Bennetts.

---

scrawny (SKRAW nee) thin and wiry
spellbinding (SPEL bynd ing) fascinating; very interesting

Discoveries   391

MINI QUIZ

Write on the chalkboard or overhead projector the following questions and call on students to fill in the blanks. Discuss the answers with the class.

1. The author and her husband spent the winter in _____.
2. They were there because they hoped to _____.
3. They had to kill their dogs because _____.
4. They lost many of their belongings when _____.
5. The author and her husband were not able to travel the Slave in the spring because _____.

Answers to Mini Quiz

1. the wilderness of Northern Canada
2. trap animals for fur
3. they did not have enough food for them
4. their tent caught fire
5. the river was frozen

ANSWERS TO UNDERSTAND THE SELECTION

1. far Northern Canada
2. from late August until the end of June
3. fur trapper
4. The author admits that she was worried about spending the winter in this area, despite her husband's cheerfulness.
5. finding enough to eat
6. They had only a few matches left.
7. A skunk gets into their tent and begins to eat their salt pork.
8. The author had not been able to eat enough while she was pregnant.
9. There was not enough food to feed the dogs.
10. Possible answer: The traps may have been heavy and awkward to carry.

Respond to Literature: Have students recount the major events of the story in diary form, as if they are one of the characters on the journey. Encourage them to write under each entry the discoveries that they make. For example, "May 3: could not go to Fort Smith because river was frozen. Discovered that travel in the North is restricted because of ice even in late spring."

WRITE ABOUT THE SELECTION

Prewriting: On the chalkboard or overhead transparency, make a sample outline, using students' suggestions.

Writing: As students work on this section independently, go around the room and help those who are having trouble. Some students may enjoy writing their paragraphs in the style of a handbook or guidebook for outdoor enthusiasts.

Revising: Have students work in pairs. Ask students to read each other's papers and make suggestions for revising.

Proofreading: Have students choose different partners to exchange papers for proofreading. Encourage students to use editorial proofreading symbols when correcting one another's papers.

UNDERSTAND THE SELECTION

Recall

1. Where does this story take place?
2. During what time of year does this story take place?
3. What is the occupation of the author's husband?

Infer

4. What hint is given fairly early in the story that this adventure may not turn out as well as planned?
5. What was the greatest problem that the author and her husband faced in the wilderness?
6. Why did the author and her husband never let their fire go out after their tent was destroyed?
7. What is the first thing to go wrong?

Apply

8. Why do you think the author's baby was so tiny when it was born?
9. Why did the couple kill their dogs?
10. Why do you think the couple left their traps behind when they returned to their cabin in May?

Respond to Literature

What did the author learn from her discoveries in "Starvation Wilderness"?

WRITE ABOUT THE SELECTION

One of the problems faced by the author and her husband in "Starvation Wilderness" was that they were inexperienced in dealing with such rugged country and climate. Imagine that you are planning a camping trip in the wilderness. What can you learn from the events of this story? Write a paragraph in which you discuss several things that you would do or not do on your trip, based on Olive A. Fredrickson's experiences.

Prewriting: Reread the story and make notes as you read ideas for your paragraph. Be especially aware of things that go wrong during the couple's adventure—you will want to learn from their mistakes.

Writing: Use your notes to write a paragraph about the way you would undertake a trip in the wilderness. Be sure to give reasons for your actions, based on the story.

Revising: Sometimes a paragraph reads more smoothly when ideas are expressed in a different order. Try changing the order in which you discuss your ideas and decide if this makes a better paragraph. Consider adding or subtracting sentences. You may want to substitute sentences or phrases also.

Proofreading: Check your paragraph for mistakes in spelling, usage, and mechanics. Be sure to capitalize proper nouns you may have used.

LPD Activity: Brainstorm and make lists of words that bring to mind these feelings:

1. panic
2. quiet
3. happiness

THINK ABOUT CONFLICT

The conflict in a story provides a set of problems for the main character or characters to overcome. How successfully the characters meet these problems determines the outcome of the story. Very often the conflict in a story provides suspense—you find yourself asking questions such as: "What will happen next?" or "Will this character survive?"

1. What is the conflict in "Starvation Wilderness?"

2. What was the outcome of the conflict?

3. What kinds of problems did the young couple have to overcome?

4. Do you think that some of these problems could have been avoided?

5. At what points in the story were you uncertain about the young couple's ability to survive?

DEVELOP YOUR VOCABULARY

You are probably used to looking in a dictionary to find the meanings of unfamiliar words. From the dictionary you can also learn the correct spelling and pronunciation of a word. You can learn the part of speech and origin of the word too. Some dictionaries include a phrase to show you how a word is used correctly in a sentence. Studying all the information in a dictionary entry will help you master a word, and make it a part of your working vocabulary.

Review the meanings of these words from "Starvation Wilderness" in your dictionary. Be sure to read all parts of the dictionary entry. Then use each word in an original sentence.

1. scow	6. stupor
2. presence	7. carcass
3. dwindle	8. thrive
4. douse	9. hoard
5. habitation	10. confirm

Discoveries

393

T393

SELECTION OBJECTIVES

After completing this selection, students will be able to

- understand rhyme
- identify a rhyme scheme
- identify discoveries about life
- relate a poem to one's own experience
- analyze rhyme and repetition in a poem
- use words with multiple meanings

More About Rhyme: Sometimes poems have words within the same line that rhyme. For example: "How sad and bad and mad it was!" (Browning) or "...O fleet sweet swallow" (Swinburne).

Cooperative/Collaborative Learning Activity: Divide the class into small groups. Assign each group a rhyme scheme. Then ask each group to write a single poem that uses the scheme. Students in the group can compose the entire poem together, or each member of the group can contribute one or two lines.

Two words rhyme when they have a similar sound. For example, *wait,* and *date* rhyme, as do *sell* and *bell.* Many poems include words that rhyme, especially at the ends of lines.

As you read a poem, you can often recognize a **rhyme scheme,** or pattern of similar sounds. You can describe the rhyme scheme with letters. For example:

> Jack and Jill
> Went up the hill
> To fetch a pail of water.
> Jack fell down
> And broke his crown
> And Jill came tumbling after.

In this nursery rhyme, the rhyme scheme is aa b cc d. Lines 1 and 2 rhyme; lines 4 and 5 rhyme with a different sound. Lines 3 and 6 do not rhyme with any other lines.

Rhyme can make a poem enjoyable to read. As you read the poems in this selection, ask yourself:

1. What is the rhyme scheme of each poem?
2. Which sounds are rhymed in each poem?

SKILL BUILDER

Write a simple poem that has the rhyme scheme aa b cc d.

Harriet Tubman, Series No. 10, Jacob Lawrence. Hampton University Museum

DREAMS

by Langston Hughes

Hold fast to dreams
For if dreams die
Life is a broken-winged bird
That cannot fly.

Hold fast to dreams
For when dreams go
Life is a barren field
Covered with snow.

---

barren (BAR un) bare, sterile

Discoveries   395

Sidelights: The first line of Dunbar's poem is the title of an autobiography by Maya Angelou: *I Know Why the Caged Bird Sings.* Students read a poem by Angelou in Unit 1. A biographical sketch of this author also appears in Unit 1.

Motivation for Reading: Ask students what they dream of doing or becoming in the next 10 to 20 years of their lives. Relate their responses to the poem of Langston Hughes by asking why dreams are important.

More About the Thematic Idea: The poems in this selection reflect discoveries about life. The first poem talks about the importance of having dreams; the second discusses the discovery of many different people within a single self; and the third poem describes the poet's discovery of the pain of being restricted in some way.

Enrichment: Langston Hughes, one of the foremost black poets of this century, is noted for his optimistic outlook about life and people. It is fitting that he would write about the importance of keeping dreams alive in one's life.

Dunbar, on the other hand, often wrote about the sorrows and difficulties of black people. His parents were former slaves, so he had close knowledge of the black person's plight. Certainly the poem "Sympathy" might well reflect the feelings of a black person, especially in the earlier part of this century.

Purpose-Setting Question: How can a person be three people in one?

More About Vocabulary: In addition to the words footnoted in the selection, you may wish to review with students the meanings of these words: bruised, fast (as in "hold fast"), barren, flings.

T395

UNTITLED

Anonymous

There were three girls walked down the road,
As down the road walked she:
    The girl she was,
    The girl they saw,
    The girl she wanted to be.

SYMPATHY

by Paul Laurence Dunbar

I know why the caged bird sings, ah me,
    When his wing is bruised and his bosom sore,
When he beats his bars and he would be free;
It is not a carol of joy or glee,
    But a prayer that he sends from his heart's deep core,
But a plea, that upward to heaven he flings—
I know why the caged bird sings!

---

plea (PLEE) appeal; request

396

Unit 4

T396

Paul Laurence Dunbar (1872–1906)

When Paul Laurence Dunbar graduated from high school, the best job that he could find was that of an elevator operator in a local hotel. His life took a decided turn for the better when his poetry was discovered by William Dean Howells, an outstanding American literary critic. Dunbar soon became the first black American to earn a living as an author.

Paul Laurence Dunbar was the son of former slaves. He grew up in Dayton, Ohio, where he was the only black in his high school class. Dunbar's literary ability was obvious during high school, as he wrote poetry and served as editor of the high school newspaper and yearbook. Some of Dunbar's early poems were published by the Wright Brothers (who built the first airplane) as they experimented with printing newspapers on their homemade press.

Dunbar's poetry often captured the humor and gentleness of the lives of black people in the rural South. He became most famous for his poems written in Negro dialect, although he wanted to be recognized for his poems in standard English.

Many of Dunbar's poems seem old fashioned today, partly because of their style, and partly because they reflect racial attitudes that have become outdated in late-twentieth century America. Yet some of his writings, such as the selection in this unit, have stood the test of time.

In addition to many books of poetry, Paul Laurence Dunbar also wrote short stories and novels. He died of pneumonia when he was only 34 years old, having done nearly all of his work in just ten years.

Discoveries 397

ANSWERS TO UNDERSTAND THE SELECTION

1. goals in life
2. "three" girls walking down the street
3. a bird in a cage
4. Without them, life becomes bleak and empty.
5. Life is empty and cold, with no growth.
6. No, but the poet sees three girls in the one person.
7. a person who is restricted in some way
8. flying
9. The bird might symbolize a black person who does not feel free to do as he or she wishes in life.
10. In "The Gold Medal" Amanda feels that people do not see her as she really is; by the end of the story she has a better idea of who she really is and a dream of what she hopes to become.

Respond to Literature: Encourage students to consider the different views of life represented by these three poems. The first poem is very positive, encouraging the reader to hold onto dreams. The second poem contains paradox—that is, the notion that a person is really many different persons, at least at different times and in different situations. The third poem is somewhat sad and less positive, for it deals with restrictions in life that may or may not be lifted.

WRITE ABOUT THE SELECTION

Prewriting: As students make their prewriting notes, ask for volunteers to share some of their thoughts with the class. This may help students who are having trouble identifying their responses to the poems.

Writing: As students work on this section individually, go around the classroom and help those who are having trouble. Ask students specific questions about the event or feeling they are trying to describe in order to help them clarify their ideas.

Revising: Have students work in groups of three or four. Within the group each member should read his or her paragraph aloud, then ask for comments from other group members.

Proofreading: Have a group of students form a "Spellcheck" team. Ask members of the class to submit their papers to the team, who will then look for spelling errors. Have the team members check one another's papers by using a dictionary.

LDP Activity: Ask the LDP students "We all have dreams about the future. What are yours? Have them make a list of words that describe the future they envision: family, home, occupation, hobbies, etc.

UNDERSTAND THE SELECTION

Recall

1. What is the meaning of the word "dreams" in the first poem?

2. What is the subject of "Untitled"?

3. In the poem "Sympathy," what is the poet observing?

Infer

4. Why does the author of "Dreams" feel that dreams are important?

5. What is the meaning of "Life is a barren field/Covered with snow"?

6. Are there really three girls walking down the street? Explain your answer.

7. What does the caged bird symbolize in "Sympathy"?

Apply

8. In "Sympathy," what might the caged bird rather be doing than singing?

9. Dunbar was a black man whose parents were slaves. How does this fact fit in with the meaning of his poem?

10. Can you apply the meaning of the untitled poem to any of the stories or plays you have read in this unit?

Respond to Literature

What discoveries about life are reflected in these three poems?

WRITE ABOUT THE SELECTION

Each of the three poems in this selection expresses something that the poet has learned about life. Which poem do you agree with most or feel about most strongly? Which poem expresses something that you have also discovered? Write a paragraph in which you relate the theme of one of the poems to your own life experience.

Cluster all the details and feeling you have that relate to the poem that you chose. Write down everything that comes to mind. You can decide what to use later.

Prewriting: Read each of the poems several times. As you read, ask yourself, "Have I ever felt this way? When?" Jot down your ideas on a piece of paper. Decide which poem you will use as the subject of your paragraph.

Writing: Use the ideas from your notes to write your response to one of the poems. Try to include specific events or examples from your life that relate to the poem you have chosen.

Revising: Add vivid words to make your ideas come alive. Substitute specific verbs for ordinary ones. For example, "My mind raced," is more exciting that "I thought."

Proofreading: Make sure that all the words you have used are spelled correctly. Look up in the dictionary any words that you are unsure of, and correct the spelling if necessary.

THINK ABOUT RHYME

The **rhyme scheme** is the pattern of similar sounds in a poem. Usually words rhyme at the ends of lines, although sometimes words rhyme within lines. Rhyme makes a poem pleasing to read.

Another technique that adds to the enjoyment and meaning of a poem is **repetition**. A poet will often repeat certain words or sounds in order to create an effect.

1. Give the rhyme scheme in "Dreams"?

2. What phrase is repeated in the poem? Why do you think it is repeated?

3. What is the rhyme scheme in the untitled poem?

4. What words are repeated in this poem? What effect do they create?

5. What is the rhyme scheme in "Sympathy"?

DEVELOP YOUR VOCABULARY

Many words in English have more than one meaning. For example, the word *bore* can mean to make a hole in something, or it can mean something or someone who is boring. When you read a word such as *bore*, you can often tell from the context what the word means. If you are uncertain of the meaning of a word with multiple meanings, you should look up the word in the dictionary.

Study these words from this selection. Tell which meaning of each word is used in the poems. Then write an original sentence to show how to use *each* meaning of each word.

1. dreams
2. fast
3. fly
4. field
5. core
6. saw
7. beats
8. free
9. wing
10. fling

Discoveries

399

Note: The TRB contains worksheets to accompany both writing assignments.

Motivation 1: On slips of paper, write the name of each selection in this unit. Put the slips of paper in a hat or basket. Have a volunteer pick a slip at random and read the name of the selection. Challenge students to write down in three minutes as many aspects of discovery in the selection as they can remember. After several selections have been chosen, have various students share their notes with the class.

Cooperative/Collaborative Learning Activity:

Writing: Have students who have chosen the same selection get together in a group. Ask each group to work together to write a paper that reflects the feelings of all group members about the selection. If students in the group have differing or contrasting viewpoints, this should be brought out in the writing. Have each group select one of its members to read its paper to the class.

Motivation 2: Make a chart to review the four elements of nonfiction: plot, point of view, tone, theme. Under each heading have students add notes that review what they have learned. For example, under "Plot" students might add, "events in a story; makes reader wonder what will happen next; may use flashback; includes conflict."

Cooperative/Collaborative Learning

Prewriting: Have students work in pairs to create their charts. Students should pair with others who have chosen the same selections, then make one chart between them.

T400

UNIT 4 REVIEW

LITERATURE-BASED WRITING

1. All of the characters in this unit have made discoveries. They have made discoveries about themselves, others, the world around them, and life. As you have read their stories, you have made discoveries also. Perhaps you discovered something about a real person, place, or event. Perhaps you discovered a new way of looking at an issue based on the message of a selection. Choose four selections from this unit and tell what you have discovered as a result of reading them.

Prewriting: Before you begin to write, decide which four of the selections had the greatest impact on you. Think for a few moments about each one and ask yourself, "What did I discover as a result of reading this selection? What new ideas, thoughts, and feelings do I have now that I did not have before?"

Writing: Use the notes from your prewriting to write about the discoveries you have made. Include how you think these discoveries will make a difference in your life.

Revising: Read your paper to make sure that it is well-organized. Does each paragraph contain one main idea? Does each paragraph have a clear topic sentence? Add or remove details to make the paragraph better organized.

Proofreading: Correct any mistakes in spelling, usage, and mechanics.

2. In this unit you have studied the elements of nonfiction in two of the selections. Now you can use these elements to analyze those selections.

First, decide which selection you feel about most strongly, either in a positive or negative way. Then compare and contrast it with the other two selections in terms of plot and story development, point of view, tone, and theme.

Prewriting: Review briefly the work that you did for the "Think About . . ." for the nonfiction sections. Then make a chart in which you write the names of the two selections across the top. List the four literary elements down the side of the chart. Fill in your chart with details about each element from the selections.

Writing: Use your chart to write a comparison of the two selections. If you feel that one selection used a particular element more effectively than the other, say so— but be sure to back up your opinion with evidence from the selection.

Revising: Add to your paper any transitional phrases that will make your ideas flow more smoothly. Examples of transitional phrases include: *first, most important, finally, next.*

Proofreading: Correct any mistakes in spelling, usage, and mechanics. Use quotation marks around titles of short selections.

BUILDING LANGUAGE SKILLS

Vocabulary

An excellent way to find the meaning of a word you do not know is to use context clues. Context clues help you figure out what a word means by the way it is used in a sentence.

Example: "I'm not an Example!" grumbled Amanda *rebelliously.* "I'm me!"

If you did not know the meaning of the word rebelliously, you could guess the meaning by the context clues. You know that Amanda is unhappy, and that she disagrees with her mother. You also can see that rebelliously must go with the word *grumbled.* Therefore, you could recognize that rebelliously means resisting authority or control.

Use context clues to determine the meaning of each *italicized* word. Then write out the italicized word with its meaning.

1. A rabbit hopped out from under the berry bush. He *nuzzled* the berry I'd spat out and ate it.

2. Why did they have to see me like this? Why did I have to look at Mom's eyes when she faced the most terrible *ordeal* of her life?

3. Across the river there was a little cabin with smoke curling out of the chimney. I can't remember that I was ever gladder to see a human *habitation.*

4. Mrs. Jones stopped, jerked him around in front of her, put a *half nelson* about his neck, and continued to drag him up the street.

Discoveries

Usage and Mechanics

When you write a sentence, it is important that the subject and the verb agree. The basic rule for subject-verb agreement is:

A **singular subject** must use a **singular verb.**
Chee *guesses* that his in-laws have become poor.

A **plural subject** must use a **plural verb.**
Chee's in-laws *guess* that Chee wants his daughter back.

The subject of a sentence is usually a noun or a pronoun. Pronouns can cause problems when they function as subjects of sentences. The pronouns *he, she,* and *it* always use a singular verb. *We* and *they* always use a plural verb. The pronoun *I* usually uses a plural verb:

I go to school.
not
I goes to school.

The pronoun *you* always uses a plural verb.

Correct any errors in subject-verb agreement in the following sentences. (Not all of the sentences have errors.)

1. You takes the food I brought.

2. The old man gives Amanda the gold medal.

3. The old man and Amanda talks to each other.

4. "This is private property—I has my rights!"

5. My grandfather look at me strangely.

401

Usage and Mechanics

Review with students the subject/verb agreement for forms of the verb *to be.* Write these sentences on the chalkboard:

1. I will be home early. Dad will be home after six.
2. Hal was late for school. You were also late.
3. I am five feet, four inches tall. You are shorter than I. Jim is taller than I.

Point out that the future tense is the same for all subjects: I will, you will, he will, we will, you will, they will. In the past tense the first and third person use *was* (I was, he was); the second person and all plural forms use *were* (you were, we were, they were). In the present tense *I* is paired with am (I am); *are* is used with singular and plural forms of *you,* as well as with the plural first person and the plural third person (you are, we are, they are); and singular third-person subjects use *is* (he is).

Cooperative Learning Activity: Have students work with a partner or in small groups to write sentences that have errors in subject-verb agreement. Encourage students to use pronouns as well as nouns as subjects. Have each group trade sentences with another group to make corrections. Then return the papers to the original group to check.

BUILDING LANGUAGE SKILLS

Vocabulary

More About Word Attack: Point out that sometimes a context clue is in the form of an in-text definition, that is, the word actually is defined in the story, if one reads carefully. Write this example from "The Gold Medal" on the chalkboard:

Up and over a gentle slope where a giant *cottonwood* offered an oasis of cool green shade she flew. Too late Amanda saw the high heap of overturned earth below the tree.
Guide students to realize that the words "cool green shade" and "tree" provide a definition of "cottonwood" as a shade tree.

Cooperative Learning Activity: Have students work in small groups to determine the answers to the three questions in the text. Then ask each group to write a similar, original question of their own. Have groups trade questions to answer with each other.

T401

SPEAKING AND LISTENING

When you make a speech about literature in your English class, you usually have some kind of script to follow. You decide what topic or selection you are going to discuss and then you follow certain guidelines to help in the discussion. Sometimes it's fun to build a lesson around a more spontaneous idea. Speaking extemporaneously doesn't mean there is no preparation. It does mean, however, that you don't have to write anything out and you don't have to memorize. It is an example of impromptu speaking.

Although this type of speaking may be new to you, you will have a bit of fun in this lesson. Read the following strategy so you'll be a well-informed participant.

1. Think about all the various selections in this unit. Focus on the characters or people to whom you've been introduced. Along with others in your class, name as many as you can. If necessary, glance back at the selections.

2. Now, choose two people or characters that have been mentioned. Go back to the selections where they can be found. Read sections of the selection that describe or give information about the character. Become familiar with things the characters say, do, feel, and how they look and act. Think of adjectives to describe the characters.

3. Finally, imagine each character as an animal. What animal would they be? To help you decide, go back to the ideas you came up with in step two. Compare the characters traits to those of an animal. Decide what animal, in your opinion, is most like that character.

That's basically it! The next part is the most fun and really the easiest. As a class, or in small groups, take turns speaking extemporaneously about "Characters or People as Animals." Limit your speaking time to a minute or less so that everyone has a chance to speak. In your talk tell about the character traits, the animal you've compared him to, and why you feel it is an appropriate comparison. Other students may talk about the same person or character; if so, don't worry. It will be fun to hear another classmate's interpretation.

CRITICAL THINKING

When reading nonfiction, it is important to be able to tell the difference between fact and opinion. A **fact** is something that can be proven or verified. For example, it is a fact that Kaw Indians go through the Ta-Na-E-Ka ritual at age 11.

An **opinion,** on the other hand, cannot be proven. An opinion is what a person thinks or believes about something. Opinions are usually based on a combination of emotions and facts. An example of an opinion is: The Ta-Na-E-Ka is not very important.

In a true story, facts include such information as time, place, details of events, general data about characters, and so on. Opinions tend to be expressed by the characters in the story or by the author's comments about the events and characters. Opinions may also be suggested by the theme or message of the story. Choose one nonfiction selection from the unit and answer the following questions.

1. What seems to be the author's opinion about the events of the story and the outcome of the story? How can you tell? Do any characters in the story voice opinions that differ from the author's opinion?

2. If you were writing a newspaper report of the events of this story, what facts would you include? How would the story in a newspaper differ from the same story written as a piece of literature?

EFFECTIVE STUDYING

An important skill that will help you do better in school is note taking. Note taking in class is important because you need to remember the information and explanations that the teacher gives. To take notes in class, use a spiral or loose-leaf notebook with enough blank pages to ensure that you will not run out of paper in the middle of class. Use the same notebook every day, so that your notes for that subject will be all together and in the right order.

As you take notes in class, try to write an outline of the lesson. Some teachers write an outline on the board; this is very helpful. Even if there is no written outline, you can tell how a teacher has organized the lesson if you listen carefully.

Sometimes as you are taking notes, the teacher will say something that you do not understand or cannot hear clearly. Write down what you hear as best as you can. Then circle what you wrote. After class or during a time when you can ask questions, ask the teacher to explain it to you.

Many students find it helpful to copy over the notes that they take in class. You can do this each night or before a test.

Discoveries

403

T403

UNIT 5: Heroes

UNIT ACTIVITY

A Continuing Unit Project: Writing Biographies

The selections in this unit are about heroes. Some of the heroes are real people; many are imaginary. Some of the heroes would be famous in the time and place in which they lived; others would be heroes only to a few people close to them. Some of the heroes might be remembered in history; others might be forgotten. Yet all these heroes have something in common—a particular quality that sets them a little bit apart from other people, that makes their lives significant in some way.

In this activity, students will write biographical sketches of the heroes they read about. For actual people, students will research the person's life and present a factual biography. For imaginary characters, students will use information contained in the selections, plus any additional details they wish to create. The only restriction is that the imagined information cannot contradict the information or inferences provided in the text.

Discuss with students some of the necessary elements in a good biography. One thing that should be clear in a biography is why the person is important enough to write about. A biography should also do more than just list the events and facts of a person's life; it should give a good impression of the person's character and personality.

Students may find it helpful to study the writers' biographies in this text as a guide to writing biographical sketches. Point out that these biographies focus on each person's contribution as a writer, while the students' biographies will focus on each character as a hero.

Have students write a biography after reading each selection in the unit. Some general questions that will help them get started include:

Who is the hero in this selection?
What makes this person special?
What facts do you know about this person's life?

What do you know about this person's character and personality?
What do you know about this person's appearance?
About how old is the hero in the selection?

If students need additional guidance, pose questions such as the following for each selection.

"Amigo Brothers"
How might Felix or Antonio be a role model for other kids growing up on the Lower East Side of New York City?

"On the Ledge"
Which person would you rather write about, Sergeant Gray or Walter?

"Terror in the North"
Would other teenagers be interested in reading your biography of Stina?

"The Secret Life of Walter Mitty"
How might you write a biography of someone who is really an antihero?

"I Have a Dream"
What additional facts would you like to know about Martin Luther King, Jr.?

"Four Native American Poems"
How might one of these soldiers be written about in a Native American history book?

"Ulysses and the Trojan Horse/Ulysses Meets the Cyclops"
What does this selection tell you about Ulysses's personality?

When students have completed all their biographies for the unit, select several from each selection to be read aloud. Discuss with the class the different interpretations that may have been given to the lives of various heroes.

"Amigo Brothers"
by Piri Thomas   (page 409)

SELECTION SYNOPSIS

Antonio Cruz and Felix Varga, best friends who have grown up together on New York's Lower East Side, are pitted against each other in a boxing match to determine who will represent their Boys Club in a championship tournament. The boys realize that the competition is putting a strain on their friendship, yet each is determined to fight as hard as possible to become the winner. Although they promise each other they will come out of the fight able to pick up their friendship where they left off, both have misgivings. While they are in training, Felix moves to stay with his aunt in the Bronx, and the boys agree not to see each other until the day of the fight.

During the fight, the two compete so savagely that the referee and trainers must pull them apart. Yet at the end of the fight, the boys leave the ring arm in arm—before the winner is announced. The reader is left to decide who became the champion.

SELECTION ACTIVITY

Have students use books and magazines about sports, as well as almanacs and other reference sources to learn about the sport of boxing. Have students work in pairs or groups to find the answers to one or more of the following questions:

1. What are the rules and regulations that govern a boxing match?
2. What are the different weight classifications?
3. Who are some famous boxing champions? Do any have backgrounds similar to Felix and Antonio?
4. What is the history of boxing?
5. Who are the current boxing champions of the world?
6. How much money do professional boxers make?
7. How does a boxer train for a fight?

"On the Ledge"
by Thompson Clayton   (page 425)

SELECTION SYNOPSIS

When the story opens, young Walter Whitfield is on the ledge of a building six stories up. As the story progresses, Sergeant Gray of the police department is able to reach Walter, both figuratively and physically. First, however, Gray must overcome his own fear of heights before he can attempt to rescue the young man. In the end, the story takes a surprising twist, and Walter ends up saving Gray from a serious slip on the ledge. Ultimately, the two make their way back to safety inside the building.

SELECTION ACTIVITY

A growing problem in the United States today is teenagers committing suicide. Have students work in groups or pairs to learn more about this problem and what is being done to remedy it. Some sources of information that students can tap include newspaper and magazine articles, recently published books on the topic, stories of famous people who attempted suicide when young (for example, the actress Rita Moreno), local mental health centers, teen-help lines, halfway houses and drug rehabilitation centers for teenagers; mental health centers at colleges and universities, doctors in private practice, and hospital mental health outpatient services.

"Terror in the North"
by Eloise Engle   (page 433)

SELECTION SYNOPSIS

Stina, a teenaged girl from Seattle, Washington, goes to Seward, Alaska, to live with her aunt and uncle after her mother dies. At the beginning of the story, Stina feels that she can never measure up to the rugged, "gutsy" Alaskans. She believes she is a coward and not an Alaskan in any sense of the word. Because of this, she declines to participate in a clean-up campaign to ready the town of Seward to receive the All-American Cities Award. Instead, she goes to the home of the Stetson family to baby-sit for their three-month-old son.

The story combines fact with fiction by introducing events related to the severe earthquake that actually occurred in the area on March 27, 1964. A young Alaskan, Dan Darby, happens to drop by to see Stina at the Stetson home. Shortly thereafter, an earthquake and tidal wave force them to flee from the house. When faced with this natural disaster, Stina proves her heroism and bravery by returning to the house to rescue the infant at the risk of her own life. As the three of them—Dan, Stina, and the baby—

are about to be rescued, Stina feels ready at last to call herself an Alaskan.

SELECTION ACTIVITY

Although earthquakes cannot be prevented, scientists are attempting to predict them far enough in advance so that people can be evacuated. Scientists are also hoping that major quakes can be predicted years in advance so that the growth of cities can be planned around these potential disasters.

Have students find out what progress is being made in this rather new field of study. One place where a great deal of attention is being given to earthquake prediction is Tokyo, Japan. Many newspaper articles have been written about the Earthquake Prediction Center in Tokyo. A considerable amount of research is also being carried out in the United States.

"The Secret Life of Walter Mitty"
by James Thurber   (page 443)

SELECTION SYNOPSIS

Walter Mitty is a timid, henpecked man who leads a boring and frustrated life. In his imagination, however, he is a hero. In this humorous selection, James Thurber has Mitty move in and out of fantasy as he goes through a typical day. In his daydreams, Mitty sees himself as a famous surgeon, the pilot of a hydroplane, and the defendent in a murder trial. The story ends with the ultimate fantasy: Mitty sees himself fearlessly facing a firing squad.

SELECTION ACTIVITY

Have students research the life and work of James Thurber (1894–1961). Thurber is well-known as an essayist, humorist, artist, and short-story writer. He began his career as a journalist with *The New Yorker* magazine in 1927. Thurber did much to establish the tone and style of this popular magazine. One of Thurber's more famous stories is "The Secret Life of Walter Mitty," which was later made into a movie.

"I Have a Dream"
by Martin Luther King, Jr.   (page 453)

SELECTION SYNOPSIS

This selection is an excerpt from Martin Luther King, Jr.'s best-known speech. It was given on a hot August afternoon in Washington, D.C. in 1963, on the steps of the Lincoln Memorial.

SELECTION ACTIVITY

Much has happened in the Civil Rights movement since Martin Luther King, Jr., made his famous speech in 1963. Among the more significant developments was the passage of important civil rights legislation during the Johnson Administration.

Have students find out how laws governing civil rights have changed over the last 25 years. Encourage them to find out in particular which laws may have been changed in their own state during this period of time. Also have students find out how certain laws (or lack of them) may differ from one state to another.

"Native American Poems"
by Teton Sioux and Omaha Indians   (page 459)

These short poems are by Teton Sioux and Omaha Indians. They poignantly describe the bravery and heroism of men who must face failure, defeat, and death.

SELECTION ACTIVITY

Although the four Native American poems are very short, they paint rather vivid pictures with words. Challenge students to create drawings to illustrate each poem. The drawings can be in the style of Native American art, or they can be in the students' own style. Display the finished drawings around the classroom, along with copies of the poems illustrated.

"Ulysses and the Trojan Horse"
by Homer   (page 465)

"Ulysses Meets the Cyclops"
by Homer   (page 474)

In this version of the well-known classical tale of the Greeks' trickery in building the Trojan horse, great detail and drama are used to engage the students' interest.

After ten years of struggle, the Trojans assume that the

Greks have given up the battle and sailed away. They view the horse they find among the reeds by the shore as a peace offering to Athena and bring it into the city—in spite of Laocoon's warning—to ensure their prosperity. Shortly, they are overcome by the Greek soldiers hidden inside.

In contrast to the story of the Trojan horse, the story of Ulysses and the Cyclops is told in the first-person. The story opens with the curious Ulysses on the island of the Cyclops. Against the advice of his soldiers, Ulysses enters the giant's cave. He and his men are sealed in, and two of the men are eaten by the giant. Ulysses, however, manages to get the Cyclops drunk and then wounds him in the eye. The crafty Ulysses then manages to get himself and his remaining men out of the cave, camouflaged as sheep. Ulysses does, however, live to regret the fact that his curiosity about the Cyclops resulted in the loss of his friends.

SELECTION ACTIVITY

Ask students to imagine that upon his arrival back in Greece, Ulysses is greeted by a team of *Eye-Witness News* reporters. What kind of interview might Ulysses give to the media, to be broadcast on the Ancient Greek Nightly News?

Have students work in pairs or small groups to stage interviews with the hero Ulysses. To gain additional information about Ulysses, students may wish to consult Homer's poems (or a synopsis of the poems), the *Odyssey* and the *Illiad*.

STUDENT READING LIST

Forbes, Esther. *Johnny Tremain*. Boston: Houghton Mifflin, 1941.

Rowe, Jeanne A. *An Album of Martin Luther King, Jr.* New York: Franklin Watts, 1970.

Walter, Mildred Pitts. *The Girl on the Outside*. New York: Lothrop, 1982.

Sperry, Armstrong. *Call It Courage*. New York: Macmillan, 1940. Paper, Collier.

Steinbeck, John. *The Red Pony*. New York: Viking, 1937.

From Globe Classroom Libraries

The Black Experience
  Black Boy by Richard Wright

OVERVIEW OF THE UNIT

The theme of this unit is heroes: likely heroes and unlikely heroes, real heroes and imaginary heroes.

In the first selection, "Amigo Brothers," two boys struggle with the difference between a public and a private hero.
Literary Skill: plot elements
Vocabulary: Spanish words
Writing: story extension

"On the Ledge" is the annotated selection. The story has two heroes, one of whom is very unlikely.
Literary Skill: elements of the short story
Vocabulary: parts of speech
Writing: character development

In the third selection, "Terror in the North," a girl surprises herself and others during an earthquake.
Literary Skill: foreshadowing
Vocabulary: synonyms
Writing: human interest stories

The fourth selection, "The Secret Life of Walter Mitty," tells the rather sad but humorous story of a man who is a hero only in his own imagination.
Literary Skill: story techniques
Vocabulary: figurative phrases
Writing: personal fantasies

The fifth selection introduces students to a real, twentieth century hero. "I Have a Dream" is an excerpt from the famous speech made by slain civil rights leader Dr. Martin Luther King, Jr.
Literary Skill: persuasive speech
Vocabulary: multiple meaning words
Writing: one's own ideas

The next selection, "Concord Hymn," depicts heroes of the early United States.
Literary Skill: lyric poetry
Vocabulary: using context clues
Writing: personal responses

The seventh selection is a group of poems that describe heroic efforts which did not always succeed.
Literary Skill: open and closed poetic form
Vocabulary: using homophones
Writing: personal experience

The next selection consists of two tales about a legendary Greek hero: "Ulysses and the Trojan Horse" and "Ulysses Meets the Cyclops."
Literary Skill: epic poetry
Vocabulary: using nouns and verbs
Writing: creating a monster story

In the last selection two feminine poets view masculine heroes.

Literary Skill: symbolism and allusion
Vocabulary: using contractions
Writing: ideas about women

UNIT OBJECTIVES

After completing this unit, students should be able to
- understand more elements of the short story: point of view, tone, symbolism, and writing techniques
- conduct an imaginary interview
- distinguish between valid and invalid inferences
- use an effective strategy for taking objective tests
- build on knowledge of literary elements in order to write both creatively and analytically
- use root words to figure out word meanings
- use new words in sentences.

Heroes

The hero can be Poet, Prophet, King, Priest or what you will, according to the kind of world he finds himself born into.

—Thomas Carlyle

Aspects of Negro Life: An Idyll of the Deep South,
Aaron Douglas.
The Schomberg Center/New York Public Library

405

Fine Arts Note

Aaron Douglas was among the artists who took part in the first Artists' Congress of New York in February 1936. This was an event in which artists united to fight against the effects of the Depression and the oppression of such dictators as Hitler. The artists produced what can be called "social art"—art done for the sake of a social cause, such as fair treatment of minorities. Out of Congress came Federal Art Projects that finally gave a voice to black American artists.

Teaching Strategy: Arrange a display of books, magazines and newspaper articles which describe various types of heroes. Include both historical and contemporary heroes who represent many walks of life: astronauts, famous scientists and explorers, political figures, sports stars, media personalities, and local heroes. Also, include some human interest stories that describe an ordinary person in a heroic action—such as rescuing a person from a burning building. After students have viewed the display, ask them which, if any, are heroes to them. Point out that their responses are based in part on their own ideas about what constitutes a hero.

AUDIOVISUAL MATERIALS

What Is a Hero? (BFA Films/Video, Inc). Shows how heroes provide inspiration and guidance for young people. 14 min, 16mm film or videocassette.

The Short Story (Guidance Association). Explains the key elements of the short story and the different techniques and objectives of various short story writers. Videocassette.

Assignments in Composition (Spectrum Educational Media, Inc.). Filmstrip or videocassette that teaches students how to write a paper using persuasive speech.

Van Wyck Brooks (Ebra Films). Discusses the elements that create great literature. 30 mins; black and white; film.

Robert Burns: Love and Liberty (Films for the Humanities). Readings from Burns's greatest lyrics. 38 mins; color; 1985; videocassette.

Margaret Atwood—An Interview (Vancouver Women In Focus) videocassette.

Contemporary Women Poets (PBS), videocassette.

Discussion: Guide students through the opening **Heroes** section of the theme discussion. Then pause to have students view the display material that you set up for the Teaching Strategy. Ask them to write down the names of three people whom they consider heroes: The names may or may not be people represented in the display. Have students put their lists aside for the time being.

Return again to the theme discussion. As you read through the rest of the material, discuss with the class each question that is raised. When you are finished, have students look again at the names of their three heroes. Ask, "How does the material that we have just read pertain to your three heroes?" Call for voluteers to relate their choices to the concepts of heroism as set forth in the theme discussion.

Cooperative/Collaborative Learning Activity. Divide the class into small groups. Challenge each group to conduct a survey in which they find out who people's heroes are. Encourage each group to survey a different population. For example, one group might survey students in their own grade, a second group might survey students in another grade, and a third might choose to survey senior citizens. Other populations that might be polled include children in elementary school and people chosen at random at a shopping mall or street corner. Have each group report their findings to the class.

Heroes.   Who are your heroes?

Do you look up to the famous athletes Florence Griffith Joyner and Michael Jordan? Is your idea of a hero an astronaut or a rock star? Perhaps you most admire someone in your own school or neighborhood who has done something courageous, such as stand up for a cause that was not very popular.

The dictionary defines a hero as someone known for great strength, courage, and daring. A hero can also be a person honored for special achievements and attributes. As Thomas Carlyle points out, heroes are shaped, in part, by the times and the circumstances in which they find themselves. For example, Martin Luther King, Jr. became a hero in a world that was ready to hear his message about civil rights. However, in the end, could it have been personal courage in the face of hostility that actually shaped the circumstances—and the times? The true nature of heroism, whether it be found in King or lesser known individuals, always has aroused great interest—even debate—among people everywhere.

The selections in this unit focus on heroes. You will meet likely heroes and unlikely heroes, real heroes and imaginary heroes.

Likely Heroes. Sometimes literature presents a situation in which a person has to choose between being a public hero and a private hero. This is the kind of situation in which two Puerto Rican boys find themselves in the short story "Amigo Brothers." In order to win a championship boxing match, each boy must beat his best friend. What would you do in a situation like this? Would you go ahead with the fight, even though it may cost you your friendship? The two boys do go ahead with the fight. Although the story ends with only one champion, both boys become heroes.

Unlikely Heroes.   There are certain actions that make a person a hero in any time and any place. One is risking one's life for another. In the short

story "Terror in the North," a high school girl who was known for being less than courageous finds the strength to rescue a baby boy during an earthquake. In the story "On the Ledge," a police officer risks his life to help a young man who is about to commit suicide. This story has a surprise ending as the police officer finds himself in need of a rescue—and a very unlikely hero emerges.

Have you ever been a hero in your own imagination? Have you ever sat and daydreamed about doing something daring or courageous? In his short story "The Secret Life of Walter Mitty," James Thurber paints a humorous and somewhat sad picture of a man whose only claim to fame is his own fantasies.

Real Heroes. "I Have a Dream" is a famous speech by Martin Luther King, Jr. King was a special kind of hero who is often referred to as a martyr. King was assassinated because of his passionate devotion to the cause of racial equality. Is there a cause that you believe in so deeply that you would rather die than give it up?

Mythical Heroes. In literature, as in life, many people become heroes during war. One of the most famous heroes in literature is a mythological figure named Ulysses, whom the poet Homer created as a great warrior in ancient Greece. You will read about two of the hero's adventures in "Ulysses and the Trojan Horse" and "Ulysses Meets the Cyclops." As you read the stories, you will discover that Ulysses's success in battle came not just from physical strength, but also from a very clever imagination. You may even discover similarities between Ulysses and personal heroes.

Who your heroes are tells a lot about you—the person you are and the person you hope to become. Perhaps you will find a hero of your own in these pages. As you read each selection, you might ask yourself, What is a hero? What do my heroes have in common with the hero in this selection?

Heroes
407

LEARN ABOUT

Plot Elements

Early in a story, an important plot problem is introduced. This is the first of a series of problems the character must solve. In a good story each problem is more interesting than the one before it. This is called **rising action.** The rising action in a story eventually leads to a climax. The **climax** is the most exciting part of the story.

Some short stories end with the climax, but most do not. These stories continue beyond the climax with a section called the **resolution.** The resolution answers any remaining questions that the reader might have and gives the story a sense of completion.

As you read "Amigo Brothers," ask yourself:
1. What is the climax of the story?
2. What plot question remains unanswered?

SKILL BUILDER

Think of a recent situation in your own life that could be the basis of a short story. List the events of the plot, then indicate which of these events would be the climax of the story. Write a few sentences to describe what you might add to the story as a resolution.

AMIGO BROTHERS

by Piri Thomas

Antonio Cruz and Felix Varga were both seventeen years old. They were so together in friendship that they felt themselves to be brothers. They had known each other since childhood, growing up on the lower east side of Manhattan in the same tenement building on Fifth Street between Avenue A and Avenue B.

Antonio was fair, lean, and lanky, while Felix was dark, short, and husky. Antonio's hair was always falling over his eyes, while Felix wore his black hair in a natural Afro style.

Each youngster had a dream of someday becoming lightweight champion of the world. Every chance they had the boys worked out, sometimes at the Boys Club on 10th Street and Avenue A and sometimes at the pro's gym on 14th Street. Early morning sunrises would find them running along the East River Drive, wrapped in sweat shirts, short towels around their necks, and handkerchiefs Apache style around their foreheads.

While some youngsters were into street negatives, Antonio and Felix slept, ate, rapped, and dreamt positive. Between them, they had a collection of *Fight* magazines second to none, plus a scrapbook filled with torn tickets to every boxing match they had ever attended, and some clippings of their own. If asked a question about any given fighter, they would immediately zip out from their memory banks divisions, weights, records of fights, knockouts, technical knockouts, and draws or losses.

Each had fought many bouts representing their community and had won two gold-plated medals plus a silver and bronze medallion. The difference was in their style: Antonio's lean form and long reach made him the better boxer, while

---

amigo (uh MEE goh) A Spanish word meaning *friend*. Other Spanish words in the story add flavor to the text but will not be defined.
tenement (TEN uh munt) low-grade housing
Apache (uh PACH ee) Native American group of the southwest
negative (NEG uh tiv) bad habit or behavior
bout (BOUT) fight
medallion (muh DAL yun) large medal

Heroes   409

Sidelights Piri Thomas knows what he is talking about when he refers to "street negatives." Thomas grew up in New York City and spent seven years in jail; it was in prison that he began to write. After his release, Thomas began to help young people who seemed likely to get into trouble. The story "Amigo Brothers" describes the kind of alternative that Thomas might recommend.

Motivation for Reading Ask students to consider this question: If you had to choose between achieving an important goal and losing your best friend, what would you do? Relate students' answers to the dilemma faced by the boys in "Amigo Brothers."

More About the Thematic Idea: In this selection the conflict that exists between being a public hero and a private hero is explored. The plot is set in motion as two best friends discover that they must fight against each other in a championship bout.

Purpose-Setting Question: Why would someone agree to fight against his best friend?

Critical Thinking: Ask students, "What does the author mean when he says that the two boys 'slept, ate, rapped and dreamt positive'?" (Their thoughts and actions were focused on achieving the positive goal of becoming boxing champions, as opposed to thinking about negative activities, such as crime or drugs.)

LDP Activity: Discuss in pairs or with the class the plot of the story.

Vocabulary: Preteach the vocabulary words. See the Comprehension Workbook in the TRB.

More About Vocabulary: Many of the words used in this story are Spanish words. If you have Spanish-speaking students in the class, you may wish to have them define some of these words for the rest of the students.

Felix's short and muscular frame made him the better slugger. Whenever they had met in the ring for sparring sessions, it had always been hot and heavy.

Now, after a series of elimination bouts, they had been informed that they were to meet each other in the division finals that were scheduled for the seventh of August, two weeks away—the winner to represent the Boys Club in the Golden Gloves Championship Tournament.

The two boys continued to run together along the East River Drive. But even when joking with each other, they both sensed a wall rising between them.

One morning less than a week before their bout, they met as usual for their daily workout. They fooled around with a few jabs at the air, slapped skin, and then took off, running lightly along the dirty East River's edge.

Antonio glanced at Felix who kept his eyes purposely straight ahead, pausing from time to time to do some fancy leg work while throwing one-twos followed by upper cuts to an imaginary jaw. Antonio then beat the air with a barrage of body blows and short devastating lefts with an overhand jaw-breaking right.

After a mile or so, Felix puffed and said, "Let's stop a while, bro. I think we both got something to say to each other."

Antonio nodded. It was not natural to be acting as though nothing unusual was happening when two ace-boon buddies were going to be blasting . . . each other within a few short days.

They rested their elbows on the railing separating them from the river. Antonio wiped his face with his short towel. The sunrise was now creating day.

Felix leaned heavily on the river's railing and stared across to the shores of Brooklyn. Finally, he broke the silence.

"Gee . . . man. I don't know how to come out with it."

Antonio helped. "It's about our fight, right?"

"Yeah, right." Felix's eyes squinted at the rising orange sun.

"I've been thinking about it too, *panin.* In fact, since we found out it was going to be me and you, I've been awake at night, pulling punches on you, trying not to hurt you."

"Same here. It ain't natural not to think about the fight. I mean, we both are *cheverote* fighters and we both want to win. But only one of us can win. There ain't no draws in the eliminations."

Felix tapped Antonio gently on the shoulder. "I don't mean to sound like I'm bragging, bro. But I wanna win, fair and square."

Antonio nodded quietly. "Yeah. We both know that in the ring the better man wins. Friend or no friend, brother or no . . ."

Felix finished it for him. "Brother. Tony, let's promise something right here.

---

sparring (SPAHR ing) practice boxing with another
elimination (ih lim uh NAY shun) in a tournament, dropped after one
   loss
barrage (buh RAHJ) huge number, as of bombs or blows
devastating (DEV uh stayt ing) carrying destruction

410

Okay?''

"If it's fair, *hermano*, I'm for it.'' Antonio admired the courage of a tug boat pulling a barge five times its welterweight size.

"It's fair, Tony. When we get into the ring, it's gotta be like we never met. We gotta be like two heavy strangers that want the same thing and only one can have it. You understand, don'tcha?''

"*Si*, I know.'' Tony smiled. "No pulling punches. We go all the way.''

"Yeah, that's right. Listen, Tony. Don't you think it's a good idea if we don't see each other until the day of the fight? I'm going to stay with my Aunt Lucy in the Bronx. I can use Gleason's Gym for working out. My manager says he got some sparring partners with more or less your style.''

Tony scratched his nose pensively. "Yeah, it would be better for our heads.'' He held out his hand, palm upward. "Deal?''

"Deal.'' Felix lightly slapped open skin.

"Ready for some more running?'' Tony asked lamely.

"Naw, bro. Let's cut it here. You go on. I kinda like to get things together in my head.''

"You ain't worried, are you?'' Tony asked.

"No way, man.'' Felix laughed out loud. "I got too much smarts for that. I just think it's cooler if we split right here. After the fight, we can get it together again like nothing ever happened.''

The amigo brothers were not ashamed to hug each other tightly.

"Guess you're right. Watch yourself, Felix. I hear there's some pretty heavy dudes up in the Bronx. *Sauvecito*, okay?''

"Okay. You watch yourself too, *sabe?*''

Tony jogged away. Felix watched his friend disappear from view, throwing rights and lefts. Both fighters had a lot of psyching up to do before the big fight.

The days in training passed much too slowly. Although they kept out of each other's way, they were aware of each other's progress via the ghetto grapevine.

The evening before the big fight, Tony made his way to the roof of his tenement. In the quiet early dark, he peered over the ledge. Six stories below the lights of the city blinked and the sounds of cars mingled with the curses and the laughter of children in the street. He tried not to think of Felix, feeling he had succeeded in psyching his mind. But only in the ring would he really know. To spare Felix hurt, he would have to knock him out, early and quick.

Up in the South Bronx, Felix decided to take in a movie in an effort to keep Antonio's face away from his fists. The flick was *The Champion* with Kirk Douglas, the third time Felix was seeing it.

---

welterweight (WEL tur wayt) boxer in a weight division between
  lightweight and middleweight.
pensively (PEN siv lee) thoughtfully
psyching (SYK ing) getting into shape mentally (slang)
mingle (MING gul) mix

Heroes

Discussion: Have students read the story up to the point where the two boys agree not to see each other until after the fight. Review with students the discussion that the boys had about fighting each other full out, as if they were strangers. Then have students comment on the boys' decision. You might begin by asking: Was the boys' decision courageous? Why? Why not? You might also ask students to comment on what they might have done in similar circumstances.

Reading Strategy: Based on students' discussion about the boys' decision not to see each other until after the fight, have students predict what they think will happen when the day of the fight actually comes.

Literary Focus: What plot question needs to be answered by the end of the story?

The champion was getting . . . beat, . . . his face being pounded into raw wet hamburger. His eyes were cut, jagged, bleeding, one eye swollen, the other almost shut. He was saved only by the sound of the bell.

Felix became the champ and Tony the challenger.

The movie audience was going out of its head, roaring in blood lust at the butchery going on. The champ hunched his shoulders grunting and sniffing red blood back into his broken nose. The challenger, confident that he had the championship in the bag, threw a left. The champ countered with a dynamite right that exploded into the challenger's brains.

Felix's right arm felt the shock. Antonio's face, superimposed on the screen, was shattered and split apart by the awesome force of the killer blow. Felix saw himself in the ring, blasting Antonio against the ropes. The champ had to be forcibly restrained. The challenger was allowed to crumble slowly to the canvas, a broken bloody mess.

When Felix finally left the theater, he had figured out how to psyche himself for tomorrow's fight. It was Felix the Champion vs. Antonio the Challenger.

He walked up some dark streets, deserted except for small pockets of wary-looking kids wearing gang colors. Despite the fact that he was Puerto Rican like them, they eyed him as a stranger to their turf. Felix did a fast shuffle, bobbing and weaving, while letting loose a torrent of blows that would demolish whatever got in its way. It seemed to impress the brothers, who went about their own business.

Finding no takers, Felix decided to split to his aunt's. Walking the streets had not relaxed him, neither had the fight flick. All it had done was to stir him up. He let himself quietly into his Aunt Lucy's apartment and went straight to bed, falling into a fitful sleep with sounds of the gong for Round One.

Antonio was passing some heavy time on his rooftop. How would the fight tomorrow affect his relationship with Felix? After all, fighting was like any other profession. Friendship had nothing to do with it. A gnawing doubt crept in. He cut negative thinking real quick by doing some speedy fancy dance steps, bobbing and weaving like mercury. The night air was blurred with perpetual motions of left hooks and right crosses. Felix, his *amigo* brother, was not going to be Felix at all in the ring. Just an opponent with another face. Antonio went to

---

lust (LUST) powerful desire
superimposed (soo pur im POHZD) placed on top of
awesome (AW sum) causing fear and wonder
restrained (rih STRAYND) held back
wary (WAIR ee) on guard; watchful
torrent (TAWR unt) rushing stream or downpour
demolish (dih MOL ish) reduce to ruins
fitful (FIT ful) uneasy; very restless
perpetual (pur PECH oo ul) never stopping; without pause

412

Unit 5

Discussion: Each fighter experiences an inner conflict as well as the outer conflict of the actual fight. Have students discuss the different conflicts presented so far in the story and predict how they might be resolved.

T412

sleep, hearing the opening bell for the first round. Like his friend in the South Bronx, he prayed for victory, via a quick clean knockout in the first round.

Large posters plastered all over the walls of local shops announced the fight between Antonio Cruz and Felix Vargas as the main bout.

The fight had created great interest in the neighborhood. Antonio and Felix were well liked and respected. Each had his own loyal following. Betting fever was high and ranged from a bottle of soda to cold hard cash on the line.

Antonio's fans bet with unbridled faith in his boxing skills. On the other side, Felix's admirers bet on his dynamite-packed fists.

Felix had returned to his apartment early in the morning of August 7th and stayed there, hoping to avoid seeing Antonio. He turned the radio on to *salsa* music sounds and then tried to read while waiting for word from his manager.

The fight was scheduled to take place in Tompkins Square Park. It had been decided that the gymnasium of the Boys Club was not large enough to hold all the people who were sure to attend. In Tompkins Square Park, everyone who wanted could view the fight, whether from ringside or window fire escapes or tenement rooftops.

The morning of the fight Tompkins Square was a beehive of activity with numerous workers setting up the ring, the seats, and the guest speakers' stand. The scheduled bouts began shortly after noon and the park had begun filling up even earlier.

The local junior high school across from Tompkins Square Park served as the dressing room for all the fighters. Each was given a separate classroom with desk tops, covered with mats, serving as resting tables. Antonio thought he caught a glimpse of Felix waving to him from a room at the far end of the corridor. He waved back just in case it had been him.

The fighters changed from their street clothes into fighting gear. Antonio wore white trunks, black socks, and black shoes. Felix wore green trunks, white socks, and white boxing shoes. Each had dressing gowns to match their fighting trunks with their names neatly stitched on the back.

The loudspeakers blared into the open windows of the school. There were speeches by dignitaries, community leaders, and great boxers of yesteryear. Some were well prepared, some improvised on the spot. They all carried the same message of great pleasure and honor at being part of such a historic event. This great day was in the tradition of champions emerging from the streets of the lower east side.

Interwoven with the speeches were

---

unbridled (un BRYD uld) uncontrolled
blare (BLAIR) make a loud noise
dignitary (DIG nuh ter ee) important person
improvised (IM pruh vyzd) made up quickly, without planning
emerging (ih MURJ ing) coming out of
interwoven (in tur WOH vun) mixed with

the sounds of the other boxing events. After the sixth bout, Felix was much relieved when his trainer Charlie said, "Time change. Quick knockout. This is it. We're on."

Waiting time was over. Felix was escorted from the classroom by a dozen fans in white T-shirts with the word FELIX across their fronts.

Antonio was escorted down a different stairwell and guided through a roped-off path.

As the two climbed into the ring, the crowd exploded with a roar. Antonio and Felix both bowed gracefully and then raised their arms in acknowledgment.

Antonio tried to be cool, but even as the roar was in its first birth, he turned slowly to meet Felix's eyes looking directly into his. Felix nodded his head and Antonio responded. And both as one, just as quickly, turned away to face his own corner.

Bong—bong—bong. The roar turned to stillness.

"Ladies and Gentlemen, *Señores y Señoras*."

The announcer spoke slowly, pleased at his bilingual efforts.

"Now the moment we have all been waiting for—the main event between two fine young Puerto Rican fighters, products of our lower east side."

"*Loisaida*," called out a member of the audience.

"In this corner, weighing 134 pounds, Felix Vargas. And in this corner, weighing 133 pounds, Antonio Cruz. The winner will represent the Boys Club in the tournament of champions, the Golden Gloves. There will be no draw. May the best man win."

The cheering of the crowd shook the window panes of the old buildings surrounding Tompkins Square Park. At the center of the ring, the referee was giving instructions to the youngsters.

"Keep your punches up. No low blows. No punching on the back of the head. Keep your heads up. Understand. Let's have a clean fight. Now shake hands and come out fighting."

Both youngsters touched gloves and nodded. They turned and danced quickly to their corners. Their head towels and dressing gowns were lifted neatly from their shoulders by the trainers' nimble fingers. Antonio crossed himself. Felix did the same.

BONG! BONG! ROUND ONE. Felix and Antonio turned and faced each other squarely in a fighting pose. Felix wasted no time. He came in fast, head low, half hunched toward his right shoulder, and lashed out with a straight left. He missed a right cross as Antonio slipped the punch and countered with one-two-three lefts that snapped Felix's head back, sending a mild shock coursing through him. If Felix had any small doubt about

---

acknowledgment (ak NOL ij munt) recognition; thanks
bilingual (by LING gwul) able to use two languages
nimble (NIM bul) quick and accurate
pose (POHZ) position; way of standing
countered (KOUNT urd) returned a blow with another blow
coursing (KAWR sing) running or flowing

Heroes 415

Reading Strategy: Ask the students to imagine what thoughts might have gone through each fighter's mind at the moment their eyes met.

their friendship affecting their fight, it was being neatly dispelled.

Antonio danced, a joy to behold. His left hand was like a piston, pumping jabs one right after another with seeming ease. Felix bobbed and weaved and never stopped boring in. He knew that at long range he was at a disadvantage. Antonio had too much reach on him. Only by coming in close could Felix hope to achieve the dreamed-of knockout.

Antonio knew the dynamite that was stored in his *amigo* brother's fist. He ducked a short right and missed a left hook. Felix trapped him against the ropes just long enough to pour some punishing rights and lefts to Antonio's hard midsection. Antonio slipped away from Felix, crashing two lefts to his head, which set Felix's right ear to ringing.

Bong! Both *amigos* froze a punch well on its way, sending up a roar of approval for good sportsmanship.

Felix walked briskly back to his corner. His right ear had not stopped ringing. Antonio gracefully danced his way toward his stool none the worse, except for glowing glove burns, showing angry red against the whiteness of his midribs.

"Watch that right, Tony." His trainer talked into his ear. "Remember Felix always goes to the body. He'll want you to drop your hands for his overhand left or right. Got it?"

Antonio nodded, sprayed water out between his teeth. He felt better as his sore midsection was being firmly rubbed.

Felix's corner was also busy.

"You gotta get in there, fella." Felix's trainer poured water over his curly Afro locks. "Get in there or he's gonna chop you up from way back."

Bong! Bong! Round two. Felix was off his stool and rushed Antonio like a bull, sending a hard right to his head. Beads of water exploded from Antonio's long hair.

Antonio, hurt, sent back a blurring barrage of lefts and rights that only meant pain to Felix, who returned with a short left to the head followed by a looping right to the body. Antonio countered with his own flurry, forcing Felix to give ground. But not for long.

Felix bobbed and weaved, bobbed and weaved, occasionally punching his two gloves together.

Antonio waited for the rush that was sure to come. Felix closed in and feinted with his left shoulder and threw his right instead. Lights suddenly exploded inside Felix's head as Antonio slipped the blow and hit him with a pistonlike left, catching him flush on the point of his chin.

Bedlam broke loose as Felix's legs momentarily buckled. He fought off a series of rights and lefts and came back with a strong right that taught Antonio respect.

Antonio danced in carefully. He

dispelled (dih SPELD) driven away; ended
feinted (FAYNT id) pretended to attack one place while really
   attacking another
flush (FLUSH) straight; even with
bedlam (BED lum) confusion
momentarily (moh mun TER uh lee) for an instant

416   **Unit 5**

knew Felix had the habit of playing possum when hurt, to sucker an opponent within reach of the powerful bombs he carried in each fist.

A right to the head slowed Antonio's pretty dancing. He answered with his own left at Felix's right eye that began puffing up within three seconds.

Antonio, a bit too eager, moved in too close and Felix had him entangled into a rip-roaring, punching toe-to-toe slugfest that brought the whole Tompkins Square Park screaming to its feet.

Rights to the body. Lefts to the head. Neither fighter was giving an inch. Suddenly a short right caught Antonio squarely on the chin. His long legs turned to jelly and his arms flailed out desperately. Felix, grunting like a bull, threw wild punches from every direction. Antonio, groggy, bobbed and weaved, evading most of the blows. Suddenly his head cleared. His left flashed out hard and straight catching Felix on the bridge of his nose.

Felix lashed back with a haymaker, right off the ghetto streets. At the same instant, his eye caught another left hook from Antonio. Felix swung out trying to clear the pain. Only the frenzied screaming of those along ringside let him know that he had dropped Antonio. Fighting off the growing haze, Antonio struggled to his feet, got up, ducked, and threw a smashing right that dropped Felix flat on his back.

Felix got up as fast as he could in his

---

flailed (FLAYLD) waved or beat aimlessly
evading (ih VAYD ing) avoiding
frenzied (FREN zeed) very excited; raving

Heroes

Reading Strategy: Ask students which fighter they think will win the fight. Why? Which fighter are they rooting for? Why?

own corner, groggy but still game. He didn't even hear the count. In a fog, he heard the roaring of the crowd, who seemed to have gone insane. His head cleared to hear the bell sound at the end of the round. He was . . . glad. His trainer sat him down on the stool.

In his corner, Antonio was doing what all fighters do when they are hurt. They sit and smile at everyone.

The referee signaled the ring doctor to check the fighters out. He did so and then gave his okay. The cold water sponges brought clarity to both *amigo* brothers. They were rubbed until their circulation ran free.

Bong! Round three—the final round. Up to now it had been tic-tac-toe, pretty much even. But everyone knew there could be no draw and that this round would decide the winner.

This time, to Felix's surprise, it was Antonio who came out fast, charging across the ring. Felix braced himself but couldn't ward off the barrage of punches. Antonio drove Felix hard against the ropes.

The crowd ate it up. Thus far the two had fought with *mucho corazón*. Felix tapped his gloves and commenced his attack anew. Antonio, throwing boxer's caution to the winds, jumped in to meet him.

Both pounded away. Neither gave an inch and neither fell to the canvas. Felix's left eye was tightly closed. Claret red blood poured from Antonio's nose. They fought toe-to-toe.

The sounds of their blows were loud in contrast to the silence of a crowd gone completely mute. The referee was stunned by their savagery.

Bong! Bong! Bong! The bell sounded over and over again. Felix and Antonio were past hearing. Their blows continued to pound on each other like hailstones.

Finally the referee and the two trainers pried Felix and Antonio apart. Cold water was poured over them to bring them back to their senses.

They looked around and then rushed toward each other. A cry of alarm surged through Tompkins Square Park. Was this a fight to the death instead of a boxing match?

The fear soon gave way to wave upon wave of cheering as the two *amigos* embraced.

No matter what the decision, they knew they would always be champions to each other.

BONG! BONG! BONG! "Ladies and Gentlemen. *Señores* and *Señoras*. The winner and representative to the Golden Gloves Tournament of Champions is . . ."

The announcer turned to point to the winner and found himself alone. Arm in arm the champions had already left the ring.

---

game (GAYM) ready and willing
clarity (KLAR uh tee) clearness
claret red (KLAR it RED) deep purplish red
mute (MYOOT) unable to talk; quiet

Discussion: Have students discuss whether they think the ending of the story is realistic or not realistic. Encourage them to give reasons for their opinions.

MINI QUIZ

Write on the chalkboard or overhead projector the following questions and call on students to fill in the blanks. Discuss the answers with the class.

1. Tony and Felix thought of themselves as brothers because _____.
2. Both boys wanted to become _____.
3. The boys are informed that they must _____ each other in the championship tournament.
4. They decide not to _____ until the tournament.
5. When it comes time to announce the winner, the boys _____ .

Answers to Mini Quiz

1. they had been such close friends for so many years
2. the lightweight boxing champion
3. fight against
4. see each other
5. had already left the ring together

ANSWERS TO
UNDERSTAND
THE SELECTION

1. on the Lower East Side of New York City
2. lightweight champion of the world
3. not to see each other until the fight
4. They knew that they would be fighting against each other in less than a week.
5. pull punches and strike at each other without hurting the other; that is, not really fight
6. helps him psych up for the fight against Antonio
7. Felix would pretend to be more hurt than he was so that his opponent would come in close; then Felix would strike him.
8. Answers may vary. Suggestion: Who won the fight is not the most important part of the story.
9. the importance of true friendship; that true friendship can withstand even the test of two friends having to fight against each other in the ring.
10. Answers will vary.

Respond to Literature: Have students discuss the idea of public heroes and private heroes. Point out that people often do things in their private lives that no one knows about, but that make them heroes to themselves or the people close to them. For example, a man might choose to spend more time at home with his children rather than run for public office or become president of a local organizaiton. Have students think of people they know who have had to make these types of choices.

WRITE ABOUT
THE SELECTION

Prewriting: Write on an overhead transparency or the chalkboard a sample story outcome.

UNDERSTAND THE SELECTION

Recall

1. Where did Antonio and Felix live?

2. What did each boy hope to become?

3. What big decision do the boys make before the fight?

Infer

4. Why did the boys feel a wall rising between them?

5. When the boys first learned that they were going to fight against each other, what were they tempted to do?

6. Why does Felix see the movie?

7. What does the author mean when he says that Felix "had a habit of playing possum when hurt"?

Apply

8. Why do you think that the author does not tell the winner of the fight?

9. What is the message, or theme, of this story?

10. Imagine yourself in Felix's or Antonio's place. Would you have been able to fight your best friend? Why or why not?

Respond to Literature

Was there more than one hero in this story? Explain why you do or do not think so.

420

WRITE ABOUT THE SELECTION

At the end of "Amigo Brothers," the announcer is about to point to the winner of the fight. Who do you think the winner is? Do you think the winner is finally notified of his victory? If so, how do you think each boy reacts? Do you think they even care who won? You choose the end; then add an episode to "Amigo Brothers" that tells what happened after the fight.

Prewriting: Make an informal outline of what you think happened after the fighters left the ring. You might want to include details about the reaction of the crowd and any further statements by the announcer. You might want to limit your ending to the reactions of the two boys on learning the identity of the winner.

Writing: Use your informal outline as a guide to help you to write the last episode to the story. You might also want to reread a few paragraphs of the original story to make a smooth connection between the author's and your writing style.

Revising: When you revise your paragraph, consider adding dialogue where appropriate.

Proofreading: Before you correct your final handwritten paragraph, decide whether you will use any Spanish words. All Spanish words should be written in *italics*. You can indicate italics by underlining the word on your paper. Also correct any errors in spelling, punctuation and mechanics.

Unit 5

For example:
"The winner is—Felix Varga!"
As the announcer says his name, the two boys turn around.
Tony lifts Felix's arm in the air as a sign of victory.
The crowd cheers; they see that in many ways, both boys are winners.

Writing: As students work on this section independently, check to see that each student has a clear idea of what the outcome is to be in his or her episode.

Revising: Have students work in pairs. Ask each student to suggest at least one line of dialogue for his or her partner's paper. Students then can decide whether or not their partner's dialogue will add or detract to their ending of the story.

Proofreading: Review with students some of the uses of italics. For example, foreign words are usually italicized, as are words that are to be given special emphasis.

LDP Activity: Discuss and write the words you think of that describe a hero.

THINK ABOUT PLOT ELEMENTS

The plot of any story has certain parts or elements. The action of a story that leads to the climax is called **rising action**. In rising action, you learn about the main characters and everything that is going to be important in the story. The rising action leads to the climax or most exciting part of the story. Then, the story moves to its conclusion. The set of actions bringing the story to its end is called **falling action**. With falling action, the story "winds down" to the resolution.

1. What is the climax of "Amigo Brothers"?

2. Does the story have a resolution?

3. In what way is this story similar to "The Lady and the Tiger," which you read in Unit 3?

4. What plot questions are introduced in "Amigo Brothers"?

5. Which plot question remains unanswered?

DEVELOP YOUR VOCABULARY

Many words in the English language are derived from Spanish. For example, perhaps you are familiar with the word *pueblo*, which in Spanish means "village." In English, the word pueblo refers to only one dwelling in a Native American village in the southwestern United States. Another Spanish word that has found its way into English is the word *amigo*, which means "friend." If you like Mexican food, you are probably familiar with a flatbread called *tortilla*. Tortilla is a variation of the word *torta*, which means "cake."

In the short story, "Amigo Brothers," a number of Spanish words appear in the text. The author uses these words to add flavor to the story. Use a Spanish-English dictionary to find the meanings of the following words from "Amigo Brothers." Then write a definition for each word.

1. panin
2. cheverote
3. hermano
4. sauvecito
5. sabe
6. salsa
7. loisaida

Guide students through the elements of a short story that are featured in the text: point of view, tone, symbolism, and techniques. Remind students that they have encountered these elements in "Amigo Brothers."

Suggested Questions

In discussing point of view, ask students what the advantages are to different points of view. For example, the first-person point of view has the advantage of telling a story through the eyes of someone who is actually in the story. The third-person point of view has the advantage of being omniscient; that is, seeing and knowing what all the characters are doing, thinking and feeling.

Next, ask students what factors influence the tone of a story. One factor is the author's intention in writing the story: Does he or she want to be humorous, serious, persuasive? Another factor is the characteristics of the storyteller. For example, if a story is told in the first person by a young person, it might be quite casual in tone. Yet another factor is subject matter. A story such as "Dead at Seventeen" (Unit 4) has a very serious tone because it is about a fatal auto accident.

Have students discuss the use of symbolism in "Amigo Brothers." Help them to see that, in many ways, the fight itself is a symbol: It represents the thing (boxing) that both boys want to do most in life, yet it also represents a threat to their friendship.

As students read "On the Ledge," have them think about the use of dialogue. Ask them to notice how dialogue is used to develop characters and to add tension and suspense to the story.

You can increase your enjoyment and understanding of a short story by remembering its four major elements. To review, they are setting, characters, plot, and theme. Now you can add to your understanding by learning about four additional elements: **point of view, tone, symbolism,** and **writing technique.**

Point of View. Every story must be written from a certain point of view. Someone, a character or speaker, must tell the story. The point of view is the position from which the story is told to you, the reader.

Most stories are written from either a first-person or third-person point of view. When a **first-person point of view** is used, the storyteller is a character in the story. He or she may be either a major or minor character. Throughout the story, this character refers to him- or herself as "I" and "me." Since everything in the story is told from this character's point of view, the action and narration are limited to what only this character can see, hear, think, know, or feel.

In a **third-person** narrative, the storyteller is not a character in the story. The storyteller must refer to each character in the story as "he" or "she." In some third-person stories, the storyteller is **omniscient,** or all-knowing. The storyteller stands outside the story but controls everything that happens. In other third-person stories, the storyteller takes a **limited point of view** by concentrating on the thoughts and feelings of only a single character, usually the main character. A third-person narrative is less personal than a story told from first person point of view.

Tone. The author's attitude toward the subject of his or her writing as well as toward his or her reader is called the tone. It may be funny, sad, light-hearted, or sarcastic. An author may use a formal, detached tone or an informal, more personal tone to address the reader. The choice of tone can even be ironic. You will recognize this tone in "The Secret Life of Walter Mitty," a story that you will read later in this unit.

FICTION

Symbolism. In literature, a symbol is something that stands for something else. For example, a Bible can be a symbol of a person's religious beliefs.

Usually the "something else" that a symbol stands for is not something that you can see or touch. Instead, a symbol represents a feeling, quality, or idea. For example, in the short story "Amigo Brothers," the boys' scrapbook of all their torn boxing-match tickets symbolizes the way the boys feel about boxing and each other.

Sometimes a symbol is an action rather than an object. In "Amigo Brothers," the two boys hug each other tightly after agreeing not to see each other until the championship fight. The hug can be seen as a symbolic gesture that tells about the two boys and their feelings.

Some symbols in a story are obvious. Other symbols are not drawn clearly. These symbols may mean different things to different people, with no one meaning being "correct."

Techniques. Authors use many special techniques to enhance a short story. Some of these techniques include dialogue, flashback, foreshadowing, description, narration, and commentary.

Dialogue helps an author to create a character. You know from your own experience that you can tell many things about a person by the way he or she talks. In a story, dialogue tells the reader what a character says and how he or she says it.

Often, events in a story are told in chronological order. Sometimes, however, an author makes use of flashback. In **flashback,** a scene from an earlier time is inserted into the story.

As you read "On the Ledge," look to see what elements of the short story are present. Ask yourself these questions:

1. What is the point of view of the story? Is the storyteller's point of view omniscient or limited?
2. What techniques does the author use? How are these techniques effective?

SELECTION OBJECTIVES

After completing this selection, students will be able to
- identify elements of the short story
- identify the heroes in a story
- extend character development
- identify various parts of speech

Radiator Building - night, Georgia O'Keeffe, Alfred Stieglitz Collection

ON THE LEDGE

by Thompson Clayton

Sergeant Gray leaned out a sixth-floor window. Eight feet to his left, on a narrow ledge, stood a young man with frightened eyes. The young man's back was flat against the building. His arms were spread wide. His fingers gripped the edges of the rough bricks.

Gray looked down and swallowed hard. Six floors below, a crowd had gathered. Somewhere down on the street a siren screamed.

If I go out there, Gray thought, *I'll fall for sure.* High places had always scared Gray. He looked over at the young man. The youth's open shirt was wet with sweat. A strong wind blew his pants tight against his legs.

"Take it easy, fella," Gray said. The youth was about the size of his own 17-year-old son. "There's a lot of people down there you could hurt if you fall."

The young man looked down. His eyes seemed to be completely white. He said nothing.

"What's your name, pal?" asked Gray.

The boy swallowed and answered. "Walt," he said. "Walter Whitfield."

"Walt, you've got a lot of guts to go out there. More than I have. You must have a big problem. You want to talk about it?"

"You a cop?" asked Walter.

"I try to be," said Gray.

"Then I don't want to talk to you," said Walter.

Sidelights: Suicide and attempted suicide are about five times more likely to occur among men than women. In recent years the suicide rate among adolescents in the United States and other Western nations has increased significantly.

Motivation for Reading: Ask students to think about what they would do if they saw someone about to jump out of a window or harm him- or herself in some other way. Relate students' responses to Sergeant Gray's dilemma in "On the Ledge."

More About the Thematic Idea: In this selection the likely hero is a police sergeant who tries to save a boy who is about to commit suicide. A very unlikely hero emerges when Gray's own life is threatened.

Purpose-Setting Question: Why would someone only 17 years old be stranded on the ledge of a tall building?

Literary Focus: Explain to students that although the story is told in the third person, the point of view is still primarily that of Sergeant Gray. This is evident because the storyteller does not describe anything that is seen, heard, or felt outide of the consciousness of Gray. The actions of other characters are described, but not their thoughts, feelings, or motivations. This point of view is called "limited third person."

Reading Strategy: Point out that although the author does not come right out and say that the young man is about to commit suicide, it is inferred early in the story. The line that most clearly indicates this is when Sergeant Gray says to Walter, "You must have a big problem."

Vocabulary: Preteach the vocabulary words. See Comprehension Workbook in the TRB.

More About Vocabulary: Most of the words used in this story are quite familiar. Based on the reading level of your particular class, you may wish to choose several wrods from the story to preteach.

LDP Activity: Students should think about who the heroes of this story are. Then discuss the reasons in groups or with partners, taking notes.

The writer now uses Sergeant Gray's physical condition as a symbolic representation.

Notice how the author uses dialogue to develop the characters of Gray and Walter.

Gray took off his cap and mopped his forehead. His head was wet and sticky. His damp shirt stuck to his back.

"Would you talk to someone else, Walter?" Gray asked.

"Maybe."

"Who, Walter? Your mother?"

"My mother's dead," Walter said. His voice shook.

"I'm sorry, Walter. Would you talk to your girlfriend then?"

"No!" Walter said angrily.

"Your brother?"

Once again Walter swallowed hard. "I might," he answered.

"What's his name?" asked Gray.

"John—John Whitfield."

"Does he live in town?"

"He has an office on Belton Street."

"Know his phone number?" Gray asked.

"No, it's in the book."

"Get it," Gray said over his shoulder to a policeman named Morely.

Morely reached for a phone book. "I'll have it in a minute," he said.

"We're calling him, Walter," Gray said with a smile. He looked down at the street. A long silver-and-red fire truck was backing into a space cleared by the police.

"I'll jump," said the boy. His teeth showed white against his tanned face. "If they raise a ladder, I'll jump."

Gray leaned out and signaled the firefighters below. They stopped and looked up. Gray waved his arms to show the firefighters they were to stop.

"All right, Walter. They won't raise it," Gray said.

"I've got Walt's brother on the phone," said Morely. "He says he's on his way."

"Your brother's coming," said Gray. "Think you can hold on?"

"I can make it." The burning noonday sun was now full on the youth's face. He licked his lips.

"Can I get you a drink?" asked Gray.

"No!"

"Anything else?"

"Only my brother," Walter replied.

Gray watched the boy's face. In the last minute the color had

Discussion: Notice that sergeant Gray continues to make conversation with Walter. Besides being a true attempt to gather information from him, why else might Gray keep up this conversation with Walter? Lead the students to discuss the possibility that Gray is attempting to take Walter's mind off jumping from the ledge—a stalling tactic.

City Night, Georgia O'Keeffe. The Minneapolis Institute of Art

Heroes

427

Reading Strategy: Have students summarize the action here. Also ask them to evaluate Gray's behavior in this crisis.

Literary Focus: What does the tone of this paragraph tell the students about the kind of person Gray is?

A hint of what Gray must do is dropped, as no one comes forward to help.

The author uses both dialogue and tone to reveal more about the kind of person Gray is.

drained away. "You feeling OK, Walter?"

"Dizzy," Walter answered.

Gray swung around to Morely. "You think you could go out there?"

"Just thinking about it scares me half to death," said Morely.

Gray's eyes looked over the small group in the room. "Any of you done any high climbing? We need somebody to go out to help that kid. He might faint."

The men looked away. Two or three young office girls looked at him with wide eyes. There were no takers. Gray turned to the window again.

Looking at the youth, Gray was surprised at the sudden change. Walter's face now looked gray. His knees were shaking.

"Hang in there, Walter," Gray said. He tried to keep his voice calm. He wished now that they had put up the ladder. Maybe Walter wouldn't have jumped.

Down in the street the crowd had grown. Besides the fire truck, there were three police cars and an ambulance.

Gray looked over at Walter again. The boy started to lean outward—away from the building. For a moment he seemed about to fall. But then he caught himself, grabbing at the brick wall. His fingers showed white under the strain.

Gray could see that Walter was about to give up. "Morely," he called, "that boy's not going to make it!"

"What are we going to do?" Morely asked, fear in his voice.

"If you'll hold on to me, I'll try to reach him," Gray answered.

Slowly, carefully, he climbed over the windowsill and out onto the ledge.

"Walter, I'm coming to help you," he said softly. Walter's mouth opened, but no sound came out.

Morely reached out the window and grabbed Gray's left leg. Gray knelt on a ledge just six inches wide. He did not look down. He began inching his way toward Walter.

Gray could see that Walter was shaking with fear. Gray had to calm him somehow.

"Walter, can you move a little closer . . . so I can reach your hand?" Gray said softly. "Take it easy . . . a little at a time."

Walter said nothing. But he was slowly trying to slide his foot toward Gray. He stretched out his hand, trying to touch Gray's. They were still two feet apart.

"I can't," Walter said, his voice shaking.

"Hold on," said Gray. His mouth felt dry. "I'm coming." He moved closer to Walter. Morely could no longer hold him.

Making a quick move, Gray reached for Walter's shaking hand. Then suddenly Gray's knee slipped. Six floors below the watching crowd gasped. Gray tried to regain his balance. He wavered back and forth. He was going over—

Suddenly he felt a hard hand. Somehow, in that terrible moment, Walter had found the strength and courage to save him.

Slowly the two made their way back to the window. Inside, they lay on the floor, drained of all strength.

"Sergeant," Walter said softly.

"Yeah, kid," Gray answered.

"I'm sorry," Walter said. Gray smiled.

It was then that he knew Walter Whitfield was going to make it.

Notice that Gray and Walter say few words to each other here, but they have reached a mutual understanding and respect.

waver (WAY-vur) move in an unsteady way

Heroes   429

ANSWERS TO
UNDERSTAND
THE SELECTION

1. on a ledge outside a sixth-story window
2. He is out on the ledge.
3. go out onto the ledge to help Walter
4. commit suicide by jumping off the ledge
5. Suggested answer: They seem to get along and care about each other, but it is questionable whether they have been very close or seen much of each other.
6. He does not want to talk to Gray when he learns that Gray is a cop.
7. very concerned and compassionate
8. Answers may vary. Most students will probably feel that he did, because he won Walter's trust and made Walter care enough to save him and come in off the ledge.
9. Answers will vary. Possible answer: Walter might have fainted and fallen to the ground.
10. Answers may vary. Suggestion: Walter was beginning to care about somebody besides himself, and to take responsibility for his actions. This is a sign of mental health.

Respond to Literature: Have students compare and contrast the heroic actions of Sergeant Gray and Walter. Both Gray and Walter attempt to save another's life. In Gray's case, however, the deed is enhanced by his willingness to put aside his fear of heights, when no one else would go out to help Walter, and to risk his life for someone he does not know. Gray's action came after a great deal of thought; Walter's action was spontaneous.

UNDERSTAND THE SELECTION

Recall

1. Where does the story take place?
2. What is Walter's predicament?
3. What does Sergeant Gray try to do?

Infer

4. What do you think Walter is planning to do?
5. What can you infer about Walter's relationship with his brother?
6. What clue makes you suspect that Walter may have been in trouble with the law?
7. How would you describe Sergeant Gray's attitude toward Walter?

Apply

8. Do you feel that Sergeant Gray said and did the right things in this situation? Why or why not?
9. Predict what might have happened if Sergeant Gray had not gone out after Walter.
10. Why does Gray think that Walt is going to make it?

Respond to Literature

Do you think that this story has one or two heroes? Explain your answer.

430

WRITE ABOUT THE SELECTION

As you read "On the Ledge," all that you learn about Walter is what little he reveals in his conversations with Sergeant Gray. Do you think that knowing more of Walter's background might help to explain why he is on the ledge? Try to flesh out Walter's character by writing a paragraph in which you give some additional information about him, such as what he is thinking and feeling as he awaits his brother's arrival.

Prewriting: Begin by making a list of questions about Walter, such as, why is he angry when Sergeant Gray mentions his girlfriend? After each question, jot down what you think might be a possible answer.

Writing: Use your list of questions and answers to develop a character sketch of Walter Whitfield. Let the paragraph reflect your idea of the kind of person you think Walter is. You must base your sketch on information from the story, but keep in mind that the purpose of your paragraph is to provide information about Walter that goes beyond the story.

Revising: Make sure that all of the details in your paragraph are consistent with the story. Eliminate or change any details that are not consistent.

Proofreading: Whenever a story uses dialogue, be sure to insert quotation marks correctly. Reread your sketch again to ensure that you have made a paragraph indention each time a different character speaks.

Unit 5

WRITE ABOUT THE SELECTION

Prewriting: Ask several volunteers to read aloud some of the questions they have about Walter. Then ask the class to respond with possible answers.

Writing: Have students work on this section independently. Help those who are having trouble by asking questions such as, If you met Walter at a party, what do you think he would be like?

Revising: Have students trade papers with a partner. Ask each student to check his or her partner's paper for consistency with the story.

Proofreading: Display on a overhead projector several examples of dialogue from familiar stories. Point out to students the correct use of indentation and punctuation. Leave the examples on display as students proofread their papers.

LDP Activity: Have the LDP students write a few descriptive words that you think desribe Walter. Then they should make up sentences about him.

THINK ABOUT STORY ELEMENTS

Four additional elements of the short story are point of view, tone, symbolism, and techniques. **Point of view** is the position from which the story is told. **Tone** is the author's attitude toward the subject matter and the reader. **Symbolism** is using an object or action to stand for something else. **Techniques** include dialogue and flashback. Dialogue—conversation between characters in a story—can reveal aspects of the speakers' personality, provide background information, or advance the plot. Flashbacks allow writers to give you important information that occurred before the events of the story.

1. Describe the point of view of "On the Ledge."

2. What is the symbolic meaning of Gray's mopping his forehead?

3. What is the tone of the story?

4. What do you learn about Gray through dialogue?

5. What do you learn about Walter through dialogue?

DEVELOP YOUR VOCABULARY

You can improve your understanding of a word and its meaning by knowing the part of speech of the word. For example, in the sentence "His damp shirt stuck to his back," the word *damp* is an adjective that modifies shirt. By knowing that damp is an adjective and by knowing that it means wet or moist, you can use the word effectively in other sentences.

Each of the words in *italics* is a noun, verb, adjective, or adverb. Use the dictionary to identify the part of speech of each *italicized* word. Then use each word in an original sentence.

1. His fingers *gripped* the edges of the rough bricks.

2. Walter had found the *strength* to save him.

3. Somewhere down the street a *siren* screamed.

4. On a *narrow* ledge stood a young man.

5. He began *inching* his way toward Walter.

6. He *wavered* back and forth.

After completing this selection, students will be able to
- understand foreshadowing
- write an episode that uses fore-shadowing
- identify characters' heroic actions
- write a human-interest news story
- analyze foreshadowing tech-niques
- use synonyms

More About Foreshadow-ing: Ask students to think about times when they have had a pre-monition or an intuitive feeling about something that was about to happen. For example, someone may have had a feeling upon re-ceiving a letter that—even before it was opened—it contained bad news. Explain that an author often tries to give the reader a similar kind of feeling in a story by the use of foreshadowing.

Cooperative/Collaborative Learning Activity: Have stu-dents work in pairs. Ask each pair to write about a single episode that involves foreshadowing. The episode may be something that actually happened, or it may be made up. When one student (from each pair) reads the episode aloud, have the student stop after the foreshadowing and ask the class, "What do you think is going to happen?" Encourage the class to respond before the student con-tinues to the conclusion.

LEARN ABOUT
Foreshadowing

Writers use foreshadowing to give the reader hints about what is going to hap-pen in a story. You can think of foreshad-owing as "clues" that encourage you to make predictions as you read. For exam-ple, in the story "On the Ledge," the author gives you several clues that Ser-geant Gray may eventually go out on the ledge to help Walter. One clue is that Gray is thinking about how scared he is of high places and about what might happen *if* he went out.

The story you are about to read is filled with foreshadowing from the very beginning. As you read "Terror in the North," ask yourself:

1. How does the opening sentence by Stina's history teacher foreshadow the events of the story?
2. How do Stina's reactions to her teacher's speech foreshadow trouble ahead?

SKILL BUILDER

Write an opening sentence for a story that has one or more details that could foreshadow the events of the plot. For example, you might write, "My sister, who is usually very talkative, is sitting silently by the window."

TERROR IN THE NORTH

by Eloise Engle

"Sometime during our lives," said the history teacher, "we all face our moment of truth."

Stina Olson sat up straight in her seat. How did he know that a problem like this had been troubling her? Could he tell just by looking at her that she was questioning what kind of person she really was?

"As history shows," he continued, "few people really know how they will behave under extreme stress. Heroism often appears in wartime. Or sometimes we find heroic deeds in peacetime, when the enemy is fire, flood, hurricane, or earthquake."

Stina Olson relaxed again. He's certainly not talking about me, she thought. I'm the world's greatest coward.

About four o'clock on the afternoon of March 27, 1964, Stina decided she would *not* go along with the others from school. They were going to help clean and paint their town, Seward, Alaska. Seward was scheduled to receive the All-American Cities Award in just one week. There were plenty of last-minute jobs to be done before tourists from all over flocked in. But this was not her concern. She was not an Alaskan in any sense of the word. She had, in fact, arrived only a few months before, to live with her aunt and uncle after her mother had died. Living in Seattle, she had always felt close to the 49th state. But now things were different. Being an Alaskan, she had learned, meant far more than just living here. Oh, it was all mixed-up. But it had something to do with a pioneer spirit, a love for the wilderness, and a little thing called "guts." No matter how hard she tried, she could not find these things within herself. So lately she had simply given up the idea of ever fitting in.

It wasn't that the people of Seward hadn't been friendly when she first arrived—the adults, that is. But the kids had a kind of "show me" attitude. At least it seemed that way to Stina. She had

---

extreme (ik STREEM) very great
stress (STRES) pressure; uncomfortable strain
Seattle (see AT ul) city in the state of Washington, the most
  northwestern of the "lower 48" states and the closest to Alaska

Heroes   433

always been self-conscious about being shorter and more slender than other girls her age. This, along with her blonde hair, blue eyes, and fair skin, took at least two years off her 16. Not being very good at sports was another mark against her.

There was the time when Dan Darby had asked her to go along with the gang on a hiking trip. She had packed a lunch and climbed into her heaviest jeans and boots. Then she started out, only nearly to collapse from fright when they reached the top of a cliff that dropped straight down into Resurrection Bay. Dan, who was almost six feet tall and just about the best-looking boy in town, just shook his head in wonder. "Boy, they sure grow 'em frail in the 'Lower 48' these days."

She forced herself to sneak another look. The city below jutted out into the turquoise-blue water. Colorful fishing boats sailed in and out of the bay. The sun shone down on the sparkling water, and Stina had to agree to the country's beauty. But that didn't help that little cowardly streak running up her spine.

"I . . . I'm going to start back down," she murmured.

"Okay, okay." Dan took her arm and guided her along the dangerous mountainside. He was quiet for quite a while. Then he said, "You'll get used to it . . . eventually . . . I think."

But she didn't. She went fishing for silver salmon and wound up seasick.

Now, at five o'clock, she headed for the Stetson house. She was to baby-sit for their three-month-old infant. She thought that she was at least freeing two adults for the clean-up job. *I'm the one behind the one behind the gun*, she told herself grimly. *Even if I don't fit in here, I can do something calm and simple like babysitting.*

The Stetsons' house had been built only two years before. It was one of the nicest in town. Stina truly enjoyed being there because of the wide view of the harbor from the living-room window.

"The baby has been fed and he's just about ready to fall asleep," Mrs. Stetson told Stina. "There are sodas in the refrigerator, and . . . oh yes, some delicious roast moose. Help yourself."

After they left, Stina settled down in an easy chair by the window. She began looking through a magazine. For some strange reason she couldn't concentrate, not even on the pictures. Her whole body felt tense. She didn't know why. Was it because twilight was now creeping over the bay? Or was it simply because she was alone and mad at herself? No, there was something more.

She shuddered and tried to think of something pleasant. But it was no use. She pushed up her sweater sleeves and

---

self-conscious (SELF KON shus) very aware of oneself; embarrassed or shy
frail (FRAYL) weak
jutted (JUT id) stuck out
eventually (ih VEN choo uhl ee) in the end; at some time
grimly (GRIM lee) harshly; sternly
concentrate (KON sun trayt) pay close attention

Unit 5

saw the goosebumps on her arms. *Now, why do I feel this way?* She glanced at her watch. Five thirty. *Something is happening somewhere . . . I know it!*

Something *was* happening somewhere. About 150 miles southeast, and about 12 miles beneath the icy green waters of Prince William Sound, powerful forces were at work on the earth's crust. Twisting, straining layers of rock began to move. The raging forces beneath the thin, rocky crust would not be stilled. The tremendous power, held back for centuries, could no longer be kept in harness. The largest single catastrophe ever to hit any state in the union began a rampage that would affect one million square miles. . . .

"Who's there?" Stina called out in answer to a pounding at the door.

"It's me. Dan." He hurried into the room carrying a large paper sack. "I can only stay a minute. I brought you some of the gang's leftover hot dogs." He looked through the bag. "And here are some potato chips and cake."

Stina was more ashamed than ever. She forced herself to laugh. "You're great, Dan. Now I won't have to eat moose for supper."

He started toward the door. "I'll try to stop in later. That is . . . if you want me to."

"Oh, I do," she blurted out. "I . . . I really don't mean to seem unfriendly. I

honestly like it here but . . ." *There was that strange feeling again!* "Dan, don't go. Please stay and have a soda."

She hurriedly poured some soda over ice. Then she set the glasses on the coffee table. But they did not stay put. The ice tinkled as the fizzing soda danced over the rims of the glasses. Stina frowned. She looked in puzzlement at Dan. Then she looked past him at the china figurines on the bookcase. These, too, were bouncing up and down. Suddenly, there was a strange and terrible sound, a sort of "Vroooooo." It came from far away or under the earth. Stina's whole body stiffened. "What . . . what was that?" she gasped.

Dan shrugged his shoulders and laughed lightly. "Oh, probably just a little earthquake. We have 'em all the time. Alaskans get used to 'em. Sit tight, and don't be afraid."

The whole house began to shake violently. Furniture fell over and slid around the room. The chimney on the roof crumbled, and now Stina began to feel seasick. "Oh, no . . . no!" she screamed, as she almost fell to the floor.

Dan wasn't laughing anymore. "It's a good strong one, I'll say that for it," he said. He grabbed her arm and pushed her toward the doorway where there would be support from overhead. "Don't panic now."

Now the pictures on the wall began to crash to the floor. Lamps sailed across the

---

catastrophe (kuh TAS truh fee) a sudden, horrible disaster
rampage (RAM payj) wild outbreak
blurted (BLURT id) say suddenly
figurine (fig yuh REEN) small statue

Heroes 435

Reading Strategy: Have students to relate, in retrospect, the feeling of uneasiness that Stina had to what is now occurring.

Softly, Vivian Caldwell

room. The floor beneath them cracked and groaned. The kitchen cupboard doors swung open, emptying dishes, silverware, canned foods, pots, and pans onto the floor. Flour, sugar, milk, syrup all crashed into a huge heap. The shattering glass and splintering house joints roared in her ears as she jerked free from Dan.

"Let go of me!" she screamed. "I've got to get out of here." This must be a nightmare. It couldn't be real. But even as she tried to get to the front door, her feet flew from under her.

It was probably less than a minute since the horrible shaking began, but it seemed as if it would never end. "Please stop," she cried. "Please!" Looking out the window she could see trees crashing down. Huge cracks ripped open the earth and horrible black mud squirted up. The ground itself was rolling in waves. In the distance she could see the dock area. "Look, Dan!" she gasped.

They stared, horror-stricken. The entire waterfront north of Washington Street slid into the bay. With it went the dock, warehouse, and huge fuel-storage tanks of an oil company. And then the other waterfront buildings north to San Juan dock, the small boat harbor—everything in sight—slipped away in underwater slides. Almost immediately, the lid blew off in another oil-storage tank area. Orange flames leaped into the air as eight tanks exploded. And in back of the flames, speeding down the bay at hundreds of miles an hour, was a huge tidal wave of sea water.

Dan grabbed Stina's arm. "We've got to get out of here. That wave is coming inland!" Somehow Stina managed to follow Dan out of the house. They scrambled up on top of some oil barrels and from there onto a neighbor's garage. "This will never hold," Dan yelled. "Here, we'll have to jump over to the housetop."

He went first, then braced himself to catch Stina. "Hurry!" he called.

She bent down to leap—and then she remembered! Oh no! Oh no! "Dan, I forgot about the baby. I've got to go back for him!"

"You can't, Stina! There isn't time! You'll be killed!"

But she could hear nothing except the pounding of her own heart. It was as if suddenly tons of strength had been pumped into her trembling body. She did not look back to the safety of the rooftop. Nor did she glance outward to the Bay, with the wall of water racing nearer and nearer. She thought only of the helpless infant whose life would be gone if she could not reach him in time. As she struggled up the broken steps of the house, she remembered the words of the history teacher. . . . Something about a "moment of truth." Yes, this was her moment of truth. She was terrified. But she was not running from her responsibility in order to save her own skin. This discovery about herself seemed to pour into her even more strength. Stumbling past broken furniture, upturned chairs, and falling plaster, she reached the bedroom. Then she snatched up the baby, wrapped him in a blanket, and ran out of the house again.

"Over here, Stina. Hurry!" Dan yelled.

Stina's throat was hot and dry. But her legs could still move, and that was what counted. She handed Dan the baby and began to climb up onto the rooftop. She saw the towering wall of water bearing down on them. Two minutes later it struck the Stetsons' house, tearing it to pieces. The garage they had been on top of, only minutes before, went next.

Beneath her, she felt the porch of the house being torn away. The bedrooms, splintering and swirling, went next. The baby, now in Stina's arms, was crying. As long as he was crying, there was strength and life in his tiny form. Stina was grateful that he could not know of his nearness to death.

"Hang on tight," Dan ordered. Suddenly the rooftop raft sailed dizzily away in the swirling water. There was nothing left of the house but the living room beneath them. As they sped on through the muddy water, she saw a raging fire in the distance. She dimly wondered if its fiery fingers would reach as far inland as their rooftop perch.

---

tidal wave (TYD ul WAYV) huge, destructive, ocean wave
bearing (BAIR ing) pressing; advancing rapidly

Heroes

437

Critical Thinking: Ask students if they think that the story is believable. Make sure that students back up their answers. Some students may feel that all or parts of the story are far-fetched—for example, why were Dan and Stina not at all concerned about their own families while the earthquake was occurring?

T437

They bumped into trees, parts of houses, and buildings. It seemed certain their raft would split wide open. Unbelievable minutes, that seemed like an entire lifetime, went by. At last they found themselves caught between trees. Dan leaped into action. He tied the roof to the trees with the television wires. Now, at least, they were anchored to something. But the waves reached as high as the attic and lapped at the roof itself.

The sixth and last of the tidal waves finally fell back. Only then did Dan risk lowering himself into the house. Stina, holding the baby, sat tight. "Be careful, Dan," she yelled.

As she waited, darkness fell. She could still see familiar objects sailing by. The moonlight reflected on a car. As it floated by like a toy, it flipped over on its side. Minutes later, the bodies of two dogs came near. She almost cried out because she thought she recognized one of them as her family's pet.

It seemed as if Dan had been gone forever. What could he be doing? "Dan, are you all right?" she called out.

La Vague
Gustave Courbet, The Brooklyn Museum, Gift of Mrs. Horace Havemeyer

"I'm coming," he answered, and swung himself onto the rooftop again. "We're in luck . . . two candles, a lighter, and a can of juice for Junior."

Stina was grateful for them. But as the heavy chill in the air grew sharper, she shivered more and more.

"Do you suppose there's some kind of insulation in the roof?" she asked. "If we could get at it, it might help to keep us warm."

"Good idea," Dan said. He began pulling up shingles and tearing out insulation with which they could wrap themselves for warmth. Then there was nothing to do except . . . wait.

"Somebody will rescue us," he comforted Stina. "Our best bet is to stay put."

"I know. I'm not afraid anymore."

"So I noticed," Dan said, smiling. "And I take back any kidding I ever did about you. Just wait till word gets around."

Down at the waterfront, the raging fires had been carried back to sea by the returning waves. Dock pilings that had been snapped off were floating upright. Coated with tar, their top sections were aflame. They looked like candles floating in the night all over the bay.

What seemed hours dragged by. Then Stina's heart leaped as she saw the beautiful gleam of approaching flashlights. There were sounds of human voices calling. "You up there. Are you all right?"

Dan cupped his hands to his mouth and shouted, "We're fine."

He peeked inside the blanket to look at the baby. Then he put his arm around Stina. "All three of us are okay," he said huskily, "thanks to you, Stina."

Stina managed a smile. Then she bent forward to yell as loudly as she could, "There are three wet, cold Alaskans up here. Come and get us!"

---

pilings (PYL ingz) wooden poles driven into the ground to form part of a wall or a foundation

Heroes

439

Reading Strategy: Have students predict what they think will happen after Stina and Dan are rescued. You can begin discussion by asking questions such as: What do you think happened to the parents of the baby? What do you think happens in Stina and Dan's relationship?

MINI QUIZ

Write on the chalkboard or overhead projector the following questions and call on students to fill in the blanks. Discuss the answers with the class.

1. The story takes place in _____.
2. Stina is babysitting when _____ occurs.
3. Visiting Stina is _____.
4. Stina decides to go back into the house in order to _____.
5. At the end of the story, Stina and Dan are _____.

Answers to Mini Quiz

1. Seward, Alaska
2. an earthquake
3. Dan
4. rescue the baby
5. reached by rescuers

1. Seward, Alaska
2. 16
3. a severe earthquake occurs
4. Compared to other young Alaskans, she found herself lacking in courage and a "pioneer spirit."
5. He seemed to like her, but was perplexed by her frailty.
6. She felt that she should have been working with the others on the town project.
7. She was probably afraid that if she looked back, she would be tempted not to go get the baby.
8. her feeling that something was wrong
9. the realization that she was not shirking her responsibility to save her own skin
10. For the first time Stina considers herself an Alaskan.

Respond to Literature: The speech by Stina's history teacher focuses on acts of courage during war or natural disasters. Ask students to think of other situations that might bring out heroic qualities in a person. You can begin by asking them to consider risks that are not physical. For example, a teenager might be a hero for standing up to his friend and convincing him not to drink or take drugs.

WRITE ABOUT THE SELECTION

Prewriting: Obtain examples from newspapers and magazines of well-written human interest stories. Read aloud or have students read several of the stories. Then discuss the elements that make up a good human interest story.

Writing: As students work on this section independently, circulate to help those who are having trouble. Ask questions that will help students focus on information that they may be omitting.

T440

UNDERSTAND THE SELECTION

Recall

1. Where does this story take place?
2. How old is Stina?
3. What happens while Stina is baby-sitting for the Stetsons?

Infer

4. Why was Stina questioning the kind of person she was?
5. What can you infer about Dan's feelings toward Stina at the beginning of the story?
6. Why was Stina embarrassed when Dan brought her left-over food?
7. Why did Stina not look back when she went to rescue the baby?

Apply

8. What caused Stina to ask Dan to stay with her at the Stetsons' house?
9. What realization about herself gives Stina the greatest strength?
10. What is the significance at the end of the story of the phrase "three wet, cold Alaskans"?

Respond to Literature

What action of Stina's illustrates the history teacher's opening statement? How realistic do you think this action is?

440

WRITE ABOUT THE SELECTION

Stina's rescue of the baby would make a wonderful human interest story for the news media. Imagine that you are a news reporter asked to cover the Alaskan earthquake. You interview Stina and Dan; then write a feature story for a newspaper or a TV news broadcast.

Prewriting: Begin by clustering the facts that must always be present in a news story: who, what, when, where, why. Use your cluster to write interview questions. Then write down what you think Stina and Dan might say in an interview.

Writing: Use your cluster and notes to write a feature story about Stina's rescue of the baby. Remember that a good news story must capture the reader's interest. Also keep in mind that when writing a news story, it is important *not* to include your own opinion, but to let the story speak for itself.

Revising: You can improve the effectiveness of your story by adding direct quotes from Stina and Dan. Make sure that you use proper punctuation when using direct quotations.

Proofreading: As you reread your story for errors in spelling, pay careful attention that recurring names are spelled the *same* way throughout the story. The name Olson, for instance, could be misspelled very easily as Olsen. Concern for small proofreading details will lend credibility to your story.

Unit 5

Revising: Students may enjoy working in small groups to role-play interviews with Stina and Dan. The interviews can help students think of quotes to use as they revise.

Proofreading: Write on the chalkboard or overhead transparency a list of proper names that appear in the story. Have students use the list to check their own spellings of these names.

LDP Activity: LDP students were newspaper reporters on the story. Find the details; who, what, where, when.

THINK ABOUT FORESHADOWING

A good story contains at least one good surprise. You know that foreshadowing prepares the reader for a surprise by giving hints about what might happen later in the story.

You know, too, that foreshadowing also involves the reader in a kind of "predicting game." Part of the fun of reading the story is seeing if your predictions turn out to be true. Answer the following questions on your ability to understand foreshadowing.

1. Why does the opening speech in "Terror in the North" clearly foreshadow the immediate future?

2. What specific situations does the history teacher mention that relate to the events of the story?

3. How does Stina's reaction to the speech foreshadow what will happen to her?

4. What definite clues about the upcoming disaster are present while Stina is babysitting?

5. What change in Dan's behavior signals the severity of the earthquake?

DEVELOP YOUR VOCABULARY

Synonyms are words that have the same, or almost the same, meaning. For example, in the sentence "Stina's action was very courageous" the word *courageous* could be replaced by the word *brave*. Brave is a synonym for courageous. The basic purpose of a thesaurus is to provide lists of synonyms for the words you look up. Some dictionaries provide synonyms after the definitions.

Consult a thesaurus or a dictionary to find synonyms for the *italicized* words in the sentences below. Decide which word could replace the *italicized* word in each sentence. Try to choose words that are new to you. Then use each new word in an original sentence.

1. The rescue required *extreme* strength.

2. The police officer knew how to work under *stress*.

3. Stina felt *self-conscious* around the other young people.

4. The teacher spoke *grimly* to the students.

5. Compared to the others, Stina was considered *frail*.

Heroes

441

After completing this selection, students will be able to
- identify story techniques
- use several story techniques to recount an incident
- evaluate character's concept of heroism
- write a personal fantasy
- analyze the use of story techniques
- use figurative expressions

More About Story Techniques: Writers use various techniques to develop a character's thought life. One such technique is called stream of consciousness.

Stream of consciousness is writing a character's thoughts as he or she has them, in whatever order and syntax. A similar technique is to present a character's daydream or fantasy as if it were an event that is actually happening. This is the technique of James Thurber in his story about Walter Mitty.

Cooperative/Collaborative Learning Activity: Have several students work together to create a single piece of writing about an event that has happened to one member of the group. Students may find it helpful if each member of the group contributes the use of a particular technique. For example, one student might write dialogue, while another writes an episode that is a flashback.

LEARN ABOUT
Story Techniques

A writer may choose to use special techniques in order to tell a story. The main tool of a fiction writer is **narration.** This is reporting the events of the story in chronological order. The purpose is to make the story clear and alive for you, the reader. **Description,** another tool of writers, brings scenes and feelings to the reader's imagination. Another technique is **flashback.** In flashback, an episode from an earlier time is inserted into the story. Writers also use **dialogue.** A simple dialogue is just two characters talking, but more characters can participate, depending on the circumstances. **Repetition** of an idea or phrase can be used to make a point clear to you.

As you read "The Secret Life of Walter Mitty," ask yourself these questions:
1. What special techniques does the writer use to enhance the story?
2. How do these techniques help make the story believable?

SKILL BUILDER

Choose two of these techniques to tell about an important event in your life. Although you are writing about a real event, you can use another writer's tool—imagination—to create appropriate effects even if they did not really happen.

Unit 5

THE SECRET LIFE OF WALTER MITTY

James Thurber

"**W**e're going through!" The Commander's voice was like thin ice breaking. He wore his full-dress uniform, with the heavily braided white cap pulled down rakishly over one cold gray eye. "We can't make it, sir. It's spoiling for a hurricane, if you ask me." "I'm not asking you, Lieutenant Berg," said the Commander. "Throw on the power lights! Rev her up to 8,500! We're going through!" The pounding of the cylinders increased: ta-pocketa-pocketa-pocketa-*pocketa-pocketa*. The Commander stared at the ice forming on the pilot window. He walked over and twisted a row of complicated dials. "Switch on No. 8 auxiliary!" he shouted. "Switch on No. 8 auxiliary!" repeated Lieutenant Berg.

"Full strength in No. 3 turret!" shouted the Commander. "Full strength in No. 3 turret!" The crew, bending to their various tasks in the huge, hurtling eight-engined Navy hydroplane looked at each other and grinned. "The Old Man'll get us through," they said to one another. "The Old Man ain't afraid of Hell!" . . .

"Not so fast! You're driving too fast!" said Mrs. Mitty. "What are you driving so fast for?"

"Hmm?" said Walter Mitty. He looked at his wife, in the seat beside him, with shocked astonishment. She seemed grossly unfamiliar, like a strange woman who had yelled at him in a crowd. "You were up to fifty-five," she said. "You know I don't like to go more than forty.

---

hydroplane (HY droh playn) a seaplane

Heroes

443

Vocabulary: Preteach the vocabulary words. See the Comprehension Workbook in the TRB.

More About Vocabulary: Point out to students that many of the vocabulary words and phrases footnoted in the story are of a particular time: World War II. Some phrases are Thurber's own invention. You may want to write each word and phrase on the chalkboard and then ask students to pronounce them.

Sidelights: James Thurber (1894–1961), who was born in Columbus, Ohio, began his career as a newspaper reporter, then became well-known as a writer and cartoonist for the *New Yorker* magazine. Later in life, Thurber lost his eyesight, but continued to write. "The Secret Life of Walter Mitty," which is probably Thurber's most famous story, is characteristic of his work in its mix of sadness and humor.

Motivation for Reading: Ask students to think about their favorite fantasies. Do they ever imagine themselves as heroes or superstars in dramatic situations? Ask for volunteers to share some of their fantasies, as a lead-in to the fantasy life of Walter Mitty.

More About the Thematic Idea: Unlike the other stories in this unit, this selection is about someone who is not a hero, but who imagines that he is. An important element in the story is that the main character never *does* anything to make his dreams come true. In fact, his own drab life is in direct contrast to his fantastic daydreams.

Purpose-Setting Question: Why would someone spend most of his life daydreaming about being a hero?

LDP Activity: Discuss in groups of two or four, or in class discussion the people Walter Mitty becomes in his fantasy: hydroplane commander, world famous surgeon, a defendant in a murder trial, a fearless World War II flier and a man facing a firing squad. These are crucial elements for the LDP students to understand.

You were up to fifty-five." Walter Mitty drove on toward Waterbury in silence, the roaring of the SN202 through the worst storm in twenty years of Navy flying fading in the remote, intimate airways of his mind. "You're tensed up again," said Mrs. Mitty. "It's one of your days. I wish you'd let Dr. Renshaw look you over."

Walter Mitty stopped the car in front of the building where his wife went to have her hair done. "Remember to get those overshoes while I'm having my hair done," she said. "I don't need overshoes," said Mitty. She put her mirror back into her bag. "We've been all through that," she said, getting out of the car. "You're not a young man any longer." He raced the engine a little. "Why don't you wear your gloves? Have you lost your gloves?" Walter Mitty reached in a pocket and brought out the gloves. He put them on, but after she had turned and gone into the building and he had driven on to a red light, he took them off again. "Pick it up, brother!" snapped a cop as the light changed, and Mitty hastily pulled on his gloves and lurched ahead. He drove around the streets aimlessly for a time, and then he drove past the hospital on his way to the parking lot.

. . . "It's the millionaire banker, Wellington McMillan," said the pretty nurse. "Yes?" said Walter Mitty, removing his gloves slowly. "Who has the case?" "Dr.

Renshaw and Dr. Benbow, but there are two specialists here. Dr. Remington from New York and Mr. Pritchard-Mitford from London. He flew over." A door opened down a long, cool corridor and Dr. Renshaw came out. He looked distraught and haggard. "Hello, Mitty," he said. "We're having the devil's own time with McMillan, the millionaire banker and close personal friend of Roosevelt. Obstreosis of the ductal tract.[1] Tertiary. Wish you'd take a look at him." "Glad to," said Mitty.

In the operating room there were whispered introductions: "Dr. Remington, Dr. Mitty, Mr. Pritchard-Mitford, Dr. Mitty." "I've read your book on streptothricosis," said Pritchard-Mittford, shaking hands. "A brilliant performance, sir." "Thank you," said Walter Mitty. "Didn't know you were in the States, Mitty," grumbled Remington. "Coals to Newcastle,[2] bringing Mitford and me up here for tertiary." "You are very kind," said Mitty. A huge, complicated machine, connected to the operating table, with many tubes and wires, began at this moment to go pocketa-pocketa-pocketa. "The new anesthetizer is giving way!" shouted an intern. "There is no one in the East who know how to fix it!" "Quiet man!" said Mitty, in a low, cool voice. He sprang to the machine, which was now going pocketa-pocketa-queep-pocketa-queep. He began fingering delicately a

[1] **obstreosis of the ductal tract:** Thurber has invented this and other medical terms
[2] **coals to Newcastle:** The proverb, "bringing coals to Newcastle," means bringing things to a place unneccessarily—Newcastle, England, was a coal center and so did not need coal brought to it.

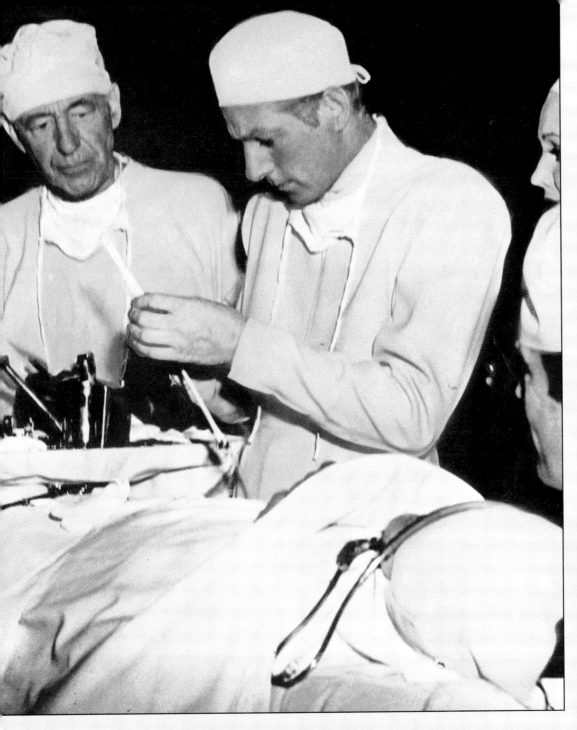

Critical Thinking: Have students contrast Mitty's real personality with his imagined version of himself. What connections might there be between them?

row of glistening dials. "Give me a fountain pen!" He snapped. Someone handed him a fountain pen. He pulled a faulty piston out of the machine and inserted the pen in its place. "That will hold for ten minutes," he said. "Get on with the operation." A nurse hurried over and whispered to Renshaw, and Mitty saw the man turn pale. "Coreopsis has set in," said Renshaw nervously. "If you would take over, Mitty?" Mitty looked at him and at the craven figure of Benbow, who drank, and at the grave, uncertain faces of the two great specialists. "If you wish," he said. They slipped a white gown on him: he adjusted a mask and drew on thin gloves: nurses handed him shining . . .

"Back it up, Mac! Look out for that Buick!" Walter Mitty jammed on the brakes. "Wrong lane, Mac," said the parking-lot attendant, looking at Mitty closely. "Gee. Yeh," muttered Mitty. He began cautiously to back out of the lane marked "Exit Only." "Leave her sit there," said the attendant. "I'll put her away." Mitty got out of the car. "Hey, better leave the key." "Oh," said Mitty, handing the man the ignition key. The attendant vaulted into the car, backed it up with insolent skill, and put it where it belonged.

They're so cocky, thought Walter Mitty, walking along Main Street; they think they know everything. Once he had tried to take his chains off, outside New Milford, and he had got them wound around the axles. A man had had to come out in a wrecking car and unwind them, a young, grinning garageman. Since then Mrs. Mitty always made him drive to a garage to have the chains taken off. The next time, he thought, I'll wear my right arm in a sling: they won't grin at me then. I'll have my right arm in a sling and they'll see I couldn't possibly take the chains off myself. He kicked at the slush on the sidewalk. "Overshoes," he said to himself, and he began looking for a shoe store.

When he came out into the street again, with the overshoes in a box under his arm. Walter Mitty began to wonder what the other thing was his wife had told him to get. She had told him, twice, before they set out from their house for Waterbury. In a way he hated these weekly trips to town—he was always getting something wrong. Kleenex, he thought. Squibb's, razor blades? No. Toothpaste, toothbrush, bicarbonate, carborundum, initiative and referendum?[3] He gave it up. But she would remember it. "Where's the what's-its-name?" she would ask. "Don't tell me you forgot the what's-its-name." A newsboy went by shouting something about the Waterbury trial.

---

[3]**carborundum** (kahr′ buh RUN dum) **initiative** (i NISH uh tiv′) and **referendum** (ref uh REN dum): Thurber is purposely making a nonsense list: carborundum is a hard substance used for scraping, initiative is the right of citizens to introduce ideas for laws, and referendum is the right of citizens to vote on laws.

Literary Focus: Discuss with students the adept way in which Thurber moves from reality to fantasy and back again. Point out that each daydream is triggered by a real-life situation. The daydream begins where the real-life incident ends—but there is always a connection. For example, as Mitty drives past the hospital, the story switches to an operating room where Mitty imagines himself to be a famous surgeon. Also point out that it is always a disagreeable encounter with reality that brings Mitty out of his daydream; for example, the daydream about the surgeon ends when the parking lot attendant yells at Mitty for being in the wrong lane.

. . . "Perhaps this will refresh your memory." The District Attorney suddenly thrust a heavy automatic at the quiet figure on the witness stand. "Have you ever seen this before?" Walter Mitty took the gun and examined it expertly. "This is my Webley-Vickers 50.80," he said calmly. An excited buzz ran around the courtroom. The Judge rapped for order. "You are a crack shot with any sort of firearms, I believe?" said the District Attorney, insinuatingly. "Objection!" shouted Mitty's attorney. "We have shown that the defendant could not have fired the shot. We have shown that he wore his right arm in a sling on the night of the fourteenth of July." Walter Mitty raised his hand briefly and the bickering attorneys were stilled. "With any known make of gun," he said evenly, "I could have killed Gregory Fitzhurst at three hundred feet *with my left hand*." Pandemonium broke loose in the courtroom. A woman's scream rose above the bedlam and suddenly a lovely, dark-haired girl was in Walter Mitty's arms. The District Attorney struck at her savagely. Without rising from his chair, Mitty let the man have it on the point of the chin. "You miserable cur!" . . .

"Puppy biscuit," said Walter Mitty. He stopped walking and the buildings of Waterbury rose up out of the misty courtroom and surrounded him again. A woman who was passing laughed. "He said 'Puppy biscuit,'" she said to her companion. "That man said 'Puppy biscuit' to himself." Walter Mitty hurried on. He went into an A&P, not the first one he came to but a smaller one farther

Critical Thinking: Have students look at the photographs of Mitty included in this story. What can they infer about Walter Mitty from the details in the photographs and the expressions on his face?

up the street. "I want some biscuit for small, young dogs," he said to the clerk. "Any special brand, sir?" The greatest pistol shot in the world thought a moment. "It says 'Puppies Bark for It' on the box," said Walter Mitty.

His wife would be through at the hairdresser's in fifteen minutes, Mitty saw in looking at his watch, unless they had trouble drying it; sometimes they had trouble drying it. She didn't like to get to the hotel first; she would want him to be there waiting for her as usual. He found a big leather chair in the lobby, facing a window, and he put the overshoes and the puppy biscuit on the floor beside it. He picked up an old copy of *Liberty* and sank down into the chair. "Can Germany Conquer the World Through the Air?" Walter Mitty looked at the pictures of bombing planes and of ruined streets.

. . . "The cannonading has got the wind up in young Raleigh[4] sir," said the sergeant. Captain Mitty looked up at him through tousled hair. "Get him to bed," he said wearily. "With the others, I'll fly alone." "But you can't, sir," said the sergeant anxiously. "It takes two men to handle that bomber and the Archies[5] are pounding hell out of the air. Von Richtman's circus[6] is between here and Saulier." "Somebody's got to get that ammunition dump," said Mitty. "I'm going over. Spot of brandy?" He poured a drink for the sergeant and one for himself. War thundered and whined around the dugout and battered at the door. There was a rending of wood and splinters flew through the room. "A bit of a near thing," said Captain Mitty carelessly. "The box barrage is closing in," said the sergeant. "We only live once, Sergeant," said Mitty, with his faint, fleeting smile. "Or do we?" He poured another brandy and tossed it off. "I never see a man could hold his brandy like you, sir," said the sergeant. "Begging your pardon, sir," Captain Mitty stood up and strapped on his huge Webley-Vickers automatic. "It's forty kilometers through hell, sir," said the sergeant. Mitty finished one last brandy. "After all," he said softly, "what isn't?" The pounding of the cannon increased; there was the rat-tat-tatting of machine guns, and from somewhere came the menacing pocketa-pocketa-pocketa of the new flame-throwers. Walter Mitty walked to the door of the dugout humming "Auprès de Ma Blonde."[7] He turned and waved to the sergeant. "Cheerio!" he said. . . .

Something struck his shoulder. "I've been looking all over this hotel for you," said Mrs. Mitty. "Why do you have to hide in this old chair? How did you expect me to find you?" "Things close

---

[4]**has got the wind up in young Raleigh:** Has made young Raleigh nervous.
[5]**Archies:** A slang term for antiaircraft guns
[6]**Von Richtman's circus:** A German airplane squadron
[7]**"Auprès de Ma Blonde"** (O preh duh mah BLON duh): "Next to My Blonde," a popular French song.

Unit 5

Clarification: The daydreaming ends and Mrs. Mitty rudely brings Walter Mitty back to reality.

in," said Walter Mitty vaguely. "What?" Mrs. Mitty said. "Did you get the what's-its-name? The puppy biscuit? What's in that box?" "Overshoes," said Mitty. "Couldn't you have put them on in the store?" "I was thinking," said Walter Mitty. "Does it ever occur to you that I am sometimes thinking?" She looked at him. "I'm going to take your temperature when I get you home," she said.

They went out through the revolving doors that made a faintly derisive whistling sound when you pushed them. It was two blocks to the parking lot. At the drugstore on the corner she said, "Wait here for me. I forgot something, I won't be a minute." She was more than a minute. Walter Mitty lighted a cigarette. It began to rain, rain with sleet in it. He stood up against the wall of the drugstore, smoking. . . . He put his shoulders back and his heels together. "To hell with the handkerchief," said Walter Mitty scornfully. He took one last drag on his cigarette and snapped it away. Then, with that faint, fleeting smile playing about his lips, he faced the firing squad: erect and motionless, proud and disdainful. Walter Mitty the Undefeated, inscrutable to the last.

Reading Strategy: Have students cite some of Mitty's imagined heroes. (a hydroplane commander, a world-famous surgeon, a defendant in a murder trial, a fearless World War II flier, and a man facing a firing squad)

Heroes

MINI QUIZ

Write on the chalkboard or overhead projector the following questions and call on students to fill in the blanks. Discuss the answers with the class.

1. In his first daydream Mitty is a _____ .
2. He is brought out of the daydream when _____ speaks to him.
3. When Mitty drives past a hospital, he dreams that he is a _____ .
4. A newsboy shouting about a trial leads Mitty to dream about being _____ .
5. At the end of the story, Mitty daydreams that he is _____ .

Answers to Mini Quiz

1. hydroplane commander
2. his wife
3. world-famous surgeon
4. a defendant in a murder trial
5. facing a firing squad

ANSWERS TO UNDERSTAND THE SELECTION

1. He constantly daydreams.
2. a hydroplane commander, a fmous surgeon, a defendant in a murder trial, a World War II flying ace, and a man facing a firing squad
3. cool, competent, and courageous
4. dull and humdrum
5. a typical shrew, who totally henpecks her husband
6. like a child and/or someone who is not all there mentally
7. not very respectfully; like someone who is bumbling and not very smart
8. They are highly skilled and respected; they are fearless; they stand apart from the crowd.
9. No. It is obvious from the story that he even cannot stand up to his wife very well. If he were willing to take real risks, he would not need so much fantasy.
10. Answers may vary. Suggestion: Mitty's life is so pitiful, a heroic death is the only escape.

Respond to Literature: Have students compare and contrast this story with "Amigo Brothers." Guide students to recognize that Tony and Felix dream about becoming heroes as boxing champions, but, unlike Mitty, they work toward their goal. Also, their dream is realistic in that they both seem to possess the talent and potential for becoming championship boxers. Continue the discussion by pointing out that when used constructively, fantasies and daydreams actually can help a person achieve a goal, but for Mitty, fantasy was an escape from the challenges of life.

UNDERSTAND THE SELECTION

Recall

1. What is Walter Mitty's secret life? Where does he live it?

2. Who are Mitty's imagined characters?

3. How do these characters behave under pressure?

Infer

4. What is Walter Mitty's life really like?

5. What kind of a person is Mrs. Mitty? How do you know?

6. How does she treat her husband? Give some examples.

7. How do other people treat Walter Mitty?

Apply

8. What do all of Mitty's imagined characters have in common?

9. Do you think that Mitty is a person who is willing to take risks in his life? Explain your answer.

10. Why do you think the author ends the story with Mitty facing a firing squad? Is it an appropriate way to end the story?

Respond to Literature

Walter Mitty is certainly not a heroic figure. Why does "The Secret Life of Walter Mitty" appear in a unit about heroes?

450

WRITE ABOUT THE SELECTION

Do you ever have a "secret life" the way Walter Mitty does? Do you sometimes imagine yourself a hero? Your assignment is to write a fantasy episode about yourself in the style of Walter Mitty.

Prewriting: Take a few minutes to brainstorm about some of your favorite fantasies. What kind of person do you dream about being? Do you see yourself as a famous athlete or movie star? Do you picture yourself as President of the United States? Do you see yourself as the most popular person in school? Perhaps you see yourself doing something brave, like rescuing a baby from a burning building. Decide which of your fantasies fits you best. Then brainstorm the details you want to include in your fantasy.

Writing: Use your prewriting outline to create a fantasy in the style of Walter Mitty. Begin your paragraph with the incident that touches off the fantasy. Then end your paragraph with the incident that brings you back to reality; invent a Mrs. Mitty if you need to.

Revising: Walter Mitty's fantasies are written in the third person with a fair amount of dialogue. They read like miniature short stories. Revise your paragraph so that your fantasy fits this same style.

Proofreading: Be sure that your reader knows when you shift from reality to fantasy and back again by clearly marking for new paragraphs.

Unit 5

WRITE ABOUT THE SELECTION

Prewriting: Have students meet in small groups to brainstorm about fantasy ideas. Ask one member of each group to jot down notes of the fantasies that are discussed.

Writing: As students work on this section independently, write on the chalkboard these phrases:

1. reality into fantasy
2. the fantasy
3. back to reality

Have students refer to the phrases as a reminder that their paragraphs should include the real incident that triggers the fantasy, the fantasy itself, and a real incident that ends the fantasy.

Revising: Have students meet in the same groups as in the prewriting activity. Ask the members of each group to evaluate one anothers' papers and suggest ways that dialogue can be added or improved to enhance the fantasy. You may want to reinforce the idea that in any creative literary effort, the writer has the ultimate say-so and may reject suggestions that do not improve the quality of the work under discussion.

THINK ABOUT STORY TECHNIQUES

Authors use special techniques to make fiction come alive. **Flashbacks** tell about episodes that happened before the story takes place. **Narration** moves the story forward in chronological order. **Description** adds details that appeal to your senses. **Dialogue,** conversation between characters, gives you, the reader information about characters, setting, and plot. **Repetition** emphasizes ideas and important points. James Thurber uses some of these special techniques in "The Secret Life of Walter Mitty."

1. What special techniques does Thurber use in this story?

2. How do these techniques enhance the story?

3. What type of dialogue is used in the story?

4. How does this technique make the story more enjoyable?

5. How do these special techniques enable the author to develop the character of Walter Mitty?

DEVELOP YOUR VOCABULARY

A **figurative expression** is a group of words with a meaning all its own. One special kind of figurative expression is the idiom, an accepted phrase, which means something different from the literal definition of the words. The meaning of the expression usually bears little resemblance to the meanings of the individual words. For example, suppose an author says of a character, "He fell head over heels in love." The expression "head over heels" means hopelessly and deeply.

Identify the figurative expression in each sentence. Then write the meaning of each expression.

1. Bringing food to my mother on Thanksgiving is like bringing coals to Newcastle.

2. I'm afraid that job will be over your head.

3. You will feel better if you get it off your chest.

4. "The cannonading has got the wind up in young Raleigh, sir," said the sergeant.

5. On his first date with Emma, he put his best foot forward.

Proofreading: Have several students submit their papers for display on an overhead projector. Proofread the papers as a class exercise.

LDP Activity: The LDP students could choose one of the imagined heroes of Walter Mitty and write a newspaper account of his exploits. Make sure students use descriptive adjectives in the article.

When is the last time that somebody talked you into something? Did that person take a stand on an issue and defend it in a logical way? Did the individual urge you to take action? If so, that person was using **persuasive speech.** The purpose of persuasive speech is to convince the listener to believe in a certain idea or to take a certain action. Strong evidence—examples, reasons, and facts—is an important part of a good persuasion. A good persuader doesn't offend by name calling but is calm, objective, and reasonable.

Writers use certain words and techniques when they want to be persuasive. Look for repetition parallel structure and quotes. As you read "I Have a Dream," ask yourself these questions:

1. What techniques does Martin Luther King, Jr. use to persuade his audience to believe in his ideas?
2. How does the first line of his speech capture the listeners' attention and make them want to hear more?

SKILL BUILDER

Imagine that you are running for an elected office, either in your school or in your community. Write a short speech in which you persuade people to vote for you.

452

Unit 5

Sidelights: This speech was given by Dr. Martin Luther King, Jr. on a hot August afternoon in 1963. The event was a freedom march to the steps of the Lincoln Memorial in Washington, DC. About 200,000 marchers heard Dr. King deliver what has become one of the best-known speeches in the last half century.

Motivation for Reading: Ask students to think about the most convincing speech they have ever heard. Encourage them to share not only the content but *why* they were moved by the speech. Then, as an introduction to the selection, ask whether they have seen TV replays of the speech by Dr. King.

More About the Thematic Idea: Dr. Martin Luther King, Jr. is a real twentieth-century hero. He gave his life for what he believed, and caused significant change to come about as a result of his efforts. The extent of King's influence on American civil liberties is illustrated by the fact that his birthday now is celebrated as a national holiday.

Purpose-Setting Question: What is your idea of the American Dream?

I HAVE A DREAM

by Martin Luther King, Jr.

I say to you today, my friends, that in spite of the difficulties and frustrations of the moment I still have a *dream*. It is a dream deeply *rooted* in the American dream. I have a dream that one day this nation will rise up and live out the true meaning of its creed:

---

frustrations (fruh STRAY shuns) unhappy feelings that come from not being able to reach one's goals
creed (KREED) formal statement of belief

Heroes   453

Vocabulary: Preteach the vocabulary words. See the Comprehension Workbook in the TRB.

More About Vocabulary: Write on the chalkboard the vocabulary words footnoted in the story. Use each word in an original sentence, then ask student volunteers to do the same, orally.

LDP Activity: Small group discussion about a time when they tried to persuade someone to do or say something that was important to them. E.g. Trying to talk a teacher into no homework the weekend of a big dance.

"We hold these truths to be self-evident—that all men are created equal." . . .

I have a *dream* today. . . .

This is our hope. . . . With this faith we will be able to work together, pray together, struggle together, go to jail together, stand up for freedom together, knowing that we will be free one day.

This will be the day when all of God's children will be able to sing with new meaning "My country 'tis of thee, sweet land of liberty, of thee I sing. Land where my fathers died, land of the pilgrims' pride, from every mountainside let freedom ring." And if America is to be a great nation this must become true. So let freedom ring from the prodigious hilltops of New Hampshire. Let freedom ring from the mighty mountains of New York. . . . But not only that; let freedom ring from Stone Mountain of Georgia. Let freedom ring from Lookout Mountain of Tennessee. . . . From every mountaintop, let freedom ring.

When we let freedom ring, when we let it ring from every village and every hamlet, from every state and every city, we will be able to speed up that day when all of God's children, black men and white men, Jews and Gentiles, Protestants and Catholics, will be able to join hands and sing in the words of the old Negro spiritual, "*Free* at last! Free at last! Thank God almighty, we are free at last!"

---

self-evident (self EV i dunt) needing no proof; obviously true
prodigious (pruh DIJ US) great; huge
hamlet (HAM lit) very small village
Gentiles (JEN tyls) originally, people who are not Jewish

Martin Luther King, Jr. (1929 - 1968)

"You are living a faith that most men preach about but never experience . . . Your name has become a symbol of courage and hope for oppressed people everywhere." These were the words that the President of Morehouse College used to describe one of the school's most famous students, Dr. Martin Luther King, Jr.

Born in Atlanta, Georgia, as Michael Lewis King, Dr. King adopted the name of the great Protestant reformer Martin Luther. After attending the local high school, King received his B.A. degree from Morehouse College, then trained for the ministry at Crozer Theological Seminary. Later he earned a Ph.D. from Boston University.

Martin Luther King's public career began in 1955, when black people in America were just beginning to protest. A black woman in Montgomery, Alabama, refused to give up her seat on a bus to a white male and she was quickly hauled off to jail. In response to the incident, local blacks founded the Montgomery Improvement Association (MIA) and elected Martin Luther King, Jr. as president.

King went on to head the Southern Christian Leadership Conference (SCLC), which fought against racism in both North and South. As he continued the fight against racial injustice, Dr. King went to jail more than 30 times; his home was bombed and shotgunned; and he himself was slugged, stabbed, and stoned. Although King refused to use or advocate violence, he himself was a continual victim of violence, even to his death.

Martin Luther King, Jr. died when he was only 39 years old. He was killed by an assassin's bullet one evening in Memphis, Tennessee. He had gone to Memphis help secure better wages and working conditions for the city's minority population.

Heroes

455

ANSWERS TO UNDERSTAND THE SELECTION

1. equality and freedom for all people
2. that someday in the United States all people will be treated as equals
3. participants in a freedom march to the nation's capital
4. There have been setbacks and difficulties.
5. The idea of equality goes as far back as the founding of America.
6. blacks and others must be treated as equals
7. He names many different states as examples where this dream must come true.
8. belief in the American dream and in the brotherhood of man
9. Possible answer: They might become more involved in fighting for or voting for laws to bring about equal rights.
10. Yes, because at the end of the speech he says "we will be able to speed up that day... when all God's children will be able to... sing... 'we are free at last!'"

Respond to Literature: Have students discuss how Martin Luther King's role as a hero was shaped by the times and circumstances in which he lived. Remind students of the Carlyle quotation that opened this unit. Also, discuss with students the idea that King had certain personal qualities that might cause him to become a hero in any time and place.

WRITE ABOUT THE SELECTION

Prewriting: You can help students think of ideas for their paragraphs by displaying newspaper and magazine articles that deal with current problems in the United States.

Writing: As students work on this section independently, help stu-

UNDERSTAND THE SELECTION

Recall

1. What is the subject of King's speech?
2. What is King's dream?
3. To what audience is King speaking?

Infer

4. What can you infer about the circumstances surrounding the cause that King believes in?
5. What is the meaning of the phrase "a dream deeply rooted in the American dream"?
6. What does King imply must happen if America is to be a great nation?
7. How does King make it clear that his dream is not just for one geographic location?

Apply

8. To what feelings in his listeners was King appealing?
9. Predict what type of action people might take after hearing this speech.
10. Would you say King expects his dream to come true? Explain your answer.

Respond to Literature

In what way was King a hero to the people who heard this speech?

WRITE ABOUT THE SELECTION

Martin Luther King, Jr. expressed his dream for America in his famous speech, "I Have a Dream. . . ." Suppose that you were to give a speech with the same title. Do you have a dream for America? Is it similar to, or very different from, Dr. King's dream? Write a paragraph beginning with the words, "I have a dream. . . ." Let your paragraph reflect something that you would like to see happen in America.

Prewriting: Take a few minutes to brainstorm about some of the causes about which you feel strongly. Perhaps you dream of the day when illegal drugs are no longer a problem. Perhaps you dream of crime-free cities. Maybe you dream of a day when no one in America is homeless. Make a list of your ideas. Then choose the one that you feel is most important to you.

Writing: Use your prewriting idea to compose a paragraph about your dream for America. Remember that your goal is to persuade your readers to agree with you and to fight for the cause you believe in.

Revising: Read your paragraph aloud as if you were giving a speech. Rewrite any parts of your paragraph that sound awkward or wordy. Then reread the paragraph aloud.

Proofreading: Be on the alert to insert a word or words that have been omitted, or delete a word that is written twice. You want your final speech to be letter perfect for ease of delivery.

dents make their arguments more convincing by challenging some of their ideas. This approach also can help point out areas where students might need to add facts or concrete examples.

Revising: Have students read their paragraphs aloud in small groups. Group members can rate one another's speeches according to content and overall effectiveness.

Proofreading: Have students trade papers with a partner to proofread.

LDP Activity: Brainstorm in class or in groups what "causes" are really important, important enough to take a stand on. What would they be willing to do to further these "causes"? Give money, make speeches, strike, die?

Then students should choose one and write a persuasive paragraph with a partner.

THINK ABOUT PERSUASIVE SPEECH

A persuasive writer knows how to capture the reader's attention and appeal to the reader's feelings. Effective persuasive writing includes examples, reasons, and facts as evidence to convince the reader to accept an opinion or to take action. A persuasive writer also knows how to use techniques such as repetition and quotations to enhance his or her persuasive piece.

1. How does King's first line capture your attention and make you want to read more?

2. What words or phrases does King repeat throughout his speech?

3. What quotations does King use?

4. Why are they effective? What examples, reasons, and facts does King use to convince you to accept his dream?

5. How persuasive is King's speech? Explain why your think so.

DEVELOP YOUR VOCABULARY

Many English words have more than one meaning. For example, the word *meet* can mean "to meet someone" or it can mean "a contest, such as a track meet." You can tell which meaning of a word is being used by noting the meaning of the entire sentence in which the word appears.

Write the correct meaning of each *italicized* word. Then write an original sentence in which you use another meaning of the same word. Use the dictionary if you need help.

1. We let the bell *ring* for five minutes.

2. John is from the *state* of Alabama.

3. He told the slave to go *free*.

4. It is my *dream* to become a professional baseball player.

5. Juan is the *head* of his family since his father died.

Heroes

457

After completing this selection, students will be able to
- understand the form of a poem
- identify and write open and closed verse
- discuss an aspect of heroism
- relate poems to personal experience
- use homophones

More About Form: The most obvious clue to the form of a poem is its rhythm. If a rhythmic pattern can be recognized in a poem, then the poem has a closed form. If there is an obviously irregular rhythm, then the form is open.

Cooperative/Collaborative Learning Activity: Choose a subject that evokes emotions. For example: success, failure, disappointment, anticipation. Pair up students and have them write a single poem about this particular feeling. The poem can be open or closed; the students should be able to explain what the form is, and why.

Return to Minute Man, National Park Service

The **form** of a poem is the outward arrangement of the poem, as opposed to the content or subject matter of the poem. Form includes such things as rhythm, rhyme, and arrangement of stanzas. In other words, form is how a poem looks as well as what techniques the poet used to write the poem.

The form of a poem can be closed or open. **Closed** form includes poetry that has a recognizable pattern. Probably when you think of poetry, you imagine a poem that is written in closed form. Most major types of poetry are closed; for example, sonnet, ballad, blank verse, and couplet. **Open** poetry has no recognizable pattern. An example of open form is free verse, which is poetry written with an obviously irregular rhythm.

As you read the four Native American poems, ask yourself these questions:
1. Which poems have a closed form? What patterns are present?
2. Which poems have an open form?

SKILL BUILDER

Write a simple four-line poem about a subject that interests you. First, write the poem in a regular rhythm and pattern of rhyme. Then try writing about the same subject using four lines of free verse.

Young Omaha, War Eagle, Little Missouri, and Pawnees, Charles Bird King. The Granger Collection

Warrior Song I

by the Omaha

No one has found a way to avoid death,
To pass around it;
Those old men who have met it,
Who have reached the place where death stands waiting,
Have not pointed out a way to circumvent it.
Death is difficult to face.

Warrior Song II

by the Omaha

I shall vanish and be no more,
But the land over which I now roam
Shall remain
And change not.

Heroes   459

Vocabulary: Preteach the vocabulary words. See the Comprehension Workbook in the TRB.

More About Vocabulary: The words used in these poems will probably be familiar to most students. You might ask students to look over the poems before reading them and have them ask about any words that they do not understand.

Sidelights: The Omahas are North American Indians of the Plains, with a Siouan language. A small number still live on reservations in Iowa and Nebraska. Their name, Omaha, means "those who went upstream."

Motivation for Reading: Ask students to think about times when they have attempted to do something and failed. For example, a student might have competed in a tennis match and lost, or came in second in a running race. Disappointment and failure—these are the normal, common feelings of competitive youth. Encourage students now to turn their minds to the wisdom of older Native Americans. Suggest in your introduction that the poems take a longer view of life—one that looks beyond "coming in second."

More About the Thematic Idea: This selection deals with a side of heroism that often is not discussed—the failed hero who fights honestly for an important cause, yet does not win the battle. Several of the poems deal with human mortality—the idea that everyone, no matter how great, eventually dies. Other poems deal with the failure and fear that can come to even the bravest person.

Purpose-Setting Question: Is it a victory to have tried and failed, rather than never to have tried at all?

Critical Thinking: Ask students if they think that land is really as unchanging as described by the poet in Warrior Song II. Guide them to understand that compared to the life of a man, land is quite permanent—yet even land can change, as is evidenced by floods, earthquakes, and other natural forces.

Buffalo Hunter, Unknown American. Gift of Harriett Cowles Hammett Grahm in Memory of Buell Hammett

Song of Failure

by the Teton Sioux

A wolf
I considered myself.
But the owls are hooting
And the night
I fear.

Reading Strategy: Have students summarize in a few words the theme or message of each poem. (Death comes to everyone; the land will remain even after a person is gone; even the great eagle is mortal; a person who thought he was brave realizes that he is afraid.)

War Song

by the Teton Sioux

Soldiers,
You fled.
Even the eagle dies.

Clarification: The eagle is considered to be the bravest and most victorious of all birds.

Heroes   461

MINI QUIZ

Write on the chalkboard or overhead projector the following questions and call on students to fill in the blanks. Discuss the answers with the class.

1. The first poem talks about meeting _____.
2. The second poem compares the life of a man to _____.
3. According to the third poem, the soldiers _____ from battle.
4. The writer of the fourth poem compares himself to a _____.
5. He says that he is afraid of _____.

Answers to Mini Quiz

1. death
2. the land
3. ran away from
4. wolf
5. night

1. fear and failure
2. defeat in battle
3. death
4. Soldiers have retreated.
5. as a fearless wolf
6. he finds that he is afraid, perhaps because of his failures.
7. Death comes to all and cannot be avoided.
8. He points out that even the bravest bird, the eagle, must die sometime.
9. Warrior Song II, because the poet speaks of his own death.
10. Answers will vary depending on students' own views and experiences with death.

Respond to Literature: Have students compare the four poems to the story of Walter Mitty that they read earlier in this unit. Help them to see that both the story and poems deal with failure, but that the messages are very different. Mitty is a pathetic character because he never attempts anything. He dreams of being a hero, but is not in reality a hero. The poems, on the other hand, describe men who did try to do something heroic. They may have encountered fear, death, and failure, but, unlike Mitty, they did make an honest attempt.

**WRITE ABOUT
THE SELECTION**

Prewriting: Have students get together in small groups to discuss their prewriting ideas on failure, fear, and defeat. Have one member of each group report back to the class with a summary of the group's discussion.

Writing: As students work on this section individually, circulate to help those who are having trouble. Help students to recall the details of their experiences, or feelings, by asking them to describe the setting, the time of year, how old they

UNDERSTAND THE SELECTION

Recall

1. What is the subject of "Song of Failure"?

2. What is the subject of "War Song"?

3. What is the subject of "Warrior Song I" and "Warrior Song II"?

Infer

4. What has happened on the battlefield in "War Song"?

5. How did the author of "Song of Failure" see himself at first?

6. How did his view of himself change?

7. What truth of existence is expressed in "Warrior Song I"?

Apply

8. How does the speaker in "War Song" make defeat seem less painful?

9. Which poem—"Warrior Song I" or "Warrior Song II"—gives a more personal view of the subject matter? Why?

10. Explain which poem expresses your thoughts most closely.

Respond to Literature

What aspects of heroism are described in these four poems?

WRITE ABOUT THE SELECTION

The four Native American poems deal with four aspects of human experience—fear, failure, defeat, and death. In one way or another, these experiences are common to everyone. You have probably experienced some if not all of them at some time in your life. Which of the poems is most meaningful to you? Choose one of the poems, and write about how it relates to a feeling or experience that you have had.

Prewriting: Take a few minutes to think about times when you have failed, have been afraid, or have been defeated in some way. Also, think about times when you have thought about death or perhaps have been touched by the death of someone you know. Then read the poems over several times, and make notes of the experiences that come to mind as you read each one.

Writing: Choose the poem that most strongly appeals to you. Use your prewriting notes to write a paragraph in which you relate the poem to an experience or feeling that you have had. Be sure you connect your experience to the poem. You might compare and/or contrast your feelings with those of the Native American poets.

Revising: If you are recounting an incident in the past tense, make sure that you use correct verb forms. Change any verb forms that are incorrect.

Proofreading: See that there are no errors in spelling, usage, or mechanics.

were. Ask students which poem they have chosen, and why.

Revising: Review some common verb forms with students. Encourage students to ask about any verb forms they are not sure of as they revise.

Proofreading: Put on an overhead projector several students' papers. Proofread the papers as a class exercise.

LDP Activity: Have the students write the theme words from these four poems. Students may wish to create a collage to illustrate one of the themes.

THINK ABOUT FORM

A poem with closed form has a recognizable rhythm, rhyme and stanza pattern; an open form poem does not. If you are uncertain about the form of a poem, it may help to read the poem out loud. If there is a regular pattern of rhythm or rhyme, you should be able to hear it. If you still have trouble, try beating or clapping the long and short sounds of each line as you say it.

1. Which, if any, of the four Native American poems have a closed form?

2. Which, if any, of the four poems have an open form?

3. Do any of the poems have lines that rhyme?

4. How does the form of "War Song" enhance the meaning of the poem?

5. Describe the form of "Warrior Song I."

DEVELOP YOUR VOCABULARY

Homophones are words that sound alike but have different spellings and different meanings. For example, *weak* and *week* are homophones.

Choose the correct homophone to complete each sentence. Then use the other homophone in an original sentence.

1. You are (*so, sew*) lucky to have an older brother.

2. I don't know (*weather, whether*) I should go to the store or not.

3. A vegetarian is someone who does not eat (*meet, meat*).

4. I'd like a piece of apple pie, (*to, too*).

5. Do you (*need, knead*) a job?

After completing this selection, students will be able to

- understand epic poetry
- create an epic incident
- discuss the qualities of an epic hero
- create a monster story
- analyze an epic poem
- use nouns and verbs

More About Epic Poetry: An epic is an adventure story that centers around one main character. This character is the hero of the story, and will show such qualities as strength, daring, cleverness, courage, and wisdom. The adventures in an epic are presented as a series of episodes. Early epics, such as the *Odyssey*, came from an oral tradition and are known as folk epics. Later epics that were written down by a single author, such as Dante's *Divine Comedy*, are known as classical or art epics.

Cooperative/Collaborative Learning Activity: Have students work in groups of four or five. Challenge each group to write a short epic indicent in which all group members are involved as characters in the story. Students may enjoy using contemporary or futuristic subject matter—such as a trip on a space shuttle—as the topic of their epic.

LEARN ABOUT

Epic Poetry

An **epic** is a long narrative poem, usually written about a historical, mythological, or religious subject. Complex and profound prose works may also be considered epics. The style of an epic is usually elevated and formal. Ancient epics were often handed down orally from one generation to another.

The two selections you are about to read are from the great epic, the *Odyssey*, by the Greek poet Homer. The first selection is written from the third-person point of view, and the second selection from the first-person point of view. You'll remember that in the first-person point of view, the storyteller is involved as a character in the story.

As you read "Ulysses and the Trojan Horse," and "Ulysses Meets the Cyclops," ask yourself these questions:

1. How does the first selection fit the definition of an epic?
2. Why is the second selection told in the first person?

SKILL BUILDER

Think of an incident you were involved in that, in looking back, you now know was part of an epic adventure. Write a brief account of the incident from the first-person point of view.

464

Unit 5

ULYSSES
AND THE
TROJAN
HORSE

by Homer
retold by Alice Delman

Across the sea from Greece, in what is now Turkey, there was once a fair, rich city, the most famous in the world. This city was called Ilium by its own people. In story and song, it is known as Troy. It stood on a sloping plain some distance back from the shore. Around the city were high, strong walls that no enemy could climb or batter down.

Inside the gates were the homes of the people. There was also a fine stone palace for the king and his sons, and a beautiful temple of Athena. Athena was the goddess who watched over the city. Outside the walls were gardens and farms and woodlands. Far in the distance rose the rocky heights of Mount Ida.

Troy was a very old city. For hundreds of years it had been growing in power and pride. "Ilium will last forever," the Trojans used to say as they looked at its solid walls and noble buildings. They were wrong. Sad changes began to take place, and cruel war cut down the pride of Troy.

The Greek armies came across the sea. They came to conquer the city. The reason was this: one of the princes of Troy, Paris by name, had done a grave wrong to Greece. He had stolen and carried away the most beautiful of all Greek women, Helen, the wife of Menelaus of Sparta. The Greeks cried for revenge. Heroes and warriors from every Greek city and town joined hands against Troy.

Of all the Greek heroes, the wisest and shrewdest was Ulysses, the young king of Ithaca. Yet he did not go willingly to war. No, he would rather have remained at home with his good wife, Penelope, and his son, Telemachus. He was far happier pruning his grapevines and plowing his fields than he could ever be in the turmoil of battle. But the princes of Greece demanded his help. Rather

---

Trojan (TROH jun) of Troy; also a person of Troy
shrewdest (SHROOD ist) cleverest, often in a tricky way
turmoil (TUR moil) disorder; unrest

Heroes

465

Sidelights: Nothing certain is known about Homer's life and personality. One of the characteristics of his poetry is that he never mentions his name or gives any biographical information about himself. Scholars generally agree that he lived in the 8th or 7th century B.C. in an Ionian region along the coast of Asia Minor.

Motivation for Reading: Ask students to think about how they would feel if they had to carry on a battle or struggle for ten years. Would they keep on going or give up? Encourage students to talk about their feelings. Relate the discussion to the long battle between the Greeks and the Trojans, follwd by the long journey home of a band of Greek warriors.

More About the Thematic Idea: The stories in this selection center around the larger-than-life mythological hero, Ulysses. It is interesting that the quality that most sets Ulysses apart from his followers is not physical strength or courage in battle (although he possesses these things), but cleverness of mind. Ulysses also demonstrates great tenderness in his love for his wife and son, and in his tremendous sorrow over the loss of some of his men to the monster Cyclops.

Purpose-Setting Question: How might a nation be tricked into thinking a war is over—when it is not?

Literary Focus: Point out to students that a characteristic of the *Odyssey* that later writers copied is that the epic begins in the middle of the action.

Also point out that although the *Odyssey* is an epic poem, it has been referred to by some experts as literature's "first novel" because of its exciting narrative and effective use of flashbacks.

Vocabulary: Preteach the vocabulary words. See the Comprehension Workbook in the TRB.

More About Vocabulary: Have students work in small groups. Assign each group several of the vocabulary words footnoted in the selection to look up in the dictionary. Then ask each group to share the definitions with the class.

LDP Activity: The LDP students should discuss and perhaps use a semantic map to show what happened in the story after Paris stole Helen. Another map might be made for a discussion on what happened after nine years of fighting between the Greeks and Trojans.

The Warrior Vase from Mycenae, Greece, C. M. Dixon.

Reading Strategy: Have students summarize the cause of conflict between the Trojans and the Greeks.

than be thought a coward, he agreed.

"Go, Ulysses," said Penelope. "I'll keep your home and kingdom safe until you return."

And so he sailed away. Forgetting the quiet delights of home, he turned all his thoughts to war.

Ulysses and his Greek warriors came to Troy in a thousand little ships with sails and oars. They landed on the beach at the foot of the plain. They built huts and tents along the shore. They kindled fires. Around their camp, they threw up a wall of earth and stones. Then they dared the warriors of Troy to come out and meet them in battle.

So the siege began. For more than nine years, the city was surrounded by determined foes. But the walls were strong, and the Trojans were brave. Fierce battles were fought outside the gates. Some were won by the Greeks, some by the Trojans. But neither side could gain a final victory. The Trojans

---

siege (SEEJ) continued military attack; blockade

Unit 5

could not drive the invaders from their shores. And the Greeks could not force their way into the city.

"Athena protects us," said the hopeful people of Troy. "While the Palladium is with us, our city can't be taken."

The Palladium was a beautiful statue that stood in the temple of Athena. The Trojans believed that it had a strange power to protect its friends.

"It's useless for us to fight longer," said some of the Greeks. "We can never win while the Palladium is in Troy."

"We've already stayed too long," said others. "Let's abandon this hopeless siege and go home."

But Ulysses wouldn't give up. On a dark and stormy night, he stole into the city. He got past the guards unseen. He crept into the temple of Athena while all the watchers were asleep. There he seized the Palladium and carried it in triumph to the Greek camp.

"Now we'll surely win," said the Greeks.

But still the Trojans persevered. Their gates were well guarded, and the siege went on.

One morning in the early summer, all Troy was awakened at daybreak. The guards on the walls were shouting: "They're gone! The Greeks are gone!"

Soon a hundred eager men, women, and children were standing on the wall. They strained their eyes in the gray light of dawn, trying to make out the hated tents by the beach and the dark ships along the shore.

"They're not there," said a guard. "There's no sign of the Greeks. Thanks to Athena, they've left us at last." Suddenly the guard pointed toward the shore and cried, "Look! There's a strange, dark object among the reeds. It's by the inlet where the boys used to go swimming. What is it?"

Everyone looked. Sure enough, there was something among the reeds. It was smaller than a ship and larger than a man. In the dim light of morning, it looked like a sea monster lately emerged from the waves.

Just then the sun rose above Mount Ida, casting a rosy golden light on sea and shore. It made every object on the beach plainly visible. There was no longer any doubt about the strange thing in the reeds.

"It's a horse!" shouted one and all.

"But not a real horse," said the guard. "It's much too large. It's a huge, ill-made image that the Greeks have left behind—perhaps to frighten us. And now I remember! For several days, there was something unusual going on behind the reeds and bushes there—workmen hurrying back and forth, and much noise of hammering. They were building this thing."

Just then Laocoön, a prince of Troy, joined them. He was an old man, wrinkled and gray—a priest of Apollo, wiser

---

persevered (pur suh VIRD) kept going by not giving up
reeds (REEDZ) tall grass that grows in a marsh
emerged (ih MURJD) came out
image (IM ij) copy; likeness

Heroes   467

Reading Strategy: Predict why this strange horse was left behind. Are the Trojans *really* safe now?

than most of his fellows. After looking long and carefully at the strange image, he turned to the crowd. "It's a trick," he said. "My children, beware of the cunning Greeks. They've made this image to fool you. I warn you to have nothing to do with it."

About the middle of the morning, Priam, the old king of Troy, issued an order. It was announced in all the streets. "Our enemies have gone," it said. "Peace and safety are ours once again. At noon the gates of the city shall be opened. At that time, our people may return to their peaceful occupations."

Then there was great joy in every corner of the city. It was as though day had dawned after a long and fearful night. How sweet it was to feel free from dread! How good to go about one's business in peace!

The women talked and sang as they began to clean their houses. The shopkeepers brought out their goods and offered fine bargains to the first buyers. The blacksmiths lighted fires in their forges, and began to hammer old spears into peacetime tools. The fishermen mended their nets. The farmers counted their rakes and hoes and plows. Everyone talked about the fine crops they would have on lands that had been idle so long.

But not all the people were so busy. Long before noon, a great crowd had gathered before the gate on the seaward side of town. They were anxious to get out of the long-surrounded city. No sooner was the gate opened than there was a wild rush across the plain toward the shore. Men as well as boys were eager to see whether the Greeks had left anything valuable behind.

They wandered along the beach, looking in every corner of the old camp. But all they found were a few bits of pottery, a broken sword or two, and a few cheap trinkets.

They kept well away from the inlet where the reeds grew. Even the boldest wouldn't go near the huge wooden horse. For Laocoön, the priest, had warned them again to beware of it. So they just stood at a distance and gazed at the strange, unshapely thing. What evil trick, they wondered, were the Greeks plotting?

Suddenly on the other side of the camp a great shouting was heard. Some Trojans who had been hunting in the marshes were seen approaching with a prisoner.

"A Greek! A Greek!" was the shout. Men and boys ran forward to see the captive and join in cursing him. The poor fellow was led by a leather thong twisted around his neck. As he stumbled along over the sand, the crowd jeered. They hit him with sticks and sand and anything they could lay hold of. The blood was trickling down his face. His eyes were

---

cunning (KUN ing) clever in a tricky way; sly
forges (FAWRJ iz) furnaces used to heat metal
idle (YD ul) unused; not busy
thong (THAWNG) strip of leather
jeered (JEERD) made fun of in a nasty way

swollen. But his persecutors, as they saw his wounds, only shouted louder. "A Greek! A Greek! Get rid of him!"

Then all at once the uproar stopped. Silence fell upon the crowd. For standing in his chariot nearby was one of the officers of the king.

"What prisoner is this? Why are you abusing him?" he asked.

"We think he's a Greek," answered the hunters. "We found him in the tall grass by the marshes. He was already wounded and half-blind. So it was easy for us to take him."

"Already wounded!" said the officer. "That's strange." Then turning to the prisoner, he asked, "How is this? Tell me whether you're a Greek or a friend of Troy. What's your name, and your country?"

"My name," said the prisoner, "is Sinon. By birth I'm a Greek, yet I have no country. Until ten days ago, I called myself a friend of Greece. I fought bravely alongside her heroes. But see these wounds. Can I remain friendly to those who maimed me and would have taken my life, too?"

"Tell us about it," said the officer. "And tell us truly. Have the Greeks

Reading Strategy: Have students predict whether Sinon is really friend or foe to the Trojans.

Wooden Horse of Troy on 7th century B.C. vase found on Mykonos, Greece, C. M. Dixon.

---

maimed (MAYMD) injured badly; crippled

Heroes 469

Discussion: What is significant about Laocoön hurling his spear at the Trojan horse? (When Laocoön threw his spear at the horse, the sounds of groans and shields came from inside. If the Trojans had paid attention to this sign, instead of dismissing it, they would have learned that Laocoön had been right all along.)

sailed home for good?" He told the hunters to loosen the thong about the prisoner's neck.

"Yes, I'll tell you," answered Sinon. "And I'll be brief. When Ulysses stole the Palladium from your temple, the Greeks felt sure the city was about to fall. Then day after day passed, and they didn't win a single fight. So they began to despair. A council was held. It was decided to give up the siege and sail for home. But great storms arose on the sea. The south wind never let up. No ship could put to sea."

"But what about the horse?" cried the Trojans. "The horse!"

"The horse," said Sinon, "was built on the advice of the soothsayer, Calchas. He told the Greeks, 'Athena is angry because her statue, the Palladium, was stolen from her temple. That's why the storms rage so fiercely. And they'll go on raging until you make a statue of a horse and leave it on this shore as a sign of your shame and repentance. Never can your ships return to Greece until that is done.'

"So the statue was built. The soothsayer said it would carry prosperity and peace wherever it went. But the Greeks didn't want it to be a benefit to Troy. That's why they built it so wide and high that it can't be taken through your gates. They placed it among the reeds by the shore. They hoped the waves might carry it out to sea."

"Ah, so that's their plan, is it?" cried the excited Trojans. "Well, we'll see

about that!" And, forgetting about Sinon, the whole company and the king's officer rushed madly to the great horse.

"Beware, my countrymen, beware!" cried the voice of old Laocoön. He struggled through the crowd. "This is a trick of the Greeks. The horse won't bring you happiness and prosperity, but misery and ruin. Throw it into the sea, or burn it to ashes. But don't receive it into the city."

With these words, he hurled his spear at the huge image. The weapon struck it full in the chest. Those who stood nearest swore that they heard deep, hollow groans and a sound like the rattle of shields coming from the monster's throat.

"To the sea with it! The sea!" cried a few who believed in the old priest.

But most shouted, "To the city with it! The city! We'll outwit the Greeks yet!"

Some ran to the city for ropes and wheels. Others hurried to make a breach in the wall large enough for the monster to pass through. Ropes were tied to its neck and forelegs. Wooden rollers were put under the platform on which it stood.

Men with axes and hoes ran forward to clear a path across the plain. Then the strongest and most willing seized hold of the long ropes and began to pull. Others pushed from behind. Still others prayed to Athena.

So they tugged and sweated, and finally the huge image began to move.

---

soothsayer (SOOTH say ur) one who foretells the future
repentance (ri PEN tuns) feeling of sorrow about one's bad deeds; regret
prosperity (pro SPER i tee) wealth; success

The Burning of Troy, Della Borla. The Uffizi, Scala/Art Resource

The wheels creaked and groaned. The shouts of the Trojans were so loud that the sound was heard far out to sea.

Slowly but steadily, the crowd advanced, dragging the wonderful horse that they believed would bless the city. The sun had set before they passed through the breach in the wall. Darkness was beginning to fall when the groaning wheels stopped. The great horse came to a standstill in a quiet corner close by the temple of Athena.

"My friends," said the king's officer, "we've done a fine day's work. Athena's horse rests near the place where it will stay. Now the happiness of Troy is certain. Go home. Tonight, for the first time in ten years, we can sleep secure."

With joyful shouts and friendly good nights, the crowd broke up. Every man went quietly to his own house. Soon the city was dark. The streets were silent and empty. And Athena's horse stood huge and wooden beside the temple wall.

About midnight, a man started to sneak out of the temple. He crept to the breach in the wall. In one hand he carried a basket of tar. In the other was a small torch that he had lighted at the temple fire. Carefully, he climbed to the top of the wall. Then he sat still and waited. Soon the sky began to grow lighter and the shadows in the city less dark. The moon rose, bright and round. The rooftops, the city wall, the plains, and the sea—all were silvered over with soft moonbeams.

The man on the wall looked eagerly

---

breach (BREECH) broken place; gap

Heroes

Reading Strategy: After students have read "Ulysses and the Trojan Horse," pause and have them predict what they think will happen to Ulysses and his men on their trip home. To heighten the suspense, you may wish to have a student read the last paragraph of the story aloud. Guide students to recognize the foreshadowing technique that is used in the phrase "where wild men lived," to set the stage for an encounter with the Cyclops.

toward the sea. What were those dark objects moving swiftly over the water toward the shore? A thousand ships. The cunning Greeks had not started for home, as the Trojans had thought. They had gone only to the island of Tenedos There they had lain all day, hidden in coves and inlets. Soon their vessels would again be beached in their old places by the empty camp.

The man on the wall was ready. He lifted his torch and dropped it carefully into the basket of tar. A bright flame rose up. It lit up the plain and the wall and the man's face. His eyes were red, his face wounded and swollen. It was Sinon.

Lights were soon seen on the ships. Then Sinon hurried down to the spot where the great horse was standing. With the flat edge of his sword, he struck its foreleg three times. There was a noise like the rattling of armor. Then a panel in the horse's chest slid aside. A man's head, in a gleaming helmet, appeared.

"Is all well, Sinon?" asked a deep voice.

"All's well, Ulysses. Our ships have landed, and our friends are marching across the plain. The foolish Trojans lie sleeping in their homes, little dreaming of what awaits them."

A rope ladder was let down, and Ulysses descended to the ground. Then fifty other heroes followed him, glad to be in the open air again. All was going the way Ulysses had imagined it would when he had planned the Trojan Horse.

"Sinon," said Ulysses, "what are

those scars on your face? Did the Trojans abuse you?"

"They abused me, but they didn't make these wounds," answered Sinon. "I made them myself, so I could persuade the Trojans to fall into our trap."

"I understand, Sinon," said Ulysses. "People call me the man of wiles! But now that title must be yours. And now, for the ending of the whole business! Follow me, my men. Let fire and sword do their worst!"

The Trojans awoke from their dreams of peace to see their homes in flames. They heard the shouts of the triumphant Greeks. They knew that nothing was left for them but captivity or death. So the long siege came to an end, and the fair rich city beyond the sea was overthrown.

Ten years had passed since the siege began. When the city lay in ashes, the Greeks set out in their ships. All sought to return to their native lands. Fondly, then, the thoughts of Ulysses turned to his beloved wife, Penelope, and his child, and the rugged hills and shores of Ithaca.

"Spread the sails, my men, and row hard," he said. "For Penelope waits at home for my return, and keeps my kingdom for me."

But scarcely were his little ships well out to sea when fearful storms arose. The vessels were tossed now this way, now that. They were at the mercy of winds and waves that drove them far, far off course. Soon they were sailing by savage shores and strange lands where wild men lived.

---

coves (KOHVS) small inlets or bays
wiles (WYLS) tricks meant to trap or deceive

Unit 5

Homer (8th Century B.C.)

The author of the next two selections may not have been able to read or write! He is called Homer. He lived nearly 3,000 years ago in Greece. We know very little about Homer's life. Legends say that he was a blind poet. His friends are supposed to have led him from city to city.

In those days, stories were listened to, not read. Long stories were often put into rhyme, or poetry form, to make them easier to remember. Traveling poets like Homer told tales that had been handed down for generations. From those who came before him, Homer learned many familiar rhymes and plots for his poems. He changed and improved the old tales and made up new ones, too. Finally, someone—maybe one of Homer's listeners—wrote down two long poems as Homer told them.

These works are called the *Iliad* and the *Odyssey*. They are considered to be the beginning of Western literature. They tell of the adventures of the Greek hero Ulysses (also called Odysseus) in the Trojan War around 1200 B.C. and his long journey home after the war.

The next two selections—in story form rather than in poetry form—come from Homer and his followers.

Homer kept his audiences spellbound for hours. So sit back and imagine that a traveling poet is telling you of amazing deeds that were done a long, long time ago.

ULYSSES MEETS THE CYCLOPS

by Homer
Retold by Alice Delman

They were giants, oafs. Living on a large island of their own, they knew no law. They went by the name of Cyclops —it means "eye like a wheel." Each of the monsters had only one—a huge, round eye in the middle of its forehead.

The mouth of a cave gaped above the water. This was the home of one Cyclops. As we rowed nearer to land, we saw him, taking his sheep out to graze. He seemed no man at all. No, he looked like a hairy mountain, rising up all alone on a plain.

We beached our ship. "Stay here and be on the lookout," I told the crew. Taking my twelve best fighters, I went ahead. With me, I brought food and wine. This was no common wine. It was a ruby-red brandy given me by the gods.

---

oafs (OHFS) stupid, awkward persons
gaped (GAYPT) opened wide; yawned

474

Unit 5

T474

I thought we might need a powerful drink like this. In fact, I knew it in my bones. We were setting foot in the lair of a beast—a wild man, all power and no law.

We scampered up to the cave. The Cyclops was still out with his sheep. So inside we went and feasted our eyes on his treasure—cheese, lambs and goats, bowls of milk.

My men crowded around me. They begged me, "Let's make off with the goats and the cheese. We ought to get back on the open seas while we can!"

Now I know they were right, but I didn't listen at that time. I wanted to see the caveman—and find out what gifts he might have for a guest like me. So we saw him. For some of my friends, it was an awful sight.

But we built a fire, ate some cheese, and waited. Towards evening, the Cyclops came back. A load of firewood was on his shoulder. He dumped it with a crash that echoed off the walls of the cave. In an instant, we all scurried to the far corner.

Next, he brought in the sheep he was going to milk. Then he picked up a huge rock and jammed it in the mouth of the cave. Two dozen wagons pulled by sweating horses could not have budged that rock.

He did his chores and fed the fire. As flames lit up the cave, his eye saw us. "Strangers," he said, "who are you? Are you good trading men? Or are you pi-rates?" His deep voice thundered against our hearts.

I answered, "We are soldiers on our way home. We ask your help. Our gods teach us to honor strangers. We beg you, great sir—do the same. Take care to please the gods, or Zeus will be angry."

From his savage chest came the answer. "You are a nitwit, trying to scare me with your gods," he said. "A Cyclops doesn't give a fig for any of them. We're more powerful. I'd never let you go for fear of Zeus—unless I felt like it. Tell me now, where did you leave your ship? Nearby?"

That was what he wanted to know! But I was too clever for him, and I lied boldly. "My ship?" I said. "It broke against the rocks of your shore. We are the only men left."

We got no pity from him. He grabbed at us. His hands caught two of my friends like squealing puppies. He beat their brains out and cut them up for his supper. He gobbled the meat like a hungry lion. We cried out to Zeus. But the Cyclops went on filling his giant belly.

Finally, having eaten enough, he lay down to sleep. Now I had the chance to act! Drawing my sword, I crept up close to him. I picked out the spot where I'd stab him. But I was stopped by a sudden thought. If I killed him, we'd all die. We could never push aside the huge rock that blocked the door. No, all we could do was moan and twiddle our thumbs till morning.

---

lair (LAIR) resting place of a wild animal; den
scurried (SKUR eed) moved quickly
Zeus (ZOOS) chief of the Greek gods

Heroes

475

Clarification: Greek laws of hospitality manadated an exchange of gifts. A host was expected to welcome his guests *and* give them gifts.

Discussion: What kind of welcome does the Cyclops give Ulysses and his men?

Soon after dawn, he did his chores. He snatched up another two men for breakfast. Then, gathering the sheep, he flicked aside the rock and went out. But in an instant, he had popped the rock back in again. He did it as easily as you'd stick the stopper in a bottle. We could hear him whistle as he climbed with his flock. Then there was silence.

What could we do? I looked around. Inside the cave lay the trunk of a fallen tree. The log was as long and thick as the mast of my ship. I chopped off a six-foot section and let my men scrape it smooth.

Next, I carved one end into a pointed spear. This my men and I plunged deep in the fire till it was as tough as iron. Finally, we dragged the weapon well back in the cave. Under one of the dung piles that lay everywhere, we hid it.

Just before evening, the Cyclops came back with his flock. Once inside, he wedged his stony door into place. He milked the sheep. He did his evening chores, caught two more men, and ate dinner.

Now was the time. I stepped forward, holding out a bowl. In it was the wine I'd brought with me.

"Here, Cyclops," I said, "have a little wine. You'll see what fine things we had in the hold of our ship."

He grabbed the bowl and drank. The drink pleased him so much that he had to have more.

"Give me another, please," he said. "And tell me your name. I'll give you a gift that will make you happy. Even a Cyclops knows grape juice from a heavenly drink like this!"

Three times I filled the bowl, and three times he emptied it. When he had gotten slow and silly, I called out to him. I spoke in friendly tones.

"Cyclops, you ask my name? My name is NOBODY. That's what my mother, my father, and all my friends call me."

"Then I'll eat NOBODY last—his friends come first. That's my gift to you."

Even as he spoke, he stumbled. He fell back and lay there with his giant head leaning to one side. Sleep captured him like any of us. Drunk, he lay there. He hiccupped. Wine dribbled from his lip, and bits of human meat stuck to his chin.

Now we drew out the rough-hewn spear. Again we thrust it in the fire. I whispered brave words to my men, urging them to get up their courage. As we pulled the spear out of the flames, it glowed red-hot. We dashed forward, raised the spear, and rammed it into the Cyclops's eye. Leaning on the spear, I twirled it till it was spinning like a drill. The eyeball sizzled. The veins popped. And the eye rolled down the giant's cheek.

Now the Cyclops roared so wildly that the cave walls shook. Full of fear, we scattered to the corners of the cave. The Cyclops yanked out the bloody spear and flung it to the ground. Then he began to roar, calling for the other Cyclops, who lived in caves nearby. Hearing him, they

---

plunged (PLUNJD) pushed something quickly into something else
rough-hewn (RUF HYOON) roughly made; not polished
thrust (THRUST) shoved

came and crowded round outside the cave door.

"What's wrong?" they called to him. "Why such a loud cry on this starry night? We can't get any sleep. Is someone stealing your flock? Has someone tricked you or hurt you?"

From inside the cave, the giant bellowed, "NOBODY! NOBODY's tricked me! NOBODY's hurt me!"

"Oh, well," they answered. "If nobody's hurt you, then we can't help." And they all went back to bed.

I was almost bursting with laughter. The name had fooled them! But now the Cyclops, groaning with pain, staggered to the door. He groped blindly and clawed away the boulder. Then he sat down in the doorway. His arms were spread wide to catch any fool who tried to escape. He was hoping I might try it. I wasn't going to. Instead, I plotted and planned. How could I outwit death?

Here's the plan I liked best: The giant's sheep were big and fat, with heavy wool. The Cyclops could see nothing. So I took some cords of willow from his bed. Standing the sheep three abreast, I tied them together. Under each three, I tied a man. Tucked up below the middle sheep, he was protected on both sides.

Last of all, I took the fattest ram, the finest of the whole flock. Myself I hid under his belly, snuggling up to his woolly curls. With the fleece wound around my fingers, I hung on. So we all breathed hard and waited for dawn.

When dawn rose, the sheep began to bustle and bleat. Their cries echoed round the cave. They moved toward the doorway, with us under them. The Cyclops, weak with pain, wouldn't let them pass. His fingers felt over the fleece of each ram. But he never found the men, hiding underneath. So he let each sheep out in turn.

Last of all came my ram, weighed down by his thick fleece—and me. The Cyclops felt him, then bent his face down. "Old thing," he said, "why are you the last to go? You never linger this way. Why now? Can you be sad about your master's eye? This NOBODY won't get out of here alive! I wish you had brain and voice to tell me where he is now. If only I knew where he hid from my anger! I'd smash him against the floor until his brains splashed all over the walls!"

Then, with a sigh, he stood aside and let us go. Once outdoors, I wriggled loose from the ram's belly. I dropped onto the soft grass. Then, going here and there, I set my men free. With many looks back, we herded the giant's fat sheep before us. We loaded them onto the ship and sailed away. But our sadness was as large as the ocean. Our sorrow was as endless as the future. We had our lives, but we'd lost our friends.

---

groped (GROHPT) felt about with the hands
ram (RAM) male sheep
bustle (BUS ul) move about busily
bleat (BLEET) make the natural cry of a sheep

Heroes

477

Enrichment: In the complete *Odyssey* the adventures of Ulysses have a happy ending. Many more things happen to him after he leaves the Cyclops but he finally returns to Ithaca, is reunited with his wife, and reestablishes himself as king.

MINI QUIZ

Write on the chalkboard or overhead projector the following questions and call on students to fill in the blanks. Discuss the answers with the class.

1. Ulysses and the Trojan Horse is about a war between _____ and _____.
2. The story takes place in _____.
3. Ulysses and his men sneak into the city inside a _____.
4. Ulysses lands on the island of the Cyclops because _____.
5. The Cyclops is a giant who _____.

Answers to Mini Quiz

1. Greece and Troy
2. Troy
3. wooden horse
4. storms blew his ship off course
5. eats people

1. a Trojan named Paris had stolen the most beautiful Greek woman, Helen
2. more than nine years
3. Their ship had been blown off course by storms as they sailed home from Troy.
4. The Greeks had left the city.
5. The Trojans believed that it had a strange power to protect its friends.
6. to convince the Trojans that he had turned against the Greeks
7. so that when Cyclops cried out, he would say "Nobody is hurting me"
8. his cleverness
9. They thought the war was over when the Greeks left the city; they brought the wooden horse into the city; they trusted Sinon.
10. He did not want to leave his wife and son to go to war; at the end of the Cyclops tale, he mourns the loss of his friends.

Respond to Literature: Have students list the heroic qualities of Ulysses, then make a bulletin board chart as a study aid. Point to the chart as you ask students if these qualities would be admired today. Compare Ulysses to some real-life heroes, such as Martin Luther King, Jr. For example, one thing that these two heroes had in common is their devotion to family, and their hesitancy to leave home or cause their wives discomfort. Yet, devotion to a cause greater than themselves led both men to sacrifice domestic comforts.

WRITE ABOUT THE SELECTION

Prewriting: On the chalkboard or on an overhead transparency, write down some possible monster characteristics, based on students' suggestions.

T478

FOCUS ON THE SELECTION

UNDERSTAND THE SELECTION

Recall

1. Why did the Greeks attack Troy?
2. How long did the war between the Greeks and the Trojans last?
3. Why did the Greeks land on the island of the Cyclops?

Infer

4. Why did the Trojans think the war was over?
5. Why did Ulysses steal the Palladium?
6. Why did Sinon wound himself?
7. Why did Ulysses tell the Cyclops that his name was "Nobody"?

Apply

8. What quality of Ulysses gave him victory over his enemies?
9. What mistakes did the Trojans make in their war with the Greeks?
10. What factors in the stories indicate that Ulysses is a warm and human person?

Respond to Literature

To the Greeks, Ulysses was the perfect hero because not only was he brave he was also intelligent. Do you think that Ulysses would be a great hero today? Explain your answer.

478

WRITE ABOUT THE SELECTION

The Cyclops is one of the first imaginary monsters in literature. Your challenge in this section is to write a paragraph in which you create a monster that would scare even the Cyclops.

Prewriting: Think of all the monsters you have seen in movies or read about. Brainstorm some of the characteristics of these monsters. Then think about the specific attributes you want to describe: appearance; where the monster lives; what the monster eats; who the monster is most likely to scare. Now add a version or two about why your monster would frighten the Cyclops.

Writing: Use your brainstorming to create a description of a very scary monster. You can write your description in the third person, or, like Ulysses, you can describe your monster from a first-person point of view.

Revising: Look at the adjectives and adverbs that you have used in your paragraph. Are these the best words you can think of to describe your monster? Add any adjectives or adverbs that you feel will make your description more vivid.

Proofreading: Because monsters naturally lend themselves to descriptive exaggeration, you may have been tempted to punctuate your writing with numerous exclamation marks. As you proofread, however, practice restraint in their use. Your writing will be more effective.

Unit 5

Writing: As students work on this section independently, go around the classroom and help those who are having trouble. As questions, similar to those asked in the Prewriting section, to help students formulate their descriptions of a monster.

Revising: Pair off students. Have them describe to their partners the special characteristics of their monsters. Encourage the partners to ask questions that stimulate the use of colorful adjectives and adverbs.

Proofreading: Have students exchange papers with a partner to proofread for correct punctuation.

LDP Activity: All LDP students should have a list of adjectives to describe monsters. They then can create a visual to show their own special monster, using the adjectives to label it.

THINK ABOUT EPIC POETRY

An **epic** is a long poem or prose piece that tells a heroic story. Ancient epics were often recited orally or sung. In some cultures, such as the African and Irish, the oral tradition continues to this day.

Point of view, as you know, is the position from which a story is told. In the first-person point of view, the storyteller is one of the characters in the story; action and commentary are limited to what that one character can see, hear, know, think, and feel. Although the impersonal third-person point of view is more common, both points of view are found in epic works.

1. How does the selection "Ulysses and the Trojan Horse" fit the definition of an epic?

2. From what point of view is this story told?

3. Who is the hero of this story?

4. From what point of view is "Ulysses Meets the Cyclops" told?

5. Who is the storyteller in this story? Who is the hero?

DEVELOP YOUR VOCABULARY

A **noun** is a word that names a person, place, or thing. For example, in the sentence, "They hid inside a wooden horse," *horse* is a noun. A **verb** is a word that expresses action or a state of being. For example, in the sentence, "The Greeks attacked the Trojans," the word *attacked* is a verb.

Review the meanings of these words from "Ulysses and the Trojan Horse" and "Ulysses Meets the Cyclops." Decide whether each word is used as a noun or a verb in the stories. Then write an original sentence that uses each word in the same form, noun or verb, as in the story.

1. turmoil
2. siege
3. persevered
4. reeds
5. emerged
6. image
7. forges
8. thong
9. jeered
10. prosperity
11. breach
12. cove
13. wiles
14. oafs
15. gaped
16. lair
17. scurried
18. plunged

Heroes

479

T479

UNIT 5 REVIEW

Motivation: Make a list on the chalkboard of the main characters in this unit. Then ask students to imagine that they are a panel of judges who must select four characters to be placed in a "Heroes Hall of Fame." Have the class vote for the four heroes they think should be awarded places. Tally the results to see which characters win.

Cooperative/Collaborative Learning Activity: Have students form proofreading "teams" in which one student checks papers for spelling, another checks for grammar, and so on. Have students submit their papers to the team for a thorough proofing.

Part II

Motivation: Write the words *tone, symbolism, point of view, and techniques* on slips of paper or index cards. Place the cards face down on a desk or table. Have a student volunteer draw a card at random. Challenge the student to make a correct statement about the element of the short story that he or she has drawn. The statement can be part of a definition, or it can be an example. Let the class decide if the statement is correct or incorrect. Repeat the process with another student, and so on, until all four elements have been discussed adequately.

Cooperative/Collaborative Learning Activity:

Prewriting: Have students pair off with others who have chosen the same selections. Ask them to create a single chart in which they both reflect their ideas. If their ideas are in disagreement, they each may wish to write in a different color pen or pencil.

LITERATURE-BASED WRITING

1. In this unit, you have read about many different kinds of heroes. You have thought about the qualities that make up a hero. Now is your chance to write about the heroes you liked best. Choose four characters from this unit for a "Heroes Hall of Fame." Write about the Heroes Hall of Fame in whatever way will describe your heroes best. For example, you may want to narrate a guided tour of the Hall of Fame, or you may want to have the heroes step from their places and tell their own stories.

Prewriting: Begin by choosing the four characters from this unit that you want included in the Heroes Hall of Fame. Then review each character's story. Cluster the details of each character's story that best illustrate why this person is a hero.

Writing: Use your prewriting cluster to develop a story entitled "The Heroes Hall of Fame." Be sure to describe the setting of the Hall of Fame.

Revising: As you revise your paper, keep in mind the point of view that you have chosen. For example, if you are writing a guided tour, then the entire story should be written in the third person. Eliminate or rewrite anything that is not consistent with the point of view that you have chosen.

Proofreading: If you have used dialogue or direct quotations, be sure you have used quotation marks and indented with each change of speaker.

2. You have studied point of view, tone, symbolism, and techniques. These are all important elements of the short story. Choose from this unit two selections; one that you especially liked and one you disliked. Then compare and contrast these works in terms of the literary elements that you have studied in order to explain why one short story is better than the other.

Prewriting: Review the work that you did for the "Think About" sections in this unit. Then make a chart that has the name of the two selections you have chosen at the top and the four literary elements down the side. Fill in the spaces on the chart with details about each element from the stories. Include everything you can think of on your chart. You can decide later if you want to use all your facts and ideas.

Writing: Use your chart to prepare a paper in which you compare and contrast the two selections you have chosen. Be sure to organize your paper so that you move logically from one point to the next, remember to prove your favorite is the superior story. You will need to do more than just point out the differences.

Revising: Transitional phrases can make your writing smoother. If you did not use such phrases as *first, next, most important,* and *finally,* add them when you revise.

Proofreading: Be sure to set off an introductory prepositional phrase that has more than three words with a comma.

BUILDING LANGUAGE SKILLS

Vocabulary

Since roots carry the basic meaning of the word, they are the foundation of developing your vocabulary. If you learn to figure out roots, you will improve your vocabulary and your reading comprehension. A **root** is a word or word part that is used to form other words. For example, the root in the word *excitement* is *excite,* which means to stir up strong feeling. Sometimes you can use the root word to find the meaning of a larger word.

Find the root in each of the following words. Use the root to find the meaning of the larger word. Check the meanings in a dictionary, then use each word in an original sentence.

1. dignitary
2. emerging
3. acknowledgment
4. dispelled
5. momentarily
6. frenzied
7. evading
8. elimination
9. devastating
10. pensively
11. waver
12. eventually
13. figurine
14. frustration
15. circumvent
16. embattled
17. seaward
18. prosperity
19. repentance
20. irresistible
21. picturesque
22. mythical
23. awesome
24. fitful
25. courageous
26. monstrous
27. relationship
28. uncontrolled
29. historic
30. gracefully

Usage and Mechanics

Using direct quotations can add to your writing. When you use a person's or a character's exact words, you must enclose the words in quotation marks. If there is an introductory expression, you must follow it with a comma. An interrupting expression must have commas before and after. A quotation that is followed by a concluding expression should end with a comma, question mark, or exclamation point.

Examples:

Introductory expression: Annie said, "The way I plan to do it is better."

Interrupting expression: "It angers me," he said, "that no one can do this right."

Concluding expression: "Get lost!" the young man bellowed.

Add quotation marks, commas, and end punctuation marks to these quotations.

1. Watch that right Tony said the trainer.

2. Stina replied You're great, Dan

3. Let go of me she screamed

4. Hang on tight Dan ordered or we'll surely drown

5. The cop snapped Pick it up brother

Usage and Mechanics

More About Usage and Mechanics: Point out that a direct quotation must end with a punctuation mark **inside** the quotes. Write on the chalkboard the following incorrect examples:

John said, "Let's go swimming".
"I can not see the road" shouted Dan.
"Yes"? she cried, "Now I know what to do"!
"Which way," asked Dennis, "should I go to get to Philadelphia"?

Point out that in the first example, the period should be inside the quotation marks. In the second example a comma or exclamation point must be added inside the quotation marks after the word *road*. In the third example the exclamation points must be placed *inside*, not outside, the quotation marks. In the fourth example the question mark should be inside, not outside, the quotation marks.

Cooperative/Collaborative Learning Activity: After students have completed exercises 1–5 in the text, have them work in small groups to create their own sentences that need quotation marks, commas, and end punctuation marks. Have groups trade papers with one another, then write answers for the exercises.

Vocabulary

More About Word Attack: Point out that because the root is often found at the beginning of a word (for example, the root in excitement is *excite*), this is not always the case. Sometimes the root is found in the middle or end of a word. Write this example on the chalkboard:

> embattled

Elicit that the root of this word is battle, and that em- is a prefix which means "in the midst of."

Cooperative/Collaborative Learning Activity: Have students work in pairs to find the roots of the words listed in the text.

1. dignity 2. emerge 3. knowledge 4. dispell 5. moment 6. frenzy 7. evade 8. eliminate 9. devastate 10. pensive 11. wave 12. event 13. figure 14. frustrate 15. circle 16. battle 17. sea 18. prosper 19. penance 20. resist 21. picture 22. myth 23. awe 24. fit 25. courage 26. monster 27. relate 28. control 29. history 30. grace

UNIT 5 REVIEW

SPEAKING AND LISTENING

One way to share vicariously a character's adventures, escapades, trials, and triumphs is to do an imaginary interview.

Part of the fun of an imaginary interview is the opportunity to identify with one of your favorite characters and to bring that character to life. Also, you have the oppor-tunity to work with a partner.

In this unit you have met a variety of heroes. It's likely that one is someone you found to be interesting. To prepare yourself for this assignment, think about selections you've read in this unit, and recall the characters in them. Then, follow these guidelines to help you prepare your imagi-nary interview.

1. Pair up with another student. Glance over the selections in the unit and choose a character who would be a good candidate for an interview. Al-though the character doesn't have to be particularly likable, it should be someone you find memorable. The more diverse and complex the charac-ter is, the more interesting the inter-view.

2. Decide who will be the interviewer and who will be the character being inter-viewed. You could change roles mid-

way if you like, or, if you choose, you could play both parts!

3. Talk about and decide with your part-ner whether you want to do a sweet and supportive kind of interview or if you prefer a hostile confrontation.

4. Next, develop at least five questions that an interviewer might ask the char-acter. The questions should reveal the character's opinions and his or her personality.

5. Make some notes on answers to the questions. Your job here is to use words the character might use. Try to emulate the character in your answers.

6. As the interviewer, practice asking the questions. Use the appropriate tone and expressions in asking the ques-tions. As the person being interviewed, practice the answers until they seem perfect. You want to sound spontane-ous, so just consult your notes; don't read them.

After you've practiced with your partner and feel confident, take your show to a larger audience. Try to keep your interview to three minutes. Following the steps above will help you to be adequately prepared.

CRITICAL THINKING

An **inference** is an understanding of something that has not been stated directly. It is based on a suggestion that the author makes "between the lines." For example, in the story "On the Ledge," it can be inferred that Walter has a decent relationship with his brother.

When trying to infer an author's meaning, it is important not to jump to conclusions. For example, suppose that you are trying to infer something about the home life of the boys in "Amigo Brothers." It would be an invalid inference to say that Felix and Antonio are from broken homes, because there is no evidence to support this idea. It would be a valid inference, however, to say that the boys live in very modest and somewhat poor economic circumstances.

Good stories, poems, and plays always ask the reader to make inferences. Choose one selection from this unit that you feel contains important inferences, and answer the following questions.

1. Consider an inference that is central to the meaning of the story. What is it? What evidence can you find to back up the inference?

2. What invalid inferences might a reader be tempted to make when reading this story? How would these invalid inferences confuse the meaning of the story?

3. What does making inferences make a story more interesting?

Heroes

EFFECTIVE STUDYING

In order to do well in school, it is important to know how to take objective tests. An **objective test** is one that requires you to recall factual information. An objective test may consist of short answer questions, multiple choice questions, or true and false questions. An objective test may also include matching exercises.

The suggestions that follow will provide a good strategy for taking such an objective test.

1. Write your name on each sheet of paper.

2. Skim through the test. Decide how much time to give each question. Notice if some questions are worth more points than others.

3. Jot down any information you want to remember in the margins of the test or on scrap paper, if this is allowed.

4. Answer the easy questions first. Circle the numbers of any questions you are not sure of.

5. Unless the directions say otherwise, give only one answer for each question.

6. Go with your first answer unless you have a very good reason to change it.

7. Go back over your test to make sure you have followed directions correctly.

8. Reread the questions and answers.

9. Make sure that you have not skipped any questions.

483

UNIT 6: Generations

UNIT ACTIVITY

A Continuing Unit Project: Illustrated Reading Log

A reading log is a learning strategy that gives students a chance to explore and express their own responses to literature. In addition, logs serve as a source of prewriting notes for other activities in the unit.

Have students create illustrated reading logs as they read this unit. After reading each selection, ask students to write in their logs. Emphasize to students that they are to write what they think and feel, not just record a recapitulation of the story.

Take some time to discuss with students the kinds of things they might write about. For example, they might jot down thoughts or questions that come to mind as they read; the relationship of the selection to the unit theme, generations; or the way the selection relates to their own experiences. Allow students about ten minutes for each entry. The entries need not be more than half a page in length.

Here are some general questions you can ask students to help them get started:

What did you learn as you read this selection?
What questions do you have?
What was the main message of the selection?
How did you feel after reading the selection?

If you find that your class needs more structure, create questions such as these for each selection.

"Andre"/"Family Album"
Which family would you rather be a member of, Andre's or the one in "Family Album"? Why?

"Bread"
Have you ever done something wrong for a good reason? What happened?

"Somebody's Son"
How do you think David's father felt about his son?

"The Medicine Bag"
What do you think Martin will tell his son about the medicine bag?

"Medicine"/"Grandfather"
How did reading these poems make you feel?

"Some People"/"My People"
Is there a group of people with whom you are proud to belong? What kind of people do you avoid?

"Otto"/"Christmas Morning I"
In what way does the "I" in the title of the second poem tell you something about the main character?

"Whale Hunting"/"Luther Leavitt"
Is the second poem really about Luther Leavitt? Explain.

Have students create covers and tables of contents for their logs, as well as illustrations. (Students who do not like to draw can cut pictures from magazines.) Have students share their logs with one another in small groups. Then collect and evaluate the logs.

"Andre"
by Gwendolyn Brooks   (page 489)

"Family Album"
by Diane Stevenson   (page 490)

SELECTION SYNOPSIS

Andre is the speaker in the poem; he talks about dreaming that he has an opportunity to choose his own parents. The speaker in "Family Album" takes the reader on a tour of the pictures in her family photograph album.

Each section in "Family Album" represents a picture in the speaker's family photograph album. Have the students choose a section from the poem and illustrate the photograph being described in that section. Ask students to read the section carefully to get a true feeling for the setting of the photograph and the mood and posture of the family member(s) in the photograph. Students should then try to capture, as closely as possible, that feeling in their illustrations. After the class has drawn their photographs, have each student display what he or she has drawn. The rest of the class may try to guess which section that student illustrated.

"Bread"
by Amado V. Hernandez   (page 497)

The speaker in this poem is a pathetic man who committed robbery, then murder, while trying to steal food to feed his sick child. Now that he is in prison, he receives the bread every day that could have saved his child's life.

SELECTION ACTIVITY

Have students compare the theme of "Bread" to the theme of the play, "Trifles," which they read in Unit 3. Discuss with students how both selections describe crimes that some people may feel were justified.

Divide the class into teams and have students take sides in a debate about the guilt or innocence of the characters in the two selections—Mrs. Wright, who is accused of her husband's murder in "Trifles," and the man in "Bread," who stole and killed to get food for his daughter.

"Somebody's Son"
by Richard Pindell   (page 501)

SELECTION SYNOPSIS

A young man, named David, has left home to "find himself" and avoid his father's insistence that he go to college. After many months traveling across the country, David writes a letter to his mother, asking her to ask his father if he can come home. He asks his mother to have tied to the big apple tree on their farm a white cloth if the answer is yes. David promises that he will be passing by the farm, which is near Baltimore, soon.

David hitches a ride from a kind-hearted man on the highway, then rides the train into Baltimore County.

As the train approaches the big apple tree on his father's farm, David cannot stand the emotional strain. He begs the person seated next to him on the train to look and see if there is a white cloth tied to the apple tree. The man in the next seat comes back with the astonished reply, "I see a white cloth tied to every twig!"

SELECTION ACTIVITY

Ask students to imagine they are a close friend of David, the boy in "Somebody's Son." While David is away from home, he sends postcards from each place he passes through. On the postcards, he describes where he is, what he is doing, and what his thoughts and feelings are.

Have students draw and write the postcards that they think David might have sent. They can use the information in the story as a starting point, but they will have to use their own imaginations to create additional information. Also encourage students to show in the postcards, which should be dated, the process by which David comes to the conclusion that he is ready to go home.

"The Medicine Bag"
by Virginia Driving Hawk Sneve   (page 511)

SELECTION SYNOPSIS

Martin, a teenaged boy who is part Native American, comes home from school one day to find that his Sioux great-grandfather has come from Dakota for a surprise visit. It becomes apparent that the old man senses that he is dying, and Martin's mother, his granddaughter, is his closest surviving relative.

At first, Martin is fearful that his friends will make fun of Grandpa, but soon he realizes that they are in awe of the colorful old man. A more serious crisis develops, however, when it becomes apparent that Grandpa plans to give Martin the Medicine Bag—a sacred leather pouch that has been passed from one male to another for many generations. Martin is afraid that he will have to wear the pouch, and endure the ridicule of his peers.

The day comes for Martin to receive the bag. Grandpa tells Martin the history of the bag and what it means to him. Then, much to Martin's surprise, Grandpa gives him the bag, but tells him not to wear it "in this place now where no one will understand."

Instead, he tells Martin to keep it until he is on the reservation. A few days later, Grandpa dies, and Martin goes to the reservation to put sacred sage in the bag as Grandpa directed.

SELECTION ACTIVITY

Obtain from the library a copy of Virginia Driving Hawk Sneve's nonfiction book, *They Led a Nation*. The book is a collection of biographical sketches of Sioux Indian chiefs who have led their people throughout the history of the tribe. Each sketch is only about a page long, with a drawing. Make enough copies of various biographies so that a different biographical sketch can be given to each student.

Have each student read the biographical sketch aloud. Also read, or have a student read, Sneve's introduction to the book. Then discuss with the class the picture of Sioux life and history that Sneve's portraits provide.

"Medicine"
by Alice Walker   **(page 525)**

"Grandfather"
by Shirley Cranford   **(page 527)**

The subject matter of these poems is a child's view of grandparents. In the first poem, a child remembers the companionship of her grandfather, who is now dead. In "Medicine," a child goes into the grandparent's bedroom, where the grandmother is taking care of the sick grandfather.

SELECTION ACTIVITY

Both of these poems paint pictures with words. The poems also lend themselves to dramatization and/or dance. (The first poem would be especially suitable to a dance interpretation.)

Have students work alone or in groups to present a visual interpretation of each poem. The interpretation can be in the form of a drawing, a painting, a clay sculpture, a dance, or a dramatization. The important thing is that the visual interpretation enables the viewer to "see" the poem come alive.

Have students present their interpretations to the class. Students who have created art works can display them around the room, and students who have chosen dance and/or drama can perform their interpretations.

"Some People"
by Rachel Field   **(page 531)**

"My People"
by Bernice George   **(page 531)**

The theme of "Some People" is the way some people are a joy to be around while others definitely are not! The theme of "My People" is the speaker's pride in being a Navaho.

SELECTION ACTIVITY

The speaker in "Some People" describes two kinds of people that one is likely to meet. In this activity, students will work in groups to create skits in which these two types of people turn up at a party.

Remind students that they must decide on a setting for the party. Then challenge them to create dialogue that is clearly "in character" for each type of person. Also encourage students to be imaginative in creating situations that will bring out both the humor and the message of the poem.

"Otto"
by Gwendolyn Brooks   **(page 535)**

"Christmas Morning I"
by Carol Freeman   **(page 535)**

The subject matter of both poems in Christmas and the gifts that children hope to receive, but do not. Otto covers his feelings for the sake of his father, while the speaker in the second poem focuses on her own disappointment.

SELECTION ACTIVITY

Have students assemble a picture album that illustrates the characters, events, and themes of these three poems. For example, students might draw pictures of Otto and his father, of Andre and his parents, and of the grandmother sewing the rag doll. After students have finished their albums, have them display them in the classroom.

"Whale Hunting"
by Sally Nashook Puk   **(page 539)**

"Luther Leavitt"
by Alfred Brower
(page 539)

Set in Alaska, these two poems describe some of the community activity that goes along with whale hunting.

SELECTION ACTIVITY

Have students work in groups or in pairs to research the whaling industry in North America. Some topics that students should consider include:

the history of the industry and how it has changed

the technology of the industry today

the problem of many types of whales being endangered species

the products obtained from whales

areas in the world where whaling is still a viable industry (this information can be presented using a map)

STUDENT READING LIST

Ryan, Betsy. *Search the Silence.* New York: Scholastic Book Services, 1974.

Gridley, Marion E. *American Indian Women.* New York: Hawthorn, 1974.

Gilbreth, Frank B., Jr., and Ernestine Gilbreth Carey. *Cheaper By the Dozen.* New York: Crowell, 1949. Paper, Bantam.

Gunther, John. *Death Be Not Proud.* New York: Harper, 1949. Paper, Perennial Library.

Houston, Jeanne Wakatsuki, and James D. Houston. *Farewell to Manazar.* Boston: Houghton-Mifflin, 1973. Paper, Bantam.

From Globe Classroom Libraries

The Teen Years
Old Yeller by Fred Gipson

OVERVIEW OF THE UNIT

The theme of this unit is generations: the succession of families, the passing on of one's heritage, and the ongoing traditions within a group.

The first selections express, poetically, how children view their parents and other family members.

Literary skill: rhythm
Vocabulary: synonyms
Writing: extend characterization

The poem "Bread" is the annotated selection. The speaker is a father who is in jail for stealing food for his hungry child. The poem suggests that society can affect the generations of a family.

Literary skill: more elements of poetry
Vocabulary: homophones
Writing: express a personal opinion

The third selection, "Somebody's Son," describes the enduring bond between a runaway teenager and his family.

Literary skill: tone
Vocabulary: silent letters
Writing: extend a story

The next selection, "Fifth Chinese Daughter," is a classic example of the generation gap. The gap that can exist between different cultures is also considered.

Literary skill: theme
Vocabulary: root words
Writing: express one's own opinion

The fifth selection, "Medicine Bag," describes the relationship between a teenaged boy and his American Indian great-grandfather.

Literary skill: elements of plot
Vocabulary: words from other cultures
Writing: express a personal viewpoint of a theme

The next two poems each express a child's view of grandparents.

Literary skill: form
Vocabulary: adjectives
Writing: set down a point of view other than one's own

The poems in the seventh selection talk about groups of people. One poem describes two kinds of people; the other is about the Navajos.

Literary skill: figures of speech
Vocabulary: figurative expressions
Writing: describe two different types of people

"The Circuit" is the eighth selection. This short story describes the transient existence of a family.

Literary skill: ideas and values
Vocabulary: adverbs
Writing: compose a litter from a story character's point of view

Two poems make up the ninth selection. Both describe the reactions of children on Christmas Day.

Literary skill: theme in poetry
Vocabulary: nouns and verbs
Writing: express a different point of view than the narrator

The last selection consists of two poems that describe the whaling activities of families in Alaska.

Literary skill: tone
Vocabulary: antonyms
Writing: revive some personal memories

Generations

My grandmothers were strong.
They followed plows and bent to toil.
They moved through fields sowing seed.
They touched earth and grain grew
They were full of sturdiness and singing.
My grandmothers were strong.

The Family. Marisol, 1962. Painted wood and other materials, 6'10⅝" x 65½" Collection, The Museum of Modern Art, New York.

UNIT OBJECTIVES

After completing this unit, students should be able to

- understand five elements of poetry: denotation and connotation; rhythm; sound; form; and symbolism
- talk about real people and imaginary characters from personally drawn notes
- understand the process of how generalizations are made
- use an effective strategy in matching, multiple choice, and true-false tests
- build on a knowledge of literary elements to strengthen creative and analytic writing
- understand how negative prefixes reverse the meaning of root words
- increase the use of new words in sentences.

Teaching Strategy: Draw a family apple tree on the chalkboard. On one of the lowest branches write "your name" inside an apple; complete the lower branches with apples for brothers and sisters. On the branches above, draw more apples, and write **mother, father, grandmother, grandfather,** and so on, in each. Ask students to copy the tree, then fill in the names of the people who can be found on each branch of **their** family tree. Point out that the trees represent several generations.

AUDIOVISUAL MATERIALS

The Short Story (Guidance Association), videocassette. Explains the key elements of the short story and the different techniques and objectives of various short story writers.

Van Wyck Brooks (Ebra Films), 30 mins; black and white; 1960; film. videocassette. Brooks discusses the elements that create great literature.

Gwendolyn Brooks (Indiana University Av Center), 30 mins; black and white; videocassette. Brooks discusses her poetry and the Chicago environment that inspired it.

Forms of Poetry (Educational Audio Visual Inc,). Read by David Allen and others; disc.

Harry Crews (American Audio Prose), two cassettes; 2 hrs. 15 mins. Interview; Crews speaks of his family's nomadic lifestyle, and the uniqueness of the South.

Indian America (East Orange, NJ Public Library AV center), color; 50 mins. Documentary narrated by Henry Fonda about the broken hopes and dreams of American Indians in which they talk about themselves and their heritage.

Discussion: Guide students through the opening three paragraphs of the discussion on generations. Then, ask them to jot down some characteristics of their own family members who are of different generations.

Read through the rest of the unit theme discussion with students, allowing time to discuss the two questions that are raised in the last paragraph. Then ask students if they can relate anything they have read to the notes they wrote about their own relatives.

Cooperative/Collaborative Learning Activity: Divide the class into small groups. Ask each group to create a family tree showing at least three generations of an imaginary set of characters. (It might help students to imagine that they are writing a short story or a novel about the characters.) Each group's tree should include such information as the name of each family member when he or she lived, and, at the bottom of the page, a short narrative about what their lives were like. For example, a group might create a family from early American history in which the grandmother and grandfather were brought over on a slave ship, their son was born in Massachusetts, and his son fought in the American Revolution.

Generations. Can you picture yourself as a grandmother or grandfather? What kind of grandparent do you think you would be? Would you, as a grandparent, in any way resemble the "grandmothers" whom Margaret Walker describes so eloquently in her poem, "Generations"? Perhaps you would be quite different. Whatever your feelings may be, the subject of grandparents is one which deserves serious contemplation. In the poem that opens this unit, Margaret Walker talks about qualities in her grandmothers that she admires. What qualities do you think your grandchildren will admire in you?

Grandparents, parents, and children make up three generations in a family. The word generation comes from the Latin word *genus*, meaning birth. The span of time that exists between the birth of parents and the birth of their children is equal to one generation.

The poems and stories in this unit are about generations—parents and children, grandchildren and grandparents. Some of the selections also touch on a larger meaning of the word generation—the idea of cultural heritage or tradition. Tradition is the handing down, from one generation to the next, a body of customs, beliefs, proverbs, stories and long established practices and teachings which are generally observed from one generation to another. The average period is roughly about 30 years between the birth of one generation and that of the next. People are products of their cultural heritages, be it black American, Native American, European, or Asian. Reading these selections will help you become more aware of your own place in the generations of your family and within your cultural group.

Parent and Child.   The generation outside of your own that you probably know best is your parents'. Have you ever wondered what life would be like if you could have chosen your parents? In the poem, "Andre," the speaker is somewhat surprised to realize that, given that chance, he would choose his own parents from the vast variety in the world.

Sometimes, being a parent can be very painful, as two poems in this unit illustrate. In the poem "Bread," a man is sent to jail because he tries to steal food for his hungry child. In the poem "Otto," you will read about a father who cannot give his children the gifts that they want for Christmas.

Probably you have heard the expression "generation gap." A generation gap exists when parents and children have trouble understanding one another's needs, feelings, and ideas. One short story in this unit offers hope that the generation gap can, at least in part, be overcome. In the story "Somebody's Son," a boy runs away from his family to find out more about life and himself. As you read the story, you will find out what happens when the boy decides that he wants to go back home again. Perhaps the story will give you insight about what people of two generations really felt about each other. How true do you find the relationship between generations in this story?

Grandparents and Grandchildren.   For many children and young adults, grandparents are special people. In the short story "Medicine Bag," a teenaged boy and his family receive a surprise visit from the boy's 86-year-old Sioux grandfather. An important part of the story is the way the grandfather passes on to his grandson a tradition of the Sioux Indian tribe.

In the poem "Grandfather," Shirley Crawford writes about her grandfather's life and death, and wonders who her own grandchildren will be. In the poem "Medicine," Alice Walker considers the realities of illness and old age as she views her grandparents.

Important Others.   Perhaps you have had significant others in your life who have been as important to you as family. In the somewhat humorous poem "Some People," Rachel Field explains why she prefers the company of some people and not others. Two short poems, "Whale Hunting" and "Luther Leavitt," present important people in the lives of two young poets.

With your family and with your cultural heritage, you are a link between the past and the future. How has your life been shaped by the generations that have come before you? What experiences and feelings do you share with the generations in these selections?

Generations   487

LEARN ABOUT

Rhythm

Rhythm is a regular recurrence of units of sound. It is rhythm that makes you tap your toes when you are listening to music. It is also rhythm that makes you feel like dancing to music.

Poems often have distinct rhythmic patterns. You can discover the rhythm of a poem by reading the poem aloud and clapping the sound of each syllable in a word as you read. You will find that accents automatically fall on certain words, as well as on certain syllables within a word.

Some poetry does not have a recognizable and consistent rhythmic pattern. This type of poetry is called **free verse.** Still, you can clap out the rhythm of each line, but each line in the poem will have a different rhythm.

As you read the two poems, ask:

1. Do both poems have recognizable rhythmic patterns?
2. What are the rhythmic patterns?

SKILL BUILDER

Choose a familiar nursery rhyme such as "Jack and Jill" or "Humpty Dumpty." Clap out the rhythm of the nursery rhyme as you say it aloud. Then see if you can fit words of your own to the rhythmic pattern of each nursery rhyme.

ANDRE

by Gwendolyn Brooks

I had a dream last night. I dreamed
I had to pick a Mother out.
I had to choose a Father too.
At first, I wondered what to do,
There were so many there, it seemed,
Short and tall and thin and stout.

But just before I sprang awake,
I knew what parents I would take.

And *this* surprised and made me glad:
They were the ones I always had!

---

stout (STOWT) having a heavy-set body
sprang (SPRANG) past tense of the verb *spring;* arose suddenly

Generations 489

Sidelights: Gwendolyn Brooks has written several poems about families in which the title of the poem is the name of the speaker. In this selection, the speaker is a boy named Andre. Later in the unit, students will read a poem in which a boy named Otto is the speaker.

Motivation for Reading: Ask students to think about how they view the members of their immediate families. How would they paint pictures of their family members in words? Where would they place themselves in that picture and what would be its setting? Then say, In "Family Album," the poet's setting is a tropical garden. As you read the poem, think about how the garden is a symbol of generational unity.

More About the Thematic Idea: In the first poem, "Andre," a boy views the generation before him, his parents. In the second poem, the speaker views herself and her sister as part of four generations of women.

Purpose-Setting Question: What would happen if children could pick out their own parents?

Clarification: In the first poem, be certain students understand that Andre is the speaker.

Vocabulary: Preteach the vocabulary words. See the Comprehension Workbook in the TRB.

More About Vocabulary: Familiarize students with the vocabulary words footnoted in the selection by asking volunteers to use the words in original sentences.

Reading Strategy: Ask students to summarize mentally the chronology of the speaker in "Family Album." (first, as not yet born; next, as a child of two; and, last, at age 12 or 13) Also, suggest to students that they identify the other characters in the poem. (the speaker's older sister; her mother and father; and her grandmother and great grandmother)

Critical Thinking: Ask students, What can be inferred about the speaker's mother at the end of "Family Album"? (Her mother has died.) Then ask, How did you draw this conclusion? (She and her sister are kneeling; also, her references to "three generations" and "a hundred years" imply that her mother has joined the grandmother and great-grandmother.)

FAMILY ALBUM

by Diane Stevenson

1

A child with only the sun
in her eyes, my sister shields her face,
hand palm out, as if to say no.

2

Alone, the garden behind her fragments
of color, my mother seems to listen.
July, 1947: I am here, too, inside,
as yet invisible, though the sun
must filter through, like blood, to me.
I must be hearing her heart.

3

At two, I sit in the grass,
legs forward, facing the sun.
On the lawn in front of me,
a dark figure approaches,
almost touching my feet.
I look up, blink, and my father
records himself, a shadow,
just out of range.

4

Florida, 1960. My sister and I kneel,
behind us three generations of women.
No son's been born for a hundred years.
Even the palms are graceful women,
and hibiscus opens its wide, red mouth.

---

shields (SHELDZ) defends; protects
fragments (FRAG munts) parts or pieces
range (RAYNJ) the area in which an object can be seen
hibiscus (hy BIS kus) a garden plant or shrub bearing large, showy flowers

Gwendolyn Brooks (1917 - Present)

Gwendolyn Brooks is one of America's leading poets, and is the only black poet to date to win a Pulitzer Prize. Her keen interest in people is expressed in her writing. She published her first poem, "Eventide," at the age of thirteen. As a wife and a mother of two, Brooks writes in the context of a full and active personal life.

Born in Topeka, Kansas, Gwendolyn Brooks has spent most of her life in Chicago. The sights, sounds, and people of Chicago's South Side became the subjects of her poems, and she has created a vibrant picture of black urban life.

Numerous honors and awards have come to Brooks throughout her career. Her first book of poems, "A Street in Bronzeville," (1945) won her critical acclaim and Mademoiselle magazine's Merit Award as the outstanding woman of the year. Brooks has received two Guggenheim Fellowships; a prize from the Academy of Arts and Letters; the coveted Eunice Tietjeans award from "Poetry" magazine; and, for three consecutive years, the Midwest Writers Conference Prize.

Although Gwendolyn Brooks's formal education ended with junior college, she has through her own efforts become extremely well-educated. In addition to being a poet, she is an expert in modern literature, an outstanding writer of book reviews, and a frequent lecturer at numerous colleges and universities.

Generations   491

MINI QUIZ

Write the following questions on the chalkboard or overhead projector and call on students to fill in the blanks. Discuss the answers with the class.

1. Andre dreams that he must choose _____.
2. He decides to choose _____.
3. The speaker in the second poem is looking at pictures in _____.
4. The first picture she sees is of _____.
5. The third picture shows the speaker and _____.

4. her older sister
5. her father

Answers to Mini Quiz

1. a mother and a father
2. the parents he has
3. family photograph album

ANSWERS TO
UNDERSTAND
THE SELECTION

1. having to pick out a mother and father
2. the same parents that he has
3. herself; her sister, mother, and father; her grandmother and great-grandmother
4. Possible answer: he realizes that he is lucky to have the parents that he has.
5. He probably learned that he really likes his parents after all—something many children think they do not.
6. inside her mother's womb
7. He was probably somewhat distant and remote—"just out of range."
8. Answers will vary. Sample answer: I chose my parents because I could tell they really loved me.
9. Answers will vary. (Students should specify their relationship to each person they name.)
10. the poet's mother, grandmother, and great-grandmother

Respond to Literature: In addition to their individual responses, you may want to have students work in groups of four on this related activity. Ask each group to create a series of four sketches to represent the four time periods described in "Family Album"; allow students to change the setting from a garden to one of their choice, but staying within the structure of the poem. When the sketches are finished, reconvene the students as a class, and ask each group, What do your sketches tell about the characters in the poem? How is the author's attitude reflected in them? If some groups have depicted the poem differently, discuss the reasons for their interpretations.

T492

UNDERSTAND THE SELECTION

Recall

1. About what does the speaker of "Andre" dream?

2. What choice does he make?

3. About what particular group is the author of "Family Album" writing?

Infer

4. Why do you think that Andre is glad about his choices?

5. Do you think Andre learned something about himself through this experience?

6. Where is the author of "Family Album" in July of 1947?

7. What can you infer about the importance of her father in the poet's life?

Apply

8. Imagine that you picked out your own parents. Why did you choose them?

9. If you were to write a poem called "Family Album," who would be the characters in your poem?

10. Who are the three generations of women that the poet refers to in "Family Album"?

Respond to Literature

Which of these poems reflects more accurately your feelings about members of other generations in your family? Explain.

492

WRITE ABOUT THE SELECTION

Each section of the poem "Family Album" is like the description of a photograph in a picture album. Based on what the poet has written, can you imagine what each member of the family is like? Write a paragraph in which you provide additional information about one or several of the characters described in the poem.

Prewriting: Across the top of a sheet of paper, write the names of the generations —grandmother, mother, etc.—that are represented in this poem. Under each name, write down your ideas of what that person might be like.

Writing: Use your prewriting list to decide which character or characters you wish to write about. You may find that your description will be more interesting if you include information about the character's relationships with other family members.

Revising: You may be able to improve your paragraph by adding a direct quote or reference from the poem. Feel free to place the quote where it will be the most effective—at the beginning, middle, or end of your paragraph.

Proofreading: If you have used a direct quotation or reference from the poem, be sure you have inserted quotation marks. The quote or reference may be so closely woven into your writing that you do not need to begin it with a capital letter. You decide. Be sure all your sentences end with periods, question marks or exclamation marks.

Unit 6

ANSWERS TO
WRITE ABOUT
THE SELECTION

Prewriting: Have students work in pairs or small groups to make their charts. In this way, the ideas of several students will be represented, and students will have more prewriting material to choose from.

Writing: Remind students that

their descriptions should stay "in character" with the way each person is presented in the poem.

Revising: Have students trade papers with a partner. Ask each student to write on a slip of paper a quote from the poem that would go well with his or her partner's paragraph.

Proofreading: Before students proofread their papers, review

with them the correct use of punctuation inside and outside of quotation marks.

LDP Activity: Have LDP students work in pairs and choose at least 2 close relatives and list the things they like and dislike about each. Also have the students consider the possibilities of trading relatives.

THINK ABOUT RHYTHM

Rhythm refers to the speed and loudness of the words in a line of a poem. Rhythm can be thought of as a pattern of long and short sounds. In a poem, long sounds occur when a word or syllable of a word is accented. Poets select words for the sounds they create. Rhythm is the music of poetry.

1. Does the poem "Andre" have a regular rhythmic pattern?

2. If so, can you describe the pattern in terms of long and short syllables?

3. One line in "Andre" has a different pattern from all the rest. Which line is it? What is its rhythmic pattern?

4. Why do you think the author made one line different from the rest?

5. Does the poem "Family Album" have a regular rhythmic pattern? What does this tell about the type of poetry it is?

DEVELOP YOUR VOCABULARY

Synonyms are words that have the same or nearly the same meaning. The words *large* and *big* are synonyms; so are the words *small* and *little*.

In each of the following groups of words, all of the words are synonyms except one. On a separate sheet of paper, write the word in each group that does not belong with the others. Then choose one synonym in each group to use in an original sentence.

1. short, stout, heavy, bulky
2. covers, shields, opens, hides
3. fragments, pieces, colors, parts
4. invisible, hidden, unseen, alone
5. look, choose, pick, select
6. glad, uncertain, happy, joyful
7. thin, stout, frail, wiry
8. under, beneath, below, after
9. take, capture, approach, seize
10. remote, near, distant, far

Another use of sound that is similar to assonance is **consonance**. Consonance is a form of rhyme in which the consonants in stressed syllables agree but the vowels do not, as in "dogged" and "dagger" or "wide" and "wade." Partial consonance is also possible, such as in "shadow" and "meadow."

Suggested Questions

When discussing denotation and connotation, use "Family Album" as an example. Ask students, At the end of the poem, what is the denotation of the word "palms"? (tropical trees with leaves spreading from the top of the trunk) And what does it connote? (a feminine dynasty)

Have a volunteer read "Family Album" aloud. Ask students to identify the rhythmic pattern of the poem. (There is no recognizable pattern: The poem is an example of free verse.)

Ask students to find a second example of alliteration in "Family Album." (No son's been born . . .")

Discuss the symbolic meaning of the verb "kneel" in Part 4 of "Family Album." Help students to see that kneeling is often associated with a religious ritual; then ask, What can you infer from the word "kneel" as it is used in the poem? (that probably the speaker and her sister are at the graves of their mother, grandmother, and great-grandmother.)

FOCUS ON...

As with many other skills, reading poetry takes practice. Your ability to understand and enjoy poetry will increase as you learn more about the various elements of poetry, including denotation and connotation, rhythm, sounds, form, and symbolism.

Denotation and Connotation. Good poets choose their words carefully, for they know that a word can often have more than one meaning. One kind of meaning is the dictionary definition of the word; that is called the word's denotation. Another meaning is harder to explain. It is the meaning that a certain word suggests or brings to mind; that is called the word's connotation.

A good example of denotation and connotation are the words *house* and *home.* Both words have nearly the same definition in the dictionary (denotation), but what the words suggest (connotation) is quite different. The word house suggests simply a building in which people live. The word home suggests not just a physical structure, but the emotional center of a family.

Rhythm. Rhythm is a regular pattern of strong and weak units of sound. Another word for strong is **accented.** In the normal flow of speech, certain syllables and words are accented. For example, in the sentence, "Father and Mother are home," the first syllables of *father* and *mother* are accented, and the word *home* is accented. The rhythmic pattern of the sentence is: strong-weak-weak/strong-weak-weak/strong.

Rhythm is part of what makes poetry enjoyable to read and to listen to. Many poems have distinct rhythmic patterns. For example, in the poem "Andre," most of the lines have a rhythmic pattern of weak-strong/weak-strong. You can discover the rhythm of a poem by reading the poem aloud and clapping each sound as you read. This will help you identify the accented and unaccented sounds.

Some poetry does not have a recognizable rhythmic pattern. This type of poetry is called **free verse.** You can still clap out the

POETRY

rhythm of each line, but each line in the poem will have a different rhythm.

Sounds.   Some ways in which poets use pleasing sounds are assonance, onomatopoeia, and alliteration.

Assonance is a type of rhyme in which the vowels but not the consonants sound alike. For example, the vowel *e* has the same sound in the words *met* and *neck.*

Onomatopoeia is the use of words that sound like the thing to which they refer. Some words that can be used this way include: *bubbly, hiss, pop, tick-tock.* In the poem, "Family Album," the use of the word *blink* can be considered onomatopoeia.

Alliteration is the repetition of the same sound at the beginning of words that are next to or near each other. The tongue twister "Peter Piper picked a peck of pickled peppers" is an extreme example of alliteration. In the poem "Family Album," the last line of the second section contains alliteration: "I must be hearing her heart."

Form.   The form of a poem is the way the poem is constructed. Form can be closed or open. **Closed poetry** includes the couplet, ballad, and epigram. **Open poetry** has no recognizable pattern. The main type of open poetry is free verse.

Symbolism.   A symbol is something that stands for something else. Symbols are very important in poetry, since poets must use "compact language."

There are many different kinds of symbols that a poet can use. Some symbols are called **universal** or **general symbols,** because they tend to mean the same thing to most people. Some symbols, called **contextual symbols,** have meanings just within the context of a particular poem.

As you read "Bread," ask yourself these questions:
1. What is the form of the poem?
2. What universal and contextual symbols are present?

Generations   495

Practical Application

Rhythm is an essential element of popular music. Ask students, What songs are currently popular? Then have them analyze the rhythmic pattern of the lyrics of several of those songs.

T495

After completing this selection, students will be able to
- understand elements of poetry
- analyze the use of specific elements in a poem
- evaluate the effect of social problems on generations
- express a personal opinion
- use homophones

More About the Forms of Poetry: Guide students to a deeper understanding of some of the closed forms of poetry. To begin, you might point out that a **ballad** is often misunderstood to be a short, simple, often sentimental song. In fact, it can be a long narrative poem that tells a story and is suitable for singing. The **lament**, also misunderstood in recent years, is of Scottish and Irish origins; it is a poetic expression of grief and sorrow, often sung, over the death of a loved one. While the **ode** was originally a short poem, in modern poetry it is a lyric of undertermined length which expresses a sentiment in exalted style. Next, point out that an **epigram** is a short, witty thought that may or may not be in poetic form. Finally, say to students, You were introduced to a **sonnet** in Unit 1. Can you name its title and tell its main identifying form? ("How Do I Love Thee?"; it is made up of fourteen lines.)

Cooperative/Collaborative Learning Activity: Organize the class into pairs. Then, ask each pair to write a ballad. Suggest that they choose an incident from their own lives that tells a complete story. Also, stress that as they write, they should decide on how to present the ballad to the class— either as a recitation or a song with musical background.

Vocabulary: Preteach the vocabulary words. See the Comprehension Workbook in the TRB.

More About Vocabulary: Introduce the words footnoted in the poem by using each word in an original sentence. Then, ask for volunteers to do the same.

BREAD

by Amado V. Hernandez
translated by E. San Juan, Jr.

He had been imprisoned
for so many years,
time was a chain around his neck
knotted up in the windings of his life.

5   A piece of bread
and a can of broth
are left at the door by the guard,
he grabs them with dirty hands.

When the wretched man
10   is about to swallow,
the tear-soaked bread drops,
rubbing against the bruise in his heart.

He remembers why
he was imprisoned:
15   he stole a box of crackers
because his sick child was groaning with hunger.

Trying to get away
from the fist of the law,
he killed his pursuer—
20   and never saw his little girl again!

Now life wears away
wearily, though now every day
he is given the bread that might have saved
his child, who died of hunger.

---

windings (WYND ingz) course of events
broth (BRAWTH) clear soup
wretched (RETCH id) miserable
pursuer (pur SOO ur) one who chases another

Generations

497

Motivation for Reading: Ask students to think about a time when they were tempted to do something wrong; for example, cheat on a test, tell a lie, or take something that belonged to someone else. Ask volunteers to share their experiences with the class. Then say, As you read the next poem, ask yourselves, Are there circumstances in which the punishment far exceeds the crime?"

More About the Thematic Idea: One message of this poem is the impact of social problems on family life. In the poem, the main character cannot afford to feed his child, and is driven first to stealing and then to murder.

Purpose-Setting Question: Is a wrong action taken for the right reason still wrong?

Reading Strategy: Ask students to summarize the events that led to the imprisonment of the man in the poem. (His child was hungry and he had no money, so he stole a box of crackers. When he was chased by police or some other law enforcer, he killed the person who was chasing him.)

Literary Focus: Have students identify the metaphor in the opening lines of the poem. ("Time was a chain around his neck/knotted up in the windings of his life.")

LDP Activity: Have LDP students discuss situations that start as a minor wrong or just "fun" and turn into a very serious problem. When the discussion is complete, compile a list of the situations that were discussed, having each team report their findings.

MINI QUIZ

Write the following questions on the chalkboard or overhead projector and call on students to fill in the blanks. Discuss the answers with the class.

1. The poem "Bread" is about a man who is in _____.
2. He is there because he _____ and _____.
3. He did things because _____
4. Each day he receives _____ at his door.
5. This makes him sad because _____.

4. bread and a can of broth
5. this is the food that could have saved his child's life

Answers to Mini Quiz

1. prison
2. stole and commited murder
3. his child was sick and he could not feed her

T497

ANSWERS TO UNDERSTAND THE SELECTION

1. a prison
2. a piece of bread and a can of broth
3. killed the person chasing him for stealing a box of crackers
4. Time weighed heavily on the man and was a bondage, since he would spend the rest of his life in jail.
5. possible answer: He is very hungry; this is all that he receives to eat.
6. He thinks of his little girl and why he was imprisoned.
7. for life
8. Answers will vary. Suggestion: the police might have been sympathetic to his plight and reason for stealing the crackers.
9. Answers may vary; he may have been so desperate to get the food to his daughter that he did not think clearly.
10. Possible answer: He might have begged; he might have asked a storekeeper to give him food in exchange for chores or other work.

Respond to Literature: Ask students to imagine that they are members of a jury asked to try the central character in the poem. Have them list the factors for and against life imprisonment. Have students make a chart as a study aid. An additional or alternative activity might be having groups of students dramatize the trial. Students could play the roles of the defendant, the judge, members of the jury, and the defendent's lawyer.

WRITE ABOUT THE SELECTION

Prewriting: Have students get together in small groups to discuss their reactions to the poem. Ask one member of each group to summarize the discussion for the class.

T498

UNDERSTAND THE SELECTION

Recall

1. What is the setting of the poem?

2. What did the guard leave outside the door each day?

3. What crime did the central character commit?

Infer

4. What is the meaning of the metaphor, "time was a chain around his neck"?

5. Why do you think the prisoner grabs at the bread and broth?

6. Why do you think he cannot swallow the bread?

7. For how long do you assume the man will be in prison?

Apply

8. What do you think might have happened if the man had not killed his pursuer?

9. Do you think that the man in the poem acted wisely? Why do you think he acted as he did?

10. How else might he have handled his problem?

Respond to Literature

What does this poem say about how society can affect generations in a family? What is this poem protesting?

WRITE ABOUT THE SELECTION

There is an unexpected twist to the poem "Bread," which is expressed in the last stanza. The prisoner stole bread to try and save his child's life; now in prison—now that it is too late—he receives bread every day. What is your reaction to this turn of events? Write a paragraph in which you express your opinion about the series of events described in the poem.

Prewriting: Read the poem several times. As you read, make notes about your feelings and reactions. Do not hold back; your emotions may be very strong.

Writing: Use your notes to write a paragraph in which you react to the plight of the prisoner. As you write, you may find it helpful to imagine first that you are the man stealing the crackers—how would you feel? Then imagine that you are the storekeeper whose crackers are stolen. Finally, imagine that you are the police or the prison guard. To add realism to your writing, you might want to include a few slang terms that you use everyday in your neighborhood.

Revising: The final sentence of your paragraph should sum up your opinion. Try writing your final sentence several different ways, then choose the sentence that provides the strongest conclusion.

Proofreading: Make sure that your paragraph is correct in subject/verb agreement. If you chose to use any slang terms, do not enclose them in quotation marks. It will only annoy your reader.

Writing: Before students begin writing, discuss the meaning of the word "irony." Point out that this poem has an ironic twist, because the bread that the man received in jail could have saved the life of his child. Encourage students to refer to this irony in their writing.

Revising: Have students trade papers with one or two other students to see which concluding sentence they like best.

Proofreading: Put several students' papers on an overhead projector. Proofread the papers as a class exercise.

LDP Activity: Have LDP students choose one of the situations from the list of situations that start out minor, but turn serious, and explain in a paragraph how they would avoid making the same mistakes.

THINK ABOUT THE ELEMENTS

Some important elements of poetry include denotation and connotation, symbolism, sounds, rhythm, and form. **Denotation** is the dictionary definition of a word, while **connotation** is the meaning or feeling that a word evokes. When **symbolism** is used, a word has a meaning beyond itself. The symbolic meaning of a word may be **universal** or **contextual**. Sometimes, poets choose words according to their sounds, using such devices as **alliteration, assonance,** and **onomatopoeia. Rhythm** is the pattern of accented and unaccented sounds. **Form** is the way that a poem is constructed.

1. What is the universal symbolism of bread in the poem? What is the contextual symbolism?

2. What is the form of the poem?

3. Give two examples of alliteration.

4. Give an example of assonance.

5. What is the connotation of the word *grabs?*

DEVELOP YOUR VOCABULARY

Homophones are words that sound alike but have different spellings and meanings. The words *beet* and *beat* are examples of homophones. If you can recognize that homophones have different spellings for different meanings, you will make fewer errors in usage.

Identify the homophone of the *italicized* word in each sentence below. Then use both words in an original sentence.

1. He took a *piece* of apple pie.

2. He *ate* the pie quickly.

3. The *bread* was on the table.

4. He had *been* imprisoned for many years.

5. It took *so* long to get home.

6. Can I get something *for* you?

7. The *time* passed slowly.

8. He tried *to* get away.

Generations

499

LEARN ABOUT

Tone

The **tone** of a piece of literature is the author's attitude toward the subject of his or her writing. Tone can also include the author's attitude toward the reader.

The tone of a story or poem can be funny, serious, light-hearted, sarcastic, or sad. An author may write in a friendly, personal way, or in a formal, impersonal way. From the tone of a story or poem, you may think that the author has an emotional feeling for the subject, or you may get the opposite impression.

As you read "Somebody's Son," ask yourself:

1. What is the author's attitude toward David?
2. How does the author address the reader?

SKILL BUILDER

Think of an incident that happened to you recently. Write two descriptions of the same incident, using a different tone for each version. For example, suppose that you decide to write about a fight that you had with a brother or sister. You might try writing the first version of the incident with a humorous tone, then writing the second version of the incident with a sad tone.

500

Unit 6

SOMEBODY'S SON

Richard Pindell

He sat, washed up on the side of the highway, a slim, sun-beaten driftwood of a youth. He was hunched on his strapped-together suitcase, chin on hands, elbows on knees, staring down the road. Not a car was in sight. But for him, the dead, still Dakota plains were empty.

Now he was eager to write that letter he had kept putting off. Somehow, writing it would be almost like having company.

He unstrapped his suitcase and fished out of the pocket on the underside of the lid a small, unopened package of stationery. Sitting down in the gravel of the roadside, he closed the suitcase and used it as a desk.

Dear Mom,

If Dad will permit it, I would like to come home. I know there's little chance he will. I'm not going to kid myself. I remember he said once, if I ever ran off, I might as well keep on going.

All I can say is that I felt leaving home was something I had to do. Before even considering college, I wanted to find out more about life and about me and the best way for us (life and me) to live with each other. Please tell Dad—and I guess this'll make him sore all over again—I'm still not certain that college is the answer for me. I think I'd like to work for a time and think it over.

You won't be able to reach me by mail, because I'm not sure where I'll be next. But in a few days I hope to be passing by our place. If there's any chance Dad will have me back, please ask him to tie a white cloth to the apple tree in the south pasture— you know the one, the Grimes Golden beside the tracks. I'll be going by on the train. If there's no cloth on the tree I'll just

---

hunched (HUNCHT) bent over

Generations

501

Reading Strategy: Have students read the opening of the story just to the end of David's letter to his father. Then ask them to predict the outcome. Ask students directly, Does David's letter indicate that there may be a favorable response from his father?

Literary Focus: Which characters in the story have a conflict? What is their conflict?

Reading Strategy: What plot question must be answered by the end of the story?

quietly, and without any hard feelings toward Dad—I mean that—keep on going.
Love, David

The sunset that evening was a violent one. Jagged clouds, trapped in cross-currents, rammed each other like primitive men-of-war and burst into flames, burning one by one into deep purple ash.

It made the boy sad to see the sun go down. He had learned that always at the moment when darkness prevails, loneliness draws closer.

A series of headlights made a domino of the highway. High beams flickered over him curiously. He put out his thumb almost hesitantly, wishing he didn't have to emerge so suddenly, so menacingly. One by one, the cars passed him, their back draft slapping him softly, insultingly, on the cheek.

Much later, turning woodenly to gaze after a car, he saw the glow of taillights intensify. Brakes squealed. The car careened wildly to a stop, and he was running down the road to capture it, his breath rushing against his upturned collar and the taillights glowing nearer as in a dream.

A door was flung open like a friendly arm reaching out to a tired swimmer. "Hop in, boy."

It was a gruff, outdoors voice. "I pret' near missed you. You ain't easy to see out there."

"Thanks, mister."

"Forget it. Used the thumb a lot myself when I was a kid."

"How far are you going?" asked David.

The man named a small place in Iowa about two hundred miles away. David settled back in anticipation of a good ride.

"Where you headin'?" the man asked him.

David glanced at him. His nose was big and jutting; his mouth, wide and gentle. His was a face formed without beauty—and without hesitation. He had a tough-friendly way of accepting David as a man, something which David was still young enough to appreciate as a fine luxury.

The boy looked out on the highway with affection. It would

---

prevails (prih VAYLZ) gains power over
careened (kuh REND) turned on one side

be a good ride with a good companion. "Home," he said with a grin. "I'm heading home."

The man heard the smile in the boy's voice and chuckled. "That's a good feelin', ain't it? Where 'bouts?"

"Maryland. We have a farm about thirty miles outside of Baltimore."

"Where you been?"

"West Coast, Canada, a little of Mexico."

"And now you're hightailin' for home, huh?" There was a note in the man's voice as if this were a pattern he understood intimately.

"Yes, sir."

David smiled wryly to himself, remembering another day. It was in the San Joaquin Valley. He was picking grapes. As usual, the sun ruled mercilessly. Grape leaves drooped. Pickers were humped in varying attitudes of defense, some with bandannas covering the backs of their necks. Even the dirt had sagged beneath the blazing heat, crumbling into limp, heavy powder.

David looked down at his feet plowing through the grayish stuff. For four hours now it seemed he had not raised his eyes from his feet. He stopped abruptly and looked back down the row, measuring his progress. He had gone maybe fifty yards.

The faint clink of scissors landing in his half-filled basket came to him and then the foreman was bawling at him, "Hey! Where do you think you're going? It ain't lunchtime yet!" David stared at his feet and the dust; and his feet were stretching out as far as they could reach, his fist was tight around the handle of his suitcase, and the dust swirling madly behind him. He didn't even stop to pick up his money.

When he reached the highway and the cars kept passing him, it was all he could do to keep from jumping out in front of them to make them stop.

"Yeah," the driver was saying now, "I know how it is." The corners of his eyes crinkled as if he were going to smile, but he didn't. "I was out on that same old road when I was a kid. Bummin' around. Lettin' no grass grow under me. Sometimes wishin' it would."

---

wryly (RY lee) humorously; twisted to one side

Unit 6

"And then, afterward," David asked, "did you go back home?"

"Nope. I didn't have no home to go back to, like you do. The road was my only home. Lost my ma and pa when I was a little shaver. Killed in a car wreck."

"That's rough," David said with such feeling the man glanced at him sharply.

The boy was staring into the night. The man shifted his grip on the wheel, deftly straddling a dead jack rabbit. He spoke softly to the boy as if he were aware he was interrupting important thoughts. "Bet you could do with some sleep."

"You sure you won't be needing me later to help keep you awake?" David asked.

"Don't worry 'bout me none. I like drivin' at night. You just lean back there and help yourself."

"Well, okay," David said. "Thanks."

Sometime later, he was awakened by a sharp decrease in speed. They were entering a town. He sat up and jerked the letter out of his jacket pocket. He had almost forgotten.

"Excuse me, sir, but would you mind stopping at a mailbox so I can mail this? I want to make sure that it gets home before I do."

"Course not," the man said. "Here's one comin' up now." He pulled over to the curb and stopped.

When the boy got back in, the man smiled kindly. "Bet your folks'll be tickled to hear from you."

"I hope so, sir." David tilted his head back and closed his eyes.

The next day, rides were slow. They were what David called "farmer rides," a few miles here, a couple of miles there, with long waits in between.

Toward nightfall, he forsook the unfriendly asphalt and swung onto a panting, slow-moving freight aimed stolidly east. As the train trundled laboriously over the Mississippi, a few drops of rain slapped the metal floor of his gondola car, and then, suddenly, he was surrounded by water, the river beneath him,

---

deftly (DEFT lee) cleverly
asphalt (AS fawlt) road pavement
stolidly (STOL id lee) dully; unemotionally
trundled (TRUN dud) rolled along; moved on wheels

Generations

505

Critical Thinking: Have students discuss the differences that exists between David and the man who picks him up on the highway. (Answers may vary. An important difference considering the theme of this story is that the man had no parents when he was growing up, while David does.)

and everywhere else, walls of rain. He crawled into a corner and huddled under some scraps of heavy paper that had been used to wrap freight.

For thirty miles, the rain pounded him, slashing his paper hut to tatters and turning his clothes into puddles of mush.

As, cold and wet, he swayed with the motion of the car, his last seven months haunted him. A spinning constellation of faces, flaring up and dying away, careened toward him. Faces of truck drivers, waitresses, salesmen, cops, employment agents, winos, tramps, cowboys, bartenders. Faces of people who had been kind to him; faces of people who had used him. They went on and on.

Well, he would never see them again. He had experienced them quickly, dazedly, as they had experienced him. He had no idea where they were now, and they did not know where he was.

Finally the rain stopped. He lunged erect, inviting the warm, night air to dry him. He looked out over the top of his racketing steel box. He faced east—toward home. They didn't have any idea where he was, either.

The train was hammering along beside a highway. He stared at the houses on the other side. How would it be at home? Would his house be like that one, the one with the porch light burning? Or would it be like that one, where the porch was dark and where over each of the lighted windows a yellow shade was pulled down firmly to the sill?

A couple of days later, in the middle of Maryland, maddeningly close to home, the flow of rides narrowed to a trickle and then ceased altogether. When cars weren't in sight, he walked. After a while, he didn't even bother to stop and hold out his thumb. Furiously, he walked.

Later, seated on the passenger train—the only freights around here ran at night—he wished with slow, frightened heartbeats that he were back on the road, headed the other way.

Three inches from his nose was the dust-stained window through which in a few minutes he would look out across his father's fields. Two different pictures tortured him—the tree with the white cloth and the tree without it. His throat closed and he could hardly breathe.

He tried to fortify himself with the idea that whether or not he still was welcome, at least he would see the place again.

The field was sliding closer, one familiar landmark at a time. He couldn't stop the train. The frenzied wheels were stamping out the end of the crescendo that had begun with the clink of the scissors in his half-filled basket of grapes. Nothing could postpone the denouement now. The tree was around the next bend.

He couldn't look. He was too afraid the cloth would not be there—too afraid he would find, staring back at him, just another tree, just another field, just another somebody else's strange place, the way it always is on the long, long road, the nameless staring back at the nameless. He jerked away from the window.

Desperately, he nudged the passenger beside him. "Mister, will you do me a favor? Around this bend on the right, you'll see an apple tree. I wonder if you'll tell me if you see a white cloth tied to one of its branches?"

As they passed the field, the boy stared straight ahead. "Is it there?" he asked with an uncontrollable quaver.

"Son," the man said in a voice slow with wonder, "I see a white cloth tied on almost every twig."

---

crescendo (krih SHEN doh) increasing in loudness
denouement (day noo MHN) the final outcome
quaver (KWAY vur) shake, tremble

Generations 507

Discussion: Ask students why they think there were so many white cloths tied to the tree. What do they think David's parents were trying to say? How did the ending of the story make them feel? Why?

Literary Focus: The climax of the story comes with the last line. Discuss why in this case it is more effective to end the story at a climatic moment. Tell students to visualize in their imaginations what happens next. Have a few students describe scenes following the last one in the story.

MINI QUIZ

Write the following questions on the chalkboard or overhead projector and call on students to fill in the blanks. Discuss the answers with the class.

1. Most of the story takes place _____.

2. David writes a letter to his _____.

3. He asks if he can _____.

4. The sign that he asks for is _____.

5. At the end of the story, David sees _____.

Answers to Mini Quiz

1. on the roads and rails between the Dakota plains and Maryland
2. parents
3. come back home
4. a white cloth tied on the apple tree
5. white cloths tied to almost every branch

ANSWERS TO UNDERSTAND THE SELECTION

1. The highways and rails between the Dakotas and Maryland.
2. his mother
3. to find out if his father will let him come back home
4. Having just graduated from high school, he's probably about 17 or 18.
5. He thinks that college is important and that David should go.
6. a good relationship. David is able to talk to her as a confidante.
7. that his parents want him back home more than he ever imagined
8. Answers may vary. Possible answer: David's father realized how much he missed David during his absence.
9. Possible answer: He recognized David as an adult for being out on his own.
10. Answers will vary but many will feel great joy.

Respond to Literature: Have students make a chart of the contrasts and similarities that exist between the man on the highway and David's father. Encourage students to make comparisons that may be inferred but not spelled out in the story. Then ask students to speculate on the kind of father the man might have been.

ANSWERS TO WRITE ABOUT THE SELECTION

Prewriting: Encourage students to freewrite the first dialogue between parents and son.

Writing: As students work on this section, go around the class. To help those who are having trouble, draw them out by asking how they would feel in David's place.

UNDERSTAND THE SELECTION

Recall

1. What is the setting of the story?
2. To whom does David write a letter?
3. What is the purpose of the letter?

Infer

4. About how old is David? How do you know?
5. What can you infer about David's father's attitude toward college?
6. What can you infer about David's relationship with his mother?
7. What message was given to David at the end of the story?

Apply

8. Do you think that David's father might have changed during the time David was away? Explain your answer.
9. Why do you think that the man David rode with accepted David as a man?
10. Imagine that you are David. How would you feel as the train came to the apple tree?

Respond to Literature

How do the man on the highway and David's parents show different aspects of the same generation? How do they show similar aspects?

508

WRITE ABOUT THE SELECTION

At the end of "Somebody's Son," David realizes that he can go home again. What do you think happens when David finally gets home? What conversations might he have with his father? His mother? His friends? Add an episode to "Somebody's Son" that tells what happens after David returns home.

Prewriting: Create an informal outline of what might happen the day David arrives home. Include details of conversations David might have with his parents and others. Take your clues from the details in the story.

Writing: Use your prewriting outline to write a paragraph that adds an additional episode to "Somebody's Son." Be sure to tell about David's feelings as he walks into his house for the first time after his absence.

Revising: When you revise your paragraph, add dialogue that makes the feelings of David and his parents clear as well as specific details that make the setting clear.

Proofreading: Read over your paragraph to check for errors. Make sure that you have used correct punctuation when writing dialogue. Remember that periods, commas, question marks, and exclamation points all fall inside the quotation marks when they are part of a character's speech. Be sure that all your sentences end with periods, question marks, or exclamation marks.

Unit 6

Revising: Have students work in threes to go over their dialogue. Suggest that for greater realism, they role-play David, his father and his mother.

Proofreading: Show some examples on the chalkboard or overhead projector of correctly punctuated dialogue. Then have students correct their own papers.

LDP Activity: Have LDP students write a paragraph about what they would tell a friend that is considering running away. Have them refer back to their partners discussion on things to consider when running away from home.

T508

THINK ABOUT THE TONE

The **tone** of a literary work communicates the author's attitude toward his or her subject. The tone of a story or poem may be humorous or serious, sarcastic or sad. Tone can also include the author's attitude toward the reader. Some literary works have a friendly, informal tone, while others have a more detached, formal tone.

1. What is the tone of "Somebody's Son"?

2. What does the tone tell you about the author's attitude toward his subject?

3. What do you feel is the author's attitude toward you, the reader?

4. In the story, David writes a letter. What is the tone of that letter?

5. What does the tone tell you about David's attitude toward his home and his parents?

DEVELOP YOUR VOCABULARY

Some English words have silent letters. For example, in the word *knife,* the *k* is silent. Words with silent letters can be tricky to spell and pronounce. Another group of words that can be difficult to spell and pronounce are words with letter combinations that sound like other letters; for example, the *ph* in pharmacy sounds like *f.*

Identify the silent letters, or the letter combinations that sound like other letters, in each word below. Then use the word in an original sentence.

1. asphalt
2. denouement
3. knight
4. knowledge
5. wryly
6. gourmet
7. write
8. whisker
9. photograph
10. physics
11. thyme
12. wreck

Generations

509

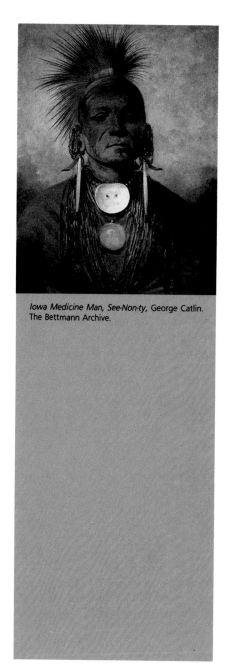

Iowa Medicine Man, See-Non-ty, George Catlin. The Bettmann Archive.

The plot is the plan or pattern of events that unfolds in a story. The important elements of plot are exposition, complication, crisis, climax, and resolution.

The **exposition** is the introduction of the plot. In the exposition you learn who the main character is and the kind of problem he or she will face in the story. Then comes the **complication**—a setback encountered by the main character attempting to overcome the problem. The decisive moment is called the **crisis** during which the main character either wins or loses the struggle to overcome the problem. The outcome of the crisis is called the **climax,** the most exciting part of the story at or near the end. Many stories end with the climax, but some do not. These stories are followed by a **resolution,** a kind of wrap-up of the story in which further questions are answered.

As you read "The Medicine Bag," ask yourself:

1. What is the plot of the story?
2. What problem is presented for the main character to overcome?

SKILL BUILDER

Choose a story in this book that you have read. Then make a list of the five plot elements as they appear in the story.

The Medicine Bag

Virginia Driving Hawk Sneve

My kid sister Cheryl and I always bragged about our Sioux grandpa, Joe Iron Shell. Our friends, who had always lived in the city and only knew about Indians from movies and TV, were impressed by our stories. Maybe we exaggerated and made Grandpa and the reservation sound glamorous, but when we'd return home to Iowa after our yearly summer visit to Grandpa, we always had some exciting tale to tell.

We always had some authentic Sioux article to show our listeners. One year Cheryl had new moccasins that Grandpa had made. On another visit he gave me a small, round, flat, rawhide drum that was decorated with a painting of a warrior riding a horse. He taught me a real Sioux chant to sing while I beat the drum with a leather-covered stick that had a feather on the end. Man, that really made an impression.

We never showed our friends Grandpa's picture. Not that we were ashamed of him, but because we knew that the glamorous tales we told didn't go with the real thing. Our friends would have laughed at the picture because Grandpa wasn't tall and stately like TV Indians. His hair wasn't in braids but hung in stringy, gray strands on his neck, and he was old. He was our great-grandfather, and he didn't live in a tepee, but all by himself in a part log, part tar-paper shack on the Rosebud Reservation in South Dakota. So when Grandpa came to visit us, I was so ashamed and embarrassed I could've died.

There are a lot of yippy poodles and other fancy little dogs in our neighbor-

---

Sioux (SOO) Native-American tribes of the northern plains of the
United States and nearby southern Canada
moccasins (MOK uh sunz) heel-less slippers of soft flexible leather,
originally worn by native Americans
tepee (TEE pee) a cone-shaped tent of animal skins, used by the Plains
Indians
Rosebud Reservation A small Indian reservation in south-central
South Dakota

Generations

511

Sidelights: Virginia Driving Hawk Sneve grew up on a Sioux Reservation in South Dakota. She has written about the Sioux Indians in both fiction and nonfiction works. This story brings out the importance of the spiritual aspect of the Sioux culture.

Motivation for Reading: Ask students to imagine that they receive a surprise visit from an older relative who lives quite far away. (Some students may have actually had this happen.) Encourage them to talk about what the purpose of the visit might be and the complications that it may have caused their families. Relate the discussion to the surprise visit from Martin's great-grandfather.

More About the Thematic Idea: In this selection, three generations are spanned when a teenaged boy is surprised by a visit from his great-grandfather. The boy discovers that it is his great-grandfather's wish to pass on to him something valuable from his Native American heritage.

Purpose-Setting Question: What might a great-grandfather give to his great-grandson to carry on the heritage of a people?

LDP Activity: Have students consider the different topics on which they do not agree with their parents. Have students list some problem areas. Make two columns and list their point of view and their parents' point of view.

Vocabulary: Preteach the vocabulary words. See the Comprehension Workbook in the TRB.

More About Vocabulary: When preteaching the vocabulary words footnoted in the story, you may want to ask volunteers to draw some of the Native American products on the chalkboard; for example; tepee, bolo, thong, moccasins.

hood, but they usually barked singly at the mailman from the safety of their own yards. Now it sounded as if a whole pack of mutts were barking together in one place.

I got up and walked to the curb to see what the commotion was. About a block away I saw a crowd of little kids yelling, with the dogs yipping and growling around someone who was walking down the middle of the street.

I watched the group as it slowly came closer and saw that in the center of the strange procession was a man wearing a tall black hat. He'd pause now and then to peer at something in his hand and then at the houses on either side of the street. I felt cold and hot at the same time as I recognized the man. "Oh, no!" I whispered. "It's Grandpa!"

I stood on the curb, unable to move even though I wanted to run and hide. Then I got mad when I saw how the yippy dogs were growling and nipping at the old man's baggy pant legs and how wearily he poked them away with his cane. "Stupid mutts," I said as I ran to rescue Grandpa.

When I kicked and hollered at the dogs to get away, they put their tails between their legs and scattered. The kids ran to the curb where they watched me and the old man.

"Grandpa," I said and felt pretty dumb when my voice cracked. I reached for his beat-up old tin suitcase, which was tied shut with a rope. But he set it down right in the street and shook my hand.

"*Hau. Takoza.* Grandchild," he greeted me formally in Sioux.

All I could do was stand there with the whole neighborhood watching and shake the hand of the leather-brown old man. I saw how his gray hair straggled from under his big black hat, which had a drooping feather in its crown. His rumpled black suit hung like a sack over his stooped frame. As he shook my hand, his coat fell open to expose a bright red satin shirt with a beaded bolo tie under the collar. His get-up wasn't out of place on the reservation, but it sure was here, and I wanted to sink right through the pavement.

"Hi," I muttered with my head down. I tried to pull my hand away when I felt his bony hand trembling, and looked up to see fatigue in his face. I felt like crying. I couldn't think of anything to say so I picked up Grandpa's suitcase, took his arm, and guided him up the driveway to our house.

Mom was standing on the steps. I don't know how long she'd been watching, but her hand was over her mouth and she looked as if she couldn't believe what she saw. Then she ran to us.

"Grandpa," she gasped. "How in the world did you get here?"

She checked her move to embrace Grandpa and I remembered that such a display of affection is unseemly to the Sioux and would embarrass him.

---

bolo tie (BOH loh TY) tie A man's string tie, held together with a decorated sliding device

"*Hau*, Marie," he said as he shook Mom's hand. She smiled and took his other arm.

As we supported him up the steps, the door banged open and Cheryl came bursting out of the house. She was all smiles and was so obviously glad to see Grandpa that I was ashamed of how I felt.

"Grandpa!" she yelled happily. "You came to see us!"

Grandpa smiled, and Mom and I let go of him as he stretched out his arms to my ten-year-old sister, who was still young enough to be hugged.

"*Wicincala*, little girl," he greeted her and then collapsed.

He had fainted. Mom and I carried him into her sewing room, where we had a spare bed.

After we had Grandpa on the bed, Mom stood there helplessly patting his shoulder.

"Shouldn't we call the doctor, Mom?" I suggested, since she didn't seem to know what to do.

"Yes," she agreed with a sigh. "You make Grandpa comfortable, Martin."

I reluctantly moved to the bed. I knew Grandpa wouldn't want to have Mom undress him, but I didn't want to, either. He was so skinny and frail that his coat slipped off easily. When I loosened his tie and opened his shirt collar, I felt a small

Memories, Amado M. Pena, Jr. El Taller, Inc.

Generations 513

leather pouch that hung from a thong around his neck. I left it alone and moved to remove his boots. The scuffed old cowboy boots were tight, and he moaned as I put pressure on his legs to jerk them off.

I put the boots on the floor and saw why they fit so tight. Each one was stuffed with money. I looked at the bills that lined the boots and started to ask about them, but Grandpa's eyes were closed again.

Mom came back with a basin of water. "The doctor thinks Grandpa is suffering from heat exhaustion," she explained as she bathed Grandpa's face. Mom gave a big sigh. "*Oh, hinh,* Martin. How do you suppose he got here?"

We found out after the doctor's visit. Grandpa was angrily sitting up in bed while Mom tried to feed him some soup.

"Tonight you let Marie feed you, Grandpa," spoke my dad, who had gotten home from work just as the doctor was leaving. "You're not really sick," he said as he gently pushed Grandpa back against the pillows. "The doctor said you just got too tired and hot after your long trip."

Grandpa relaxed, and between sips of soup, he told us of his journey. Soon after our visit to him, Grandpa decided that he would like to see where his only living descendants lived and what our home was like. Besides, he admitted sheepishly, he was lonesome after we left.

I knew that everybody felt as guilty as I did—especially Mom. Mom was all Grandpa had left. So even after she mar-

ried my dad, who's a white man and teaches in the college in our city, and after Cheryl and I were born, Mom made sure that every summer we spent a week with Grandpa.

I never thought that Grandpa would be lonely after our visits, and none of us noticed how old and weak he had become. But Grandpa knew, and so he came to us. He had ridden on buses for two and a half days. When he arrived in the city, tired and stiff from sitting for so long, he set out, walking, to find us.

He had stopped to rest on the steps of some building downtown, and a policeman found him. The cop, according to Grandpa, was a good man who took him to the bus stop and waited until the bus came and told the driver to let Grandpa out at Bell View Drive. After Grandpa got off the bus, he started walking again. But he couldn't see the house numbers on the other side when he walked on the sidewalk, so he walked in the middle of the street. That's when all the little kids and dogs followed him.

I knew everybody felt as bad as I did. Yet I was so proud of this eighty-six-year-old man, who had never been away from the reservation, having the courage to travel so far alone.

"You found the money in my boots?" he asked Mom.

"Martin did," she answered, and roused herself to scold. "Grandpa, you shouldn't have carried so much money. What if someone had stolen it from you?"

---

thong (THAWNG) a narrow strip of leather

514   Unit 6

T514

Grandpa laughed. "I would've known if anyone tried to take the boots off my feet. The money is what I've saved for a long time—a hundred dollars—for my funeral. But you take it now to buy groceries so that I won't be a burden to you while I am here."

"That won't be necessary, Grandpa," Dad said. "We are honored to have you with us, and you will never be a burden. I am only sorry that we never thought to bring you home with us this summer and spare you the discomfort of a long trip."

Grandpa was pleased. "Thank you," he answered. "But do not feel bad that you didn't bring me with you, for I would not have come then. It was not time." He said this in such a way that no one could argue with him. To Grandpa and the Sioux, he once told me, a thing would be done when it was the right time to do it, and that's the way it was.

"Also," Grandpa went on, looking at me, "I have come because it is soon time for Martin to have the medicine bag."

We all knew what that meant. Grandpa thought he was going to die, and he had to follow the tradition of his family to pass the medicine bag, along with its history, to the oldest male child.

"Even though the boy," he said still looking at me, "bears a white man's name, the medicine bag will be his."

I didn't know what to say. I had the same hot and cold feeling that I had when I first saw Grandpa in the street. The medicine bag was the dirty leather pouch I had found around his neck. "I could never wear such a thing," I almost said aloud. I thought of having my friends see it in gym class or at the swimming pool and could imagine the smart things they would say. But I just swallowed hard and took a step toward the bed. I knew I would have to take it.

But Grandpa was tired. "Not now, Martin," he said, waving his hand in dismissal. "It is not time. Now I will sleep."

So that's how Grandpa came to be with us for two months. My friends kept asking to come see the old man, but I put them off. I told myself that I didn't want them laughing at Grandpa. But even as I made excuses, I knew it wasn't Grandpa that I was afraid they'd laugh at.

Nothing bothered Cheryl about bringing her friends to see Grandpa. Every day after school started, there'd be a crew of giggling little girls or round-eyed little boys crowded around the old man on the patio, where he'd gotten in the habit of sitting every afternoon.

Grandpa would smile in his gentle way and patiently answer their questions, or he'd tell them stories of brave warriors, ghosts, animals: and the kids listened in awed silence. Those little guys thought Grandpa was great.

Finally, one day after school, my friends came home with me because nothing I said stopped them. "We're going to see the great Indian of Bell View Drive," said Hank, who was supposed to be my best friend. "My brother has seen him three times so he oughta be well enough to see us."

When we got to my house, Grandpa was sitting on the patio. He had on his red shirt, but today he also wore a fringed

Discussion: Have students discuss why they think the medicine bag was so important to Grandpa. What do they think the medicine bag represents? What traditions and objects pass on from generation to generation in their own families?

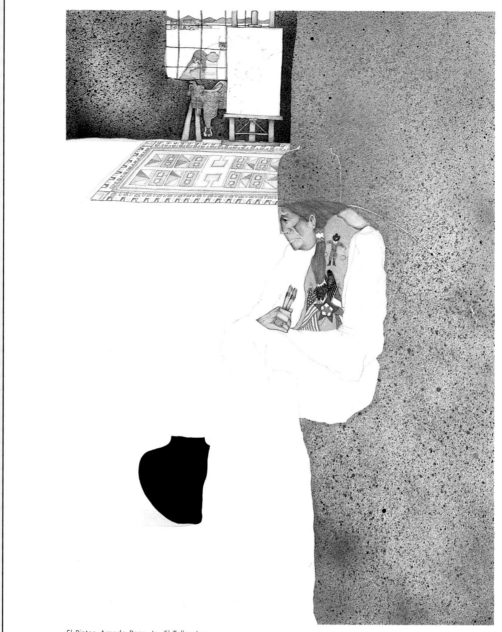

El Pintor, Amado Pena, Jr.. El Taller, Inc.

T516

leather vest that was decorated with beads. Instead of his usual cowboy boots, he had solidly beaded moccasins on his feet that stuck out of his black trousers. Of course, he had his old black hat on—he was seldom without it. But it had been brushed, and the feather in the beaded headband was proudly erect, its tip a brighter white. His hair lay in silver strands over the red shirt collar.

I stared just as my friends did, and I heard one of them murmur, "Wow!"

Grandpa looked up, and, when his eyes met mine, they twinkled as if he were laughing inside. He nodded to me, and my face got all hot. I could tell that he had known all along I was afraid he'd embarrass me in front of my friends.

"Hau, hoksilas, boys," he greeted and held out his hand.

My buddies passed in a single file and shook his hand as I introduced them. They were so polite I almost laughed. "How, there, Grandpa," and even a "How-do-you-do, sir."

"You look fine, Grandpa," I said as the guys sat on the lawn chairs or on the patio floor.

"Hanh, yes," he agreed. "When I woke up this morning, it seemed the right time to dress in the good clothes. I knew that my grandson would be bringing his friends."

"You guys want some lemonade or something?" I offered. No one answered. They were listening to Grandpa as he started telling how he'd killed the deer from which his vest was made.

Grandpa did most of the talking while my friends were there. I was so proud of him and amazed at how respectfully quiet my buddies were. Mom had to chase them home at supper time. As they left, they shook Grandpa's hand again and said to me.

"Martin, he's really great!"

"Yeah, man! Don't blame you for keeping him to yourself."

"Can we come back?"

But after they left, Mom said, "No more visitors for a while, Martin. Grandpa won't admit it, but his strength hasn't returned. He likes having company, but it tires him."

That evening Grandpa called me to his room before he went to sleep. "Tomorrow," he said, "when you come home, it will be time to give you the medicine bag."

I felt a hard squeeze from where my heart is supposed to be and was scared, but I answered. "OK, Grandpa."

All night I had weird dreams about thunder and lightning on a high hill. From a distance I heard the slow beat of a drum. When I woke up in the morning, I felt as if I hadn't slept at all. At school it seemed as if the day would never end and, when it finally did, I ran home.

Grandpa was in his room, sitting on the bed. The shades were down, and the place was dim and cool. I sat on the floor in front of Grandpa, but he didn't even look at me. After what seemed a long time he spoke.

"I sent your mother and sister away. What you will hear today is only for a man's ears. What you will receive is only for a man's hands." He fell silent, and I felt shivers down my back.

"My father in his early manhood," Grandpa began, "made a vision quest to find a spirit guide for his life. You cannot understand how it was in that time, when the great Teton Sioux were first made to stay on the reservation. There was a strong need for guidance from *Wakantanka,* the Great Spirit. But too many of the young men were filled with despair and hatred. They thought it was hopeless to search for a vision when the glorious life was gone and only the hated confines of a reservation lay ahead. But my father held to the old ways.

"He carefully prepared for his quest with a purifying sweat bath, and then he went alone to a high butte top to fast and pray. After three days he received his sacred dream—in which he found, after long searching, the white man's iron. He did not understand his vision of finding something belonging to the white people, for in that time they were the enemy. When he came down from the butte to cleanse himself at the stream below, he found the remains of a campfire and the broken shell of an iron kettle. This was a sign that reinforced his dream. He took a piece of the iron for his medicine bag, which he had made of elk skin years before, to prepare for his quest.

"He returned to his village, where he told his dream to the wise old men of the tribe. They gave him the name *Iron Shell,* but neither did they understand the meaning of the dream. The first Iron Shell kept the piece of iron with him at all times and believed it gave him protection from the evils of those unhappy days.

"Then a terrible thing happened to Iron Shell. He and several other young men were taken from their homes by the soldiers and sent far away to a white man's boarding school. He was angry and lonesome for his parents and the young girl he had wed before he was taken away. At first Iron Shell resisted the teacher's attempts to change him, and he did not try to learn. One day it was his turn to work in the school's blacksmith shop. As he walked into the place, he knew that his medicine had brought him there to learn and work with the white man's iron.

"Iron Shell became a blacksmith and worked at the trade when he returned to the reservation. All of his life he treasured the medicine bag. When he was old, and I was a man, he gave it to me, for no one made the vision quest any more."

Grandpa quit talking, and I stared in disbelief as he covered his face with his hands. His shoulders were shaking with quiet sobs, and I looked away until he began to speak again.

"I kept the bag until my son, your mother's father, was a man and had to leave us to fight in the war across the ocean. I gave him the bag, for I believed it

---

vision quest (VIZH un KWEST) a search for a revelation that would aid understanding
Wakantanka (wah kan TANGK uh) The Sioux religion's most important spirit—the creator of the world
butte (BYOOT) the top of a steep hill standing alone in a plain

The Banjo Lesson, Henry Ossawa Tanner. Hampton University Museum

would protect him in battle, but he did not take it with him. He was afraid that he would lose it. He died in a faraway place."

Again Grandpa was still, and I felt his grief around me.

"My son," he went on after clearing his throat, "had only a daughter, and it is not proper for her to know of these things."

He unbuttoned his shirt, pulled out the leather pouch, and lifted it over his head. He held it in his hand, turning it over and over as if memorizing how it looked.

"In the bag," he said as he opened it and removed two objects, "is the broken shell of the iron kettle, a pebble from the butte, and a piece of the sacred sage." He held the pouch upside down and dust drifted down.

"After the bag is yours you must put a piece of prairie sage within and never open it again until you pass it on to your son." He replaced the pebble and the piece of iron, and tied the bag.

I stood up, somehow knowing I should. Grandpa slowly rose from the bed and stood upright in front of me holding the bag before my face. I closed my eyes and waited for him to slip it over my head. But he spoke.

"No, you need not wear it." He placed the soft leather bag in my right hand and closed my other hand over it. "It would not be right to wear it in this time and place where no one will understand. Put it safely away until you are again on the reservation. Wear it then, when you replace the sacred sage."

Grandpa turned and sat again on the bed. Wearily he leaned his head against the pillow. "Go," he said. "I will sleep now."

"Thank you, Grandpa," I said softly and left with the bag in my hands.

That night Mom and Dad took Grandpa to the hospital. Two weeks later I stood alone on the lonely prairie of the reservation and put the sacred sage in my medicine bag.

sage (SAYJ) plant belonging to the mint family

Clarification: Have students explain the significance of each item Grandpa puts into the medicine bag.

520

Unit 6

T520

Virginia Driving Hawk Sneve

(1933-Present)

Writer and teacher Virginia Driving Hawk Sneve grew up on a Sioux reservation in South Dakota. Her knowledge of Sioux life and heritage has played an important role in her writings, which include novels, short stories, and nonfiction.

According to Ms. Sneve, the Sioux history was an oral one, with stories handed down by word-of-mouth from one generation to another. As a result, written records of historical events are difficult to find. Time, she explains, is less important to the Indian than to the white man, for Indians are more concerned with the dramatic significance of an event—and its impact on their lives—than with when it occurred.

In addition to several novels and many short stories, Ms. Sneve has written a collection of biographies of Sioux leaders entitled "They Led a Nation." In this book, she points out an interesting fact—that the word "chief" is not a Native American word. "Chief" is a word coined by non-Native Americans to refer to the leader of a Native American tribe. Yet Sneve often uses the word "chief" in her stories, because she feels that for her readers it evokes "a picture of stoic greatness, unflincing courage, and . . . manly beauty and strength. To use another word for these men would be to rob them of their glory."

Generations   521

ANSWERS TO UNDERSTAND THE SELECTION

1. Martin, a teenaged boy
2. Martin's great-grandfather
3. He has told her friends tall tales about Grandpa and is afraid his friends will laugh at him.
4. He knew that he was not going to live much longer.
5. He said it would not be right to wear it in this time and place where no one would understand.
6. He was embarrassed, angry (at the dogs barking at Grandpa), and he felt like crying.
7. The sexes seemed to be quite segregated, with things like the medicine bag not known to women; the relationships within a family were very formal, with little display of affection.
8. Cheryl was totally glad to see him and readily brought her friends home. Martin cared for Grandpa but had mixed feelings about his visit, and was afraid to bring his friends home.
9. Cheryl, being younger, did not feel the peer pressure that Martin did and, accordingly, was less concerned about what other people thought.
10. Before Grandpa's visit, Martin admired Grandpa for his "tall tales." At the end, Martin admired Grandpa for his courage to travel to Iowa alone and for his devotion to his family and his heritage.

Respond to Literature: Have students think about reasons why many Sioux Indians choose not to continue traditions such as the medicine bag. Remind students that in "Ta-Na-E-Ka," the author mentions that many Kaw Indians had given up the Ta-Na-E-Ka ritual. Also ask students in what way Martin's great-grandfather has

T522

UNDERSTAND THE SELECTION

Recall

1. Who is the main character and story-teller in this story?
2. Who comes to visit?
3. What problem does this present for the storyteller?

Infer

4. Why did Grandpa travel to Iowa?
5. What indicates that Grandpa knew how Martin felt about wearing the medicine bag?
6. What different feelings did Martin have when he saw his grandpa walking down the street?
7. What can you infer about the relationships between men and women in the Sioux culture?

Apply

8. Compare Cheryl's initial reaction to Grandpa with Martin's reaction.
9. How do you account for the difference?
10. What qualities in Grandpa did Martin admire at the beginning of the story? What qualities did he come to admire?

Respond to Literature

Why are Martin and his family especially important to Grandpa in terms of generations?

522

WRITE ABOUT THE SELECTION

The short story "Medicine Bag" has several important themes. One of these themes is the importance of family traditions and cultural heritage. Another theme is Martin and Grandpa's very successful bridge of a three-generation gap. Yet another theme is the blending of white and Native American cultures, both in terms of the iron shell in the medicine bag and in Martin's mother marrying a white man. Which theme is most meaningful to you? Write a paragraph in which you express your opinion about one of the themes in the story.

Prewriting: Reread the story and list any theme you discover that was not mentioned above. Then choose from all the themes the one that has the most meaning for you. Cluster facts, details, and ideas about the theme you chose.

Writing: Write a paragraph in which you express your opinion about the theme that you have chosen. Your opinion can be positive or negative; it can be based on your own experiences or the experiences of people you know.

Revising: What point of view have you used for your paragraph? If you have written in the first person, try rewriting your paragraph in the third person, and vice-versa. Decide which version is most effective.

Proofreading: Make sure that all of your sentences have a subject and a verb. Correct any sentence fragments by rewriting them as complete sentences.

Unit 6

given up something of the old ways. (By telling Martin not to wear the medicine bag in a time and place where no one will understand)

ANSWERS TO WRITE ABOUT THE SELECTION

Prewriting: As a class exercise, create a prewriting cluster on the

chalkboard or overhead transparency.

Writing: Some students may find it helpful to ask themselves these questions as they write about theme: What did I learn as a result of reading this story? What did the main character learn? What problems did the main character go through and overcome?

Revising: Have students trade papers with a partner. Ask students to read both versions of his or her partner's paragraph, then offer an opinion as to which is better—first-or third-person point of view.

Proofreading: Review the use of subjects and verbs by putting a student's paper on an overhead projector. Have the class identify the subject and verb in each sentence.

THINK ABOUT THE PLOT

Without a plot, there would be no story. The events that happen in a story make up the plot. The main elements of a plot are **exposition, complication, crisis, climax,** and **resolution.** In a well-written **story,** every event and action is important and related.

1. What is the exposition of the plot in The "Medicine Bag"? Where in the story does it occur?

2. What complication is introduced into the plot? How does this add to the problem of the main character?

3. What is the crisis of the story?

4. At what point does the climax occur? What is the outcome for the main character?

5. Does the story have a resolution? If so, what do you think it adds to the story?

DEVELOP YOUR VOCABULARY

Several words in the short story The "Medicine Bag" relate specifically to the Native American culture. Some of the words, such as *moccasins,* have found their way into everyday speech. Words from other cultures have also found their way into the English language. For example, you are probably familiar with the word "igloo," which is a house built of ice used by Eskimos.

Find the meaning of each word. The cultural origin of the word is given in parenthesis. Then use each word in an original sentence.

1. tepee (Native American); also teepee
2. siesta (Spanish)
3. amigo (Spanish)
4. cafe (French)
5. cabana (Spanish)
6. pueblo (Spanish)
7. marionette (French)
8. marina (Italian)

Generations

523

1. The great-grandfather Martin had bragged about came to visit; it occurs in the third paragraph.

2. Grandpa plans to give Martin the medicine bag. Martin is afraid he will feel embarrassed to wear it.

3. Answers may vary. Some may feel that the crisis is when Martin's friends come to see Grandpa; others that it is when Martin is told to take the medicine bag.

4. When Martin bends over, thinking that he will wear the medicine bag. At this moment, he is spared the embarrassment of wearing the bag, for his great-grandfather understands his different life-style.

5. Yes. It indicates that shortly after Martin receives the bag, Grandpa dies. Martin goes to the reservation and puts the sacred sage in his bag.

ANSWERS TO DEVELOP YOUR VOCABULARY

Original sentences will vary.

1. cone-shaped tent made of animal skins
2. nap taken in the middle of the afternoon
3. friend
4. small restaurant
5. a beach shelter resembling a cabin with an open side facing the sea
6. people; an Indian village in the Southwest
7. wooden puppet with strings
8. place near the water where boats are kept

LDP Activity: Have students choose one situation from their list of embarrassing moments and describe this situation in a paragraph.

After completing this selection, students will be able to
- understand form
- use closed form to write a couplet
- discuss relationships between children and grandparents
- write from a different point of view
- analyze the form of a poem
- use adjectives

More About Form: An interesting form of poetry is concrete poetry. In concrete poetry, the arrangement of the words on the page contributes to the meaning of the poem. Sometimes the words form a picture, as in a poem about Christmas written in the form of a Christmas tree. At other times, the arrangement of words simply creates a feeling. In this selection, the poem "Medicine" uses words in this way.

Cooperative/Collaborative Learning Activity: Have students work in pairs to write two couplets. First, have one student write the first line and the other write the second line. Then have students switch roles to write the second couplet. Ask that they choose the one they like better for class presentation.

LEARN ABOUT

Form

The form of a poem is the way the poem is constructed. The two main types of poetic form are **closed** and **open.** Closed form includes most established forms of poetry, such as the couplet, the ballad, and the epigram. A **couplet** is a pair of lines that, together, form a complete unit —either because of their meaning or because of end-rhyme. A **ballad** is a short narrative poem that is written in four-line stanzas that rhyme *abcb.* An **epigram** is a short, usually witty, poem, dealing with a single thought or event. Usually, it is composed of either one couplet or two couplets (also called a **quatrain**).

The main type of open poetry is free verse. **Free verse** is, as you have already seen in several poems, verse that has no regular rhythmic pattern.

As you read the poems in this selection, ask yourself:

1. What form of poetry do you recognize in "Medicine"?
2. What form is "Grandfather"?

SKILL BUILDER

Write a couplet that consists of two lines that rhyme. The couplet should express a complete thought; for example, I'd like to go to bed and rest/ But I must study for a test.

Medicine

by Alice Walker

Grandma sleeps with
my sick
       grand-
pa so she
5   can get him
during the night
medicine
to stop
   the pain
10   In
   the morning
     clumsily
      I
   wake
15   them

Her eyes
look at me
from under-
       neath
20 his withered
arm

   The
medicine
  is all
25   in
her long
  un-
   braided
      hair.

---

clumsily (KLUM zuh lee) ungracefully
withered (WITH urd) powerless; incapable of action

Generations

Sidelights: Alice Walker (1944–) is an American novelist, poet, and short-story writer whose works deal with personal and family relationships. Walker is the author of the acclaimed novel, *The Color Purple*. She has also written a collection of feminist writings, *In Search of Our Mothers' Gardens*.

Motivation for Reading: Have students recall the discussion of generations in the opening pages of this unit. Read again, or have a student read, the opening quote by Margaret Walker. Discuss the way the poet views her grandmothers. Then relate the discussion to the poems in this selection.

More About the Thematic Idea: In this selection, two poems provide different views of grandparents by their grandchildren. In "Medicine," the speaker views the relationship between her grandmother and grandfather. In "Grandfather," the speaker recalls the relationship that she had with her grandfther, who is no longer alive.

Purpose-Setting Question: What do children remember most about their grandparents?

Literary Focus: Have students respond to the placement of words on the page in the poem "Medicine." Ask them if they feel that the arrangement of words adds to the meaning of the poem, and why.

Vocabulary: Preteach the vocabulary words. See the Comprehension Workbook in the TRB.

More About Vocabulary: Familiarize students with the vocabulary words footnoted in the selection. Use each word in an original sentence, then ask for volunteers to do the same.

LDP Activity: Have students choose their favorite grandparent and list adjectives to describe that grandparent. If the students prefer to choose a favorite aunt or uncle that is fine. Be sure they discuss why this person is a favorite.

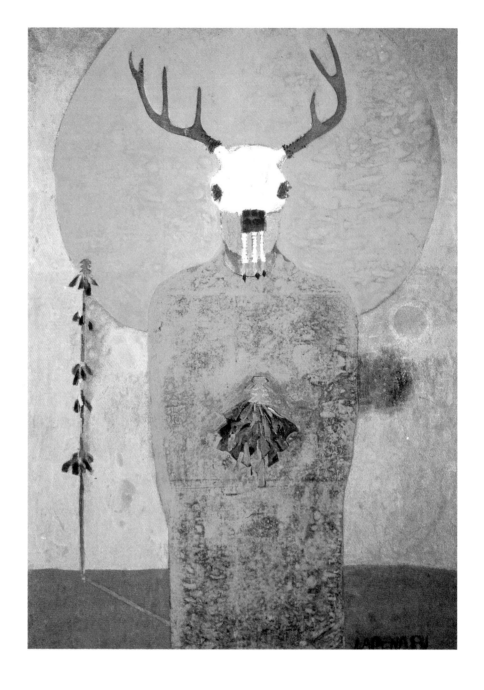

Grandfather

by Shirley Crawford

Grandfather sings, I dance.
Grandfather speaks, I listen.
Now I sing, who will dance?
I speak, who will listen?

5   Grandfather hunts, I learn.
Grandfather fishes, I clean.
Now I hunt, who will learn?
I fish, who will clean?

Grandfather dies, I weep.
10   Grandfather buried, I am left alone.
When I am dead, who will cry?
When I am buried, who will be alone?

Reading Strategy: Have students summarize in the poem "Grandfather" the things that the speaker and his or her grandfather did together. (sang, danced, talked, went hunting and fishing)

MINI QUIZ

Write the following questions on the chalkboard or overhead projector and call on students to fill in the blanks. Discuss the answers with the class.

1. In "Medicine," the grandfather needs medicine to _____.
2. _____ gets the medicine for him.
3. In the morning, the medicine is in _____.
4. In "Grandfather," the person who has died is _____.
5. The person who is left alone is _____.

4. the speaker's grandfather
5. the speaker

Answers to Mini Quiz

1. stop pain
2. grandma, his wife
3. grandma's long hair

1. the poet's relationship with her grandfather, and her interest in who her grandchildren will be

2. death of the speaker's grandfather

3. The speaker's grandfather is sick, and her grandmother is caring for him.

4. Who will view her the way she viewed her grandfather, when she is the grandparent.

5. They seemed to be close companions—real partners.

6. Probably quite young; a child

7. They appear to be very close and devoted to each other.

8. the relationship between speaker and grandfather; the relationship between the grandmother and grandfather.

9. No. One may infer that the speaker does not yet have children or grandchildren, as she seems to wonder who will view her as a grandparent.

10. Answers may vary. Possible answer: If the medicine was put on his arm, it got in her hair as she slept under his arm.

Respond to Literature: Ask students to speculate about how the speaker in "Medicine" feels in the presence of her grandmother and grandfather. (Possible answer: the word "clumsily" suggests that maybe the speaker felt awkward in their presence, perhaps because of grandpa's illness, or becauseof the closeness between the grandmother and grandfather.)

Prewriting. Have students get together in small groups to discuss the poems and other possible points of view. After a short time, bring the groups back together

UNDERSTAND THE SELECTION

Recall

1. What is the subject of the poem "Grandfather"?

2. In this poem, what event has occurred?

3. What situation is described in the poem "Medicine"?

Infer

4. In "Grandfather," what question is the speaker asking?

5. What kind of relationship existed between the poet and her grandfather?

6. Can you guess the approximate age of the speaker in the poem "Medicine"?

7. What can you infer about the relationship between the speaker's grandmother and grandfather?

Apply

8. What relationship is most important in the poem "Grandfather"? In the poem "Medicine"?

9. Do you think that the speaker in "Grandfather" has children? Why?

10. How do you think the medicine got into the grandmother's hair?

Respond to Literature

How do these two poems give different views of grandparents and grandchildren?

528

WRITE ABOUT THE SELECTION

Each poem "Grandfather" and "Medicine" is written from the grandchild's point of view. How do you think the same stories might be told from one of the grandparent's point of view? Write a paragraph or poem in which you speak from the point of view of the grandfather in Shirley Crawford's poem, or from the point of view of one of the grandparents in Alice Walker's poem.

Prewriting: Decide which poem appeals to you more. Then begin to make notes about how the grandparent might tell the story. Ask yourself: What tone would the speaker use? What aspect of the story would the grandparent emphasize? Take your cues from the details in the poem.

Writing: Use your prewriting notes to write from the grandparent's point of view. Be sure to include in your poem or paragraph the grandparent's view of the grandchild.

Revising: Try writing in the same form as the original poem. If you are writing based on Crawford's poem, use couplets. If you are writing based on the Walker poem, use free verse.

Proofreading: Check your paper for errors in spelling. Then compare your form to the original. If you chose free verse like Alice Walker, for example, you may want to change where a line breaks. Do not forget to place a period at the end of the poem.

Unit 6

and ask one member from each group to summarize their group's discussion.

Writing. If students are writing poems, make sure that they have a clear idea of what form they are using. If they are writing paragraphs, make sure they have a clear idea of who the speaker is, and whether the point-of-view is first or third person.

Revising. For those students who chose writing in the same form as the poem, have them read their poems aloud to a partner. Ask students to evaluate the effectiveness of their partner's use of form.

Proofreading: Choose several students' papers as examples of each type of form. Put the papers on an overhead projector and proofread them as a class exercise.

LDP Activity: Have LDP students write a paragraph explaining why they chose a particular relative as their favorite.

THINK ABOUT THE FORM

The **form** of a poem is its outward structure. The two main types of poetic form are closed and open. **Closed** poetry includes such forms as the couplet, ballad, and epigram. **Open** form includes free verse and concrete poetry, in which the arrangement of letters and words in the poem relate to the content—for example, a poem about Christmas written in the shape of a Christmas tree.

1. Is the form of "Grandfather" closed or open?

2. Does the poem resemble a couplet, ballad, or epigram? If so, how?

3. What rhythmic relationship exists between various lines of the poem?

4. Is the form of "Medicine" closed or open?

5. How does the form the poet uses in "Medicine" reflect the speaker's age?

DEVELOP YOUR VOCABULARY

An **adjective** is a word that describes a noun or pronoun. An adjective answers one or more of the following questions about the word it describes: What kind? Which one? How many? How much?

In a sentence, an adjective usually comes before the noun it describes. Sometimes, however, an adjective comes after the noun; for example, *Juan is sick.* The adjective *sick* describes Juan.

Review the meaning of each adjective listed below. Then use each adjective in an original sentence.

1. alone
2. sick
3. withered
4. long
5. unbraided
6. sparkling
7. interminable
8. personal
9. fancy
10. exciting
11. weary
12. patient
13. respectful
14. sacred

Generations

529

T529

After completing this selection, students will be able to
- understand figures of speech
- use figures of speech to describe a person, place or thing
- recognize the importance of heritage
- write a fantasy encounter
- analyze figures of speech in a poem
- use figurative expressions.

More About Figures of Speech:

Figures of speech are words and expressions that are used in ways that are out of the ordinary. While it is true that some figures of speech have become cliches, such as "tower of strength," good poets usually use figures of speech that are quite original— and that is part of the appeal of their poetry.

Cooperative/Collaborative Learning Activity:

Divide the class into small groups. Ask each group to think of as many metaphors and similes as they can that have become part of everyday speech. For example: tower of strength, pillar of the community, hard as a rock, light as a feather. Once groups have finished, make a list of common metaphors and similes on the chalkboard or overhead transparency for class review.

Tocito Waits for Boarding School Bus, Grey Cohoe. Private Collection

LEARN ABOUT
Figures of Speech

Figures of speech are specific forms of figurative language. Most figures of speech compare two unlike things. Two important figures of speech are similes and metaphors.

In a **simile,** words such as *like* or *as* are used to make a comparison. For example, you might say, "Riding in Grandpa's old car was like riding in a roller coaster."

In a **metaphor,** a comparison is made directly, without using like or as. For example, to say "My father is a tower of strength" is a metaphor. The phrase "tower of strength" describes a quality of the father.

Similes and metaphors add meaning by providing vivid imagery in describing a person, object, place, or idea.

As you read the poems in the next selection, ask yourself:

1. What similes or metaphors are used by the poets?
2. How do these figures of speech add meaning to the poem?

SKILL BUILDER

Look around you wherever you happen to be right now. Choose five objects or people that you can see clearly. Write a simile or metaphor to describe each.

530   Unit 6

Vocabulary: Preteach the vocabulary words. See the Comprehension Workbook in the TRB.

More About Vocabulary: Familiarize students with the vocabulary words footnoted in the selection. Remind students that they came across the word "hogans" in Unit 4, when they read "Chee's Daughter" and "Navajo Chant."

Some People

by Rachel Field

Isn't it strange some people make
  You feel so tired inside,
Your thoughts begin to shrivel up
  Like leaves all brown and dried!

But when you're with some other ones,
  It's stranger still to find
Your thoughts as thick as fireflies
  All shiny in your mind!

My People

by Bernice George

I am a Navajo; the Navajos are my people.
They live in the hogans upon the dry desert,
With a little shade house and a sheep corral.
It is nice and peaceful there away
5 From the city street.
There were the sad, dark years for my people,
But my people didn't disappear.
They started rebuilding, increasing
In population.
10 I am proud that the desert floor,
The lonely hogans,
Have made me thoughtful and
Respectful of my people.
I am proud to be born in my people's land.
15 I shall never forget my home and people.

---

shrivel (SHRIV el) wither, dry up, become wrinkled
hogans (HOH gunz) Navajo houses made of branches, clay, and sod
corral (kor RUHL) a fenced-in area for keeping livestock

Generations   531

Sidelights: In 1868, the Navajos were given a reservation that has grown to 16 million acres in Arizona, New Mexico, and Utah. The Navajos have the largest tribal newspaper in the US and the first Indian-operated college, Navaho Community College.

Motivation for Reading: Ask students to describe the kinds of people that they enjoy being with. Have them list some of the characteristics of these people, such as sense of humor, optimistic attitude, and so on. Then ask, How do these people make you feel about yourself? Relate students' responses to the poem "Some People."

More About the Thematic Idea: The poems in this selection refer to groups of people rather than to specific generations. The poem "My People" discusses the importance of the speaker's heritage. The poem "Some People" describes two types of people that are likely to be met every day.

Purpose-Setting Question: How does heritage affect the way a person feels about himself or herself?

Literary Focus: Have students identify the rhyming pattern in "Some People." (abcb)

Critical Thinking: Ask students what they think the poet in "My People" is referring to when she speaks of the "sad, dark years for my people." (probably the years when the Navajo Indians were first forced to live on a reservation.)

LDP Activity: Have LDP students list unique people they know or have known. These lists should contain ones they liked and disliked. The key word is "unique."

MINI QUIZ

Write the following questions on the chalkboard or overhead projector and call on students to fill in the blanks. Discuss the answers with the class.

1. In "Some People," the first type of person the poet tells about are those who make you feel _____ .

2. The second type of person makes your thoughts _____ .
3. The speaker in "My People" is a _____ .
4. The speaker's people live _____ .
5. The speaker says that she is _____ to be born on her people's land.

Answers to Mini Quiz

1. tired inside
2. as shiny as fireflies
3. Navajo
4. in the desert
5. proud

1. the way different people can make a person feel inside
2. the poet's pride in her heritage as a Navajo
3. a Navajo who was born on Navajo land
4. those who spark creative thoughts in others, and those who shrivel up others' thoughts
5. the way the Navajos rebuilt after hard times; they way they have continued to live in their peaceful life-style
6. probably not, although it is not totally clear in the poem
7. Answers may vary. Probably she is refering to some period when the Navajos were either persecuted or confined to a reservation.
8. the contrast between people who make you feel good inside and those who do not; the contrast between dry leaves and fireflies
9. Answers may vary; students should realize that the poet must have met many people before she set up the two categories.
10. The poem contains many facts about the Navajos but it also contains some opinion, as the poet presents these facts in a positive light and emphasizes her own pride in and respect for her people.

Respond to Literature: Ask students to think of a group of people outside of their families with whom they feel connected. The group might be friends, neighbors, a club, a sports team. Then have students list the aspects of this group that makes them feel happy or proud to be a part of it. Relate the discussion to the poems in this selection.

UNDERSTAND THE SELECTION

Recall

1. What is the subject of the poem "Some People"?

2. What is the subject of the poem "My People"?

3. Who is the speaker in "My People"?

Infer

4. What two groups of people does the poet describe in "Some People"?

5. What qualities of her people does the speaker admire in "My People"?

6. Can you infer whether the speaker in "My People" is with her people now?

7. What do you think the speaker means when she speaks of "sad, dark years for my people"?

Apply

8. What contrasts are made in "Some People"?

9. What personal experiences might have led the poet to write "Some People"?

10. Would you say that "My People" contains facts or opinions about the Navajos? Explain your answer.

Respond to Literature

In what way does the poem "My People" speak about generations?

WRITE ABOUT THE SELECTION

The poem "Some People" describes two different types of people. What do you think it would be like to meet each of these people at a party? How would they make you feel? Write one or two paragraphs in which you describe an encounter with each type of person described in the poem.

Prewriting: On a sheet of paper, make two columns. At the top of one column, write *Type 1;* at the top of the other, write *Type 2.* Under each heading list characteristics of the imaginary persons you are going to describe; you may, instead, want to base your descriptions on actual people you have met.

Writing: Use your prewriting notes to write one or two paragraphs in which you describe meeting at a party the two types of people described in the poem "Some People." Be sure to include details about the setting of the party. You may also wish to include dialogue.

Revising: Read over your paper and think about the tone you have used. Is your paper serious or humorous? Try adding specific verbs and vivid descriptions to make your paragraphs more interesting.

Proofreading: Make sure that each sentence in your paper begins with a capital letter and ends with a period, question mark, or exclamation point. If you have used direct dialogue, remember to insert quotation marks.

Prewriting: As a class exercise, use students' suggestions to make a prewriting chart on the chalkboard or overhead transparency. Encourage students to share personal experiences about actual people they have met who fit into one of the two categories.

Writing: Encourage students to use dialogue in their paragraphs. Point out that it is largely the things a person says that make us feel a certain way in their presence.

Revising: Ask for one or two volunteers to share their papers with the class. Place the paper on an overhead projector, then have the class assist you in revising the paper.

Proofreading: Have students trade papers with a partner to proofread.

LDP Activity: Have LDP students choose one individual from their lists of unique people and write a paragraph explaining why they liked or disliked this person.

THINK ABOUT FIGURES OF SPEECH

Figures of speech add meaning to a poem by providing vivid images that help you see things in new ways. Two important figures of speech are similes and metaphors. A **simile** likens two different things by using the comparing words *like* or *as*. A **metaphor** likens two different things directly, without using a comparing word.

1. State two similes that are used in "Some People."

2. What two images are conveyed by these similes? Are the images similar, or are they opposite?

3. State a metaphor that is used in "Some People."

4. What image is conveyed by this metaphor? How does it add meaning to the poem?

5. Does the poem "My People" use similes or metaphors? Can you think of a reason for this?

DEVELOP YOUR VOCABULARY

A **figurative expression** is a group of words that has a meaning of its own—a meaning that will be different from the meanings of the individual words. For example, suppose you say, "The answer was on the tip of my tongue." The expression "tip of my tongue" means that you were just about to say the answer.

Identify the figurative expression in each of the sentences below. Then write a sentence explaining the meaning of each figurative expression.

1. He was running around like a chicken with its head cut off.

2. The story was about a woman with shattered hopes and broken dreams.

3. Keep a stiff upper lip.

4. I think it would be best to talk and get it off your chest.

5. Donna decided to go home and curl up with a good book.

Generations

533

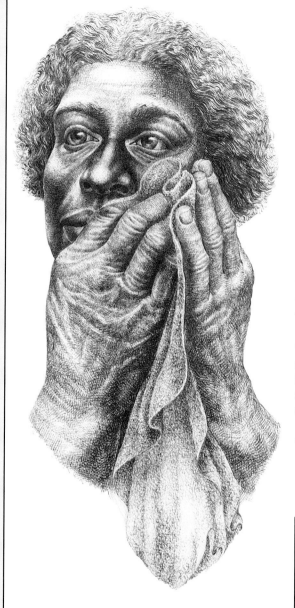

LEARN ABOUT
Theme in Poetry

You have learned about the theme of a short story. It is important to realize, however, that not only short stories have themes. Theme is also an important element of poetry.

Like storytellers, poets write because they have something to say. The **theme** of a poem may be what the poet values or feels deeply about. Two poems that you will read illustrate the poets' values in a few lines. In "Otto," the theme tells of a child's sensitivity to his father's difficulties. In "Christmas Morning I," the theme concerns a child's relationship with a grandparent.

As in a short story, it is important not to confuse the theme of a poem with the subject. The **subject** of a poem is simply the topic. Keep in mind that two poems may have similar subjects, but very different themes.

As you read the poems "Otto" and "Christmas Morning I," ask yourself:
1. What is the theme of each poem?
2. Are these themes similar or quite different?

534   Unit 6

OTTO

by Gwendolyn Brooks

It's Christmas Day. I did not get
The presents that I hoped for. Yet,
It is not nice to frown or fret.

To frown or fret would not be fair.
My Dad must never know I care
It's hard enough for him to bear.

Christmas Morning I

by Carol Freeman

Christmas morning i
got up before the others and
ran
naked across the plank
floor into the front
room to see grandmama
sewing a new
button on my last year
ragdoll.

fret (FRET) become worried or upset
plank (PLANGK) long, thick boards

Generations

535

Sidelights: Gwendolyn Brooks is sometimes referred to as a "people's poet" because she writes about the kind of people that one might see on the street any day. Brooks' view of herself is that of an ordinary person—even after many years of fame and literary prizes, she is likely to describe herself as "just a housewife."

Motivation for Reading: Ask students to think about a time in their lives when they did not get a present they had hoped for. Encourage students to share their experiences and talk about their feelings. Also encourage them to consider the reasons why they did not get the gift. Relate students' responses to the feelings of the speakers in "Otto" and "Christmas Morning I."

More About the Thematic Idea: The understanding of a child for his father is the theme of the poem "Otto." The relationship of a child with her grandmama and, probably indirectly, the other adults in her family is the theme of "Christmas Morning I."

Purpose-Setting Question: Can a child understand that the hoped for Christmas present is less important than a family's love?

Literary Focus: Ask students to find the examples of alliteration in "Otto." (not-nice/frown-fret/never-know)

Literary Focus: Have students identify the rhyme scheme of "Otto." (aaa, bbb)

Critical Thinking: Ask students to speculate about what the child in "Christmas Morning I" was hoping to find when she got up before the others. (Possible answer: She was probably hoping to find presents that she wanted; instead, she was surprised in another way.)

MINI QUIZ

Write the following questions on the chalkboard or overhead projector and call on students to fill in the blanks. Discuss the answers with the class.

1. The poem "Otto" takes place on _____.
2. Otto did not get _____.
3. He does not complain because _____.
4. The setting of "Christmas Morning I" is _____.
5. The speaker in the poem sees _____.

Answers to Mini Quiz

1. Christmas Day
2. the presents he wanted
3. He does not want to hurt his father.
4. a house early on Christmas morning
5. her grandmama sewing a button on her old ragdoll

ANSWERS TO UNDERSTAND THE SELECTION

1. on Christmas Day
2. A boy named Otto.
3. Probably the poet.
4. That the burden of providing Christmas presents is difficult, and that it would be unbearable for him to know of his son's disappointment.
5. probably his father's
6. That for Christmas she is going to get last year's rag doll with a new button.
7. disappointed
8. Both take place on Christmas Day, and both express a child's feelings about his or her presents.
9. Yes. Both children are disappointed by their Christmas presents. The first poem, however, expresses the child's understanding of the parent's dilemma.
10. Possible answer: The family could not afford to buy new presents.

Respond to Literature: Have students identify the different reactions of the two children. Then ask them which child they like better or find more admirable. Also ask them which child they most identify with, and why.

ANSWERS TO WRITE ABOUT THE SELECTION

Prewriting: As they work on this section, students may find it helpful to freewrite some conversation between the father or the grandmother and other family members.

Writing: As students work on their poems or paragraphs, go around the class and help those who are having trouble. Suggest to students that they imagine themselves in the position of the father or grandmother as they write.

UNDERSTAND THE SELECTION

Recall

1. When do both poems take place?

2. Who is the speaker in the first poem?

3. Who is the speaker in the second poem?

Infer

4. What does Otto understand about his father?

5. About whose feelings does Otto care most?

6. What does the speaker in the second poem infer when she sees grandmother sewing?

7. How do you think the speaker will feel about her Christmas presents?

Apply

8. In what way are both poems similar?

9. Do both poems express similar feelings? Why or why not?

10. Why do you think that the grandmother of the speaker in the second poem was sewing a button on last year's ragdoll?

Respond to Literature

What do these poems have to say about the relationships between children and parents, and between children and grandparents?

536

WRITE ABOUT THE SELECTION

Each poem in this selection is spoken from the child's point of view. What do you think the speaker's father would have to say in the first poem? What do you think the grandmother would have to say in the second poem? Write a paragraph or poem in which you tell either story from the parent's or grandparent's point of view.

Prewriting: Decide which poem you want to write about. Then read the poem several times and try to imagine that you are the father or the grandmother. Write down your ideas about how this person might feel. Also write down any additional details that you might want to add, such as the family's financial circumstances.

Writing: Use your prewriting notes to write a poem or paragraph from the father's or grandmother's point of view. Be sure to include the older person's view of the child or grandchild. Take your cues from the details in the story.

Revising: As you revise, consider using dialogue in your paragraph or poem. You can also present a character's thoughts in the form of dialogue.

Proofreading: If you chose to write a poem, reread it now with careful attention to your punctuation at the end of each line. You may choose whatever you want—a comma, period, nothing at all—as long as you keep in mind that end-of-line punctuation plays an important part in *how* a poem is spoken.

Unit 6

Revising: Have students work with a partner. Have each pair role-play conversations between the grandmother or father and other family members. Students can then use ideas from the conversations to write the dialogue.

Proofreading: Have students trade papers with a partner. Ask students to read their partner's poem aloud, paying special attention to punctuation. Then have partners discuss how the punctuation might be changed or corrected to improve the way the poem is spoken.

THINK ABOUT THEME IN POETRY

The **theme** of a poem expresses what the poet values, feels, or thinks. Often a poem communicates an insight that the poet has gained about life, about others, or about self. Like the author of a short story, a poet may state the theme clearly or leave it for you to figure out for yourself. Since poetry involves many fewer words than a short story, it is more likely that the theme will be suggested, rather than spelled out.

1. What is the theme of "Otto"?

2. What is the theme of "Christmas Morning I"?

3. What is the subject of each poem?

4. Would you say that the subjects are similar or different?

5. Would you say that the themes are similar or different?

DEVELOP YOUR VOCABULARY

A **noun** is a word that names a person, place, or thing. A **verb** is a word that describes action or a state of being. Some words can be used as both nouns and verbs. For example, the word *dare* can be a noun: "He took the dare and dove into the water." The word dare can also be used as a verb: "I dare you to tell Father what you told me." The meaning of words that can be used as either nouns or verbs depends on their use in a particular sentence.

Each of the following words can be used as a noun or as a verb. Write original sentences that illustrate both uses of each word.

1. call
2. frown
3. bill
4. present
5. care
6. bear
7. pass
8. throw
9. turn
10. button

Generations

537

After completing this selection, students will be able to
• understand tone
• use tone to change the meaning of a poem
• evaluate character's feelings
• write about a childhood memory
• analyze the tone of a poem
• use antonyms

More About Tone: One literary critic says that tone is what "colors" a poem and gives it "atmosphere." Tone is also closely associated with mood. The tone of a poem can convey a mood that is somber, giddy, serious, or lighthearted.

Cooperative/Collaborative Learning Activity: Divide the class into small groups. Have each group choose a poem or a paragraph from a short story to read aloud. Then ask each member of the group to read the poem or paragraph in a different tone of voice. Have students discuss how the meaning of the piece is changed by the tone of voice in which it is read.

LEARN ABOUT

Tone

The attitude of a poem is called the **tone.** The tone indicates the speaker's feelings toward the subject and, possibly, also toward the reader.

You can understand better the concept of tone if you think of the way tone of voice can change the meaning of spoken words. For example, if a person says in a friendly tone of voice, "That is a great dress you have on," you know that you are being given a compliment. If, however, someone says the same sentence in a sarcastic tone of voice, you know that you are being insulted.

As you read the poems in this selection, ask yourself:

1. What is the tone of each poem?
2. What does the tone tell you about the speaker's attitudes?

SKILL BUILDER

Read the following sentences silently. Then try reading each sentence aloud using various tones of voice. Write down how the meaning of each sentence is changed by the way it is spoken.

Where are you going?
The weather is supposed to be warm and sunny.
You are an hour early!
I am going out to take a walk.

538

Unit 6

Vocabulary: Preteach the vocabulary words. See Comprehension Workbook in the TRB.

More About Vocabulary: As you review the vocabulary words footnoted in the selection, have students locate Alaska and the Bering Sea on a map.

LDP Activity: Have LDP students consider the fact that many of their ancestors did not live in cities and they may have earned their livings in very different ways than their parents. These relatives may have lived in other countries. Have students list some of their relatives, where they lived and how they earned their livings. Students may need to "interview" parents to find out the information on grandparents they may never have met.

Whale Hunting

by Sally Nashook Puk

My daddy goes whaling in the Bering Sea
I'm just a girl, he can't take me
My brother joins the whaling group
They caught four this year
for muk-tuk soup.

Luther Leavitt

by Alfred Brower

Luther Leavitt is a whale hunter.
last year
they got a whale
we went
to the blanket toss
I never
got a chance to go
on the blanket
cause there were too many kids.

---

whaling (HWAYL ing) hunting whales
Bering Sea (BIR ing SEE) part of the north Pacific Ocean between
    Alaska and Siberia

Generations   539

MINI QUIZ

Write the following questions on the chalkboard or overhead projector and call on students to fill in the blanks. Discuss the answers with the class.

1. In "Whale Hunting," the speaker's _____ and _____ go whaling.
2. The speaker cannot go because_____ .
3. Whales are used to make _____ .
4. When Luther Leavitt got a whale, people celebrated with _____ .
5. The speaker was left out because _____ .

Answers to Mini Quiz

1. father, brother
2. She is a girl.
3. muk-tuk soup
4. a blanket toss
5. There were "too many kids."

T539

ANSWERS TO UNDERSTAND THE SELECTION

1. Alaska, near the Bering Sea
2. a celebration of a successful whale hunt
3. whale hunting
4. a blanket toss that seemed to involve the community
5. She does not particularly like being a girl.
6. She is not able to do what her father and brother can do.
7. It seems to be important to both her family and community.
8. It is really about the child speaking, because it deals with his or her feelings about the event.
9. Both feel left out of an important event.
10. envious

Respond to Literature: In both poems, a child feels left out of an important event. Have students list the similarities and differences in the situations of the two children. For example, the child in the first poem is excluded because of gender, and this exclusion is probably permanent. The child in the second poem is excluded because a particular event is crowded; he or she may very well not be left out of a similar event in the future.

WRITE ABOUT THE SELECTION

Prewriting: Ask for a volunteer to have his or her prewriting cluster displayed on an overhead projector. Encourage students to ask questions of the person to bring out additional details. Then give students a few more minutes to add details to their own clusters.

Writing: Remind students that they are to compare their memory with one of the poems, not just relate an incident. Encourage them to use comparison words such as like, as, unlike, and so on.

T540

UNDERSTAND THE SELECTION

Recall

1. What is the setting of the first poem?
2. What is the setting of the second poem?
3. What occupation is discussed in both poems?

Infer

4. What in the second poem tells you that catching a whale is an important event?
5. What can you infer from the first poem about the speaker's feelings about being a girl?
6. Why do you think the speaker feels this way?
7. Why is whaling important to the speaker in the first poem?

Apply

8. The second poem is entitled "Luther Leavitt," but who is the poem really about? Explain your answer.
9. In what way do the speakers in both poems have similar feelings?
10. How do you think the speaker in the first poem feels toward her brother?

Respond to Literature

What aspects of generations are illustrated by these two poems?

540

WRITE ABOUT THE SELECTION

In the poems, two children express their observations and feelings about events connected with whale hunting. Most probably you have never lived in a place where people whale hunt, but you may have childhood memories that are similar to those of the speakers in other ways. For example, perhaps you had to stay behind as your brother or sister joined a parent or grandparent in doing something important. Perhaps you were the only child who did not win a prize at a party. Write a paragraph in which you compare a memory from your childhood with one of these poems in.

Prewriting: Take a few minutes to cluster incidents that you remember from childhood. Write down your ideas and any details that you can remember.

Writing: Choose the incident that you remember most vividly or about which you feel most strongly. Then use your prewriting cluster to write a paragraph in which you compare and contrast this incident with the incident described in one of the poems.

Revising: As you revise your paragraph, make sure that your feelings about the incident are clearly communicated. Often, adding adverbs can help to communicate feelings. Use parallel structure to make your comparison logical and organized.

Proofreading: Check your paper for correct grammar, spelling, and punctuation. If you are writing in the past tense, make sure that you have used correct verb forms.

Unit 6

Revising: Have students work in pairs to revise. After students have read their partners' papers, have them suggest adverbs and other descriptive words that can be added.

Proofreading: Have students proofread their papers in groups of three. Ask one member of each group to be the spelling "expert," another to be the grammar "expert," and the third to be the punc-

tuation "expert." Have each "expert" proofread the group's papers for that particular kind of error.

LDP Activity: Have students choose one relative from their list compiled earlier. Have students write a paragraph describing their relative's profession and where this particular relative lived. Have them use at least 7–10 adjectives and adverbs, and underline them. Help

them become aware of how much descriptive words can do to help bring out images.

THINK ABOUT TONE

The **tone** of a poem indicates the speaker's attitude toward his or her subject. The tone can also indicate the speaker's or poet's attitude toward the reader. Some elements that contribute to the tone are the formality or informality of the poem's language, the rhythm, the choice of certain words, and the energy or "pace" of the poem. Sometimes, tone will change within a poem, especially if the poem is long.

1. What is the tone of "Whale Hunting"?

2. Which line in "Whale Hunting" displays the tone most clearly?

3. What is the tone of "Luther Leavitt"?

4. In which part of the poem is the tone most evident?

5. How might the tone of the poem be different if the speaker had been able to go on the blanket?

DEVELOP YOUR VOCABULARY

Antonyms are words that have opposite, or nearly opposite, meanings. *Short* and *tall* are antonyms, as are *thin* and *fat*. In the poem "Luther Leavitt," the speaker says that there were "too many kids." An antonym of the word *many* would be *few*. The phrase would have exactly the opposite meaning if the word *few* were substituted for the word *many*.

Two words in each group below are antonyms. Write the antonyms on a separate sheet of paper. Then write a sentence using the first antonym in each pair. Rewrite each sentence using the second antonym, and see how the meaning of the sentence changes.

1. knowledge, thoughtfulness, ignorance, consideration

2. tired, rude, polite, quick

3. difficult, hidden, confusing, easy

4. politely, hesitantly, eagerly, slowly

Note: The TRB contains work-sheets to accompany both writing assignments.

Part I

Motivation: Ask students to think about the last time their extended family got together. The occasion may have been a holiday, such as Thanksgiving, or it may have been a wedding, funeral, or birthday celebration. Ask students to share some of their experiences, impressions, and feelings about this event. Relate the discussion to the writing assignment in this section.

Cooperative/Collaborative Learning Activity: The following activity can be used during the prewriting section, or it can be used after the completion of the writing section. Divide the class into small groups. Ask each group to role-play the conversations that group members have written, as if they were characters in a play.

Part II

Motivation: Have students discuss the things that make a particular poem appealing to them. At first, encourage students to express freely their feelings about what makes a "good" poem. Then relate the discussion to the literary elements that students have studied. Try to help students see that much of what they like in poetry is the effective use of these elements.

Cooperative/Collaborative Learning Activity: Divide students into teams of five to eight. Have each team put their papers together to form a small literary magazine. Each team can provide additional copy to introduce or conclude the magazine; teams can also include illustrations or short biographies of authors.

T542

LITERATURE-BASED WRITING

1. All of the stories and poems in this unit have been about generations. Imagine that four of the characters from this unit meet at a family reunion, and the conversation turns to the importance of family history and tradition. What might these characters say to one another? Write the conversation of the four characters as a dialogue for a story.

Prewriting: Choose the four characters that you feel you know best. You will have to decide how the four characters might be related. For example, perhaps one character is the distant cousin of another character, or one character has married into the family of another character. Maybe, one character comes to the reunion as the boyfriend or girlfriend of another character. Freewrite their conversations, thinking of questions that they might ask one another, and the answers that might be given.

Writing: Use your freewriting as a basis for your dialogue. Be sure to describe each character's facial expressions and tone of voice. Introduce your dialogue by describing the setting of the reunion.

Revising: As you revise your paper, make sure that the personality of each character stands out clearly. Add details and descriptive words wherever possible to make each characterization more vivid.

Proofreading: Check your paper to make sure that you have used quotation marks correctly. Remember that a new paragraph must begin each time the speaker changes.

542

2. You have studied five important elements that can be used to analyze poetry: denotation and connotation, rhythm, sounds, form, and symbolism. Choose two poems from this unit about which you feel strongly. Compare and contrast the works according to the literary elements you have studied.

Prewriting: Review the work that you did for the "Think About the_____" sections for the poems in this unit. Then make a chart that has the name of the two poems that you have chosen at the top and the five literary elements down the side. Fill in the spaces on the chart with details about each element from the poems.

Writing: Use your prewriting chart to write a comparison of the two poems. You might enjoy writing your paper as if you were a literary critic writing for a newspaper or magazine.

Revising: Try to include in your paper both positive and negative statements about each poem. Add a sentence or two that states how well you think a particular poet uses such devices as symbolism, sounds, or connotation.

Proofreading: Check your paper for correct punctuation. If you used colons or semi-colons, make sure that they are used correctly. Also, check to be certain that you used either a question mark or an exclamation mark at the end of a sentence in which a period would be inappropriate.

BUILDING LANGUAGE SKILLS

Vocabulary

A **prefix** is a letter or combination of letters added to the beginning of a word or word root to change its meaning. A negative prefix acts like the word *not* and changes the meaning of the word from positive to negative. For example, the word *inconsiderate* is formed by adding the prefix *in-* to *considerate*. The word inconsiderate means not considerate. In addition to *in-*, some commonly used negative prefixes include *un-, dis-, il-, ir-,* and *im-*.

Identify the negative prefix and root word for each *italicized* word below. Then write a definition for each word.

1. It would be *inappropriate* for a girl to hear of these things.

2. She was wearing a very *unusual* hat.

3. The boy lost something that was *irreplacable*.

4. Grandfather was *immobilized* by the injury.

5. It would be *impossible* for Roberto to go to school.

6. He *disregarded* his father's remarks and kept on walking.

7. Some of the farm workers were *illiterate*.

Usage and Mechanics

A **conjunction** is a part of speech that makes a direct connection between words or groups of words. Some common conjunctions include *and, or,* and *because*.

Two kinds of conjunctions are coordinating conjunctions and subordinating conjunctions. **Coordinating conjunctions** connect similar words or word groups. The following are examples:

It was a thoroughly happy *and* relaxed time for everybody . . .

Should she *or* should she not?

Subordinating conjunctions connect two complete ideas by making one of the ideas less important than the other. Some subordinating conjunctions are: *after, as, even though, since, unless,* and *wherever.* Here are some examples:

When I woke up this morning, it seemed then right to wear good clothes.

He stole a box of crackers *because* his sick child was groaning with hunger.

Find five sentences from the selections that use conjunctions. Identify the conjunctions and state whether they are coordinating or subordinating. Then identify the words or word groups that the conjunctions connect. Use the five sentences as models to write five original sentences.

Usage and Mechanics

More About Usage and Mechanics: Write these sentences on the chalkboard:

I will give her either a sweater or a skirt for her birthday.

I will go out, even though it is raining.

Point out that in the first sentence, "or" is a coordinating conjunction because it connects similar words. Elicit that in the second sentence, "even though" is a subordinating conjunction because it connects two ideas by making one idea less important than the other.

Cooperative/Collaborative Learning Activity: Have students work in small groups to write original sentences that use conjunctions.

BUILDING LANGUAGE SKILLS

Vocabulary

More About Word Attack: Point out that identifying a negative prefix and the root word can help students figure out the meaning of a particular word. Write this example from "Somebody's Son."

"Is it there?" he asked with an uncontrollable quaver.

Elicit that the negative prefix changes the meaning of controllable to not controllable.

Cooperative/Collaborative Learning Activity: Refer students to the questions in the vocabulary section of their text. Then, have students work in small groups to find the answers. Have them check their answers in a dictionary. (in/appropriate; un/unusual; ir/replacable; im/mobilized; im/possible; dis/regard; il/literate)

SPEAKING AND LISTENING

You have read about many interesting real people and some colorful imaginary charac-ters in this unit. If you were asked to name the most notable real person in this unit, who would it be and why? Also, if you were asked to name the character who seemed to be the most interesting, who would it be and why? Think about these questions as you prepare to talk about literature.

1. Think about the people that you have read about in this unit. Choose two, one real and one imaginary, who seem to stand out from all the others. Write their names on 3×5 cards.

2. On each card write as much as you can recall about the person or character whose name is on the card. Limit yourself to two minutes per card, but try to remember as many things as you can. Write without stopping if possi-ble, and do not worry about complete sentences.

3. Try to fill up both sides of the card. In writing about the character, you will want to consider such aspects as mem-orable qualities, personality, impor-tance to the story, and whether or not he or she was a stereotype or an unusual character. In writing about the real person, you probably will want to include such information as personal life, personality, and contributions to family or community.

4. After you have filled your cards, sit with a group of your classmates. Decide whether you will discuss characters or real people, or a mix of both. Then take turns round-robin style to discuss the characters and real people you have chosen. Use your 3×5 cards to assist you. Limit your dialogue to about one minute.

5. If someone in your group has chosen the same person or character, try not to repeat anything already said. In-stead, add to his or her dialogue. You will be surprised how something an-other person says can jar your memory so that you recall something new about that person or character.

Now that you have read these five steps, go back to the beginning and prepare yourself to talk about characters from literature. Once you meet with your group, you will want to spend enough time together so that everyone has a chance to share ideas.

CRITICAL THINKING

A general conclusion drawn from particular details is called a **generalization**. For example, suppose that all the children on your block play a certain game. You might make the generalization that this game is popular among children.

Sometimes, when you read a piece of literature, you will be tempted to make a generalization based on what you have read. It is important that you recognize whether such a generalization is accurate or inaccurate. For example, after reading the short story "The Medicine Bag," you might come to the conclusion that the Sioux place a great deal of importance on passing traditions from generation to generation. This would be an accurate generalization. However, suppose that after reading the story you come to the conclusion that all Sioux children fear their grandparents might embarass them. This would be an inaccurate generalization.

Choose a selection from this unit that suggests several generalizations. Use the selection to answer the following questions:

1. What generalizations are suggested by this story or poem? What specific details support these generalizations?

2. What inaccurate generalizations might a reader make based on this selection? Why are these generalizations inaccurate?

EFFECTIVE STUDYING

It is important to know how to take three types of tests: matching, multiple choice, and true-false.

In a matching test, first read the instructions. Notice whether an item in either column can be used more than once. Also, note if some items in a column may not be used at all. Begin by matching the items that you are sure of. If each item is used only once, it is possible to match some of the remaining items by the process of elimination.

In a multiple choice test, answer the question in your own mind before you look at the choices. Eliminate the choices that are obviously wrong. Then choose the remaining answer that seems best.

In true and false tests do not mark a statement true unless it is totally true. If you know that a statement is true only in some cases, it is probably false. Be aware of limiting words such as *always, never,* or *only.* Also be aware if a statement has two parts joined by a word such as *because.* One or both parts might be true, but the relationship between the two parts might be false.

Mark each statement "true" or "false."

1. In a multiple choice test, only one answer to each question can be correct.

2. You should mark a statement true as long as it is true some of the time.

A Career to Consider

After reading the poem "My People," students might be interested in a career as an anthropology field worker. Anthropology is the study of the physical, social, and cultural development of humans. An anthropologist will study a particular people, such as the Navajo Indians, and trace their origin and development throughout history.

An anthropology field worker is a person who assists an anthropologist by gathering information in the field. A field worker may work anywhere in the world. Since field work can be rough, an anthropology field worker must be in good physical condition and able to adapt to extremes of climate and terrain. Educational requirements for anthropology field workers vary according to the particular job; the minimum requirement is a high school diploma. Students who are interested in this career should contact the anthropology department of a local college or university.

GLOSSARY

PRONUNCIATION KEY

Accent is the force or stress given to some words or syllables in speech. In this book, accent is indicated by the use of uppercase letters. Words of one syllable are always shown as accented. Thus, if the word *hand* were pronounced, the pronunciation would be printed *(HAND)*. In words of more than one syllable, the syllable that gets the main accent is printed in uppercase letters. The other syllable or syllables are printed in lowercase letters. If the word *handbag* were pronounced, the pronunciation would be printed *(HAND bag)*. The phonetic respellings are based on the pronunciations given in Webster's *New World Dictionary*.

Letter(s) in text words	Letter(s) used in respelling	Sample words	Phonetic respelling	Letter(s) in text words	Letter(s) used in respelling	Sample words	Phonetic respelling
a	a	hat	(HAT)	i	u *or* uh	possible	(POS uh bul)
		bandit	(BAN dit)				
a	ay	ate	(AYT)	o	o	hot	(HOT)
		makeup	(MAYK up)			bottle	(BOT ul)
a	air	stare	(STAIR)	o	u *or* uh	gallon	(GAL un)
		daring	(DAIR ing)				
a	ah	dart	(DAHRT)	o	oh	go	(GOH)
a	u *or* uh	about	(uh BOUT)			open	(OH pun)
				o	aw	horn	(HAWRN)
						malt	(HAWLT)
e	e	belt	(BELT)			ballroom	(BAWL room)
		denim	(DEN im)	oo	uu	book	(BUUK)
e	eh	ingest	(in JEHST)			football	(FUUT bawl)
e	ih	delight	(dih LYT)	oo	oo	move	(MOOV)
		result	(rih ZULT)			pool	(POOL)
e	u *or* uh	darken	(DAHR kun)			ruler	(ROO lur)
		perhaps	(pur HAPS)	oi	oi	point	(POINT)
e	ee	he	(HEE)			boiler	(BOI lur)
		demon	(DEE mun)	ou	ou	pout	(POUT)
i	i	hit	(HIT)			output	(OUT put)
		mitten	(MIT un)	u	u	up	(UP)
i	ih	distress	(dih STRES)			upshot	(UP shot)
		gravity	(GRAV ih tee)	u	uh	support	(suh PAWRT)
i	y	dime	(DYM)	y	i	rhythm	(RITH um)
		idle	(YD ul)	y	ee	lazy	(LAY zee)
i	eye	idea	(eye DEE uh)	y	y	thyme	(TYM)
i	ee	medium	(MEE dee um)				

abhorred (ab HAWRD) hated, dreaded

abrupt (uh BRUPT) sudden; a little rude

acrid (AK rid) bitter to the tongue

aggressors (uh GRES urz) those who make the first move in a quarrel

amorous (AM uh rus) full of love

anatomy (uh NAT uh mee) (*as used here*) body

apologetic (uh POL uh JET ik) filled with apology; suggesting that one is sorry

attorney (uh TUR nee) lawyer. A county attorney is a lawyer responsible for bringing criminal charges against someone.

authorities (uh THAWR uh teez) people with official power

avarice (AV uh ris) greed

banter (BAN tur) good-natured teasing

barbaric (bahr BAR ik) wild and cruel; not yet civilized

bedlam (BED lum) confusion

belt (BELT) area; region

beseech (bih SEECH) ask earnestly

bilingual (by LING gwul) able to use two languages

blunt (BLUNT) having a rounded point

bolt (BOHLT) run away fast

brawl (BRAWL) noisy fight

bustle (BUS ul) move about busily

caravans (KAR uh vanz) in Great Britain, camping trailers

carcass (KAHR kus) body of dead animal

casually (KAZH oo uh lee) in an off-hand or indifferent way

catastrophe (koh TAS truh fee) a sudden, horrible disaster

chaperone (SHAP ur ohn) older person who supervises an unmarried couple

civic (SIV ik) having to do with good citizenship

clarity (KLAR uh tee) clearness

client (KLY unt) person who pays for a duty performed

coincidence (koh IN suh duns) two or more related events accidentally happening at the same time

companion (kum PAN yun) a friend

comprehensible (KOM pree HEN suh bul) understandable

comprehension (kom pree HEN shun) understanding or knowledge of something

confide (kun KYD) tell as a secret

contagion (kun TAY jun) spreading disease

corral (kuh RAL) a fenced-in area for keeping livestock

correspondence (kawr uh SPON duns) exchange of letters

covert (KOH vert) hidden or disguised

creed (KREED) formal statement of belief

crocus (KROH kus) spring flower

cuddling (KUD ling) holding and petting

cupboard (KUB urd) a closet fitted with shelves for holding cups

deception (dih SEP shun) trickery; action intended to fool another person

demonstration (dem un STRAY shun) any happening that can be observed

dénouement (day noo MAHN) the final outcome

dictatorial (dik tuh TAWR ee ul) forcing one's beliefs upon someone else

dignitary (DIG nuh ter ee) important person

dismaying (dis MAY ing) losing courage or confidence

doff (DOF) take off or discard

douse (DOUS) soak with water

elimination (ih lim uh NAY shun) in a tournament, dropped after one loss

emerged (ih MURJD) came out

endure (en DUUR) put up with

entitled (en TYT uld) have as a claim or right; empowered

eventually (ih VEN choo ul ee) in the end; at some time

exclusive (iks KLOO siv) private and expensive

explicitly (eks PLIS it lee) very clearly

extreme (ik STREEM) very great

facetiously (fuh SEE shus lee) jokingly, especially at an inappropriate time

fanatical (fuh NAT ih kul) incredibly devoted, to the point of being unreasonable

fantasy (FAN tuh see) daydream; idea created by the imagination; something imagined

faze (FAYZ) confuse; weaken

felon (FEL un) criminal

fiancé (fee ahn SAY) husband-to-be

fitful (FIT ful) uneasy; very restless

fond (FOND) affectionate

fortnight (FAWRT niyt) two weeks
frustrations (frus TRAY shunz) unhappy feelings that come from not being able to reach one's goals

gaped (GAYPT) opened wide; yawned
gaudy (GAWD ee) showy; bright-colored
genial (JEEN yul) pleasant; good-natured
gopher (GOH fur) a rodent that digs into the ground
gory (GOR ee) bloody
greed (GREED) a great desire for wealth or material things
grungy (GRUN jee) shabby or dirty

habitation (hab ih TAY shun) a building to live in
hamlet (HAM lit) very small village
heritage (HER ih tij) what is handed down to a person from ancestors
hesitating (HEZ ih tunt lee) pausing in doubt
homesteaded (HOHM sted id) occupied government land as a home
hummocks (HUM uks) areas of fertile, wooded land, higher than the surrounding swamp

idle (YD ul) unused; not busy
impeach (im PEECH) accuse
improvised (IM pruh vyzd) made up quickly, without planning
indolence (IN duh lens) laziness
inexorable (in EKS uh ruh bul) unable to change or control
instinct (IN stingkt) a natural tendency; unconscious skill
interminable (in TER muh nuh bul) endless
invalid (IN vuh lid) sick person

knobby (NOB ee) lumpy

lagoon (luh GOON) a shallow body of water, usually connected to a larger one
lamentable (LAM en tuh bul) distressing, sorrowful
lust (LUST) powerful desire

malnutrition (mal noo TRISH un) poor health condition caused by not having enough of the right kinds of food
marina (muh REE nuh) large area set up for docking boats

martyrdom (MAHR tur dum) ready to die or suffer for a cause or belief
medallion (muh DAL yun) large medal
mingle (MING gul) mix
mint-condition (MINT kun DISH un) brand-new
mores (MAWR ays) manners or moral customs of a social group
mortgage (MAWR gij) loan given to purchase a house
motive (MOHT iv) reason to act
murky (MUR kee) clouded; unclear
mute (MYOOT) unable to talk; quiet

nimble (NIM bul) quick and accurate

oafs (OHFS) stupid, awkward persons
omelet (OM lit) eggs beaten up, fried, and folded in half when done

pallet (PAL it) bed
paramour (PAR uh muur) lover
pensively (PEN siv lee) thoughtfully
perpetual (pur PECH oo ul) never stopping; without pause
persevered (pur suh VIRD) kept going by not giving up
perverse (pur VURS) stubbornly difficult or contrary; wrong; improper
pleasantries (PLEZ un treez) lively, agreeable talks
pneumonia (noo MOHN yuh) disease of the lungs; caused by an infection, and results in swelling and soreness
poltergeist (POHL tur gyst) a noisy ghost
portly (PAWRT lee) heavy, but dignified
potion (POH shun) a drink with special powers, such as medicine or poison
presence (PREZ uns) nearness; being there
prodigious (pruh DIJ us) wonderful; of great size; power; monstrous
profane (proh FAYN) show disrespect for holy things
purge (PURGJ) get rid of

quilt (KWILT) a bed cover made by stitching a layer of cotton between two layers of fabric

rakish (RAYK ish) stylish
reconnaissance (rih KON uh sens) quick survey of information

reeds (REEDZ) tall grass that grows in a marsh

relentless (rih LENT lis) without pity; harsh and cruel

repelled (rih PELD) put off

restorative (rih STAWR uh tiv) something that brings back consciousness or health generally; a medicine

rickety (RIK it ee) feeble; shaky

righteous (RIH chus) morally right, virtuous

ritual (RICH uu ul) ceremony; tradition; a set pattern

rival (RY vul) one who wants the same thing as another person

sarcastic (sahr KAS tik) sneering or ironic, and meant to hurt feelings

scowl (SKOUL) frown and look angry

scullery (SKUL er ee) a room for cleaning and storing dishes and pots

scythe (SYTH) a long, curved blade fixed at an angle to a long, bent handle and used to cut down grass or grain

self-centered (SELF SENT urd) selfish; concerned with oneself

self-conscious (SELF KON shus) very aware of oneself; embarrassed or shy

sharecropper (SHAIR krohp ur) a farmer who works land owned by another and receives part of the profits.

serene (suh REEN) calm; peaceful

shields (SHEELDZ) defends; protects

shrewdest (SHROOD ist) cleverest, often in a tricky way

silhouettes (sil oo ETS) outline drawings filled in with a color, usually black

sires (SYRZ) fathers or forefathers

sluggish (SLUG ish) lacking energy; slow, inactive

snatches (SNACH iz) grabs suddenly, rudely, or eagerly

somber (SOM bur) gloomy; grave; sad

spellbinding (SPEL bynd ing) fascinating;

stout (STOWT) having a heavy-set body

stride (STRYD) long step

stupor (STOO pur) dazed or dull state; loss of feeling

superstitious (soo pur STISH us) too much fear of the unknown

surged (SURJD) rolled; swelled up

surplus (SUR plus) amount left over when a need had been met

tarpaulin (tahr PAW lin) a waterproof sheet used to protect

telephoto (TEL uh foht oh) a camera lens that is able to make faraway things appear large

tepee (TEE pee) a cone-shaped tent of animal skins, used by the Plains Indians

theory (THEE uh ree) guess based on

thrive (THRYV) grow healthy and strong

timid (TIM id) shy

tolerant (TOL ur unt) willing to accept views different from your own

traditional (truh DISH uh nul) following old customs

transmitter (trans MIT ur) radio device that sends out signals

trifles (TRY fulz) anything of little value or importance

turret (TUR it) small tower on top of a building

unnerved (un NURVD) took away courage; terrified

utterances (UT ur un suz) spoken words

vague (VAYG) not clear; hazy

varmints (VAHR munts) animals regarded as troublesome

vegetation (vej uh TAY shun) plant life

vestal (VES tul) virtuous, pure

virtuous (VUR choo us) honorable

welterweight (WEL tur wayt) boxer in a weight division between lightweight and middleweight

whimsical (HWIM zih kul) humorous in an odd way

woes (WOHZ) misery, sorrows

womb (WOOM) stomach or uterus; any place that holds or generates something else

wryly (RY lee) humorously; twisted to one side

zealously (ZEL us lee) eagerly; fanatically

INDEX OF FINE ART

INDEX OF SKILLS

INDEX OF TITLES AND AUTHORS

Index of Titles and Authors

ACKNOWLEDGMENTS

Unit 1: Harold Matson Company, Inc—for "The Love Letter" from *Eleven Great Horror Stories* by Jack Finney, copyright 1959 by Jack Finney; Delacorte Press—for "Up on Fong Mountain" excerpted from the book *Dear Bill Remember Me? and Other Stories* by Norma Fox Mazer, copyright 1976 By Norma Fox Mazer, reprinted by permission of Delacorte Press; Harper & Row Publishers, Inc.—for "Where Are You Now, William Shakespeare?" (pp 35–43, with deletion), from chapter 2 in *Me, Me, Me, Me, Me: Not a Novel* by M.E. Kerr, copyright 1983 by M.E. Kerr, reprinted by permission of Harper & Row Publishers, Inc; Macmillan Publishing Co. Inc—for "What is Once loved" from *Alice-All-By-Herself* by Elisabeth Coatsworth, copyright 1937 by Macmillan Publishing Co., Inc., renewed 1965 by Elizabeth Coatsworth Beston; Random House, Inc.—for "Greyday" from *Oh Pray My Wings Are Gonna Fit Me Well* by Maya Angelou, reprinted by permission of Random House., Inc; Southern Music Publishing Co. Inc.—for "I Dream a World" from *Troubled Island* by Langstom Hughes & William Grant Still, copyright 1976 by Southern Music Publishing Co. Inc., used by permission, all rights reserved; Vanessa Howard—for "Reflections" by Vanessa Howard. **Unit 2:** Scott Meredith Literary Agency—for "Appointment at Noon" by Eric Frank Russell, reprinted by permission of the author and the author's agent, Scott Meredith Literary Agency, Inc., 845 Third Avenue, New York, New York 10022; Wesleyan University Press—for "Incident in a Rose Garden" from *Night Light* by Donald Justice, copyright © 1967 by Donald Justice, reprinted by permission of the publisher; Scholastic, Inc.—for "Boy in the Shadows" from *House of Evil* by Margaret Ronan, copyright © 1977 by Scholastic, Inc. Reprinted by permission of the publisher; Dramatists Play Service, Inc.—for *Sorry, Wrong Number.* Copyright © 1952, 1948 by Lucille fletcher, reprinted by permission of the Dramatists Play Service, Inc. and the author; Harold Matson Company, Inc.—for "Thus I Refute Beelzy" by John Collier, copyright 1940 by John Collier, copyright renewed 1967 by the author, reprinted by permission of Harold Matson Company, Inc.; E.E. Cummings—for "hist, whist", reprinted from *Tulips and Chimneys* by E.E. Cummings, copyright © 1973, 1976 by Nancy T. Andrews, copyright © 1973, 1976 by George James Firmage; Gerald Duckworth & Co.—for "Overheard on a Saltmarsh" by Harold Monro from *Collected Poems* by Harold Monro, reprinted by permission of the publisher, Gerald Duckworth & Co.; Don Congdon Associates, Inc.—for "Of Missing Persons" by Jack Finney, copyright © by Don Congdon Associates, Inc.; The Society of Authors—for "The Listeners" by Walter de la Mare, the Literary Trustees for Walter de la Mare and The Society of Authors as their representative. **Unit 3:** John Curtis Publishing Company—for "The Getaway" by John Savage, reprinted from *The Saturday Evening Post,* copyright © 1966 by The Curtis Publishing Company; Susan Glaspell—for "Trifles" by Susan Glaspell from *Modern Drama in America, Vol. I,* reprinted by permission of the Estate of Susan Glaspell; Charles Scribner's Sons—for "Rattlesnake Hunt" from *Cross Creek* by Marjorie Kinnan Rawlings, copyright 1942 Marjorie Kinnan Rawlings; copyright renewed © 1970 Norton Baskin, reprinted with the permission of Charles Scribner's Sons; Charles Scribner's Sons—for "Earth" from *The Bashful Earthquake* by Oliver Herford, reprinted with the permission of Charles Scribner's Sons; Charles Scribner's Sons—for "Earth" from *The Gardener and Other Poems* by John Hall Wheelock, copyright © 1961 John Hall Wheelock, reprinted with the permission of Charles Scribner's Sons; Poetry Magazine—for "The Bat" by Ruth Herschberger, copyright 1951 by Ruth Herschberger, reprinted by permision of the author, Macmillan Publishing Company, Inc.—for "The Bird of Night" from *The Bat-Poet* by Randall Jarrell, copyright © 1963, 1964 by Macmillan Publishing Company, Inc. Reprinted by permission of the publisher; Frederick H. Rohlfs/Quentin Reynolds—for "A Secret for Two." Copyright © 1936 by Crowell-Collier Publishing Company, reprinted by permission of the Estate of Quentin Reynolds. **Unit 4:** Scott Meredith Literary Agency—for "The Gold Medal" by Nan Gilbert, reprinted by permission of the author and the author's agents, Scott Meredith Literary Agency, Inc., 845 Third Avenue, New York, NY 10022; Eve Merriam—for "Conversation With Myself" from *It Doesn't Always Have to Rhyme* by Eve Merriam, copyright © 1964 by Eve Merriam, reprinted by permission of the author; Barlenmir House, Publishers—for "Happy Thought" from *Street Poetry and Other Poems* by Jesus Papoleto Melendez, copyright © 1972 by Barlenmir House, Publishers; Scholastic Inc.—adapted from "Ta-Na-E-Ka" by Mary Whitebird, from Scholastic Voice, December 1973, copyright © 1973 by Scholastic Inc. Reprinted by permission of the publisher; Field Newspaper Syndicate, Ann Landers—for "Dead at Seventeen" from the Ann Landers column, copyright © Ann Landers, Field Newspaper Syndicate, and *The Waterbury Republican;* Harold Ober Associates—for "Thank You, M'am" by Langston Hughes, reprinted by permission of Harold Ober Associates Incorporated, copyright © 1958 by Langston Hughes; Xerox Education Publications—for "Chair" by Cheryl Miller Thurston from *Read* Magazine, reprinted by permission of *Read* Magazine, copyright © 1981 by Weekly Reader Publications; University of Washington Press—for the untitled poem beginning "A bee thumps . . ." by Robert Sund from *Bunch Grass;* copyright © University of Washington Press; Crown Publishers, Inc.—for "Starvation Wilderness." Adapted from *The Silence of the North* by Olive A. Fredrickson and Ben East, copyright © 1972 by Olive A. Fredrickson and Ben East, used by permission of Crown Publishers, Inc.; Alfred A. Knopf, Inc.—for "Dreams" from *The Dream Keeper and Other Poems* by Langston Hughes, reprinted by permission of the publisher. **Unit 5:** Alred A. Knopf, Inc.—for "Amigo Brothers" from *Stories from*

ART CREDITS

Illustrations

Unit 1: pp. 2, 3: Michael Garland; pp. 36, 39, 41: Judith Lombardi; p. 82: Sterling Brown; p. 100: Andrea Arroyo. **Unit 2:** p. 110: Jack Stockman; p. 112 Gary Underhill; p. 123: Marlies Merk-Najaka; p. 126: Maggie Zander; pp. 136, 144, 149: (tinting) Donna Day; p. 162: Stella Ormai; p. 164: David Palladin; pp. 168, 170, 172, 175, 177: Yoshi Miyake; p. 180: Mike Eagle; p. 183: Michael Bryant; pp. 186, 187, 191: Doug Schneider; pp. 200, 203: Alex Bloch; **Unit 3:** p. 214: Michael Garland; pp. 216, 220: Den Schofield; pp. 224, 227, 230, 235, 237, 240, 246: Bert Dodson/Bookmakers Ltd.; p. 280: Steven Hunt; p. 284: Amand Wilson; **Unit 4:** p. 315: Karen Kupper; p. 316: David Dircks; p. 332: Eva Auchincloss; pp. 336, 338, 340, 344: Rupert Baxter; p. 349: Karen Bauman; pp. 368, 369, 373: Dick Smolinski; p. 376: Gary Underhill; p. 394 Michael Bryant; p. 396: Robert Pasternak; **Unit 5:** pp. 406, 407: Pat Cummings; pp. 408, 413, 417, 419: Paul Lackner; pp. 442, 445, 447, 449: (tinting) Donna Day; p. 455: Merlies Merk-Najacka; pp. 464, 465: William Hunter-Hicklin; p. 489: Robert Martin; **Unit 6:** p. 496: Jack Stockman; pp. 500, 503, 507: Yoshi Miyake; p. 524: Richard Leonard; p. 527: Bradford Brown.

Photographs

Unit 1: p. 20: Photo Researchers; p. 48, 50, 54, 57, 61, 65, 69: The Museum of Modern Art/Film Stills Archive; p. 77: Historical Picture Service; p. 77: Berlitz/ Tony Stone Worldwide; p. 80: Naoki Okamoto/Visions; p. 83: AP/Wide World Photos; p. 83: H. Armstrong Roberts; p. 91: Eve Arnold/Magnum; p. 96: Photofest; **Unit 2:** p. 136: H. Armstrong Roberts; p. 144: H. Armstrong Roberts; p. 149: H. Armstrong Roberts; p. 151: Courtesy of Lucille Fletcher; p. 151: H. Armstrong Roberts; p. 165: Harry Ransom Humanities Research Center, University of Texas, Austin; p. 195: AP/Wide World Photos; **Unit 3:** p. 272: R. Smith/H. Amstrong Roberts; p. 276: H. Armstrong Roberts; p. 281: National Aeronautics and Space Administration; p. 294: John Gerlach; p. 300: Courtesy of Professor John Hedgecoe; p. 302: Gjon Mili; **Unit 4:** p. 397: Ohio Historical Society; **Unit 5:** p. 452: Flip Schulke/ Black Star; p. 453: Dennis Brack/Black Star; p. 455: Flip Schulke/ Black Star; p. 473: Northwind Picture Archives; p. 473: The Bettmann Archive; **Unit 6:** p. 488: Tony Stone Worldwide; p. 491: Bill Tague/The Contemporary Forum; p. 519: The Heard Museum; p. 521: H. Armstrong Roberts; p. 538: Rosamond W. Purcell.

Art Credits